TALBOTT'S COVE

A SMALL TOWN ROMANCE COLLECTION

KATE CANTERBARY

VESPER PRESS

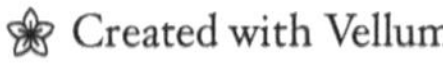 Created with Vellum

FRESH CATCH

ABOUT FRESH CATCH

Take a vacation, they said. *Get away from Silicon Valley's back-stabbing and power-grabbing. Recharge the innovative batteries. Unwind, then come back stronger than ever.*

Instead, I got lost at sea and fell in love with an anti-social lobsterman.

There's one small issue:
Owen Bartlett doesn't know who I am. Who I really am.

***

I don't like people.

I avoid small talk and socializing, and I kick my companions out of bed before the sun rises.
No strings, no promises, no problems.

Until Cole McClish's boat drifts into Talbott's Cove, and I bend all my rules for the sexy sailor.

I don't know Cole's story or what he's running from, but one thing is certain:

I'm not letting him run away from me.

This is a work of fiction. Names, characters, places, and incidents are the product of the author's imagination or are used fictitiously, and any resemblance to actual persons, living or dead, business establishments, events, or locales is entirely coincidental.

Copyright © 2018 by Kate Canterbary

All rights reserved. No part of this book may be reproduced, stored in a retrieval system, or transmitted in any forms, or by any means, electronic, mechanical, photocopying, recording, or otherwise, without prior written permission of the author.

Trademarked names appear throughout this book. Rather than use a trademark symbol with every occurrence of a trademarked name, names are used in an editorial fashion, with no intention of infringement of the respective owner's trademark(s).

Editing provided by Julia Ganis of Julia Edits.

Proofreading provided by Marla Esposito of Proofing Style.

Cover design provided by Anna Crosswell of Cover Couture.

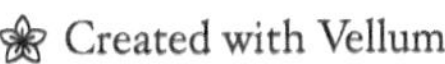 Created with Vellum

PREFACE

I want you to know
one thing

You know how this is:
if I look
at the crystal moon, at the red branch
of the slow autumn at my window,
if I touch
near the fire
the impalpable ash
or the wrinkled body of the log,
everything carries me to you,
as if everything that exists,
aromas, light, metals,
were little boats
that sail
toward those isles of yours that wait for me.

from "If You Forget Me" by Pablo Neruda

For Nick and Erin,
the ones who started it all.

1

———

ADRIFT

adj. Floating without being either moored or steered.

Cole

"OH, FOR FUCK'S SAKE!" I yelled, pounding my fist against the sonar system's housing. It was the only tool I knew to be functional, but now the screen was black. "Fuck, fuck, *fuck*."

This was bad. I was officially in the shit, and more shit than my usual.

Abandoning the boat's failing navigation system, I stormed into the captain's quarters for my laptop and tools. It was dark in there, darker than at the helm, and it heightened my senses. The summer air was thick and close, and sweat was rolling down my back. My belly was rumbling with hunger and my eyes were bleary from straining to spot rocks and land through the heavy veil of night.

I wanted air conditioning, whiskey, sushi, and a good night's sleep. In that order.

"Un-fucking-likely," I murmured as I returned to the boat's control center.

The screen indicated I was minutes away from reaching my destination at Newburyport Harbor, but the sea and shore were dark. Too dark to be anywhere near a port city.

If not for the lighthouse shining in the distance, I would think I was miles from shore.

"If this is what I get for investing in start-ups," I muttered, "then start-ups can go fuck themselves."

I snorted at that notion and set to unscrewing the control panel. If it weren't for start-up investors, I wouldn't have been the youngest billionaire in history. But founding an all-things-internet company and making it a household name wasn't as golden and glossy as the media made it seem.

According to the company's public statements, I was on sabbatical. It was a good cover story, and my spokeswoman managed to weave in some cozy anecdotes about my childhood love of sailing to make it feel even more authentic. It was handy that I did love sailing. Or, I *had* loved it, back when my summers were spent helping my uncle build custom boats in Morro Bay. But that was a lifetime ago.

The truth was that my board of directors had ejected me from the CEO's seat after my latest initiative fell below Silicon Valley's expectations. Project DaVinci was supposed to turn the industry upside down. Instead of doing that, it was a gigantic flop that yielded nothing worthy of my company's name.

All told, the billions spent on that endeavor were nowhere near as painful as the landslide of bad press.

This was the first time I'd *ever* taken a true vacation, one without a whiff of work, since founding the company in my apartment three blocks from Harvard University's Cambridge, Massachusetts campus. I wasn't one for lavish holidays or extreme adventures. I was like all the other Red Bull-addled programmers who found it easier to admire smartly constructed code than the natural world.

I hated this PR-inspired bullshit walkabout. If it wasn't for my desire to keep my stock prices from plummeting, I would've thrown a bigger fit when the board stripped me of my control and saddled me with a lame title. Chief Innovations Officer was a long, hard fall from CEO.

I was known for that—fit-throwing. I wasn't especially proud of it, and I'd worked my ass off to get my temper under control in the early years of my success, but it still followed me. Any glimmer of impatience was filed under my storied tyrannical management style known widely as Scream, Fire, and Throw. There had been tell-all books written by people who didn't care about violating nondisclosure agreements. The ass-lickers called it a new, disruptive style of leadership. The haters petitioned Amnesty International to add me to their watch lists.

Over the years, I'd changed. But that didn't rewrite my history. For an environment that evolved by the nanosecond, the half-life of bad behavior was eternity.

I'd matured from the slouchy geek who'd changed the way people spent their time on the internet. I was still arrogant and more condescending than necessary, but now I kept all of that close to my bespoke vests. My chief of staff, Neera Malik, beat some corporate manners into me and helped me recognize the negative impact of my punk-ass attitude on investors, stock prices, and the Valley's mercurial moods.

I'd never realized how much my behavior mattered. I'd always thought my work could—and *should*—speak for itself. But I'd learned the hard way that how I handled things mattered mightily. I didn't have to like it. I didn't have to agree. But I did have to deal with it if I intended to stay in this business.

And for all that work, I was lost and alone on the North Atlantic. The money, the connections, the pseudo-fame, the illusion of power... none of it could help me now. I was the only one who could help me. I was on my own here.

The nav system was on the fritz, the electrical panel was shooting sparks, and in trying to find the flashlight, I walked straight into the stainless steel server tower.

It had been almost twenty years since I'd sailed. Now, with blood running down my face in the dark, I was failing at this, too.

And then the pirates arrived.

2

———————

OLD SALT

n. Someone who has sailed for many years. An experienced mariner.

OWEN

THERE WAS a sailing vessel in my cove.

I was reading on the porch, alone save for the Japanese beetles watching me from the other side of the screen. Contentment came in the form of drinking my beer and settling into some Whitman until I noticed a light at the mouth of the cove. I gave it a long, weary stare before setting my book down.

With annoyance growing heavy on my shoulders, I pushed to my feet. This area was remote, far outside the typical routes of the luxury yachters and sport fishermen. The only visitors in these parts were locals, and they didn't come calling at this hour of the night.

That left only two options for this vessel. It was either off course or trespassing.

Now, I didn't own the water, but all the solid ground ringing the shore belonged to me. Regardless of whether this sailor had lost his way or was looking for a quiet spot to drop anchor for the night, he'd be going through me first.

I offered my old rocking chair a baleful stare before marching out of the porch. The beetles scattered as the screen door banged shut behind me. I thundered down the narrow wooden staircase that connected my home and the adjoining lighthouse to the dock. An aging skiff was moored there, opposite an equally old lobster boat.

Before casting off, I squinted over water. The intruder was drifting closer, and making no obvious attempt at turning back or signaling for aid. These waters were protected. Endangered species lived in and around the rocky coast, and vessels with that size and hull structure would leave a wake big enough to disrupt those fragile colonies. Not that I cared about the boat, but it was also in danger. If it came much closer, it was liable to run aground and that was even worse news for the conservation zone.

Time to show this sailor the way back to open water.

"It's too damn late for this shit," I groused as I turned over the skiff's motor. I could count the hours until a new day started and I was hoisting lobster traps and ferrying the day's catch to the fish markets up and down the seacoast. But this was *my* cove, and mine alone. I'd see to its preservation, as I had for nearly two decades, even if that left me tired and cranky tomorrow.

I was tired and cranky most mornings. I blamed my temperament on the backbreaking work of being a lobsterman who was doing everything in his power to survive, but there was more. Life on the ocean wasn't easy, and as the years passed, I was more and more convinced I was destined for a solitary existence.

And that made sense. I didn't like most people and hated sharing a bed. My philosophy was simple: get in, get your business done, get out. No need to complicate matters. No reason to go hog wild with those online dating schemes. Putting my information out there, on the internet, didn't sit well with me. It seemed like a big black hole of bank accounts and sexual preferences, and I didn't want to get sucked into that garbage.

No, I preferred the order and structure of my life without any of that. People, dating, the so-called digital age—I didn't need it, not when it was easy enough to dedicate one night every now and then to random hookups outside this small town.

In, out, over.

"Oh, for fuck's sake," I grumbled when I noticed the trespassing boat's lights flicker off. That wasn't a good sign for anyone.

I circled the vessel twice, the skiff's motor puttering as I slowed. It was more than enough notice for the crew, and any seaman who knew his shit would've acknowledged my presence by now. None of this felt right.

With a huff, I tossed my buoys overboard and climbed onto the trespasser's deck. I called out to the captain, hoping for a quick chat about shoreline species conservation and directions to the nearest marina.

Instead, I found myself staring down the barrel of a shotgun.

"Welcome to Talbott's Cove," I said. "Now, lower the firearm, Captain."

"I know maritime laws, and I know I did *not* invite you aboard," a hard voice said. It was hard, but there was a quiver behind it.

In one deft movement, I had the gun in hand and ammunition tumbling to the deck. "No," I said, "you did not. However, you're drifting northwest and minutes away from running aground. If that wasn't enough, you're in an ecological preserve that's only open to small crafts. You're looking at a ten-thousand-dollar fine, and on top of that, you've fucked up my night."

I hadn't gotten a good look at the shotgun-wielding captain. It was too dark in the cloudy moonlight to see more than shapes, and the man was sheltered by the mast's shadows. But now, as he stepped forward, his eyes wide with fear, I realized a few important things.

To start off, he was injured. His forehead was split with an ugly gash, his preppy polo shirt soaked with blood, and his hands were shaking.

Next, he was strong; stronger than I'd expected for a man who let his weapon make introductions. His chest and shoulders were broad, his biceps strained against his sleeves, and his thighs were thick and powerful. His hair was light, somewhere between blond and brown, though his eyes were dark. I'd place him in his early thirties, but no more than ten years younger than my thirty-nine.

Last, I was immediately attracted to him. I couldn't articulate why I found this man pulse-quickeningly sexy, and I didn't want to dwell on that reaction either.

"You need to get out of this cove," I said. He almost recoiled at the vicious snap in my words. That was one of my many problems. I was a mean sonofabitch when I wanted to be.

The captain waved at the boat. "Power's out," he said with a pathetic shrug, "and that controls everything. Motherboard on the navigation system is fried. And..." He turned his face to the night sky. "Not enough wind to catch the sails."

I stared out at the calm sea. "What about the crew? They can't bust out some duct tape and get things back in order?"

He shook his head. "No crew," he replied. "It's just me."

Well, that made no fucking sense. A boat like this, a captain dressed like that, these were the conditions for an unreasonably large crew. The one percent didn't sail solo.

"Fine. I'll radio the Coast Guard. They'll tow you to Portland," I said, my eyes drawn to the tight white polo again. He was fit as fuck, but it was the manicured, thoughtful kind of fit. It wasn't the product of hard labor but of discipline and, most likely, a lot of money. I couldn't decide how I felt about that. Forcing my attention from his chest, I sneered at his shiny new Sperrys. "Or Bar Harbor. That's probably more your speed."

"Is that where I am?" he asked. "Maine?"

He yanked a bandana from his back pocket and pressed it to his forehead. A swell of warmth moved through me, and I itched to snatch the fabric away and care for this man myself. That was another one of my problems: for all my curmudgeonly ways, I gave a shit. I didn't know how to turn off my feelings or shutter my concern. It was always there, waiting for someone to smother. Someone to drive away with my endless desire to dote.

"You're thirty miles north of Bar Harbor," I said. "So, yes. Maine."

"Bar Harbor is the opposite of my speed." The captain chuckled, but his words spoke nothing of humor or levity. "Is there anything closer? Look, I know I'm a pain in your ass right now and I admire your loyalty to the mollusks and plovers. Honestly, I do. But you can't even imagine the ration of shit I'll get if I wander back to civilization like this." He gestured to his injured face, and then the deck. "Not tonight. Just, I... please. There has to be another way."

I couldn't help myself. "I can tow you to the town harbor."

The captain's body sagged in relief. "Thank you. Seriously. I'm a fan of conservation, and if I could've prevented it, I never would have drifted into this cove." He lifted the bandana and palpated his forehead, frowning when his fingers came away bloody. He folded the fabric in on itself before returning it to the contusion. "Any chance I'll find a grocery store open at this hour? Motel?"

I glanced at my watch, the hands glowing in the inky night. Sure, I could wake up the young couple who ran the village's one and only inn, but...No. They had a new baby. They had enough on their hands without me banging on their door. There was no need for that.

"Unlikely," I said. I rasped out an impatient breath. There was no way this would end well. Not for me, not for my cove, not for my cock. "I have...some extra room. It's not much but you're welcome to it," I said. "Though you should know I keep my firearms under lock and key. I'll expect the same of you."

"Yes. Yes, *of course*," he replied. "I can't believe you'd do that for me. Thank you."

I waved away his comments. "It's nothing," I said. I meant it. I wasn't one for houseguests but I wasn't one for turning away folks in need either. "Just—just don't be irresponsible on the water. You're not the only one you're putting at risk, you know."

He shook his head slowly, his fingers still pressed to the injury. "I know. I'm an idiot. That's probably obvious by now," he said softly, almost to himself. "My systems failed, and I was lost and confused."

"Lost and confused is one way to put it," I said under my breath.

"I've never pulled a gun on anyone before. That's gotta count for something, right?"

"Not as much as you'd think," I replied.

"I thought you were a pirate," he continued, his words dissolving into a groan. "Last month I listened to a podcast about the rise of pirate activity around the world, and that was the first place my mind went. An idiotic place, but the first."

I laughed then. A deep, true laugh, and my houseguest's lips turned up in a rueful smile. "How about you get some gear and then you come with me? Sound good?"

"That sounds amazing," he said, his voice loaded with relief. "Thank you."

"Don't mention it," I said with a quick shake of my head.

I meant that. If he offered even one more drop of vulnerability, I was bound to wrap my arms around him and claim him as my own. And that wouldn't do. Not at all. I couldn't pour all of myself into a man who was certain to up and leave without as much as a backward glance. Just like the rest of them.

I returned to the skiff in search of a winch, and kept my back to the captain. I didn't want him to see the smitten smile tugging at my lips.

3

____

BACK AND FILL

v. Trim the sails of a vessel so that the wind alternately fills and spills out of them, in order to maneuver in a limited space.

Cole

I WOKE up with a skull-ringing headache.

It took me a moment to place my surroundings, but the wash-worn linen under my head smelled of soap and sea in a rough, humble way that brought to mind the great redwood of a man who boarded my boat last night.

He'd said his name was Owen Bartlett when he ushered me to this room.

Owen of the big, capable hands.

Owen of the quiet, knowing eyes.

Owen of the "Good night, and...we'll need that head of yours looked at if it doesn't stop bleeding soon."

He didn't have to bring me back here. He could've left me to the Coast Guard and motored away without a backward glance. He was ready to kick my ass last night, but there was kindness and generosity punching through his grouchy veneer.

I rolled out of bed, groaning as the pounding in my head intensified. I would have flopped back onto the mattress, buried my face in the pillows, and surrendered to the headache if my bladder wasn't a second from bursting. I fumbled across the hall and into the bathroom.

Once relieved, I set to washing the dried blood from my face. The cut only looked terrible, as if I was an extra on *The Walking Dead*. There was swelling, and bruising running down my nose and over one cheek. As per usual, I'd inflicted a sizable amount of damage on myself.

Staring into the mirror, I realized I was almost unrecognizable.

I'd been on the covers of countless magazines—everything from *Forbes* and *Newsweek* to *Rolling Stone* and *Nylon*—and while I wasn't as identifiable as George Clooney or Justin Timberlake, most people knew I was *someone*. A memorable face, but not memorable enough to stop traffic.

But Owen didn't have to know I was *someone*. Maybe this was my chance to be no one again, if only for a couple of days.

After showering and changing into a fresh set of clothes, I dug my glasses from my bag. The pounding in my head made it impossible to see straight. Next, I fumbled through the pockets for my phone. There were missed calls, voicemails, emails, and text messages lighting up my notification bar, and I ignored all of it. I didn't need any of that noise right now. Instead, I called the small firm that built most of the components on my boat, and requested a full complement of replacement parts.

They were extremely apologetic, even offering to send their top craftsmen out to repair my boat personally. I didn't want that. They'd work too damn fast for my purposes here, and while I didn't know much about this region, I knew a crew of custom boat fabricators from California would garner too much attention. Since they didn't want negative press any more than I did, they agreed to shipping the components and keeping this quiet.

They thought I was doing them a favor by staying low profile. They thought I was only concerned with protecting my investment in their firm rather than protecting my anonymity. It was funny how these situations worked. How people focused on the things they were getting out of an arrangement before considering how the arrangement harmed or benefited others. People were, as a matter of course, self-absorbed assholes and I knew that to be a fact because I had significant experience in the self-absorbed asshole business.

But that was all the navel-gazing I needed for today.

Next, I tapped open my secure text messaging app. I'd built it myself, and it was the only thing I trusted for communication with my team.

That forced a bitter laugh from my chest. It wasn't clear to me whether I had a team anymore. Would my successor scoop them all up in a greedy power grab but strip them of their projects and priorities, leaving them to linger in corporate purgatory? CEOs called in to replace founders had a habit of doing that. They were also known for cleaning house and firing anyone connected to the old regime. Industry reporters liked to cloak it as "establishing culture" or "realigning core value pillars" but the reality was that new leadership hated the idea of semi-loyal servants. They wanted people who'd kiss the rings and bow, and they didn't care if they terminated all senior staff and vaporized institutional knowledge in the process.

But I didn't need a staff. Not really. The next steps were all on me.

I scrolled through the messages, ignoring most of them. There was one notable exception: Neera Malik. The most amazing thing about Neera was that she didn't need me. She wasn't hitching her wagon to my stars, she had no interest in climbing over me, and she was competent to the extent that I knew she'd solve most world issues if someone gave her a crack at them.

Honestly, I was just waiting for the day when the United Nations called her up and requested her immediate presence to address global hunger, or broker some peace deals. And she'd have that shit managed within a few weeks. She was actually that good.

She was also one tough motherfucker but too stoic and reserved in her motherfucking for most to notice. Her story was simple, and more uncommon than anyone wanted to believe. Born in South Carolina shortly after her family emigrated from India. Grew up poor and socially isolated. Went to Stanford on a patchwork quilt of grants, scholarships, work-study, and loans. Odd jobs at odder start-ups in the Valley for a few years. Back to Stanford for business school. Found herself the unlikely right hand to a tech giant CEO after he judged her team in a case study competition and hired her on the spot. She left him and his company in better shape than either deserved, and then moved on to me shortly before my IPO.

None of that happened every day, and there was no underestimating Neera's drive and grit. She was proper like a white-shoe law firm, and had a knack for distilling issues down to their most essential parts. Whatever *the thing* was, she knew it long before anyone else and she knew how to tell me that without sending me into fits of rage.

Neera also knew how to tell me that the fits of rage had to stop, and —magically—imparted that information without bringing about another fit of rage. She gave it to me straight, and I appreciated that. We didn't pussyfoot around.

At one point—ages ago—there was chatter of us being romantically involved after we'd attended some local events together. But not *together* together. We simply traveled in the same vehicle and people assumed we were fucking in the back seat and boardroom. We had a good laugh at that.

Neera knew I was gay, but it wasn't the talk of the town. I didn't hide my sexuality when asked about it directly, but I didn't want it to precede me. I didn't want to be the gay CEO, the gay guy in tech's (mostly) straight guy world, the one who should expect interviews to include questions about coming out rather than the company's newest innovations. I didn't want my dick involved in my business, and that meant making sure my dick was no one's business.

As for Neera, I still didn't know who or what did it for her. Aside from offering the basics of her background, she didn't share many details from her private life. I took most of my clues in that area from her. Really, I took most of my clues in all areas from her.

So, I had to respond to her message.

Neera: May I ask: where are you?
Cole: The Atlantic.
Neera: That's a vast area.
Cole: The American side.

Neera: Still vast.

Cole: I've been gone for less than a week. I'm no Magellan but I don't think I could've sailed from New York to Brazil in that time.

Cole: The most logical explanation is that I'm somewhere in the northeast Atlantic, and I'm comfortable leaving it at that.

Neera: Do I need to have you tracked?

Cole: I'd love to see you try.

Cole: As if I haven't buried everything traceable beneath thousands of redirection layers.

Cole: It would take any in-house team months to peel it all back and even then, it's not like I'm on public Wi-Fi.

Neera: Very well.

Neera: Do you have an idea as to when you'll be returning to California?

Cole: Has my presence been requested?

Neera: Your presence is always appreciated.

Cole: That is not accurate, and you know it.

Neera: I'd beg to differ.

Cole: Wait. Does the new boss expect me to show up for morning huddles?

Cole: Because fuck that shit.

Cole: I haven't seen a job description for the Chief Innovations Officer but I'm pretty sure I can't innovate if I'm wasting away in huddles and structured conversations with rigid agendas.

Cole: If you so much as mumble the words "dilemma protocol" or "wagon-wheel consultancy" I will burst into flame right now.

Neera: That sounds like a lot of effort. Save the flame for another day.

Neera: You know the team enjoys when you spend time on campus.

Cole: The team is a little over 57,000 people and the campus is roughly the size of a Hawaiian island.

Neera: Perhaps the smaller one, yes.

Cole: They don't all enjoy me.

Neera: So, you're still dissatisfied with the organizational shifts. Understandable.

Cole: Dissatisfied isn't the word that comes to mind.

Neera: Understood.

Cole: I'll keep you posted. All right?

Neera: Yes. Please do.

I BLEW out a breath and powered down my phone. My belly was rumbling, and I figured it was time to show my face. I wandered down the seaside home's hallway in search of my host. It was a long, narrow expanse of knotty pine and stone that reeked of family with its wide old hearth and country kitchen. The window over the sink was adorned with little white curtains. Tiny anchors dotted the edges, and though the embroidery's color was long since faded, they hung straight and proud, as if carefully ironed just the other day.

That was the way of this home: old, lived-in, loved.

I expected to find a rosy-cheeked woman rolling out dough for biscuits or some hazel-eyed children, perhaps a Newfoundland pup eager for a belly-scratching.

But I found none of it.

Discovering that I was alone, I helped myself to a banana. It was late in the day—I'd slept long past breakfast and lunch—and I hadn't eaten since early yesterday.

"I see you're alive."

I turned, my mouth stuffed with a chunk of banana, and saw him. A sun-bleached Red Sox cap shielded most of his face. Owen of the gravelly voice and ripped-to-fuck body.

Men like him didn't exist in my world. They just didn't look like this, not even when they worked at it. They were products of CrossFit, "clean" eating, style consultants, image strategists. And Owen couldn't compare to any of that.

Thank God.

He wasn't affected by anything other than his environment, and I figured he liked it that way.

Fuck, *I* liked it that way.

Owen pointed to my face. "Stopped bleeding," he said. "Still looks like hell."

I nodded, gulping down the banana. That left the limp peel pinched between my fingers, and while I should've been focused on disposing of it, I couldn't tear my eyes off Owen. The hair poking out from under his ball cap was dark, nearly black, with a hint of white at the temples. His eyes shone green, and his skin was dark and freckled from endless hours in the sun.

"Yeah, well..." I said, my voice trailing off. I didn't know what to say but I wanted to keep talking with him.

"Do you think you need a doctor?" he asked.

I lifted my hand to my forehead but then realized I was still holding the damn banana peel. "No, no," I said. "It's fine. I'm fine. Everything's fine."

Owen chuckled, and his shoulders lifted along with the deep chest rumbling. "You're sure about that?"

I wasn't sure. I had a business to reclaim and new programming ideas to test, but for the first time since high school, I wanted to slow it all down. I wanted to take a break.

Not the bullshit PR cover-up sabbatical, but a vacation.

In Maine.

With a fisherman who didn't know anything about me.

"Yeah," I replied. "I'm good. Really good."

"Right."

Owen drew his fingertips over the dark scruff on his jawline, and shook his head as he watched me for a long moment. I had no idea what he was thinking, but I wanted to know. I wanted to know everything.

Grumbling under his breath, he crossed the room in long strides and plucked the peel from my hand. He called over his shoulder, "How about I give you that ride down to Bar Harbor now?"

No. *No.* This was crazy. Even if he looked like rough-palmed sex, he was straight. Probably. Maybe. Aw fuck, I couldn't tell. The longer I thought about it, the easier it was to convince myself that he was gay and a huge, husky gift to me from the sea. From Poseidon himself. But it wasn't like I had enough game to make anything happen. I'd earned my born-again virgin chip some time ago.

"I'm trying to keep a low profile," I started. He was in front of me again. Close enough to touch. Definitely close enough to pick up the scent of salty air and sunscreen. *Oh, Jesus, take me now.* "Is there any chance you'd rent that room?"

Owen crossed his arms over his chest, and the grim line of his mouth turned firm.

"There's what—five, six more weeks until the end of summer? What would that run? About thirty grand?" I fumbled for my wallet, knowing I had cash in there. "I don't have it all, but here's a couple hundred, a decent deposit."

At that, Owen laughed. It was a startled, uncomfortable sound. I wasn't making a great case for myself, what with me waving a fistful of cash around. I was desperate, and that much was obvious.

"More?" I asked. "That's not a problem. What's the going rate in this region? Whatever it is, I'll triple it. I don't want to take advantage."

I knew summer shares weren't cheap. I'd buy the whole fucking house—the town—if I could stay here. And stay with him. Even if that was more ill-fated than my attempt at sailing solo. Regardless of whether Owen was as straight as a mainsail and wouldn't give me a second glance, I needed to stop being Cole McClish, boy genius, tech wunderkind, dethroned CEO. Just for a little while.

"Put your money away," Owen warned.

His voice was deep and low, all coarse vibrations that I was hungry to hear against my skin. It was absurd to think he'd reciprocate, but that didn't stop me from wanting. From hoping.

"Look, that came out all wrong. My boat is in bad shape. You saw it. It probably needs a system overhaul before I can get out of the harbor. The replacement parts, they have to be custom ordered from a small supplier in California. They're a niche operation, and let's just say they aren't up to full capacity yet. And I'm going to need some specialized tradespeople who can handle the electrical work. It's a complicated situation," I said, holding my palms out in front of me.

Owen yanked the cap off and ran his hand through his hair. He blew out a breath and tossed the cap on the butcher block countertop. "Are you running from something?" he asked.

"No," I said with a forced laugh.

Most definitely. I'm running from the reality that I'm not meant to manage the day-to-day affairs of the company I founded. I'm running from the failure of my latest project, and the failures of five before that one. I'm running from the fear that I might have lost the vision that launched my career. I'm running from all the mistakes I can't seem to shake. I'm running from the cliché of being a sad, lonely boy billionaire.

"Of course not," I continued.

Owen wasn't buying it. "You're not in trouble with the law?" he asked. "Or...something like that? Crazy ex-wife? Child support?"

I knew it then, with absolute certainty. Whether he liked me or loathed me was a direct response to this stripped down version of myself. My money, my relative fame, my history—none of those factors could cloud his perspective. I had a blank slate.

"No. None of that. Not at all," I said. It sounded believable this time. "I'm taking some time to reevaluate my business and my priorities, and wanted to get off the grid. I'd be doing that right now if my navigation and electrical hadn't shit the bed." I gestured to him, my gaze as honest as I could manage given my lies of omission. "I'm serious about paying you."

Owen looked around, his eyes prowling over every surface in the kitchen save for me. I wasn't sure whether he was debating with himself or evaluating whether I'd fucked up the precise order of things in here. He was a right-angle enthusiast. Everything just so.

"I'm not going to take your money," he said at last. He scrubbed his palm over the back of his neck, and oh what fresh hell was this life. I needed to feel *my* hand on his neck right now. "But I could use some help."

Please say you need help massaging away some knots in your neck, or a charley horse.

"You name it," I said. I was really rooting for that charley horse. Maybe we could get to the bottom of the gay/straight question, or unbox some bi-curious feelings.

"My deckhand leaves for school this week," Owen said. "He goes to the University of New Hampshire. It's early, but he works in the dorms now. Some kind of advisor. He found out about this a few days ago. Or, he *told* me a few days ago. He's a bonehead, so good luck to UNH with him."

I blinked, not sure I understood my place in this story. "You need a deckhand?" I asked eventually.

I knew he worked on the water. Hell, there was a coffee table fashioned from a lobster trap in the other room. An anemometer on the back deck. Framed photos of boats and crews decked out in yellow rain gear lined the hallway walls. Curtains embroidered with anchors. Throw pillows in the shape of seashells. This place was fisherman central.

"Yeah," he replied. "Think you can handle that?"

"I'm better with..." What the fuck did I do well? I was terrible with people, moody as shit, and hated matters of business and finance. I could code, and had the personal phone numbers of several other billionaires who alternately wanted to kill me and commiserate with me. "Technical things."

His eyebrows arched. "You had a tough time with the technical things on that boat of yours."

"Ah, yeah," I said, rubbing my temples. "Different kind of technical."

"Decking isn't hard. You'll learn," Owen said. His gaze landed on me for a long beat, and I would've fidgeted under his watch if I hadn't enjoyed it so much.

Fuck yeah, I'll learn.

"How about a steak?" He moved to the refrigerator and then the pantry, piling food and dishes in the crook of his thick arm as he went.

Soon he had the materials laid out on the counter in neat rows. All right angles. I wanted to ask how often he cooked for two, whether there was someone special in his life. This wasn't a bachelor pad. It was a *home*, a place soaked with family, comfort, tradition. The idea of Owen living here by himself filled me with sorrow. He didn't even have a dog to keep him company.

Maybe there was someone, and he saw no reason to share that information with me right now. Fair enough. It wasn't as though I was being transparent about my life either.

"Why won't you let me give you any money?" I asked from the opposite side of the kitchen island.

Owen was busy seasoning the meat, and didn't look up when he spoke. "It's not necessary," he said. "If you really need to get rid of thirty grand, give it to the Maine Lobster Conservancy."

"Is that what you fish?" I asked. Watching Owen prepare food was like ballet, but instead of the dancer and *Swan Lake*, it was a hot fisherman and red meat. Breathtaking. "Lobster?"

He nodded, and pointed his elbow toward the romaine lettuce. "Can you manage a salad? Are you as reckless with kitchen knives as you are with shotguns?"

I sighed as I reached for the cutting board and salad bowl. I wasn't living that one down any time soon. "Since we've established you're not a pirate, I'll be fine."

"Arrrrr," he barked in a stunningly bad pirate voice. I wedged in beside him at the counter and chopped the lettuce. "Ye can't be sure."

4

———————

SPINDRIFT

n. Spray blown from the crests of waves by the wind.

Cole

"SO, AH, IT'S COLE," Owen started, "right?"

I set the plates on the table and glanced up at him. "Yeah," I said, a whip of defensiveness in my words. There was no reason for it, other than my harebrained attempt at pretending to be anyone but myself.

Owen placed the salad bowl on the center of the table and pulled large wooden spoons from his back pocket. He'd tucked them there when we'd gathered the dishes and cutlery in the kitchen before transporting everything to the porch. "Just Cole? Like Cher? Or Rihanna?" He peered at me. "I guess you could make that work."

He sat at a small, weathered table, and I followed. My last name was stuck in my throat, thick and paralyzing like a mouthful of too hot coffee. The miserable part was that the coffee had to go somewhere—I had to swallow or spit—even if both options were equally unpleasant.

"McClish," I said quickly. It was more of a croak, a rough, guttural sound that I'd never be able to intentionally re-create.

Owen nodded, and busied himself with dressing the salad. I braced for the impact of recognition, the ten-second delay in which he'd put the pieces together and wonder aloud where he'd heard that name before. And then I'd be screwed.

"All right then, Cole McClish," Owen said as he heaped servings of salad, potato, and steak on our plates. He waved at me, an indication that I should eat. "This is a nice salad. Pretty spiffy how you cut those cucumbers."

"Yeah," I mumbled, staring at a forkful of lettuce and tomato. "Glad you like it."

Owen bobbed his head as he chewed. "Mmhmm."

He didn't offer another word. Not even a murmur. He really, *really* didn't know me. I couldn't believe that I had this incredible gift, this moment to be the version of myself that I wanted instead of the one I'd become, and I was experiencing it with a man too fascinating and desirable to be real. A breath whooshed past my lips, fast and ragged like I'd taken a kick to the chest. I covered it up with an exaggerated cough, and then dug into my dinner.

I worked hard at keeping my gaze trained on my plate as I didn't want to stare at my host. I mean, I *wanted* to stare and there was a whole lot of goodness to stare at, but I was still treading water here. I didn't know Owen and—as I'd discovered—he didn't know me, and that meant I had to exercise some of those manners Neera beat into me.

"Beautiful, isn't it?" Owen asked, shaking me from my thoughts.

"Yes," I agreed automatically. I'd been staring at the crescent-shaped cove without seeing, my thoughts deep in debate over whether he hauled in those lobster traps shirtless. God, I hoped so.

"I don't have a lot of material requirements," he continued, "but I don't think I could live here without a porch." He pointed his beer bottle at the floor-to-ceiling screens that separated the deck from the elements. "You just can't appreciate this view from indoors."

I wiped my hands on a napkin and tucked it beside my plate. "How long have you lived here?"

Owen sipped his beer, his head moving from side to side as if he was digging back through memories to find the start of his life in this remote corner of the world.

"A little more than fifteen years now," he said. He leaned out of his chair, jerking his chin in the direction of the slim lighthouse nestled into the high point of the cove. "One family maintained the lighthouse for almost two hundred years. The DaSilvas. They worked on the water, of course. But the younger generation wasn't interested in the upkeep. Didn't want to get involved with lobstering either." He rubbed his chin, pausing for a beat. Owen stared at the rocky cove as he spoke, and his words cooled with a bit of melancholy. "I know it's not for everyone, but it's not right for traditions to die out like that."

"Is lobstering a family tradition for you?" I asked.

"No, not my family, but I seem to think anyone who has lived on these shores has a bit of it in their bones," Owen said.

I nodded though I didn't understand his logic. The world wasn't composed of people who felt compelled to follow their parents' footsteps anymore. There was no occupation-via-birthright.

"My mom was a high school guidance counselor before she retired. My dad worked in logging before he lost his hand," he continued. He offered a half smile with that tidbit, and I had to fight back an uncomfortable laugh. "Everyone who works in logging long enough loses something. Thankfully, it wasn't his head."

"I can understand why you wouldn't follow in his footsteps," I said. "The desire to keep your limbs and all. How did you get into lobstering then?"

"I bought this land, and the boat, from the last lobsterman in the DaSilva family," Owen said. "He took me on as a summer deckhand when I was twelve, and taught me everything." He met my gaze. "It's important work. Most people don't think much of it, but it's important to care for the sea." He gestured to the lighthouse again. "Times might change, but some things should remain the same."

"And it's only you here?" I asked, tempting him to tell me there was more to his life than lobsters and screened-in porches. He nodded. "For the past fifteen *years*? That's insanity. I'd lose my fucking mind if I was alone this much. Do the walls respond when you talk to them, or is the conversation one-sided?"

"I like it that way," he said, each word rougher than the one before. "I enjoy being alone." He stared at me, his eyes narrowed in warning. "I prefer quiet. I hope that's not a problem for you."

I bobbed my head, in agreement or acceptance or some acknowledgement that I wasn't to question Owen's life choices any further. I was the guest here, and if I wanted to stay a guest, I'd shut the fuck up.

So much for those manners.

"The work on your vessel," he started, his voice low and heavy, "it will take weeks? Or months?"

Thanks to the kindness of the harbormaster, my boat was docked in Talbott's Cove's marina. Despite my willingness to pay above the market rate for his trouble, he rented the slip for pennies. I didn't understand this town or these people.

"Weeks," I replied, but quickly thought better of it. I was forever overcommitting on outcomes, underestimating timelines. "Although that depends on a few factors. It won't take too long to get the parts, and I think I can do some of the work myself—" Owen snorted. It was as if he knew I had a history of overpromising, too. "I'll have to hire contractors for the electrical system. There's no telling how long that could take."

Owen looked out at the water, nodding slowly. "All right."

After that, we ate in silence, the only sounds coming from waves lapping against the shore and beetles hissing as they doddled around the exterior lights. We cleared the table, and then washed and dried the dishes without sharing a single word. Once the kitchen was tidy—and right angled—Owen headed to the porch, book in hand.

He stopped at the door, his head turned in my direction but his eyes cast down. Avoiding me. "We hit the water before sunrise," he said. "Four fifteen. Be ready."

With that, the door snapped shut behind him. The message was clear: I wasn't to follow.

I heeded that message, but I also lurked in the kitchen. The view from the window over the sink allowed me to watch as Owen settled into a chair, swept his gaze over the horizon, and thumbed open his book.

So many contradictions in one man. He craved solitude but offered me—a stranger as strange as they came—a temporary home. He grunted and growled as his primary means of communication but stocked his bookshelves with great works of literature *and* read them. He believed in tradition but didn't seem concerned with passing his on to another generation.

I studied him for several minutes, and debated joining him out there. But I knew that urge was selfish—I wanted to be close to him. Figure him out. Crawl inside his mind. Then, crawl into his lap.

Instead, I returned to the room where I'd slept last night. I closed the door behind me and pivoted in a slow circle, taking in the red, white, and blue quilt, whitewashed pine walls, and rustic chest of drawers.

I wasn't special here. I wasn't gifted or talented, or remarkable in any way save for my ability to fuck things up. Part of me wanted to leave. Order a private plane to the nearest airstrip and get the fuck out of this small town before Owen realized he was better off without a roommate.

But another part—a bigger, hungrier part—wanted to stay. To be here and be no one in particular. To live like a regular person.

I stripped down to my boxer briefs and slipped between the sheets. I needed to rest up if I was going to work on a lobster boat first thing tomorrow.

5

RED-TO-RED

adv. The condition in which two sea-going ships travelling in opposite directions pass each other on their port sides

OWEN

COLE DIDN'T KNOW the first thing about fishing.

That was obvious when I found him inspecting my traps before sunrise this morning. He'd opened and closed them, studying the mechanism like he'd never encountered anything like it, or he thought I'd be quizzing him later.

I couldn't understand why someone who didn't know fishing or boating would set out on a solitary sailing journey. The fact that he hadn't crashed that boat of his into any underwater rock formations or another vessel was nothing short of miraculous. And he'd been out there all alone. None of it made sense to me. I didn't know what he did for a living—he'd said he owned a firm that was "in tech" and left it at that, though he indicated he had enough flexibility to take an extended summer vacation.

Must be nice.

I'd watched him from the house, leaning against the kitchen sink while sipping coffee. Barely two days had passed and I was in over my head with this man. Never mind the fact that everything inside me ached when I was around him, but he pushed me. He found my soft spots and zeroed right in.

Maybe it only seemed that way. Maybe I was overly sensitive after Cole's comments about my life of sea and solitude. And maybe I was drowning in my own needy, hungry hormones.

I'd tucked that thought away, right along with the erection throbbing behind my zipper, and went to work. I knew what I was doing when I was out on the water, and not even the presence of this beautiful man and his questions could shake my focus.

But then he fell overboard.

"I sure as shit hope you're better at those technical things," I said as I reached out to grab his hand. How he'd fallen was a mystery to me. All I knew was that he was on the deck one minute and in the water the next.

"I am," he snapped as he gained his footing on the deck. He bent at the waist, his hands propped on his knees, and took several ragged breaths.

I fisted my hands to keep from touching him. I didn't know what else to do with myself. I wanted to skim my fingers down his chest, feel the rasp of his scruffy jaw against my palm, brush the salt water from his skin, strip away his soggy clothes. "What the hell happened? Do you need to wear a life vest? You know, you seem to have a lot of accidents."

Cole gestured to the horizon. "It's choppy out here," he said. "I lost my balance when you pulled to the left."

The breeze was stirring up some whitecaps, but they were wimpy. "Just wait until hurricane season hits," I said with a laugh. "You'll understand *choppy* then."

"Fantastic," Cole grumbled. He looked down at his soaked shirt, another slim-fitting polo with an alligator over his heart, and shook his head. Then, because the deities loved and hated me in equal measures, he peeled off the offending shirt.

Fuck me.

All the humor in my body dried up and blew away. *Poof.* Gone. In its place—and the place of every other emotion I could summon—was desire. Stick-to-your-ribs, prickle-the-back-of-your-neck, hot-and-sweaty-all-over, headboard-banging desire.

Cole stood there, his legs braced and his chest bare, and wrung the ocean from his shirt while I watched. In all honesty, I was gaping. It was rude and gratuitous, and I had a schedule to keep, but I couldn't stop myself.

He was blond and golden in a way that reminded me of Zack Morris, *Endless Summer* movies, and The Beach Boys. Freckles dotted his shoulders. There was a thick patch of hair on his chest, and a fuzzy trail running between his washboard abs. His shorts were dripping wet and plastered to his legs, and my chest swelled at the giddy hope he'd take those off too.

"Any chance you have an extra shirt lying around?" Cole asked, meeting my gaze. "I realize that I've demanded quite of a bit of your hospitality, what with requiring another rescue on top of everything else, but I'd be extremely appreciative."

I blinked at him. Twice. Gulped, and then cleared my throat. "What?" I asked.

Cole swept his hand down his torso. "My shirt is wet," he said, careful to enunciate each syllable. "Do you have one I could borrow?"

A growl unfurled in my throat. "What about your shorts? Those are wet, too."

He glanced down, shrugging. "An astute observation, Owen. But I didn't figure you'd have an entire wardrobe on board," he replied.

My previous deckhand, the college kid, didn't talk much. He knew the routine and did his job with limited commentary, and we both enjoyed that approach. He had his big-ass headphones and a steady stream of whatever the kids were listening to these days, and I had the waves, the wind, the radio. It worked for us. It worked for *me*.

But now I had Cole, and he came with an endless supply of questions —he wanted to know every little thing about lobsters, fishing, boats, oceans, tides, and Maine—and chatter. All these quips and smartass comments flew at me like a swarm of greenheads in July, and I couldn't keep up because I was busy imagining the taste of his skin.

And praying that he was gay. Hell, I'd be happy with bisexual. I'd scrub the memories of all those pretty young bi boys I'd met in Bar Harbor and Kennebunkport over the years. The ones who sucked cock like they'd declared it their major. The ones who preferred to sneak around because their parents wouldn't understand. The ones who only wanted to play in secret, the ones who led straight lives, the ones who were all for equality but refused to see themselves in the Pride flag. The ones who always went back to Yale or Penn, and their girlfriends, come September. The ones who returned summers later for their posh, picturesque weddings to those same Ivy League girlfriends. The ones who taught me to stick with one-night stands and no last names because my heart was too tender for anything real.

Yeah, I'd forget all the promises I'd made myself.

And it wasn't about being bi or pan or any other identity. It was about the shame that came with being a summer vacation secret. If Cole was any shade of queer, I'd be all over him. I'd be his.

When I didn't respond, Cole continued. "No sweat. I'm SPF'd. I can go without a shirt," he said, clapping his hands together.

I finally found my words, and they were harsh and low. "We have a schedule to keep," I said. "And we could do with less drama, McClish."

He held his hands out and quirked his brows up as if to say *Who, me?* He was cute when he wasn't busy wielding a shotgun or indulging his quarter-life crisis. He was charming in a half-smiling, eye-twinkling, chatty-Chad way. If I didn't keep my jaw clenched and my words to myself, there was no telling what would happen.

No, that wasn't true. Inaccurate. Erroneous. Completely false.

I knew what would happen. I'd laugh. Smile. Maybe even blush. I'd bend to Cole's light like a tulip to the sun, and for a few blessed moments, everything would be perfect.

But it wouldn't last. None of this would last, and it didn't matter that I had no idea what *this* was.

Cole crossed the deck and collected the hook-headed pole used to grab hold of the trap lines. He turned, the warm sunlight celebrating every line and curve on his chest, and a noise slipped from my lips. I couldn't hear much over the pulse pounding in my head but it sounded like *Ohhh-mmm-ahhh.*

"I'll grab this one," he called. He leaned over the edge of the boat, his taut body stretching as he yanked the buoy closer. It was a thing of beauty, and it would have been a glorious moment if Cole wasn't seconds away from taking another dip in the ocean. He still didn't understand how to keep himself balanced against the weight of water.

I raced to his side but it was already too late. He lost his leverage and pitched overboard trying to regain it.

"Fuck me," I muttered under my breath.

Cole swam to the surface and shook the water from his hair. "I don't know what happened there," he said.

He looked up at me with bright eyes as if he was unaware that he'd upended my life in the short days since his arrival. As if he could take a header into the water—twice—without me wanting to spank and then swaddle him. As if he didn't know I'd spent the past two nights squeezing my eyes shut and forcing my brain to focus on anyone but him while bringing myself to silent, unsatisfying orgasms. As if I could survive this newfound companionship without coming apart at the seams.

"I don't know how any of this happened," I said through a sigh.

6

ARC OF VISIBILITY

n. The portion of the horizon over which a lighted aid to navigation is visible from seaward.

Cole

THIS TOWN—IF you could call the tiny collection of homes, boats, and roads that—was charming. Small and storybook quaint, and humble. The people here were decent, honest, salt of the earth. All the things snotty dickheads like me said about people who lived simply and worked the land and sea.

And no one gave a shit about me. At least that was how I was interpreting the reception I'd received in the past few days. The folks in town were curious about Owen's houseguest, sure, but they were more interested in my boat than my origins or identity. The sailors and fishermen in the area wanted the lowdown on my vessel, and they accepted me without qualification.

I couldn't decide whether I'd overestimated my celebrity or underestimated the allure of a beautifully crafted sailboat. It had to be some combination of both.

That, and the realization that Silicon Valley was a weird little jungle gym composed of ambition and backstabbing, gossip, and crazy wild money. We in the Valley—and sometimes, California as a whole—liked to believe we had it right. We knew the way, and everyone else just had to hurry the hell up. But living in Talbott's Cove and working the decks forced me to reconsider all that. I was beginning to believe that this was right, and the Valley was missing out on something essential.

It was a learning experience, this past week with Owen. We were both particular, but Owen erred on the side of anal retentive perfectionism, and I didn't understand that shit. I was a night owl, and I figured a lifetime on the water had formed Owen into an early bird. He was a Red Sox fan, and—apparently—I was wrong.

But it was a good week. *Great* week. I learned things I'd never considered—separating lobsters based on size and sales channel, tying knots for every conceivable purpose, maintaining a lighthouse—and basked in the warmth of Owen's approval every time I got it right. He was an antisocial grump to be sure, but that didn't make him any less of a good man. And he was *good*.

When finished hauling in his lobsters for the day, Owen turned his attention to fishing tuna, haddock, cod. He sold some directly to restaurants along the coast, but he delivered most of it to a farm-to-table co-op program that distributed fresh fish to nursing homes, veterans' hospitals, and public schools. He was a member of the Talbott's Cove town council because—according to Owen—he wasn't going to let some yahoos take over.

The guy practiced what he preached, and there was something about that—about being a man who I could respect and admire—I found devastatingly sexy. I had to drag my gaze away from his thick, powerful arms every time he pulled a trap up from under the sea. Or when he planted his feet wide on the deck, his shoulders tight and his long stare traveling over the water like he was a ruler appraising his kingdom.

Owen was strong and sure, and I wanted him. In every possible way.

If I was even half as strong or sure as Owen, I would've told him I was attracted to him. I would've told him I wanted to kneel at his feet and rub my cheek on his thighs, and beg for the privilege of serving him.

But I wasn't, and I didn't.

I rationalized it all away as fear of wrecking the good things I had going here, but that wasn't it. I was afraid of rejection. *His* rejection. I preferred to be the one who did the rejecting—as fucked up and shallow as that was—and I didn't know how to make the first move.

Oh, I thought about those first moves. Thought about them all the fucking time.

The old stretch-an-arm-around-the-shoulder bit while watching television. Some flirty dinnertime chatter about how he liked his meat. Another fall overboard—intentional this time—and another excuse to peel off my shirt.

I mentally choreographed every one of those moves, but never executed any of them. The rejection would kill me, and kill this idyllic break from my reality. Instead, I followed Owen everywhere he went. Less lost dog, more cat in quiet heat. It was painful, all this self-denial, but Owen declining my advances would hurt more.

The worst part was the ticking clock. The knowledge that my time in Talbott's Cove was limited. Work on my boat was slow and spendy, but it would end right along with the summer. Not that I brought up my departure, and Owen didn't ask.

Neera: Any update on your expected return date?
Cole: Not that I have planned, no. I believe I was instructed to take the summer. My understanding of meteorological summer is that it ends on September 1. If we're talking astronomical summer, it ends on September 22.
Cole: Thusly I won't consider a return until sometime between or after those dates.
Neera: Are you still on the Atlantic?
Cole: Is my name still on the masthead as founder?
Neera: I sincerely hope that isn't a serious question.
Cole: Wasn't sure how quickly things would change.
Neera: You're exceptionally argumentative.
Cole: If that's what you want to call it, fine, but I'm just doing what you

recommended. I'm out of the picture, not making noise or starting problems, and I'm not interfering with my replacement.

Cole: I can't see how that's problematic.

Neera: It's not. I only wanted to get a sense of your timing so I could best support your return.

Cole: I'm working on something new. I don't want to talk about it yet but I'll keep you looped in when I have something to share.

Cole: Does that work?

Neera: I'll make it work.

SLACK TIDE

n. A short period when the water is completely unstressed and there is no movement in the tidal stream, before the direction of the tide reverses.

Cole

"MAY I JOIN YOU?" I asked, leaning through the doorway to the porch.

Owen was kicked back in his chair, a book in his lap and a tumbler of whiskey by his side. If there wasn't an interesting ball game to watch after dinner, Owen often settled on the porch and I holed up in my room. I'd made good progress with a handful of new ideas I was testing out, but I was climbing the walls tonight.

I didn't mind the routine we had going here—awake before dawn, on the water all morning, fish markets followed by work fixing up my boat in the afternoon, dinner around sunset, bed shortly after—but I needed something more tonight. Back in California, most of my days were spent talking. Taking calls, sitting in meetings, hearing from my coders, arguing with my board. There was always someone or something that required my attention, and being here with Owen was still strangely quiet for my tastes.

Gesturing to the open seat beside him, Owen said, "Yes, but I have some conditions."

I stepped onto the porch, thankful for the slight drop in temperature from the heart of the house. The air was still heavy and thick, the day's heat and humidity continuing long after sunset. Only the slightest breezes blew in off the water, and they were laced with the pungence of seaweed and marsh.

"Anything," I said, dropping into the open rocking chair. Before coming to Talbott's Cove, I would've ascribed rocking chairs to grandmothers and nurseries, and nothing much else. But these were just right.

"No questions," Owen said. I bit back a groan at that. "You've asked all the questions necessary, and I need a break." I opened my mouth to reply, but he held up his hand. "No. No, this isn't an opportunity to ask why. Just live with it."

"I'll try," I said, rocking back in the chair. I could see why Owen enjoyed this. It was just like being on the water. "It would be really terrible if I died of curiosity though."

Owen snarled and set his book on the table beside him. "How would that even happen, McClish?"

I held out my hands, shrugging. "I can think of a number of ways," I started, "but I'll keep them to myself. I don't want to bother you."

He hissed out a breath and I was convinced he grumbled, "Oh, for fuck's sake."

I had to suck my lips between my teeth and bite down to keep from laughing. "We don't need to talk," I said. "We've got the ocean and the stars, and there's no need to talk. This is great. You do you, Bartlett."

I glanced over at him. He was sighing and grumbling as if I was causing him physical discomfort. At least he couldn't turn himself on with those sounds. I did not possess the same immunity. With my hands folded over my crotch as casually as I could manage, I gazed out over the water and focused on identifying all the constellations I could find. It was good, distracting work, and it would've kept me distracted if not for Owen's huffing and snarling.

Such a moody one, this Owen Bartlett.

"All right," he said, finally breaking free of his sigh-a-thon. "How would one *die* of curiosity?"

"Marie Curie comes to mind," I mused. I leaned forward, my arms braced on my thighs, and studied the Japanese beetles congregating on the screens. The yellow glow of the porch's overhead light attracted them, but the screens held them off. They were small, pea-sized, but their low hiss called to mind the sound of old-fashioned dial-up. I imagined they were sweltering, too.

"How do you figure?" Owen snapped. "She discovered radium."

"Oh, yes, and polonium," I agreed. "It killed her."

He reached for his whiskey and took a hearty gulp. "Right. You're not discovering new elements tonight."

"And the cat." I sat back, nodded toward him.

The lighthouse blinked on the far end of the cove, the brightness illuminating his features. My fingers ached to trace the scruffy line of his jaw, stroke my thumb over his cheeks, scratch my nails along his scalp. My skin was flushed from the unrelenting heat but now I was *hot*. Hungry, too.

Owen waved his glass in front of him. "What cat?"

He was getting riled up, and I loved that shit. A few days ago, I pretended I didn't know the difference between flat head and Phillips head screwdrivers for the simple pleasure of his exaggerated reaction.

"The one killed by curiosity," I replied. "*That* cat. Poor bastard."

Owen sighed as he shook his head, but it morphed into a chuckle. Soon, his shoulders were shaking as he laughed. I laughed too. I couldn't help it. The deep, full-bodied sound was contagious.

"I don't know about you, McClish," he said as he patted his belly. "I just don't know."

"What do you want to know?" I asked.

We hadn't ventured into the realm of discussing more than the basics of my life, and that was good enough for me. Owen knew I owned a technology firm—didn't think it was necessary to mention that it was the biggest one in the world—and I lived in California. The rest of it was just details, and I couldn't find a reason to share them with Owen. It wasn't that he wouldn't care or wasn't interested, but that I didn't want to spend all of our time talking about me. He and this quaint town were the most interesting things I'd ever encountered, and I wanted to soak up all of it.

He considered his whiskey for a moment before saying, "You're from California? That's where you grew up?" He sipped, and then shot me a sharp glance. "It would explain a lot."

He didn't look at me long, and that was fair. I wasn't much to look at. Bruised, swollen, blood dried black around the laceration. I rarely indulged in vanity but I wasn't accustomed to being hideous.

"I am," I said carefully. I longed for a drink to occupy my mouth and hands. I hadn't thought that far ahead before venturing out here. "But—I mean—not the California most people associate with California."

Owen regarded me over his glass, an eyebrow bent. "There are multiple Californias?"

I murmured in agreement. "Northern and Southern," I said. "But there's more to it than that. It's a collection of ecosystems more complex than anything contained within conventional notions of statehood." Both of Owen's eyebrows were arching up into his hairline now. "When people think of California, they think of Los Angeles and San Diego. Surfing, beaches, girls roller-skating in bikinis. But that's not the whole story. You have the South Coast but also the North and Central Coasts. There's the Sacramento Valley, the San Joaquin Valley, and *The* Valley. There's the Cascades, the Sierras, and the Inland Empire. And then there are the big cities. Bay Area, Los Angeles, and San Diego."

"That was an extremely long way of telling me that California is a big place," he said. "This is why you're not allowed to talk."

I leaned toward him and rapped my knuckles on the arm of his chair. "I forgot about Orange County. Add that to the list."

"Is that where you live?" Owen asked. "Or where you're from?"

He grabbed the front of his t-shirt and fanned himself with the fabric. I thought about inviting him to take it off. Strip down. If that didn't offer enough relief, we could wade into the water and hold each other under the ripe moonlight and...*ahhhh*. I went from zero to pervert in three seconds flat.

I bobbled my head, trying to shake that idea loose. "No and no," I said, laughing to stifle a growl of desire. "Like I said, people associate California with beaches and bikinis, but that's not how it is for everyone. I grew up about three hours east of San Diego, right along the Colorado

River and the Arizona border. It's hot and dry and mostly flat, and the only kind of trouble you can get into out there is stupid trouble."

"You speak from experience," Owen said. "Nearly running your boat aground isn't your first brush with being a damn fool, I take it."

Why did I enjoy this man's insults so much? I couldn't explain it, but I wanted him to keep going. Pick apart my privilege-soaked preferences and deride my expensive polo shirts. Tear down my quirky-for-the-sake-of-wonky mannerisms. Strip it all away.

"If you're asking whether I hacked into Agua Fria High's student information system and deleted all of my unexcused absences from skipping ninety percent of my calculus classes—" I held up my hands and then let them fall. "Then, yes, I might've found myself in a bit of trouble."

"Of course," Owen muttered.

"But I'll have you know," I added, "I only got caught because I took the final exam. The teacher didn't recognize me. I should've skipped that too, and then hacked back into the SIS to give myself a grade. Should've. Didn't. Me and my goddamn morals."

Owen stared at me for a long moment, his eyes narrowed and his brow crinkled. "Are there any consequences in your world, McClish?"

"There are," I said, breaking away from his gaze. "There are definitely consequences." I cleared my throat as I sneaked a glance at him. His attention was on the stars now. "Anyway, I live in Palo Alto."

"Which is in the Bay Area," Owen supplied. "Near San Francisco."

"Right," I said. "My sisters are all over the place. One in Denver, the other outside Baltimore. My mom lives in Palm Springs now. I tried convincing her to check out Balboa Island or Marina del Rey, but she prefers the inescapable heat. I only visit her in the winter. I can't deal with summer in the desert. I feel like I'm trapped in a dehydrator and turning into beef jerky."

"You'd make for some fine jerky," Owen said, laughing.

"As would you, Bartlett," I replied. There was no humor in my tone, but I couldn't hold back the smile.

"I'd gnaw on you," he continued, eyeing my torso.

My heart was in my throat, thumping fast as I tried to breathe, swallow, think.

What the actual fuck was happening here? Was he...hitting on me?

No. Of course not. This was an awkward bit of humor gone astray, not a revelatory moment where we simultaneously flashed our queer cards.

Or maybe it was exactly that moment.

"I'm not a piece of jagged, dried-out meat," I said indignantly. "I'm tender, juicy meat."

Nothing ventured, nothing gained.

"Yeah, you are. You're some fine cut of meat." Owen barked out a startled laugh and pushed to his feet. "Whoa. Okay. Now I know I'm drunk," he said. "Get some sleep, McClish. Another early day is coming our way."

I nodded and babbled something in response, but I couldn't stop hearing his words in my head. *I'd gnaw on you.* It wasn't clear what I'd gained there, but I was satisfied with the venture.

8

———————————

BETWEEN WATER AND WIND

n. The part of the ship's hull that is sometimes submerged and sometimes above water by the rolling of the vessel.

OWEN

I CAN'T KEEP this up for much longer. Something has to give.

That was what I was telling myself as I stomped around the deck and growled at the sunny sky. The sky hadn't offended me in any notable way but I was in a mood. The kind of mood that could turn milk sour and burn holes in the rug without much effort. The kind of mood born from telling Cole I wanted a taste of him and then going to bed needy and alone.

But then it got worse when I saw him reeling in a trap, and leaning too far over the starboard side while he did it.

Please, Jesus, don't let him fall in. I don't possess the strength for his bare chest today.

"Keep your feet planted, McClish," I called, jerking my chin toward the starboard side buoys. The sun was high overhead, and only here, miles from the shore, did the breeze extinguish August's humidity. "If you go for a swim, you're dragging your ass out of the water this time."

"Would you shut the fuck up?" Cole replied. "I got it."

I tossed several more traps into the water while Cole wrestled one up. The first time he'd hoisted up a trap filled with live lobsters by himself, he'd fumbled it back into the water with an uncomfortable howl. Today, he was better. He knew what to expect this time, and he didn't flinch when reaching in to sort the sellable lobsters from the ones who deserved more time under the sea.

He looked better, too. The bruising on his face had cooled to a sickly yellow-green shade, and he seemed relaxed. That first night, when his boat was stalled in the cove, probably wasn't the standard by which to judge Cole McClish, but the hard work and hot sun were doing him good. I could tell, and I couldn't help but look every chance I got.

After some time in Cole's company, I'd learned a few things about the curious stranger who'd drifted into my cove. He couldn't fish worth shit but I'd admit he wasn't the worst sailor. He just ignored his instincts in favor of the nav systems and sonar. It was as if he trusted the machines more than he trusted himself. We couldn't be more different in that respect. To me, the machines were unreliable. They were bound to fail, and they'd fail when I needed them the most. I didn't want to put my faith in anything I couldn't trust completely.

He also talked all goddamn day, and his approach to tidiness was distinctly untidy. It was a damn good thing he was hotter than the sun itself because there'd be no surviving his chaos otherwise.

He was avoiding something or someone but I didn't want to know. I wasn't asking any more personal questions. I cared but I couldn't go there again. I couldn't discover that he had a woman or a family out west, or even a home to which he was eager to return. I could only manage Cole the stranger, void of context or complications. Or cute stories about his hatred of desert climates.

When he set another trap and dropped it off the side of the boat without hesitation, my chest surged with pride. He'd learned all that from me.

"You didn't even cry with that one," I said as I traversed the deck. "We'll make a lobsterman out of you yet."

I clapped him on the back at the exact moment as he pivoted toward me, and that left us in an unexpected embrace. His chest was hard against mine and he was breathing heavy and I couldn't move. Wouldn't. Wouldn't for anything.

My hand continued patting his shoulder. How could I stop? How could I push him away when the only thing I truly wanted was to feel his skin under mine?

Cole's fingers were curled around my forearm as if he was bracing himself, but instead of maintaining a polite distance, he leaned into me. His shoulder was on my chest and his breath was on my neck, and *I want you more than I've ever wanted anyone* was on my tongue.

Neither of us made a move to break away for a long, confusing beat that twisted with more heat and affection than I could handle without embarrassing myself right now. He smelled good, like sunscreen and sweat. I wanted to memorize that scent, and everything else about the way we fit together.

I didn't want that to *mean* something, but it did. It meant everything to me.

Clearing my throat, I eventually drew my hand back and gazed at the water. "Need to make some deliveries up the coast," I said, still watching the waves as I stepped away from him. I wasn't ready to look at Cole, and I didn't. I returned to the controls without a backward glance because I couldn't trust myself to meet his eyes without revealing the depth of my desire for him. "Go put that catch on ice."

"THIS IS AN EXCELLENT BURGER," Cole said. "The last time I had a burger, it was made of mushrooms, lentils, and pumpkin seeds."

"That's a crime," I replied. "Tell me who did that to you. I'll make him pay."

Cole chuckled around another bite. "Plant-based eating is increasingly popular in my world," he said. "I'd forgotten that meat is delicious. I'm getting really spoiled here. And fat."

He patted the blue polo shirt over his flat belly, the one I'd seen bare too many times to forget. The afternoon sun was scorching, and once the day's catch was out of pinching range, he peeled those shirts right off. He was golden and sculpted, and I only allowed myself brief glances.

"You've been kind to let me stay here, Owen," he said. He shrugged, kicking the emotion out of this moment. "Much more of this home cooking and good conversation, and you're going to ruin your reputation as a pirate."

"Fuck off, McClish," I murmured.

A smile pulled at my lips. This companionship *was* nice. The domesticity, too. Looking after someone fed an urge that I'd otherwise ignored, and there were moments when caring for Cole satisfied me more than anything I could imagine between the sheets. I liked our dinners on the porch together, even his nonstop questions and chatter. We often sat out here long after the meal was over, drinking beer and admiring sunsets. I didn't mind that our evenings put me behind on my reading, even if I told my houseguest otherwise. Whitman could wait. Thoreau, too.

Cole tipped his beer bottle to his lips and shot an anxious glance at me. "You know...you don't have to wait on me. I won't get into trouble around here." He turned his attention to the cove before continuing. "I'm sure you have friends. A girlfriend, or you know, someone you like to spend time with. You don't have to put your life on hold because I'm hanging out at your place."

I reached into the ice chest between us and grabbed two more longnecks. It wouldn't be Maine if you didn't have beer available indoors and out.

"I'm still worried that you're going to accidentally shoot yourself," I said, knocking the bottle caps off. Another mouthful of cold beer washed down my internal debate. I wasn't ashamed of myself, and while I didn't hide my sexual orientation, it wasn't something I offered up. I favored gay bars, Pride events, situations where it was implied. Where I didn't have to hide. Where I was with my people, my family. Not my blood relations, but my true family.

Even after more than twenty years of comfort in my queer skin, I didn't savor coming-out conversations. But I'd done basically that this afternoon, with that hug. I was still feeling every spot where his body had connected with mine. There was no mistaking the heat between us, and I couldn't be the only one feeling it.

Here goes nothing. "No girlfriends. I'm not interested in women."

Cole cocked his head to the side as if he'd misheard me. "Does that mean you prefer men?" he asked, his brow furrowed. He looked like a puppy who couldn't find his ball. "Or do you consider yourself asexual? Not that a lack of interest in women is indicative of asexuality. You could identify any number of ways. It's a spectrum."

"I'm gay, if that's what you're asking," I replied.

Cole's mouth fell open as my words registered, but he rapidly schooled his expression. "That's cool," he croaked.

Fuck. Fuck it all.

"Is that going to be a problem for you?" I asked, studying his reaction.

"No," he said.

It was a little too forceful, as if he knew he was walking the line between acceptable responses and honest ones. It would be a real shame if he was a bold-faced homophobe. Couldn't have that. I gave no quarter to the haters.

"No," he repeated, pushing his glasses up his nose. "Not at all. You just caught me by surprise." He threw his hands up, then pressed his fingers to his eyelids. "Shit, that's not the right thing to say. I don't have to prepare myself to respect anyone's sexual orientation. No one should need an adjustment period to accept another human being. It's not like you're telling me you keep a bag of your ex's old hair with you at all times."

"No worries," I said. I meant that. Eventually, there'd be a time when we led with curiosity rather than assumptions about sexual identity, race, faith, ability...all of it. But today wasn't that day, and considering I had a roof over my head, food in my belly, and the sea in my backyard, I could cope with humanity's shortcomings. "Are we good?"

"No—I mean, yes—we're cool. Yes." He scrubbed his hands over his face and then picked up his beer, gazing at the bottle like sweet salvation. "If you're seeing someone, please don't change your routine on my account. You're welcome to bring, ah, him around."

I watched his throat bob as he guzzled his beer, and while I felt better that I'd cleared the air between us, I'd be lying if I said I wasn't disappointed that he didn't offer up his own big gay announcement. That would have improved this conversation considerably. It also would've helped me understand the constant fizz and pop of tension I felt when he was nearby. It would've explained the way my body reacted to his touch today, and his starring role in all of my fantasies.

But this was the way of it for me. I was forever falling for men who had neither the room nor interest in their lives for me, then hating the world for a time. That was why I didn't do *this*. I didn't get to know men, and I didn't bring them home or let them into my world. I kept it clean and easy. A night in the city, a bar or club, a guy I'd never see again. A boozy weekend in Provincetown with a handful of bears who knew what I needed and expected nothing come Monday. It was better when it didn't mean anything to me. When I didn't care.

"I'll keep that in mind," I said, the words rough as I forced them out.

"Come on," he said, gesturing inside. "The game is starting soon, and you're miserable if you miss the first pitch."

I shook my head at that, sweeping away my dark and broody thoughts. "I like to watch the entire game. That doesn't mean I'm miserable if I miss the first pitch," I said. "That you can live on highlights alone means you were dropped on your head as a baby."

"But the games are so long," he whined.

"Baseball is meant to be appreciated in its complete form," I countered. "You need to realize that life shouldn't be condensed down to a couple hundred characters, McClish."

He stopped gathering our plates to glance at me. "Wait. Was that a Twitter reference? I thought you were taking Thoreau's *Walden* approach to life, but you're a down-low Tweep, aren't you?"

Cole extracted a great deal of pleasure from ragging on my low-tech lifestyle. "That sounded like a gay slur, McClish."

"Not even a little bit," he said, laughing as he walked to the kitchen sink. He set the dinner dishes in the basin, stacking them just as I'd instructed. "I'll wash tonight."

"I don't know anything else about Twitter," I confessed, grabbing a dish towel off the oven door handle and slinging it over my shoulder while he filled the sink with water and soap. "I don't understand what all those internet things are about, or why anyone uses them."

"Ultimately, you don't need any of them," Cole said, his hands deep in the soapy water. "It's basically a study in herd behavior."

I accepted the plate he handed me and set to rubbing it dry. "Come again?"

"Yeah," he said, running a scrubbing brush over a handful of forks and knives. "Social media is inherently dehumanizing. Most platforms peel back the artifice of human communication and reduce people down to basic instincts. There's a reason the internet is filled with porn."

"Oh," I murmured. I'd heard that, about the porn, but I was old-fashioned. I liked my dirty DVDs, and the adult toy store I frequented in Portland had a hearty supply. "That's interesting."

"People on Twitter are like cats," Cole continued. "They knock shit over because why the fuck not?"

"Seems like a great use of time," I replied.

"People on Facebook are dogs at the dog park. They're running around in circles, looking for belly rubs, and barking when they're happy, sad, angry, and confused." He handed me another plate. "People on Tumblr are raccoons. They only come out when it's dark and they love trash. There are a few on Reddit, and they're toads. They make a lot of noise and then disappear when someone wants to interact with them on a meaningful level. And the people on Instagram, they're squirrels. They love shiny things and never stop fidgeting."

"Fascinating," I said. I dried another plate and then got to work with the utensils. "You're saying there's nothing good about any of it? It's all terrible people and toxic behavior?"

"No, of course not," Cole said. He was scrubbing the sink now, and he was only doing that because I'd given him a hard time about leaving the basin dirty a few nights ago. He hadn't noticed the bits of potato or salad dressing residue, but that shit annoyed the hell out of me. "People find each other, despite geographic distance and social factors that would've otherwise kept them apart. There are communities of support and affinity, groups mobilizing for important causes, and collaboration that would've never been possible before internet access flattened and condensed the world. There are moments when the very best of humanity is on display, but there are also moments of the absolute worst. For all the good, there's plenty of bad."

"And this is how you make your living?"

"It is," Cole said with a rueful laugh. "If not for the cats and dogs, and raccoons, toads, and squirrels, I'd have nothing." He looked up and hit me with a paralyzingly sweet smile. "I certainly wouldn't be here."

"To the cats and dogs," I said, raising an empty glass.

He reached across me for one of the upturned glasses I'd set on the countertop after drying, and his arm rubbed against my abdomen in the process. It was nothing much, just a quick touch not unlike many we'd shared while washing dishes every night this past week, but it was different now.

"To the cats and dogs," Cole repeated.

I choked back a groan before he lifted his glass and we toasted a world I didn't know.

We finished cleaning up in silence and shifted toward the living room when the kitchen was in good shape. There were a couple of minutes before the game started, and Cole was surfing through the channels. He had an aversion to watching the evening news, one I didn't understand but didn't mind indulging.

"You really should let me rewire your setup," Cole said, gesturing to the footage from football's preseason training camp. "Get a DVR, and some expanded access for games outside your market. You'll appreciate it come football season."

"Sit down and enjoy the damn game," I said, pointing at the sofa.

"Every minute of it," he said. "But—one more thing. You could fast forward through commercials, you know. I can't imagine you enjoy all the promos for Canobie Lake Park and Jordan's Furniture."

"That's where you're wrong," I said. "I love that shit, and it's no secret that Water Country has the best jingle."

Cole turned to me, stone-faced. "We're going to agree to disagree on that point."

We settled into an amiable banter of cheers, groans, and curses punctuated with comfortable silence. I'd been alone for years and rarely considered what it would be like to have a partner, but playfully arguing with Cole about the Red Sox showed me what I could have. What I wanted.

The game went into extra innings, and though I wasn't built for too many late nights followed by early mornings, I wasn't interested in abandoning my position on watching the entire game. I was a stodgy bastard like that.

But Cole's hands were folded low on his belly, right above his crotch, and through the thin fabric of his athletic shorts, I could make out the shape of him. And *oh fuck*, it was a nice-looking shape.

There was nothing overtly sexual about his position, yet I yearned for the right to reach over and take my man in hand. He was close enough to touch, and I didn't think I could endure extra innings tonight with that temptation.

When it was clear the Sox were taking home an easy win, I clicked off the television and stood, brushing my palms down the front of my cargo shorts. I'd never been one for spontaneous erections, but beer and too-thin athletic shorts and this proximity to Cole brought me damn close. My cock was heavy and aching, and I needed to find some relief far away from my guest's watchful eyes.

"We'll hit the water early," I said, desperate to keep my mind on topics that didn't involve imagining the rasp of Cole's unshaven jaw against my inner thighs.

He nodded as he collected the empty beer bottles. He was meticulous about recycling, and had gone so far as to lecture me about the impact of plastics on marine life. Somehow he knew as much, if not more, about preserving the seas than I did.

"Yeah," Cole said. "That works for me."

He sounded distant, and not because he was busy tidying the kitchen. He was distracted. "Everything okay, McClish?" I asked.

He folded a dish towel into precise thirds and set it on the counter with a pat, and then glanced up with a forced smile. "Great."

I didn't know him, not well enough to read his every mood and twitch, but I had the distinct sense that he *wasn't* great. "Good," I said.

Cole patted the towel again and reached for a glass. "Yeah," he replied, watching me while he filled his glass with water. He drank it down, his eyes still trained on me.

Not unlike sitting beside him on the couch, there was nothing loudly attractive about drinking water but I couldn't save myself from the pull of his body. It was a vortex sucking me in. I wanted to touch him and taste him, and I wanted him to love it as much as I knew I would.

But that wasn't my life. That wasn't how it went for me.

"Listen, man," I said, gesturing toward him. "You can tell me if something's bothering—"

"Not at all," Cole replied quickly. "I'm preoccupied with some work issues. A lot on my mind." He tapped his temple as if to confirm the location of his troubles. They were not in his shorts as I'd hoped. "Things I'm trying to sort out. Problems, bugs. That's all." He nodded several times, and I was certain he believed the repetition was critical to convincing me. "I'm going to tackle some of that."

He patted the towel again.

"Yeah," I replied.

He moved around me, slipping down the hallway with little more than a hasty "Good night" as his chest brushed against my back. I didn't press the issue. I wanted to, but I didn't know what or how to press. And more importantly, I needed a very cold shower.

CONSTANT BEARING, DECREASING RANGE

n. The condition when two vessels are approaching each other from any angle that stays the same over time. Also known as a collision course.

Cole

Neera: You'll notify me before you do anything substantive, right?

I BARKED out a laugh when I read those words.

I'd been closed up in my small room for a matter of moments before reaching for my phone in hopes of a distraction from Owen. Not that I wanted a distraction, of course, but it wasn't like I could throw myself at him. As thrilled as I was to hear of his preference for penis, I couldn't drop my shorts and ask if he wanted a taste of mine.

It was also possible that he wasn't interested in me. Two gay men could live under a shared roof without devolving into a fuck festival. Although it would certainly help if one of those men was up front about his sexuality when peach-ripe opportunities presented themselves.

I shook my head, astounded by my own absurdity.

Neera: Real estate purchases, public appearances, search and rescue teams, the like? I'd rather not have a repeat of the Appalachian incident.
Cole: Of course. But I'll remind you that you thought the Appalachian incident was going to be great, and the search and rescue team was totally unnecessary.
Cole: Further, I haven't gotten a haircut without your input in almost a decade.
Neera: Please don't consider this an invitation or suggestion to repeat the Appalachian incident. I can speak for the senior leadership and board of directors when I say getting lost in the Smoky Mountains at night again is ill-advised.
Cole: No, nothing Appalachian in my future. I'm quite content where I am.
Neera: And yet you won't tell me where that is, what you're doing, or when you'll be back.
Cole: Only because I'm 100% certain you'll charter a plane and come check on me.
Cole: That would be great but I need some time and space to work everything out.
Neera: Some habits are hard to break.
Cole: Like managing up?
Neera: You're allowed privacy and secrets, but you're also allowed to trust people.
Cole: I do. I trust you implicitly.
Cole: I also trust the person I'm staying with, and I want to protect that person's privacy as well.
Neera: Oh.
Neera: Okay. All right. I understand.
Cole: Let me get this straight. I'm allowed to have privacy only if it involves human companionship?
Neera: Yes, that's correct.

THAT YIELDED ANOTHER LAUGH. I could've gone a few more rounds with Neera but I set my glasses on the bedside table, then switched my phone off and tucked it away in my duffel bag. My head wasn't in the right place to chat with her tonight. Based on my conduct earlier, I wasn't in the right place to chat with anyone.

Years ago, back when my company was first taking off, I sat for a live television interview. *Train wreck* wasn't an adequate representation of how poorly it went. I had an asshole answer for every question. I drummed my fingers on the armrest, rolled my eyes, and sighed audibly. I couldn't get comfortable in the chair so I shifted and repositioned to the point of distraction, and then snapped at the interviewer when he asked if I was all right.

That hot mess was a shining achievement compared to the way I handled Owen this evening.

All the opportunities in the world were in front of me, and I skipped over every one of them. I could banter and bullshit all day long but that was it. That was all I had—bullshit. All systems were go, the bases were loaded, the stars were aligned...and I blew it. Not only did I blow it, I came off like an apathetic dickhead. I said all the wrong things, laughed like an idiot, and rolled deep in the awkward pauses.

It was true. I didn't know how to get out of my own way.

With a groan, I pushed off the bed and headed to the bathroom. I had to wash up for the night, and then I was determined to sleep off today's indiscretions and start anew tomorrow. I could manage that. I could even sit Owen down after we delivered the day's catch and tell him about my—

"Unnnnnnf."

I stopped in the hallway, my hand frozen an inch from the bathroom door handle, and I heard it again.

"Mmmmm."

It took only a moment to place that sound and the unmistakable rhythm of skin shuttling over skin. The air went out of my chest and everything in my body turned hot, my skin prickling with awareness because Owen was masturbating within inches of me.

A decent guy would've retreated immediately and given Owen the privacy he deserved. I wasn't that guy, and I didn't think I could move from this spot if a family of tiny purple ponies paraded down the hall and asked for directions to the carnival.

I leaned forward, closer to Owen and the noises I wanted to memorize and keep in a special, secret place. If I couldn't invite myself into his self-love session—because I possessed *some* decency—I was going to listen real hard.

Not trusting myself to remain standing without support, I rested my forehead against the doorframe. That was when I noticed it. The door had been warped by years of close proximity to the ocean air, and shutting it all the way required a firm shove. Owen hadn't given it that shove.

Only a thin sliver of him was visible, but that was more than enough. The vanity light shone down on his dark hair, bathing him in a warm glow. His shirt was rucked up around his chest and his shorts were barely out of the way, as if he'd surrendered to this need with haste. His hand gripped the edge of the sink, his knuckles white. His other hand moved in a lightning-quick blur that demanded my cock's full attention.

I was hard and ready, and I had to make a decision. I could stand in this hallway while Owen jerked it on the other side of the door, or I could go back to my room. There was one more option, of course, but I didn't have the balls to push the door open and observe this act to completion.

"*Ohhh*," he groaned. "Oh *fuuuuck*."

There was a flash of white that obscured my view for a moment. When it cleared, I found a towel gnashed between Owen's teeth, muffling his noises. Seeing him desperate like this triggered something inside me, and before I could think better of it, my fingers were curling around my cock.

I thrust into my palm in time with Owen but my pleasure was secondary. I was only concerned with him. His movements, his noises, his need. It was glorious, and I couldn't contain my groan when he slowed to long, twisting strokes that offered a glance at his thick erection.

Owen's eyes popped open and his gaze darted to the door. He caught sight of me, and answered my groan with a gasp.

Then all the words I knew in this language flew out of my mouth at once. "I was just going to—err, you know, I was going out. I was leaving.

The house. For a bit. And then coming back. It's a great night for a walk. I mean, I figured I could leave. Now. I could leave and go for a walk. Or something like that. Now that I think about it, there's a podcast I've been meaning to listen to, and I have noise-canceling headphones. I can walk with the headphones. On my head. I won't hear anything at all. Except the podcast. I'd hear that. But you know what? I'm exhausted. Just beat. I mean—no, not that. I'm not beating anything. No. What I meant is that I'm sleepwalking. I've been told I sleepwalk. I never remember it. I don't remember anything. I won't remember any of this." I took a breath while Owen blinked at me. "This is a dream."

The tension between us jolted me back, away from the bathroom. I stumbled into the safety of my room, and shut the door behind me. I stared at the bed while my breath stuttered out in jagged bursts and my heart slammed into my ribs like it was trying to break free. My cock, unaware that this peep show had taken a turn for the incredibly awkward, was throbbing against my belly. It wasn't the kind of erection I could ignore either. I had to do something about this unless I wanted to be miserable and aching all night.

Owen's bedroom door slammed shut, and through the thin walls, I heard him moving around. I groaned again, but this time I was groaning in response to my uncanny ability to fuck things up.

As if he understood the difference, Owen chuckled. It was low and exasperated, like he couldn't believe what I'd done now.

"Sorry," I shouted at the wall.

There was another chuckle and I heard drawers opening and closing. "Go to bed, McClish," Owen replied.

Obeying this command, I stripped off my clothes and slipped between the sheets. My dick was pitching a tent that could comfortably sleep a family of four and their elderly beagle, but I forced myself to listen to the night instead of my body's drumbeat of arousal.

There were crickets and cicadas chirping in tandem and woodland creatures engaging in their nocturnal rituals. The trees rustled and the ocean lapped against the shore, and—and I heard it again. I heard *him*.

I would've missed it if not for the creaking bedsprings playing backup to his moans. Right on cue, my cock throbbed in response. I was in bad shape here. Harder than humanly possible, leaking all over the sheets, and now I had to listen while he finished the job. I was one self-indulgent second away from flopping on my belly and rutting into the mattress without concern for the current level of weird between me and Owen.

"Go to bed, Bartlett," I called.

"I *am* in bed," he shouted back. "Something's keeping me up."

I swallowed a laugh as it dawned on me. I'd announced my presence before Owen could finish, and I had to imagine he was in as much distress as I was. And I was imagining. I couldn't stop thinking about the way he touched himself. There was a frantic quality to it, as if his entire existence hinged upon finding his release.

"Sorry about that," I said.

Another garbled noise drifted through the wall from Owen's room, and my fingers found my shaft. I couldn't help it. Just couldn't help it.

"Enough apologies," he yelled.

I closed my eyes and dragged my palm up, twisting over the crown the same way Owen had. Indulging in this small dose of relief, I allowed myself to believe I was showing him what I wanted. Or it was him stroking me. Or it was my hand on his cock, and I was showing him I knew how he liked it. Then the fantasies collided, and it was all of it at once. In my mind, I gave him everything and he gave just as much in return. Cocks, hands, mouths; there was no limit.

My hips were rocking up, surging as I pumped into my hand. The motion sent the headboard knocking against the wall and the bedsprings creaking, and then I heard a very clear command from Owen. "Don't stop."

My whole body shuddered, and a grunt caught in my throat. It didn't matter whether his order was intended for me. That was how I was taking it, and I was too lost in lust to consider anything else.

"Fuck yes," I replied. I shoved my shoulders back into the mattress as I stroked harder, and the headboard hammered against the wall. "Yes, yes, *yes.*"

It was a little over the top, sure. I wasn't ashamed to say there were some theatrics involved in that porn star wail. I was putting on a show, and Owen was too.

There was a thump followed by a groan that was distinctly Owen, and I could almost feel him watching me. Just as I'd watched him.

"Don't stop," he repeated, his voice rough. He sounded closer, as if he was speaking directly to the barrier between us. And there was no doubt his words were meant for me. "Don't you fucking stop."

We were no longer performing solitary acts on dueling stages, separate, and simultaneous only as a matter of coincidence. We were sharing this now.

Another thump sounded above my head, and I envisioned Owen bracing himself there as he stroked. His head would hang low, his chin resting on his chest and his eyes screwed shut as he focused on finding his release. Sweat would dot his forehead and heat would crawl up his neck and cheeks. He'd snarl and gasp as he edged closer, and slap his palm against the wall each time he denied his orgasm. Of course he'd hold back. He'd wait for me. He didn't know how to be selfish.

"Let me hear you," he rasped.

Get in here. The words were dancing on the tip of my tongue but I didn't have the backbone to say them. I couldn't disrupt the forward trajectory of this moment by requesting a left turn.

"Don't go quiet on me now," Owen said, his words huffing out in strained snarls.

"I need to come," I moan-whined.

"Maybe I'll let you," he replied.

My body was rigid with tension, every muscle held tight, and his response was a current of heat down my spine and around my cock. The challenge he levied—wait for his permission—fit like a too-tight suit, but I craved his approval more than my comfort.

"Please," I groaned, my hips jerking off the mattress as I thrust harder.

He growled, but offered nothing more.

I needed more, and I was going to get it.

I forced a breath from my lungs. My legs parted as I imagined Owen settling there, his hand gliding over his cock as he watched me. He pressed his free hand to the back of my thigh, pushing it to my chest until I was spread open for him. A feral smile tugged at his lips as he gazed at me, like he was categorizing every inch and devising methods of sexual torment. His fingers trailed down my leg and around the base of my cock. It was the lightest touch, one that seemed too gentle and measured for a man like him. But then two fingers were in my crease, then they were inside me, then I was seeing stars. Nothing gentle or measured about it.

"Oh, fuck," I sighed.

My bicep was burning and I wasn't certain I could feel some of my fingers anymore. The grip I had on my shaft was unforgiving, but I was too far down this path for any of that to matter. I was right there, teetering with little more than a toehold on my orgasm, my sanity, my consciousness.

"Owen," I gasped.

Even in this state, calling for him seemed like a step over the line. But the man between my legs, the Imaginary Finger-Fucking Owen, was nodding, granting me permission to fall over the edge.

"Give it to me now," he commanded. "Right now."

In my mind, Owen was still kneeling between my legs, the hand on his cock moving in time with the fingers in my ass. That sharp grin was still in place, and it deepened each time he traced my prostate. Instead of grinding my teeth in blissful agony, I melted into that all-the-shivers-and-goose-bumps sensation. He whispered "Mine" every time I quivered under his touch, and I nodded in agreement.

One spurt after another landed on my belly, my shoulder, the pillow. I heard a shuddering breath from Owen, and then he pounded the wall several times as he snarled and hummed. I could picture him spilling into his hand, his chest heaving and his lips parting as he growled through his release.

I was crying out and convulsing, and clinging to the quilt as if it could keep me from drifting away. But it was as though these things were happening outside of me, and I was observing them from a detached distance. Inside, I was sliding into the deep mellow of an earth-rocking orgasm. Static filled my ears and my eyelids were too heavy to lift, and every muscle in my body eased until I was nothing more than a blob of satisfied jelly.

I hated the slimy, squishy feel of semen drying on my skin but I didn't possess the strength to clean it off. I couldn't even lift my arm and reach for a tissue from the bedside table.

Bedsprings squealed on the other side of the wall, and I knew he was tucked in for the night. A part of me—not a small part—hoped he'd trudge over here with his palm full of jizz and ask me what I planned to do about it. Hoped he'd flip me over and force me facedown on the mattress. Hoped he'd drag his thick fingers through my hair and curl up beside me.

"Good night, McClish," Owen called.

He sounded drowsy and loose, and I liked it. I wanted to get him in this state again.

"Good night, Bartlett," I replied.

A warm, sated smile tugged at my lips as I drifted off. Before sleep pulled me under, a voice in the back of my head asked, *What did we just do?*

10

FULL AND BY

adv. Sailing with all sails full and lying as near the wind as possible.

I SLAMMED the refrigerator door shut and moved to the pantry. "Too late to make chili," I said to myself. "Too late for *good* chili."

"There's a whole haddock packed in ice," Cole called.

He was perched on the countertop, his legs hanging loose and his arms braced behind him. His skin was glowing from another sunny day on the water and his hair wind-blown. He looked like an offering, and I could only shoot quick glimpses in his direction or suffer a full-body spasm of need. Again.

I didn't know what the hell had happened last night. One minute I was lusting over athletic shorts, the next I was pressed flat against my bedroom wall and racing to keep up with Cole's strokes. Then there were his sounds and my sounds and *oh my God*. I didn't know how I was supposed to feel after masturbating with my presumably straight house-guest, so I felt a bit of everything. Excitement, anxiety, affection, amusement, shock. All of that, and a little bit of shame.

Shame wasn't an emotion I allowed myself but I couldn't think about last night without simmering in embarrassment. *How did I let it go that far? What was I thinking?* That was just it—I didn't think. Not with the head on my shoulders.

And now I'd spent the day trying to look Cole in the eye and talk about lobsters like last night was nothing more than a weird dream. Wasn't that the truth. I didn't even know this man, not really, and I was allowing myself to build these sandcastle feelings. It was dangerous, and I knew better. Summer love wasn't for me, and neither was this man. He wasn't here to stay, and he wasn't here for me. He was running away from something I didn't want to explore, but I couldn't help myself from wanting to care for him. Ease his troubles.

I snorted at that thought. His *troubles* weren't the only things I wanted to ease. I was in it with this guy, and it wasn't just me. Cole had participated too. He didn't instigate it but he certainly took an otherwise excusable situation to another level.

Even as evening settled down around us, I didn't know where I stood —*we* stood—after last night. I had an educated guess, of course. We'd shared some beers with dinner and a few more while watching the game, and liquor often blurred sexuality's not-so-tidy boxes.

Liquor was a champ when it came to taking the blame.

Not that there was much blame to go around. Jerking off with a wall between us wasn't arrow-straight, but it wasn't a subscription to the Bear of the Month club either. There was room on the rainbow for everyone.

And now I was rationalizing. Might as well explain it away before my hopes climbed all the way up and started planning some kind of future with Cole. How fucking ridiculous was that? There wasn't going to be any of that. His boat would be fixed soon enough, he'd set sail, and then I'd be right back where I always was—wondering why I'd given every-thing to someone who couldn't spare anything for me.

Not this time. No future, no *us*.

When I woke up this morning, hard, mortified, hungry for more, I decided I'd handle this the only way I knew how—hunkering down in my foul mood. I'd pushed Cole away with grouchy scowls and short-tempered barks all day. Avoided discussion of last night so hard I started to wonder whether it actually happened. Feigned disinterest in his chatter though I was silently soaking it all up. Busied myself with the radio, the engine, the maps—anything to keep my eyes off him. I pushed him away before he could push me.

And that approach had worked well enough while my hands were busy hauling in traps and navigating the coastline, but the sea couldn't save me now. The house seemed impossibly small, the walls and ceiling pressing in close, and I couldn't escape Cole.

Thus I was taking my sweet-ass time in the pantry. I hoped he'd get bored soon enough and leave me in peace, but that didn't appear to be happening.

"Do you want me to get it?" he called. "The haddock?"

"Not in the mood," I called over my shoulder. "For haddock."

Important clarification. With a sigh, I pawed at a jar of preserved tomatoes from last summer, and I considered the dishes I could throw together with them. It saved me from thinking about stepping between Cole's legs and demanding his attention. I could do that. I could run my hands up his thighs, grab his waist and jerk him close. Force him to look me in the eye while my dick was pressed against his belly. Force him to account for his actions, and then beg him to give me more.

I could. I wouldn't.

"Is that allowed?" he asked. "Aren't fishermen honor-bound to eat fish all day, every day?"

"No," I said as I emerged from the pantry. "Some of us are vege-tarians."

"I doubt that," Cole replied.

I did too but I enjoyed baiting him like this. Real talk—I enjoyed baiting him in all situations. Last night came to mind. But he was adorable when argumentative, all furrowed brows and aggressive gestures. Couldn't get enough of it.

He had an unshakeable belief that he was always right, and it didn't matter whether he knew anything of the topic at hand. He walked on miles-deep layers of confidence and arrogance, but I suspected I was among the lucky few to have witnessed his vulnerability too.

And then I reminded myself—once again—that he was leaving soon. He didn't have to say it. I knew. Work on his boat was coming along, and as soon as some high-tech piece of equipment came in from California, he'd set sail. I couldn't deal with the prospect of losing my new friend and the subject of my desire, and I wouldn't allow myself to ask him about it.

Avoidance, my coping mechanism of choice.

"It's true," I said. "There are entire coalitions of vegetarian fishermen —and women, of course—and they're gaining in popularity. I imagine they'll outnumber the carnivores within a decade." I gave him an earnest nod. "It will make catering at the conferences a real challenge."

Cole's forehead wrinkled as he scratched his chin. He'd taken to letting his sandy beard grow out for several days before trimming it down to scruff, and that beard had a starring role in my favorite fantasies. I'd imagined it on my neck, my chest, between my thighs. Fantasies vivid enough to wake me with an erection that seemed to throb his name.

Cole held up his hands, shaking his head. "I'm not buying it this time, Bartlett," he said. "I've gone along with one too many fish tales. I'm calling horseshit—no, *fish shit*—on this one."

"Look into it," I replied with a stiff laugh.

I set several jars and cans on the counter beside him. My fingers itched to stroke his thigh. See if it was as taut as I'd dreamed. Instead, I tossed a can of black beans from hand to hand. "Since we didn't make it to the market this morning, we're low on provisions," I said. "I can whip up—"

"Let's just go out now," he said, shrugging.

There were many things Cole still didn't understand about my world. Most notably, the closest twenty-four-hour grocery store was an hour away. "The market in town is closed," I said.

"I know that," he replied impatiently. "We'll hit the little tavern instead. It's a short walk, right? It's just through the woods. Come on, you deserve a night off from cooking. Let me take you out. My treat."

A surprised laugh bubbled up from my chest. "Are you asking me on a date, McClish?"

Cole blinked at me and then glanced away. I forced another laugh as the question went unanswered for longer than I could manage.

"I mean—" I started.

"Yeah," Cole said at the same time, a devilish grin pulling up the corners of his lips. "I'll be a perfect gentleman."

I crossed my arms over my chest and eyed him. My heart was pounding away, frantic and filled with cocksick hope. It required substantial effort to keep my expression neutral. "Couldn't if you tried."

Cole hopped off the countertop. "Now I can't let that challenge go unanswered." He glanced down at his t-shirt. "Give me a minute to make myself presentable."

"You're gonna need more than a minute," I said to his back as he walked away.

I had to curl my fingers around the edge of the countertop to restrain myself from following. I wanted, with every ounce of me, to watch him strip his clothes off. I'd sit on the edge of the bed, staring while he revealed more and more of his perfect California surfer boy skin. I couldn't imagine sitting there for long. Once he was bare, I'd drag my fingertips up his thighs, over his hips, around his backside. I'd press my chest to his back and nudge my cock between his cheeks. Make it clear what I had for him. And I had so much.

Without thinking, I thrust my hips forward, slamming hard into the cabinets. I cried out in a messy mix of pleasure and pain. The drawer handle speared into my balls, deflating my erection and driving an uncomfortable shudder through my body.

"Aw, fuck," I said, groaning. With a hand between my legs, I rubbed away the ache. I couldn't erase the fantasy behind my eyes—and the reality of it down the hall—but it helped. Closing my eyes, I pushed a breath past my lips and imagined Cole's hand caressing me.

"Hey. Are you okay, Bartlett?"

My eyes popped open and I put both hands up. "What?" I snapped, staring at him on the other side of the kitchen. "What do you want, McClish?"

"Whenever you're ready," Cole started slowly, "we can go."

"I'm ready," I replied.

I wasn't ready. I wasn't ready for any of this.

WATCHING

v. When a fisherman's buoys are visible on the surface of the water due to a slack tide.

OWEN

"WHAT IS the difference between baked stuffed lobster and the lazy man's lobster?" Cole asked, drumming his fingers on the tabletop. "You know, this is like ethnographic research. I should be taking notes."

"I'm sure California is dying to know all about the way real Mainers live," I replied.

"I'm sure of it," he murmured. "Foodie blog post waiting to happen." He snapped his fingers and pointed at the menu. "No vegetarian fishermen welcome here unless they're willing to settle on a side salad. Can't imagine that would satisfy you."

Cole's eyebrow arched up as he spoke and it didn't matter what he was saying because I only wanted to grab him by the neck and kiss him. All I heard was *satisfy*, and that was it.

"It's just a bowlful of chopped iceberg," I said through clenched teeth. "A slice of cucumber. Maybe a chunk of tomato."

"Like I said, that wouldn't do much for you," he replied, gesturing toward me. "You're not a side salad guy."

I met his gaze and held it for a long, challenging beat. I didn't give up so much as a blink.

"Probably not," I finally conceded. "Neither are you."

He leaned back against the booth, slowly nodding as he crossed his arms over his chest. "I see you've finally figured that out," he murmured. "Good."

What the fuck are we talking about right now? The air around us was incendiary, and nothing else existed. Not the buzzing tavern, not my issues, not his impending departure. It was just us and all the tension in the world.

And I couldn't handle it. I couldn't sit here and go round after confusing round with this guy when all I wanted was to feel his skin under mine.

"The lazy man's lobster is a regular steamed lobster, but the meat has been removed from the shell. It's lazy because you don't have to crack the shell to eat it," I said, all the words rushing out in a burst. "The baked stuffed is in the shell and stuffed with breadcrumbs." I spared him a quick glance and went back to my menu. "You'd like the swordfish. Get that."

"Would you repeat that?" he asked. "I need to write this down. I'm going to take this concept back to Silicon Valley and find someone to open a seafood restaurant with ninety-four different lobster preparations. Poke bowls are out, Maine lobster is in." He nodded several times. "I'll make a killing on it, but first you need to explain the rest of this menu to me. What in the world is a steamer?"

"It's a clam. One that's been steamed," I said. "No more questions."

"I'll hire you as my crustacean expert," he said. "Give you a cut of the profits."

"No more questions."

"I'll call it the Owen Bartlett House of Lobster," he continued.

"No, you won't."

"I will," he said. "I will and you'll be famous. Everyone will want to know the true story of this legendary lobsterman and I'll have to tell them about Talbott's Cove. You'll have reporters camped outside your house and sailing into your cove."

I rolled my eyes. "You're not supposed to threaten your date."

"You know, this isn't the first time I've received that feedback," he mused.

"Not surprising," I murmured.

Cole returned to his menu, humming and quipping as he reviewed The Galley's seemingly infinite seafood offerings, and he didn't notice Annette Cortassi approaching our booth.

Annette was sweet like maple syrup, and I believed her picture was in the dictionary right beside the entry for "girl next door." She was the best of the best people and this town was better because she was part of it, but she harbored the belief that she could flip me like a split-level house.

She was convinced we'd end up together as soon as I gave her a fair chance, and I was convinced she was delusional in that regard. I didn't think she took any specific issue with my sexuality but I was certain she saw me as subject to the power of her pussy.

The implication that I'd abandon everything I knew to be true about myself was rather insulting, but she'd learned that trick from my mother. It drove me crazy, but I chose to ignore Annette's advances. I didn't hold them against her either. No reason to make an issue out of it when I was sure she'd get the hint soon enough.

My mother was still getting the hint, but that was another issue for another day.

"Quite the pleasant surprise to see you this evening," she said when she stopped at our table. "I never see you out after sunset anymore."

Her fingertips trailed over my shoulder, and I bit back the desire to shake her off. She met my scowl with a sunny smile that glowed with real warmth, and then turned her attention to Cole.

"Is this the new deckhand I keep hearing about?"

"I prefer fishery intern," he replied, offering his hand. "Cole."

"Cole," I said, gesturing between him and Annette. "This is Annette—"

"Such a pleasure," she interrupted, taking his hand between both of hers. "It's wonderful to have you here, Cole. I hope you're enjoying your time in the Cove."

Jealousy flared hot and fast, and I wanted to snatch his hand away from her.

"Annette owns the bookstore around the corner," I said, not allowing him the time to reply.

It was rude but I didn't care. He was here with *me*. We were having dinner *together*. This wasn't an opportunity for this town's single women to rub all over my friend. My deckhand. Houseguest. Whatever the fuck he was, he was mine and not theirs.

"That I do," Annette chirped. "I can get you anything you want."

Cole leaned back against the booth as he blinked up at her. Then his eyes flicked over her body. It was quick. If I hadn't been watching, I would've missed it. I wish I'd missed it.

"Anything, huh?" he asked. "That's impressive."

"Anything at all," Annette replied. "You name it, I'll get it."

"It's funny," he started, his knuckles running along his jaw, "I can't remember the last time I read a physical book. I'm an e-book convert."

Annette offered him a patient-but-mostly-impatient smile. "There's nothing like holding a book in your hands," she said. "Maybe you could stop by some time, and we can have a little chat about your interests. I might be able to recommend something new. Something you didn't expect you'd enjoy."

I was ready to flip the table. Just lift that fucker up and throw it across the fucking room. And then I'd tell everyone listening that he was moaning in *my* ear night last night, after *I* gave him permission. It was my name he was calling when he came because he belonged to me.

I'd do it, too. I really would. I couldn't sit here and watch all these days of falling for a man who wasn't meant for me come crashing down because the town sweetheart whipped out her vagina and wielded that thing like a Venus flytrap.

"I'll keep that in mind," Cole said. His tone was pleasant, almost fond. As if he not only knew what she was implying but was actually making note of her invitation.

The hell you are.

"What about the book you're getting me?" I asked, dragging her attention away from him. "Where's my special order, Annette?"

It was such a fucked-up move. I didn't want her—of course not—but the attention she was paying Cole had me seething with jealousy.

"Oh, don't you worry, sugar," she replied, reaching out to squeeze my forearm. "It's due in next week." She tapped her chin and pursed her lips. "Come see me a week from Thursday. It should be in by then. We can take a look at the new arrivals, too. There are a few you might like. I'll set them aside. Wouldn't want anyone getting to them first." A group of women called to Annette from the bar, and she waved to them in response. "I have to get back. It's girls' night. You know how it is."

"Not really," I said flatly.

Cole caught my gaze and lifted his brows. "Not at all," he added.

Annette glanced between us and threw back her head with a hearty laugh. "You two are a hoot. Just a hoot. I love it. You must be having a whole lot of fun together," she said before aiming a manicured finger in my direction. *If you only knew, Annette. If you only knew.* "Next Thursday. I'll stay open late for you."

We watched while she retreated to her group, and I shot a glimpse across the table before turning my menu to the draft beer list. "So, that's Annette."

"Dude." Cole barked out a laugh. "She's going to *stay open late for you.*"

The implied meaning was heavy in his words.

"She has a few ideas about things." I blew out an irritable sigh. "I don't agree with all of them."

"That's not an idea, my friend. That's a heat-seeking missile." He glanced to Annette's group at the bar. Every woman was staring right at Cole—even the married ones—and if they didn't get their ovaries off him, I'd throw the fuck down. "She wants to climb you like a tree."

"There will be none of that," I murmured, shaking my head as I reread the beers. As if I didn't have this list committed to memory after a lifetime in this town.

"Yeah, I figured as much." Cole dropped his arms to the tabletop, laughing. "But she's under the impression you're bending her over a stack of books next week."

"For fuck's sake, McClish, don't you think I know?" I snapped. "That's why you're coming with me."

"You're looking to me for protection?" he asked, tapping the mint green polo shirt stretched tight across his lean chest. "I thought I wasn't allowed around knives or shotguns."

"You're not," I replied. "But I need a buffer. I haven't been alone with Annette in ten years."

He chuckled. "Based on the scene I just witnessed, she hasn't received the message you're sending."

Bringing my fingers to my forehead, I rubbed my brows until some of the frantic energy built up inside my mind dissipated. I couldn't handle all this lust, jealousy, and aggravation in one evening. I wanted to drop my head into Cole's lap and let him drag his fingers through my hair until I forgot my name. I wanted him and that want was infinitely greater than sexual desire. I wanted to fuck him straight through the summer but I also wanted to wrap my arms around him and never let go.

"I mean, she seems nice," Cole continued, "in a willfully blind sort of way. But then again, maybe she thinks you're playing hard to get. You aren't exactly an open book, my friend."

"Fuck. You're right." I whistled for the bartender's attention. "JJ," I called to him. "Double whiskey on the rocks." I glanced back at Cole and found an expectant grin on his face. I held up two fingers. "Make that two double whiskeys."

"I hate to be obvious," Cole started, "but is she aware that she isn't your type?"

"Yes." I spun the salt shaker between my palms. "I don't hide who I am."

"I wouldn't expect you to," he replied quickly. "But that only confirms my original suspicions about darling Annette."

"Which were?" I prompted.

"The bitch has balls," he said, laughing.

"No, she's..." My voice trailed off. "She's a good person. The trouble with living in the same small town your entire life is that everyone knows your story, and everyone forms opinions of their own. And they're not alone. I know everyone else's stories, too. I have opinions about many of them." I tipped my head toward the bar. "Lincoln, the guy with the

Patriots hat? I've seen him at gay bars in Portland. Often enough to know he likes the leather and Levi's scene. He's married with two kids. Then there's Fitzy, the big guy blue t-shirt? His son is going through an opioid addiction treatment program. Third time. His wife doesn't want the son back in the house after treatment on account of him stealing everything out from underneath them and selling it to buy pills. Fitzy comes here most nights to keep from arguing with her about it, and I can't say I blame him. And you've got Brooke-Ashley over there. She went to college somewhere down south, somewhere fancy and presti-gious. Graduated the top of her class, found herself a big job in New York City, the whole deal. But she moved back home two years ago, and hasn't said a word about it to anyone. Some people say something terrible happened to her. Others say her father has symptoms of early-onset dementia, and she gave it all up to care for him at home." I spread my hands out in front of me. "She decided to go by Brooke when she moved away, but everyone around here still calls her Brooke-Ashley. That's how it goes in small towns."

Cole rested his elbows on the table and it required profound restraint to keep from tracing the muscular lines of his forearms. "Which opinion has Annette formed about you?"

I stared down at the salt shaker because I couldn't manage another glimpse at Annette's crew. I didn't want to get thrown out of The Galley for fighting women. "It's her position that, because I went out with a girl or two in high school, I'm not *thoroughly* gay. You know, that there's a chance I could go straight for the right woman."

JJ set two glasses on the table, making no effort to keep the liquid from sloshing over the sides. "Good luck with this," he said as he walked away.

Cole shook his head as he mopped the spilled liquor with a paper napkin. "What's with all the gold star pedants these days? My God. They're worse than the evangelicals with their concern-trolling."

"I don't know, man." With a shrug, I gulped my drink. Every ounce of that liquor was going to backhand me in the morning but I didn't care about that tonight. "But she's not the one for me."

Cole considered his glass and took a quick sip. "Good to know."

"Yeah? Why?" I asked as jealousy boiled up again. "Is she your type?"

He tipped his head to the side, a half-smile tugging at his lips. "No. I'm not into the perky-bubbly-pushy cheerleader types," he said.

"Why not?" I asked. The whiskey was already going to my head, and I could feel my words getting loose. "Everyone likes cheerleaders, with the skirts and everything."

"Not me." Cole leaned across the table, his knuckles rubbing against the back of my hand as he shifted, and he tipped his head toward me with the same half-smile he used to reject pretty cheerleaders. Every nerve in my body was pulsing at his barely there touch. "I'm not interested in women, Bartlett."

I blinked at him, frozen as he threw my exact words back at me. Every conversation, every memory of him stripping off his shirt on the boat, every sound he made last night filled my mind, and I realized this guy didn't know how to make things easy on me. He was secrets and mysteries, and one complicated mess after another. He was single-handedly ruining my quiet, comfortable existence with his questions and noise and obscene abs, and that was before I knew he was an option. Prior to this conversation, he was a short-term condition. A crush bound to end as quickly as it started.

But now—now that he'd aimed that smile at me and stroked my hand and invited me into one of his quiet truths—he was an affliction.

"Owen, say something," Cole said, his voice tinted with the same untethered panic I experienced last night. His gaze fell to the table, and he shifted his knuckles away from my hand.

"You couldn't have mentioned this earlier?"

Cole ran his hand over his jaw. "Didn't seem like the right time," he said, not meeting my eyes. "But I've wanted you since you took me home like a stray mutt."

"Yeah, I really would've appreciated this information much earlier," I said. "Last night comes to mind."

He had the decency to stare down at the tabletop while his cheeks reddened at the mention of our exchange. "You got me so hard last night," he whispered. "I needed your help."

Stunned silence didn't begin to describe my current state of existence. I could still feel his fingers on my wrist, his touch seared into my skin like a tattoo. I dragged my tongue over my parched lips. Reached for my whiskey but then put it down. Grabbed my napkin but then tossed it aside. "Sounded like you were doing just fine on your own."

"Only because I was imagining your hand on my cock," he replied. "And...elsewhere."

I locked my fingers around his wrist and tugged him back. The only words I could pull together were, "I didn't tell you to let go."

"Okay," he said, gulping. The sight of his throat bobbing turned my cock to stone. "I won't."

"Good. That's good." Without looking away from him, I called, "JJ. Another round over here."

12

HARDEN UP

v. To turn toward the wind; sail closer to the wind.

OWEN

"WAIT, WAIT A MINUTE," Cole hissed, his arms outstretched at odd angles as he stumbled over his feet. "Look."

I reached for the maple tree to my right, needing somewhere to lean. Leaning was easier than staying upright. "What am I looking for?"

It was late and we were drunk, but the worst part was that we'd spent the evening flirting with each other like young lovers and now I was about to explode on him. Cole knew it, too. He wanted it. The sparkle in his devious grin, the way his gaze bathed me in heat, his inability to go more than a minute without brushing his hand against mine. He wanted this as much as I did or...or he was one hell of a cockteasey drunk. God, I hoped it was the former.

"The fireflies," Cole whispered. "The louder we get, the longer they'll hide. They don't like a lot of noise or movement. Or light. But I know they're out here. Let's wait. They'll come back."

"Yeah," I replied, transferring most of my body weight to the maple.

"I've seen them plenty of times." I yawned. "Is this what does it for you? Finding fireflies? You should've told me that two weeks ago."

Cole crouched down low, and he was quiet for a long moment. "I went to Tennessee once. There's a researcher there, an old woman who specializes in the Smoky Mountain Synchronous Firefly." He stood, turning in a small circle. "*Photinus carolinus*," he added, as if I required that detail. "The males, they flash in a synchronized rhythm. It's a mating call. But they only live in certain regions."

"Like, the Smoky Mountains?" I asked around a laugh.

"Well, yes," he replied. "And a few other regions in southern Appalachia."

"Can't picture you in southern Appalachia," I murmured. Cole was too busy tracking fireflies to hear.

"I brought a group of my—uh—businesspeople to the Appalachian Trail," he continued. "I had this big idea about sparking some childlike wonder and nostalgia for the ways things used to be. You know, summer camping trips. The great outdoors."

"And fireflies," I offered.

"And fireflies," he repeated. He gestured for me to follow him. I reluctantly pushed away from the tree, but the motion sent me colliding with his shoulder. His arms went around me, his palms settling on my belly and the small of my back to keep me steady. "Easy there, big guy."

"I'm good, I'm good," I said, righting myself. But my body was aglow where he'd touched me. I patted his shoulder—a gesture of thanks—but lingered a couple of seconds too long. Not long enough.

"Some species of firefly are dying out," Cole said. Apparently he didn't require full minutes to process my touch before forming words. Lucky Cole. "Skyglow, the phenomenon of constant brightness from cities, highways, and screens, interferes with their ecosystems. And I took a bunch of businesspeople—the kind who built their careers on technological advancement—into the Smoky Mountains to catch a look at some fireflies."

"Did that work out as intended?"

"Not at all," Cole said, laughing. "The researcher, she wouldn't allow us to bring any phones or tablets—like I said, screens are part of the problem—or flashlights."

His words hitched as he stumbled over an exposed tree root in the path. I dropped my hand onto his shoulder again, and kept it there this time.

For safety. Of course.

"There'd been a forest fire the previous season, and some of the trails were gone. We didn't get lost because this researcher knew the forest like the back of her hand, but the journey didn't go as planned. We didn't get to see any fireflies, not really. There was some twinkling in the distance, but the fire did a number on their population." He sighed, and I squeezed his shoulder in response. "They missed the point I was trying to make."

"You're getting some fireflies now," I whispered.

Cole didn't respond. He was staring into the woods, pointing and murmuring in delight as he spotted another zip of light.

"It really is something when you think about it," he said. "Adult fireflies are only active for about two weeks. They live for almost two years but they spend most of that time eating bugs and hanging around, not doing much of anything. Just waiting and waiting for that snap of time when they have to find a mate, and then they only have two weeks to get the job done."

"Seems like a lot of pressure," I said.

"But isn't that the way? You spend forever waiting for the right time, but then the right time is over before you know it." Cole shrugged, and I gulped down a groan at the feel of his muscles rising and falling beneath my touch. "That's probably why they have extremely active sex lives."

"Someone should have an extremely active sex life," I muttered.

"Once they find a mate, it takes almost an hour to transfer the sperm," Cole said. It sounded like he was reading from a textbook. A sexy textbook about horny fireflies. Or something.

"Sounds good to me."

"Once it's done, the sperm transfer, the male stays around to ward off competitors. He doesn't want anyone else getting in there." He shrugged again, and if I was sober, I'd think he rubbed his cheek against my hand. Then again, if I was sober, I wouldn't be massaging his shoulder in the woods at night. I would've moved this conversation somewhere with beds. And lube. "They're territorial fuckers."

"Me too," I said. Not sober, not sorry.

Cole stopped, and pointed toward the woods. It was dark back here, completely hidden from the lighthouse's steady beacon, and that darkness awakened a whirl and flow of tiny stars. They blinked in the quiet beat of an ancient universe to which we were guests, voyeurs in a mating ritual that mirrored my own wants.

"I get it," I said slowly. "The nostalgia. It feels pure. Or, as pure as any booty call can be."

"That wasn't what I wanted my team to walk away with, but it's true," Cole replied. "I wanted them to think micro—the fireflies—and macro—us—but they weren't picking up on any of that."

He sighed and this time he definitely rubbed his cheek on my hand. That scruff. *Ah.*

"They're flashing us their happy little dick pics," Cole said. "This is just a whole lot of dick announcing *I'm down to fuck.*"

"We're basically watching a glow-worm orgy," I said.

"I know," he whispered. "It's awesome until you really think about it."

"You should've told that team of yours about the sex. That got my attention."

"Should we give them some privacy?" Cole asked.

I started to respond but instead of speaking, I pressed my lips to his neck. My hand moved from his shoulder to his chest, and I dragged him closer to me. I should've stopped. Should've pushed him away, put this on hold, and figured out what the fuck we were doing because the heat between us was increasing by the second and I was a breath away from losing my thoughts—every one of my damn thoughts—and letting need guide the way. But I didn't do that.

For once in my life—twice, if we were counting last night's indiscretions—I did what I wanted rather than thinking about the implications and repercussions. I brought my hand to Cole's face, turned him away from the glow-worm orgy, and kissed him.

In the back of mind, I knew...one wrong move and this could end with some awkward moments and hard feelings, and I didn't want either for us. He was an unexpected friend, and one I wasn't ready to lose.

He twisted in my arms, his lips returning to mine, his hands shifting down to my waist, his knuckles stroking the small of my back in the most precious way, and I fell over the edge of reason. It was like those seconds between barreling over the bow and splashing down in the ocean, when all sense of balance and equilibrium went wild before recalibrating as the water took over.

I cupped his face and pressed my lips to his in a kiss that was too tortured, too desperate to be the kind of kiss he deserved. We clawed at each other, pushing and pulling and grabbing in a battle for touch that would have no end.

"Tell me we're doing this," he panted against my lips.

"What is *this*?" I asked. I needed him to spell it out. Draw the map and show me the course. There could be no miscommunication here. "What do you want?"

Cole pressed his face to the crook of my neck, his lips exploring my skin as his hand traveled down until it squeezed my cock. It was exactly as firm and confident as I'd imagined last night. Before I found him outside the bathroom, and after.

"I want this," he said, releasing a hot breath on my neck.

Grabbing his shoulders, I pushed him back far enough to catch his eyes. My touch was rough, nearly punishing, and I would have regretted that if it weren't for the blissed-out sigh on Cole's lips.

Yesssss.

"Say it," I ordered, my hold on him tightening.

"I want you. So much that it hurts," he said, his words tumbling out in a gasp.

There was only one way to ease this pain. Without a word, I backed him up against a tree and dropped to my knees. My hands were curled around his hips while I pressed my face to his heat. He was thick and hard behind his shorts, and I dragged my scruffy chin over the fabric to feel the length of him.

"Do that one more time and I'm gonna come in my pants," Cole said, his words slurring around a hiccup.

"Are you too drunk for this?" I asked. I was unbuttoning his shorts while I asked, but I still asked. "I don't want you to regret this tomorrow."

Cole shook his head but it had the effect of shaking his entire body. I had to lash my arms around his waist to keep him from hitting the ground. "Nope," he drawled. "I'm a sloppy drinker. It's my worst trait. That, and my penchant for screaming at the people who work for me. But anyway. No, I'm completely lucid under this. I can't turn it off. I've tried. Once, in college, I tried to get drunk enough to find women attractive. Like, sexually. I mean, women are beautiful but—"

"Is there a point?"

I shoved his boxer briefs down and his cock swung free. It tapped my cheek, and though I wanted more than anything to get my hands on him, I waited. I didn't know where that Herculean strength sprang from, but I appreciated the hell out of it now.

"Yes, there's a point, Owen," he replied, exaggerating every word like a sassy teenager. "It's that there's nothing I can do to turn off my mind. That's the trouble with having an extremely high IQ. It's one of the highest ever recorded."

"Don't make me gag you," I said, then thought better of it. "Unless you'd like that."

"No, I wouldn't," he said. "But if you don't suck my dick right now, I'm gonna think you don't know how to."

I shook my head but took pity on him, wrapping my fingers around his shaft before brushing my lips over the crown. He was thick and warm, and he smelled like the most hedonistic heaven I could imagine. "Always something to say."

Cole's hands landed on my shoulders, and he gripped me hard. "Do that again," he ordered.

I thought about teasing him. If this was a random hookup, I would've. I usually answered demands with more torment. Same with pleading and begging. But rather than wanting to assert my control, I wanted to give Cole what he needed. Even if that meant ceding some of that control.

"Please, again," he begged.

"Anything," I whispered, laving my tongue over him. I learned the contours of him, licking up and down his length, around his crown. It didn't take long—maybe a minute or two—but for me it was an epic journey. I was Magellan here, and I was intent on mapping my new world.

Cole's hands slipped up my neck and into my hair, his hips pumping as I worked him. The woods seemed to close in, the night joining forces with the noises of nature and the raw smell of earth to surround us. It was primal, as if the woods were calling on me to make this man mine.

The cloak of darkness offered a voyeuristic sanctuary, a secret as long as we didn't mind the audience. The damp soil beneath my knees, the lightning bugs and beetles fluttering around us, the creatures lurking in the distance, the whisper of trees and the roar of the sea—it all rose up like an unblinking chorus.

I swallowed him down, inch by inch, and sighed in delight when my nose brushed against his pelvis. His scent was different here, richer. In the back of my mind, I knew I'd never be able to venture into these woods without recalling his scent. I wasn't prepared to deal with that thought or the possibility that this man could mean something—maybe everything—to me, and shoved it far away while I worked on showing off the best of my blow job skills.

And when it came to skills, I had them. No one racked up a decade's worth of meaningless sexual encounters without learning their way around a topflight blow job.

Cole's fingers tightened around my hair. "I'm," he started, his voice pitching high while my fist moved him fast and my tongue rolled along the underside of cock. His back arched away from the tree. "I'm—*mmm* —yes."

I hummed in response and dragged my free hand away from his hip and between his legs. My touch was light and gentle as my fingertips ran up his thigh, over his sac, and between his crease. I was as surprised as anyone that I could not only manage light and gentle but enjoy it, too.

I was good at rough, hard, fast, and I guess that fit. I was a big guy who worked on lobster boats. Of course I'd fuck as rough and hard as I worked. But—no. No, that didn't fit. A man possessed more facets than his profession, and I knew that to be true because I wanted to lay Cole on my bed, massage every inch of his body, and take him as soft and sweet as he could bear. And then I wanted him to do the same to me.

"*Ohhh.*"

I glanced up and found Cole's head tilted back against the tree, his eyes screwed shut and his chest heaving. Even in the darkness I could make out a rosy flush across his sharp cheekbones. I wanted to tell him he was beautiful and goofy and erotic, all at once. I wanted to watch the way my words affected him. I wanted him to give me his words, and I wanted them to come from the same confusing places as mine.

But I didn't. I went on sucking him, stroking him, speaking my desires the only way I knew how. This night offered no place for my heart and its flowery notions, and I could live with that as long as I could spend it with Cole in my arms.

I pushed a finger inside him and he cried out, a sound that was at once desperate and vicious. His balls were tight and heavy against my wrist, and I doubled down on my efforts, swallowing him deep while I massaged that magical spot.

"What the fuck are you doing to me? What the running fuck is happening right now?" Cole hissed. "This is what a supernova feels like. Or breaking the sound barrier. Or cold fusion. Maybe dark matter. I don't know much about that but—"

He didn't finish that thought because he popped off like a shot down my throat. He went on sighing and groaning as I licked every drop and then mapped his skin with my lips. Minutes passed while he fought to catch his breath, his fingers still tight around the strands of my hair.

My cock was throbbing to the point of pain. It was like one of those old cartoons where a character knocked himself in the head with a hammer, and the resulting goose egg pulsed white to red, white to red. A snarl was building in my throat and I was ready to pounce. Tear his clothes, spin him around, bend him over, take what I wanted. Needed.

As much as my body wanted that, my heart didn't. Regardless of whether I'd recently blown his mind, I couldn't bring myself to unleash that kind of self-serving desire on him. It was silly, really. This was a summer fling at best; a one-night stand at worst. He was leaving and I was staying, and there was no sense winding myself up with emotional ideas. But I was already wound up, long past silly, on my way to lovesick.

Cole's grip on my hair loosened. "I hope you're not done with me."

I kissed the jut of his hipbone and shook my head, stealing another lungful of his scent. "Not even close," I replied.

Cole blew out a breath as a growl rattled in his throat. He dragged his fingers over my scalp and canted my head to meet his hungry gaze.

His eyes were hooded but sober as a sermon. He tipped his chin down. "Zip me up."

Taking orders wasn't my style but serving Cole was. I'd been serving him since the minute he'd drifted into my cove, and I wasn't about to stop.

"A 'please' wouldn't be too hard, would it?" I asked, dragging my teeth over the same hipbone I'd adored seconds ago. "Or am I just someone to put your dick away for you, little prince?"

Cole fisted my hair, snickering. "I've said it about nine thousand times tonight."

I sucked a mark into his skin and then pulled his boxer briefs up, careful to snap the waistband when they were in place. "If you know what's good for you, you'll keep saying it," I murmured. "You can be bossy or bratty, but not both."

"I think you like both."

His shorts were in a heap around his ankles, and I did my best to shake the dirt and forest miscellany from them before sliding them up his lean legs. "You don't know what I like."

Cole wrapped his hand around my bicep and hauled me up from the ground. "I'm gonna find out." He busied himself with pinching the seams of my t-shirt and straightening my clothes. He ran his hands from my shoulders to my fingertips, and then pressed his palm to my aching cock. "Real soon."

All the strength in the world couldn't keep me from whispering, "Please."

13

HARDEN IN

v. To haul in the sheet and tighten the sails.

Cole

THERE WERE steps between that spot in the woods and Owen's bedroom, many of them, but he took my hand and guided me down the path, and everything else drifted away. I wanted to take a picture of us, just like this. My man, holding my hand as he led the way. *My man.* Now, that was a rare thought.

Once we were behind closed doors, he attacked my clothes. Unbuckle, unzip, unbutton, off. When my boxers hit the floor, Owen stepped back and stared at me, drinking in my bare skin.

Before modesty could get the better of me, I gripped my cock at the base and gave it a lazy stroke. A growl rumbled up from his chest and his brows lowered in warning. His breath was coming in quick, rough pants that worked me like a seductive lullaby. I knew nothing beyond hunger, absolute starvation for this man.

"Off," I said, reaching for his t-shirt.

"Now you're thinking," he replied. "Thought you were just going to make me watch while you jerked it. Not that I'd complain but that wasn't what I had in mind."

I yanked the shirt up and over his head, and then moved on to his shorts but I was a disaster. At least one button was sacrificed to the cause and I gave up trying to maneuver the zipper around the substantial bulge of his erection. Bypassing the zipper altogether, I dragged the garment down his hips and sighed in relief when he was free of it.

"Shit. Sorry about that," I mumbled. "I'm not great in the dark. Or with undressing. That's not what I meant. No, I mean, obviously I know how to get undressed. I'm just not experienced when it comes to taking off someone else's clothes. It's not one of my skills. I might be a born-again virgin."

Owen—God love him—chose that moment to cross his arms over his thick chest.

"You say that like it's a bad thing. It's not. I'll teach you anything you need to learn," he said, his dick pointing straight at me. He reached out, his knuckles skimming down the line of my jaw. "You did just fine, little prince."

I didn't know what it was about his acceptance and affection, but it gave me wings. I wasted no time backing him to the bed, flattening him against the quilt, and taking his cock in my mouth. I couldn't remember the last time I'd sucked someone off but what I lacked in talent, I made up for in enthusiasm. I was eager to have this—and him—and I packed years of need and loneliness, desire and relief, into every roll of my tongue.

I sucked him deep and hard, and his hands were everywhere. Tight around my shoulders. Rubbing my scalp. Stroking my jaw. And then his hand found mine. Our fingers laced together, our eyes met. Seeing him there, his eyes narrowed as I brought him to the edge, his hips rolling against the bed as he fucked my mouth, it turned me on like nothing else.

And it had Owen erupting like a geyser.

"You taste like the ocean," I murmured after I'd swallowed every pulsing spurt. "I liked it."

"That's the right answer," Owen said, a sated laugh ringing in his words. His hand was on my shoulder and he squeezed, pulling me closer. "Come here. I want to play with you a little before I fuck you."

I peered up at him from between his thick thighs. "What?"

"Is that all right?" he asked, edging up on an elbow. "Or do you need to take a break?

"No." I was kneeling at his feet, my arms around his waist and my cheek pillowed on the warm skin above his knee where his tan and freckles faded away. He smelled like sex and dirt, and it was the truest moment I'd ever lived. This was the only place I wanted to be. If I closed my eyes and concentrated on the thrum of his pulse under my ear, I could keep this. "No," I repeated.

Owen sat up, his brows furrowing as he moved. "No, it's not all right?" he asked, his fingers rubbing the back of my neck. "Or no, you don't need a break?"

I tilted my head to get a better look at him. "What? I didn't catch any of that."

He hummed to himself and pushed his fingers through my hair. "Are you sure you're not too drunk for this?"

I shook my head. "Not drunk at all. Not anymore."

Owen hooked his arm around my torso and hauled me onto the bed. "That helps, I suppose."

I sat beside him and rested my head on his shoulder. "I'm just a little —I don't know. Dazed?"

"Dick drunk?" he offered.

"Probably, yes." I laughed, and waved toward his crotch. "How could I not be? With all that?"

"I'm glad you enjoyed it," he said, laughing. He kissed my forehead and dropped his hand onto my chest, pushing me back. "Get on your belly. I want to spend some time with your ass."

That was all I needed to hear. It was *everything* I needed to hear. I crawled to the middle of the bed, my skin burning under the heat of Owen's gaze. His fingertips brushed over the back of my calf and up my leg. A shiver started at my shoulders and moved through my body.

"Something you like?" Owen asked.

One finger traced the seam of my knee. His touch was barely there but the anticipation only doubled the impact. "Mmhmm," I murmured against the quilt. The rhythm was slow but purposeful. He wanted me to know how he'd tease me elsewhere.

The mattress dipped at my waist. He planted his hand near my shoulder, brushed his lips over my neck. "Then I'll keep going," he said, his breath warm on my skin.

I shivered again. "Please."

Owen dragged his lips down my spine, licking and kissing as he passed each notch. "You're fucking golden," he whispered.

"And you like that?" I asked. "That I'm golden?"

I felt him nod, his scruff scraping over the tender part of my flank. Goose bumps rippled over my skin. "Love it," he murmured. "I've always wanted my very own California boy."

For the first time, I glanced back at him. He didn't notice. His cock was jutting out from his body. He was thick and throbbing, the head shiny with a dot of arousal. "I can't believe you're hard again," I said.

"Why not? Haven't you seen yourself?"

He moved to my waist, his hands locked around my hips, and hiked me up. His palms smoothed down my back and over my ass, his thumbs sliding between my crease with enough pressure to have my breath shuddering out.

"Not from that angle," I replied.

"It's a good angle." Owen laughed as he squeezed my backside, each finger triggering a rush of need like cracks in a dam. "Then again, you're hot from every angle."

His grip tightened and then—*oh, fuck*—his tongue swiped over my flesh. "Oh, my God."

A growl was the only response I received. He went on tormenting me while I clawed the quilt down and flung pillows to the floor. It was all I could do.

"This ass is so sweet," Owen said. He reached between my legs, gripped my shaft. "I'm gonna tear it up."

His fingers moved down my cock with quick, light strokes. It wasn't enough, and he knew it. He chuckled as I thrust into his fist, trying and failing to find more friction.

"Now, please," I said.

"This," he said, his thumb stroking the head as he kissed up my spine, "*this* is what I was thinking about last night. You, on my bed. Naked. Panting. Pleading."

"Did you think about fucking me at any point?" I asked. "Because that would be great right now."

Owen laughed. "Yeah, I thought about that all night." He patted the mattress around me, searching until his fingers closed around the condom packet. I heard the rip, then the glug of lube into his palm, then the rasp of his short beard on my lower back. "Ready?"

"Very." I squirmed, desperate to feel him inside me. "Don't tease me, Owen. I can't, I—" The words caught in my throat as he pushed into me. He felt like iron, hard and unyielding. My body burned, vulnerable and hot as I forced myself to breathe through the stretch and sting.

"If you think I have the strength to tease you, you haven't been paying attention," Owen said. "If anyone's the tease here, it's you."

He rested both hands on my waist, his thumbs massaging my lower back while he inched inside me. Every thrust drew a gasp from my mouth and then a quiet prayer for more. He leaned down when he was fully seated, and brushed his lips over the base of my neck.

Tears sprang to my eyes, not from pain but the emotional impact of opening myself to a man for the first time in years. As if he was dragged under the same overwhelming wave, Owen kissed my neck and shoulders. "Okay?" he asked, his hips moving faster now. "Is this good?"

"Yes great please more don't stop," I begged.

He kissed me again, and then I sensed him pulling away. "Good," he said.

The heel of his palm pressed the base of my neck, his fingers sliding, fisting in my hair. He had me anchored there, my cheek flat on the mattress and the sheets balled in my hands. My lips were parted on an infinite moan as he pounded me.

He was going at me hard, there was no doubt about that, but it was perfect. I didn't know it when I set out on this summer journey, but I needed this. Not a fling, not a rough hookup, but Owen. I needed him to dirty me up, take me apart.

Reaching around, Owen took my length in hand. "I'm there," he said, his words nothing more than a groan. "Need you there, too."

I couldn't put thoughts together right now. All I could manage was a murmur and a nod, and a hard thrust onto his cock. I was full beyond belief, every inch of my skin electrified with sensation.

"For a born-again virgin, you know how to work that ass. Show me," he ordered. "Show me how you like it, baby."

My eyes were barely open, my lips parted, my body slick with sweat. I brought my hand to my erection, wrapping my fingers around Owen's, and showed him what I wanted. "This," I said, the word muffled against the mattress. "Just like—"

The pressure of our hands, his cock, his body over mine, it hit me at once. I fell apart, came back together, and then fell all over again. I heard him roar and pant, I heard him yell my name like no man had ever yelled it before, and I felt his body go slack against mine. He ran his hands over me, rubbing and squeezing me as he went. I couldn't manage more than the occasional moan or sigh, and I hoped the sloppy, sated grin on my face said it all.

"I'll be right back," Owen said, his lips pressed beneath my ear. "You stay right here."

"Don't think I can move," I mumbled.

The mattress shifted as he rolled away from me. Then, the floor creaked under his feet, a sudden reminder that I wasn't actually floating on a cloud of warm marshmallows but in this man's seaside cottage, sweaty and used in the best way. And I knew—once again—that I didn't want to be anywhere else.

Owen returned a few minutes later, a damp cloth in hand. He cleaned me up and fixed the bedding, all while I smiled up at him.

"You look like a Renaissance painting," he said, tossing a pillow at my head. "A slutty Renaissance painting."

"The best kind," I said.

He tugged the sheets up to my waist and slipped in behind me. He said nothing. I wanted him to respond, tell me he liked it when I was a little slutty. I wanted some recognition that he enjoyed teasing me as much as I enjoyed teasing him. I wanted something, anything to confirm that we hadn't made a huge mistake.

"Are you all right?" Owen asked, his hand skimming down my flank.

"I'm good," I said. "This was good."

Owen started to say something but stopped himself. I need him to say something. Eventually, he curled his arm around my waist and blew out a breath. "Get some rest, McClish. The sun's up in a few hours."

It wasn't what I needed, but it was something.

ABOVE BOARD

n. On or above the deck; in plain view; not hiding anything.

Cole

OWEN WAS AWAKE FIRST. I didn't have to look outside to know he was on the dock, readying the *Sweet Carolyne*, because recent days had taught me he was a creature of habit. A habit that excused him from acknowledging that we'd spent the night curled around each other. It was simpler this way. Simple was good, at least for today.

But as the dawn broke into day, I was increasingly confused about where things stood. It wasn't like Owen was the kind of guy who enjoyed sitting down for tea and sorting it all out. That was another place where we deviated. My brain preferred the precise, and without it, I was edgy and untethered. Aside from the tug of my sore, satisfied muscles, it was an ordinary outing on the water followed by a trip to the local market, and dinner on the porch, and the entire time, I wanted to scream, "*What is going on with us?*"

Of course I didn't. I'd made it to thirty-four years old without experiencing a relationship of any substance. Dating in Silicon Valley was fraught with complications. People were drawn to me for my money, my status, my power, but never once for *me*. On most days, I doubted that anyone in the Valley knew me at all. Sure, I was the CEO—err, former CEO—with the temper and the track record of transforming the industry, but that wasn't the sum of my parts.

But Owen...he didn't know the CEO. He didn't know any of it, and in that, he was the only one who knew me.

And that was what made the possibility of Owen telling me it was a one-night thing the worst scenario. That he didn't want more, or didn't want more of *me*, and it would be finished for us.

Instead of talking through my issues, I'd skipped the preseason NFL game and retired to the guest room to work on some programming projects after dinner. It was an out for Owen. If he didn't want anything more than a deckhand, I wasn't going to force the issue.

My phone blew up with notifications every time I powered it on, but I ignored all of them tonight. Neera's messages were the only ones that interested me. That, and I required a distraction.

Neera: People are starting to ask questions about your vacation. I don't have anything to tell them.
Cole: Are they wondering if it's permanent?
Neera: Some, but not all. A few questions about whether you're working for the government. A few questions about whether you're working against the government. Others have asked if you're writing a book, starting a new company, in rehab, planning a run for office.
Neera: It's mostly BS. Not difficult to shut down.
Cole: Good.
Neera: It would be easier if I had the real story and didn't look as clueless as everyone else. You know the bloggers and reporters come to me before going to the PR team.
Cole: You know what they say about secrets.
Neera: Three people can keep them so long as two are dead.
Cole: There you go.

BUT THEN, not long after I'd opened my laptop and dived into coding headspace, Owen barged into the room wearing only his boxer briefs. I blinked twice as I dragged my glasses down my nose because *holy fuck*, that man was beautiful. He was a bear. A big, angry bear.

He beckoned me toward him with a hot stare. "Why aren't you in bed?"

I ran my hand over the quilt beneath me in what I hoped to be an illustrative response.

"My bed," he clarified.

"*Your* bed?" I repeated. "You mean—"

"Get your ass in there right now," he barked. "What are you even doing in here?"

I gestured to my laptop. Did he want to know the specifics of the program I was developing? That didn't seem likely. Owen was one of a dying breed that lived happily without the quicksand of the internet. He preferred walking inside the bank to speak with a teller when making a transaction. He relied on maps and tide charts rather than modern—and surprisingly finicky—navigation systems. He even had an old-fashioned rotary phone on the kitchen wall. Before I'd arrived, there was no internet access in his home. I'd fixed that, of course, but I wasn't troubling him with those details.

"Working," I said, and I hoped it didn't sound overly evasive.

A sound rumbled in his throat that sent shockwaves through my body. "I meant," he started, rubbing the back of his neck, "why the fuck are you working in *here*? Why aren't you next door?"

My eyes darted to the screen for a moment, hoping to find the words between the lines of code. I could offer an excuse about needing quiet or my gear but knowing that he wanted me again—that he wanted me *at all* —changed things. It gave me a bite of confidence I'd never known I was lacking.

"I didn't know you wanted that," I said.

Owen cocked his head, squinting at me. "Was there something vague about my dick in your ass this morning?"

Gulp. I could still feel his weight on me, his hands on my hips, my groans into the mattress.

"But—but—you didn't say anything. You haven't said anything all day.

I've had no idea what you want and what you're thinking," I said. "For all I know, it was a one-and-done thing for you."

"More like four," he quipped.

"What?" I asked, shaking my head.

"I meant," he started, "last night was more like four-and-done."

I ran my hand through my hair. "I didn't know you'd want that again."

"Do you?" he asked, his gaze darting away from mine.

"Yes," I answered. "If you do."

"Okay." He nodded decisively. "Good."

"Yeah, it's great that it's good and all, but this has been really confusing," I said, my voice raising. "You could've given me—I don't know—any indication of what you were thinking as to prevent me from creating insane scenarios in my head."

"Is that what you need?" Owen asked. His words were slow and soft, like he'd wrapped them in a blanket especially for me. "Me talking about things?"

"Yeah. I need you to tell me what's going on, even if it's nothing. I need you to be up front with me."

I bobbed my head in an effort to force back the reminder that I wasn't giving Owen any of the things I demanded. He didn't know the truth about me, and I should've told him sometime before my cock met the back of his throat.

"It's not nothing," he growled. "How could this be nothing?"

I looked back to the screen, the one place I always knew what to do and how to communicate, but before I could formulate a response, Owen was wedging himself beside me on the bed.

"Put this thing away," he said, his voice husky in my ear.

I obeyed. Of course I did. How could I do anything but exactly what Owen wanted when his lips were ghosting over my neck and shoulders?

His big hand settled on my chest and tugged my shirt up, over my head. He drew his knuckles down the centerline of my abs and dipped just below the waistband of my shorts. His fingers didn't move any farther down, instead stroking the fine trail of hair and stirring me to life.

"Did I not take care of you, my little prince?" Owen asked.

I'd never found myself on the receiving end of a pet name before, and I'd never imagined I'd like it. But I did. I liked it a lot.

Open-mouthed kisses covered my chest, and I felt myself unraveling like a tightly bound spool of thread. My head dropped back to the pillow, my legs parted, and all the weight I'd been carrying in my chest transformed into desire.

"Ah, no, you...you're amazing," I said, my eyes closing as his tongue found my nipple. "But it's complicated for me. There are a few things we should talk about."

I didn't want to withhold the truth any longer. He deserved to know that I wasn't just me, but me plus a worldwide empire, a mind-boggling fortune, and an entire blogosphere dedicated to reporting on my every eyebrow twitch.

Owen shook his head against my belly. "You're thinking too hard," he said, dropping kisses up my torso. "But you're probably right. I'll go first, and I won't tease you while I do it." He sat up and folded his hands in his lap.

"But I enjoyed the teasing," I complained. "Please, tease away."

"After," he promised. "I had a physical in June, and my blood work checks out. I haven't been with anyone since then, but I understand if you want to use condoms anyway."

"Oh, yeah," I said, reminding myself that normal people had conversations like this when they were sleeping together. "I'm good, too, on the health stuff."

"And you prefer bottoming?" he prompted. "Or did I read that wrong?"

"No, you're right," I said, swallowing a lusty sigh. I didn't know how I was going to pivot this discussion.

"Have you ever topped?"

"Yeah." I jerked a shoulder. "A long time ago. College. Not since."

"Would you do it again?" Owen asked. "If I asked you?"

I watched while he traced the line of hair running down my chest and past my belly button. "You'd want that? With me?"

"That's the second time tonight you've questioned my interest in you," he said, his gaze trained on my skin. "I can't decide whether you can't see yourself with a guy like me or you don't realize you're one helluva catch."

I ran my finger over the crease in his forehead. "What do you mean by that? A guy like you?"

"You know what I mean."

Owen glanced up from the spot he'd claimed on my abs and met my gaze with an arched eyebrow. Our backgrounds weren't the same, I knew that. But if he wanted to make something about the differences between us—economic, social, geographic—he was going to have to use his words and tell me that. I wasn't going to accept any assumptions on the matter, not when I believed these differences were exceedingly manageable. We'd made it this far without finding ourselves tangled in a different world knot. Why make one now?

When I shook my head, he blew out an impatient breath. "Dammit, McClish. A guy who wants you to fuck him. All right?" He rubbed his lips along the waistband of my boxers. "I'm just a guy who wants your cock. Can you live with that? Can you find it in yourself to bend me over and nail me one of these days?"

"Yeah, I can live with that," I replied with a snort. "Just let me know when you want to get nailed."

A grin pulled at the corner of his mouth. "I will," Owen promised. He scooted down, between my legs, and pressed his face to my crotch. He nuzzled my cock, his chin and lips stroking me through my boxers. The friction was unreal. When his hand slipped under my hip to nudge my back channel, I almost sprang off the bed.

That was all I could take. My cock was hard, my skin tight and hot, and I was nearly cross-eyed with need but I didn't want to be deceptive. It wasn't right, and Owen deserved to know who he was fucking.

"I want you right now," I whispered, "but we should talk first."

"We've done enough talking," he said, his fingers hooking around my shorts. "I've wanted you since you tried to shoot me off your boat, and if you didn't know it then, you knew it when you started whipping your shirt off in front of me every afternoon. End of discussion."

He shifted to slip out of his boxer briefs, and the motion sent his thick cock slapping against his belly. I reached forward, hungry for it— for *him*—and led him down with a firm grasp on his length.

"It's hot out there," I murmured, dropping a kiss on the corner of Owen's mouth.

He gave me *don't I know it* eyes. "*You're* hot out there."

He reached between my legs and trailed his fingers along my crease. I'd surrender everything in the known world to feel him there, more gentle than any man his size had a right to be, for the rest of my life. And it wasn't just his touch. It was his everything.

"I need," I said, groaning when Owen's fingers pressed between my cheeks as he took me in his mouth. All the fucks, *yes*. My eyes drooped shut, and stars and rainbows danced behind my lids. "We need to get the lube from your room. You're too big for me without it."

He looked up, confused. That had the unfortunate effect of separating his mouth from my erection.

"You don't have any?" Owen asked.

I shook my head as a whiny groan rattled in my throat. My hips jerked upward, seeking his attention. I was shameless when it came to him.

"We need to work on your preparedness," he said.

I looked away, not sure how to respond to him. "I didn't expect to get laid this summer," I confessed. "That wasn't even on my short list of priorities."

Owen brought his palms to his thighs with a decisive nod. "Well, you're getting laid tonight. Tomorrow night, too. Then there's next week, and the week after that. If you're up for it, of course. If Maine is on your short list of priorities."

I needed this, for as long as I could get it. I'd give up everything if it meant more time with Owen. I sat up on my knees and roped my arms around his waist. "It's my only priority."

Owen's gaze darkened as he stared at my mouth. His palm cracked over my ass, and as I yelped in surprise, he said, "Go get in *our* bed."

I'd never chased after a man before, but when Owen marched down the hall, his erection slapping against his belly loud and proud, I wasn't ashamed to say I power-walked myself right after him.

"Get comfortable," Owen ordered, pointing to the bed. He was digging in a bureau drawer, his back to me. I turned down the blankets and slipped between the sheets, but I couldn't tear my eyes off his body. His shoulders were like a mountain range.

"What are you doing?" I whined. I was losing my mind watching him like this, the muscles in his ass flexing every time he shifted on his feet. It was like watching two puppies wrestling under a blanket. My legs parted and my hand went to my erection. I needed some relief.

"Looking for the good lube," he replied. "I figure you're worth it."

I kicked the sheets off. Too hot, too much. "You better believe I'm worth it."

"This drawer is a mess," Owen grumbled. "I can't believe I let it get this bad."

"I can't believe you're talking about messy drawers right now," I complained. "I *am* naked."

Owen shifted, his eyes glazing over when he caught sight of me in the center of his bed, cock in hand. "That you are," he murmured. "And what a sight you are, my little prince."

I blinked, and then I noticed it. In one hand, Owen held three dildos. In the other, two metal butt plugs of differing sizes. "Umm. What the hell are we doing with all that?" I asked.

He glanced down at his hands, his eyes widening as he assessed the toys. "Nothing," he replied with a laugh. He dumped them back in the drawer and then slammed it shut. "We'll play with those some other time."

I gulped. "We will?"

"If you want." Owen yanked open the top drawer on the bedside table. "There it is," he said to himself. He tossed a bottle of lube to the bed and climbed up beside me. "I really need to organize this stuff."

"You have a lot of toys," I said, dragging my fingertips down his chest. "*A lot* of toys."

"Does that interest you?" He smiled when I nodded in response. "Good. Now, get your hands off that dick. It's mine."

Owen nestled between my legs and pushed my thighs back. I watched while he poured lube into his palm, and slicked his fingers and my crease. Cool liquid between my legs had me tensing back a shiver. I gasped, clenching as his fingers pressed into me, cold and thick.

"Relax, baby," he murmured. "You want this, right?"

And yeah, I did. I really fucking did, and I breathed through the pressure as Owen stretched me. His touch was firm but careful, and he was always asking what I needed. He had half his arm up my ass but he was respectful about it.

Fuck. This man. I was damn lucky to get lost in his cove...and then his bed.

I was in love with his fingers. It was just crazy, filthy love with those fingers. I could live out the rest of my days with nothing more than the sexual torment this man brought to me, and I would be content.

Correction: I *was* content. I needed nothing more.

"If you're gonna leak all over the place," Owen started, dragging his chin up my throbbing length, "I'm gonna have to lick you clean."

"You should," I replied. "It's your fault."

"And I'm happy to take responsibility," Owen said, laughing.

He swirled his tongue over the spot of arousal on my belly, and then took my cock in his mouth. He sucked and stroked in a slow, steady rhythm that had me moaning like a foghorn.

"Need to fuck you," he whispered against my thigh.

I nodded in response. I wanted that too, but there was no reason to rush. My cock couldn't get any harder. It wasn't possible. And I was wrong; there *was* reason to rush and it had a lot to do with the orgasm winding its way down my spine. His teeth nipped at my inner thigh, and I was damn near floating when he bit down while his fingers circled my prostate.

"Oh my hell yes please," I cried.

Owen chuckled as he reached for the lube he'd left near my shoulder. He nudged my thighs open as his slippery fingers found my prostate again, and a hungry, desperate cry caught in my throat. "Get inside me," I growled. "Give it to me. Don't make me wait anymore."

I watched the rise and fall of Owen's chest as his cock replaced his fingers. When he pushed past my resistance, my gaze scraped up his body to his gorgeous face to see bliss softening his features. He leaned forward, his heat wrapping around me like a blanket as he braced his elbows on either side of my head. My hands went to his shoulders and my ankles to his ass as he thrust into me. His cheeks were flushed, his eyes hazed over with heat.

"Is this good?" he asked, flattening his hips against me. "Are you all right?"

I nodded, no words available to me. I was only capable of taking it, of taking him, and wanting him to take all of me in the process. Owen eased back, dragging his cock from me on a slow, torturous path. Our eyes met and then shifted downward, and we watched as he disappeared inside me again.

"Ah, *fuck*," he hissed.

He was fucking me slowly now, all rolling hips and long, heavy thrusts, and I was about to lose my mind. I reached between us, suddenly frantic to find my release, and stroked my cock.

"No no," Owen said, moving my hands to his waist before taking my cock. "This is for me."

"But I need—"

"I know," he said, cutting me off with a kiss. "I know, little prince. But this is for me."

His grip was unforgiving, but his gaze. *Fuck,* that gaze. That was what got me. It was like he was staring straight into me, knowing me and begging me to know him in return. "Take it," I whispered. "Take all of me."

His thumb passed over my crown as he stroked into me. For a minute there, I went cross-eyed.

I'd never experienced sex like this before. There was the insanely good fucking component but that wasn't the whole story. It was the feeling of it all. The emotion behind every thrust, the intention in every kiss, the promise in every breath we shared. This kind of sex was an affirmation, and an ever-growing part of me knew I could scavenge the earth and not find anything else like it. Like *him*.

"Don't say something like that unless you mean it," Owen replied. "Because you better believe I will."

He did. He had me flying apart within minutes, one hot spurt after another.

"Your turn," I rasped, my eyes glued to his abs as they rippled with each glorious thrust. "You gave me everything I wanted, Owen. Now I want you to take what you need."

His eyebrows arched, and a smile tipped up one side of his mouth.

He pulled out and jerked himself with the same force he'd offered me. It was a blur of movement and guttural moans, and he huffed out a long, filthy string of curses as his release hit. He spilled—and spilled and spilled—all over my belly.

"Look at you," he breathed as the last spasms spiraled through him. "Just look at you."

Owen swirled two fingers through the mess on my belly. I was warm all over, filled with a hot new happy that felt too good to be mine. "Come here," I whispered, pulling him to my side. "Just stay right there."

"Nowhere else I want to be," he murmured, his lips on my neck and shoulder.

I lived a pretty big life. I'd traveled the world and met celebrities, heads of state, and more billionaires than I could count. Even though there were moments when I wanted to kick it all to the curb, I had it good. But none of that life compared to Owen's head on my shoulder or his bare skin warming mine.

15

TACKING

v. To change course by turning a boat's head into and through the wind.

OWEN

WHERE OUR FIRST week of sleeping together was an overwhelming rush of new, urgent and rough in the best ways, we'd now eased into the lazy indulgence stage. There was no rush, no awkward moments. We had a feel for each other now, and we knew this wasn't ending at sunrise. That made all the difference.

Also, several nights of flat-out fucking combined with unrestricted touching throughout the day took some of the edge off. I could curl around Cole while our breathing eased and our bodies cooled, and not lose myself in another heady swirl of lust. It was a good thing I found that restraint, too. The afterglow left him chatty, but it wasn't his usual noise. He confessed his desires, shared secrets, told stories I was certain had never before seen the light of day.

It was another piece of Cole I was fortunate enough to claim as my own, and I relished these dark, quiet moments when we could shed everything and be the most raw versions of ourselves.

In all this glorious honesty and openness, a few critical details were missing. The reason for his extended summer vacation never came up. Details about his life in California were off the table. He rarely talked about his work, and when he did, it was to vent his hatred for corporate culture.

I knew I shouldn't but I preferred it this way.

I loved the fantasy of Cole. The version of him that came without strings or complications. That version didn't have a life and a business waiting for him on the other side of the country. That version wasn't going to gather up his pastel polo shirts and sail away.

If I could hold onto the fantasy, I wouldn't have to cope with the reality that I'd fallen for a man who could never be mine. Not really. I didn't need to know the inner workings of his world to know it wasn't mine. He could enjoy the hell out of a summer in Talbott's Cove, but that didn't mean he had any intention of permanently relocating here. Just another one of my sandcastle dreams. I was getting ahead of myself, planning our future together when I didn't know if he shared a fraction of my feelings.

I knew I was good for a fun time in the summer. That was how it went for me. I went starry-eyed and lovesick, and they went back to their lives in the city. Summer loves only led to autumn heartbreak, and that was why I needed the fantasy.

I blinked that thought away as I stared at the ceiling. It was another hot, humid night and the ceiling fan only moved the oppressive air around. By all accounts, it was too hot for sex, for cuddling, for anything more energetic than lying flat on the bed and breathing. But none of that registered. It was as if my body didn't care to process anything but the feel of Cole's fingertips sliding over my hip. His head was on my chest, his arm around my waist, and his legs tangled between mine. The quilt was in a heap on the floor and the sheets were clinging to one corner of the mattress.

This, right here, was my heaven.

"Have you ever been with a woman?" he asked.

I shook my head. "No. Came close once," I admitted. "After that situation, it was pretty obvious I wasn't interested in the hetero scene." I brushed his damp hair off his forehead. "You?"

"Not...quite," he said.

"Go ahead and explain that one," I said, laughing.

Cole dragged his hand up my belly to the center of my chest and drummed his fingers there. "I was a little slutty in college."

"Slutty or experimental?" I asked.

He bobbed his head for a second, humming while he considered this. "Slutty," he replied with a laugh. "But also, experimental. Sluttily experimental, I guess."

"Was it fun?" I asked.

Cole hesitated. "Yeah, most of the time. Going away to college was a big change for me. I didn't know who I was back then, or how to be comfortable with myself. I was out then but I didn't know how my sexuality fit into my identity. I didn't know what it meant to embrace the feelings I'd had for so long, and then experience them with someone else. I didn't how to accept and embrace myself as a gay man. There were days when I struggled with it. I mean, I didn't walk around with a Pride pin on my jacket."

"You don't do that now," I said.

"And neither do you," he argued.

I stared at Cole, willing him to meet my eyes, but he didn't. "Fair enough," I replied. "Where does the experimentation come in?"

"College was like an all-you-can-eat sex buffet," he said. "Most of the time, it was with men, but there was one time with a woman. Sort of. Not completely."

I didn't want to hear this. I didn't, but I did. The thought of Cole with other men—a buffet of men, no less—twisted my gut. Cole with women was a different form of pain. I could hold my own when I was competing with gay guys for his affection, but I was powerless when it came to women. "All right. This woman. What's her story? Were you out with her?"

"I wasn't, no. I was still figuring out how to say it, believe it, own it back then. I made some mistakes along the way." He hesitated. "We were friends though it was clear she wanted to be more. She flirted with me all the time and always had a reason to touch me—"

"That's fantastic," I grumbled. This jealousy of mine, it knew no reason.

"She was all the right things—nice, funny, smart—but I wasn't into her," he said, ignoring me. "Not at all. Objectively, I knew she was beautiful and sexy—"

"Of course she was," I said under my breath.

He speared me with an amused smirk. "She was beautiful and sexy but I still wasn't into her," he continued. "She started seeing a guy. I figured she'd shift her attention toward him but it didn't work out that way. Instead, she wanted the three of us to hang out."

"Because they both wanted to fuck you," I said, not at all surprised by the bright streak of possession racing through my blood. "Right? Isn't that the way it worked out?"

Cole continued tapping his fingers against my breastbone, studying my skin without responding.

Eventually, he heaved out a sigh and said, "I didn't recognize that to the be the case at first, but yeah. That's what happened. Basically." He sanded his fingers through my chest hair. "It was just one time. I didn't do anything with her. Not really. The guy, though, he wanted to play. He was pretty enthusiastic about me introducing him to his prostate. She was cool with that but I'm certain she imagined herself as the star of the evening rather than the minor player. Looking back, I think she wanted to start a stable." He layered his hands over my heart, dropped his chin there, and met my eyes. "That was my first and last time with a woman. If you can even call that being *with* a woman. She went out of her way to avoid me after that. The guy hit me up every time he was lonely and drunk."

"I hate her," I said. "I'm not fond of him either."

Cole rolled away from me as he shook with laughter. "You shouldn't," he said between gasps. "It was several lifetimes ago. I hadn't thought about her in years."

"Yeah, well, I'm still not happy with her." I reached for him and caught hold of his backside. "Get back here," I ordered, pinching until he yelped.

"That's going to leave a mark," he said, glancing over his shoulder. "Remind me to never activate your jealous side."

"I'll kiss it better," I promised. "Sorry. I didn't expect you to tell me about a threesome with a side story about you fingering some virgin ass."

"Tell me about the time you came close with a woman, and I'll excuse it," Cole said, returning to his spot at my side. "Was it Annette?"

I clapped my hand over my eyes. "God. No," I said, groaning. "Not Annette." I shook my head and indulged in another groan. "I took one of Annette's best friends to the prom, Jenna, and then made a valiant effort at engaging in post-prom traditions. It was a disaster."

"I didn't even go to the prom," Cole said. "Never mind the after-party."

"You didn't miss anything," I promised. "I didn't want to go. My mom forced me. She picked out the tux, the corsage, the girl—"

"Wait a damn second," he interrupted, holding up his hand. "What did you just say? About your mother and the girl and the picking out?"

I pulled a pillow out from under my head and pressed it to my face. "My mom set me up," I replied, hoping the pillow would suffocate me quickly.

It didn't. He plucked it from my hands and tossed it across the room. "Why?" he asked.

"Let me ask you this," I said, sitting up against the headboard. "When you came out to your family, how'd that go? How did they react?"

"We're going to do that?" he asked. "We're going to trade coming-out stories now?"

"Answer the question, Cole."

He shifted to sit beside me, blinking at the sheets while he considered my question. "I didn't come out, not exactly," he admitted. "My dad and I were stuck in traffic one afternoon. He asked if I had any questions about safe sex, and whether I'd thought about my sexual orientation. That's why he said. *Sexual orientation*. At first, I was too stunned to say anything. No one had ever been that direct with me. Plenty of kids teased the shit out of me, and there was no shortage of bullies in school, but no one had ever stopped to ask me about my identity. They'd always made assumptions. Once I recovered from the shock, I told him I had thought about it, and I was attracted to men. He nodded, and lectured me on the limitations of condoms for twenty minutes."

A grim smile pulled at my lips while I bobbed my head. "And your mother? Your sisters? How did they take it?"

Cole shrugged. "My mom ordered a bunch of books about Stonewall, the AIDS crisis, and gay memoirs. She insisted we read and discuss them together. We watched *And the Band Played On.* That all sounds depressing, but it wasn't. I mean, not too depressing." He folded his hands in his lap. "My sisters baked me a Bundt cake."

"Yeah, that wasn't my experience," I said with a rueful laugh. "My dad was cool but my mom was convinced I was going through a phase. She said I was confused, and I didn't know what I wanted because I'd lived in this small town for too long. I didn't like the girls here because I'd grown up with them, and viewed them as sisters."

"That's terrible." He reached over and took my hand. "I'm sorry."

I shrugged off his words but laced our fingers together. "Honestly, I believe she meant well. She didn't see how I could know my sexual identity when I was a fifteen-year-old kid who'd never kissed a girl—or boy. She thought it was an exposure issue, and once I got some exposure, my outlook would change. That's why she was always setting me up on dates and telling girls I was just shy. She meant well," I repeated. "She just didn't understand."

"That doesn't make it any easier to swallow," Cole said. "Good intentions do not erase or excuse harmful actions."

"It's okay. I don't walk around with that rain cloud over my head," I said. "I might have Annette chasing after me, but I'm not deeply traumatized or anything."

"Hang on a second," Cole said, holding up a finger. "You've dated in this town, right?"

I barked out a laugh. "No," I said. "Never. This place is far too small for me to hook up with the locals. Hell, no."

"And that, my darling, is why Annette thinks you're free game," he said. "Think about it. Your mom told everyone you were confused, you don't date locally, and you're a gentleman of a certain age. Knowing all that, I'm not surprised the vagina vultures are circling."

"Gentleman of a certain age," I repeated. "Not sure how I feel about you calling me old, McClish."

"Shut up. It looks good on you," he said, dragging his gaze over my chest. "You need to shut it down with Annette. I see it from her perspective now, and you really need to shut it down."

I groaned. "Yeah, that sounds wonderful."

Cole shifted to face me. "Does she understand now? Your mom?"

I held my hands out as if I was weighing my thoughts. "Yes and no," I replied. "She was a guidance counselor at the local high school—"

"And she called it a phase. I'm dying a little inside right now," he murmured.

"After she retired from the high school, my parents moved to one of those master-planned communities for active adults not far from Miami," I replied. "She says she's learned a lot about 'the gays' living in south Florida. She recently asked if I had a drag name, and whether I liked twinks. Apparently, her hair stylist would be perfect for me."

"I'm dead," he murmured.

"She means well," I said, as much for Cole's reassurance as mine. "Even if she should've handled it differently when I came out, she didn't throw me on the streets. She didn't send me away to conversion camp. Talking about drag names isn't the best entry point but it's her way of reaching out. If there's one thing I've learned in my time on this planet, it's that I can't wait for people to be perfect. I can't reject them because they don't know the best way to open a discussion on my queer life. I can want more and demand more, but I'm not going to refuse them when they're trying."

"I wouldn't have expected that much tolerance from such a grumpy guy," he said.

I hooked my arm around his leg and yanked him closer. "What are you talking about? I'm not grumpy."

Cole snickered, bumping my ribs with his elbow. "No, of course not. You're salty. Surly. Moody. Curmudgeonly."

"Now you're just being mean," I said with a huff.

"Hardly," he quipped. "You don't like people."

I planted my hand on his chest and pushed him down to the mattress. Rising to my knees, I straddled his thigh. My cock was thick and heavy, and pulsing as I rutted on him. "I like you."

His abs dipped as a laugh moved through him. "Oh, what a relief," he replied. "One last question for you."

"It's never the last question," I grumbled.

He ran his knuckles up my arm with a soft laugh. "Maybe not," he conceded. "But *are* you into twinks? I want to know if I should be worried about this hair stylist. Or dieting."

I smiled down at him, all rippling muscles and golden skin, and shook my head. "No," I said, flattening my palm on his trim waist and dragging it up to his broad shoulders. "I'm not. I like my man thick," I said. "I'm gonna keep you that way."

16

———

SNARL

adj. The condition when two or more lobster lines become tangled.

Cole

Neera: Could we schedule a check-in? Phone or video?
Cole: What would you like to discuss?
Neera: The usual. Goals, accomplishments, issues.
Cole: Nope.
Neera: Pardon me?
Cole: I'm not doing that. I don't have a work plan so I don't have goals, accomplishments, or issues to report back.
Neera: I thought you were developing something.
Cole: I am. But I'm not tying myself to timelines.
Neera: I see.
Cole: You say that when you don't see at all and just want to throw something at my head.
Neera: I wasn't attempting to imply that. I apologize.

Cole: No need to apologize.
Neera: Is there anything I can do to support you?
Cole: Not really. I'm being innovative. Isn't that my new job?
Neera: You're still dissatisfied. Still understandable.
Cole: If that's what you want to call it, that's fine.
Neera: What are you calling it?
Cole: I'm not. I'm just going about my life without agonizing over titles and hierarchy. There are more important things.
Neera: Such as?
Cole: Now that I think about it, there is something you can do.
Neera: I see you haven't lost your skill for deflection.
Cole: I'm going to send you a list of NGOs in need of some signal boosting. Some oceanic conservation nonprofits. Make it big but not connected to me.
Neera: I'll get right on it.

***

OWEN RAISED a hand toward the setting sun, waving at a passing lobster boat. The captain returned the gesture.

"That's the O'Keefe boat," he said, tipping his chin toward the green and white vessel. "They live north of town."

He ran his hand over my shoulder and I leaned into his touch. It was different now that we weren't working our asses off to avoid each other as a poor form of lust concealment. I enjoyed the easy affection he offered, and the freedom to reach for him whenever I wanted. It was a weightlessness I'd never before experienced, and it forced me to realize the ways in which I'd narrowed my life back in California.

I didn't date, I didn't flirt, I didn't have sex. There was no romance, no intimacy. I'd convinced myself I needed it that way. My existence was far too complex to add any human variables, and I was hardened by the fear of betrayal. Books featuring the sordid details of my company's inner workings—and my colorful leadership style—routinely landed on bestseller lists. Click-baity blogs went crazy every time I dined at a restaurant, splashing photos of me and my party. They'd make ridiculous comments about the people I was with and analyze the hell out of my meal. If they were lucky, they'd get a quote from a server about how much of an asshole I was that night.

There was no room in my world—the world I left in Silicon Valley—for a simple relationship. I couldn't determine whether I could change that world, make room. Whether Owen would be able to carry the weight of that world on his broad shoulders.

If I indulged in fanciful thoughts, I'd allow myself to believe I was meant to find Owen, and Talbott's Cove. I was meant to lose my title, leave California under the cover of PR bullshit, and nearly crash my boat on Maine's rocky coast.

If any of that was true and not merely the thing of fairy tales and dreams, I was also meant to tell Owen the truth about me and trust that his feelings wouldn't ebb. All this time in this cozy seaside town, all that had changed between us, and I still hadn't put my cards on the table with Owen. Not the ones that mattered, the ones revealing my true identity.

But it wasn't for lack of trying.

There was always something. An important ball game. A town council meeting. A breakthrough on one of my projects. A debate about nothing. A devious grin that turned into blowjobs behind the boat's bridge. Of course I could've put a stop to everything and forced him to listen but I didn't. With each passing day, it became more difficult to speak the truth when I'd let it linger in the shadows all this time.

When I was in college, one of my professors liked to say, "The longer you put off a task, the harder it is to get started." I couldn't remember the class but that adage stuck with me. I couldn't stop thinking about it, and watching the interest compound on this long overdue conversation.

"It's Thursday," I murmured. "Annette's staying open late for you."

Owen squeezed my shoulder, and I rubbed my cheek against his knuckles. "Don't remind me."

"Come on," I said, laughing. "You're a tough guy. You can handle a sweet little book mistress who hides her fangs incredibly well."

"Not sure about that," he said under his breath. "The fangs, that is. She's a nice lady. She means well."

"Another one with the good intentions." I ran my hand down his back and slipped beneath the worn fabric of his t-shirt. "I'm sure there's a nice guy—one who likes vag—who will make her very happy."

Owen snickered. "Add that to your list of projects. Get on the dating websites and find Annette's perfect match. I'm sure you can make a spreadsheet or something. All scientific." He shifted to face me, a thoughtful wrinkle across his brow. "What are you working on? You never talk about your projects."

I cut my gaze toward the ocean as I answered, "Nothing you'd find interesting. Interfaces and apps, that kind of thing."

That was the truth. Mostly. It wasn't inaccurate. It only omitted a few details.

He nodded and turned his attention to the boat's controls as we headed in the direction of the fish market. I kept my hand on his back, right up against the strong dip where his torso disappeared under his shorts. I loved dragging my fingers through the dark patch of hair there.

"I am interested," he said quietly. "Just because I don't do the internet thing doesn't mean I don't care about your work."

"Oh," I managed, the sound sticking in my throat like a fish bone. "Oh, I know. I didn't mean to suggest—"

"You didn't," he interrupted, his words tempered with charity and patience. Two things Owen rarely offered. Two things I didn't deserve. "I know I've been something of an ogre about my low-tech lifestyle, and I'm sure it made you feel as though I didn't value your work." He stared at the docks in the distance as he chose his words. "I didn't mean to make you feel unwelcome in any way. I'm sorry."

I couldn't believe this. If anyone was due to deliver an apology, it was me.

"You were not an ogre," I shot back.

"You can say it," he replied with a baleful shrug. "I was an ogre. It happens."

This was it. This had to be it. The last straw.

"Actually, we should talk about my business," I started. "There are a few things you should know."

Owen kept his gaze trained on the docks behind the fish market as he maneuvered around other lobster boats. "Yeah, if that's what you want," he said. "Let's finish up here and then you can give me the whole song and dance." He shot me a quick glance. "Will there be any singing or dancing? I get the impression you've got moves, McClish."

"What gives you that idea?" I replied, feigning a truckload of indignation.

Owen chuckled. "The way you move your hips when you like what you're getting. The way you shake your ass when you want my attention."

Was there anything that escaped Owen's notice? There couldn't be.

"Ass shaking aside," I started, sliding a hand down to give his rear end a squeeze, "we're going to the bookstore next."

I was stalling. Definitely stalling.

"The only reason you're pinching my ass is because you want me pounding yours," he warned.

I didn't respond until he stared at me for a moment. "Are you waiting for me to deny it?" I asked. "If so, you're going to keep on waiting."

"Such a smart mouth on you. Where'd you say you went to school?"

"I didn't," I replied. "It's act one in the performance. You'll have to wait to find out, but not until after we visit your dear friend Annette."

"Then after that," he said, steering the boat into one of the empty slips. "It's not like you're going anywhere, right?"

"Right," I murmured.

"Toss those buoys over, would you?" Owen asked, pointing to the dock. "Go ahead and shake that ass a little while you do it."

* * *

"WHAT DOES ANNETTE HAVE FOR YOU?" I asked as we walked through Talbott's Cove's tiny downtown. "Other than a major crush and the names of the five children she wants to have with you."

"You're not funny," Owen murmured, shaking his head while he growled like an angry bear.

"You're cute when you're irritable," I replied. "Lucky for me, you're always irritable."

I glanced at the lovingly maintained sidewalk planters and window boxes on each storefront. This town, with its tavern, general store, inn, and short string of shops dotting the streets around the harbor, defined quaint. It was something out of a magazine, or one of those free calendars realtors liked to send their clients with idyllic scenes from far-off locations. Places that didn't seem real.

"Something about American Revolution battles," Owen said. He shoved his hands in his pockets and jerked his shoulders up as he spoke. "The untold stories and whatnot."

"You like history," I said, studying Owen for any reaction or gesture of agreement. I received none. "And literature."

"Do we really need an inquisition right now, McClish?"

Ah, my beast. There he was.

"I made two observations, Bartlett. That's hardly an inquisition. It would be an inquisition if I asked you to defend your preference for Whitman over Keats, or Melville over Joyce. An inquisition would be me asking you to explain why you'd want to explore the battles of the American Revolution when you probably covered them in high school, whereas you probably did not learn about the Belgian Revolution of 1789. A true inquisition would force you to attribute the success of the American Revolution to one influential individual—not George Washington—and compare that person to—"

"Enough," Owen roared as he ground to a halt. He tossed up his hands, ripped his baseball cap from his head, and ran his hands through his hair. "I'm not in the mood to choke on your huge IQ right now."

I continued for several steps before stopping and pivoting to stare at him. His hands were perched on his hips and I could almost see the waves of frustration radiating from his body. If I didn't know him better, I'd think he was about to go Hulk Smash on this town. But I was beginning to believe that I did know him, and I knew he liked it when I pushed him. When I forced him to interact with me despite his desire to retreat into his thoughts. When he needed to get out of his head—and his worries about damaging Annette's feelings—for a minute.

"But my huge dick?" I asked, waving toward him. "You'd choke on that?"

"Like it's my job." Owen advanced on me, swallowing up the sidewalk in two long strides, and snatched my hand. "Let's get this over with. You'll get your inquisition later."

I followed him into the small shop, a bell tinkling overhead as we entered. I zeroed in on Annette as I crossed the threshold. She was behind the counter, her dark hair spilling over her shoulders, making her white dress appear strapless. It was the sexy angel look, and she was nailing it.

A customer stood on the other side of the counter, nodding while she spoke and held up each item in his pile, turned it over, opened the jacket, then patted the front cover. It appeared that she was telling him the secrets behind every book, offering up the special details only a book-seller would know.

If I wasn't busy stewing in jealousy over her baseless stake on my man, I'd want to get to know her. The lady was high octane, and I liked that. I respected it. I also had the distinct impression she had dirt on everyone in this small town, and I respected that, too.

"We'll just wait," Owen said, glancing at Annette before turning away. "I'm sure it will be only a minute."

"She talks with her hands," I said under my breath. "Five bucks says it will not be a minute."

"Shut up," he whispered.

The space was flooded with sunlight and books, paperbacks and hardcovers overflowing from every surface. A quick scan of the covers told me I wasn't the subject of any of these books, and that was a relief. Cheerfully painted terra cotta pots and baskets marked the new release section. Hand-drawn signs announced sections for every subgenre. Maine was well represented. There was local history, local cookbooks, local fiction, local nonfiction, local photography, even local romance.

"See anything you like?" Owen asked, squeezing my hand. "Oh—right. You don't read real books."

"That kind of incendiary language is unnecessary," I replied, smirk-ing. "Since you know all the best reads around here, pick something out for me. You know what I like."

His answering smile was dark, almost feral. "Yeah, I do." He inclined his head toward the opposite side of the shop, tugging my hand. "Let's see what we can find for you, little prince."

We crossed the small sales floor toward a section cheerfully labeled with a hand-lettered pennant banner as mystery and suspense. Owen stood behind me, one hand on my waist while he skimmed his free hand over the book spines. His breath was warm on my neck and the scruffy tickle of his beard sent a shiver through my shoulders.

"This is going to be good," I said. "We'll have a little book club situation going. Can we have wine and cheese with our literary conversations?"

He tugged a paperback from the shelf, ignoring me. "This might work," he said, almost to himself. "Cybercrimes. International intrigue. A bit of a love story."

"That's what I like?" I asked, arching back to press my ass to his crotch. "Tech stuff and spy games? Sounds like my day job."

"You forgot the part about the love story," he replied, his words rougher than they were a moment ago.

I laughed. "None of that in my day job."

Owen's arm curled around my torso, his fingers sliding barely beneath my shorts. He pressed his lips to my neck. "Good," he said. "You should save that part for your summer vacation."

I almost replied, telling him that I *had* saved the love story for this summer vacation, and that he was playing a starring role.

But Annette called, "It's my favorite fishermen!" and the words dried on my tongue.

With a sigh, I dropped my head back to Owen's chest. He pulled his fingers from beneath the waistband of my shorts but I clamped my hand over his, stopping him. "Where do you think you're going?"

"I'm not going to molest you in public," he snapped.

Annette rounded the counter, her perky smile melting into a confused grimace as she approached.

"You've done it before." I hooked my hand around the back of his neck, pulling his face closer. "Kiss me," I ordered. "Right now."

Owen didn't hesitate. His lips met mine with a kiss that started sweet and turned molten in seconds. But neither of us forgot we were in this shop, not more than a few feet from the woman who'd been crushing on my man for ages. With one last peck and a hungry growl, he broke away.

"Hey, Annette," Owen said.

His pinky finger was still in my shorts, and in some small, strange way, that was a victory for us.

Annette hugged a hardcover book to her chest and she blinked at us. Repeatedly. Her gaze followed Owen's hold on my body, each blink growing longer and more exaggerated. It was as though she was trying to erase the image in front of her by closing her eyes and wishing it away.

A fraction of me felt badly for her. I didn't need to have a long balance sheet of heartbreak behind me to know she was watching a relationship end. Even if that relationship was one-sided and nonexistent.

"Good to see you, Owen," she said, a dejected sigh weaving through her words. "You too, Cole."

"You have a great shop," I said. "Awesome selection, fantastic layout."

"Yeah, I try," she said. She glanced away and touched her fingertips to her brow, brushing aside a lock of hair. "Is there anything I can help you find?"

"I think we're good," I replied at the same moment Owen said, "Cole wants a few mystery novels. Can you recommend some?"

"Oh," Annette said, surprised. "Oh, sure." She took one hesitant step forward, another, and then she was scurrying around the store.

"Look what you did now," I whispered to Owen. "You activated her hummingbird setting."

"Me?" he asked, his head swiveling as he watched Annette. "This is definitely your fault."

"Only because I wouldn't let you lead this woman on for another decade," I replied. "We could've paid for your book and left, but you laid down the bookish lady challenge instead and now she's trying to prove a point."

She flew around us, snatching up books and tucking them under her arm as she stomped. "Let me pick out some books for your new boyfriend, Owen. That's what I do, make everyone else happy. Sure! Mysteries. Fantastic! Everyone else gets their happy and I get to pick out books. Fabulous!"

"So," I murmured. "This is really happening."

"It is, and I don't like being the asshole in her story," Owen said to me.

"Mysteries. I love a mystery. Sometimes I think I live in a mystery. You know, the *what is happening in my life?* mystery. Because I sure as hell don't know." She slammed a pile of books on the counter. "Can I get you anything else?"

"No, this is plenty," I replied while Owen said, "Did that special order come in?"

From her position behind the counter, Annette seemed to deflate. Her shoulders fell, her jaw unclenched, her grimace wilted into a frown. "Yeah, Owen, it did," she said. "I'll need a minute, okay?"

She didn't wait for a response, instead smoothing her hands down her skirt, turning around, and heading for the back room.

"It would've been easier to let her think we had a chance," Owen said, loosening his hold on me. "That would've been better than this."

Owen shook his head and walked toward the butcher block counter where the cash register was located, leaving me to chase after him.

"No, it would *not* have been better," I replied. "You can't continue that way. It's not right, and it's not fair to you."

"It's fine and—"

"It's not fair to me," I interrupted. "It would be one thing if she had a simple crush on you. But it's not a simple crush. It's not the same as that girl at the fish market in Bar Harbor who eye-fucks you every time we stop in. Hell, I've seen half the women on the seacoast undress you with their eyes. That's a different story. It's temporary. This is hitching her hopes to your dick and waiting for you to learn to like the feel of it."

Owen stared at me, his expression impassive as always. Then, "Okay. You're right," he said. "But you should know the other half of the women on the seacoast undress *you* with their eyes."

Annette emerged from the back room, a book in hand and smudged mascara under her eyes. "Here we go," she said, adding the paperback to our towering pile.

"Annette," Owen started, "about all of this. I didn't mean to make you uncomfortable. If I did, I'm...I'm sorry."

She waved away his words with both hands, shaking her head. "No apologies needed. I wasn't thinking. I wasn't being smart," she said. Then, softly, "I knew but I still hoped."

They stared at each other, Owen with his furrowed *I don't want to hurt you* brows and Annette with her big, tear-filled Disney princess eyes. A different iteration of me would've offered a pithy remark, something intended to cut the tension and trivialize the moment. I couldn't do that. I cared about Owen, enough to march him into this face-off. Instead, I scanned the immediate area and found a display of Maine coastline photography books. I grabbed three copies.

"This looks like something my mother would love. My sisters, too," I announced.

Annette dragged her gaze away from Owen only to shoot me the most unimpressed glare in the modern history.

"My mother loves a good coffee table book," I continued. This much was true. "She likes to dig through the clearance piles at her local book-store. For reasons I don't understand, she hates paying sticker price for anything. Unfortunately, she doesn't live in a region where bartering is part of the cultural norms. She lives in Palm Springs. It's hotter than hell there. Come to think of it, I have a funny story about that."

It was Owen's turn to scowl at me. The upside? They weren't locked in some Romeo-and-Juliet-but-one-of-them-is-gay trance anymore.

"My mother plays tennis with a former Catholic priest," I said, waving my arm as though I was holding a racquet. "They play tennis and then drink boxed wine spritzers. White zin and store-brand seltzer. I don't know how they found each other or why he left the priesthood, but it's sufficient to say they're good friends now."

"Please tell me there's a point to this," Owen said.

Ignoring him, I continued, "The priest—rather, former priest—has an old story about missionaries traveling west. The Church would send one party of missionaries after another to the desert, but they couldn't convert anyone. When asked why it was so difficult, one of the mission-aries explained the people in that region didn't need religion because half the year gave them everything they needed to know about heaven and the other half gave them everything they needed to know about hell."

"Great," Annette said, still unimpressed.

Chuckling, Owen roped his arm around my waist. "You talk too damn much."

"I'll just ring these up and you two can be on your way." She glanced up, working hard at a sunny smile that just wasn't there. "Will these be together or separate?"

Owen caught my eye, smiling despite Annette's increasing distress. "Together." He bowed his head toward my ear, whispering, "When we get home, I'm gonna torture you for several hours."

I was all too happy to oblige. "You should do that," I said, keeping my voice low. "Torture. Punish. Subjugate. Whatever you want."

Owen's gaze shifted to Annette and then back to me. "Don't say that," he murmured. "You don't know what I'm thinking."

"That will be one-forty-four fifty," Annette said, glancing between us.

I grinned. "I have an idea," I replied to Owen, pulling my wallet from my back pocket. I handed her my credit card without tearing my eyes away from him. "I have several ideas, actually. I'm in favor of all of them."

17

KEEL

n. The longitudinal structure along the centerline at the bottom of a vessel's hull, on which the rest of the hull is built, in some vessels extended downward as a blade or ridge to increase stability.

OWEN

THE MOON WAS high in the sky, a cool breeze was blowing in off the water, and a choir of cicadas screeched in the distance. My body was spectacularly sated and my man was wrapped around me, still purring from the pounding I'd given him.

This life, it didn't get much better.

Drunk on that milky afterglow, I stared at Cole's blond hair and sun-kissed skin and willed myself to withhold the declarations of love and forever I itched to give him. It was too soon for any of that, and if he didn't enthusiastically reciprocate, I doubted I'd recover from the blow.

Instead, I dug into my plentiful stores of jealousy, asking, "What changed for you?"

"What? When?" he asked. His words were rough, his voice raw from hours of begging and moaning.

Lord, I liked that. I liked the marks I'd sucked into his neck, chest, thighs. I liked the beard rash between his legs. I liked the red, swollen shape of his lips. He'd be sore tomorrow, his body used in delicious ways, and I'd like that, too.

For as much as I enjoyed the evidence, I enjoyed caring for him more. Soaping him up in a steamy shower. Rubbing him down with thick creams and herby balms. Kneading his tender muscles. Kissing it all better.

I patted his backside. "You said you were slutty in college, but then you wind up in the Cove and you're a born-again virgin. What changed?" I asked.

"Mmhmm." He nodded, his scruffy chin scraping my chest. "I founded a technology firm, one that gained a certain amount of ubiquity. Most people think it's all about hatching a new idea and then watching the cash roll in, but that isn't a tenth of the truth. That new idea has to stay new, stay fresh. It has to evolve faster than its users, and it has to anticipate needs. Shareholders expect innovation but they also demand robust earnings. There are always disasters. Every day, a new crisis."

I nodded, but I didn't know what to say.

"And I've...I've made some mistakes," Cole said. "Years ago, when I was just starting out, I trusted someone. I shouldn't have done that."

I shifted to catch his gaze. "Who do I have to kill?"

Cole offered a weak laugh. "It's in the past. It doesn't matter now."

"The past has a way of staying present," I said.

"Especially when there's litigation involved," Cole said. "We were close. Friends, then lovers, and then he was an essential member of my team. He took confidential information about my business—about me—and sold it to the highest bidder." He blew out a heavy sigh. "I've had a few hookups since then but nothing more than that."

A surprised breath burst from my lips. I didn't know what I expected Cole to tell me, but it wasn't that. "Are you kidding me? Someone did that to you?"

"That doesn't even scratch the surface, babe." He shook his head against my chest. "This can't make much sense without the full context," he said. "Silicon Valley is a complex place, and my firm—

"Cole, stop," I interrupted. I wanted to know just enough, but not everything. "I understand what you're saying. You don't have to explain all the bits and pieces to me."

He tipped his face up, his brow wrinkled as if he'd misheard me. "I don't?"

I stared out the window for a long moment. When I was a kid, I believed all manner of sea monsters lived in the Atlantic's deep, cold waters. They were out there, swallowing up boats and fighting whales and sharks. In my kid brain, I convinced myself that I was safe as long as I could see the shoreline. Monsters never dared to enter the tidal zone.

That was how I felt about Cole, and the life he led separate from me. If we stayed on familiar ground, we'd be safe.

"You own a technology firm," I said.

"Fifty-one percent of it," he added. "My founding team and the shareholders own the rest."

"You own most of a technology firm," I started, "and a dickhead guy screwed you over. That's all I need to know."

Even after all these years working the water, part of me still believed in the great, unknown sea monsters. Beasts that would sneak up and strike without warning.

"Are you sure about that?" Cole asked.

"I am. I want Cole, the lost sailor. The man overboard. The guy who intrudes on my jerkoff sessions," I said with a chuckle. "Let's not muck this up with too much reality. Okay?"

Cole tipped his face up and stared at me, his lips folded in a tight line and his brows still wrinkled. For a second, I thought he was going to call me on my bullshit. Hold up my objections as illogical and unreasonable, and something I'd never accept if he tried to pull the same maneuver. But he pressed his palm to my heart, gave me a quick smile, and said, "Okay."

"Okay?" I repeated.

"Yeah, talking about corporate shit stresses me out," he replied. "I'd rather hear about you. Why hasn't some guy snapped you up? You're one helluva cook, you bathe regularly, and you have the baddest sex toy box. That's the full bear package right there."

I dropped my head back on the pillow and stared at the ceiling while a soft laugh rolled through my chest. "Maybe I don't want to be snapped."

"Everyone wants to be snapped," Cole replied. "There's no one in the world who doesn't want it. We want it in different ways, at different times, but we still want it. *Need* it, even when we say we don't. We want to be accepted, cherished, adored. We want someone to recognize our messy, complicated souls, and love us for those messes and complications."

"Maybe," I conceded. "But some people just want to get fucked while they're on vacation."

"Are you talking about me?" Cole pushed off my chest and glared down at me. "You know I didn't even bring lube with me. I didn't come here expecting to get fucked."

I hooked my arms around his torso and returned him to my chest. "No, I'm not talking about you, silly boy," I said. "But you're not the first guy to spend the summer in Maine. Too many times, I've fallen hard for some pretty young thing, only for him to leave at the end of the summer without a backward glance. It's vacationland for them, and vacations never last."

Cole planted small kisses along my sternum, humming as he went. "I'm sorry, babe."

"They always went back to their girlfriends, too," I grumbled.

"I hate them," he hissed. "They didn't deserve you, or your gold-medal dick."

I wrapped my arms around him as a laugh rocked through me. "Gold-medal dick? *That* good?"

Cole snorted. "You know I'm not going to be able to sit for a week," he said. "Aside from those pretty young things, hasn't anyone else tried to keep you?"

"I don't want to be kept," I said, immediately hating the tense of my words. *Didn't* want. *Didn't.* But I couldn't take it back now, and I couldn't color my relationship history to suit my purposes. "There's a vibrant queer community in Portland. The West End side of downtown has some great bars and restaurants, and I meet up with friends about once a month. Sometimes, I hookup with a fuck buddy. It's not a big deal."

Cole was silent for a moment, then he asked, "Am I your fuck buddy? Is that what we're doing?"

I sanded my fingers through his hair, hoping my touch could speak all the words I wasn't ready to say and he wasn't ready to hear. "No. You're my little prince."

He nodded. "I can live with that."

18

———————

SEXTANT

n. A navigational instrument used to measure a vessel's latitude.

Cole

Cole: Another request.
Neera: What do you have for me?
Cole: Can you push an independent bookstore package for the homepage?
Neera: Of course. Any other parameters?
Cole: Good bookstores. Not pretentious, snotty joints but community-based, inclusive, representative. All that good stuff.
Cole: Make sure Harborside Books in Talbott's Cove, Maine gets top billing.
Neera: Should we mention you're a fan of that shop?
Cole: Nope.
Neera: Understood.
Cole: If there's an opportunity to run some content on women entrepreneurs or female-owned businesses, get that one on the list.

Neera: Consider it done.

Cole: Thank you.

Cole: And thank you for keeping the questions at a minimum.

Neera: I apologize if this is too forward but...are you all right?

Cole: Great. Why?

Neera: It takes you days to reply to messages, and that's highly atypical.

Neera: You're also calmer than I expected.

Cole: Were you expecting me to give a ranty interview to Fast Company or show up at the campus with Dumbledore's Army to oust my replacement?

Neera: Somewhat, yes.

Neera: Are you planning something like that?

Cole: No.

Neera: That's it? No?

Cole: Yeah. No. I have other things on my mind right now.

Neera: Does that include some new programming?

Cole: I'm staying out of trouble. You do the same.

Cole: No. Forget that. You could use some trouble in your life.

Neera: Pardon me?

Cole: Do something fun. Get away from the Valley. There is a whole wide wonderful world outside the Valley.

Neera: So I've heard.

Cole: Get out of the office. It will do you good.

Neera: Says the man who had to be forced onto a luxury sailboat.

Cole: I never appreciated how good it is to get away until I was required to do it.

Cole: Before you say anything, no, leadership retreats in Banff or Sun Valley don't count. Neither does the Appalachian incident. Those were all work. This place is different. It's good for me.

Neera: Thank you for that clarification.

Cole: It occurs to me that you might enjoy some forced time off. Should I fire you? Would that help?

Neera: We've talked about this. It's not acceptable to threaten termination in casual conversation.
Cole: That's right. My bad.

19

———————

HEELING

v. To be tilted temporarily by the pressure of wind or by an uneven distribution of weight on board.

Cole

THE LONG SUMMER days were giving way to later sunrises and earlier sunsets, and the woods behind Owen's house were turning fiery and golden. Autumn was right around the corner, and it dawned on me that I hadn't paused to admire the passing of a season since childhood. These days, I couldn't miss it. Everything about my life—*our* life—in this quiet town was tuned in to the nature's every turn.

I used to think I knew what I wanted, and I knew where I wanted to be. The brightest, most forward-thinking mind in Silicon Valley. The dominant force in my industry. People hanging on my every word. Big house, fast cars, influential friends. More money than I'd be able to spend in a hundred lifetimes.

Somewhere along the way, the operative features of my life lost their relevance.

Being demoted had something to do with it, but losing my way in the

North Atlantic and sailing to Owen and the Cove claimed a large share of the responsibility. After six weeks here, I knew it to be true. If I hadn't found myself here, I would've spent a few weeks on the water, raging my way from one seasonal town to another while I cooked up a plan to retake my company.

I would've done it. Abandon the boat, fly back to California, storm into the office, and argue the shit right out of my replacement. I would've screamed, thrown things, caused a dreadful scene. And for several precious moments, I would've felt better, too. Vindicated, even.

But that tantrum wouldn't have made a damn bit of difference. It would've only confirmed for my board of directors that they'd made the right call.

Now, from the comfort of Owen's guest room, I was thankful for the upheaval I'd experienced this summer. I was no longer resentful of the board's decision to remove me as CEO. With my fingers flying over my keyboard as I blew through line after line of the best code I'd constructed in years, I appreciated their decision. They saw everything I wasn't willing to accept—my inability to care about every little financial indicator, my fraught relationship with strategic decision making, my curious management style—and enacted changes I never would've made on my own.

Most of the time, I was the smartest guy around. I was used to that. It'd always been that way. There was nothing I couldn't accomplish if I worked hard enough, stretched my skills, learned something new. Knowledge was my belief system, and the one that convinced me I could do anything and everything.

The only trouble with knowledge was that it never stopped to ask if I wanted to do everything.

I didn't, and recognizing that truth was like taking my first deep breath in decades. My head cleared, my senses sharpened, and my heart pounded with the promise of my man's unyielding affection. This was where I belonged, and I wanted to celebrate that. Get out of the house, go places, see people, let them see me. See *us*.

For all the time we spent joined at the hip, I wasn't convinced the people of Talbott's Cove saw us as a couple. I meant to change that tonight.

I saved my work and yanked the noise-canceling headphones off. I pushed my glasses to the top of my head and stretched my arms out in front of me.

Once I stowed my gear, I left the bedroom and went in search of Owen. I found him in the kitchen, his hands braced on the countertop while he stood, reading the local newspaper. Instead of standing beside him, I roped my arms around his waist, pressed my chest to his back, and nuzzled his neck. "Let's go out," I murmured.

"You're rubbing your dick on my ass and you want to go out?" he asked. "Seems contradictory, McClish."

"I want to go out with you," I insisted, my lips sliding under his ear.

Owen barked out a laugh, the sound reverberating through his body and into mine. "You want to take me on a date?" he asked over his shoulder.

I stole the opportunity to drop a kiss on his lips. "We enjoyed ourselves the last time we went out. Let's do that again."

"Are we going on a date?" he asked, reaching back to grip my neck. "Or do you want to get naughty in the woods?"

"Yeah, I want to take you out on a date," I replied with a purposeful roll of my hips against his backside. "And I want to show off my man."

He chuckled, a rough, rich sound that went straight to my cock. "Show me off? Why?"

"I want everyone to know you're off the market."

"What would that involve?" he asked. "I don't think JJ at The Galley would put up with you blowing me on the bar."

I rested my forehead between his shoulder blades, laughing. "I wouldn't blow you on the bar," I replied against his shirt. "I'd do it in a booth. Like a gentleman."

"Good to know," Owen replied, a laugh ringing in his words. "So, we're doing this? We're going on an actual date?"

"A real date with date-ish things," I said. "I'll pull out your chair for you, we'll engage in pleasant conversation, and maybe I'll let you kiss me goodnight at the door."

"By 'kiss you at the door,' do you mean fuck you in the woods?"

I slipped my hand between his legs, stroking him over his shorts. "I see no problem with that interpretation."

He reached back and squeezed my ass. "Go pick out a shirt for me. I want to be presentable for my date."

I nodded against his back but didn't let him go. "Are you sure about this?" I asked. "You don't mind being *with me* in the village?"

Owen was quiet for a long moment, his fingers still gripping my backside. Eventually, he said, "No. I don't hide who I am, and I don't want to hide you."

SWINGING THE LAMP

v. Telling sea stories.

OWEN

WE WALKED TO THE VILLAGE, following the worn path through the woods. Fingers of sunlight cut through the canopy, turning the woods into a bright, breezy stroll absent of the dark seduction we'd shared all those weeks ago.

"How's the project going?" I asked, shooting a glance at Cole as we neared the end of the trail. "It seemed like you were really focused today."

He bobbed his head. "It's good. Really good. I'm making a lot of progress."

I hesitated. I hated to tempt fate by inquiring about his work. "What happens when you finish?" I asked. "Does that mean—will you go back to California when you're done?"

"That's the beauty of the internet, Bartlett," Cole said, a bright smile stretched across his gorgeous face. "I can do this from anywhere in the world."

It was an answer but it wasn't. It didn't escape my notice that I was exceedingly sensitive about this topic, too. Any waffling from Cole, and I was bracing for impact.

"As long as you don't mind," he added. "I don't want to overstay my welcome."

"I am getting free labor out of you," I said. "It's not good labor but it is free. I can't complain."

"Such a grumpy motherfucker," he murmured.

I held The Galley's door open and gestured for Cole to enter. "Isn't this the way we're supposed to do it?" I asked. "Since we're on a date."

"If this is a date," Cole started, "you should check out my ass while I walk by."

He walked through the doorway, glancing over his shoulder to verify I was ogling him. "I don't need an occasion to check out your ass," I said, sliding my hand into his back pocket. "But since you asked, you're looking fine as fuck in those shorts."

I'd never stopped myself from touching him, not since I'd gained the right. I'd never given much thought to who might notice, but tonight was different. I wanted everyone to notice.

He smiled over at me, preening a bit, but my gaze was on the woman tucked into the far corner of the bar with an open book at her elbow. It had been weeks since that exceedingly awkward exchange with Annette in the bookstore. We'd seen her around town, of course, but our paths hadn't crossed. Until now.

Cole followed my stare, humming in acknowledgement. "She seems busy," he said. "We should leave her alone. If she wants to chat, she'll stop by."

Nodding, I walked with him to an open booth. We sat facing each other, his hand over mine, and debated beers.

"I want to try the shandy," he said, his brows furrowed in thought as he studied the menu.

"Please don't," I replied. "It's not right to mix beer with lemonade. It's a crime against reason."

"But I don't like hoppy beers," he argued. "The ones you drink, they're like liquid pinecone."

Absently, he ran his thumb over his bottom lip. I wanted to jump across the table and do the same, if for no other reason than I hadn't felt that lip in the past half hour.

"Then try a Belgian wheat. If you're nice, JJ will throw a slice of orange in there for you," I said. "It will taste the same if you close your eyes."

Cole glanced at me, his lips quirking up into a smirk. "Are we still talking about beer?"

I barked out a laugh. "Mostly," I replied. "The same could be said for balls."

"That is false." He pointed at the menu, a silent command to focus on my ale of choice rather than his mouth.

"All right," I said after the waitress took our drink orders. A Juliet Imperial Stout for me, a Night Swim'ah for him. "Let's date night the shit out of this."

"Do you come here often?" Cole asked, fighting a grin. He couldn't manage a straight face. He winked and God help me, it unleashed a rush of butterflies in my belly. I was in it deep with this man. "Forget that. Tell me about yourself, Bartlett. Tell me things you've never told me before. All the things we skipped. The basics. What d'you do for fun?"

I held out my hands and then let them fall. "Reading. I like books, but you already know that."

"But I don't know why you like it," he said. "Start there."

"I blew off school when I was a kid but now I wish I'd paid more attention," I said. "If I knew then what I know now, I wouldn't have pissed away my time."

"We're never given things when we want them," Cole said. "It's the universe's way of fucking with us."

"Something like that," I said, laughing.

Cole reached for his beer, asking, "When was the last time you took a vacation? I can't imagine lobstermen observe traditional holidays. The lobsters don't give a fuck whether it's Christmas or Columbus Day, right?"

"It can be challenging, yeah. But I got away a couple of months ago,"

I replied. "I sail down to Provincetown—that's in Massachusetts, on the far end of Cape Cod—every year for Pride. The past few years, I've rented a house with a bunch of guys. It's always a good time in P-Town. Parades, events, shows. It's a trip I never miss."

"Why? What makes it important?" Cole asked.

"It's like coming home, but instead of parents and siblings, it's people who welcome and accept you in the most thorough way. And you've slept with most of them at one point or another." I ran my knuckles over my jaw as I watched him take in this information. The hard set of his jaw and thin line of his lips told me he wasn't a fan of my past exploits. "Have you ever been to Pride?"

He blew out a breath, his expression turning pensive. "No, I haven't." He reached for his glass but didn't drink. "I've never known how I'd fit in. If I'd fit in."

"Trust me, you and your slim-fit polo shirts will fit right in," I replied, laughing. "Maybe...you could come with me next June. We could go together."

"Yeah. Maybe," he said, bobbing his head slowly. "These friends of yours—the ones you've slept with—would we stay with them? Is that what we'd do? A bunch of us in a house? Musical beds, perhaps?"

I crossed my arms over my chest. "Is that your way of asking whether I'd share you?"

Cole lifted a shoulder while he drew lines in the condensation on his glass. "I'm just trying to understand how it goes," he replied.

"No, it wouldn't be like that," I said, dead serious. "If we bunked with my buddies, I'd bite your neck and piss a circle around you to make my intentions clear. Hell, I'd do that regardless of where we stayed. Your fine ass wouldn't leave my sight."

His cheeks flushed red, and I liked that. He bit his lip to hold back a smile, but it didn't work. I took his hand in mine just to feel an ounce of that electricity.

"All right. Good to know," he said. "Aside from that celebration, do you get away from the Cove much?"

"I take long weekends when I can," I said. "It seems like I'm always going to weddings. Back before marriage equality was passed nationwide, it was legal in Massachusetts. Many of my friends went there to get married, so I was always sailing down to the Cape." I glanced down, suddenly feeling shy. "I did the internet minister thing a couple of years ago. I've officiated for some of my friends. A few people in town, too."

Cole blinked at me, silent for longer than comfortable in this type of conversation. "That's—that's amazing," he replied.

"You really think so?"

"Yes," he said, slapping both hands on the table. "I want to hear all about this. How did you start?"

I rubbed my neck, thinking back. "It all started when some friends from Portland were planning their wedding and they couldn't find an officiant they liked. They wanted someone who knew them and actually gave a shit about them taking this step in their relationship. For reasons I still don't understand, they decided I was the guy for the job."

"And you kept going?" Cole asked. "After that wedding, you kept officiating?"

"Pretty much," I said. "I didn't set out with the intention of starting a side hustle in the wedding business, but I'm happy to take part in these special days."

He shifted, leaning out of the booth and peering around the tavern. "I want to know who you've married here," he said. "You've got me hooked on townie gossip."

I held out my hand, ticking off each couple on my fingers. "The harbormaster and his wife. It was the second marriage for both of them. If you believe the rumors, they filed for divorce because they were cheating on their partners with each other. Now," I said, pausing, "I can't tell you whether those rumors are true but I know they got together right after their divorces, and they were engaged a month later."

"Huh," Cole murmured. "He's a nice guy. I haven't met the wife."

"She's a physician's assistant a few towns south of here." I held up another finger. "The couple that runs the inn. They bought the old motel about eight, maybe nine years ago, and fixed it up. They don't have any family. They moved up here for a fresh start after a gruesome tragedy. I don't know the particulars, only that it was bad. It seemed only right to offer my services to them."

"Whoa," he murmured. "I can't believe you've never mentioned this. The innkeepers with the horrible history *and* you moonlighting as a minister. All this time, and you've kept this incredible side of yourself hidden."

I took a sip of my beer as I considered Cole's comment. "I'm not like most people," I said carefully. "I don't feel the need to post all my thoughts and experiences on the internet, or see anyone else's thoughts and experiences. I'd rather take my time to understand someone piece by piece. I don't want to condense anyone down to a blurb or caption. I want to hold and treasure every piece, and I want someone to do the same to me."

Cole brought his fingers to his eyelids. He laughed, but I couldn't imagine why. Unless he thought I was an antiquated fool. That was entirely possible.

"I am so happy we're doing this," he said, dragging his hands down his face. "I'm truly amazed by you, and I want to hear more."

My eyebrows arched up. "Really?"

"Let me hold and treasure this piece of you," he said. Warm sensation rippled down my spine with his words. "Okay?"

"There was a couple I met a few years ago," I said, resting my head back on the booth. "Two of the strangest people I've ever met but I've never forgotten them."

"What made them so strange?" he asked, his face split in a warm smile.

I shook my head, still struggling to put those two into words even after several years. "To start, they were wandering around the docks in Wellfleet at four in the morning. He's a doctor, she's some kind of scientist, and they wanted me to take them on as deckhands for the haul. At first, I thought they were high on Ecstasy or something. Turned out, they were just really fucking weird."

"You are always short-staffed, aren't you?"

I waved him off. "I don't work the water when I'm outside of the Cove, but there's an old timer down there who had a hip replacement that year. A bunch of us pitched in to help him out so he could cover his costs. It was just one weekend. I didn't need a full crew for that."

"Okay, now that we've established you're the nicest guy in the world," Cole said, gesturing to me, "tell me about this strange couple."

"From the first moment, they were like magnets. Chemistry so intense I could see it radiating off them. What they had, it was palpable. Part of me was jealous," I admitted. "But the other part of me was happy I was able to stand in the presence of real, limitless love. Even if they were annoying."

"You married them? On the boat, at four in the morning?" Cole asked. "How did that work, legally? If they were wandering around the docks, they couldn't have had a proper marriage license."

"I married them while the sun rose over Cape Cod Bay. It was one of the coolest ceremonies," I said. "It wasn't legal, but that wasn't an issue for them. They belonged to each other and it didn't matter whether they had the documentation to back it up."

Cole laughed. "Now I'm jealous of them, too."

"The strangest part came last year," I continued. "It was December, a couple days before Christmas, and they showed up at my door. I still don't know how they found me."

"That *is* strange," he said.

"They wanted to make it legal," I said. "I married them again. This time, I did it in the middle of my kitchen."

"Knowing how you react when people show up at your house uninvited," Cole mused, "you must really like weddings."

"Only certain weddings," I replied. "I only marry people I can see staying together for the long haul. I've passed on officiating for folks who didn't seem right for each other, or ready for the commitment. The ones who just want a party. The ones who need something to do. The ones who think it's the next milestone they should check off in their life. I don't want to be associated with any marriages that end, you know?"

"Does that mean you believe everyone has a lobster?"

"A *what*?" I asked.

"You know, a lobster," Cole said, laughing. "From that episode of *Friends*. Lobsters mate for life, and they walk around holding claws—"

"Lobsters do not mate for life," I argued. "Female lobsters take turns with the dominant male in a given area."

"Huh. That's a very different type of relationship than the one I'd imagined," he said, his brow wrinkling. "That pokes some holes in my theory."

"Setting aside biology for a minute, I do believe it," I said. "Everyone has a lobster, but you have to haul up a lot of empty traps before you find it."

"Isn't that half the fun?" Cole asked with a smirk.

"If you had to estimate," I started, reaching for my beer, "how many broken hearts did you leave back in California?"

Cole rocked back with laughter. "I don't need to estimate," he said. "It's zero."

"Oh, great. You're one of those assholes who doesn't even realize he's beaten the shit out of someone's heart," I replied. "That doesn't bode well for me."

"I am not one of *those* assholes," he said, still laughing. "I'm an entirely different breed of asshole. The kind who works too much and never has time for relationships. After a while, not having time for relationships turns into forgetting how to be in relationships. Then that turns into forgetting how to speak to people who don't work for you. Not long after reaching that point, your virginity grows back and you start researching the monastic approach to life."

"Or sailing to Maine?" I asked.

"Well, yes," Cole replied with hesitance. "But I took to the water because I needed time away from my business. Things weren't going well. No, that's not accurate. The business is strong, really strong—"

"I've seen your boat, babe," I replied, my tone right on the edge of salty and surly. "You also offered me thirty grand to stay in my nine-by-nine guest room. You don't have to pull out your earnings statement."

"All fair points." He nodded to himself before continuing, "But now you have me wondering. How many broken hearts do you have to your name?"

"I don't do hearts," I lied. "My history is of the no-strings variety."

Cole stared at me for a long beat, his gaze inscrutable. "I'm not sure I believe that," he said. "You bring fish to nursing homes. You drive yourself crazy with budgets and regulatory guidance for the town council. You ask after Fitzy's son when everyone else avoids the topic. You marry the innkeepers because they don't have any family. You take in lost sailors even when they fuck up your nights." He shook his head. "You're all heart, Bartlett. All strings."

"Maybe," I conceded. "But I haven't broken anyone's heart. I'm certain of it."

"Not yet," Cole replied. "You seem like the kind of guy who would have a dog. You're the grumpiest motherfucker I've ever met but that crusty shell only hides a sweet, gooey center. Like crème brûlée. So, tell me. Why don't you have a dog?"

"I did," I said softly, glancing down with an aching sigh. "I did, and she was the best dog in the world. Sheilagh. She was the best girl."

"Oh," he murmured. "Oh, shit. I'm sorry. I shouldn't have brought it up."

"It's okay." I shook my head and looked away. "She lived a long life, and she really was the best girl. Before the arthritis took her legs, she loved coming on the boat with me every day. She loved the water. She'd run up and down the deck, barking at the seagulls. I knew...I knew when it was time. I just didn't have the strength to put her down."

"I'm sure." Cole reached across the table and took my hand. "That must have been a difficult time."

I shrugged. "She loved catching rays at the lighthouse. She'd lie down in front every afternoon, when the sun was right overhead."

He regarded me for several moments, his hand warm over mine and his eyes crinkled with concern. "It's a nice spot," he said.

"I left her at the house when I went out on the water one day," I continued, "and when I got home, I couldn't find her. Then I knew. I knew she went to the lighthouse, and—and she was gone." I gulped down a knot of emotion. "She didn't want to be a bother to anyone. She wanted to nestle into her favorite spot on a sunny day and close her eyes."

Cole's hand retreated, and he scooted out of his side of the booth. He came around the table, settled beside me, and brought his arm around my shoulders. "Owen," he whispered. "I'm so sorry."

"I buried her there, at the lighthouse. On the side with all the beach plum bushes." I ran my free hand down my face. "Cried the whole damn time," I admitted with a laugh.

"Have you thought about adopting another dog?" he asked. "Not that you can replace Sheilagh."

"I have thought about it." I jerked my shoulders. "But whenever I think about it, the time isn't right. Puppies are a lot of work, and I—I don't know that I can do it."

"You need a dog," Cole said. "And I need to stop with the depressing questions."

We sat there for several minutes, Cole's arm tight around my torso and his lips pressed to my temple. It was then I noticed the quiet in the tavern. Glancing up, I found the citizens of Talbott's Cove watching us. JJ was frozen behind the bar, a rag in one hand, a dripping glass in the other. A group of waiters were clustered nearby, their arms crossed over their chests. Patrons sat motionless, their forks still and eyes wide. Even Annette stopped reading long enough to glance in our direction.

"We have an audience," I whispered to Cole.

I felt him smile. "I know."

JJ shook free from his stare and set down his towel and glass. "There's nothin' to see here," he shouted, his Down East accent thicker than ever. "Eat ya food, mind ya business. All of you now. If ya want to gawk at my customers, get the hell outta here."

A gust of relief blew through me. I'd never expected anything short of acceptance from these people, but the world was packed with contradiction. Good people often made hateful choices. Friends turned their backs and families closed their doors. It mattered that JJ was willing to speak up for us, more than I'd expected.

I cupped Cole's face and kissed him. It was quick—as quick as I could be with him—and when I pulled back, life in The Galley was back to normal. "Thanks for coming over here," I said. "I like having you next to me."

His eyebrows arched up. "You like easy access to my dick."

"I enjoy both of those things," I said, laughing as I dropped my hand to his thigh. "I'll think about it. A dog. I need some time."

Cole shook his head. "I know how you are," he said. "You need to think everything through."

"You should know Sheilagh used to sleep on the bed with me," I said. "If she was still alive, she would've climbed on top of you and slept there."

"Cozy," he murmured. "Hey. That's interesting." He jerked his chin toward the far end of the bar. I craned my neck to see a man at Annette's side. "Who's that?"

"Jackson Lau," I said. We were flat-out staring now, and we weren't the only ones. All the eyes that had once been on us were now trained on them. Talbott's Cove operated an equal opportunity gossip mill. "The town's chief of police."

Jackson pulled his wallet from his back pocket, thumbed out some cash, and dropped it on the bar. He brought his hand to her lower back and tipped his head toward the exit.

"It looks like they're...friendly," Cole said. "And by 'friendly' I mean he's fucked—"

"*No.*" I speared him with a sharp glare. "This is one situation where I don't want your filthy thoughts."

With her lips pursed, Annette hopped off the barstool and shoved her book into a tote bag. She went to sling it over her shoulder but Jackson relieved her of it first. She scowled at him. I couldn't explain the genesis of this feeling, but I was proud of her. I wanted to high-five her, and tell her to make him work for it.

"Yeah, they're very *friendly*," I said.

"See? It was a good thing that you broke up with her," he said.

I rolled my eyes. "I didn't break up with her."

"Close enough," he replied.

Jackson and Annette crossed the restaurant, his hand low on her back and a town's-worth of eyes following them. She glanced in our direction as they passed, and offered a small smile.

"That is interesting," I said under my breath, waving to her in response.

"I'm just glad she's found her own man and stopped pining over mine," Cole said.

I swiveled away from Annette and Jackson to face Cole. "What?" I asked.

He lifted his beer to his lips, smiling. "You heard me," he replied. "You know I'd bite your neck and piss a circle around you, too."

My heart slammed into my throat so hard I was certain I'd choke on it. "Yeah," I said. Then, quietly, "It's nice to hear you say it, little prince."

ALL NIGHT IN

v. Having no night watches.

Cole

TONIGHT WAS similar to the last time we walked through the woods under the close-aired darkness. Similar yet loaded with difference. We walked hand-in-hand now, not rebelling against our connection but accepting it, cultivating it, sharing it. We didn't need alcohol to loosen our lips and embolden our actions. We knew the path would lead us home, and from there, it would take us to bed—together. It was good, and this was right.

We stumbled down the path—not as a result of liquor, though it had some hand in this—clinging to each other as we broke out in fits of riotous laughter. "I couldn't tell whether JJ was going to hop over the bar and drag us out by the scruff or launch into a slow clap," I said.

"Such an odd moment," Owen said with a chuckle. "Did you see the look Brooke-Ashley gave him? She rolled her eyes so hard they still haven't come back around."

"True story," I murmured. "It was nice of the O'Keefes to drop by and say hello, even if they were a little awkward about it."

"Yeah, they're kind people," Owen replied. "They've had a few tough years, and they've struggled, but they'd still give you their last slice of bread if you asked for it."

I still didn't understand this town or the people in it, but neither were a puzzle in need of solving.

Owen turned, pinning me with a fierce stare. "But I don't want to talk about them anymore," he said.

"Okay," I replied. "That's fine. Maybe you can compliment my ass some more. That's what you're supposed to do on a date."

"I don't want to play pretend anymore," he said, his words quick and sharp. "I want to be real with you now."

"We are real," I said, confused. "Of course we're real. This entire night has been real. We weren't pretending to be on a date, Owen. We actually were on a—"

"I don't want you to go," he interrupted, "when the summer ends."

Boom. Just fucking *boom* went my heart.

"Say something." He stepped closer, pressing his chest to mine. If his declaration wasn't enough to stun me into silence, his cock, hardening under his shorts, did the trick. "Tell me what you're thinking."

"I—*ohhh*—yeah," I stammered, widening my stance and arching toward the firm ridge of him. He rocked against me, grinning as I groaned. "I can't think when you do that, baby."

"Try, for me, baby. Try. Promise me you'll stay." Owen's hips were bucking against me in a lazy rhythm. We groaned at that, and I was ready to come all over us. It could have been the friction, but it was mostly his words. "Say something," he repeated, the order taking on an edge of anxiety.

"Yes, I want you," I replied with a needy groan. The dry friction of his clothing-covered dick rubbing against mine made it impossible to do anything other than sink into these sensations. "Of course."

"That's right," he said, growling.

"I want to stay," I continued, the loose tooth of my life outside this town wiggling under these words. "I want to stay here with *you*. But I should tell you—"

"The only thing you have to tell me is how you want me fucking you," he said as he pushed me against a tree.

A gasp burst from my lips as the trunk bit into my back. With a shaking hand, I reached for Owen's jaw. I canted his face up, wanting to see the wild in his eyes. "Not this time," I whispered.

My hand still gripping his face, I stepped away from the tree. I curled my fingers around his belt and jerked his hips flush with mine. I wanted him like nothing else. So much that it hurt. But I also wanted this—him, us, these woods—and I couldn't bring myself to stop.

"What do you think you're doing, McClish?" he asked.

My eyes drifted shut while I basked in the pleasure of his shaft rubbing against mine. Even through layers of clothing, the sensation was unreal. "Could I make you come?" I asked. "Just like this?"

Owen's hand shifted from my waist to my backside. He held me, squeezing just a bit. "You could smile at me, and I'd fall apart," he whispered. His fingers skimmed down my ass, pressing and rubbing like a dream. "I think you know that."

"I don't," I said, my voice tight as I held back a groan. With all the strength I could gather, I positioned him against the tree, pecked a kiss on the corner of his mouth, and dropped to my knees. "My turn."

This time, I handled both his button and zipper without incident, and yanked his boxer briefs down. He loved it when I played with him a bit, teased, but I'd do all that some other time. Tonight, I was hungry for him. Hungry for a piece to call my own.

Owen's hand skimmed up the back of my neck. "Baby, no. You don't have to."

"I want to," I said, my eyes trained on his thick shaft. With his thighs trembling and flexing under my hands, I dragged my tongue up his cock. He was hot and delicious, and I wasted no time taking him in my mouth.

"Goddamn," Owen hissed.

I pushed a finger inside him, just past the rim, and he howled. Actually fucking *howled*. His hips jerked away from the tree trunk, thrusting into my mouth. His hands were in my hair and his thigh was stiff under my free hand. He was leaking and twitching in small, quick pulses. Just like waves at low tide.

I kissed down his length and across his sac. "Good?" I asked, glancing up at him.

"Would it be cliché to tell you I love you right now?" he asked. "Because I do. I really fucking do."

My world lit up then, a riot of heat and joy, and a fullness, like being swaddled in a tight embrace. The words were burning on my tongue, but I couldn't offer them in return until I was certain he meant them. Owen wasn't one for hyperbole but I had to be sure.

"No clichés," I replied, smiling against his thigh. "My blowjobs are *that* good."

"Get up here," Owen ordered, hooking his hands under my arms and urging me off the ground.

When I pushed to my feet, he took my face in his hands and kissed me hard. He nipped at my tongue, bit my lip, and I bit right back. His pants were still tangled around his ankles, and I stole this opportunity to slide my fingers along his seam.

"I want to fuck you right here but I don't think tree sap makes for the best lube," I said.

I felt Owen smile against my neck. "Let's not do that," he said. "The tree sap lube, that is. I quite enjoy natural products, but that's over the line for me. The rest of it sounds great."

I rubbed my free hand up and down his chest, pawing at him. "You want me to fuck you?"

"The answer to that question has always been yes," he said. "Always will be."

After another biting kiss, I turned him around in my arms. My hips rolled against his backside, my cock right between his cheeks while I stroked him. I was cross-eyed and crazy with lust, and *this close* to spitting into my palm and fucking him raw.

Rarely did I feel the desire to take a man like this, but with Owen, I had a desperate, panting need that I felt rising up from deep within me. I wanted to have him, be *with* him in every place possible way, brand him as my own.

"That settles it," I said. "I'm taking my man home now."

22

―――――――――――

OUTWARD BOUND

adj. Leaving the safety of port, heading out to open ocean.

OWEN

THIS WAS *THE* NIGHT.

The one when I came out—all the way out—to the town.

The one when we made a tradition out of blowjobs in the woods.

The one when I confessed my love for Cole and didn't have a nervous breakdown when he laughed off my words.

And also the one when Cole led me into the bedroom, stripped me naked, and guided me to the bed so he could tease me with his tongue for approximately nine years while I dissolved into a bright, shimmering disaster of love and need and hope. Now, I was gasping and quivering, on the verge of goddamn tears as he pushed inside me. It wasn't pain that dampened my eyes but an ache, a spasm far inside me that only grew as I watched his cock sliding into my body. I loved this man, I loved him more than I understood.

"How's that?" Cole asked, shifting his hips a bit as he inched in. His eyes were hooded, his teeth pressed into his lower lip, his breath coming in shallow pants. "Tell me it's good because you feel amazing."

"Good, good," I said, gasping as he stretched me. My cock was weeping all over my belly but I couldn't focus on anything but the glorious pressure between my legs. "Keep going. You're doing great, baby. You're perfect."

He stared at me, smiling like he knew a secret, and I was absolutely helpless. But I was the one with the secret. My sweet, silly man with his clumsiness and his arrogant streak. He was everything to me, and I was dying to be everything to him.

Cole ran his hand up the back of my thigh, pushing it closer to my chest as he seated himself. He closed his eyes and dropped his head back. For a moment, neither of us moved. He blew out a breath and gripped my thighs hard, as if he needed an anchor to hold himself back. I didn't want that.

"Come here," I whispered, beckoning him closer. His dick was inside me and somehow, he was too far away.

Cole nodded and positioned my legs around his waist. "Oh, fuck," he murmured, his eyes rolling back as he found a rhythm. "I mean it. You're amazing. I'm never bottoming again."

"That's not an option," I said. I reached for him, first grabbing his flanks, then his shoulders, and finally lashing my arms around his torso when we were chest-to-chest. My lips found his neck, and I breathed a content sigh because I had him. Inside me, around me, everywhere. "I love fucking your ass. You're not taking that away from me."

"And I love *you*," he started, "so I won't."

A laugh burst from my lips, unbidden. He was thrusting into me now, slow and hard, but that pleasure was a distant second to the one seizing my heart.

"You made me wait," I said, smiling up at him. "You walked me home, licked my ass for half-a-fucking-hour, and waited until you were balls deep inside me to say that." I arched up to meet his lips, hoping my kiss would tell him how much he pushed me, and how much I needed those pushes. "I love you."

Cole grinned, nodding. "I know," he said, reaching between us to wrap his fingers around my cock. "Would it be cliché of me to come right now? Because I'm damn close."

I shook my head, the words tangled up in a knot of emotion heavy in my chest. I *loved* this man, and he...he loved me, too. Those words weren't ones I'd heard before, it wasn't a feeling anyone had reciprocated.

The fast slide of his hand over my length kept me on the edge but it was the blissful sighs stuttering past his lips as he slammed into me that did it. That pushed me over, broke me apart, and patiently sewed me back together again.

Tonight was *the* night but that didn't mean it was the only night. This could only get better.

23

ROGUE WAVE

n. A large, unexpected and suddenly appearing surface wave that can be extremely dangerous.

OWEN

IT WAS LATE SEPTEMBER, and I was in Portland for the monthly meeting of the Maine Lobster Conservancy's board of directors. It was true what they said about the squeaky wheels getting the grease, except this squeaky wheel had been nominated for a board seat after complaining about the issues long enough. I still preferred the ocean to the office but it was rewarding to know that I was making some small difference.

But this meeting couldn't adjourn quickly enough. Tomorrow marked the eight-week anniversary of Cole's arrival in Talbott's Cove, and we were starting the celebration with a special dinner tonight.

These weeks had been nothing short of magical, and I wasn't the kind of guy who threw words like those around. With Cole, I felt things I'd never before experienced. I wanted things, too. Things I'd never thought available to me.

Love. Family. Forever. And I really wanted it all with him.

So I was laying it all out there tonight. I was loading him up with the best steaks and wine I could find, and I was telling him that I wanted to make this official. It was time for him to move in, all the way. We could convert one of the extra bedrooms to a proper office. He could get rid of his place in California. Obviously, he could run his business from Maine. He'd managed just fine for almost two months.

He'd move in, we'd fix up an office, and we'd have a life together. And maybe...maybe we could plan a trip down to Cape Cod next summer to exchange vows. A visit to P-Town would do him good.

That *maybe* had my heart plotting an escape from my chest because *maybe* had to be *yes*. Had to be.

Cole was in charge of dessert tonight. I was hoping that consisted of nothing more than a dollop of whipped cream on my fiancé's dick.

Repairs finished on Cole's boat early last week, but that event came and went with little fanfare. It was an amazing craft—now that it wasn't on the fritz and running aground—and we took it for a sail down to the Isle of Shoals over the weekend. It was a nice break from our usual routine, one we needed. Life was great, but it was busy. The lobster season was hitting its peak, and Cole was spending more time on work projects when we weren't hauling in traps.

Even though it meant a decrease in our time together, I understood that Cole needed to work. That he'd been able to spend the summer working my decks was a gift, one I knew wouldn't last forever. He had a conference call a few days ago, and though I didn't mean to eavesdrop on the entire thing, I found myself addicted to his authoritative tone. It didn't matter what he was saying. I liked in-charge Cole. I wanted more of him.

Instead of staying to talk shop after the meeting, I hustled out and headed to downtown Portland. My grocery list was long, and I had exactly seven minutes to find everything I needed and get on the road if we were going to eat before Thursday Night Football kicked off. It was situations like these that made me reconsider Cole's desire to install one of those DVR things.

He was gentle like that, always nudging me to try new things but never forcing. He didn't care that I hated bourbon or reading books on electronic screens, or that I preferred the butt plug in *his* ass. I wasn't as gentle. The solitary life I'd once considered adequate was now filled with affection and laughter, but that hadn't beaten the cranky bastard out of me.

Perhaps that was why I was sighing like a moody teenager and drumming my fingers on the grocery cart while the woman ahead of me handed the cashier a wad of coupons thicker than the Bible. Food, our future, football, fucking. That was the plan for tonight, and Coupon Cathy was screwing up my schedule with her thriftiness.

Craning my neck to find a quicker line, I found myself staring at the last person I expected to find in Portland: Cole. Except it wasn't him, not the Cole *I* knew. It was a polished-up, slick-haired, fake-smile, suit-and-tie version of him with "Where In The World Is Cole McClish?" printed across his chest.

Why is my man *on the cover of a magazine and why the fuck are people wondering where he is?*

I snatched the magazine from the rack and flipped to the article about Cole while I steered my cart to the short order line. I didn't care whether I had many more than ten items. If the cashier noticed, she didn't care either. Maybe I was the one who didn't notice as the only thought in my head was an infinite loop of *I thought I knew him* while I read.

Paying, leaving the store, getting into my truck, driving home—I remembered none of it. I did, however, remember every word of that cover story about Cole. I couldn't handle this. I'd given this man everything, all of me, and I'd thought I was getting all of him in return.

But there was always more to Cole's story. Secrets, histories, situations I didn't understand and couldn't bring myself to explore. But I'd convinced myself reality wasn't too far divorced from the fantasy. He was wealthy and accomplished, and held enough sway to take the summer off without issue. I could handle that. His reality was a slim fraction of the one I'd imagined, one that foreclosed all possibility of a future for us.

There was no place for me in a world that involved epic fortunes.

I was a tough guy, a strong guy. Being a lobsterman did that to me, and being alone for all these years did it, too. I didn't consider myself sensitive or delicate, but everything about this fucking hurt. Throughout the ride back to Talbott's Cove, I kept a fist pressed to my chest to hold back the rising ache.

He was on the couch when I arrived, his long legs stretched out, computer on his lap, glasses perched on his head. I was all out of words, and couldn't offer more than a slammed door in greeting.

"Hey, what's..." His voice trailed off when I turned the magazine toward him. "Oh, *shit.*"

"That's it?" I barked. "All you've got for me is *oh, shit?* You're a fucking billionaire and you've invented, like, the *entire internet*, and you never thought any of that was worth mentioning? You didn't think I deserved a heads-up on that one?"

Cole closed his computer and stared at the floor. Seconds that felt a whole fuckton like hours passed without a word.

"I'm sorry." He stood, wincing at the magazine as he approached me. "I didn't mean for it to happen like"—he glanced at the magazine that hung from my hand like an old-timey wanted poster—"that. But you said you didn't want to know. I tried to tell you."

Somewhere along the way, I'd stopped thinking of him as a fantasy. I allowed myself to forget the corners of his life he kept from me, and in that forgetfulness, I believed he could be mine.

Never once had I braced myself for the kind of status and acclaim that would put his face on magazines. It wasn't a matter of our worlds being different anymore.

"There's a difference between knowing you're wealthy and important, and *this*." I shook the magazine at him. It didn't matter that I'd asked him to spare me the details of his life on the West Coast. That I asked for the lies. "I know my world is nothing like yours. I've always known that. I had no idea you're the master of the online universe. You're fuckin' internet royalty."

"That's an exaggeration." Frowning, he folded his arms over his chest. "I'm not internet royalty."

"The fuck you aren't," I cried.

"Royalty suggests power by bloodline." He shrugged. "I wasn't born into this. I'm more of an alchemist."

"Oh, my God, Cole," I shouted. "Shut the hell up."

He was decent enough to stop talking and hold up his hands in surrender.

"The article said you were in search of a 'creative lightning rod' and a 'spiritual, strategic reawakening,' whatever the fuck that means. What was this to you?" I asked. "Some kind of experiment? Head up to Maine, fuck a lobsterman, and find your next great idea?"

"Of course not," he said. "I was wrong. I should've told you, and I wanted to tell you so many times."

"But you decided to keep right on hiding instead," I roared. "You're good at that, aren't you? You ran away from Silicon Valley after some app that didn't work. That's why you're here, right?"

"None of that matters, Owen," he argued. "You're the only one who knows me, the real me. You have to believe me."

I turned away from him, shifting my gaze to the ocean. "I thought I knew you, but that article makes it clear that I don't."

"I can tell you right now that article is bullshit. There are news stories and blog posts written about me every day. Entire books about me, my company, my approach to business. I know this is all new to you, but—"

"I'm not stupid, Cole," I interrupted.

He brought his fingertips to his forehead and rubbed his temples. "That's not what I was saying. I was wrong, Owen. I should've told you. Held you down and forced you to listen. But I loved that you knew me, the guy who drifted into the Cove, not the internet royalty." His lips quirked up in a rueful smile. "You found me and you took me in when I was lost and lonely. You accepted the guy who fell overboard. The one who required a lesson on dishwashing and pestered you with a thousand questions. I wanted you to love *that* guy, and not the one with an industry on his shoulders."

"I *did* love that guy, but I can't love this guy," I said, gesturing to the magazine.

"Goddamn it, Owen," he yelled. "Don't say that. Don't fucking say that."

Summer love was never meant for me. It wasn't mine to keep. I built sandcastle dreams and the tides washed them away every time.

"I think you should go."

Cole's eyes drifted shut, his head fell forward, and his shoulders slumped. For an instant, my heart ached to comfort him. And goddamn him for that. Even at my most gutted, I still wanted to care for him.

These four walls were soaked with memories of these past eight weeks—of *us*—and I couldn't drown in them, not now. I dropped the magazine and marched to the porch. The sea would soothe me tonight.

"Don't be here when I get back."

24

CUT AND RUN

v. The fast but expensive practice of sailing away quickly, either by cutting free an anchor or by cutting ropeyarns to unfurl sails from the yards.

Cole

Cole: Did you know about TechToday's cover story?
Neera: I did not. They didn't reach out to me or the communications shop for comment.
Cole: But you knew it was released? And didn't think I needed to know that?
Neera: Yes, I knew it was released.
Neera: No, I didn't think it was worth notifying you. It was unremark-able. Dozens of similar stories have been printed in recent weeks.
Neera: Is there an issue?
Cole: Issues, plural.
Neera: Understood. How can I help?
Cole: I'm going to need your assistance.

Cole: Get my replacement on the phone.

Neera: I'll take care of it.

Cole: Get a pilot and a jet ready. If the next day doesn't shake out the way I'm hoping it will, I'm going to need a ride home.

Neera: May I ask what's happening in the next day?

Cole: I'm begging the love of my life to take me back despite my extremely long list of flaws, inadequacies, and missteps.

Neera: Very well. Where might this jet be picking you up?

Cole: I'm in Talbott's Cove, Maine.

Neera: Forgive me for asking but if things do go as you're hoping, do you anticipate staying there?

Cole: I'd like to. If he lets me.

Neera: Then I'll do whatever I can to make that happen.

Cole: Thank you. I appreciate it, N.

Neera: That's what I'm here for.

Neera: I figured you'd find one spot and stay there for the summer. I'm happy you found that spot, and someone to share it with.

Cole: What?

Neera: The bookstore you asked me to feature is in Talbott's Cove. And the oceanic nonprofits you asked me to signal boost are also in Maine.

Neera: I also received an invoice from the sailboat fabricators last week. It referenced delivering parts to Talbott's Cove Marina.

Cole: You knew? All this time, you knew where I was and you didn't come find me?

Neera: You didn't want me to find you.

Neera: I believe you were busy finding yourself.

THERE WERE benefits to being a billionaire. I didn't worry about having a roof over my head or food on the table. The health and well-being of my parents, sisters, and nieces and nephews was secure.

And whenever I needed to make a call without the benefit of mobile service, I had a satellite at the ready.

With a secure connection in place, I explained my issues with that *TechToday* click-bait bullshit to my acting CEO and PR team. There was none of my usual Scream, Fire, or Throw. Not when I was fighting to keep the tears out of my voice.

Apparently, the newer, calmer Cole was absolutely terrifying because they were snapping to attention and suggesting every countermeasure imaginable, short of putting a hit on the journalist. The acting CEO was even amenable to my proposals, and that right there was progress.

For all that I could solve with money, there were several things I couldn't. One of them—my grumpy, growly bear—was somewhere in Jericho Bay by now. Knowing Owen, he'd sooner tuck his big body into the *Sweet Carolyne*'s cramped quarters and spend an uncomfortable night at sea than risk seeing me again.

He wasn't wrong. I hadn't shown myself worthy of his presence, not when I'd let months pass without telling him everything. There were opportunities to put it all on the table, and I should've ignored his request to the contrary. I pushed him to be honest and real with Annette, even when staying hidden was the easiest route. I should've taken some of my own advice. Instead, I usually seized those opportunities to suck his dick or get bent over the kitchen table. I always wanted him wrapped around me, and I knew talk of my other life wouldn't give me that. I knew it would come between us because it came between me and everything.

But that didn't mean I was accepting it, not this time. Not with Owen.

I sat on the dock for hours, long after the sun had slipped past the horizon. The lighthouse blinked out a golden beam, a silent reminder that I wasn't alone in watching over the water. My ass was sore and my heart was heavy, but I was staying right there until Owen returned.

When the boat's light cut through the darkness, an hour or two before dawn, I found him staring at me, his gaze hard and hurt.

"I told you to leave," he yelled from the deck. He turned away, busying himself with lines and buoys.

"That's tough shit, Owen," I called as he stepped onto the dock. "We need to talk."

He froze, his fists on his hips and his head hanging low. "Please," he said, his voice strained. "I can't do this."

I wrapped my hand around his bicep and pulled him close. "I fucked up and I was wrong but I love you, and you can't just toss me back into the sea."

Sighing, Owen looked out at the dark waters of the cove. "Your life... it's not here."

One of his greatest powers was his stoicism. He could hear my most sacred, private words and respond with little more than an impatient exhale. A blink. But I knew him, and I knew there was more to him than that. He wanted to be loved as much as I did, and he wanted me to keep pushing. His walls might be tall, but I wasn't afraid of the climb.

"It can be," I said.

That caught his attention, but holy Jesus, I wanted to hold him tight when he gave me that sad, pouty bear face.

"I mean that. I can stay. My life can be anything I want it to be. Anything we want."

His eyebrow winged up, unconvinced. "It seems that you're needed back in Silicon Valley."

"I'm not going back to the Valley, at least not permanently. I kinda hate it there." I shrugged, and he continued watching me with *what are you talking about?* eyes. "They'll be fine without me, and I can build apps to make working remotely more seamless." I dropped my hands to my waist, my hip cocked. "There's also the issue of my boyfriend living in Maine, and long distance just won't work for us."

"Then...what are you going to do?" he asked.

I brought my palm to the back of his neck. "Being here helped me realize that I didn't like managing the business. I'd always known, but...it was the only thing I had, you know? Now I know I'd rather mess around with crazy ideas and fix wonky code issues, and none of that requires me to spend any time in the office. I can do it anywhere, as long as I'm with you."

Owen didn't say anything for a long, painful minute where I was more interested in drowning myself than having him turn me away again. But finally—*fucking finally*—he wrapped his arm around my waist and dropped his head to my shoulder. "This probably means you're going to want that Wi-Fi stuff in the house now, huh?"

I laughed and rubbed my hand down his back. "I installed it in July," I said.

He lifted a shoulder but didn't respond immediately. "I let myself think this would work out, you know, with us. That I could ignore your life before me, and we could live in this little bubble. Then I saw that magazine, and..." He sighed, and that warm puff set off a ripple of goose bumps over my neck. "And I felt like a fool. That's why I wanted you to leave. Not because I didn't want you."

His words were the sharpest arrows.

"I mean it, Owen. I'm so sorry. Tell me how I can make it up to you."

"No more secrets," he murmured. "And you could say yes when I ask you to marry me."

"Yes," I said. "Yes now, and yes always."

EPILOGUE
REEF KNOT

n. Joining two ends of a single line to bind around an object.

OWEN

FIFTEEN MONTHS later

"WHAT IS THIS UNHOLY MESS?" I asked from the doorway as I shook out of my sleet-soaked coat. A nor'easter was blowing in tonight.

Cole glanced up at me but quickly returned to the measuring cups and mixing bowls on the countertop. "I thought you'd be out for another two hours," he replied.

"You didn't answer my question," I said.

"You didn't stick to your schedule," he answered, pushing his glasses up his nose. His fingers were dusted with flour, leaving a white smudge on his dark frames.

Once I'd shucked off my cold, wet outerwear, I padded into the kitchen to get a look at the chaos brewing there. "It smells good," I remarked, glancing at the sheet trays cooling near the oven. "Whatever it is."

"I made gingerbread," Cole said as he poured sugar into a mixing bowl.

I took another look around the kitchen. "For the entire town?"

"For a gingerbread house," he replied. "I'm constructing a scale replica of the house. And the lighthouse." He tapped the measuring cup against the bowl before turning on the mixer, the shine of his wedding band catching my eye. I couldn't fight the grin that surfaced every time I noticed it on his finger, or the obscenely sweet photo of our first dance that was framed and hung above the fireplace. "I'm making frosting now."

We were a few days away from our six month anniversary. We'd intended for our wedding to be a small affair, but I discovered my definition of "small" deviated from Cole's by fifty percent. In the end, it was a bit larger and more lavish than I would've selected for myself but getting married wasn't about me alone. If there was one thing I'd learned since Cole drifted into my life, it was that *we* mattered more than *I*.

"Um," I started, running my hands through my hair, "if you needed something to do, you could've helped me haul in traps. Were you bored or something?"

Cole still accompanied me on the boat most mornings, but not all the time. There were days and nights when he was too deep in his work to look up, and I respected the ebb and flow of his mind's machinations. When I left this morning, he appeared lost in his coding. No cakes in sight.

"I was working and now I'm baking," Cole answered over the whirring mixer. "It's the holidays, and I wanted to do something festive. Since we spent last year in Palm Springs with my mother—"

"Where we did *not* dehydrate into jerky," I said.

He glared at me over the mixer. "Since we spent last year in Palm Springs," he continued, "I wanted to start a tradition of our own this year."

"You were bored," I murmured.

Cole was between projects, and having that kind of time on his hands often led to him falling down curious rabbit holes. He tried his hand at gardening last summer. It yielded a handful of tomatoes and one amusingly girthy zucchini before he abandoned it to start building a new app. That product met with massive success.

The Talbott's Cove Effect. That's what Cole called it. Everything he created here was a hit.

As much as he loved being here, there were still moments when it was difficult for him to cede control to the people back in California. Those moments occurred only when he was locked in a power struggle over issues and details I didn't understand. Reliably, Neera talked him off those ledges.

She visited us in the Cove every month or so. She'd fly in for a weekend, and she and Cole would spend two hours working at the kitchen table. Then the three of us would hit the water. For reasons I still didn't understand, the lady enjoyed sorting lobsters. She was good at it, too. It only took a quick overview of the process and she sorted more quickly—and more accurately—than her boss.

Cole traveled to Silicon Valley from time to time, but he spent the majority of his time here in Maine. We'd flown out there—on a goddamn private jet, no less—a few months after everything hit the fan with his so-called disappearance last year. His company was introducing a new product, the one he'd developed while working as my deckhand, and he wanted me to join him for the launch party.

Before we'd arrived, I wanted to hate everything about California and his world there. It was fucked up, it was immature, it was irrational. The good news was that it didn't last.

Cole's house was big, modern, and boring, and I fucked him on just about every surface I could find. That seemed like the right way for him to say goodbye to that era of his life. Since he only visited California a few times each year now, he ditched the gigantic mansion and downsized into a penthouse apartment. If anyone could call a penthouse downsizing.

Palo Alto was different from Talbott's Cove for sure, but it was amazing. It was fast-paced and overflowing with people, and I loved it. I loved the vibe, the places, the weather, even the people who wore sneakers with business suits.

I'd worried I'd be intimidated by the people from his company, or they'd resent me for keeping him on the East Coast. None of that happened. They were fun and fascinating, and interested in hearing about our life in the Cove. One weird dude asked me about bringing a group out on the water for some lobster boat team building, and Cole damn near pissed himself laughing about that. Later, he told me I could indulge the offer, yell at some executives all morning, and charge six figures for my time.

I wasn't ashamed to say I gave it serious consideration.

If Talbott's Cove hadn't been inundated with wealthy businesspeople —and their tourism money—I would've gone along with that ridiculousness. But ever since Cole announced he'd be staying in Maine, the tech types had been flocking here. My sleepy seaside town was becoming the next Sun Valley.

The local inn was always booked, and some of the locals had taken to fixing up their homes and listing them on short-term rental websites for obscene rates. The O'Keefes were able to pay their daughter's college tuition after renting out their house for the summer *and* pay off their mortgage. JJ sprung for a new can of paint and added some kale salads to The Galley's menu. No one ordered them but it was an amusing gesture. The town council was slammed with proposals for restaurants, shops, hotels. It was madness.

The Cole McClish Effect. That's what I called it. Everyone wanted to catch some of the magic he found here.

"Yes, I hit a wall with my work but I also wanted to surprise you with a new tradition," Cole started, pinning me with a sharp glance, "but it seems you chose this as the one and only day you'll deviate from your schedule."

"The fish weren't biting," I said, laughing. "That's often the case when winter storms move in."

He looked up, his lips parting, and stared out at the sleet and dark clouds. The visibility was low and the waves high. Based on the surprise washing over his face, he hadn't noticed until now. Absentmindedness was one of Cole's most adorable—but also infuriating—traits. I was certain the earth could open up and swallow everything around him, and he wouldn't notice until his ass caught on fire.

"You went out in that weather?" he asked, incredulous.

"Yes, sweetheart, I did." I pointed to my dripping hair. "That's why I'm soaked. Unlike some people, I don't make a habit of falling overboard."

"I haven't fallen over in"—Cole turned his gaze to the ceiling while he murmured to himself—"three or four months."

"It's almost a record," I replied.

Rolling his eyes, Cole scraped the sides of his mixing bowl with a spatula. "You didn't have to go out," he said. "You know I don't like it when you're on the water in bad weather."

It was my turn to roll my eyes. "You didn't notice the weather until now."

"That has no bearing on whether you should've been out there," Cole replied. "You could've looked outside, seen the storm, and gone back to bed. I would've joined you for that."

Lightening my fishing and lobstering load was one of Cole's side projects. To his mind, money wasn't an issue, and I didn't need to work the water every day. I agreed with him—to a point. Unlike years past, I wasn't compelled to go after other catches during lobster's slow season from January to June. I didn't sweat over expenses when the market prices dropped. But I wasn't interested in lightening the load any more than that. My objection was less about not wanting to be a kept man and more about enjoying my work. It was grueling but I still loved it, and I didn't want to abandon it.

Change wasn't easy and I didn't take to Cole's money overnight, but it wasn't a major point of contention for us. There were moments when I found his wealth staggering. Paralyzing, even. But I didn't want that to become a rock in the middle of our relationship. That took work. I had to practice dealing with the shock associated with spending loads of money as easily as he did. I rolled with it when Cole wanted to spend a month on a private island in Belize after the launch of one of his newest developments, and when he bought out an entire hotel in Palm Springs when we traveled there for the holidays last winter. Instead of getting caught up in the disparity between our income levels, I admired my husband's ass in short shorts.

"I had traps to pull in." I reached over, turned off the mixer, and held up a hand to silence Cole's protest. "Just be quiet for a minute. Please."

I glanced down at his apron, covered in floury handprints, and then back up at his face. There was a dark smudge on his cheek—probably molasses—and a bit of sugar sparkling on his brow. He was a beautiful mess, and I was the luckiest guy in the entire state.

"Don't look at me like that while I have gingerbread in the oven," Cole warned. "Save those bedroom eyes for later, babe."

I pressed my lips to his and sighed when his tongue darted out. He tugged me closer, until only our clothes separated us. "What about kitchen eyes?" I whispered against his jaw. "Can I have those?"

"What?" he asked, breathless as I dragged my denim-covered erection over his. "What are you talking about?"

I laughed, the tight sound bursting from my mouth in quick, strangled puffs. "I need to warm up, and you have one helluva hot ass. Do I have time to bend you over the countertop before the next cake comes out of the oven?" The words had barely passed my lips when the oven timer wailed. "*Fuck.*"

Cole shook with silent laughter. "To answer your question, babe, no."

Before I could pry myself off him, I heard paws skittering down the hall. "Here comes trouble," I murmured.

Last winter, we rescued a three-year-old mixed breed dog from the local no-kill shelter. We waited until after the new year, when things settled down from Cole's big launch and we returned from our extended holiday in Palm Springs. I wasn't sure I was ready for another pup, but when we walked past Sasha's kennel, everything changed. Her sweet face and happy spirit stole our hearts.

"She snoozes until the timer goes off," Cole said. "Then she's my shadow. She's on crumb patrol."

"I don't doubt it." An eager, fidgeting mass of dog wedged between our legs, paws stamping and tail wagging. I reached down to scratch her head. "What's this? You'll wake up for gingerbread but not me?"

With a whine, she plopped down on her bottom, her tail thumping against the hardwood. She was part Irish Setter, her coat a warm, glossy red, but the rest of her lineage was unclear. She had the temperament of a Labrador, the strength of a Boxer, and the lapdog sensibilities of a Maltese.

The oven timer pealed again, and Cole slipped out of my hold. "Since you won't be bending me over the countertop, you can help me with the gingerbread lighthouse," he said.

I crouched down to give Sasha some love. "What do you mean I'm not bending you over?" I asked.

"We're building this lighthouse, Owen," he warned. "We're going to have some traditions, and you're going to damn well enjoy them."

With a low groan, I pushed to my feet. Sasha nudged my leg with her nose, and I responded with another head scratch. She huffed and stalked toward Cole, more interested in sniffing out those crumbs than anything I had to offer. I stared at my husband from across the kitchen, smiling when he fed her a bit of gingerbread.

There was a time when I filled my life with quiet and order. When I'd accepted solitude as my only companion. But now my dog was begging for scratch-made baked goods. My man was inventing holiday traditions. My finger wore a shiny new ring. My home was full of noise, clutter, and chaos.

"I will, Cole," I said. "I promise I'll enjoy it all."

And my heart, it was overflowing with the kind of love I'd never imagined for myself.

THANK **you for reading *Fresh Catch*! I hope you love Cole and Owen. If you enjoyed this visit to Talbott's Cove, you'll love Annette and Jackson in** *Hard Pressed*.

Dear Jackson,

I'm leaving you this note because I know you're very busy and I don't want to waste the town sheriff's time. Lord knows I've already wasted enough of it.

Thank you for taking me home last night and...everything else. I made you a basket of wild blueberry muffins for your trouble. That seemed like the appropriate baked good for getting naked in your living room.

I wasn't myself last night. I didn't mean to kiss you or fondle your backside or ask all those intimate questions. Thank you for pretending to enjoy it.

It was very noble of you to sleep on the couch while I was starfished on your bed. I couldn't help but notice it's quite large. The bed, that is. I swear, I didn't notice anything else when I let myself out this morning.

As you know, Talbott's Cove is a ridiculously small town and there's no chance we can avoid each other. Not that I'd want to avoid you, of course, but I'm not sure I can look at you without thinking of the forty different ways I made a fool of myself.

Instead of avoidance, let's try to be friends. We'll forget all about last night...if that's what you want.

Please burn this note after you read it—

Annette

P.S. I whipped up some cinnamon buns, too. Please enjoy them. I'm not sure why, but I couldn't get buns out of my mind today.

HARD PRESSED ***IS AVAILABLE NOW!***

Join Kate Canterbary's Office Memos mailing list for occasional news and updates, as well as new release alerts, exclusive extended epilogues and bonus scenes, and cake. There's always cake.

Visit Kate's private reader group to chat about books, get early peeks at new books, and hang out with over booklovers!

If newsletters aren't your jam, follow Kate on BookBub for preorder and new release alerts.

HARD PRESSED

ABOUT HARD PRESSED

Dear Jackson,

I'm leaving you this note because I know you're very busy and I don't want to waste the town sheriff's time. Lord knows I've already wasted enough of it.

Thank you for taking me home last night and...everything else. I made you a basket of wild blueberry muffins for your trouble. That seemed like the appropriate baked good for getting naked in your living room.

I wasn't myself last night. I didn't mean to kiss you or fondle your backside or ask all those intimate questions. Thank you for pretending to enjoy it.

It was very noble of you to sleep on the couch while I was starfished on your bed. I couldn't help but notice it's quite large. The bed, that is. I swear, I didn't notice anything else when I let myself out this morning.

As you know, Talbott's Cove is a ridiculously small town and there's no chance we can avoid each other. Not that I'd want to avoid you, of course, but I'm not sure I can look at you without thinking of the forty different ways I made a fool of myself.

Instead of avoidance, let's try to be friends. We'll forget all about last night...if that's what you want.

Please burn this note after you read it—
Annette

p.s. I whipped up some cinnamon buns, too. Please enjoy them. I'm not sure why, but I couldn't get buns out of my mind today.

Praise for *Hard Pressed*

"Hard Pressed is a charming and deeply satisfying blend of humor, passion and emotion, and frankly, it's downright huggable." ~ USA Today

"...every book of [Kate Canterbary's] I've picked up since has been better than the last, especially her latest, Hard Pressed." ~ Hypable

"This is my first Kate Canterbary book and I freaking loved it! I read this book in a day and see myself rereading in the future." ~ Stephanie Rose, Author of the Second Chances Series

"This story was an absolute delight! It was so charming, swoony and sexy and I loved everything about it!" ~ Goodreads Reviewer

"Hard Pressed is one of my favorite reads so far this year!" ~ *Goodreads Reviewer*

"...it floors me every time I read one of Kate Canterbary's books just how unbelievably intelligent she is. But most importantly, I just love her stories." ~ Goodreads Reviewer

"Hard Pressed was the perfect Kate gateway book for me, because it checked all manner of boxes - sexy af, swoony, smart and brilliantly funny. So damn funny." *~ Goodreads Reviewer*

"Hard Pressed is just another stellar example of the brilliance that is Kate's stories." ~ Goodreads Reviewer

"...sweet, sexy, quirky and so damn beautiful, I want to read it all day every day for the next 5 years." - *Goodreads Reviewer*

For best friends who scream obscenities in restaurants.

And Mary and Paul, and Mel and Sue.
On your marks, get set, bake!

1

———————

ELASTICITY

n. Capable of recovering shape after stretching.

Jackson

FOR FIVE MINUTES EVERY MORNING, my life was pure agony.

On most days, I went out of my way to avoid her. I scheduled myself for early patrols or wellness checks on some of my elderly residents. Anything to get out of the station. It was a necessity. I couldn't see to the public safety of this town with my dick harder than a nightstick.

I knew because I'd tried. The squad was too small for briefings from behind a podium. When it came to positioning a clipboard or the sheriff's standard-issue campaign hat over my crotch, I found I could only hold that pose for a few minutes.

Oh, I'd tried to hide it, but the only solution was staying away from the station and the sweetheart of Talbott's Cove, Annette Cortassi. The bookstore she owned on Main Street was no more than fifty yards from my desk and I had a front row seat for her morning rituals.

Annette walked down the street as if surrounded by moonbeams and unicorns, her smile radiant. I didn't know it for sure, but I'd put money on her being the homecoming queen back in high school and Miss Congeniality, too. I'd also put money on her making it her life's work to torture and torment me. She was a devil in angel's clothing, I knew that to be fact.

Since my first days in this sleepy fishing town, an outsider in every sense possible, it was the spunky brunette shopkeeper who'd stolen my attention. Annette knew how to wear the shit out of a summer dress. That woman's bare calves were a public safety hazard. And her ankles. *Fuck*. Since when were ankles sexy? They were bony joints, for Pete's sake. But all it took was the sight of her walking through the village in strappy sandals to turn me on.

As if the ankles weren't enough, her round hips swayed like a hypnotist's pocket watch. I couldn't avoid the sight of her sun-kissed skin or her waterfall of dark, wavy hair if I tried. More than once, I'd found myself gazing after her, hands clenched, jaw on the floor, and a puddle of drool beside it.

Annette was the brightest star in the Talbott's Cove sky. Every time I caught sight of her, I was powerless to look away. And that was why I couldn't look *at all*.

I was a newcomer here, still working my way into the good graces of the natives. They didn't know me yet and they didn't trust me either. Bedding the town sweetheart wasn't the way to those good graces, no matter how much she enjoyed it. And she'd enjoy it. I wouldn't have it any other way.

But that didn't matter. For the time being, I was sleeping alone. A temporary vow of chastity was the right thing to do. The town deserved my full attention, and my predecessor had made it clear I was to lead by example. No boozing, no gambling, no skirt-chasing. Not unless I wanted a one-way ticket back to Albany.

I wasn't much of a boozer, gambler, or skirt-chaser, but I heeded the previous sheriff's warnings nonetheless. Getting this job was a big step up for me. It was an even bigger step *away*.

In the span of a couple of months, I'd left my job and sold my home in upstate New York and headed for this town on Maine's rocky coast. It was a bold move, but a necessary one. I wanted to find a different pace of life, and somewhere I could do important work and make some small difference.

I didn't say it in job interviews or mention it in conversation, but I also wanted to belong somewhere. Maybe, eventually, belong to some*one*.

I shot the clock on my SUV's dashboard a bitter glare. I'd already looped the town twice this morning, fielded complaints about a pair of foxes lurking around the Lincolns' chicken coop, helped the innkeepers fix a section of their back fence that went down last night, and mediated a dispute between fishermen over some missing buoys. So far, a productive morning and yet I still had fifteen minutes before Annette would be tucked inside her shop.

I'd only managed to speak to her a handful of times. It wasn't nerves that kept me away but a complete inability to look at her without wanting to step into her personal space and smell her hair. I didn't understand that reaction and a part of me resented Annette for surfacing it. Hair-smelling. What kind of witch was she?

Instead of doing or saying something I'd regret, I kept my distance. This small town didn't allow for any true distance but I didn't have to watch her scrawl the quote of the day on the shop's chalkboard sign or arrange and rearrange potted plants on the sidewalk.

Just the thought of her kneeling down to write in one of her gauzy sundresses drew a knot of want low in my belly. She was beautiful and alluring in the most simple, honest ways. Hell, she couldn't jot down a Dickinson quote without lighting a fire inside me from across the street.

But I couldn't get Annette messy and dirty. I couldn't make her scream my name. Not unless I was also ready to wife her up, and I wasn't sure about that. I couldn't casually date her with the entire town watching—and they would watch—and chances were good I couldn't casually fuck her either. She looked altogether too by-the-book for fuck buddies, and there was no room for a tomcat sheriff around here.

That left me killing time by patrolling the town's back roads and praying the lovely book mistress was on time today. My cock couldn't take any mix-ups this morning.

2

SCALD

*v. **To heat a mixture of liquid just below the boiling point.***

Annette

THURSDAYS WERE GOOD SALES DAYS, especially in the summer. It was close to payday and people liked to stock up for the weekend. Sometimes the direct deposit was already burning up their bank account, and getting their hands on a beach read made the weekend seem that much closer. It was a mind game, of course, and I was the queen of those. I'd spent the better part of a decade pursuing a man who'd never want me. Not because I wasn't fun or smart or interesting or beautiful but because I was rocking a vagina and he preferred penis.

Not exactly the sort of thing I could fix with the right dress.

Yeah, I was the queen of mind games. Years ago, somewhere in the doldrums of being in my early twenties and frustratingly single, I'd convinced myself Owen Bartlett could be mine if I worked hard enough.

Silly girl, silly games.

On any other Thursday in July, I would've stayed open late and enabled those weekend dreams. The town's inn was fully booked, as were several rental houses and cottages within walking distance of my book-store. Summertime in the Cove brought tourists and tourists brought money.

But it was close enough to closing time and I was shutting this place down because I needed hard liquor and wallowing. It wasn't every day that a crush I'd harbored for years—years!—blew up in my face. It wasn't just a crush. It was a dream—an *illusion*—I'd cultivated so thoroughly that it was my reality. I'd never stopped to ask whether I was operating on bad assumptions or shoddy information. Or playing a damn mind game with myself.

Instead, I devoted years to slowly pursuing a man who would never want me. I'd known this, of course, in the dark part of my mind where I hid truths too true to speak. I knew and I chose to ignore it until faced with him cuddling his boyfriend in my shop.

I wasn't surprised to see Owen with his new deckhand Cole in the mystery section, but I blinked several times as I saw him wrap his arms around Cole's torso. My brain couldn't make sense of this image at first and cycled through all the non-romantic possibilities. Bro hugs, back cracking, Heimlich maneuver, spontaneous team yoga session. All valid options. But then his hand teased under the waistband of Cole's shorts and I couldn't look away. Not even when Owen kissed Cole's neck and everything inside me turned to quicksand.

I wanted to scream, "What are you doing to him? What the fuck is going on?" but instead I sent up a prayer for a swift and graceful end to this visit and called, "It's my favorite fishermen!"

I wasn't sure how I managed that. I desperately wanted to know what the hell was going on, even more so when Cole let out an impatient sigh and dropped his head back to Owen's chest. That was the only acknowl-edgement of my presence. They carried on a whispered conversation as I rounded the counter and approached them.

I wasn't sure how I walked without stumbling. I wasn't one for theatrics but when Owen kissed Cole, my knees had the strength of jelly and a ten-ton boulder landed in my gut. I stood there, too stunned to speak, to look away as they shared this moment. There was no mistaking the intimacy they shared. It was true and deep, and it was a side of Owen I'd never known until now. Seeing him share it with someone else ripped me right in half. I grabbed the newest political tell-all off the shelf and pressed it to my chest just to keep myself intact.

"Hey, Annette," Owen said.

It took me a minute to find my words. In that time, Owen didn't loosen his hold on Cole. It was as though he wanted me to see this, in all its crush-killing glory. He wanted to make his intentions clear.

"Good to see you, Owen," I said, forcing a smile I didn't feel. "You too, Cole."

"You have a great shop," Cole replied. "Awesome selection, fantastic layout."

I'm gonna have to talk now. I'm gonna have to play nice. And I'm gonna need a big bucket of vodka when this is done.

"Yeah, I try," I said, looking away as I rolled my eyes. I wanted to believe he was sincere but I was too busy hating this entire conversation. Hating everything, my bad judgment most of all. "Is there anything I can help you find?"

For the love of pinwheels and popsicles, please say no.

"I think we're good," Cole replied.

Thank you, thank you, thank you.

A second later, Owen said, "Cole wants a few mystery novels. Can you recommend some?"

Would it be wrong to say no?

"Oh. Oh, sure." I took a step forward, prepared to rattle off my standard mystery recommendations, but something snapped inside me. There was an actual snap, like a rubber band stretched past its limits, and everything it once restrained tumbled loose. The force of that snap propelled me forward and I whirled around the shop, plucking paperbacks as I went. "Let me pick out some books for your new boyfriend, Owen. That's what I do, make everyone else happy. Sure! Mysteries. Fantastic! Everyone else gets their happy and I get to pick out books. Fabulous!"

Cole and Owen went on cuddling and whispering like they were cozied up on a picnic blanket, and they missed all the impatient glares I shot in their direction. A girl could only take so many hits in one day before trotting out some first-class sass.

"Mysteries. I love a mystery," I said, the edge in my voice sharp enough to cut stones. "Sometimes I think I live in a mystery. You know, the *what is happening in my life?* mystery. Because I sure as hell don't know." My arms were overloaded with books and I needed to get rid of these guys. I dropped my haul of recommendations on the counter. "Can I get you anything else?"

Please, please, please say no.

"No, this is plenty," Cole replied.

Of course, Owen asked, "Did that special order come in?"

Argggh.

The damn special order. My deus ex machina. For years, we'd played the special order game. It'd served me well. Owen came in looking for a book, something old, obscure, or odd. Often, it was all three. And I got it for him, every time. He'd come in to pick up his newest read and we'd get to talking about books and history and everything else. To him, it must've been casual conversation with the book lady. For me, it was proof that we had something, even a little something.

Now, that special order was killing our little something with fire.

I sighed, and the effort pulled my shoulders down. I couldn't find a smile to save my life. "Yeah, Owen, it did," I said, annoyed with him, myself, everything. "I'll need a minute, okay?"

I didn't wait for a response, turning toward the storeroom and power-walking my ass behind closed doors. When I was alone and separate from the catastrophe on the other side of the wall, I brought my hands to my eyes as I choked out a sob. It was a gasp followed by tears that poured down while I gulped for air.

It was ugly, and it was gross. My makeup was melting off my face and my nose was running like a faucet, and I didn't even know why I was crying.

Yeah, I was hurt, but hurt for a hundred different, ridiculous, contradictory reasons. I couldn't even land on one reason and hold it up as proof that I was allowed to feel this way. Instead, I had a collection of missteps and mistakes, assumptions and inferences. It added up to a tiny disaster but it was coming down around me like a monsoon.

I could hear Owen and Cole talking on the other side of the door. Their happy little love fest was going on its merry way while I snot-sputter-laughed at the idea of sneaking out the back door. I'd do it, too. I could leave them there while I found that bucket of vodka to fade the warts and hairy moles of my life.

But I'd known Owen Bartlett my whole life and his mother was my high school guidance counselor. Small town manners—and a long-standing fear of Mrs. Bartlett—had me snatching his special order off the shelf, wiping away the tears, and pulling myself together. I'd get through this sale and then I'd drown myself in vodka.

When I emerged, I found Cole and Owen with their heads bent together, whispering to each other in a way that squeezed my heart. I wanted to share that kind of intimacy with someone who adored me the way Cole adored Owen.

"Here we go," I said, slapping the paperback down. I wasn't trying to be ranty. It was just flying out of me too fast to pull it back.

"Annette," Owen started, "about all of this. I didn't mean to make you uncomfortable. If I did, I'm...I'm sorry."

His words were meant to smooth my obviously frayed ends but they only irritated me further. Owen didn't have to apologize for me being a fool. I did this all by myself.

I shooed his words away with both hands like they were annoying mosquitos. "No apologies needed. I wasn't thinking. I wasn't being smart." I glanced at the man beside Owen and felt the tears fill my eyes again. "I knew," I said with a vague gesture toward them, "but I still hoped."

Owen stared at me, his brow crinkled and his lips folded into a grim line. I stared back at him, my brows arched up in silent question, but he said nothing. I didn't have to be the love interest in his life to know he was desperate to make this better. I'd sat through enough town council meetings to know how he operated.

"This looks like something my mother would love," Cole announced, piling several copies of a local photography book onto the counter. "My sisters, too. My mother loves a good coffee table book."

He prattled on about his mother and several other things which I thoroughly ignored. I plowed my energy into ringing up their order rather than reveling in the newfound adoration they had for each other. I managed to ask a few rudimentary questions and charge Cole's black card—who the hell was this guy?—before shoving them out the door and flipping the locks. The lights were off, the front shades drawn, and I made quick work of stowing the cash in the safe before dashing out the back door.

I didn't bother fixing my makeup or cleaning myself up before heading to the village tavern, The Galley. It didn't matter tonight. If they weren't already, the people of this town would be abuzz with news of Owen's beau soon enough. They'd have something to say about him shacking up with a man and then they'd have something to say about me chasing after him since shortly after high school. Then they'd share knowing glances about me being thirty-three years old and having only this bookstore to call my own. Around here, there was always something to say.

I could almost hear it now. "Poor Annette," they'd coo. "My heart just breaks for her. All those years she spent pining over Owen and come to find out, he's gay. What will she do now?"

"Vodka will solve this," I said to myself. "Vodka always comes to the rescue."

I pushed The Galley's heavy wooden door open and headed for the bar. The tavern was packed with people but I ignored all of them.

"JJ," I called, catching the bartender's attention as I settled onto a stool. "I need something strong."

"What d'you mean?" he asked, not looking up while he towel-dried a glass. "Like, a hammer? I don't got a hammer, honey."

"No, not a hammer." I sucked in a breath and blinked furiously to keep my tears from spilling over. Why was I crying? No need for that. I was a big girl with big panties and big vodka. "Some shots."

"Only shots I do are Jäger and whiskey. That whatcha want?"

The tears were flowing now, and I didn't care. I was furious with myself and hurt by my own hand, and I couldn't hold it all in anymore. "What about a German Chocolate Cake shot?" I asked, thinking back to my last foray into shots. Bachelorette party, Portland, blinking penis necklaces. "Or a Wet Pussy? Or a Slippery Nipple? Rim Job?"

He cracked the towel against the bar like a whip. "Try again, honey. None of that shit here."

I sniffled, and said, "A drink. I want a strong drink."

"Do I look like a mind reader?" He spared me a quick glance. "You're going to need to be more specific."

He was trying to break me, right here in front of everyone. I was sure of it. "Um, I don't know. Can you make me a cosmo?"

JJ went on rubbing his dishrag around the rim of a pilsner glass. "I can," he started, "but I don't want to. I don't do girly shit."

"For fuck's sake, JJ," I snapped. If I wasn't brimming with frustration at his refusal to give me the one thing I wanted right now—when nothing else in my world was working—I would've cried a river and floated away. Instead, I wiped my face and shot him an exasperated glare. "Shake up some vodka and some juice and keep them coming. If you can't deliver on that simple request, I'll hop behind the bar and do it for you."

JJ inclined his head, studying me with a surprised smirk for a second, and then shrugged. "Vodka and juice. All right." He set the pilsner down and reached for a martini glass. "Where are your girls tonight? Shouldn't you be mixing wine spritzers with Mitzi and Titzi? Where's Carley and Barley?"

"I don't have friends named after grains," I said. "You know that."

"But you do mix wine spritzers." He snickered as he filled a shaker with vodka and ice. "Where's Bam Bam?"

I reached for a cocktail napkin to manage the excessive tears-and-snot situation. It was woefully inadequate. "Brooke-Ashley doesn't like that nickname," I replied, reaching over the bar for more napkins. "I don't know where she is, but she told me this morning she was busy tonight."

He snickered again. "I bet she is," he said. He set the martini glass in front of me and stabbed a finger in my direction. "If your drunk ass gives me any trouble, I'll toss you out."

I rolled my eyes and scowled as hard as I could, which wasn't saying much. I didn't scowl too often. "You've known me your entire life, JJ," I said. "You know I have zero-point-zero trouble in me."

That earned me another snicker. "Famous last words."

3

DOCKING

v. The process of slashing or making incisions in the surface of bread or rolls for proper expansion before baking.

Jackson

THE CALL CAME in a few minutes shy of midnight, while I was checking out the high schoolers' usual late-night drinking-and-hookup haunts, and the request was quick.

"Could use your help down here, sheriff," JJ Harniczek barked.

"Be there in five," I replied, pulling a U-turn as I spoke.

The barkeep grunted in response before ending the call. It was polite by Harniczek's standards.

When I arrived in town three months ago, Harniczek made quick work of introducing himself and setting expectations. The man made it clear he was the unofficial law in these parts, and he kept the people—the drunks and everyone else—in line. He kept tabs on everything above board, under the table, and anywhere in between. He could handle most issues but if ever he called upon me or one of my deputies for assistance, he expected a prompt response. For a man in his early thirties, Harniczek knew his business and everyone else's too.

That made this call—direct to my mobile phone, no less—alarming.

Three months in a small town like this was nothing. I was a tourist as far as the natives were concerned. A few of them were doing their damnedest to test the boundaries, not unlike a rowdy group of tenth graders conspiring against the substitute teacher. They wanted to see what I'd put up with but the real test was whether I'd last. Others were more welcoming. Many paid calls to the station, offering their well-wishes on my new post or inviting me to their homes for supper. All in all, the people of Talbott's Cove were kind and gracious, if not a touch suspicious of the New Yorker taking up residence in their tight-knit community.

I'd only been summoned to the tavern on two other occasions, and one of them was to help trap a posse of raccoons out back. I trusted Harniczek, and I had no quarrel with his role around here. If anything, I was thankful for it.

The barkeep was an institution in small, insular communities like this one. I wasn't about to challenge that, or any of the other institutions. They needed me but I needed them just as much. Their approval and acceptance were critical, and not only because my job depended on securing the majority of the town council's votes each election year.

There was the harbormaster who doubled as the gossipmonger, old Judge Markham who puttered in his garden and yelled at seagulls, and the antisocial lobsterman who headed up the town council.

Another institution: Annette Cortassi, the beautiful book mistress busy twisting a long curl around her finger while she mouthed the words to Stevie Nicks's "Edge of Seventeen."

I made my way through the empty restaurant and toward the bar, my thumbs hooked under my tactical belt and my gaze on Annette. Her hair was a mess, half of it spilling out of the bun on the top of her head. Her eyes were shiny and red, with dark makeup was smudged on her cheeks. She'd been crying. I didn't like that. I didn't like any of this.

Something was wrong and I wanted to make it better for her. It wasn't my job, not the one I was sworn to carry out, but the one I desired more than I dared to understand.

I glanced at JJ Harniczek, taking in his ever salty scowl. "What seems to be the issue here?"

"It's not a mystery, sheriff," he replied. "The girl's blitzed."

Turning my head to stare at the woman who drew me in like a force field, I watched as she propped her head on her hand. She mumbled the song's chorus while her eyes drifted shut for a long moment. She was a wreck and drunk as a skunk—probably twice the legal limit—and a minute away from sliding off the barstool.

"I can see that," I said, stepping behind Annette. I held my hand a few inches from the small of her back, prepared to catch her if she took a dive. "You don't call me up every time you overserve a patron, JJ."

"I don't overserve anyone," he snapped. "They don't know their limits."

I pinned him with a sharp look. "That's not my interpretation of the law."

Impatient, he shook his head and waved me off. "Just get her outta here. I got things to do tonight. I don't have the time to hustle her home or spend another hour listening to her cry over spilt milk."

I cut a glance toward Annette and then back to JJ. "Mind telling me more about this spilt milk?"

"Dammit, sheriff," he grumbled. "I said I don't got time tonight."

Nodding, I replied, "Understood. I'll have time to fine you for overserving, but you get where you need to be going."

He pivoted to shelve a glass, muttering under his breath. I didn't catch the entirety of the comment but it wasn't complimentary. Something about wishing my mother had swallowed me when she had the chance.

When he turned back, he said, "Best I can tell, Bartlett let her down easy and she didn't see it comin'."

"Um, no, I did not." Annette snorted out a laugh and reached for the martini glass in front of her. "Bring me the alcohols, JJ. All the alcohols."

I snatched the nearly empty martini away and handed it to JJ. "Let's get the lady some water."

JJ gave me a wan look while he shoveled ice from a bin under the bar top into a cup. "Yes, let's. There's nothin' I'd enjoy more than gettin' *the lady* another beverage."

"What's this about Captain Bartlett?" I asked, glancing between the bookseller and the barkeep.

Owen Bartlett lived on the far end of Talbott's Cove, made his living as a lobsterman, and was a powerful member of the town council. He'd asked hours of tough questions when I interviewed with the council for this job, and he was one of my biggest supporters now that I was sheriff. He led with his principles and believed in contributing to his community, and I admired those qualities.

But I couldn't square the idea of Bartlett and Annette. Not when I knew Bartlett was gay and living with internet billionaire Cole McClish. Mr. McClish seemed to be keeping a low profile this summer, and not splashing his fame or wealth around the Cove. I was thankful for that small gift. The last thing I needed was the media storming my beaches or news helicopters circling the harbor.

"He doesn't want me. No one ever wants me," Annette wailed. She tipped the glass of water back but grimaced when the liquid hit her tongue. "This isn't liquor and that is a problem."

"The sheriff is cuttin' you off," JJ announced. "Adios, honey."

With one hand low on Annette's back, I leaned across the bar toward JJ. "Kindly explain to me what the fuck is going on here."

He glanced at the wall clock and then back at me. "Are you payin' this girl's bar bill? If not, it's closing time."

I reached into my back pocket and thumbed out two twenties. "This should cover it for tonight."

"Barely," he muttered.

"Tomorrow we'll have an official visit to talk about overserving," I continued, tossing the cash on the bar, "and shaking down law enforcement. Good?"

JJ scooped up the bills and nodded. "Great," he said. "As far as I know, our girl here wasn't going with Bartlett but she wanted to be. They had words this evening. He told her it wasn't happening." He paced the length of the bar and switched off the overhead lights. "End of story, time to go, farewell and good night."

As the bar descended into near darkness, Annette wobbled on the stool and spilled the glass of water down my tan uniform trousers. "Oh, shit," she yelled.

I hissed as the icy cold seeped into my clothes and shocked my skin.

She lost her grip on the glass and it rolled down the bar, a wobbly, ominous echo in the dusk while she patted my crotch with a wad of cocktail napkins. Between the ice bath and the surprise fondling, my cock had no idea what to do. It was a true "Should I stay or should I go?" conundrum in my pants, and I was helpless to stop her. She had one hand braced on my thigh while the other worked me over, and the only reasonable response to this was sliding my palm up her spine to the back of her neck. Without conscious thought, my fingertips pressed into her soft skin, my thumb stroking the graceful column of her neck. A rush of newfound intimacy washed over me, hot and welcoming, and it was almost enough to forget everything else in the world save for Annette.

Almost.

In the distance, I registered a quick whistling sound. At the same time, I realized I couldn't hear the glass rolling down the bar anymore and—*crash*. It hit the floor and shattered, and JJ let out a string of curses laced with complaints about having better things to do with his night.

The crunch and clatter of glass shook me from my momentary paralysis. "Annette," I barked, reaching for her hands. The ones with enough knowledge of my anatomy to sculpt a perfect replica. *Jesus Christ.* This was wrong. I was in uniform and on the clock, and she was past the point of making informed decisions. So fucking wrong. Regret pulsed through me as I pulled her away from my crotch. Regret that I had to end this. Regret that I'd let it get this far. "It's good, it's fine. You can stop."

"You can both stop," JJ called. "Like I've said, it's closing time."

My fingers were still wrapped around her wrist and I wasn't inclined to change that. "Let's get you home," I said, peering down at her bright, wide eyes. "Are you steady enough to walk?"

She met my stare with a studious one of her own, dragging her gaze from head to toe and then up again. She paused on my face and I knew she was working to make sense of my features. It was a flicker, nothing more than a half second.

And I didn't mind Annette's close study.

"Of course I can walk," she replied, hopping off the stool.

If I didn't have a hold on her wrist, she would've hit the floor when she swayed on unsteady feet. I yanked her closer to me and locked an arm around her waist. "Are you sure about that?" I asked.

"Right now," she started, her words punctuated by a hiccup, "I'm not sure about anything."

"Believe me," I murmured as I steered her toward the door, "neither am I."

Getting Annette out of The Galley was a challenge. She was a stumbling, bumbling disaster, all incoherent rambling and singing, and moments of weepiness that edged dangerously into full-on crying. Couldn't have that. I wouldn't be able to stand it.

It was dark, the empty streets illuminated only by the harbor lights. With my arm tight around her waist and my fingers splayed over her belly, I steered her toward Harborside Books. She lived in the apartment over the shop. "Sounds like you're having a rough night," I said. "Is that right, Miss Cortassi?"

"Owen and I have more in common than I thought," she announced. She leaned into me, her hand on my chest. I hated myself for reveling in her closeness. It was unprofessional and it was irresponsible to carry on with these thoughts while she was under the influence. I knew better and I had to do better. "We both like dick."

I let out a surprised laugh. I liked the way "dick" sounded on her tongue. It was bold and unashamed, and I was falling under this woman's spell. I couldn't help myself and I couldn't stop smiling down at her. "Do you now?"

"Oh, yeah," she drawled, pushing away from me. The second she was gone, I wanted her back by my side. She stood on the sidewalk, motioning both hands toward her mouth. I wasn't sure what she was doing but it loosely resembled her jerking off two guys. Or shaking a set of tambourines. Couldn't be sure. "I love dick. The bigger the better. All the dicks. I should call Owen and talk to him about dick. We can compare notes. And techniques! That will be fabulous. Dick, dick, dick."

I stepped toward Annette, not trusting her to stand on her own. That, and I was enjoying this more than I should. "Let's save that for another day. Okay?" She didn't respond. "How about we get you upstairs? Where are your keys, ma'am?"

"Oh, Lord," she said, groaning. "Don't ma'am me. My day's been bad enough."

I shook my head once. "I don't understand the objection," I said under my breath. "How would you prefer I address you?"

"Annette would be fine," she said. "Book Lady if you can't remember."

"How could I forget?" I asked. I gazed down at her, meeting her humor-filled smile with my serious stare. "I mean that sincerely, Annette. How could I forget?"

"I don't know," she said with a shrug. "It happens, or whatever."

She pushed away from me to study her reflection in a storefront window. Her hands lifted as she shook out her loose curls and I had to exert real energy to keep myself from walking up and smelling her hair.

"I wouldn't forget," I said. She wasn't listening. She was shoving her hands down the front of her dress and adjusting her cleavage. Scooping one breast up, plumping it in the cup of her bra, then delivering the same service to its twin. *God help me.* "I won't forget any of this."

"That's funny," she said, her voice flat. "I'm trying to forget."

"About that," I said, stepping to her side. "Time to go home. Lead the way and I'll follow."

She couldn't produce her wallet or keys, or any idea where she left them. The choices available to me weren't good. Either I was picking the lock to her apartment above the bookshop or I was taking her home with me. Neither situation was conduct becoming a sheriff.

On the off chance she'd left her door open—not uncommon in this town but worrisome nonetheless—I tried helping her up the back stairs without allowing my touch to turn into anything more than supportive. It would've been easier to throw her over my shoulder or cradle her in my arms, and I would've enjoyed it a lot more. But my hands hovered at her waist, barely there.

But the door wasn't open, and there were no potted plants or decorative bullfrogs hiding a key. Now we were faced with a trip down the stairs.

"I'll go first," I said, gesturing down the steep incline. "You stay right behind me. I don't want you falling."

"Yay," she grumbled. "The indignities of this day won't quit."

With my torso twisted toward her, I took several steps, my hand outstretched if she required assistance. "Are you doing all right?" I asked when she wobbled onto the next riser.

"I'm so far from all right, I'm all left," she replied.

I shifted to glance down at the stairs, and then a petite pile of girl slammed into my back. Before I could make sense of this, her arms tangled around my neck and her legs around my waist. Her breath was warm on my neck, and when I moved just a twitch, her lips brushed over my skin.

"Careful there," I said. "You're too fragile to be launching yourself at people."

"I am fragile," she whispered. "Please don't leave me in the drunk tank for the night. Don't...don't leave me."

It didn't matter that Talbott's Cove didn't have a drunk tank, or that inebriated citizens who posed no danger to themselves or others were rarely arrested for public intoxication. The lady didn't want to be alone, and I wasn't about to contradict her desires. I wrapped one hand around her ankles and another around her wrists, the least I could do to hold on to her, and continued down the stairs.

"Okay then," I announced, mostly to myself. "You can sleep it off at my place."

"That's almost as bad as the drunk tank," she muttered.

"Not that bad," I replied with a laugh. "Is there someone you'd like me to call? Somewhere else I can take you? What about your fam—"

She cut me off with, "Nope. Going to your house in the middle of the damn village is less awful than calling my family."

"You're sure?" I asked. I stroked her wrist as I crossed the street, wanting her to say yes. She murmured in agreement, her head still on my shoulder.

When I first moved here, back before I understood much about life in Talbott's Cove, I rented a house near the town center. It seemed like a great location, with glimpses of the ocean and a short walk to the station. What I didn't account for was having the entire town in my front yard. Residents liked to pop in with a plate of pot roast and pota-toes—not that I complained about that, of course—or to gather my opinion on Old County Road's traffic issues. Others simply made my comings and goings their business. It wasn't uncommon for me to step into DiLorenzo's, the local diner, and field questions as to why my lights were on past midnight. They wanted to know if I was sleeping well enough, if I had company, if I was tracking safety issues. Apparently, I was the only guy around here who fell asleep on his couch, not more than ten minutes into the local news.

I had to force all of that from my mind as I hiked up the hill toward my house with Annette Cortassi plastered to my back and her lips on my neck. I was thrilled to have a near-moonless night.

Once inside, I shifted her off my back and into a chair.

"You sit here," I ordered, unbuckling my duty belt. "I have to—uh—handle a few things."

First order of business: adjusting the erection hammering away at my trousers. Next up, pulling every curtain shut. That would probably set off alarm bells of its own with the locals, but that was an issue for another day. Once the house was adequately buttoned up and my gear and firearm were stowed in the safe, I poured a glass of water for Annette and snatched a banana from the fruit bowl.

That was when things went pear-shaped.

Annette wasn't in the living room anymore. She was right behind me, standing in the middle of my kitchen, bare-ass naked. My fingers tightened around the banana. "Annette," I warned. "What—what are you doing?"

"I might be fragile," she purred, swaying a bit as she stepped closer to me, "but that doesn't mean I always want to be treated like I am."

I was working hard at keeping my eyes above her chest. I had a peripheral awareness of her nudity but I'd yet to allow myself the kind of long, quenching gaze at her lush curves. Goddamn, I wanted to look. I wanted to drop to my knees and press my face to the soft lines of her belly, drag my fingers up her calves and grab her ass like I meant it. I wanted to feel her spine arch under my hands and her body tighten around me. I wanted to get lost between her legs and never, never find my way out.

Clumps of pulverized banana filled my palm, and I turned away. "I'll get you something to wear," I said over my shoulder. I tossed the fruit in the garbage and then rinsed my hands at the sink, but I knew she was watching me. I felt the intensity of her stare on my skin, and I wanted to give it right back to her. I wanted it more than anything.

Turning, I said, "Annette—"

She wasn't hearing it. She flew into my arms and pressed her lips to mine, and for the second time tonight, I was paralyzed. Dumbstruck and frozen in place. But then my body and brain returned to me in pieces. I sighed into her kiss, forgetting my job, my duty, myself. She tasted of liquor and juice, and something succulent and special all her own. I couldn't help myself. I curled my arms around her torso, backed her against the refrigerator, and rocked myself into the valley of her parted legs.

I stayed right there, trapping her between the hard lines of the refrigerator and my body while I drank in every ounce she offered up. I couldn't even process the glory of her naked skin under my hands. It was one gift too many.

Annette broke away first, turning her head a few degrees and hiccup-giggling against my cheek. Then her hand slithered down my back and she slapped my ass.

At first, I was stunned into silence. That was becoming my default reaction to this woman. But then I remembered she was sloppy drunk, and I wasn't the type of man who capitalized on that condition.

Her palm cracked over my backside again, and another hiccup-giggle rang out. "You're so...hard," she whispered.

I surrendered to her words rather than my judgment and rutted against her core. If she wanted to know something about hard, I was happy to illustrate. "You have no idea," I replied. "Not a clue."

She tipped her head back against the refrigerator and gazed up at me, her lips parted and her eyes unfocused. "Whoa," she murmured. So beautiful and so drunk. *"Whoa."*

Right then, my responsibility came down on me. It was lightning fast and there was no way I was coming back from it this time. Not tonight.

I tossed Annette over my shoulder and blocked out the sensation of her smooth thigh against my cheek. No, that wasn't true. I was keenly aware of her thigh. But I wasn't letting myself enjoy the thigh.

"Please tell me we're going to a bedroom," she called. "That would be fabulous."

"We're going to a bedroom," I replied, "and I'm putting you to bed. Alone."

"That's the story of my life," she whined, dragging her fingertips up and down my flanks. Goddamn, that felt good. I could die happy after nothing more than a night of her hands moving over my skin. "Me, in bed, alone. It's never my turn."

I wanted to argue with her, insist that she'd get more than a turn from me as soon as she sobered up. But it occurred to me that she was offering this information under drunk cover, and chances were good I wouldn't hear the same tune tomorrow. Annette had been pleasant to me since my arrival but hadn't given me much more than passing, platonic glances. She wanted someone right now, and I was that person only because JJ called me in to collect her. If he'd walked her home, he could be receiving the same treatment. He could've been the one getting her hungry kisses and gently demanding touch.

That idea did terrible things to me. *Terrible.* I tightened my grip on her thighs and gritted my teeth as I stomped through the house, barely fighting off the urge to throw her down and make her crave me the way I'd been craving her.

I could do it too. I'd lay her down on my bed. Make her comfortable. Kiss my way from those sexy ankles to her full lips, the ones that looked even more delicious now that I'd tasted her sweet smile. I'd skip the places she wanted me most. I'd make her wait the way I'd waited for her. She'd ache and squirm and beg, and then I'd hike her legs over my shoulders and show her everything I'd held back. And then she'd know. When I was deep enough to steal her words and everything else save for screams, she'd know I'd wanted nothing but her for months.

Instead, I set her on my bed and only allowed myself an extra moment with my hands on her body before turning away. I couldn't meet her hungry, needy gaze again. Not without tearing my pants off and feeding her my cock. I moved toward the door but couldn't leave. I stood there, my hands gripping either side of the doorframe while I stared unseeing down the hall. I needed this moment to gather myself, pull the loose threads of desire tight and sew them up. Set aside the urge to forget myself and take everything she was offering.

"Where are you going?" she asked. Her voice was small, almost child-like. "I want you to stay with me. You're not leaving. Are you?"

Go ahead and flay me open, woman. Go right ahead and gut me where I stand.

"No," I choked out. There was no way in hell I could walk away now. "Just going to grab some water for you." I shot her a glance over my shoulder. That was a huge fucking mistake. She was tucked back against my pillows, her knees drawn to her chin and her ankles crossed. It was a modest pose, her most private places covered, and I didn't believe there could be anything more intimate. Or anything that could make me want to crawl to her on my hands and knees more. I wouldn't be able to look at those pillows again without wanting her right there, exactly like that. "Put your head down. I'll be right back."

I stood in the kitchen for several minutes, my hands curled around the lip of the countertop while my cock thrummed against my zipper. I had to remind myself I didn't know Annette, not beyond her reputation as the town sweetheart and everyone's favorite book mistress. But that bright, joyful woman, the woman who had a smile and buckets of patience, wasn't the one begging me to join her in my bed right now. The slightly heartbroken and fully drunk woman was asking, and there was a world of difference between the two.

With a growl aimed at any number of frustrations, I grabbed the glass and headed back down the hall. I was busy playing out several scenarios in my head and finding the side of right in each one. I could hold her for a bit, and kissing wasn't off the table, but it couldn't go any farther until she was sober. If she really wanted something more, well, I'd just handcuff myself to a chair, tell her what to do, and watch from a distance. It would probably result in a broken wrist and equally broken chair, but I'd do it if it kept that lonely, vulnerable bite from her voice.

I was so busy with those plans that I missed the sound of Annette snoring like a chainsaw. Water sloshed over the rim of the glass as I stut-tered to a stop at the door, and I choked down a laugh. This woman was something else. Within minutes she'd gone from the picture of sweet sin to classic drunk chick. Her hair was tangled around her face like a veil, one leg was over the blankets, and her hands were pillowed under her head. She was just as alluring as always, but now she wasn't Miss Congeniality or the white-sundress-wearing book mistress of my fantasies. Now she was a real woman, raw and flawed, and miles away from the pretty girl on the town's pedestal. If it was possible, I liked this version even more because she saved it for me.

That was the story I was telling myself.

I set the water on the side table and tucked a wastebasket next to it in case that liquor came back to haunt her, and then pulled the quilt over her shoulders. The breeze off the water was cool and damp tonight, and I didn't want her waking up with a chill. I did my best to brush her hair from her face but sensed I was doing it wrong when she batted my hand away between snores.

"Sleep well, Annette," I whispered. "See? I told you I'd remember."

With a t-shirt and pair of athletic shorts in hand, I left Annette in my bedroom. It was odd stripping off my work clothes in the middle of the living room but it was one more thing I was ignoring for the time being. This entire evening was odd but while I collected her abandoned clothes and set them in my bedroom, I kept telling myself I was doing the right thing. Even if we both wanted me in that bed right now, it was best for me to find rest elsewhere.

My couch wasn't meant to sleep men like me. Not intentionally. It was too short, and the arms were bad pillows, and the fabric itched the patch of skin exposed when my t-shirt rode up. Worse than all of that was the erection throbbing against my belly.

Since I couldn't do anything about it—I mean, I *could*, but I wasn't going to—I folded myself into a tolerable position and yanked an afghan over my legs. Nothing to kill a boner like Gramma's orange and blue afghan. That lady never quit with the Syracuse pride.

And the blue, it was especially fitting.

4

____

RECONSTITUTE

v. To restore to a former condition by adding water.

Annette

I WOKE NAKED. That was my first clue that my evening had gone horribly, horribly wrong. The second clue was that I had no idea where I was.

My hair was a ratty disaster and I could smell the vodka seeping out of my pores. When I sat up to take in my surroundings, the contents of my stomach sloshed like a snow globe and I reconsidered ever moving again. I could stay here, in this strange bed, and make a new life for myself. Easy peasy. No need to account for my mistakes.

Carefully, I turned my head to glance at the framed photographs atop the dresser. I couldn't make out the fine details from this distance but I knew I was looking at a graduation photo. It wasn't a simple cap-and-gown setup though. It was military or...Oh, shit.

That was a police academy graduation photo and I was naked in Sheriff Lau's bed and oh my god how did I bring this many disasters upon myself in a twenty-four-hour period without earning some kind of medal? Where were the roses and cupcakes for being a prize train wreck? Because I wanted both, and the sash, too.

My only consolation was that I was naked and alone, and yes, that was better than being naked with Sheriff Lau. Only vodka used my body last night, and that was preferable. It was bad enough Owen dumped me...or whatever it was that went down between us...but I'd have to pack up and move to a new town if I'd drunkenly bedded the new sheriff. I didn't drunkenly bed anyone. Ever. I didn't possess the language to make those kinds of advances or negotiate those terms.

Then I caught sight of my sundress. It was neatly folded on the dresser, and my bra and panties sat right beside it. I stared at my clothes for a minute, wondering where I'd left my purse. As I dusted off hazy memories of yesterday, every minute of last night came rushing back to me. The bar, the cosmos, the water down his pants, the piggyback ride to his house, the kiss, the ass slapping—my god!—the way I'd begged him to take me to bed. The way I'd begged him to stay.

My embarrassment was much larger and far more powerful than my hangover, and it propelled me out of bed in a flash. I finger-combed my hair, threw on my clothes, and made the bed. I couldn't leave an unmade bed behind. I couldn't do it at my apartment, and I couldn't do it after inviting myself into the sheriff's bed. With the stealth of a cat burglar, I flattened myself against the hallway wall and tiptoed toward the door. I knew the sheriff was going to be around here somewhere, but I wasn't prepared to find him washed up on the couch.

He had one arm bent over his head, the other under his t-shirt, flat on his belly. Dark golden skin peeked out from where his t-shirt was rucked up and I spent a solid minute studying the muscled cuts on his torso. I thought those things only appeared while flexing but Jackson was as loose as linguini this morning.

His sandy blond hair was roughly tousled, as if he'd spent the entire night running his hands through the thick strands. He was a tall guy, too tall for this couch by at least six inches. Both legs dangled from the arm at angles I couldn't imagine were comfortable. There was a truly hideous blanket tangled around his legs but I couldn't spend a second wondering why anyone would knit such an atrocity after I caught sight of the tent in his shorts. At first, I didn't believe it was an erection. I'd never seen anything that, *ahem*, proud. I assumed it was something else. Maybe he had a cell phone in his pocket or...some zucchini. Sure, those were crazy options but no crazier than the possibility he was working with *that* kind of equipment.

As I stared at him, I was reminded of him pressing me against the refrigerator and fitting himself between my legs. His dark eyes had clouded over with need when he ground into me. I'd felt every inch of him then, and I'd—I'd slapped him. Yes, I'd slapped this man's ass and I'd done it more than once.

"Oh my god," I breathed.

With a shake of my head, I slipped out the front door. It was early, even for a fishing community that lived and died by the dawn. I had to pick my way through the woods ringing the village to get back to my shop. It wasn't the most direct route, but I couldn't risk a walk of shame past the docks. Also, I had to stop every few minutes to vomit into the bushes, and that kind of local news would make it back to my parents in nine seconds flat. My mother would be on her knees at St. Cecelia's, lighting candles for the salvation of my soul. My father would threaten to pack up my apartment and move me back home. Somehow, I couldn't have that.

I made it back to my apartment and fished the extra key out of the loose cedar shingle near the door. I had several hours before I was due to open the shop for the day—I wasn't even going to think about the condition I left it in yesterday—but I was too edgy and overwrought for sleep. That was the smart choice but it was too late to start with that now. Not when I could flip on *The Great British Bake Off*, drool over baked goods I'd never seen before, and tune out the world. I needed to forget a few things this morning.

I happened upon the Bake Off last winter. I didn't watch much television and couldn't justify spending money on a monthly cable bill, but I'd turned to public television after three weeks of mega snowstorms that shut down the seacoast. I was out of books to read, as impossible as that seemed, and I was going crazy in my little attic apartment. I found this charming import from the BBC that featured a dozen amateur bakers competing in a trio of challenges each week. It lacked all the snark and sass of most reality programming and focused instead on the baking itself.

To that point, I hadn't baked more than some Duncan Hines brownies on my own. I was Italian-American and I bled my grandmother's red sauce, but the kitchen had never interested me. It always felt like an event that belonged to my mother and older sisters, and never me. I was always too young to help, and when I wasn't too young, I was too clumsy, too disorganized, too something. If ever I was involved, they made sure I knew what I was doing wrong.

My mother and three sisters had their world, and I had mine. I didn't begrudge them anything, but that was always the way of it. That was the strange price for being the youngest by eleven years when my sisters had a year or less between them, all born before my mother's twenty-first birthday. If anything, they'd all grown up alongside my mother and spoke in a shorthand I didn't understand. How could I? They shared too many common experiences for me to reach their level. They were English teachers at the regional junior high school, their classrooms all together in a row. At one point or another, every kid in this area had one of the Cortassis.

But it was more than the years between us and my decision to get a degree in teaching but never use it. My parents had three girls in quick succession and they wanted a boy. My dad had taken over the family plumbing business from his father, and while he'd never turn one of us girls away if we wanted to partner up with him, he had it in his head that he'd pass the business on to his son. Cortassi and Son. That was how it went. Except...it didn't go that way at all.

They waited until they could afford another kid, an addition on the house, and a year off from school for my mother. They waited for a boy and that was one challenge I'd never best.

To be fair, my parents didn't lock me in the cellar because I didn't come with a penis. They didn't do much of anything. I wasn't abused or ignored, but I wasn't what they'd hoped for and that was plain to see. They cared for me and loved me in their own stilted, unsatisfied ways, but even when I was a child, I had the sense I was a consolation gift... and a problematic one at that.

They looked at Nella, the oldest, with pride and affection. She was smart and well-spoken, and even though a thick mean streak ran through her, she was always ready with clever ideas.

Then there was Rosa, the one they often called the middle child, and she was beautiful. She had other qualities but she didn't need them. She could live a long, happy lifetime on her appearance alone. That knowledge left her a bit vain, a bit self-absorbed, a bit cruel.

Lydia was the youngest of the original three, and they adored her feisty, outgoing nature. She could strike up a conversation with anyone and make that person feel like the center of the universe. But Lydia was terrible to people behind closed doors, tearing them to shreds over the slightest offenses.

My parents had a smart one, a pretty one, and a chatty one. That left me as the difficult one. I wasn't explosively rebellious or anything, but I had ideas that differed from my sisters' and parents'. I preferred getting lost in books to anything else, and my sisters went to book club gatherings for the wine. I had to make my own mistakes, and my sisters were content to take direction and advice without question. I liked the rustic village of Talbott's Cove, and my sisters and parents were quick to move several towns away for newer construction, Dunkin' Donuts drive-thrus, and better shopping. I wanted to be my own boss, and my sisters and mother believed I was denying my destiny as an English teacher. I rotated between preparing the same four meals for dinner every night, and my mother and sisters once compiled a cookbook based entirely on family recipes for a church fundraiser.

Anything from the kitchen was the domain of Mom, Nella, Rosa, and Lydia. It was surprising, then, that I'd latched onto the Bake Off. But it was a distant relative of my mother's ricotta cheesecake or tiramisu. This show was about slightly obscure tortes and unusual pastries, and other creations that didn't know a home in my mother's Italian kitchen. It sucked me in, and not long after those winter storms cleared, I started experimenting with recipes. My apartment had a postage stamp of counter space but I made the most of it. I'd gained a few pounds in the process, but I considered them fun, happy pounds.

I watched as the bakers organized their ingredients for a new challenge but couldn't keep my mind from wandering back to Jackson. I had to *do* something about this. About him. He'd come into the shop a few times since his arrival this past spring. He was polite but reserved, like he was only coming in to make sure I wasn't cooking meth in the storeroom. We'd talked about books—he liked sports memoirs—and he'd always left me with some pointers about security or safety issues he'd noticed. It was easy and free of complications such as unwelcome ass-grabbing or stripteasing.

Of course, I'd noticed he was attractive. He went running on the beach at sunrise. Shirtless. It was impossible to miss him and his orange shorts. And it wasn't just me, it was everyone else in a thirty-mile radius.

Sheriff Lau was the topic of conversation at my mother's Easter dinner after he'd visited the junior high to speak to the students about the dangers of four-wheeling in the woods. The way my sister Antonella —she went by Nella with family, Antonella with everyone else—told it, teachers were swooning left and right. Some of them were contemplating low-level crimes to get his attention. It was generally agreed upon that Sheriff Lau could stop and frisk any of them, any time.

But he wasn't *just* attractive. Anyone could be attractive. That didn't make them kind or respectful or compassionate, and Jackson checked all those boxes. I hadn't put conscious effort into cataloging his qualities because I'd had my eyes on Owen and other dead ends, but my entire life revolved around this town and the people in it. I knew Jackson mowed Mrs. Mulcahey's lawn when her husband broke his arm two months ago, and her grandson couldn't do it until after his college final exams. I knew he helped the Fitzsimmonses get their son into one of the good opioid treatment programs in Portland. And he took me to his home when I was drunk and sad.

"Muffins," I said to the empty room. "I'll make him some muffins."

I had blueberries because it was July in Maine and everyone had a barrelful of blueberries right now. Two bushes grew wild in the space behind my shop, and I wouldn't be able to eat them all if I tried. But I could cram them into these muffins until they were more molten blueberry, less cake. And there was nothing sexy or suggestive about a blueberry muffin. Not even a perfect blueberry muffin. They were safe and simple, and the most neighborly of the muffins. Neighborly was the closest thing to "sorry about sexually harassing you last night" as I was going to get with blueberries, flour, and sugar.

I threw myself into baking, first doubling and then tripling the recipe as I decided to load up a basket with muffins and walk it over to the station. It wasn't a gesture for Jackson's benefit alone but all the law enforcement officers and firefighters there. They were going to be double-fisting those muffins and all would be right with the world. Maybe then I'd be able to stop thinking about his lips on mine, and the way it felt when I was certain he was kissing me just as much as I was kissing him.

Drunk memories were liars. They told stories and invented truths, and I couldn't rely on them. But...he'd pressed me against the refrigerator—maybe a cabinet or a wall, I wasn't sure—and *kissed me*. Really kissed me. Like he'd wanted to kiss me and he wasn't merely putting up with crazy drunk girl antics. He'd held me, too, and more than the steadying hand of a man who dedicated his life to looking out for others.

Drunk memories were liars but Jackson Lau's touch was the truth.

When the last tray of muffins went into the oven, I stared at the mountain of dirty dishes in my sink. It should've been a reminder that for every action there was an equal and opposite reaction—and I had to deal with my damn reactions—but all I could think about was caramel sauce. Sauce meant for drowning thick, chewy, cinnamon buns. With pecans. And caramel sauce, too.

Without giving another thought to the dishes, I dug into my refrigerator for the chunk of dough I'd left in there a few nights ago, and then cleared off my two-seat kitchen table. It wasn't ideal for stretching dough the way good buns deserved, and neither was storing dough indefinitely, but they did the job well enough.

I didn't have enough dough to make a full pan, but I was happy with the limited edition. If the muffins were for the first responders, the buns were all for Jackson. The thought made my heart leap with anticipation, and I had to fight back a grin while I coaxed the sugar into caramel. I wanted him to have this, something I'd made all by myself, and I wanted it to say a million different things.

Thank you for giving me a soft place to land. Sorry about rubbing my ass all over your house. I hope we can be friends even though I attacked you. Thank you for shutting down all of my attempts at seduction. Have a muffin; now please forget all the things I said when I was drunk. Did you mean to kiss me back? Would you do it again?

While the muffins and buns cooled, I stepped into the shower. Like everything else in my apartment, it was tiny. This space was little more than a converted attic but it was plenty for me. I didn't need a soaking tub or proper closets or full-size windows. Those things were all nice to have, much like retirement plans and stand mixers. But I could make do with what I had.

When I was finished, I toweled off and wrapped myself in a short robe printed with flamingos. With my damp hair falling across my face, I thumbed through the greeting cards I hoarded in an old boot box. I had a serious compulsion where cards were concerned. If I saw something cute or thoughtful or punny or emotional, it didn't matter whether I had a need or purpose. I had to have them.

Of course, there was no greeting card appropriate for my current situation. Not even the blank ones with art or photographs on the front were right for this. Every card invited too many opportunities for accidental symbolism. Flowers were too sensual, too suggestive. Driftwood on the beach was just as bad. The one with a bowl of glistening cherries and a wooden spoon made my cheeks heat with embarrassment, among other things. Abstract art was out of the question.

Close to losing my patience and ready to blow off the entire muffin plan, I found a package of recipe cards. I wanted to believe I'd get into the habit of writing recipes down on nice, orderly cards rather than scribbling notes on the side of printouts or relying on my phone, but I'd never followed through on that plan. Now I had one hundred cards trapped behind shrink wrap, waiting for a reason to exist.

Kinda like my vagina.

Blowing out a heavy breath, I tore into the plastic and carefully slipped one card free from the deck. Then I thought better of my ability to get it right on the first shot and pulled out two more. With my flamingo mug filled with coffee and sugar, the cards, a pen, and a hardcover book in hand, I climbed out the window and settled onto my sliver of a deck. It was big enough for me, a beach chair, and a handful of terracotta pots. I'd only managed to keep the mint alive but I was still calling this a kitchen garden.

This narrow parcel of outdoor living space was perfect. I could see for miles out here, and there was nothing better than an ocean breeze. And early sunrises followed by impossibly late sunsets were the best parts of summertime in Maine. The sun was bright, and already far above the horizon, though the day was young. The shop wasn't due to open for another two hours and the sheriff didn't settle into his desk until after his morning patrol for another three hours.

I knew that only because my shop was on Main Street, a stone's throw from the station, and I couldn't *not* notice. It wasn't just the sheriff; I noticed everyone's routines. Maybe that made me the town creeper but I didn't care. I'd rather be the kind of person who noticed everything than the kind who noticed nothing. That was my little way of being the change I wanted to see in the world. I wilted a bit whenever someone forgot the details I'd shared in our last conversation or asked the same questions every time we talked. Those exchanges always dimmed my shine and I always walked away wondering why I wasn't memorable.

Considering I made good observation my corner of the market, it was shameful that I'd failed to notice the most basic things about Owen Bartlett. It seemed I could notice things as long as they didn't impact me. And that—*that* was the wound I was feeling today. I wasn't aching over the loss of Owen as a love interest, probably because he'd always existed as a future prospect, a hypothetical. I should've stepped back and examined my flirtations with him ages ago, but it was easier to soothe myself with the idea that I'd always have Owen. Even if he was never mine.

I sipped my coffee and wished I'd brought a muffin with me, but I wasn't putting everything down and monkeying my way back inside now. Climbing out here was no simple task and I had a history of spilling coffee or cocktails in the process. And I was stalling. Putting off the sorry-and-here-are-some-muffins note I had to write. If I didn't, they'd be mystery muffins and the sheriff would march on over to my shop and demand to know the meaning of all this. Or he'd read all the way into those *muffins* and *sticky buns*, and we couldn't travel down that road today.

I'd sample my creations after I found the right words for Sheriff Lau.

My first attempt wasn't awful but it wasn't awesome either.

Sheriff Lau,
My deepest apologies for my behavior last night. I wasn't myself. Thank you for
coming to my rescue. The town is lucky to have you.
The least I could do was bake some muffins and rolls for you to show my appre-
ciation.
Best wishes,
Annette Cortassi

I REREAD the words with a scowl. They weren't *right*. They met the basic criteria for an apology note, and the overall message was appropriately concise, but the whole thing tasted bitter, like an over-ripe cucumber.

And that brought to mind the feel of Jackson's body pressed against mine, the hard planes of his chest, and the undeniable ridge of his erection.

I realized I wasn't scowling anymore. A breath parted my lips as I shifted through foggy memories of his hands on my naked body, his ragged breath in my ear, his hips rocking against me as he searched for a small dose of relief.

I did that to him, all of it. I'd also stripped down to my skin and thrown myself at him. I wasn't sure how much feminine pride I was allowed in this situation. He was a man, and as much as I loved and respected men, most were consistently reliable in their reaction to bare breasts. Hell, my tits were terrific. I would've been miffed if he hadn't popped some wood.

A small part of me wanted to acknowledge it. I wanted to signal to him that things took a turn for the intimate for both of us and I wasn't one hundred percent clear on my feelings there. I knew I was zero percent clear on his feelings.

On the one hand was the erection, the way he touched me, the way he kissed me back.

On the other hand were drunk memories, and they were liars.

"None of this is helping," I muttered to myself.

Shuffling the next card to the front of my pile, I started a new note. I was aiming for a personal tone, something that quietly said, "Hey! You've seen me naked! Maybe you liked that?" but striking that balance was tough.

Dear Sheriff Lau,

Thank you for escorting me home last night. Unfortunately, it seems that I didn't make it to my home and I am sorry for any difficulty I caused you. I had a bad day and drank too much, and somehow that became your problem. I apologize for that. I don't like being anyone's problem.

I know muffins and rolls can't solve everything and they probably won't make you forget any of the inappropriate and invasive things I said and did last night, but they're the best I've got. I hope you enjoy them and I hope we can put this weird night behind us. I know you haven't been in town long but I can promise you, I don't get sloppy-and-stripping drunk very often. Or, ever.

I'm a grown-ass lady and I can handle my liquor except for when the guy I thought I'd marry (eventually) shows up at my store with his boyfriend. It's not fair to say I thought we'd get married. It was more like a backup plan. Like, a back-way-up plan. I thought we'd get together at a certain point if neither of us were married or in a serious relationship, but I'd never run that plan by him. I didn't want to be his problem. I wanted to be the girl who was there if he wanted me.

That sounds pathetic. That's even worse than sloppy-and-stripping. I'm not pathetic and I can handle my liquor. It was a bad day and I learned many things I'd been ignoring or pretending I didn't know. Thank you for being there when I needed someone, even if I don't like needing people. I doubt that matters to you. I was a hot, drunk mess and you kept me safe. I imagine this is all part of your job description and just another day at the office for you.

Enjoy the muffins.

Annette Cortassi

I BARKED out a mortified laugh as I read over this draft. This was personal but it was also awful. I could be embarrassed without being a sad, single girl cliché. And this was the saddest.

Staring out at the sparkling blue ocean, I drank the rest of my coffee and debated short and sweet notes like, "Thanks for all your help!" or "Sorry about all the trouble last night. Enjoy some baked goods." Those were much easier approaches. I wasn't lacing anything between the lines and he wasn't getting the story of my life.

But I couldn't get over the feel of him, the pressure. Even through the heavy fog of vodka, I remembered his touch. It wasn't a cautious hold, as if he was preventing me from falling over. It wasn't friendly either. It was purposeful, as if he was telegraphing his intentions. His desires. No man had ever touched me that way.

I'd embarrassed the hell out of myself and probably Jackson, too. And I owed him an apology. Somehow, I had to wrap each of those sentiments up and tuck them into a bakery basket.

Leaning forward on my rickety little chair, I caught sight of the clock inside my apartment. I had half an hour to finish this damn note, get dressed, drop off the basket at the station, and then open the shop. That was all the motivation I needed to get it right this time.

Dear Jackson,

I'm leaving you this note because I know you're very busy and I don't want to waste the town sheriff's time. Lord knows I've already wasted enough of it.

Thank you for taking me home last night...and everything else. I made you a basket of wild blueberry muffins for your trouble. That seemed like the appropriate baked good for getting naked in your living room.

I wasn't myself last night. I didn't mean to kiss you or fondle your backside or ask all those intimate questions. Thank you for pretending to enjoy it.

It was very noble of you to sleep on the couch while I was starfished on your bed. I couldn't help but notice it's quite large. The bed, that is. I swear I didn't notice anything else when I let myself out this morning.

As you know, Talbott's Cove is a ridiculously small town and there's no chance we can avoid each other. Not that I'd want to avoid you, of course, but I'm not sure I can look at you without thinking of the forty different ways I made a fool of myself.

Instead of avoidance, let's try to be friends. We'll forget all about last night...if that's what you want.

Please burn this note after you read it—

Annette

p.s. I whipped up some cinnamon buns, too. Please enjoy them. I'm not sure why, but I couldn't get buns out of my mind today.

I DIDN'T ALLOW myself the time to reread this draft, instead folding it in half and penning his name on the front. I returned inside, marched straight for the basket, and set the note right in the center. The other drafts I slipped inside the hardcover book, and left it on the counter.

The morning sun and ocean breeze had dried my hair, and I pulled on the first sundress I found in my closet. Dresses were my favorite. One piece of clothing, no worries about matching tops and bottoms. It didn't get any better than that. Then again, dresses that required neither dry cleaning nor ironing were better. I didn't mess with either of those chores.

I slipped into a pair of cute sandals, grabbed my spare set of shop keys, and hooked the basket around my elbow.

I didn't allow myself any time to reconsider the muffins or the note, instead greeting other shopkeepers and neighbors as I walked down Main Street. It wasn't strange for me to come calling with an armful of goodies. Ever since I'd started watching Bake Off and teaching myself how to prepare pastries, I was always delivering something to someone.

"Good morning," I said when I reached the station's front desk. "I made some muffins this morning and couldn't possibly keep them all to myself. I thought the new sheriff might like to try some wild blueberries."

"Of course," Cindy, the station manager said. "He'll be in by ten. He does morning patrol first, then paperwork."

She went to high school with my grandmother. They played bridge together every Thursday and she came into the store each week for a new stack of romance novels, the smuttier the better. That was small town life for you. It was a wonder she didn't mention how grown-up I looked these days or that she was happy my teenage acne had cleared up so nicely.

She gestured to the corner office, and then swiveled away from her desk. She tapped a cane against a thick plastic boot on her leg. "Take that back to his office, wouldya, dear? I had bunion surgery last week and I'm slow going."

"No problem," I said, plucking two muffins from the basket and setting them on her desk. "Let me know how these turned out."

"I'm sure they're outstanding," she called as I walked through the station to Jackson's office.

I didn't allow myself to think about being in his space, instead smiling and greeting officers and firefighters on my way. The door to Jackson's office was ajar and I elbowed my way through. It was sparse and tidy, not unlike his home, and it smelled like him. I didn't know how to describe the scent—woodsy? male? were there any words that didn't remind me of erections?—but I liked it.

I liked it enough to know I had to put the damn basket down and get the hell out of his office.

Something about this man made me want to take off my panties.

5

———————

KNEAD

v. To combine dough by hand on a hard surface.

Jackson

I READ the note once more but not for content. No, I knew what it said. I'd read it forty times if I'd read it once. This time through, I focused on the line and swoop of her letters. Her penmanship was simple, direct. No time wasted on flourishes like dotting the *i*.

I wasn't going to let this note—or last night—go unaddressed. But more importantly, I wanted to see Annette again. Hell, I'd wanted to see her this morning but she foreclosed that possibility. Not that I blamed her. It grated on me and it drove me mad with worry but I understood her reaction. If the tables had been turned and I woke up after a night like that, I'd probably tuck tail and run, too.

I didn't have to glance out the windows to know evening was settling in and it was long past quitting time for me. My inbox was as empty as I was going to get it today and my deputy was on duty for the night. By all accounts, I should've been kicked back on my patio with a beer by now.

But I couldn't go home. Not yet. Not after Hurricane Annette left her mark all over my house. Not after suffering several heart attacks when I found her gone this morning. Not after receiving the best blueberry muffins in the world—or so I was told—and a note loaded with mixed messages.

And I didn't have to look in the direction of Annette's shop to know the door was open and the lights were on.

I hadn't been able to keep myself from staring across the town center all day. I'd wanted to go to her the minute I arrived at the station and found the treats she'd left for me, but I knew we required the type of time and privacy that a busy Friday morning in July couldn't deliver. So, I waited. I paced my office, gazed out the window, went on unnecessary patrols around town, always looping past her shop.

I hated that she'd left my house before I woke up this morning. I'd barely slept on that rigid torture device of a sofa and I couldn't fathom how she'd snuck out without my notice. Discovering she was embarrassed about last night—and thinking I *pretended* to enjoy her—was another round of torture. We couldn't have that. It took everything in me to keep from marching across Main Street and setting her straight. It was a damn good thing I'd been due in court this afternoon. I needed every distraction I could find.

But through it all, I was conflicted. Annette's head and her heart were all over the place. I couldn't blame her for that. As recently as twenty-four hours ago, she had romantic feelings for Owen Bartlett. Even if he'd closed the door on those possibilities, it wasn't right to assume she'd shed that skin overnight. Any advances she made toward me were a product of Owen's rejection rather than an attraction toward me.

But I couldn't deny the way she set my pulse racing every time she smiled at me. I couldn't deny my attraction toward her, or that I'd felt it since my first day in Talbott's Cove.

I glanced out the window around sunset and caught sight of Annette through her storefront. She was with a customer, her hands doing all the talking. With a smile, I read the note again.

We'll forget all about last night...if that's what you want.

I tapped the card on my desk, nodding to myself. I didn't want that.

With that decided, I pushed away from my desk, grabbed the empty basket, and strode through the station. A wall of hot, humid air hit me when I stepped outside. Thankfully, I'd left my suit coat in the office. I wrenched my tie loose, flipped open the buttons at my collar, and rolled up the sleeves of my dress shirt. Before coming here, I'd believed coastal Maine enjoyed mild, breezy summers. That was occasionally true. It wasn't true tonight.

As I walked toward her shop, I watched two customers exit with bags in hand. They didn't notice me as they chatted about their purchases and headed toward The Galley. I'd devoted too much time to staring out my window today to have that talk with JJ about overserving his patrons, but I'd make time soon.

I pushed open the door to Harborside Books, a small bell tinkling overhead to announce my arrival.

"Just one second," Annette called from behind the counter. She was crouched down low and I couldn't see what she was doing. "Just plugging in my phone. I forgot to charge it today—and last night, for that matter —and I just remembered that now. Actually, I just found my phone now. I guess I'd left it in the receipt tape box. Funny, I don't remember going in there yesterday. I hope the world didn't fall apart today. If it did, it couldn't have been that bad since we're fine but you never know. Anything I can help you find this evening?"

I set the basket on the counter and planted my hands on the wooden surface. I couldn't begin to catalog the number of worries she just invented for me. Instead, I studied her dark curls as she wrestled with an overloaded power strip. That was the first thing I'd noticed about her—I was obsessed with her legs but her curls straddled the line between damn cute and fucking sexy.

"You can help me find the woman who made the most incredible cinnamon buns I've ever tasted," I said. "I'd like to thank her for her generosity, among other things."

"The—oh," she stammered, her head snapping up and connecting with the edge of the counter. "Oh, shit. That hurt."

"You're a whole lot of trouble, Annette," I muttered as I joined her on the floor. I brought my hands to her face, squinting at the red mark on her forehead. "How bad is it?"

"Not bad," she replied, her eyes cast down. "Just took me by surprise. I'm all right, sheriff."

"Jackson. You call me Jackson," I ordered. I wanted the openness and honesty of last night. I didn't want the nice girl who said all the right things and lathered everyone in cheerful platitudes. I didn't want her at all. "Now, tell me. Where do you keep the ice around here?"

She turned her head, silently forcing my hands away from her face, and pushed to her feet. She put several steps between us and busied her hands with a small flower pot filled with pens. I almost laughed at the idea of her being shy around me when she'd stripped down and stood naked in my kitchen last night, but this was the side of her I was getting today. Shy, and jumpier than a cat in a roomful of rocking chairs.

I hated it.

"No need for ice. Just a little bump. It won't even bruise," she said, still focused on the pens. They had softball-sized fake flowers attached to the ends. I didn't get it but I wasn't about to ask. I knew something about sticking to my priorities. "I'm glad you liked the rolls. I made the caramel myself."

I was a modern man. I believed in equal pay for equal work and every one of women's rights and choices. I didn't entertain any notions of women belonging in the kitchen. But something about Annette announcing she'd made the caramel herself sent a ripple of rightness down my spine. I'd kneel at her feet if it meant I'd get a taste of her fresh caramel.

"I *loved* the rolls," I corrected, brushing my palms down my thighs as I stood. "The guys demolished the muffins before I could get a hand in there but I heard they were also exceptional."

Finally, she glanced up and met my gaze, a smile pulling at her lips. "I'm happy they went over so well," she said.

I shook my head and stepped closer to her. "Let me be clear, Annette. Grown men were shoving muffins in their face as if they hadn't eaten in weeks. A fistfight almost broke out in my bullpen over those rolls. The rookie resorted to picking crumbs out of the basket. It was mayhem. I almost turned the fire hoses on them."

Laughing, she abandoned the pens. "I'm sorry you didn't get a muffin. The wild blueberries are amazing right now. I should've made more."

I wagged a finger at her. "Don't say that. Don't take the blame when you haven't earned it. You had no way of knowing my staff was full of heathens."

She lifted a shoulder and let it fall. "I saved a few muffins. I might have some stashed in the storeroom if you'd like."

I spread my hands wide in front of her. "Would I like? I'd fuckin' love. Lead the way."

Her pale blue dress swirled around her legs as she moved toward the back of the shop. The fabric looked soft, maybe a bit stretchy, and all I could think about was dragging it up her thighs. I'd bend her over the counter, shove that dress up to her waist, discard her panties, and then fill her with one glorious thrust. I could see her lips parting on a sigh, her eyelids drifting shut, her cheek pressed flat against the surface.

"Jackson?"

"Wh-yeah?" I asked, the majority of my brain busy cultivating my newest fantasy.

I blinked twice and glanced around the storeroom. It was a compact space with floor-to-ceiling shelves, a battered kitchen table, and a small desk up against the far wall. I'd expected a mountain range of books but this was painstakingly ordered.

She grinned and seemed to gulp down a laugh. "I asked if you wanted any coffee," she said. "I have tea and water, too."

"Water," I croaked. "Water would be great."

Annette gestured toward the table. "Have a seat," she said.

I heeded her request but sitting only consumed a handful of seconds. After completing that task, I didn't know what to do with myself. I couldn't pin her to the table and claim her panties as my prize. Not yet. Not until I drew out the woman who slapped my ass like the vixen I knew she was last night.

"Annette, I—"

"Did you finish that basketball book? The one about the Larry Bird-Magic Johnson rivalry?" she asked, blowing right past my attempt to revisit the events of last night. "I've sold that book to a couple of people, and always heard positive things about it. The author has several other titles if you'd like me to order them for you."

Annette set the glass of water and a plate in front of me, a fist-sized blueberry muffin in the center. Then she joined me at the table with a mug. "No muffin for you?" I asked.

She waved off my question. "I'm good. I had one before the evening rush."

"Okay." I shrugged as I broke the muffin in half. "I haven't finished that book yet. I'm sorry. I have it on my bedside table—"

"I know," she interrupted. Her words were quiet and husky, just as I imagined they'd be when I pushed inside her and she told me how full she felt. "I saw it there. That's why I asked."

I stared at Annette, my heart hammering as I stood at this cross-roads. I didn't want to make the wrong move and I didn't know what she wanted.

"I'm sorry about last night," she continued. "I'm sorry I wrecked your evening and I'm sorry I was such a mess."

"Don't be," I replied. She started to interrupt but I held up my hand. "No, Annette. You can apologize for sneaking out of my house without saying goodbye and that's about it."

"Then I'm sorry for sneaking out," she said, laughing. "But I know you didn't have to bring me home with you and put me to bed. You could've—I don't know—done something else. I'm sure you don't take every drunk chick in Talbott's Cove home with you after last call."

"You're right about that," I said. "I don't take women home. You're the first woman I've had in my house. I could've sent a deputy to The Galley to pick you up and get you settled for the evening."

"But you didn't," she said.

I nodded. "I didn't do that. I wanted to take you home."

"You wanted to take me home," she repeated.

"Yes, Annette," I replied. "I wanted to take you home. I don't regret anything and it kills me that you're upset about it."

She sat back in her chair, crossed her arms over her chest, and glared at me for a long, uncomfortable beat. I had no idea what was going on.

"You're placating me," she said eventually.

There were many things I'd expected Annette to say in response. That wasn't in the top one thousand. "I'm—I'm what?" I asked.

"Placating me," she repeated. "You know all about my personal drama and you're using it against me."

"I-I-I, uh...what?" I stammered. I couldn't stop shaking my head. "No, that's ridiculous. If anything, I've spent the past twenty-four hours trying to pretend you weren't lusting over the lobsterman."

"And why is that?" she asked.

She had no idea. Not a fucking clue. Even after insisting I'd wanted to take her home, she still didn't get it. That I was starved for the mere sight of her. "For one, it's a waste of your time and energy," I said, spreading my hands out before me.

Annette flinched, bringing a hand to her chest and rubbing the exposed skin above her heart. "Ouch."

That gesture had the unfortunate consequence of directing my attention to her breasts. Her gorgeous, slightly more than a handful breasts. The ones swaying against the soft fabric of her dress as she rubbed. I wanted to reach in and stroke my thumbs over her nipples. I was damn near salivating at the thought.

"I don't say that to add insult to injury," I continued. "I'm sorry."

Glancing away from me, Annette said, "It's fine. What was two?"

"Two?" I repeated.

"You said wasting my time and energy on Owen was your first point. Surely, there's a second point that you're looking to present. If not, thank you for returning the basket and have a good evening."

Her ankles were obscene. Her hair was soft and wild all at once. Her big, dark eyes were straight out of an animated princess movie. Her dresses launched the filthiest dreams of my life. But it was her mind— the one thing I hadn't been able to watch from my office—that had me twisted ten ways to Tuesday.

"You're right, I do have another point," I admitted. "I don't want you lusting over the lobsterman and I don't want to forget about last night."

Annette's lips parted as she blinked at me. "I don't want any romantic pity," she said. "I don't need it, thank you very much."

"Pity?" I repeated.

She nodded. I shook my head in earnest. She nodded again.

I picked up the forgotten muffin and pointed it toward her. "I'm gonna eat this while I try to make sense of you. I need a quiet moment with the muffin. Okay?"

She rolled her eyes and re-crossed her legs, and I couldn't believe this was the same shy woman who couldn't look at me minutes ago. Or the same seductress who'd pushed the limits of my restraint last night. There was far more to the town sweetheart than I'd realized. And I liked all of it, even if she was driving me mad with this argument.

I bit into the muffin and promptly discovered a new level of ecstasy. "This is fucking amazing," I said around another mouthful. "This is blueberry muffin heaven. It's not even a muffin. It's a blueberry acid trip orgasm."

The scowl and angry glint in her eyes melted, and a warm smile took its place. "Yeah?"

"Fuck yeah," I replied. "Now I understand why the guys went crazy. These things are life altering. It's like I've just now learned what a muffin should be."

Annette threw back her head and laughed at that. "That's a bit much, don't you think?"

I devoured the other half of the muffin and she was quick to set another on the plate. "Not at all," I said. "I'll never again waste my time on inferior muffins. Not when I can knock on your door and beg for more."

She stared at me for a moment and her gaze dropped to my mouth. She started to say something but then pressed her fingertips to her lips and glanced away.

"What?" I asked. "After last night, I think we should be comfortable with each other."

"Easy for you to say," Annette replied. "You were fully clothed."

"Yes, well," I started, shooting her a pointed look, "it sounded as though you got an eyeful of something on your way out. Or did I read that wrong?"

Shrugging, she offered an innocent smile. "Maybe a little something."

"Maybe not so little," I said, leaning back in the chair and manspreading like it was my job. "Whatever you want to tell me, I want to hear."

"You're wearing a suit today," she said, tipping her head toward my navy trousers.

"You like?" I asked between bites.

Her curls rustled as she shook her hair. "It was just an observation. It doesn't matter what I think about your clothing."

"No? Not at all?" I asked as she continued shaking her head. "It matters to me."

She tossed up her hands with a frustrated grumble. "It's not what you usually wear. That's the only reason I brought it up."

"I was in court this afternoon. It was a short hearing so I gave the suit a shot." I shrugged, aiming an easy smile at Annette. Her lips turned up in a grin but her gaze dropped to my mouth and I had to stifle a hungry groan. It was all I could do to smother the desire to drag her into my lap and finish what she started last night.

"It works for you. The suit." Annette leaned forward and gestured toward my face. "You have a little something," she said, staring at my mouth again. "Some blueberry."

I jerked my chin toward her. "Get it for me."

She hesitated but then edged closer. Her thumb passed over the corner of my lip and I couldn't stop looking at her mouth. I wasn't sure who moved first but her hands were in my hair and my arms around her waist, and then she was in my lap and our lips crashed together in a frantic rush. Every second throbbed like a strobe light. My tongue stroked over hers and my hands were sliding up her flanks, her thighs, her ass. But it wasn't enough.

A quiet thought spiraled up from the back of my mind, one that nearly dragged me right out of the moment. *I'll never be able to have enough when it comes to Annette.*

"Does this feel like pity to you?" I asked, rocking my erection against her. "D'you still think I'm placating you?"

She dragged her teeth down my neck and stars sparkled behind my eyes. I'd never wanted to rip a dress or any article of clothing before but I needed it like I needed oxygen. *Annette, naked, now.*

"I don't know what I think," she whispered against my skin. Her hands traveled down my shoulders to rest on my chest, and after a breath, she pushed me away. It was the slightest push but there was no mistaking it. "I don't even know you."

I gazed at her, my hands still gripping her ass, and waited for direction. I knew what I wanted and I had a good idea what she wanted, too, but I wasn't about to announce that. There was no reason to bully my way into her panties or insist that she surrender to my wishes because I'd make it good for her. It didn't matter whether she was sorting through some complex issues right now. To my mind, a real man waited for his woman to be ready and willing. There was nothing sexy about cajoling a woman into something, even if she enjoyed it in the end. Even if she loved it and begged for more. Sex wasn't about saying "I told you so." I wanted my woman how and when she was ready for me, and nothing less.

"That's all right," I said. "There's no rush to—"

Annette grabbed my shirt and yanked me to her, her knees squeezing my waist as her mouth found mine. I held her close and kissed her until we were breathless. When she edged back again, I knew it was time to go.

I brushed her hair off her forehead and kissed the corner of her mouth. "I like you. I've liked you for a long time. I don't think it's crazy to say you like me, too. When you're not hollering at me, of course. But you're figuring things out and you don't need me pawing at your ass right now."

I kissed her again because—for this fleeting moment—I could, and I couldn't stay away from her.

"I want to know you, Annette," I said, my forehead pressed against hers.

"I was naked in your kitchen last night," she said, laughing. "How much more do you need to know about me?"

"Naked is only one form of knowledge," I replied, "and I'm sure you're an opponent of judging books by their covers."

"You want to get between my pages?" she asked, her eyes sparkling.

"Like you wouldn't believe," I said. "But I also want to be your friend, Annette. Let me do that."

"What kind of friend, sheriff? The kind with benefits?" she asked. "Or something else?"

"Is that what you want?" I asked.

Annette started to respond but bit her bottom lip instead. Then she said, "I'm not sure."

"When you figure it out, let me know," I said. I wanted to kiss her again but I knew I wouldn't stop if I did. Instead, I brushed my lips over her forehead. "I should go. Keep that cell phone charged, would you?"

"I'll work on it," she said, settling back in her seat.

"Good," I replied. "Lock the door behind me."

I didn't allow myself another word, instead dragging my gaze over her body and shooting her a heated smile as I backed out of the storeroom. When the front door bell chimed overhead and I stepped onto the sidewalk, my chest lurched at the reality of leaving her.

I'd never felt starved and sated all at once.

6

———

CRIMP

v. To seal the edges of two layers of dough with a fork, tool, or fingertips.

Annette

I DIDN'T LET myself think about Jackson while I baked that night. Instead, I plowed my focus into my pie crusts and fillings, and the Bake Off reruns playing in the background. That combination soothed my senses and lulled me into a Zen state where the implosion of my romantic life didn't seem too bad. And I couldn't dwell on my desire for Jackson when I was busy folding butter into dough.

But I didn't have to think about Jackson to know why I pushed him away when his kisses were heaven and his eyes were hunger. I pushed him away—*twice*—because I didn't trust myself anymore.

I used to be chock-full of confidence. I knew what I was doing and where I was going, and the path was clear. Striking out on my own, opening this shop, putting everything into making it a success, and... Owen. Confidence struck again, telling me I could have anything—and anyone—if I worked hard enough. Never once did I stop to ask whether

I should be doing that work. I believed the world was mine for the taking, and with that arrogance, I took a man who'd never belong to me.

I didn't know what to believe anymore. I'd allowed myself to believe Owen harbored feelings for me—small, sapling feelings that would require time to grow, but feelings nonetheless. But that was a lie perpetrated by my boundless belief in myself, one that succeeded at forcing Owen into an awkward position and humiliating me.

It was a belief in myself but also a slow-rumbling awareness that I had to take anyone I could get, regardless of how poorly we fit together. When I stepped away from the awkwardness and the humiliation, I was forced to see some unpleasant truths. Owen wasn't meant for me and I knew that. I'd known it for ages but I'd allowed myself to believe there was a chance for me because I hadn't seen him date anyone, ever. Aside from grossly disregarding his preference, I was also telling myself I was only worthy of the scraps. That I could live with a love that came from me wearing someone down rather than authentic affection. That I didn't deserve someone who wanted me enough to pursue me.

I wasn't sure where any of that came from. Maybe it was my upbringing; maybe it was something I created. Maybe it was both, or neither. I'd spent so long hustling to make my way and do everything on my own that I didn't know how to accept anything that came without concerted effort. It seemed too good to be true.

Now, I couldn't trust my reaction to Jackson. I didn't know how to abandon the world I'd built around Owen and then construct a new one around Jackson, and I wasn't convinced I should. It was easy to force him into the space Owen vacated, but that seemed like a recipe for disaster. As if disaster wasn't a big enough problem, I didn't *want* to slide Jackson into Owen's slot. They weren't interchangeable cogs but creatures with their own shapes and angles. Jackson would never take Owen's place and he wouldn't fit if I tried.

If I was hopping on the truth train and riding all the way to revelation station, I'd see that I didn't know what I wanted or needed. I knew these little pies were delicious and there was a good chance I'd be wiping some wild blueberry filling from Jackson's lip tomorrow, but I didn't know anything beyond that. I couldn't get myself to choose past the point of my thumb brushing over his lip. I saw all the paths—friends, fuck buddies, dating—but I was afraid the ground would collapse beneath me if I took a step forward.

But if Jackson took that step, I knew I'd follow him down whichever path he chose.

I slipped two trays of mini pies into the oven and set the timer. Again, I ignored the dishes, flopping onto the sofa with my phone instead. It was charged, as per Jackson's request. I didn't spend much time on my phone. The cell signal in this area was wobbly and I hated notifications with the fire of a thousand suns. My social media energies were reserved for the shop, and I was a lazy texter, often forgetting to respond to messages for hours.

Case in point: a truckload of messages had piled up from my friend Brooke over the past two days. Brooke and I went to high school together but we barely knew each other back then and didn't become friends until she moved home to Talbott's Cove after a decade away. She lived at her childhood home with her father, Judge Markham. He'd retired from the bench years ago but he was still Judge Markham around here, much in the way many of us gave directions based on landmarks that no longer existed. "Turn right where the Zayre's used to be," or "Around the corner from the old market, the one they turned into the sporting goods store but that went out of business and now it's Planet Fitness."

Brooke, or Brooke-Ashley as she was known in high school, was my opposite in every way. Tall, blonde, slim, super stylish. If I was the kind of lady who used the word *chic*, I'd use it to describe Brooke. But beyond those basics, she was bold and brash where I favored subtly subversive. She was salty when I leaned into killing with kindness. She lived for big risks and bigger payoffs, and I found owning a small business to be more than enough risk.

The one thing we had in common was our single lady status. At the ripe old age of thirty-three, we alternated between wanting to get married right-fucking-now and giving convention the finger. Brooke was a pro at shutting down the well-intentioned fix-up attempts by everyone in this town with an eligible son or grandson. I loved the girl through and through.

I'd never expected to claim Brooke-Ashley Markham as my best friend but I wouldn't have it any other way. Unfortunately for her, I was a terrible texting partner.

Brooke: Could it be any more humid and miserable around here? This weather actually makes me miss NYC subways in the summer and those smell like piss and corn nuts.
Brooke: Okay. Fine. We don't have to talk about the weather.
Brooke: Do you want to get lunch this weekend? We could wear complementary Lily Pulitzer dresses and drive down to Kennebunkport and drink wine and call it lunch. As you do.
Brooke: To be clear, I want the wine. Food is unnecessary.
Brooke: Excuse me, ma'am, but did I just see your cute ass walk of shame its way down the street?
Brooke: I need an explanation for this. If I don't get one, I'm going to start inventing my own.
Brooke: Nope. Can't do it. I tried but I can't figure out why Little Miss Angel Cake would be sneaking home before dawn. That is not your operating system.
Brooke: Serious question, no judgment: do you need some Plan B? I stocked up before I left NYC because I wasn't sure rural Maine had its women's health shit in order.
Brooke: I've done some light recon but no one has any intel for me. I'll never understand how this town can alternate between high-powered rumor mills and cones of silence.
Brooke: I mean, they'd cone of silence all over you. You're like the town mascot.
Brooke: No, you're not a mascot. Mascots are weird. You're more like our Good Witch.
Brooke: Or something like that. You're just pretty and happy and everyone loves you.
Brooke: Does that make me the Wicked Witch?
Brooke: Shit.
Brooke: Now that I think about it...I kind of hate you. We can't be friends.
Brooke: In other news, Dad wanted meatloaf for breakfast, lunch, and

dinner, and he insisted I serve his mashed potatoes with an ice cream scoop so I'm going to need you to talk me through this walk of shame situation before I start eating the wallpaper.

I PRESSED the phone to my chest and laughed for a solid minute.

Annette: So many questions but let's start with this: why were you awake and watching the streets at 4:30 in the morning?
Brooke: Because I'm a muthafuckin' beast?
Annette: Yes, but also...?
Brooke: Hong Kong's market closes at 4 a.m. EST. Singapore at 5.
Annette: Oh, right. I don't understand how you keep those hours.
Brooke: Funny story because it seems like YOU keep those hours, too.
Annette: It was just the one time and it won't happen again.
Brooke: Wait a hot second. Why isn't it happening again? It should definitely happen again!
Brooke: Also it would be wonderful to grab some details like who, where, how it was, length and girth. The basics.
Annette: Because I wasn't being smart. I made some bad decisions.
Brooke: Was it bad-bad decisions or bad-very good decisions?
Brooke: No, don't answer. Just tell me the damn story before I get an eye twitch.

THE OVEN TIMER trilled and I abandoned my phone to collect my little pies. Dark purply-blue liquid bubbled up between the crust's lattice lines and the scent of sweetness filled the air. I'd prepared a small batch this time and they were just for Jackson.

When I had them seated on the cooling rack, I returned to the sofa and Brooke.

Annette: Sorry about that. I had to take some pies out of the oven.

Brooke: How the holy fuck are you baking in this weather? Dad's house has central air conditioning and I'm still sweating like Whitney Houston on stage. I have to wear a bra just to keep the tit sweat under control.

Annette: There is such a thing as oversharing, dearie.

Annette: I have a breeze off the water. It's not much, but it helps.

Brooke: Back to the story and make it snappy, please. I'm due for my two hours of sleep soon.

Annette: I got drunk at The Galley, Sheriff Lau took me home, I stripped in his living room and did rude things to him, and then passed out in his bed.

Brooke: YOU FUCKED LAU?!?

Brooke: Well done. I knew we'd make a hunter out of you.

Annette: I didn't fuck him. I was really drunk and really stupid, and I kissed him. And then I spanked him.

Brooke: I'm going to need some time to process this information.

Brooke: Processing finished. Tell me about his cock. It's huge, right? It's gotta be.

Annette: I was the only one naked, but based upon certain interactions, yeah, I'd say it's huge.

Brooke: YESSSSS. So, what's next? When are you seeing him again? I need this kind of live action drama in my life.

Annette: I don't know. He's so polite and respectful, it makes my teeth hurt. He wouldn't fuck me when I was drunk, and when I saw him tonight he made it clear he wasn't going to fuck me until I had my head on straight. Which it is not. So it's probably a good thing I didn't go there with him.

Brooke: You saw him tonight?!? You saw him tonight. Of course. Go ahead and live your life without informing me. It's fine. I'm fine. Whatever. I'll just drown myself in rosé and mashed potatoes. IT'S FINE.

Annette: I made him some muffins this morning to thank him for... everything. And he came to the shop tonight. I didn't go looking for him.

Brooke: Bullshit.

Annette: What?

Brooke: Pardon me, ma'am, but your crockery is full of bullshit. Those muffins were like a trail of breadcrumbs. You basically hiked up your skirt and said "come and get me."

Annette: Even if I did, he said he wants to be friends.

Brooke: Question. Did he say this with a straight face and/or a soft dick?

Brooke: Don't answer that yet. More important question: why did you get drunk at The Galley without notifying me first?

Annette: It's late. We'll talk about it another time.

Brooke: Now you have to tell me. I won't be able to sleep until you do.

Annette: Owen came by the shop yesterday.

Annette: With his boyfriend.

Brooke: Ah. I see. I'm going to extrapolate for a moment.

Brooke: Owen comes into your shop with his boyfriend and you go on a bender therefore you must've been hanging on to your Owen+Annette4Ever dreams despite compelling evidence that he doesn't prefer XX chromosomes. With that bubble burst, you got naked and handsy with the sheriff, and unloaded some part of this ridiculousness on him. Given that knowledge, he won't touch you with his ten-inch pole because first, he's a decent guy who knows better and second, he's afraid of catching your crazy.

Annette: Is there a question?

Brooke: Were you seriously holding out for Owen Bartlett?

Annette: I thought it was within the realm of possibility, yeah. Realms can be big places.

Brooke: And you failed to mention that to me at any point since I've been back in town? Perhaps because you knew I'd whip that insanity right out of you?

Annette: It never came up.

Brooke: Serenity now.

Brooke: You're not asking for my advice but I'm giving it anyway. Buckle up, buttercup.

Brooke: Go on with your bad self. Stop shaming yourself over naked shenanigans with the sheriff. I'm violently jealous over those shenanigans and I expect detailed reports on his dick. Stop trying to follow a plan. Plans are fucking useless because life will always jack that shit up. I speak from experience. Stop trying to force guys to fit your plans. Men are square pegs, and while they're all about the round hole, they're never

going to stop being square. Either embrace the square or find a
new one.

Annette: You want me to fuck Jackson?

Brooke: One of my favorite things about you is that you do your thing
and you don't apologize. You're nice about your thing but you still do it
like a badass. So, I hate that you're losing your mind over this right now.
I want you to do what you want and not worry about it being wrong.
And someone should be getting laid around here.

Annette: I just don't know what I want.

Brooke: Then fake it until you figure it out.

SOMETIMES, my ideas were bigger than my lady balls.

Everything sounded fantastic in my head but I couldn't quite execute
those ideas. When I was in high school, I had this big idea to read one
hundred books over the summer. Not any one hundred books, but the
ones a fancy newspaper said everyone should read before they die. To
make matters even more special, I decided I'd also analyze those books
much like the newspaper's in-house reviewer did. I'd be witty, eloquent,
and excessively referential, and traffic would overwhelm my clunky little
WordPress blog.

I didn't make it through ten books. They were boring or pedantic or
far removed from any point of relatability, and I gave up. The only
person reading my reviews was my grandmother, and that only reminded
me that I wasn't finding the reach I'd expected. On top of that, I was
stuck inside, racking my head for pithy comments and wrangling code
while I wanted to be kicked back on the beach with books I didn't hate
reading.

Looking at the pies I'd baked for Jackson, I couldn't help thinking
about that summer. No one knew I'd spent the night weaving strips of
dough into a textbook basket weave pattern and coaxing blueberries into
glossy perfection.

I could just as easily deliver these pies to Brooke's house or drop
them off at the barbershop around the corner. Those boys never refused
free food.

But just as I knew I didn't want to keep reading those books, I knew I wanted to see Jackson again. I wanted him to look at me like I was as delicious as yesterday's sticky buns. I wanted those things but I didn't want it to mean anything. There was a limited number of things I could manage in a given day and the expectations associated with wanting Jackson weren't on my list. I just didn't have it in me. I could do this as long as I didn't build it up into a huge project like my one hundred books and their pithy reviews.

If the expectations didn't exist, the risk didn't exist either.

Still, those pies taunted me all day. They were in the storeroom, secure in a glass container, but they taunted me from all the way back there. With every lull between customers, I found myself pacing down the sidewalk to look for Jackson's town-issued SUV in the station parking lot. Each time I found it there, I debated dashing over to deliver my pies. I figured I'd drop them at the reception desk and retreat, insisting I couldn't leave the shop unattended for long.

That was my tidy little plan, but somehow the day slipped away from me. When I finished with my last rush of customers, I glanced toward the station and found the sky streaked with pink, purple, and gold. It wasn't my typical closing time but I grabbed my pies and flipped the front sign on my way out.

I didn't stop to fix my hair or check my teeth for leftover bits of spinach from my lunch salad. I didn't need to do any of that because I was walking in and then walking right back out. No visiting. If Jackson wanted to talk about pie or anything else, he knew where to find me.

It was just another one of my mind games.

I pushed through the station doors and waved to Cindy at the reception desk. "Hi! How are y—"

She cut me off with a wobbly wag of her cane. "Go on back," she said, winking in the direction of my pies. "He'll be thrilled to see you, I know it."

I sputtered to a stop, blinking as I processed her words. "No, that's fine. I don't want to bother—um—anyone. I'm just dropping—"

"No can do, my dear," she hollered, waving that cane around like a drunk bride with a penis wand. "He told me to send you right back the next time you dropped in."

That stopped me fast. The only reason he'd say that was if he expected me to pay him visits and that—that was the kind of expectation I was trying to avoid. "He said *what?*"

"He's expecting you," she replied as she answered the phone. "Talbott's Cove Public Safety Office, you got Cindy here. How can I assist you this evening?" When I didn't move, she whacked her cane against the side of her desk and covered the receiver with her palm. "Go on. Don't stand there all night. You know the way."

I glared at the office door in the back corner of the station. It was slightly ajar. "Wouldn't want to keep him waiting," I murmured as I marched through the station. It was nearly deserted, with only two deputies busy at their computers. It didn't take me too long to slip inside Jackson's office. "Since when am I on your list?" I asked as I leaned back against the door.

Jackson's head snapped up from studying the documents on his desk and his gaze landed on me. His eyes softened a bit and the hard line of his lips melted into a smile. "Since always," he replied.

Without looking, he closed the file in front of him and pushed to his feet. His hands dipped into his trouser pockets. Another suit, the coat abandoned on the ancient rack in the corner. His sleeves were rolled up to his elbows and his collar open. No tie today.

"It's good to see you again, Annette," Jackson said. "I wasn't sure I would."

He beckoned me forward. At least ninety-four percent of my body wanted to follow his command. Maybe more. That little stronghold in my head wouldn't allow it. Instead of going to him, I deposited the pies on his desk and dropped into one of the empty chairs. He stared at me for a moment, his jaw working and his eyebrows lifting as he watched me cross my legs. "And yet you told Cindy to send me back. You must've had some idea I'd show up here again if you told her that."

Jackson reached for the Pyrex dish and pried off the lid. "What did I do to deserve this?" he murmured, looking inside.

"Nothing in particular," I said, as flippant as I pleased. I didn't know why but this man brought out my sassy side. My inner bitch, if you will. That, and the desire to drop my panties the minute he leveled me with one of those stern stares. It sounded ridiculous but one look from him and some ancient, cavelady part of me was ready to hand over my undies and take what he had to give. "Why am I on your list?"

He pointed at me with a pie. It looked miniscule in his big paw. "The better question is why wouldn't you be on my list?"

I motioned between us. "I know this is really fun, us repeating questions back to each other for five minutes and all, but I'd appreciate an answer."

"I like you," Jackson said, "even when you're busy hollering at me." He bit into the pie, sighing and murmuring his praise as he devoured it. "How do you do this? What's your secret? I couldn't bake a pie like this with the aid of ten pastry chefs and your magical back alley berries."

"Answer my question or I'll feed the rest to the firefighters." I reached for the dish but Jackson snatched it away. "I'll do it."

"You wouldn't dare," he replied, the dish cradled in the crook of his arm like a newborn baby.

"I would," I countered. I had to work real hard to ignore the throb of enthusiasm from my ovaries at the idea of Jackson and babies. *Oof.* "I would and I'd make you watch."

He narrowed his eyes at me. "You're cute but you're cruel. You hide it behind that pretty smile and those fuck-hot ankles—"

"Excuse me, my *what*?"

"—but there's some evil hiding under those dresses. Those fuckin' dresses." Jackson nodded as if he'd proven an essential point and popped another pie in his mouth. "You're on my list because I want you there. If you come to the station, I won't have you waiting for me if I can help it."

"Gotta get those pies and muffins hot from the oven," I said with a stiff laugh.

"If that's what you want to believe, sure, Annie," he replied. "The treats are good but you're better."

I didn't know how to respond to that, instead rubbing the pad of my thumb over my fingernails. "Okay," I murmured. "I'm happy you like them. I played around with a new recipe and that design on the crust. It's fun. Not a big deal, really. Just something I do in the evenings. I like experimenting with baking and I can't eat it all myself."

Jackson stared into the dish for a moment, his brows winging up as he studied the lattice pattern. "It is a big deal and I'm glad you came up here," he said. "I wanted to see you but it seemed like you were busy most of the day."

"How—I mean, what?" I stammered. "What do you mean? How did you know that?"

He swiveled his chair to the side and gestured to the large, wide window. "If I want to see you, I need only look out the window."

The station's slightly elevated position offered a broad perspective on the village and a straight shot to my store. It could've been creepy, Jackson observing me from atop this hill, but it wasn't. It was overwhelmingly arousing. Of all the vast and interesting things he could've watched—Main Street, the harbor, the Atlantic Ocean stretching off into the horizon—he watched me shelving books and ringing up sales. How in the world did I compare to an entire ocean?

Finally, I said, "I never realized you had such an amazing view."

He studied me, his gaze rolling over every inch as if he was remembering me naked. His eyes seemed to darken and heat. That was all it took. I had to tuck my hands under my backside to keep from flinging my underwear at him.

His throat bobbed as he swallowed the pie. I'd never thought of swallowing as a sexy action before but this man was something else. The longer I spent with him, the more I liked him. And everything about him, right down to swallowing.

"I do," he agreed, his stare bringing pink to my cheeks. "It's gorgeous."

I smiled at him in response, glancing to his lips. I was real smooth. My seduction game was on lock. "You wear that pie well," I said, gesturing toward his mouth.

That was it. The extent of my game. No wonder I was still single.

Jackson grinned, wise to my play. "Get it for me."

Drumming my fingertips on the edge of his desk, I said, "You're all the way over there."

He shrugged. "Then you should come over here."

"That hardly seems necessary," I replied.

"You're right," Jackson said, nodding. "It's hard and necessary."

"That's not what I said," I argued, a laugh taking the sting out of my words. "You know it."

Another shrug. "It's what I heard." He brought his hands together, brushing off the crumbs. "You're a mile away. Get over here so I can have a look at you."

I glanced to the door at my back, suddenly aware of the privacy afforded by Jackson's enclosed office. I pushed out of the chair and rounded his desk, my gaze anywhere but Jackson. I needed all of my attention on walking without incident.

When I reached his side, I leaned back against the desk and finally looked him over. His hands were loose on the armrests and his legs spread wide. His trousers stretched tight across his thighs and I dedicated a long, long moment to studying those thighs and the unmistakable bulge beneath his belt. I glanced up, a shy grin on my face. All I had to do was take this itty-bitty step.

"Where's your head at today?" he asked, his voice low.

"Right here," I replied. That was the best I could do. I couldn't handle anything serious. I was fresh off a long-term, one-sided, mostly imaginary relationship and I couldn't dive into the dating game and its associated bullshit right now. But I could be here, with this man who made swallowing sexy, and I could want him. I didn't have all the answers yet but I could want him and it could be as simple as that.

I leaned in to wipe a buttery crumb from Jackson's scruffy chin, and he answered that gesture with a kiss to my inner wrist. A wave of tingles rolled over my skin and a tiny gasp passed my lips. I stood there, frozen as he pressed his lips to my pulse again. I felt that kiss everywhere. It grazed the back of my neck, tugged at my nipples, and brought a rush of heat between my legs.

"Jackson," I breathed.

"Annette," he replied with a growl.

Take charge. Take me.

As if he heard my silent pleas, he stood and hauled me close, wrapping his arms around my waist and seating me on his desk. With a hand steady on the back of my neck, he kissed me hard. He was aggressive, and I liked it. I *needed* it. My hands scraped up and down his flanks, my fingers digging into his soft tissue in silent demands to claim more of him.

His teeth scraped over my lower lip while he filled his palms with my breasts. My head fell back as I groaned and I decided I didn't care whether I knew any of the answers. I wanted this man and if the hard cock trapped beneath his clothing was any indication, he wanted me, too. And then he kissed me again, and my hands found their way to the throbbing length behind his trousers.

"Annie, I want—"

"I don't know what it is about you," I whispered, reaching for his belt.

"Whatever it is, you're welcome," he replied with a laugh.

That burst of levity turned into a frantic fumble to get rid of the layers between us. Skirt up, trousers down, panties off, his fingers on my clit. His mouth was on the pulse in my neck and his cock was in my hand, and—

"Wait," he panted. "*Wait*."

7

———

GRATE

***v. To reduce a food into small bits by rubbing it against the sharp
teeth of a rasp.***

Jackson

I COULDN'T DO THIS. There was no way I could take her on my desk. I
didn't care whether it was late and most of the crew was gone for the day,
we'd still have to be quiet. She deserved more than I could offer her here.

"Wait," I said, groaning. "Wait. Annie, wait."

She reared back, her eyes wide and her touch gone. "What? What did
I do? What's wrong?"

"This is too quick," I argued. We were on my *desk*, for fuck's sake. I
was all for indecent but this was unnecessary. I had a perfectly good bed
a few minutes' walk from here. "Let me do this right. Let me treat you
right."

She pursed her lips and cut her glare to the side, unimpressed.
"Really? That's what you want?" She aimed a glance at the heavy erection
bobbing against my belly. After a beat, she took me in hand, stroking just
enough to keep me hard and hungry. "I must've misinterpreted this."

Why was I doing this? Why couldn't I follow my instincts and fuck her like I'd dreamed? Why couldn't I take what she was offering without second-guessing?

"I don't have a condom," I replied, my fingers circling her clit. She was so wet. So wet. She'd slipped off her panties but now I regretted missing out on doing it for her. I wanted the pleasure of stripping her clothes off, watching her body reveal itself to me. None of this was *right*. Not for our first time together. "If you really want this, you'll want it in ten minutes when I get you into my bed."

A cloud passed over her eyes and I knew I'd pushed her too far. I'd forced her to consider what she truly wanted again, rather than what felt good in the moment. And hell, I was all for the feel-good option but I could wait until she was certain about it for more than a minute.

"I shouldn't have—we shouldn't have done this. I should go." She dipped her chin and reached for my trousers. Pulled them up, tucked me in. "Perhaps our paths will cross some other time."

Annette went to slide off the desk but I wasn't ready to watch her go. I leaned forward, caging her in with my hands on either side of her hips, and brushed my lips down her neck. "You were going to let me fuck you on this desk two minutes ago. That requires something stronger than 'perhaps.'"

After a long pause, she tipped her face up to me, a smile quivering over her lips. "Enjoy the pies, sheriff. I'll see you around town."

She pushed off the desk, scooped up the panties she'd kicked off, and marched to the door without a backward glance.

"The next time I have you under me," I called, loud enough for her to hear but too low for my deputies on the other side of the wall, "it won't be on a desk."

She dropped her hand to the doorknob and inclined her head to the side. "Good night, sheriff."

8

─────────────

CUTTING IN

v. The process of quickly combining flour and dry ingredients with fat, usually butter.

Annette

"WAIT A SECOND," Brooke cried, tearing her sunglasses from her face. "You *left*? You had a cock in your hand and you *left*?"

"Yes?" I answered, shrinking behind my glass of sangria. I didn't have much else by way of cover out here on the day-drinking deck at Arundel Wharf in Kennebunkport. It was another warm July day, the sun high overhead and a cloudless sky stretching on for miles. That meant this harborside restaurant was packed and everyone was hearing about my questionable dick-juggling skills.

"I can't fucking believe you. When there's a hot cock in your hand, you fuck it. It's the law," she yelled. People around us turned to stare but Brooke waved them off. "Oh, please. You're fine," she called over her shoulder. "Learn to eavesdrop less obviously."

I folded my arms on the table and gestured her closer. "If you keep screaming about cock, we're not going to be allowed to come back here," I whispered. "Turn down the volume a touch, okay?"

Rolling her eyes, Brooke sat back in her seat. "I just can't believe you left him there in that," she started, motioning toward her crotch, "*condition.*"

"Would you listen to yourself?" I demanded. "I leave one guy with blue balls and it's a crime against humanity. You leave half the men in New York City in the same condition and it's a point of pride. Please, explain to me how the situations are different."

Brooke tipped her sangria back and drank deeply. "First things first, I'm the baddest, beastiest bitch New York's ever known. I can't help it when men find that arousing and run after me with their sad little dicks hanging out. But most importantly, I didn't care about any of those guys. Hell, I couldn't even keep track of their names when I was with them."

I stared out at the water and the boats moving through the harbor. It really was the perfect summer day, the kind of day I stored up in my memories to save me in the winter. "I don't care about Jackson," I said.

"You know what's awesome?" she murmured. "How you're so bad at lying. Say that again—about how you don't care for him. Maybe this time you'll be able to look at me while you do it. Oh, and also? Try to say it as if you believe it, too, and you're not asking me a damn question."

I shot a sharp glance across the table. "Okay, fine," I said. "I care about Jackson. He's my neighbor and I see him around town but—"

"Oh my fucking god," Brooke said, groaning. She pushed her sunnies to the top of her head and rubbed the bridge of her nose. "I love you but I also want to slap you. Really hard. Not some quick tap but a full slap, the kind that leaves a handprint on your face and knocks this bullshit out of your head."

"I'd slap you back," I muttered.

"I'd fucking hope so," she replied, tugging up the top on her strapless sundress. "Girl, what is your malfunction? Why are you avoiding that fabulous slab of man?"

"Oh, I don't know," I said, lifting the pitcher of sangria to top off our glasses. "Perhaps it's because I barely know him and I can't hook up with him and then avoid him for the rest of my life."

Brooke shook her head, sending strands of pale blonde hair over her shoulders. "You'd only have to avoid him if you do something unforgivable. You know, like calling out the wrong name or kneeing him in the balls or passing gas while he goes down on you. You get that, right?" Not waiting for a response, she barreled on. "And don't quote me on this but I'm mostly certain you won't have to announce your sexytimes at the monthly town council meeting. I know Talbott's Cove is behind the times but I don't think it's necessary to present courtship plans to the community anymore. So, to recap, call him now and tell him you're ready to come to your senses."

"Great info. Thanks bunches."

I guzzled my drink. It was all I could do. I was out of explanations for Jackson, for Brooke, for myself. All I knew was that my head had told me to leave, my heart had been on the fence, and my vagina had screeched at me to stay. And that was the crux of it for me, this internal war of wills.

It was go-for-flight with my lady bits, of course. They hadn't been the center of someone else's attention in ages. My heart was still bruised from Owen and my poor judgment, but it also beat a little harder, a little faster when Jackson was near. But with every one of those hard, fast beats, the ache of my semi-imaginary breakup shot through my chest. My brain was taking neither shit nor prisoners. It didn't like the idea of me jumping into it with Jackson and was lobbying hard for me to take it slow, get to know him, keep my panties on.

My major organs were locked in a staring contest.

"Please, just explain to me why you dropped the cock," Brooke said. "I'm actually very curious about this and if you don't tell me now, I will probably hound you for the rest of your natural life. Maybe longer. I've heard there's a witch in Salem, Massachusetts who communicates with the dead. She might be able to tell me, once and for all, why you rejected Jackson Lau *after* you got your hands on his jewels. So, it's fine if you don't explain this shitshow to me now. The witch will get it out of you after you're gone. And that might be very soon because I'm going to strangle you if you keep pussyfooting over a man who is clearly obsessed with you."

I glanced at her, the afternoon sunlight bouncing off her hair. Her sunglasses were enormous, straight out of Jackie O's accessory drawer, and her dress's deep blue and lime green print made her skin look like buttercream. It was amazing how someone so beautiful could also be so relentless.

"He's not obsessed with me," I argued.

"Uh huh, sure, okay," Brooke replied, bobbing her head.

"He's not," I insisted. "He's a really nice guy. He's just being nice."

"Did you realize the juice wasn't worth the squeeze?" Brooke asked. "He's got the meat but not the motion?"

"I can't believe you just said that out loud," I muttered. "It's one thing to think it but entirely another to say those words in the middle of a busy restaurant. I don't understand your brain."

"Few do," she replied. "But can you blame me for asking? You're not giving me anything. You tell me you went to his office with pie— which is the pastry equivalent of come-fuck-me heels—and things quickly heated up. Then you dropped his dick like a hot potato? I can't square that circle, sister. I can't do it. Set me straight or plead insanity."

I tugged my lower lip between my teeth as I considered this. The answers, they weren't the kind of truths I could get my arms around on the first try. I wanted Jackson, there was no mystery there, but it wasn't that simple. I didn't know how to want him while guarding my emotions and I didn't trust myself with those emotions right now.

"He said he wanted to take me back to his place," I started, plucking each word with care, "and he wanted to do things the right way."

Brooke blinked at me for a solid minute. "You're not helping your case here, hun," she said. "Look, I'm all for the quick-and-dirty-on-the-desk routine. I love the Q-and-D. But him saying he wants to take you home, do it right...that's a big neon sign informing you that he wants to go downtown and spend a little while visiting each neighborhood."

"What—what are you talking about right now?" I asked. "Honestly, I'm confused. I thought I knew where this was going but—"

"Vagina licking," she roared.

That drew several surly glances from the people around us.

"I'm sorry," I called to the table beside us, motioning toward Brooke. "She's not...she's not well. It's a condition."

Ignoring me, she continued, "If he only wanted to get his dick wet, he would've fucked you on the desk. I continue to be baffled by your rejection of this guy."

"To be fair," I replied, "he said no before I said no."

"He didn't say no," Brooke argued. "He said, 'Let's go back to my house so we can play Jane and Tarzan.' The difference is remarkable." She signaled to the waiter for another pitcher of sangria. "It's worth noting that we have sufficient amounts of time and liquor to continue playing logical fallacy games but I'd love to hear the real story. The one you're hiding under a mountain of horseshit."

"I'm scared," I confessed. "I'm scared that I'm going to start things with Jackson and—"

"Hate to break it to you, honey," Brooke interrupted, "but you've already started."

"Brooke," I warned.

"Annette," she replied, matching my tone. "I'm just calling you on your shit. It's all I'm really good for."

That wasn't true but I'd deal with her comment later. "I'm scared that things are going to progress with Jackson," I started, shooting her a pointed look, "and I don't know if I'm ready for that. I don't know what I want. I don't even know him. I just don't trust myself to make the right decisions."

Brooke stared at me for a long beat and then said, "You're over-thinking this. Forget about Owen Bartlett and the beautiful, fictitious babies you were going to have with him. The best remedy for that nonsense is getting laid. You're taking a simple situation and making it all kinds of extra. Stop worrying about everything. If you don't climb him like a jungle gym in the next few days, I'm going to do it."

I slammed my drink on the table as white-hot possessiveness zipped through me faster than I could comprehend. "You wouldn't."

Shrugging, Brooke continued, "I'll dig the Louboutins out, put on one of the two dresses that make me look like I have tits and an ass, and bring him some of my *pie*."

I could see it now. Her tiny waist wrapped in a mere scrap of fabric and her long legs made even longer by the most treacherous heels in her closet. She'd go for the full red lip, too. She always knew how to pull that off whereas I looked like a kid playing with Mom's makeup.

But I couldn't see Jackson's hands on her. As much as I attempted to torment myself with the sight of Brooke in Jackson's arms, I couldn't get there. In trying to mentally pair my best friend with the guy I couldn't get out of my head, I found myself toggling through the memories of his hands on me. The way he squeezed my waist when he picked me up and set me on his desk. The way he'd gripped my thighs when he'd tossed me over his shoulder. How he was rough but tender.

Despite the day's heat, a patch of goose bumps broke out on my skin. I refused to acknowledge the tightening of my nipples. They were on their own.

"Listen, girl. If you don't want to take what he's offering, someone else will," Brooke continued. "And that someone else will be me." She smiled at me, shrugging. "What? Is that a problem for you?"

I still couldn't see them together but even the thought of Brooke's hands on Jackson turned me inside out. Working hard to keep the cave-lady screech out of my voice, I said, "Uh, yeah, it is." I shifted to face her. "Keep the Louboutins on the shelf and stay away from the cherry red lipstick."

"Really? Because I thought you weren't interested," she said, waving her *I had no idea* hands at me. "You've spent the entire afternoon telling me how it wouldn't work out and you didn't have feelings for him. Since you walked away and refuse to consider going back, I am left to infer that he's free for the taking."

Most people underestimated Brooke. They saw the hair, the face, the body first, and they assumed she was nothing more than a real-life Barbie doll. Head full of plastic, right? Wrong. She was whiz-bang smart and worked harder than anyone I knew. And she had the biggest heart. It was wrapped in barbed wire and kept on ice but huge nonetheless.

I tapped her elbow to grab her attention from the men a few tables away. "I'm going to say something and I need you to know it comes from a place of love."

Brooke rolled her hand, urging me to proceed. "Quickly, sweet pea. I need to get back to eye-fucking those guys."

"Sometimes you're a manipulative bitch."

She threw her head back and let out a throaty laugh. "Sometimes?

That is literally on my business cards. 'Brooke Markham, Manipulative Bitch and Hedge Fund Manager.'"

"Is that what you do?" I asked.

"For fuck's sake, Annette," she muttered. "First you tell me I can't sink my hooks into your man meat and now you're saying you don't know the basic details of my professional life? I'm beginning to think we're not friends but acquaintances who drink and complain together."

"There's nothing wrong with being acquaintances who drink and complain," I said, raising my glass to meet hers with a *clink*. "Acquaintances who say things to each other that no one else will say, and not hate each other too much because of those things."

That was the straightforward but also convoluted truth. Adult friendships were complex. Ours certainly was.

"Stop it. I don't do sentimental," she whined. "And don't forget— we're basically the only thirtysomething single ladies in town. This is friendship born from scarcity."

"Of course," I replied, nodding along with her snarked-up version of reality. "Okay, this calls for a new law. If I've had his penis in my hand, you're not allowed to go after him. Bare, not over the clothes."

"Does that allow for dry humping?" When I leveled her with a scowl, she asked, "What? It's an important clarification."

"We're too old for dry humping," I said. "We're not seventeen anymore and we don't hookup with men in the back of someone's mom's minivan."

"Fine," she replied with a dramatic eyeroll. "Care to legislate anything else?"

I shook my head, laughing. "That's all for today. I can't handle much more than Jackson."

Brooke edged her sunglasses down and peered at me over the frames. "But you'll *handle* him?" she asked, the suggestion weaving through her words.

I held up both hands in surrender. "I don't know. I don't know what's going to happen. He might not want me handling him anymore." As I said it, I remembered Jackson telling me the next time wouldn't be on a desk. I had to fold my lips together to keep from bursting into a silly grin. "You'll stay away from him and I'll take it as it comes."

"Excellent," she said. "Taking, coming. All good things. You need more of both in your life."

"Only me?"

Brooke shot me a wide-eyed scowl. "Uh, no. We both need it. The world would be a happier place if we were getting it on the regular. That's why I need to return my attention to those snacks on the other side of the deck. Let's see if we can get them to buy us some more drinks."

I glanced at the group of guys, each in a different colored pastel polo shirt. They were young, probably early twenties. Cute but far too fresh-faced for me. I needed a bit of age on a man. Some experience, some wisdom. "Starting a harem?"

"Don't you know that term is outdated and pejorative?" she snapped. "It's polyamorous love puddle now."

"Oh, right," I murmured. "Yeah, you should have one of those. Definitely. But I'm going to stick with the one dick if you don't mind."

"That's what I'm screaming about," she shouted, drawing the attention of the surrounding patrons again. She looked around, grinning. "What? I didn't even say *cock* this time."

9

MACERATE

v. To soften or become softened by soaking in liquid.

Jackson

THREE DAYS WENT by without a word—or a crumb—from Annette.

It was strange, really, having a relationship with a woman that started with her getting naked, peaked with me refusing to fuck her, and then declined to wondering whether we'd see each other again. Was it even a relationship at this point? It had to be. I wasn't entertaining any alternative designation.

I'd thought about going after her when she left my office. Who wouldn't? But there was the slight issue of my dick being harder than an iron spike and her arousal all over my fingers. I wasn't fit for public appearances. It was bad enough my station manager, Cindy, was already starting a wedding registry and drafting a list of baby names. I couldn't make matters worse by chasing Annette through the village while everyone watched from their decks and screened-in porches.

Instead of going after her, I waited...and waited. I'd held out hope that she'd drop by with some baked goods just to keep the pattern going.

No such luck. Over the past few days, I'd managed to work hourly loops down Main Street into my routine.

Yeah, I was checking up on her. Part of me was hoping she'd notice me driving by her shop a time or fifty and come outside to holler at me.

Thankfully, I didn't have to wait much longer. I caught sight of her pawing through a display of fresh peaches at the local market and I wasn't too proud to admit I stared at her for a full minute or two from the far end of the produce section.

I hadn't planned on grocery shopping tonight but now I was thrilled about running out of eggs. Her dark hair spilled over one shoulder, curtaining her face while she studied the peaches. Sniff, squeeze, inspect.

I envied the shit out of that fruit.

After drinking in a good, long look at her, I was able to move again. Quick strides had me out of the leafy greens section and closing in on the seasonal fruits. I sidled up next to her, my elbow bumping hers as I reached for a peach. She glanced up at me, her automatic smile shifting into an eyebrow-arching smirk.

"Sheriff," she said, giving me a quick once-over. Her gaze swept across my shoulders, seeming to pause at the sheriff's office emblem on my sleeve. "Funny seeing you here."

"Is it? Funny?" I asked, my words innocent. "Should I take that to mean you believe I subside on your baked goods alone? Or that I haze my rookies, making them shop for me?"

"Of course not," she murmured. "It's just that I've never seen you here. I figured you used one of those delivery services as you have your hands full."

"My hands haven't been full for three days," I replied under my breath. "Know anything about that?"

"Sure don't," she replied, reaching for another peach. Sniff, squeeze, inspect.

"Well then," I said with a shake of my head. "I do my own shopping. I'm not sure any of the local markets offer delivery, and none of the big chains come out this far."

I held out a peach for her and damn near burst into flames when she leaned down to inhale its fragrance, her breasts grazing my forearm in the process.

Her eyes fluttered shut and her smirk transformed into a joyful smile. "Mmm. Yes. This one." Nodding, she took the fruit from my palm and added it to her cart.

What a treat it would be to please this woman as much as a ripe peach.

"So," I started, clearing my throat, "why all the peaches?"

Annette bobbed her head from side to side as she reached for another peach. "I'm working on some new recipes. Scones, tarts, a few other things. I haven't been able to nail them but I think that's because stone fruit wasn't in peak season when I tried. Since the entire market smells like ripe peaches, I figured this was the time to try again."

"Need any help?" I asked.

She glanced up at me, surprised. "With what? Baking?"

"Yeah," I said. "Or anything you want. Put my hands to work."

She laughed but leaned closer to whisper, "Your hands will probably find their way under my skirt and away from the dough."

It was my turn to laugh. "Is that how it is, Annette? I can't be trusted?" She jerked a shoulder up in vague agreement as she continued inspecting the fruit. "I'll remind you that I've never had the pleasure of stripping your panties off you. Maybe I'm not the one who can't be trusted."

She'd always beaten me to it, one way or another.

"Believe me," she murmured, shooting me a side-eye glance. "I've considered that angle."

She abandoned the peach display and I was hot on her heels. It occurred to me that following Annette around the town market at this hour was bound to catch the attention of the locals. I was torn between slowing my steps and forgoing all concern for the rumor mill. In that split second, I settled on the best of both. I allowed her the space to walk without me hovering over her but accepted that anyone watching would be able to read my intentions from a mile away.

"You can't survive on scones alone. Let me cook dinner for you," I said when I caught up to Annette in the dairy case. She was loading butter into her cart. "Then you can teach me about baking."

She started to object, her lips already pursed and her curls rustling against her shoulders as she shook her head, but then she stopped herself. "How big is your oven?" she asked.

I replied with the type of conviction reserved for horsepower and dick size. "Huge."

ANNETTE MET me back at my house and piled her groceries and baking tools on my kitchen island. Once I had my firearm stowed, I stood to the side, my hands clasped behind my back, and allowed her a minute to unpack her bags and organize her goods. That seemed to be an adequate amount of time to wait before getting my hands on her.

When her materials and ingredients were sorted, I caught her around the waist. "You're coming with me," I growled, backing her up against the refrigerator.

My lips brushed hers and all the tension I'd been carrying the past few days vaporized. *Poof.* It was gone and in its place was a heavy cloud of desire. Her hands fisted in my tan uniform shirt as I kissed her, tugging me closer. I kicked her feet apart and pressed myself to the notch between her legs. There was no denying the immediate reaction I had to her kiss, her body, her presence in my home, and she deserved to know how she affected me. When we finally came up for air, she was breathless and trembling in my arms, her eyes unfocused and her lips swollen. I wasn't much better.

"What was that for?" she asked, tilting her head to look up at me.

"Do I need a reason?" I asked, still rocking against her. She felt like a dream, even through these layers.

"I guess not but we really have to stop going at each other with questions. Someone has to answer at some point," Annette said, dropping her head to the side. It offered me the space to savor her there and it wasn't long before my fingers were itching to feel her skin.

I tugged her skirt up, fisting the fabric at her hips. I was dangerously close to her panties. This wasn't what I had in mind. I figured I'd kiss her and quench my body's need to have her close. But it wasn't enough. I'd had her kisses, her embraces. I wanted more. That led me to an obvious conclusion. I wasn't walking away from this refrigerator until I'd MacGyvered an orgasm out of her.

No touching the undies, no problem.

"Here's a question you can answer," I said, groaning as I pressed into her heat. No longer was this a simple matter of friction. I was rutting on her now. We were so close, separated only by thin layers of fabric. Her panties, my trousers. Nothing else. If it was possible, this was more indecent than the moment we shared in my office. "Is this all right? Do you want me to stop?"

She shook her head and her hair cascaded around her, covering her face. "Don't stop."

"But is this all right?"

"Mmhmm" was her only response. That, and she dragged her nails up my back and over my shoulders. My shirt should've muted her touch but much like everything else between us, it heightened the sensations. The fabric teased my skin in the wake of her fingers and a hot, dizzy feeling plowed through me like a head rush.

"You're such a tiny thing," I whispered, stroking her thighs as my hips bucked against her center.

"Not really," she replied, her words low and husky, as if she'd just woken up. "I'm nowhere near tiny."

"Ah, but you're tiny to me," I said, my lips at the crossroads between her neck and shoulder. "I told you the other night, you're fragile."

She hooked her leg around my waist and canted her hips up to meet me, desperate to find the rhythm she needed. "Does that mean you're afraid you'll break me?"

I shook my head, murmuring my disagreement. "I know how to handle you, Annie."

"Tell me how you'd handle me," she said. "Please."

"You don't have to beg me. Not ever," I answered. I wrapped my arms around her, boosting her up for better leverage, and thrust into the notch between her legs. The warm spot there was growing wetter by the minute. "I'd push a finger inside you, and then another. I wouldn't have to warm you up because you're always hot for me. Aren't you, beautiful?" A broken gasp slipped from her lips as she nodded. "When I couldn't bear the sight of your round ass rocking on my hand anymore I'd get my cock out. Slide right in, all the way."

"Oh my god," she panted. "Jackson."

"Yes, Annie?" I continued rutting into that sweet spot between her legs but never delved beyond the cotton barrier. In a sense, she hadn't granted me that permission. The occasional chastity and uneven boundaries we'd established were nothing short of illogical but this wasn't the time to renegotiate. She wanted to know how I'd fuck her and I intended to illustrate that...without touching her underwear.

"I'm—I'm close," she whisper-shrieked.

"I know, beautiful," I replied, picking up speed. The refrigerator was rocking along with us now, creaking on its casters and shuffling against the adjoining cabinets. "You're going to give it to me."

"Tell me," Annette started, "what happens after you—you're inside me."

I figured I'd be shocked. I figured I'd wade in some incredulity that sweet, bookish Annette was dredging my depths for filthy stories. But I wasn't. This was Annette, sweet, smart, welcoming, generous—and dirty. To me, it made sense. I wouldn't want her any other way.

"You'd scream for me," I said, growling as my cock flexed the way it did when I was on the edge. I was ready. So fucking ready. "You'd scream when I slammed into you and then you'd scream when I pulled out to do it again. You'd keep screaming as I held you down."

"And you wouldn't stop," she said between cries. I felt her nails scoring the skin at my collar, those little bites of pain like whips urging me forward. "Wouldn't stop for anything."

That was it. I'd held out long enough and the roughly whispered pleasure in her voice was too much. Just too damn much. "No, beautiful, I wouldn't stop until I pumped everything I had into you and you were all out of screams and until you couldn't stand on your own."

Her hands clawed at my back and shoulders, desperate to find something to hold on to. "Oh my god, yes," she panted. "I want more, Jackson. *More*."

Who was I to refuse the lady? I would not. No, not even if I was dangerously close to coming in my pants. We were rushing headfirst toward that outcome and for the first time in all my ejaculating years, I wasn't looking for an alternative. Her nails were raking down my back, her legs were tight around my hips, and her pussy was soaking straight through my trousers to my boxers. I was exactly where I wanted to be right now.

"As much as you want, for as long as you want, Annie," I vowed.

As I edged farther into her cotton-covered heat, my orgasm shot down my spine and released into my boxers. For a minute there, I was certain my brain scrambled. My vision shorted out and my ears filled with static and my hips went on pumping. I couldn't stop, even if I tried. My body was dead set on giving her everything I had and some of the things I didn't, and I couldn't stop until she was satisfied.

"But you wouldn't be finished," she said, her voice pitching high and dragging me back to consciousness. She convulsed against me, her legs tightening as she dug her heels into my ass. It hurt but it was worth it. "Would you?"

Her body pulsed under my cock as she shuddered and came apart. I kept rutting, slower, less urgent, but I couldn't bring myself to stop. As this point, I needed this as much as she did.

"Not even close. Then I'd take you into the bedroom," I rasped, "and fuck you right through the mattress. Like I want to fuck you through this refrigerator right now."

Another spasm coursed through me, a spurt for good measure, and I was done. From the feel of the vibrations moving through Annette's body, she was right there with me.

Neither of us spoke for several minutes as we caught our breath. That orgasm wrung everything out of me. I needed a big bottle of Gatorade, an entire pizza, and a night curled around Annette. Not in that order but all at once. Naked lady, food, electrolytes.

Slowly, the world around us came back into focus. The breeze was cooler now, damp. The smell of fresh peppers and tomatoes scented the kitchen air. Peaches, too. The refrigerator fan clicked on for a bit and then off. I was a wet, sticky mess from my belly button to my balls. My grip on Annette's waist was fierce and my face was buried in her hair, and life was good.

"Whoa," she whispered, loosening her death grip on my shoulders. *"Whoa."*

"I love it when you say that." I kissed her neck, sucking a bit to draw another gasp from her lips. "Good whoa?" She laughed and the movement had me throbbing against her again. My hips still bucked lazily, not ready to abandon the cause. "Don't answer, just keep laughing. Your body feels amazing."

"Good whoa," she confirmed. "Really good."

I loosened my hold on her waist and then dragged my fingers up her thighs. I followed the line of her panties, tracing from hip to backside. I wanted to get rid of them.

"Hey, Jackson?"

I smiled against her neck. I liked this woman. I liked her a whole lot. "Yeah, Annette?"

"You're touching my panties," she sang.

"Yes, I am." I chuckled into her hair. "Am I wrong in thinking you're enjoying this?"

"Not wrong," she said on a sigh.

"That's what I like to hear," I replied.

She dragged her nails up and down my forearm. It was heaven. "But that's not the issue. You said you could touch me without going anywhere near my undies and I believe I've disproven that theory."

"In that case, I'll be wrong any time you want it." I tucked her hair over her ears and dropped a kiss on her temple. This time, I was the one to pull away first. Given my condition, I had to. My boxers were rapidly shifting from pleasantly wet to uncomfortably soggy. "I'll be right back," I said, crouching down to catch her eyes. "Are you all right?" She pressed her fingertips to her lips, nodding. "Okay. Stay right there. Don't move a muscle. Got it?"

I stared down at her, waiting for a response. Her lashes brushed her reddened cheeks and she kept her fingers on her lips. Eventually, she inclined her head to the side and said, "Got it."

I stepped away from Annette and the loss of her heat sent a shiver through my shoulders. As I marched down the hall, I unbuckled my trousers and opened my shirt, ready to toss both in the hamper when I reached my room.

It didn't take long to clean up and change into a fresh pair of boxers and shorts, but every minute felt like one too many. I wanted to be back in the kitchen, pressed up against Annette and whispering every depraved thing I'd ever thought into her hair. She smelled like sweetness there; vanilla, sugar, spice. That scent gave me ideas, ideas that flew in the face of everything I believed. I wanted her in the kitchen, wearing nothing more than a frilly apron and her feet bare. I wanted her sitting in my lap and feeding me pie.

"I'm losing my damn mind," I murmured to myself as I zipped my shorts.

When I rounded the corner into the kitchen, I was faced with two facts.

One, Annette was still here. Given our history, I wasn't convinced she'd stick around when the afterglow faded. This was good news.

Two, she hadn't followed directions. She was busy slicing a tomato as if she owned the place. This was also good news. I wanted her to feel like she owned the place. I would've enjoyed some direction-following, but I'd survive.

Tugging a t-shirt over my head, I asked, "Didn't I tell you not to move a muscle?"

She eyed my torso for a beat, studying me as if she was deciding whether I met her criteria. I hoped to hell that I did. "You said something," she replied, waving the knife. "I don't recall the specifics."

"I'll forgive you this time." I grabbed two bottles of beer and knocked the tops off. "But only because the refrigerator is not the most interesting place to hang out."

She took the beer I offered, remarking, "Nor is it the most comfortable."

I smoothed my hand down her back and tugged her closer. "Did I hurt you? Was that too much?"

"I'm good," she replied, glancing up at me with a tight grin. Then she blinked, and a wall came down. We weren't discussing the refrigerator games any further. "Let's get this dinner going, okay? What can I do? These tomatoes were too good to miss so I got started on them."

We worked together to prepare the meal and chatted about our days. I'd grown accustomed to living alone and this domestic back-and-forth was like speaking a language I'd learned years ago and nearly forgotten. I liked that language. I wanted to speak it more often and I wanted to speak it with Annette.

"What is this?" Annette asked, pointing inside the refrigerator.

I followed her gesture to the shelf of plastic-wrapped plates and jerked a shoulder up in response. "Food," I answered.

"Yeah, sure," she replied, still pointing. "But what's the story? These aren't your dishes."

She wasn't wrong. I had a rainbow of dishes and plastic food storage containers, none of them mine. "They are not," I replied slowly. "But I intend to return them to their rightful owners."

"But...but what is this all about?" she asked, inspecting a plate of pork chops and cauliflower. Lord, I hated cauliflower. I didn't have the heart to tell Mrs. Mulcahey that but I hadn't eaten a bite of cauliflower since I was a kid. Not even those weird purple and yellow cauliflowers my mother grew in her garden. I was no fool. Being purple didn't make it any better. "There's a story here and I don't think I can close the refrigerator until I hear it."

I set my knife down with a quiet groan. "The ladies in this neighborhood, they bring me meals. Dinner plates, zucchini breads, a Crock-Pot of meatballs. It's always something. I didn't ask them to," I added when Annette's brows shot up. "They just come by with a plate or two."

And a story about their single daughter or sister or friend being perfect for me.

"It's more than I can eat," I continued, "but I don't want to insult them."

Annette dragged her gaze away from the chops to eye me up and down. "You seem like the kind of guy who can manage an extra plate or two without complaint," she said. "You have that eats-raw-eggs-for-breakfast look about you."

"I'm taking that as a compliment," I murmured, returning to the cutting board.

"By all means." Annette retrieved a few items from the refrigerator and set them beside me. "Should I expect Meals on Wheels to stop by tonight?"

I shook my head. "I doubt it. They've probably activated the phone tree and alerted everyone to prioritize the other bachelors this evening."

"Ah, got it," she replied, bobbing her head. "They know I'm here. I figured the mother hens would keep eyes on you, sheriff, but I had no idea they were spoon-feeding you, too. It's making me rethink the muffins and pies I've sent your way."

"Don't say that," I murmured. "I love your baking but it's a distant second to you."

She laughed and flattened both hands on the countertop. It reminded me of her hand on my cock. I couldn't help it. We'd shared nothing more than a few minutes in my office, but in my mind every second stretched on for hours. I remembered the heat of her palm, the tight curl of her fingers around my shaft, the confident way she stroked me. It was amazing—*she* was amazing—and I'd pumped the brakes.

Oh, how I'd regretted that decision. I regretted it when I went to sleep, aching and alone. When I woke up painfully hard. When I jerked off in the shower. When I glanced out my office window at her shop. Basically, all day and all night.

"Did you hear me?" Annette asked, forcing me out of my memories.

"No, I'm sorry," I said, running a hand down my face. "What did you say?"

She peered at me, her lips pursed as if she was holding back a laugh. "I said, does it bother you that people know I'm here? That they're forming their own conclusions and spreading it up and down the seacoast?"

Shaking my head before she finished speaking, I replied, "No. Not at all. Does it bother you?"

It wasn't until then that I realized I didn't mind the constant gaze of the townspeople if it meant I could steal time with Annette. Just a few days ago I was worried about keeping a squeaky-clean reputation but how could this be wrong? Sure, my thoughts were dark, filthy sins but my neighbors didn't have to know that.

I'd also considered that I couldn't court Annette's attention without getting serious as required by the "no tomcat sheriffs" rule around here. But I wasn't concerned about that now. I didn't have a different woman in my house each night and the serious part didn't scare me. Not anymore. If anything, I craved it. Seeing Annette out in the village or busy in her shop drove me mad. I could look but I couldn't touch.

I wanted the right to go to her, to be with her, to call her mine.

"It doesn't bother me because people talk about people all the time. It's just what they do around here," she said. "It's no different from anywhere else. We all know each other so it seems like everyone is meddling in each other's lives. They're not. It's the same as everyone in a circle of friends talking about each other. I don't mind the talking. I get it. It's human nature."

I blinked, waiting for the "but." Because it was coming. Her tone was too hesitant for any other word to follow.

"But"—and there it was—"I don't want to give people the wrong idea. I know I can't control anyone's ideas but I don't want anyone getting carried away with some notion that we're, you know, a thing."

I set my knife down and watched her. "And that would be a problem?"

"Maybe not a problem," she said, a little exasperated. "But a situation."

"And you're not ready for another situation?" I asked.

She gave a curt shake of her head but didn't meet my eyes, instead kept her focus on the cutting board. "No. Not entirely," she said.

I grabbed a dish towel, needing something to keep my hands occupied. "No situations," I said. I wound the fabric around my palm like a tourniquet. It was all I could do to hold back the argument burning on my tongue. "That's not a problem, Annie. I don't need any situations either."

WE ATE outside on the back patio, flanked by citronella candles to keep the bugs at bay. Annette was quiet, more than I'd expected. Then again, few of my expectations panned out when it came to her. I'd wanted her to curl up in my arms and let me protect her from everything beyond us, but she didn't want that. Not yet.

Annette pointed to a thin beam of light to the south with her fork. "That's the old Talbott's Cove lighthouse. Owen Bartlett took it over when he bought the land where it sits."

"Is that so?" I asked. Discussing Captain Bartlett—and Annette's relationship with him—wasn't my preferred topic.

"Yeah," she murmured, oblivious to my displeasure. "Up on the hill, overlooking the town, is the Markham house. You can see the roofline from here, and the flag pole, too. Their property extends way back into the woods. There's a dairy barn out there, a bunch of old cabins, even a cemetery. Their family has lived on that land for centuries. Judge Markham retired about five years ago and he wasn't thrilled about that. It's a complicated situation with him. His daughter Brooke —she's an only child—moved home from New York City not too long ago."

I allowed her to ramble as if she was telling me something new. I'd made it my business to know every patch of land and resident in this town, and enough about their comings and goings to know when something wasn't right.

I knew about Bartlett's billionaire houseguest within hours of him arriving in the Cove. I had an eye on the Nevilles' inn, too. I was still piecing together the whole story but I knew they'd survived a gruesome attack that killed Cleo Neville's immediate family years ago, and one of the perpetrators was still at large. I'd been keeping extremely close tabs on the Fitzsimmonses' property. There was no telling when their son would leave rehab and I wanted to be prepared. I was hoping for the best and rooting for the kid to kick his addiction once and for all, but I also knew the reality of the opioid epidemic. I'd seen it in Albany and I was seeing it here, and it wasn't getting any better.

"And over there is the mouth of Dickerson Creek, which used to be part of the old Dickerson Farmstead," she continued, gesturing toward the forest. "The high school kids hike up there in the summer and drink beer after Eskimo King closes down for the night. The Creek, not the Farmstead, that is."

"Thanks for the clarification."

"Anytime," she replied, tipping back her beer. "I know this is a small town but there's a lot more than meets the eye."

"Do you doubt my ability to handle the town's safety?" I asked with a chuckle.

"What? No. Of course not," she replied. "What makes you think that?"

I gestured toward her. "You've been schooling me on the people and places of Talbott's Cove for the past ten minutes and I have to assume you're doing that because you don't believe I know how to find my way."

"Oh, I—I," she started, tapping her index finger against her lip. "Sometimes I lapse into tour guide mode. It helped when I first opened the bookstore and out-of-towners would ask general questions like, 'What's good around here?' and I'd just tell them everything I could think of."

"I've heard that about you."

Annette leaned back, stared at me for a second, then nodded slowly. "Is that what people say about me these days?"

"They've said you're uncommonly beautiful, intelligent, and generous with your time and knowledge," I said.

She waved away my words. "You're confused. That wasn't me. It was one of my sisters. Or all of them, blended together and averaged out," she added.

"Excuse me, ma'am, but I'm capable of vetting my own intel," I countered. "And I'm sitting right here, in the presence of your uncommon beauty and boundless knowledge. I'd say it's a fair assessment."

"Are you flirting with me, sheriff?"

I tossed my hands up in the air. "Finally, she notices," I said to the night sky. "I'm telling you, when I first arrived, *everyone* told me you knew the nooks and crannies of this place better than anyone else. If I wanted to know what was up, they said I should get the pertinents from you."

"Oh, really?" she asked. I nodded. "Why didn't you ever stop by to get those pertinents?"

"I did," I said, laughing. "Several times. I discovered I couldn't talk to you for more than five minutes without wanting to touch you." I dragged my knuckles down her bare arm, not missing the slight sigh she released. "Why are you nervous right now? That's the reason for tour guide mode, isn't it?"

The breeze rustled her hair as she shrugged. "Yeah, it looks that way," Annette replied. "I am nervous. I've never been with someone without also having plans. I don't know what this is and I don't know what to do with it. Even with random hookups or friends with benefits, I had a plan. I knew where it was going and where it wasn't."

She glanced at me, her eyes shining bright in the near darkness. God, she was gorgeous. The kind of gorgeous that hid behind homecoming queen smiles and epic blueberry muffins and the simple act of being nice to people. The kind most people missed because she distracted them with books and stories about old farms and piles of local gossip.

"Do you need a plan?" I asked.

Annette lifted her hands and then let them fall to her lap. "I don't trust myself to make plans right now, not after everything that's happened in the last week or so," she replied.

At first, I assumed she was talking about us and everything from her naked confessions to this evening. Then I realized she was talking about Bartlett. I fucking hated that. I liked the guy but I couldn't deal with this unrequited love bullshit. Not even for a minute.

Through clenched teeth, I asked, "What happened with all that?"

She shook her head, frowning. "I don't want to get into it. It's complicated."

I leaned forward to catch her hooded gaze. "Not complicated. Not really." She started to protest but I continued, "You're a smart chick. As you just illustrated, you know everything about everyone in this town. Of all the people in the Cove, you would've known the deal with Bartlett."

She leaned back in her chair and crossed her arms over her chest. Clearly, I wasn't making the progress I'd intended for this evening.

"Yes," she started, "but—"

"Nope," I interrupted.

"But," she continued, "Bartlett and I go way back. I've known him since forever and I wasn't really sure about—about, you know. His mom said it was a phase and—"

"Now that's fucking obnoxious," I muttered.

"And he took one of my friends to homecoming—"

"A million years ago," I said. "Here's what I don't understand."

"Oh, great," she muttered, rubbing her forehead.

"Why do you think that was good enough? I'm serious," I added when I caught her eyeroll. "Like I said, you're a smart chick and you have fuck-hot ankles. Why were you willing to rubber-stamp a relation-ship with a man who wasn't fighting off bears for the pleasure of your company?"

"There are no bears out here," she said, unimpressed. "Not usually. But it was good enough for—"

"Please don't finish that sentence," I interrupted. "I beg of you. Don't tell me that you'll hold out for a guy who isn't interested in you."

"Just rub salt in the wound," she said under her breath.

That stopped me. I wasn't trying to be hurtful. "I'm not trying to do that. I'm only trying to understand why you'd undercut yourself like that for Bartlett."

Annette blew out a breath and shook her head slowly. "I don't know, Jackson. I guess I need to spend some time soul-searching. Shall I leave to do that or am I allowed to finish my beer?"

Ah. There it was. The edge of Annette's patience. Even town sweethearts had one.

"Listen, I shouldn't have brought it up. You don't have to defend yourself to me. Whether you're making plans or not making plans, I can roll with it. It's your choice and I understand where you're coming from now."

Annette peered at me the way I'd probably peer at someone who made several hairpin turns in a single conversation. "What about you? How do you feel about plans?"

I reached for my beer bottle, needing something to keep my hands busy. Jerking a shoulder up, I studied the label and said, "Nah, no plans here. I should've said this the other day but I'm not looking for anything serious."

I tipped back my beer, a futile attempt at washing away the taste of my lies. If she'd asked me a week ago, it would've been true. I hadn't been looking for anything serious, anything that diverted my attention from the job and the reputation I wanted to build here. But now I understood why she was the town sweetheart, an institution like JJ growling at patrons and Bartlett pulling in lobsters. She was one of a kind, and she deserved to be treated that way.

By me.

"I'll drink to that," Annette replied, holding her bottle up to mine in a toast. "Now, let's make those scones."

10

———————

SWEATING

v. To heat fruits or vegetables slowly in a pan with a small amount of fat so that they cook in their own juices.

Annette

JACKSON HAD IDEAS.

Big ideas. Relationship ideas. He claimed he didn't but that was a special slice of bologna.

I couldn't tell up from down right now and everything I felt with him seemed distorted, as if I was experiencing my life through fun-house mirrors. Aside from my issues—and my constant desire to dispense with undergarments while in his presence—he wanted me in a way I didn't comprehend. I'd never been on the receiving end of attention—*desire*—like this and I didn't trust it. It seemed too much, too fast, too good to be true. Yeah, he brought out my inner stripper, the one who lived right beside my inner bitch, but sexual chemistry wasn't everything.

The reality was that I felt things for Jackson. Sexual things, emotional things, connection things. But he was the first man in ages to offer me a bit of attention, some affection. As I'd already learned, I could go for actual years with little more than a few special book order conver-sations. This avalanche of emotions was nothing more than Jackson tuning into me and turning me on. It didn't mean anything.

Right?

Right. Of course. I had this under control.

The scones, though, not as much. We had the dry ingredients measured and sifted—not without leaving plenty of floured handprints on each other—and most of the wet ingredients ready to roll. It had only taken us two hours to accomplish these initial steps. The operative ingre-dient here, the peaches, wasn't making things easy on us.

"Like this," I said, bumping Jackson with my elbow to get his atten-tion. "Peel the skin off gently so you're not bruising the fruit."

"No bruises," he murmured, watching as I worked the skin off a peach.

This time, I nailed it. The last two tries weren't as smooth. "Now, you try it."

He held the fruit in the palm of his hand while he scored the skin with a paring knife, sectioning it into quadrants. From there, he worked his thick fingertips, of which I was intimately acquainted, along the knife's lines. He edged the skin away with care and precision, even when the fine flap slipped out of his grip or tore in uneven swaths.

But the problem I'd discovered with peaches—good peaches, ripe peaches—was the juice. A peak-season peach would sop all over your hands once cut, and this crop was no different. Just when Jackson was about to tug the last bit of skin from around the stem, the fruit went flying.

"That fucker," he muttered, grasping after the peach even as it sailed across the kitchen and landed near the back door with a sloppy *thud*. "That fucking fucker." Shaking his head, he turned to me, his hands coated in peach juice. "I'm the worst helper you've ever had, aren't I?"

I snorted out a laugh. Ladylike, truly. "You're the only helper I've ever had," I said as I went on a retrieval mission. "You might be fumbling the star ingredient—"

"Don't forget me mixing up teaspoons with tablespoons," he added.

"And that," I agreed, "but I'm not complaining. Help is help, and I'll take it."

Jackson tore a handful of paper towels off the roll and passed them to me. "You don't test out recipes with your family? Everyone's told me that your mom's quite the cook."

"Nope," I replied, an entire lifetime's worth of exclusion packed into one word. "We have different kitchen philosophies. Better to keep them separate than start a holy war, you know?"

"Let me make a deal with you," Jackson said, holding open the garbage pail while I deposited the runaway peach and the paper towels necessary to clean up its trail. "You do the baking, I'll wash the dishes."

For every action there is an equal and opposite reaction.

I didn't know why that thought burst into my mind like an annoying pop-up ad but it was there now and I couldn't force it away.

"Sure," I said, turning back to the countertop. I couldn't look at him. I didn't trust myself to meet his gaze without agreeing to his demands and that was a bridge I couldn't cross right now. "That would be awesome. I hate washing dishes. I usually fill up the sink and leave everything soaking in there for days. It's not until I need something and there are no alternatives that I'm compelled to wash anything."

Jackson slung a dish towel over his shoulder as he leaned against the island. "We have a deal," he said. "One last question for you, Annie."

Still concentrating on the peach in hand, I asked, "What's that?"

"Am I coming home with you tonight? Or would you rather I come over tomorrow to"—I swear on my life, his voice dropped a full octave and my undies fell off all by themselves—"wash you up?"

"Hmm," I started, "let me think about that."

The peach bobbled out of my grip, first popping into the air and then bouncing off my inner arm when I tried to reel it back in. Instead of containing the fruit, I volleyed it toward Jackson. Bless his heart for trying but he only made matters worse when it slipped out of his grasp and hit me square on the clavicle. It followed the line of my chest down, rolling to a sticky stop right between my breasts.

Jackson and I stared at the half-bald peach sitting just beneath the neckline of my dress before glancing up at each other.

"You're not allowed to distract me while I peel peaches," I shouted.

At the same time, Jackson said, "Now you really need me to give you a good washing."

I wagged a finger at him, and then reached in to retrieve the peach. "At this rate, we're not going to have any scones before three in the morning," I said, handing him the fruit for disposal. "This shit would never happen on *The Great British Bake Off.*"

"I don't know what that is but I think we could put this stuff in the fridge and try again tomorrow." Jackson shrugged as he tossed the peach away. "It's a tough job but I'll roll up my sleeves and lick the peach juice off you." He hooked his thumb over his shoulder, toward his bedroom. "Just take off your clothes and I'll do all the work."

"You're rather gallant, sheriff," I said. I was like a three-year-old—sticky, sugary, in need of a nap. "But it's late and I should go. We have a bit more time until peach season ends."

He nodded as if he understood but I knew he didn't. To him, I was getting over a non-relationship and being ridiculously cautious with my heart. My vagina, too, but mostly my heart. He didn't understand my mind games, my mental gymnastics, my struggles to accept affection when it wasn't hard fought. But he was a nice guy, a gentleman, and he respected the boundaries I laid down.

"I'll walk you home," Jackson said, shoving his hands into his pockets. It was as if he realized the touchy-gropey-kissy portion of the evening was over. "Don't think you can argue this point with me either. You probably know everyone on this street and the location of every crack in the sidewalk but that doesn't mean I'm going to let you walk through town by yourself at this hour. I'll see you home, Annie, whether you like it or not."

I hummed in response, not confident in my ability to reply without overturning my plan to leave. Jackson was tricky like that. He seemed like the average good guy, all nice and polite with his ma'am-ing and charitable lawn mowing and collecting drunk girls from bars. But underneath the good guy veneer was a man who wanted to keep a woman as his own. He stewed with a desire to protect and serve that woman but he also wanted to belong to her. It traveled through his words and gestures, his stares and touches, and it was potent enough to run off with my thoughts. It made me believe that a man could want me—just me, just as I was—and that belief lodged a knot of confused emotion in my throat.

My head couldn't keep my heart straight—or maybe it was the other way around.

I reached for the bowl of cracked eggs but Jackson beat me to it. "I've got this. I'll have it for breakfast, since you claim I chug raw eggs," he said, gesturing with the bowl toward the epic mess we'd created in his kitchen. "Whenever you decide to revisit the scene of these crimes, I'll have everything waiting for you, and I swear I'll stay out of the splash zone until it's time to hit the pots and pans."

With my hands washed and my baking tools stowed in my tote bag, I laced my fingers with Jackson's and let him walk me home. In the harbor, sails jangled against masts. A dog barked in the distance and beetles hissed at the street lights. The midnight air was cool with a hint of damp sea breeze, the kind of air that folks referred to as "good sleeping weather." It was a blessed reprieve from the past weekend's wave of hot, humid days and equally unpleasant nights.

This would've made for the perfect weather to sleep with Jackson. I knew he'd be my personal furnace. My big grizzly. I bet he was a compulsive cuddler, too. He'd chase me right to the edge of the bed and then lock me in his strong arms all night.

I didn't know whether I was a cuddler or not. I'd never lived with anyone but my family and college roommates, and I didn't snuggle with any of them. I'd never had serious relationships either. I was always making big plans, always climbing.

Climbing didn't leave much time for cuddling.

We walked down the street and into the village without a word, and I was thankful for the quiet. It helped ground me in my decision to slow this—this flirtation. It was barely more than that, if I didn't include the nakedness and the one time in his office when we were *this close* to having sex and then the time he said the dirtiest things I'd ever heard spoken.

Just a flirtation. One that was dry humping its way out of control. *Dry humping.* My word. How did that even happen? I wasn't telling Brooke about this. She'd rake me over the seventeen-and-in-a-minivan coals.

When we reached the alley behind my shop, I gestured toward the building as if he didn't know where we were and said, "This is me."

"It is," Jackson said, bobbing his head as he surveyed the area.

"Okay, well," I said, my voice trailing off. "Thank you for the walk. And dinner. And attempting to bake scones with me." I hiked my tote higher on my shoulder, a move that separated my hand from his. "I should go. Up. Go upstairs. To the apartment. Where I live."

Chuckling at my inability to produce complex sentences, Jackson announced, "I want to see you to the door."

I lifted my clasped hands to my lips as I searched for the words to send this man away. He was one of the good ones, I knew it. Too good.

"That's okay. I can't get lost on a single staircase," I said, regret thick in my words. "Jackson, I think"—I glanced to the sky, the moon and stars, and the dark expanse of the ocean for guidance but found none —"I think we should stop seeing each other like this."

Shocking the shit out of me, Jackson replied, "I concur."

"You do?" I snapped. I wasn't expecting him to agree this easily. If I was honest, I'd hoped for a tiny bit of protest. A lady needed hope, right?

He ran a hand down his face as he laughed. "I don't want to walk you home at midnight."

"Well, you insisted so that's not my problem," I replied, flicking my fingers at the street behind him. "I would've been perfectly fine on my own."

Jackson rubbed his brow, laughing. "I don't want to wonder whether I'll bump into you at the market," he continued. "I want to get your phone number from you and not from questionably ethical uses of my office. I want to have dinner with you and then I want to spend the night with you. I want to spend a lot of nights with you. As many as you'll give me. I want to watch you bake and then wash your dishes for you. I want to give the people around here something to talk about because the only dirty secrets we keep are the ones in the bedroom, you hear me?"

Without conscious thought, I took a giant step toward him. It was the wrong direction but I couldn't help myself. "I want you to have that," I said, "with someone who wants it, too."

We stared at each other for the longest minute since humanity started measuring time. It stretched on and on as he stared at me, stern as always, and I did everything in my power to keep from taking his hand and walking him up the stairs with me.

It wasn't about me wanting him anymore. Feelings and expectations were wrapped up in this now, and I couldn't handle those.

"You have really big feelings and I don't know how to deal with that," I said, a little breathless. "My entire world has tipped and twisted in the past week and you're fast-forwarding ahead with these—these *plans*." Jackson gave me a slow blink but no other response. "I'm squarely in no-plans mode and you're—hell, you're picking out new dust ruffles."

Another slow blink.

"Jackson, say something or leave. Staring at people in the dark is creepy."

The sails went on clanging and that dog was still barking, and Jackson just blinked at me.

"I don't know what a dust ruffle is," he said. "I don't believe I've picked one out."

I ran my hand through my hair, sighing. "We're in different places. That's all I'm trying to say."

"I understand that you're not ready," he replied. "But know this: I'm not going anywhere. I'm right here, waiting for you."

"I speak from experience when I tell you waiting isn't a winning strat-egy," I said, a rueful grin spreading across my lips. "Don't waste your time repeating my mistakes."

His eyes crinkled as he stared at me. "I don't see it that way."

"Find someone who doesn't make you wait, Jackson. It's not worth it."

Jackson took a breath and glanced away, his eyebrows inching upward. "I have to disagree with you there," he replied. "You might know this town and everyone in it, but you don't know me. If you did, you wouldn't try to change my mind when I already know it. You'd know I'm not a dumb cop fixated on somethin' pretty. You'd also know that I have enough patience to wait for what I want and enough sense to know when it's worth waiting for."

He leaned in, sliding his hand through my hair, and brushed his lips over mine. It was quick but earnest, making promises I realized he intended to keep.

"Good night, Annette," Jackson said, dropping a kiss on my forehead.

The forehead kiss hit me hard. Somehow, it was more intimate than the straightforward lip lock and it left me aching for more. And that —*that* right there—was the worst part of this. I couldn't believe anything I felt. Wanting more, wanting to leave, wanting anything; all of it came at me like the first steep ascent on a rollercoaster. I didn't know what waited after the peak and I couldn't pry my fingers away from my face long enough to find out.

"Good night, Jackson," I replied, lifting my gaze to his. "I'll see you around town."

I already knew I was going to bake for him, see him, kiss him again. I knew it as well I knew my own name. Despite all the doubts and distortions in my mind, I wanted Jackson Lau.

And he wanted me, too.

A smirk pulled at the corner of his lips. "If I don't see you first."

Brooke: I just watched Jackson walk you home. Then he walked back to his house.

Brooke: Why, pray tell, was he doing that?

Brooke: Is it my turn with him? Is that what's happening? We're going to time share his ass? Full-on sister-wife this thing?

Brooke: If that is the case, it's in our best interest to draw up an agreement now. Terms, conditions, operational standards.

Brooke: I'll get started on the documents.

Brooke: Okay. Done. I had something similar sitting on my hard drive and it was easy enough to change the key details.

Brooke: I assume you're fine with alternating weekends because I'm all about hard partying Saturday nights followed by lazy Sunday mornings and it would suck if I couldn't have him for those consecutive days.

Annette: What the hell are you talking about?

Brooke: Sharing Jackson.

Annette: Oh my god.

Brooke: What?!? It makes perfect sense.

Annette: I sent him home. He wants...lots of things.

Brooke: And by that you mean...anal?

Annette: OH MY GOD. Brooke!

Brooke: Am I right or wrong? I'm...I don't know how to interpret that response. It could go either way, really.

Annette: He wants a relationship. He wants something serious and official and, I don't know, long term.

Brooke: So...not anal?

Annette: It didn't come up, no.

Brooke: But you can't rule it out.

Annette: Again—OH MY GOD.

Brooke: Okay, settle down, Angel Cake.

Brooke: Remind me why you have a problem with relationships? Because I distinctly recall us drinking Moscow mules in Bar Harbor two months ago and planning our weddings.

Annette: It just seems like this thing with Jackson is too good to be true.

Brooke: You're being stupid.

Annette: Thanks, love.

Brooke: Seriously. You're letting this Owen shit weigh you down. Stop it now.

Annette: I am working on it, you know. I'm not trying to be this way.

Brooke: But you're going to see him again, right?

Annette: Yeah.

Brooke: Does he know that?

Annette: Maybe. Not sure.

Brooke: Good. It's good to keep men guessing.

Brooke: But since I have you here, could we talk about a time share arrangement?

Annette: Was I not clear last weekend? I'll fucking end you if you touch him.

Brooke: Okay, all right, fine. It's not a big deal. I'll just shred the documents I prepared.

Brooke: We really did make a hunter out of you.

BUN WASH

n. A sugar syrup solution brushed onto yeasted buns on removal from the oven to impart a glaze or assist in the dusting of sugar.

Jackson

I STEPPED up to the counter at DiLorenzo's Diner and tucked my thumbs under my tactical belt. Before arriving in Talbott's Cove, where the sheriff's department sported tan uniforms right out of the seventies, I hadn't worn a tactical belt in years. Once I'd climbed a few ranks with the New York State Police, I traded in the uniform for suits, but muscle memory always took me back to my earliest days on the job.

Waving to the diner's namesake, Joe DiLorenzo, I turned down the radio clipped at my shoulder. "What's good today?" I called.

"Hiya, sheriff," Joe said. "It's all good. What? You think I'd serve you shabby chicken salad? This isn't New York."

This was our back-and-forth. I asked him about business, he made a playful jab at New York. If I was lucky, I got a side-eyed question about when I was heading back there. These locals, they didn't think I'd last.

"And thank god for that," I replied.

"I'll have your order up in a couple of minutes. Can I get you something cold to drink while you wait?" He glanced at the coffee pots and soda fountains behind him. "I've got a fresh batch of lemonade today. Some iced tea, too. What'll it be?"

"If it's no trouble, could you mix the tea and lemonade? Half and half?" I asked.

"Trouble?" he muttered. "What kinda joint would I be running if I couldn't mix a drink? You think that hack Harniczek is the only one in this town with a good pour? Please."

"I never doubted you." I stifled a laugh when Joe went on muttering about the price of an iced lemonade tea in New York. To his mind, everything outside the Cove was grossly overpriced.

Joe slid a plastic cup and straw across the counter before ducking back into the kitchen, still muttering. This time, he was fed up with taxes. I didn't disagree with him there. His absence gave me a moment of unexpected quiet. When I visited local establishments on non-official business—namely, lunch—I often found myself bombarded with town gossip, safety concerns, and random gripes.

Today was different. The diner's lunch counter was mostly empty and the handful of patrons seated in booths were busy with their food and newspapers. They paid little attention to me beyond a quick nod or wave, and that seemed like a milestone of sorts. Rather than peppering me with questions to ensure I was tending to the town's concerns, they ignored me. Either they were too famished to leave their turkey club sandwiches or they trusted me to do the job.

"If you don't get your fine ass to that bookstore, I'm gonna fuck you up."

Alarmed, I pivoted in search of the low, smoky voice and found Brooke Markham. She stood behind me, hipshot, arms crossed over her chest, and a glare sharp enough to cut glass. I blinked, quickly taking in her impossibly tight pants that cut off below the knee and the baggy tank top that demanded I buy her brunch.

"I beg your pardon, ma'am?"

"Get your ass to the bookstore," Brooke said, biting out each word. "It's not complicated, dude. Go to her. I don't care what bullshit she fed you. She's lying. She wants to see you." She uncrossed her arms and waved them at me. "Also, she's a terrible liar. I'm assuming you're at least minimally competent, which means I'm also assuming you're capable of recognizing when Angel Cakes Cortassi lies her ass off."

"I'm sorry, ma'am," I started, but Brooke was quick to interrupt.

"Save your *ma'am* for someone who appreciates that shit," she snapped. "Perhaps the bookstore."

It was my turn to cross my arms and level the glares. "*The bookstore* isn't a fan of it either," I replied.

"The bookstore doesn't know what she's talking about," Brooke said, stepping into my space. "I know the bookstore is throttling your bandwidth. The bookstore thinks she needs time to sort through some issues." Her nostrils flared as she blew out an impatient breath. "The bookstore needs a push in the right direction because the bookstore doesn't believe she deserves a slab of prime rib like you."

"Prime rib?" I repeated, failing to hold back a chuckle.

"Oh, shut up," Brooke said, pulling a sour grimace. "You know you're hot as fuck. You're like six-five, two-fifty, jacked to shit, and your tan is a goddamn Coppertone commercial. Aside from all that, you have hand-cuffs and say things like, 'it can and will be held against you.'"

I gestured toward her, openly laughing now. "Keep going. I thrive on positive feedback."

She rolled her eyes but the motion wasn't isolated to her face. It seemed to ripple through her entire body. Every last inch of her hummed with annoyance.

"If you don't turn around and go straight to the bookstore, I will fuck you right up," Brooke said, leaning closer to stab her finger against my chest.

"Ow," I yelped, rubbing my solar plexus. "Was that a finger or a claw, Wolverine?"

"I'd call you a pussy but those things can take a beating and keep on fighting. You need to get to that bookstore. Today. Now. Run really fast, reverse time, and save me from this blasted conversation. If you don't, I'll tell everyone you don't like shellfish. They'll run you out of town with pitchforks and fire." She caught my arched eyebrow and continued, "Try me. When it comes to protecting my people and launching disinforma-tion campaigns, I'm your worst nightmare."

"You play dirty," I said, careful to keep my voice low. This conversation needed to stay between us.

"If you think this is dirty, I won't abuse your tender mind with details of my more effective tactics. But if you ever want to know what really happened to the Sheppard Stevenson investment banking house before the housing market bubble burst, I know where the bodies are buried and I keep the shovel close by."

I studied her for a moment, taking in her white-blonde ponytail and diamond stud earrings. "The things you say, Miss Markham, they make me wonder whether I should call for a search warrant."

She reached into her tank top and retrieved her mobile phone. I didn't know whether bras now came equipped with pockets and it didn't seem like the proper time to ask.

"Do as you're told, sheriff," she murmured, busy typing and swiping.

I stared at her for a moment, not sure I understood anything I'd heard in the past five minutes. "What are you? Ex-CIA turned small town mafioso or something?"

"Worse," Brooke said, her eyes widening as she smiled up at me. "Ex-sorority president turned hedge fund manager." She regarded me as I accepted my order from Joe. "Go to her. I won't tell you again."

"Thank you for the advice, ma'am," I said. "I'll take it under advisement."

She narrowed her eyes and returned her hands to her hips. "Never speak of this conversation again."

From halfway out the door, I asked, "What conversation?"

She turned her head, just enough to stare at me from the corner of her eyes. "Very good. We'll keep you. Now, go. I have egg salad to retrieve."

12

———————

DISSOLVE

***v. To stir a solid food and a liquid food together to form a mixture
in which none of the solid remains.***

Jackson

DESPITE BROOKE'S ORDERS, I gave Annette space.

She needed some more time to get her head on straight and I allowed it.

Today, though, this was a different story.

Instead of dodging the station and Annette's morning rituals, I turned the tables on her. Armed with coffee and donuts, I headed to her shop a few minutes before she usually arrived. I needed that time to straighten myself out. I needed to pull it together and fortify if I was going to carry on a conversation with the beautiful book mistress.

I'd spent the past few nights reliving every moment of Annette up against the refrigerator. God damn, I needed to get her on a bed. Kitchen appliances were the wrong surface for worshipping quirky women.

I was unaccustomed to wanting a woman like this. Don't get me wrong, women were amazing and delicious, and I'd desired several over the years, but that was nothing compared to the run-through-a-wall-to-get-to-her desire I felt for Annette. This was a pull unlike any other, one that wasn't entirely comprehensible. I didn't understand how she could draw me to her, body and soul, as if she was my true north.

In reality, I barely knew Annette and she definitely didn't know me. It seemed that we'd skipped over those steps, and maybe that was the problem at play. We were operating on inadequate knowledge. We needed to talk...and stay away from refrigerators.

When the lights flipped on inside the shop, I parked myself near the door to catch her attention. But she spotted me long before she reached the door, pausing in the middle of the sales floor. Today's sundress was long and white with thin black stripes rounding the bottom of her skirt. No ankles to be seen but it was angelic and sexy as hell, all at once.

She shook her head at me but couldn't fight off a smile.

I could work with that—slightly exasperated but generally pleased to see me.

Rapping my knuckles against the glass, I called, "Open up. I brought breakfast." I held up the cup carrier and pink bakery box as evidence. "Can't eat these by myself. It's a bad stereotype waiting to happen."

At that, she started toward me. Once the storefront window lights flicked on, the lock unbolted, and the sign turned over, she pulled the door open. The chimes tinkled overhead and I tightened my hold on the breakfast goods. It was that or risk dropping them while I dragged her into my arms because these past days and nights without her were a special brand of agony.

"Good morning," she said, stepping aside to let me in. "This is a surprise."

"A good surprise," I said, moving toward her. "Right?"

"Good, yeah," she said. It sounded like a concession. "It's also an awkward surprise."

"How so?" I asked. I was undeterred. Nothing she had to say was slowing me down.

"Come with me," she ordered.

"With pleasure." I trailed after Annette, captivated by the sway of her full hips. I was a slave for this woman and she didn't even know it. It didn't compute that I'd followed her into the storeroom until she plucked the coffees from my hand.

"Thanks for this," she murmured, taking a sip of cold brew.

I ran my hand down her back, starved for the feel of her. "I wasn't sure how you liked your coffee," I confessed. "But I asked around. Found out you like it cold and sweet."

Annette glanced up at me, her eyes the same shade as the beverage in her hand. "You asked around?"

"I did," I said, bobbing my head as I stroked her back. I didn't want to stop touching her. Not today, not ever. "Found out you like old-fashioned cake donuts, too. Chocolate."

"Dust ruffles," she murmured.

"No dust ruffles," I insisted. "You must think I'm pretty bad at my job if I can't query a local merchant without powering up the rumor mill."

Annette sipped her coffee, her eyebrow arched especially for me. "That is not my suggestion, no," she said. "You might know your detective work but I know this town, and I know everyone and their auntie will be in here this afternoon looking for juicy bits."

"Lucky for you, I picked up coffee and donuts for most of the shopkeepers on Main Street. Everyone and their aunties will have several stops on the juicy bits tour today." She rolled her eyes but she smiled while doing it. "Just doin' my part to keep the local economy chugging along, ma'am."

"Appreciated." Annette set the coffee down and turned toward the small refrigerator tucked into the back corner. "Seems like we've both put a lot of effort into donuts."

She returned, handing me another one of her Pyrex containers. I pulled the top off and stared at the powdered sugar lumps. "And these are...?"

"My awkward donut holes," she replied, pinching one between her fingers. Raspberry jam dribbled out. Some very primitive corner of my mind found that arousing. I didn't want to understand it. "My kitchen is too small for a full-scale donut operation so I went with the holes instead. I could make regular donuts but I'd have to fry them one by one and that would take hours. It's a new dough for me, a sweet brioche. I hope they came out well."

Annette held the not-quite-round ball to my lips and I accepted, gripping her wrist to lick her fingers clean in the process. "Delicious," I murmured. "But I have one question for you."

She watched as I sucked on her index finger, her eyes hooded, lips parted. "Anything," she whispered.

"Is this awkward because we both brought donuts or because you made them for me and I trampled all over that by showing up here with your favorite old-fashioneds?"

She blinked up at me as pink dashed across her cheeks. "I wanted to work on making a good brioche," she said, a touch of defensiveness in her tone. I sucked harder. "A-a-a-and I thought you might like them. I-I knew you'd like them."

"That's right, beautiful. You know what I like," I replied. "Another question."

"I only agreed to one," Annette argued.

"I'm asking anyway," I said, lashing an arm around her waist. God, she smelled good. "If I hadn't come here this morning, were you going to walk yourself over to the station?"

"Maybe," she replied with a shaky breath. "I might've fed the fire-fighters instead."

"Evil, evil woman," I whispered. I took the dish from her hand and set it on the nearest surface. "You wouldn't do that, not even to spite me."

"You don't know that," she said, shrugging. "For all you know, I like making you suffer."

"Oh, I'm well aware of that fact, beautiful." With both hands on her waist, I picked her up and set her on the table. "What do you think I've been doing the past two nights?"

"Reading that book you've had on your nightstand for months?" she quipped.

I pushed her legs apart and stepped between them. "Yes, that's exactly it," I replied. "Unfortunately, it's been a worthless distraction."

Annette's hands skimmed up my chest and over my shoulders. "Sounds like you need to get between some different pages."

I leaned down, my lips a breath away from hers. "Sounds like I need to get some fuck-hot ankles between my sheets."

"Just the ankles?" she asked, shooting me a sharp glance. "Are you sure you're not some kind of serial killer posing as a small town sheriff? Seems like a good cover."

"Not a cover. Not a serial killer. Not just the ankles," I said, kissing the corner of her mouth between each statement. "I want the whole package and the peach down your dress, too. Hell, Annie, I want it so much. I just need you to want it, too."

"I made you donut holes." She inched closer, nipping at my bottom lip. "That has to count for something."

I covered her lips with mine, sighing into her as she opened for me. My tongue stroked over hers, tasting coffee and sweetness. I'd planned on coffee and conversation, but Annette annihilated my best intentions. She always did, and I was the fool who still hadn't learned my lesson.

"It counts," I said against her lips. "It would count for more if you admitted you were walking your fine ass to the station and feeding me these donut holes in the privacy of my office."

Annette paused for a moment, blinking at my neck. Then, she said, "Yeah, I was bringing them over."

I could see her there, sitting on my desk with her legs spread while she hand-feeding me her best creations. Then I'd lay her back on the hard surface and taste her sweetness until she was shaking and writhing. I'd take her right there on my desk and let her scream down the walls. No one would doubt what was happening and no one would doubt she was mine.

"Now, admit you wore this dress because it is the most unholy piece of clothing in your closet and you like making me jizz in my pants."

Her palm shifted to my crotch and she stroked me over my trousers. We could talk later. We had all the time in the world so long as she kept touching me. I wasn't much for conversation before noon anyway. I bucked into her hand, every inch of my body tightening as my head fell back on my shoulders and I let loose a growl too animalistic to be human.

I wasn't the kind of man who lost control. I didn't lose my temper or find myself at the end of my rope too often. I worked hard to keep a cool head. But a few minutes with Annette canceled it all out. I was ready to riot if it meant getting my hands on her.

"I knew you'd like it," she purred. "You love it when I wear white. That, and no one will notice the powdered sugar all over me."

"The last time you wore white, you didn't let me admire you for long," I said. "Not that I minded you getting naked at my house. If you recall, I've been inviting you to do that again."

"Ah, yes," she said, sighing. "You should know I've had some rough nights as well. I've had a lot on my mind."

"I want to hear all about that." I growled into her neck, still rocking into the heaven that was her hand on my dick.

She laughed at that, the vibrations moving through her body and into mine like an electric shock. "Ah, but some things are best left unsaid."

There were so many reasons to step back, straighten myself out, and return to the plan. Aside from the fact we were in a glorified closet, I came here to talk with Annette. I wanted to build a connection beyond our history of complicated interactions. I wanted to make it work with her.

But my cock was a single-minded master and the cradle of her thighs felt like the only place I'd ever truly belonged.

"Annie," I said, grunting as I pressed into her heat.

"Yes, Jackson?"

I pushed her skirt up to her waist and out of my way, and then dragged my hands up her thighs. With my fingers twined around either side of her panties, I asked, "Are you with me, beautiful?"

The nod came first, then the words. "Yeah. Yes. I am," she whispered, her eyes dark and hungry.

"All the way?" I continued. "We're doing this, you and me? You're not going to tell me you need time to figure things out and show me the door when we're finished?"

Her shoulder jerked up. "That depends on how well you finish."

"You don't have anything to worry about there," I murmured, tossing her undies to the floor and wrapping an arm under her backside. Her hands went to my belt while I tugged the top of her dress down to reveal her breasts. "I've been waiting to lick these tits for ages. They're like perfect cupcakes with cherries on top. Bet they taste like vanilla sugar, too."

"You're ridiculous," Annette said, laughing.

"Completely," I agreed. Goddamn. This woman was so much *fun*. "Since I have to concentrate on your tits, I'm gonna need you to get these pants off me before you cause another accident."

"That wasn't my fault," she said. "Not entirely."

She pushed my trousers down and curled her hand around my cock while I tongued her nipples. She tasted like all the things I loved about her. It wasn't a flavor, it was a feeling.

I dropped kisses onto each of her breasts before working my way back to her lips. "There's a condom in my wallet. Grab that for me, beautiful."

She reached into my back pocket and retrieved the billfold. Instead of going for the rubber and tossing everything else aside, she took a moment to study my driver's license and glance at the cards inside. All while her other hand stroked me to within an inch of sanity.

"How long have you had this?" Annette asked, pinching the condom between two fingers. "I have an IUD but I like to cover all the bases."

"It's new. You can check the expiration date," I said, the words turning into groans as her grip tightened. "With the exception of last week, I'm always prepared."

"Are you always such a Boy Scout?" she quipped, tearing the packet open with her teeth.

"Put the goddamn condom on me," I ordered, my jaw clenched. I couldn't take another minute of this hand job or her smart-ass comments. The combination was lethal. "Do it now, Annie." Her eyes widened, sparkling as if she enjoyed my rough tone. If that was the case, I had plenty more where that came from. "Now or I'm fucking you without it."

She kept her gaze steady on me while she rolled the condom down. Once it was in place, we stared at each other, our lips no more than a breath apart. She gave me the tiniest of nods and I pushed inside her.

The first moment was heaven. Annette cried out, I buried a groan-turned-growl in her neck. She rocked into me, I nearly blew it all right then. It was so good, terrifyingly good. Good because she felt like absolute perfection but terrifying because I knew I was a goner for this girl. I was gone when I started lusting over her ankles but this was some higher-level cosmic soul mate shit.

"Keep yourself still, beautiful," I barked, my hand flat on her back.

"Don't want to," she replied, her ankles locking at the base of my spine as her body rolled against mine. "Can't make me."

I dragged in as much oxygen as I could but it wasn't enough. My body was diverting all resources toward moving in Annette and as long as I could do that, nothing else was necessary.

"Yes, I fucking can," I snapped, sliding my fingers down the seam of her ass.

She clawed at my back, her nails blunted by my shirt. I hated that shirt for existing. I wanted it gone. I wanted me and Annette, and a bed and all the time in the world, and I wanted everything else to go the hell away.

I pressed two fingers to her ass. Her entire body shuddered against me. "See? I made you do that."

I slammed into her like I was trying to prove a point. Maybe I was. Maybe I wanted her to know we were better together than either of us could've guessed.

"Right there, right there, right there," she gasped.

"If you'd stop squirming for a second, I'd get you right there," I said, squeezing the cheeks of her ass hard.

"You love my squirming," she argued.

She was right. I loved the way her compact body fit with mine and how her hips matched my rhythm without faltering. And now, with her thighs clenched around me and her hands fisted in my hair, I loved the way she clung to me while I fucked her mindlessly. I was coming apart piece by piece, splintering with her every whisper and plea.

"Jackson," Annette cried out. *"Jackson."*

Her lips found my neck and stayed there as I drove into her, too consumed by these sensations to respond with more than my body's instincts. Oh, this hurt. Everything ached, straight down to my bones. My body was fevered, my blood pounding in my veins. My muscles were pumping hard, pushing, pushing, pushing. Tightening as I held myself off, spasming as I surrendered to the pain. I couldn't hold on another minute without cracking right in half.

The front door chimes sounded at the same moment I blasted into the condom, shooting hard enough that I wondered how it could stay intact. Annette pressed her palm to my mouth, muffling my roar. I went rigid, every last inch of me, as I emptied myself into her. It was like a dam bursting.

"I'll be right with you," she called, running both hands through my hair. "Just give me a minute. Or five."

The customer replied with some comment I couldn't hear over the fuzzy noise in my ears.

When the last spurt pulsed through me, I laid Annette back on the table, dropped my head between her breasts, and closed my eyes. I needed to deal with this condom but I was sleepy-sated and didn't think I could peel myself from this heaven for anything. Not when I was still half hard inside her and thinking up ways we could make this table work for us one more time.

I could pull that off. Bend her over, flip that skirt up, slap her ass, hold her down just the way she liked. Yeah, that would do just fine.

"What are these little growls all about?" Annette asked, her fingers making magic on my scalp.

"Thinking about fucking you on this table," I mumbled.

"We just did that," she said.

"Mmhmm. I want to do it again."

She traced the tendons in the back of my neck, dissolving every ounce of tension stored there. "I like that idea."

When I gathered my senses, I pushed up on an elbow and pressed a kiss to her lips. "Please tell me we have time for that. Also, I need you to tell me I imagined someone coming into the shop."

"Nope, that really happened," she replied.

I shook my head against her chest. "This wasn't what I had in mind when I came here this morning," I said, glancing at up her.

"Are you sure about that?" Annette asked, her lips pursed in the best pout ever. Loved that pout.

"Actually, yes," I replied. "But then I saw you in this white dress and you had little donuts for me, and I am powerless when it comes to you and your pastries."

Her eyebrow arched up. "My baking isn't intended to turn you on."

I gave her a quick shake of my head. "Neither are your ankles, beautiful. You just can't help it."

13

PROOFING

***v. The period of time the dough must rest after dividing and
rounding.***

Annette

Brooke: I was on the front porch just now, staring at the ocean and wondering how my life managed come apart at the seams like the last days of Rome, and who did I see sneaking out the back door of your shop but Sheriff Lau.

Brooke: I have to assume he was leaving after a quick morning romp and I am impressed.

Brooke: I have a multitude of questions but I am still impressed.

Annette: Thank you.

Annette: And your life hasn't fallen apart. You're doing awesome.

Brooke: Don't distract me from the topic at hand but you're wrong, my life is a Shakespearean tragedy and I am never more than five minutes away from floating myself down a damn stream like Ophelia.

Annette: Why don't we unpack that for a second?

Brooke: No. No. I'd rather hear about your quickie, please. The thrill of your life is the only thing keeping me going.

Annette: I'm still processing but here's what I know for sure. It didn't seem quick.

Brooke: Ohhhhhh that's the best kind.

Annette: It was incredible. I've never had sex like this before. I'm smiling like a lunatic and my belly feels like cotton candy.

Brooke: Does this mean you've completely foreclosed the possibility of a sister-wife setup? If there were any two women who could make it work, it would be us.

Annette: I love you but if you say that again, I'll tear your eyes out.

Brooke: Fair enough.

Brooke: When are you seeing him next?

Annette: I'm not sure. He got a call and had to go check on something near the Nevilles' inn.

Brooke: That place is fucking haunted.

Annette: No disagreement here.

Brooke: You didn't articulate next steps? Didn't establish expectations going forward? He just zipped up and zipped out?

Annette: I could barely speak when he kissed me goodbye. I was in no condition to formulate action plans.

Brooke: He really knows what he's doing, huh?

Annette: My head is fizzy like sparkling water, my chin is still trembling, and I can't feel my lips. Aside from sex in the storeroom, he brought me cold brew and chocolate old-fashioneds and said really sweet things. I almost told him I loved him.

Brooke: I wouldn't blame you. I love him for you.

CONFIDENCE WAS A TRICKY THING.

For years, I'd believed my big aspirations for my tiny bookstore were within reach if I worked hard enough. If I did the right things and put in the time, people would come. Even when I only sold a handful of books each day, I kept on believing my work would pay off.

That confidence moved me forward when I was barely covering my expenses and my family wanted me to give it up for a reliable income. It pushed me out of my disappointment when I couldn't snag big-name authors for an in-store visit during their book publicity tours. It picked me up when I couldn't convince the locals to join a book club unless I was offering free food and wine.

And it was that confidence that had me nodding in smug agreement when I woke up this morning to find my sweet little shop listed as one of the best independent bookstores in the country.

The country.

At first I thought it said *county* and that seemed plausible. But then I noticed the next bookstore on the list was in Culver City, California and realized this list had nothing to do with my county. Repeated mention of works by local artists, photographers, and diverse authors I stocked here had me thinking back to Cole, Owen's deckhand boyfriend. He'd gushed about one of my Maine photography books. Bought several copies, too. With his fancy black card, the kind reserved for professional athletes and movie stars and other special people. When I followed the article's threads back to the beginning, I discovered it was first posted on a small site two weeks ago. Only days after Owen, Cole, and all the vodka in the Cove.

But I shook that coincidence off. The shop was inundated with customers today and I wanted to focus on that rather than the strange sequence of events leading to my shop being full. People came from Bar Harbor, Kittery, even Portsmouth, all touting the online article that was now trending on all the local news sites.

My shop had never seen traffic like this. I had to call in my part-time sales clerks, Jane and Yosefina, just to keep up with the mad rush. I barely had a minute to pee but I found a few moments to wonder whether Jackson was watching me from his office. I hoped he was watching. I hoped he was still thinking about me and us and yesterday morning. I wanted it even when wanting scared the shit out of me.

That confidence, it sure was tricky.

Around noon, I took a call from someone at an internet company wanting to help me develop an online storefront. I'd never considered such a thing. It came at the perfect time, since I'd spent the morning juggling customers in-store and fielding calls requesting many of the local books and gifts I stocked here.

By four o'clock, the Portland newspaper had called to schedule an interview. They were working on a series about female-run businesses and wanted to come up to Talbott's Cove to visit.

Shortly before closing time, Jackson appeared in my shop, his height and heft sucking up the oxygen around him. My gaze scraped over the long lines of his body without conscious thought. He was dressed in sheriff's garb today. I couldn't decide which look I preferred, the suit or the uniform. He seemed more comfortable in suits but more authoritative in the uniform.

As I watched him scanning the shop, his gaze passing over each customer before landing on me with an easy smile, I realized I craved both his comfort and his authority. Even when I didn't know what to believe or where to stow my trust, Jackson wrapped me up in his steady strength. I liked that. I didn't understand it or know the right way to embrace it, but I liked it.

He lifted his fingers to his head, tipping an invisible hat toward me. "What's going on here?" he mouthed from across the room.

I held up my hands and let them fall to the counter. When I registered a pinch in my cheeks, I realized I was grinning at him like a madwoman.

I was roused from my staring contest when a customer bustled up to the counter with a pile of books the length of her arm. "Do you have the next book in this series?" she asked, holding a paperback up. "I couldn't find it but I wasn't sure if you had a special supply in the back."

"I can check. Give me a minute." I caught Jackson's eye over her head. He winked, as if he knew I was thinking about yesterday morning. I was never looking at my grandmother's old kitchen table the same way again.

Once I was alone in the storeroom, I pressed my hand to my chest and surrendered to shuddering breaths. Of all the things that had happened today, it took Sheriff Lau tossing a wink in my direction to get my heart hammering against my ribs and my lungs begging for oxygen. Not to mention the heat between my legs and the ever-present urge to drop my drawers. I stood there a moment, cataloging my body's reaction to this man.

A hat tip, a smile, a wink. That was all it took.

After collecting a few books, I returned to the counter and finished the sale. Jackson was tucked into the nonfiction corner with a new political hardcover. I watched him while he flipped through the book, stopping every few pages to skim the text. And I wasn't the only one watching him. Nearly every customer shot glances in his direction, taking in his broad shoulders and the height that forced everyone to crane their necks.

I signaled for Yosefina to take over the sales counter and then made my way to Jackson. When I reached his side, I tapped the book cover. "Getting between some new pages?"

He shifted, turning his back to the shop as he studied the shelves. From the other side of the shop, I was certain it appeared we were carrying on a quiet but book-centric conversation.

"Haven't thought of anything but getting between your pages since I left here yesterday morning," he said, his voice low and rough. "I'm sorry I had to run out like that. I've been keeping my eye on a situation and ended up dealing with it all day, and—"

"No apologies," I interrupted. "I had customers and it was nine o'clock in the morning and it just wasn't the time."

Jackson looked away from the shelves, his gaze landing on my lips and sliding down the v-neck of my blue wrap dress. "It damn well better be the time soon," he said. "I haven't been able to think of anything but bending you over that counter since I walked in."

I dragged my tongue over my parched lips. "You should tell me about it. To get it off your mind."

A switch flipped in Jackson, shutting down his cool, calm sheriff vibe and turning on the starved, sexual man I was beginning to adore. His jaw locked, his lips pulled up in a naughty smirk, his nostrils flared. He was verging on snarling bull and I couldn't help but lean closer to him.

Jackson shot a glimpse across the shop. "Turn off all the lights. Lock the doors. Get you behind the counter," he said, each statement rushing out in a huff. "Skirt up, underwear down. Wrap your fingers around the edge of the counter because you'd need to hold on to something." He dragged his knuckle from the base of my throat to the valley between my breasts. "Get my cock out and slide inside you, fuck you, lose my damn mind on you."

A choked sob slipped past my lips and I didn't try to cover it up. There was no point. My nipples were tunneling their way through the fabric of my bra and dress, my cheeks were flushed, and my chest was heaving with erratic, choppy breaths.

I turned my head toward Jackson but didn't meet his gaze. I couldn't. If I took one look at his hot, hungry eyes, I was going to climb him like a jungle gym and demand he take me right up against the boring-as-hell political manifesto books.

"This place will be cleared out in ten, maybe fifteen minutes," I said.

"And yet we could be upstairs in your apartment in three," he replied. "Decisions, decisions."

"My apartment is small," I cautioned.

I didn't know why I said that about my sugar-cube-sized apartment. It seemed like I should warn him that me and my existence were less than he was anticipating. Even if I'd wowed him with muffins and pies and a tumble on the back table, I didn't want to escalate his expectations. I didn't want to disappoint him.

"But it has a bed?" He shuffled, causing his elbow to brush my arm, and a tiny purr rumbled in my throat.

"It does," I replied.

"That's all we need," he said. "I've been waiting to get you in bed for months."

"More like weeks," I said, stealing glances over my shoulder at the remaining customers.

"Months," Jackson repeated, pressing his hand to my belly. "Believe me, Annie, it's been months."

His fingers stretched from the bottom of my bra's underwire to the top edge of my panties. He stroked me in tiny circles and lit a line of heat down my torso. I was aching for him, my core throbbing and clenching while my shoulders were strung tighter than ever before. The slightest tap could split me in half and leave me in shards on the floor.

The door chimes sounded and I shot another glance over my shoulder. The shop was nearly empty, only two customers still perusing the shelves. On any other evening, I would've been right there, chatting them up and staying open long past the official hours. Tonight, after dropping into the deep end of crazy-good publicity, I was shutting this place down.

"All right, here's the plan," I said to Jackson. "Go on upstairs. The door's open and I'll meet you there in five minutes."

"The door is open? Why would that be the case?" he asked, separating his warm hand from my belly.

"Because I left it open," I said. "I burnt some orange brioche rolls last night and needed to air the place out."

Jackson shook his head as he backed away from me. "We'll talk about that later," he promised. "The burnt rolls *and* the unlocked doors. And the pepper spray I want you to keep in your bag."

"Later," I said, holding up my hands in surrender. "We'll talk about everything."

I MANAGED to hurry the stragglers along, lock up the cash, send Jane and Yosefina home, and secure the shop in three minutes. I moved with the singular purpose of getting upstairs and getting under Jackson. It didn't matter whether it was loaded with complications or weighed down with all my doubts and issues. Right now—tonight—I was setting all of it aside. I could want Jackson and have him without getting lost in the thicket.

If I kept telling myself that, it would be true.

I climbed the stairs and pushed open the screen door to find Jackson standing in the middle of my apartment and his sheriff's belt slung over the back of a kitchen chair. He seemed too big for my cozy home, too male for my flamingos-and-pink-pineapples décor. But he crooked his finger at me and I went to him, dropping my phone, bag, and keys to the floor.

Too big, too male, too right.

"That was six minutes," he said, tracing the line of my dress's v-neck.

"I know, I know," I replied with a sigh. My fingers went to his short-sleeved uniform shirt, attacking the buttons as I groaned about my most talkative sales clerk. "Jane usually works a few weekend hours for me and was able to come in today because, you know, a million people came through the shop. Yosefina too but she's antisocial so that's good. But Jane wanted to talk about those million people and didn't realize I was trying to, uh, I mean—"

"Go home and get fucked?"

I stopped unbuttoning, flattened my hands on his hard chest, and looked up. "Yeah. Yes. That. She didn't understand that and I wasn't prepared to explain it to her."

"She didn't need an explanation. We're the only ones who need to know." Jackson reached for the tie at my waist, loosening it with one finger. When it fell away, he loosened the internal tie. My dress hung open, revealing my mismatched panties and bra. He ran his knuckles over the rise of my breasts and down my belly. "*Annette*," he rasped.

I went back to working his buttons and opening his trousers, my gaze steady on the barely covered wall of muscle in front of me. After everything we'd shared, this was the first time I was getting my hands on his naked skin. Anticipation hummed through my veins, electrifying every touch and breath.

"Mmhmm?"

"Am I allowed to touch your panties tonight?" he asked. "Because I want to. I want to twist them around my fist and rip them off."

I pushed his shirt over his shoulders, letting it fall to the floor. A white cotton t-shirt separated me from his chest and I pushed it up, driven by my need to touch him. All of him.

"Annette," he prompted.

"What?" I murmured, busy tugging the t-shirt over his head. When it was free, I smoothed my hands up the hard ridges of his abs and across his chest. There was a dusting of golden hair there, barely dark enough to stand out against his skin. But I loved the feel of those coarse strands under my palms. "Oh, this is nice."

"All right, that's it," he said, bending down and hoisting me over his shoulder. He marched through my apartment and into the bedroom, yanking off my undies as he went. "Won't be needing these."

With more care than I expected from him right now, he set me on the bed and freed the dress from my shoulders.

Jackson pointed toward my bra as he kicked off his shoes, socks. "Get rid of that," he ordered.

He pushed his trousers down, stepped out of them. Only his boxers remained, and the huge erection stabbing at the fabric.

"Annette," he said, dragging my gaze away from his crotch. "The bra. Lose it."

He dropped his knee onto the bed and my legs fell open. I reached back to wrest open the clasp then flung my bra aside. I was naked and waiting, my most intimate places revealed to him. But it wasn't self-consciousness (hello, belly rolls) or doubt (what if I wasn't good in bed?) that sent a herd of buffalo stampeding through my stomach. It was that I knew I could love him and maybe I already did.

And wasn't that hysterical? After everything I'd experienced in the past couple of weeks and all my efforts to curtail my attraction to Jackson, I was carving out a spot for him in my heart. I already knew it was a deep, yawning cavern, a space he'd grow into over the years. Yep, it was absolutely hysterical because even as I went on making room for him, I didn't trust myself to give him the keys. It belonged to him but I couldn't let him take ownership.

Not yet. Not until I understood us better, knew it was real. I was the queen of mind games, after all. I'd carved out space for a man before. I'd handed him the keys, too. I wasn't going to be so giving this time. It wasn't like we were in any rush. Nope, no rush. We had all the time in the world.

"Jackson," I said, holding out my hand. The way he stared at me, I was amazed the bed wasn't on fire.

He shucked his boxers and crawled toward me, his cock heavy and hot as it bobbed between us. I reached for him, needing an anchor. "You feel so good," he murmured, thrusting into my fist. "You're stunning. Do you know that? Looking at you now, I can't believe how beautiful you are."

"It's not like this is the first time you're seeing me naked," I said, laughing.

"It is," he replied. "It's the first time I'm looking."

A breath shuddered out of me as Jackson pressed his lips to mine. It was a sweet kiss, slow and generous, but the need vibrating between us was enough to register on the Richter scale. He knew this, too, and pulled my hand from his cock.

"No more. No more, beautiful. I don't want to come on your belly. Not this time," he whispered against my jaw. "Let me get a condom."

"We don't have to," I said, wrapping my arms around his waist to keep him in place. "I've been tested and I have an IUD and if you wanted—"

"Fuck yes. Yes, I want," he roared, his fingers finding my clit. He circled me there, unhurried at first then quicker. Much more quickly. "I don't know what to do with you right now, Annie. I want everything. I want to lick you for hours. Suck on your nipples and fuck you with my fingers. Feed you my cock. Tease you and find out what you like. Flip you over, fuck you from behind while I grab that round ass of yours. Flip you back over, wrap your legs around my waist and fuck you slow. I want it all and I don't know where to start."

I canted my hips and locked my legs around him. "Let's start at the end of that list and see where it takes us."

Jackson took that recommendation and ran with it, sliding inside me with one magnificent drive. He stayed there, his body rigid and his breath coming in ragged pants. Then, after dropping his forehead to my shoulder, he started to move. His hips pumped in quick jabs, in and out, in and out. I dug my heels into his backside, urging him deeper. I wanted longer drags, harder thrusts.

"Like this?" he asked, pulling out and then grinding into me.

"Yes," I said, forcing that single word into thirty syllables. "You feel so good, Jackson. It's *so* good. I'm so full. Don't stop."

"That's funny," he said, chuckling against my shoulder. "You make it seem like I'd electively leave your pussy paradise."

"Is that what we're calling it?"

Jackson nodded, grunting when he rocked inside me again. He forced his arms under my back, holding me tight. "I'm not trying to be one of those guys who says it's better without the rubber but fuck me, you are fucking perfect right now. I don't want this to end."

"It doesn't have to," I whispered, my fingers scrabbling over his back, desperate to hold on to him as my body dissolved like sugar over high heat. Something about his grip on me, the way he gathered me up like I was fragile but fucked me like I was unbreakable, it tripped me into the immediate orgasm zone.

"Come on, beautiful," he murmured as the first wave of spasms rolled through me. I felt his teeth on my neck, my shoulder. Kisses all over. His cock moving in me, my muscles rippling around him. Clinging to him. His body went stiff as he sank into me again, his cock twitching and jerking as he emptied himself in me. "I've got you. Just let go."

And he did. He had me and the cavern in my heart, too.

14

CRUMB

n. The soft inner part of a loaf of bread or cake.

Jackson

"HOW DO YOU BAKE HERE?" I asked. Wearing only my boxers and the lazy grin of a guy who just had incredible sex, I stretched out my arms, almost certain I'd be able to touch two walls from the center of Annette's apartment. I couldn't but I wasn't far off. "It's...it's tiny."

Annette's home was just like her: small, pink, and hemmed in with some awkward ceiling angles. And there were flamingos everywhere. Embroidered on little pillows, printed on mugs, painted in watercolor. The short, silky robe she was wearing.

"It's not that bad," she argued, twisting her hair up into a bun. "It works for me."

The kitchen and living room were separated by nothing more than a big footstep, and the dining room was a corner. Her queen-sized bed was tucked into an alcove to create the illusion of privacy. As much as I liked her, it wasn't big enough for the two of us. Or, more specifically, it wasn't big enough for me. That, and I kept knocking my head on the sloped ceiling.

"Your stove, it's tiny. The oven, too." I motioned toward the miniature appliances, the ones I'd expect to find in a child's play house. "How do you bake here? It must've taken you hours to bake all those muffins."

"Not really." She shrugged and moved toward the refrigerator. Also child-sized. "How about...hmm. Let's see what we have in here."

She opened the door and peered in while she stroked the top of her foot against the back of her calf. This common movement was sensual and intimate, and it had me crossing the room in two steps to wrap my arms around her waist.

"Hello there." She dragged her nails down my forearm. Loved that sensation. "You just can't leave me alone around refrigerators, can you?"

Kissing her neck, I murmured, "So what?"

"Just an observation," Annette replied with a laugh. She bent at the waist, forcing her backside against my cock. Without conscious thought, my hands shifted to her waist and my hips rocked forward. "Fridges really turn you on, huh?"

"It has nothing to do with the appliances," I said, a low growl rumbling in my throat. "All about you."

She didn't say anything for a long moment and I forced myself to be still, even as I craved her friction. Then, "I have cheese, rye bread, too. I made it the other night so it's not the freshest but it's good. I know I shouldn't keep it chilled but it's been so warm recently. It would've turned stale and moldy in a hot minute if I didn't refrigerate it. I also have a Sussex pond pudding with apples but that recipe didn't turn out anything like I anticipated."

I didn't know what Sussex pond pudding was and I wasn't about to ask. "Rye bread it is," I said.

"I have beer, too," she offered. "Grab some, will you?"

Our arms loaded down with bread, its accompaniments, and beer, we returned to her bedroom. The blankets and pillows were in a heap on the floor and the top sheet clung to a single corner but we nestled in with our snacks, no care for the linens.

Annette handed me a slice of bread topped with a hunk of cheddar, a dollop of sweet, spicy mustard. It looked like art. Everything she did was beautiful, thoughtfully precise. For the first time in my life, I wanted to stop what I was doing and photograph the food I was about to eat because sharing this with everyone seemed necessary. I wanted to say, "My lady made this. She made it from scratch. Isn't she something?"

And it didn't escape my notice that she served me before fixing her own slice. That was Annette's way.

"Is that okay?" she asked, pointing toward the bread. The bread I'd been staring at for a solid minute while I fantasized about Instagram captions. "I can make you a slice without mustard."

I leaned over, kissed her temple. "It's great," I said. "It's the prettiest piece of bread I've ever seen."

"Thank you for that but it's not particularly pretty," she said. "I didn't score the dough correctly and the bake was a bit uneven. I think the loaf was too big for my oven so the heat didn't distribute effectively."

"You know my oven's huge," I said, working damn hard to hit that innuendo. "You're welcome to it any time."

"Your oven is amazing," she said with a breathy sigh. My cock was interpreting that sigh as a point in its favor and I took no issue with that. "But, you know, that's—it's very nice of you to offer."

"But?" I prompted.

She was busy assembling her own slice. "But I can get along fine with my own," she said. "I don't want to trouble you."

"What troubles me is you leaving your home open for anyone to walk in," I said.

"Oh, stop it," she said, waving away my concern. "Nothing like that happens in the Cove."

I traced the line of her jaw with my index finger, drawing her toward me. "That's what everyone says until something happens. Don't leave your front door open all day, Annette. Don't leave the back door to the shop open either."

"Jackson, I've lived here my entire life. I know this town inside and out. You could blindfold me and drop me in the woods at midnight, and I'd find my way home without a scrape. Hell, I can identify most of the residents by the way they jingle coins in their pockets." She pinned me with a sharp look. "I know this town."

My finger still on her chin, I said, "I don't doubt that. I don't doubt you, beautiful. But I know a few things, too, and this town isn't as safe as you think it is."

She blinked, nodded. A flash of surprise passed through her eyes. "Okay. I'll work on it."

"And I'm getting you a can of pepper spray. You're going to keep it with you." I kissed her then, mostly because I couldn't get enough of her lips but also to head off her disagreement.

When we parted, Annette reached for the beer bottles on the window ledge. She passed one to me before taking a long drink from hers.

"What made you come here?" She ran the back of her spoon over the slice of bread, distributing the mustard to every corner. There was an eroticism to her ministrations, something captivating about the capable way her hands moved. "What about Talbott's Cove appealed to you?"

I felt my cock lengthening, hardening as I watched her drizzle more mustard over the slab of cheddar. Why was mustard drizzling sexy? What was it about the way she twirled that spoon over the bread and cheese that made me think of the kind of sex that resulted in broken bedsprings and scratched backs? It took real effort to respond to her question when I wanted to force her legs apart and taste her sweetness.

"I field this question a fair amount," I managed.

"I'm sorry," she said, biting into her slice. "I didn't mean to pry."

"No, it's fine. I like it when you pry. Talbott's Cove isn't the kind of town that brings in a lot of newcomers, and people are curious," I said. I sampled my bread—heaven. I still wanted to feast on Annette but that would keep while we talked. "I usually tell people that I wanted to work in a town where I'd know all the residents."

"But that's not the truth?" She licked a spot of mustard off her thumb and I couldn't hold back my growl. "Or, not the entire truth?"

"Yeah, not the whole truth," I admitted, staring at my beer. The beer wasn't licking its thumb or sitting cross-legged in a short robe with nothing but skin beneath. The beer was safe. "The whole truth isn't a good look for a sheriff."

"I'm sure it's a good look for the man I'm sleeping with," she said.

"Is that what I am?" I squinted at her, not understanding her. "Is that all?"

Her words, they stung a bit. I didn't want them to but they did. I didn't know what I wanted her to say but I wanted to be more than the man she was sleeping with. And I would be. It was just going to take some time.

"Tell me your story," Annette insisted, patting my knee. "We'll save the labels for later. They go better with breakfast. I'll make you some cinnamon rolls with fresh caramel sauce."

"Fuck, yes," I said, laying both hands over my belly. "All right, well, since cinnamon rolls are on the line, I better get on with this." I laced my fingers around the bottle and stared at the ceiling, silent for a long moment as I gathered the words. "There was a missing persons case a few years back. A little boy disappeared, and the circumstances were highly suspicious. Conflicting stories from the parents, physical evidence that couldn't be explained away. Something about that case stuck with me. I couldn't let it go. Even when the evidence dried up and the trail went cold, I couldn't stop thinking about that kid and the gut sense that someone who knew him did something terrible to him. It kept me up at nights, interfered with my cases, drove me damn near crazy."

"That's awful," she murmured. "I'm so sorry, Jackson."

I forced down a mouthful of beer, trying to push images of the crime scene from my mind. Tried, failed. This job had a way of changing people, and that case changed me.

"It hit me hard when his body was discovered. Harder when the forensic evidence pointed toward the father," I said.

I'd never forget the anger that flashed through me like a bomb blast after finding that boy's remains. The anger stayed with me, too. Followed me around for weeks, months. I'd always accepted that some violence was senseless but I couldn't accept this. For a time, I doubted whether I wanted to live in a world with the kind of savagery that had killed that boy.

"It hit me harder than any other murder investigation. I had some time off shortly after that. If I was smart, I would've seen the department's counselor and got my head straightened out, but I didn't. I hopped in my truck and drove east until I hit the ocean. Then, I headed north. It was an unintentionally scenic road trip through Rhode Island, Massachusetts, New Hampshire. I stopped in small towns along the coast, and by the time I crossed the border into Maine, I knew I needed to get out of the city for good. Part of it was the case. The other part of it was realizing I did want to work in a town where I knew every single resident."

"One small step toward saving the next kid?" she asked.

I blew out a breath but didn't respond until Annette ran her fingertips down my arm. "I realize that I can't prevent every crime, but in a town like this, I can keep an eye out for the signs." I shifted to the side, gazing at Annette. "What makes you stay here?"

A deep laugh rumbled up from her belly. "When I'm not chasing after unavailable men and getting sloppy drunk and generally embarrassing the hell out of myself, I like it here. I like the people, the community, the way this place changes slowly but surely."

"Why are you still beating yourself up about that?" I asked. I dropped my hand on her thigh, needing some physical connection to her.

She avoided my gaze as she worked on another round of rye bread extravaganzas. "Because I'm probably banned from The Galley for life and I acted like an emotionally unstable drunk girl, and both of those things are embarrassing."

"That's not what I'm talking about," I said. "I think you know that."

Annette turned back toward me, a slice of bread in her outstretched hand. "Because I'm not so different from the town, Jackson. I change slowly but surely."

15

———————

CREAMING

v. Beating sugar and softened butter together to form a lighter, aerated mixture.

Annette

AUGUST PEACHES WERE the best peaches.

This was the first summer I was paying attention to peach quality but I knew this month's crop was as good as it got. Last month's peaches—the one that ended up down my dress—didn't compare to the beauties coming out now. Since they were so damn good, I couldn't stop testing new recipes. My kitchen was filled to the rafters with cobblers and crumbles, crostatas and cakes. And that didn't include the pastries I'd distributed around town.

I'd shipped a peach and almond tart off to Brooke's house on Monday and a peach and raspberry yogurt cake to the Fitzsimmonses on Tuesday. Jackson took a basket of cinnamon peach turnovers to the station on Wednesday and my sales clerk Jane got a peach and blueberry bread pudding on Thursday.

It was hard to believe I'd baked this much in one week. It helped that

I had Jackson hauling in big sacks of sugar and flour for me and washing the dishes while my creations were in the oven.

As much I adored the kitchen at his house, I never managed to bring all the things I needed. Either it was the good sifter or the board scraper I always misplaced, or the paring knife I liked better than the rest. There was always something missing.

That was part of the reason I ended up back at my apartment after baking at Jackson's house. The other part was my own crazy mind game where I refused to accept I was falling for him but inventing a world of feelings based on good sex and well washed dishes. That crazy mind game was cool with the sex and the dishes but everything came to a screeching halt at the notion of spending the night at Jackson's house. That was the hard limit, the third rail.

It didn't make sense but neither did my fantasy relationship with Owen.

I allowed myself to believe it didn't have to make sense. Love didn't make sense. Hell, life didn't make sense. Why did my thoughts have to follow a logical sequence? They didn't and it wasn't worth my time to dwell on the roundabouts and contradictions in my head. Not when I could enjoy the time we had together and hope it all worked out for the best.

I hadn't planned on baking this afternoon but a thunderstorm rolled in and canceled my beach plans. I didn't take many days off from the shop but liked to reserve some Fridays and Saturdays throughout the summer. Not always the whole day but even a few hours away was worth it. Good for my tan, better for my soul.

I washed the frosting from my fingers and dried my hands on a towel while inspecting my latest bake, brown butter peach cupcakes. They stood in neat rows and columns on my cooling racks, perfect rosettes of luscious peach-scented cream cheese frosting on top.

I studied them for a moment, my hands still curled around the dish towel, then glanced to the clock. Jackson was still at the station. He'd be there a little while longer.

I stepped toward the window and looked to the sky. Only drizzle and lake-sized puddles remained. The worst of the storm was on its way north.

Seemed like the right time to deliver a snack.

I KNOCKED on the door to Jackson's office and wiggled the glass container filled with cupcakes when I poked inside.

My stars, he was a sight. Legs open as if he was giving a master class in manspreading, his tan uniform trousers pulled taut over his tree trunk thighs. Phone tucked between his ear and shoulder, a pen trapped in one hand, the other wrapped around the nape of his neck. With his arm bent behind his head and that short-sleeved sheriff's department shirt, it looked like his bicep was carved from stone. And now that I'd caught his attention, his dark gaze traveled over me, his eyebrow arched.

Jackson beckoned me closer as I shut the door behind me. He usually kept his door ajar but if history was any guide, we'd want it closed. The station was mostly empty but Cindy was out there and I wasn't taking any chances.

"Are you sure?" I whispered, pointing to the bullpen behind me. "I can come back later."

"Don't you dare leave," he said, his hand over the mouthpiece. His tongue poked out, tracing his lip as he studied my white sundress printed with green palm fronds. "Stay. Let me finish up this conference call but stay."

I moved toward the open chairs but he shook his head and motioned for me to come around the side of his desk. He repeated the gesture when I stood there, staring at him.

"Why am I going over there?" I asked.

"Because I want you over here," he mouthed.

With a saucy smirk, I rounded Jackson's desk and handed him the cupcakes. "Thought you might need a treat." I crossed my arms over my chest and leaned back against his desk, waiting for his reaction.

He didn't open the container. Instead, he set it aside and tapped his palm against the wooden surface of his desk. "Sit," he ordered. I gave him an *are you serious?* head tilt but he tapped the desk again. "Sit."

With an exaggerated eyeroll, I edged myself onto the surface. Jackson responded by grabbing me by the hips and dropping me right in front of him. He leaned back in his seat, his jaw tight and his eyes hooded as he looked me up and down. It felt like an appraisal. Then he nodded, brought his free hand to my ankle. His thumb stroked half moons into my skin.

"Eat," I said, my fingers drumming on the lid.

Jackson glanced at the container but responded with a curt shake of his head. I loved his stern sheriff vibe. He was such a soft, sweet teddy bear under the stares and head shakes and that made me love the stern even more.

I watched while he listened to the call, his brows sliding together or climbing up his forehead in reaction. Every few minutes he'd chime in with a comment or reach for his pen and scribble on the pad beside me. At one point, he scowled at the phone, rolled his eyes, and then dropped his head back against the chair.

Definitely time for a treat.

I pried open the container and scooped a dollop of frosting off the lid. I held out my finger to him, not at all surprised when he curled his hand around my wrist, tugged me forward, and licked every drop of frosting. His teeth scraped over the pad of my finger, sending electricity up my spine and through my limbs.

"You were in the kitchen without me," he whispered, pressing a kiss to the inside of my wrist.

"Don't worry," I replied. "I left all the dishes in the sink."

Jackson dipped his chin as his dark gazed settled on me. "Good girl," he mouthed.

Was it any wonder I couldn't keep my undies up around this man?

He reached for his pen, poised to write something, but then dropped it to the pad. "Thank you. I appreciate any insight the Bureau can offer on this matter," he said into the phone. "That's all. We'll be in touch if this matter continues to develop. Thank you again."

Jackson slammed the phone down, shot to his feet, and shoved his fingers through my hair.

"Look at you. Coming into my office in your pretty little dress with all your sweetness. Sitting on my desk like an angel waiting for permission to sin. Just look at you."

His lips hovered over mine as he watched me, waiting for a reaction.

"I thought you could use a break," I said, my gaze shifting from his eyes to his mouth. "And I know you like cream cheese frosting."

"Don't give me that," Jackson said. "You could walk in here with an empty potato sack and I'd still want to see you, beautiful."

I tilted my head up to meet his mouth, barely brushing my lips over his. A growl sounded in the back of his throat and his hands moved over my shoulders, down my back, up my flanks. He kissed me fast, almost aggressively. The desk was hard under my backside and I heard a crack of lightning off in the distance but none of it distracted from the way his tongue rolled over mine and he branded me with his kiss.

But then Jackson dropped into his chair and ran the back of his hand over his mouth. I was wild eyed and panting like a pack mule when he pointed at my dress and simply said, "Up."

"What?" I asked, my hands pressed to my chest to keep my heart from bursting free.

"The dress," he said, pointing. "I want it up."

I reached down, grabbing for the skirt's hem. I lifted it past my knees but stopped there. "Why?"

Jackson pushed the fabric to my waist but paused, his eyes narrowing as he stared between my legs. Eventually he glanced up, saying, "You brought me a treat and now I'm going to eat it."

I laugh-gasped as he tugged my undies down and tucked them in his pocket. *Oof.* I wasn't going to recover from the gleam in his eyes when he pocketed those panties. It was confident but also a little arrogant, like he knew what he was doing and he knew I wanted it too.

Jackson brought his hands to my thighs, pushing them apart as he scooted closer. His scruffy chin scraped the tender skin of my inner thighs and I cried out. It was a strange noise, somewhere between a yelp and a moan but also a little bit of *Oh, more, please, yes.*

Jackson glanced up at me, his eyes dark as night and his grin feral, and he said, "You'll get what you need, beautiful, but only if you're quiet. Can you do that for me?"

I nodded like a bobblehead doll.

He pressed his palm to my chest, forcing me back on my elbows, and then his head disappeared between my legs. I waited for what seemed like nineteen hours before I felt two fingers trailing over me. It was the lightest touch but the anticipation had my shoulders jerking up to my ears and my head falling back. Those two fingers continued tracing me from clit to core while he showered my inner thighs with kisses and tiny bites.

Every time his teeth closed around my skin, I was certain I was going to melt into a puddle and slide right off this desk. But then he released me and a thousand itty bitty fireworks went off in the exact same spot. It was a wild rush of heat and want and explosion.

It was making me crazy.

I was ready to tell Jackson that I couldn't take much more of this teasing but then those fingers parted me and he said, "You look fucking delicious."

His tongue swept over me and my elbows gave out.

Right there, that was it. I was done. Stick a fork in me. *Done.*

"Jackson," I whispered, reaching down to get a hold on his hair. There was something I wanted to say to him but I couldn't produce words when he was sucking on my clit. Just couldn't do it.

He pushed two fingers inside me and I had to layer both hands over my mouth to keep from moaning. His fingers moved in me, teasing over that perfect spot again and again. And his tongue on my clit and his scruff on my thighs. *Oh, hell.* There was no way I could stay quiet. This was too much. Far too much.

Desperate for a moment without his tongue and fingers and beard tormenting me, I twisted my fingers around his silky hair. He wasn't having it. He shook his head as he murmured his dissent.

"Jackson, you're killing me," I hissed.

His fingers stilled. He turned, kissing my inner thigh. No bite this time. "Good killing? Or bad killing?"

"G-g-good," I stammered. "Good killing. Great killing. Gonna lose my mind killing."

Jackson nipped at my thigh, setting off another itty bitty explosion before returning his tongue to my clit. But he didn't go back to business as usual. No, he redoubled his efforts. Leaving little bites all over my legs, my mound. Sucking my clit like he wanted an imprint of it on his tongue. Curling his fingers inside me until I went cross-eyed.

He did these wonderful things but he tortured me while doing it.

Backing off when my hips started rocking in a rhythm with his fingers. Lapping at my clit when I wanted more circling or sucking. Leaving kisses on my folds instead of the little fireworks I was craving.

It was possible I could stir up a thunderstorm from nothing more than the electricity coursing through my body. Everything was amazing but the type of amazing that was almost awful. This *hurt*. My core clenched around his fingers. My abs spasmed as if I was completing my hundredth set of crunches. I was coiled tight and vibrating, my body far past the point of desperation. I was convinced I was going to snap right in half if I didn't come soon.

Just when I was ready to tear off Jackson's trousers and sink down on his cock, his thumb pressed against my back channel and I went off. A switch flipped and a roar of heat blew through my body. It went on and on, one bright, burning pulse after another.

"That's right," he said, his fingers still moving as the waves rolled through me. "That's what you needed. Isn't it, beautiful?"

He gathered me in his arms and lifted me from the desk, settling me on his lap. His cock was hard against me. Hard and impossibly thick. Though I didn't believe my body was ready for rough chair sex, I loved the way he wanted me. I rocked against him, drawing a growl from him.

"I can't have you the way I need you right now, Annie," he whispered, his lips pressed to the tender skin below my ear. "But when I get home tonight, that's how I'm taking you. Understand?"

I nodded, not sure I could manage much more. This was the kind of sex that required a warm bath, a heavy blanket, and a bottle of wine afterward. I probably didn't qualify for any of those things since it wasn't technically sex, not in the traditional sense. But dammit, I was having that wine. And a moment sprawled on the sofa with my arm over my eyes, too.

"I missed you today," he said.

I sighed at that. No one had ever missed me before. "That's why I baked cupcakes for you," I said, as if that explained everything.

"Because I missed you?" Jackson asked.

I shook my head. "No," I replied with another sigh. "Because I missed you too." I shifted back to glance up at him. "But also, I had all these peaches and I had to do something with them."

"Entirely reasonable," he said, laughing. "Why don't you spend the night? That way, you won't have to miss me tomorrow morning."

My thighs burned against the fabric of his trousers, each one of those bites throbbing as the endorphins subsided.

"Not tonight," I said with a decisive nod. When he stared at me, his brows pinched and his lips turned down in a frown, I continued, "Give me tonight to miss you and just imagine the new things I'll bake up for you. I promise, it'll be worth it."

Jackson dragged his finger down the line of my jaw and said, "You know you don't have to bake me anything. Right? I don't ask to spend time with you so you'll feed me."

"I know," I said, running my teeth over my bottom lip.

I knew that. I believed it. I wasn't using pastries with Jackson the same way I used special order books with Owen. It had taken me the past couple of weeks to get to this point but I believed it now.

"But maybe," I added, cutting myself off before I could finish. "Maybe next week. Maybe I could spend the night then. Or the week after, or something like that."

That was what I needed. A due date. A timeline for ending this crazy mind game. I could figure out whether I was falling for him or falling for more of my old bullshit.

"If that's what you need, Annie, that's what you'll get," Jackson said, patting my backside.

Goddamn. I wanted this to be real. I wanted it more than anything.

16

———

BEATING

***v. The process of thoroughly combining ingredients and
incorporating air to make cakes light and fluffy.***

Jackson

I WAS DRINKING coffee in my kitchen, my feet bare and shirt draped over the back of a chair when my phone vibrated across the countertop. Even though Talbott's Cove was a town built on early mornings, only a few people would call me at this hour. Either there was an emergency or my mother wanted to chat.

A quick glance at the screen informed me there was no emergency.

"Hi, Mom," I said between sips. "Up with the roosters as always?"

"I'll sleep when I'm dead," she replied. "There's no sense lazing about. I just don't understand what people *do* in bed all morning. I can't lie there while the sun shines."

"Don't I know it," I murmured. "Since the sun has been shining for"—I glanced at my watch—"twenty minutes, what kind of trouble have you found for yourself today?"

"I don't find trouble, Jackson," she said, immediately impatient with me. "Trouble finds me."

"Don't I know it," I repeated.

My mother was born with the energy of ten rabbits, the work ethic of five horses, and the strength of two oxen. It sounded hyperbolic but it was the straight truth. Bonnie Lau was incapable of slacking off. She kept a garden that most considered a small farm, worked as a certified nursing assistant at an assisted living facility outside Albany, and regularly volunteered for a dozen or so charitable organizations. Meals for shut-ins, rides for veterans, knitted caps for preemies—she did it all.

"Well, I just talked to your sister," Mom announced, a pinch of purpose in her voice. She was in family update mode. That was preferable to interrogation mode. "Rachel decided to extend her stay in Belize through the new year and will be joining Teach For America next summer."

"Are we sure she's in the Peace Corps and not just chilling on a beach in Belize?" I teased. "If I was in Belize, I'd be on the beach."

"She's involved in important community health outreach programs," my mother replied.

"Of course," I continued, still ribbing her about Rachel's yearlong visit to Central America. My younger sister shared my mother's boundless energy and drive to do good, but she also had a touch of wanderlust. "And sneaking in a bit of beach time. Who wouldn't?"

"It's a good thing you're my favorite son," she said. "I wouldn't put up with this malarkey if you weren't."

"Only son, Mom," I replied. "I'm your only son."

I took another sip of my coffee while I prowled through the refrigerator for something to eat. If only I had some scones or donut holes...and an equally delicious woman to share them with. Unfortunately, that woman didn't enjoy spending the night here. Which wasn't to say she didn't visit. No, she was here almost every evening. She'd come over and I'd defile her on any solid surface we could find, and then we'd cook dinner together and she'd bake. But she always left at the end of the night.

She was immune to all persuasion efforts, even ones that included me on my knees with my head under her skirt. She wasn't having it and I accepted that as another one of her craggy boundaries I wasn't to cross. Even if we'd been going about the sex-dinner-baking-no-sleepovers routine for more than a month now, it was more important for me to keep Annette in my life than break through that boundary. She'd come around in good time, I was sure of it.

"Like I said," Mom countered. "We'll have a party for Rachel when she comes home next spring. I hope you can sneak away from Maine for a few days but I understand if you can't."

I settled on a banana and resolved to bring lunch to Annette this afternoon. Given some of my meetings at the county and late conference calls, it was going to be a late lunch if I could call it that. Then, I'd bring her home with me and take another run at those peach scones.

"As soon as you give me a timeframe narrower than 'next spring,' I'll put it on my calendar. Shouldn't be a problem."

I hesitated, wanting to add that I'd be bringing a date to Rachel's party. But that was a gamble, one I wasn't certain I wanted to take. I was all for confidence but I knew my limits. Even if Annette and I found a rhythm that worked for us, it didn't mean she wanted to drive down to New York and meet my entire family.

"Might as well spit it out," Mom said. "I can hear you hemming and hawing from three hundred miles away."

"I met," I started, uncertain, "I met someone." Mom paused for a moment, drawing in a breath as if she was about to speak but then stopping and humming to herself. "What? Is it that unfathomable?"

"No, not *unfathomable*," she said slowly. "Just surprising. The last time we talked, you said you weren't looking."

I chuckled at that. "I was *not* looking," I agreed. "But someone came into my life and I couldn't look away." Again, I paused. "If it works out and the timing is good for her schedule, I'd like to bring her home with me when Rachel returns."

I heard pages flipping and drawers closing on the other end of the line, but still no response.

"You're giving me a complex with all the murmurs and pauses, Mom."

"Are you working this weekend?" my mother called, her words spoken away from the phone. "I can't find your class schedule anywhere. It must've sprouted legs and walked off because I keep it right here and it's not right here."

My dad taught at a technical college outside Albany. It would've been a typical Monday through Friday gig if he didn't sign up to teach during every extra session the college offered its students.

When I was a teenager, I thought he took on these additional courses because my parents were hurting for money. Around my fourteenth birthday, I had a man-to-man talk with him and promised to get a job so I could help out. He laughed at me. A good, long laugh complete with tears rolling down his face. He explained that more cash was always nice but he taught those courses because he enjoyed his students that much.

"It's right there," my father shouted in the distance. "Put your glasses on, Bonnie Marie. It's staring you in the face."

"Just tell me if you're teaching," she shouted back.

"Open your eyes, woman," he replied. "I'm not teaching but that schedule is going to jump up and bite you on the nose."

"Everything all right down there?" I asked.

"Everything is perfect, Jackson. Don't you worry," she said. "I was just checking my schedule to see if I could rearrange a few things and it looks like I can. Isn't that great?"

"Rearrange what? What's happening?" I asked around a mouthful of banana.

"We can come visit you this weekend," Mom said. "Dad's not working and I can trade shifts with Mary Louisa Thompson because she owes me several favors. We don't have to wait until next spring to meet this woman, the one you're seeing. We can meet her this weekend and that's perfect timing because we're going to the Maciases' lake house next weekend and then there's the wedding for what's-her-name's daughter, the one with the unfortunate avocado allergy. No guacamole at that wedding, I'm guessing. But this is the best timing and I can't wait to meet this lucky lady of yours. What's her name? You know what, why don't you give me her number. I'll give her a call and introduce myself. We'll get along famously, I know it."

"I'm gonna need you to slow down there, Bonnie," I ordered. "Slow way down. These are some high octane plans. I understand that's your mode of operation but I'm going to need you to dial it back several notches. Things with this woman—"

"At least tell me her name," Mom begged.

"Annette," I replied. "Things with Annette are new. I need some time before I unleash the full force of Bonnie on her."

She sniffed but I knew she wasn't offended. She wasn't one quick to take offense. "Jackson, did you hear yourself? You said she came into your life and you couldn't look away." She huffed out a sigh. "I can appreciate that you want me to slow down even if it doesn't sound like you're heeding that advice. I want to get her on the phone, have a little chat. I want to know all about her, her work, her family. So many questions. And I'd like to find out how many grandbabies she's going to give me."

I leaned my forehead against the refrigerator as I groaned. *What have I done?*

"We'd love to meet her, Jackson. Don't you think it would be great if we drove up for a visit?" she asked. "We'll take it easy, I swear. It's just that you've never said anything like this before and I want to meet the woman who caught your attention."

"This weekend might be a bit soon. I'm not sure where this is going or if it's going to last. Give me a month," I said, but quickly thought better of it. "Or two."

"You're such a pragmatist," she said, a bit exasperated.

"Someone has to be," I murmured.

"Are you sure I can't call her?" Mom pressed. "Just a quick chat to let her know how excited I am to meet her. When I'm allowed. In a month or two."

"Put the guilt trip away," I said. "When the time is right, I'll make sure you get your fill of Annette."

"It's like you don't even trust me to place a phone call," she said. "You must like her if you don't want me embarrassing you with stories about you being the fattest baby in upstate New York."

"While I'm sure she'd love a story about my baby pudge, she's really busy," I said, hedging. "She owns her own business and has been teaching herself to bake and I'm trying to take as much of her free time as she'll—"

"Oh my god, I love her already," Mom said with a yelp. "Jackson, I'm so happy for you. This is the first woman you've mentioned in ages and I just want to give her the biggest hug because I know she's special to you."

"Yeah, she is," I agreed, smiling to myself. "I hate to cut this short but I have to hit the streets and check on my town, Mom."

"Well, I'm glad I caught you this morning," she said. "I'll make sure to call around this time again."

"Oh, wonderful," I murmured.

"Tell Annette we can't wait to meet her and we already adore her," she continued. "I hope you're eating fresh vegetables and keeping your checkbook balanced."

"As always," I said, shrugging my shirt over my shoulders. "Stay out of trouble."

"Why should I start now?" she replied with a hoot.

"MY MOM WANTS TO MEET YOU," I said as we lazed in bed, our breath still ragged and the sheets tangled around our feet. I rolled to the side and planted a kiss on Annette's shoulder. "She wants to come up with my dad for a weekend next month."

She reached back from where she lay on her side, her palm grazing my leg. "We're meeting the parents?"

Focused on tasting the entirety of her shoulder, I brushed her wavy hair out of my way and kissed my way around. "If you want," I replied, as noncommittal as possible.

I was catching feelings.

It wasn't a new thing. I'd been catching them right from the start. But those feelings were bigger now, heavier. They blew right past attraction and lust and orbited around love.

Love. I was falling in *love* with this woman.

"I wouldn't mind," Annette answered as she trailed her nails down the length of my thigh. It felt amazing, like a million tiny tingles rushing out in the wake left by her touch. "What did you tell them? About me? I guess I'm assuming you told them anything at all. Maybe you didn't. That's also fine."

I dragged my teeth over the ball of her shoulder, nipping her skin just enough to draw a squeak from her lips. "I told my mother that I met someone," I said simply. "Is that all right?"

"Yes, of course," she replied. "I hope it's not a problem but I haven't said anything to my family. We have a wonky relationship. I don't offer too many details. They find everything I do problematic anyway so I try to keep my distance. It's easier on everyone that way."

My brain was still rattled from the last orgasm, but my cock didn't care. Nope, it was basking in the glory of Annette's fingers on my thigh —so close but also so far—and throbbing to life. With each pass of her nails, my body slipped into the old rhythm of rocking toward her softness, her heat. Soon I was stiff again, my cock hurting for the relief only she could offer.

"Not a problem at all," I said through a grunt. "There's plenty of time. I'm not going anywhere."

It didn't make sense that someone as devoted and generous as Annette would have a strained family life. I should've asked for details on her family situation but couldn't see through this thick fog of want. Should've pushed her to explain how a family could sustain itself with a principal member keeping her distance and rationing news of her life. Instead, I set it aside with a mental vow to revisit it later.

"Good," she murmured, her palm sliding over my ass cheek. "I like you right here."

I looped my arm beneath her, flattening my hand on her belly. *Oh, fuck.* I wanted to have her just like this, our bodies side by side and the sweat barely dried from our last round. I wanted to watch my cock shuttling into her and then dragging back, her inner muscles clinging to me as I retreated. I wanted to watch her tits bounce and sway as I thrust into her and feel the vibrations of her moans and pleas. And then I wanted to wrap my arms around her spent body and fall asleep with her.

"I want you," I said, my words spoken to her skin. "Now. Just like this."

I felt her nod before I heard her response. "I'm never making those kouign-amann cakes, am I?"

"Maybe not tonight." I pulled her leg back to rest on top of mine. "But there's always tomorrow."

I ran my fingers over her cleft, groaning at the rush of wet waiting for me. Her nails dug into my ass cheek, clawing as I circled her clit. "It's been five tomorrows," she murmured. "But I'm not complaining."

She urged me closer, her nails scratching over my backside like the strike of a match. My cock twitched against the small of her back. My skin was pulled tight over my shaft, swollen and needy from root to tip.

"Come here, Jackson," she said, patting my thigh. "Come fuck me."

Canting my hips, I drove into her with one rough thrust. This angle was glorious. It was enough to bring those three little words to the tip of my tongue and I was only able to choke them back when I closed my teeth around her skin, marking her just the same.

"Just like that," she said, her words snapping out with each thrust.

I locked both arms around her torso, holding her close and still as I pounded into her. The minute she sensed my control over her body, a flood of hot, slippery arousal washed over my cock. She wanted me to play rough and possessive but she wanted me to cherish her while I did it.

"Yeah? This is what you need, Annie?" I dragged my palm up her belly and cupped her breast, plumping it, circling her nipple.

Her answer came in the form of a purr, her body shuddering under my grasp. Her inner walls fluttered around me like the wings of a thousand butterflies and it took every last shred of strength to hold back my orgasm another second. That was all I needed, one fucking second to pump into her before I let go.

"I need you," she whispered. "You're all I need. All I want."

Her words hit a trigger inside me, a place distant and primal. I pushed into her one last time, already brainless and on my way to boneless as the first spurts blasted out of me. Goddamn, I never wanted to leave this bed. The world could burn down around us and I'd stay here, buried in Annette. I didn't want the world to burn down but I was damn interested in staying here with my woman.

"I can't believe I've never asked you this but," Annette started, her voice dreamy, "why did you get into law enforcement?"

I pressed my forehead to her shoulder. "Annie, sweetheart," I said. "I can hear my pulse right now. I can't see straight. Don't get me wrong, I'm happy for it. But I'm working on keeping myself from drooling all over you. I'm not sure I'm up for meaningful conversation." I squeezed her backside. "Not unless you're telling me how I rocked your world."

"Oh, you did," she replied. "You rocked it so hard I'm hanging off the edge of the bed and staring at your police academy graduation photo."

"For Christ's sake, Annie," I muttered, scooting back to the middle and yanking her with me. "You should've said something. You were damn near on the floor."

"I did. Just now," she said, laughing. "I figure we would've gone over together so it would've been fine."

"Yeah, fine," I grumbled. "All you need is me fucking you off the bed and then falling on top of you." Annette rolled away from me and smothered a laugh into a pillow. "All right, I'll tell you but you need to bring your sweet ass back here." I patted the mattress.

"I knew you'd be a cuddler," she said, edging closer.

I had a smartass response at the ready but discarded it as I thought better. "I haven't always been a cuddler," I said. "This is a new development."

Annette nestled her head under my chin and I looped my arm around her shoulder. "Okay. Is that your way of telling me you want to talk about past loves or is it more a matter of learning how to stay warm now that you're a Maine-iac?"

I kissed the top of her head but didn't respond for a minute. In my mind, there was no one before Annette and no one after. I was hoping to hell it was the same way for her. "Neither?"

"That's a relief because I've gotta tell you, I don't know that I can listen to your greatest hits at the moment. Not after"—she swirled her finger between us—"everything. You might be in bed with me but that doesn't mean I want to hear about all the other women who came before me. Literally."

I kissed her head again, a broad smile stretched across my face. "Same."

After several minutes of silence, Annette leaned up on an elbow to glance at the clock. "I should head home. It's getting late."

I blinked at her, silently wishing for another hour with her. It wasn't about the sex, although it helped that we'd checked that box more than once tonight. I wanted to be with her, talk to her while we fell asleep, see her first thing in the morning.

"Sure. I'll walk you home." Annette held up her hand to protest but I swatted it away. "Don't," I warned. "I can deal with you leaving but I can't deal with you walking the streets alone at night. Say what you want about smashing the patriarchy and my toxic masculinity, but by god, I'm walking you home."

Annette tugged her dress over her head, no bra. That sight alone had me half hard again and ready to throw her back on the bed. Instead, I tucked my hands behind my head and watched her tend to her hair in my mirror. She was beautiful in the best ways. It wasn't the obvious type of beauty that anyone could spot from fifty paces. It was an easy smile and an easier warmth. It was hair that couldn't decide whether to curl or wave and did a little of both. It was thick, delicious thighs that parted like the pages of a book, opening to my favorite chapter. It was the quietly devastating way she took me into her body and turned my cock into her slave.

"Okay," she said, meeting my gaze in the mirror. "I guess I won't chip away at the patriarchy tonight."

"Thank you," I said, pushing up from the bed. My shaft slapped against my belly, still damp from her, still buzzing with pleasure. "You're sure I can't convince you to stay a bit longer?"

Aside from the chest-clutching shock of realizing I was thirty-seven years old and falling in love after less than two months with Annette, I had it good. I'd never had more satisfying sexual experiences since...ever. My belly was full of sweet pastries, my body and soul were well-tended, and life could only improve if a certain brunette book mistress would stay in my bed long after the sheets cooled.

Her eyes dropped to my cock, flaring when she realized I was primed for her. "Again?" she gasped.

"Well, you're not wearing a bra," I said, lifting my hands and letting them fall to my waist. "And you're fucking amazing, so there's that."

Annette gestured to the window, in the direction of the village and her apartment. "But I, um, I was going to..." Her voice trailed off as she glanced between my erection and the panes of glass.

"You could stay," I suggested, my words as neutral as I could manage. It'd been almost a week since the last time I'd broached this topic but I wasn't trying to rush things. As far as I was concerned, I had Annette in a manner no one else did and that was plenty for me. I didn't require declarations or anything grand, not when I knew she was pulling herself out of a bad spot with past relationships. I had her now and the rest would follow. "You have stayed here before. It wasn't so bad."

She barked out a laugh and covered her face with her hands. "That was a very different situation, Jackson."

I coiled my fingers around my shaft and gave it a light tug. "Not different at all," I replied. "This"—I tipped my chin down the length of my torso—"is exactly the same. It hurt so bad that night, Annie. So bad. Do you have any idea how hard I was for you? How much I wanted to crawl into this bed with you and feed you my cock? How much I wanted to taste you? How much I wanted to touch you and hold you?"

She stared at me, unblinking, as I stroked. Her pink tongue darted out to wet her lips once, twice. Then a new purpose flashed in her eyes and she stalked toward me. She covered my hand with hers, learning my grip and rhythm.

"My turn," she whispered, pushing my fingers aside as she dropped to her knees.

I wanted this—fuck yes, I wanted this—but I didn't. I wasn't going to come in her mouth and then walk her home. I was going to keep her in my bed, filled with my orgasms and held tight through the night. Just the way she needed.

I hooked my hands under her arms and yanked her back up. "No, I don't want that. Not tonight," I clarified.

"I thought blowjobs were always a good idea. Kind of like bacon." Stricken, Annette edged away from me. "I'm sorry."

Closing the distance between us, I reached for the hem of her dress but she pushed my hand away. "No apologies, Annie. Just stay. Please. I haven't done a decent job if you can walk out of here on steady legs."

Her gaze pinged to the ceiling, the clock, the windows. Anywhere but me. I didn't know what it was going to take for her to trust her instincts. They were in there, lurking right beneath the surface, waiting to replace this doubt with action.

"I never said my legs were steady," she whispered. "You've done a completely decent job. You've never left me with steady legs."

I crossed my arms over my chest, nodding. "All right. I'll take that. But I've never fucked you to sleep before. That's a damn shame."

Annette bunched her skirt in her hands, slowly lifting it up and over her head. "Then maybe it's time we try that."

When her dress hit the floor, I lunged for her, tumbling to the bed with her above me. I rolled her, settling in the notch between her legs. My cock, that mindless servant, flexed toward her heat as I leaned down to meet her lips, lacing a silent "I think I love you" every kiss.

DUST

v. To lightly sprinkle a dry ingredient such as flour, meal, or powdered sugar on a baked good or other surface.

Annette

Brooke: Where can I get a complete Thanksgiving dinner in the middle of August?
Brooke: I don't mean the ingredients. I'm talking about the fully cooked meal. Especially the goddamn mashed potatoes. I want to order it and have it delivered to the house. I could probably send someone to pick it up but I'd rather have it delivered.
Annette: Harris Farms might do that for you in November but I'm not sure they're taking orders now.
Annette: Why?
Brooke: You wouldn't believe me if I told you so I'm not going to tell you.
Annette: Okay. Sure. Nothing weird about that.
Annette: Do you want to meet up tonight? We could go somewhere

outside of town where people don't know us and they won't ask personal questions while taking our drink orders.

Brooke: I'd love to but I can't.

Brooke: Tell Jackson to take you on a real date. You two spend too much time fucking each other's brains out at his house.

Brooke: I can't believe I just said that.

Annette: Same.

Brooke: You can't believe it because you think I say the first things that come into my mind. I can't believe it because I am now realizing I think two people can spend too much time having sex.

Annette: Jackson is at a town council meeting tonight.

Brooke: Boring. If I wasn't stuck here, I'd definitely get dinner with you tonight.

Brooke: But you should go. It'll be fun.

Annette: You just said town council meetings are boring.

Brooke: You know how to have fun with them. Bring a flask, make a game out of it.

Brooke: Better yet, make a sexy game out of it. Put on something cute and cross your legs a lot. You won't be able to walk right when Jackson's done with you.

Annette: I do have some lemon squares here...

Brooke: I don't know how that figures into my recommendation but go for it, babe.

Annette: I was experimenting with recipes last night.

Brooke: Is that something kinky? Because we can be friends and we can talk about sex but I'm going to need you to warn me if we're blowing past vanilla and discussing all the flavors.

Annette: No, dearie, it's not kinky. I made lemon, orange, and key lime curds and then made different pastries with each one. I had a lot of assorted citrus squares left over when I was done. Jackson took the orange squares to the station this morning and I dropped the key lime off with the Mulcahey's house but now I have leftover lemon squares in my kitchen. I could probably bring them to the town council meeting.

Brooke: I hope these assholes appreciate you and your squares.

Annette: They do.

Brooke: All right, then. Put on something cute. Pack up your squares. Go distract that man.

Brooke: And tell me all the dirty details tomorrow.

Annette: I always do.

Brooke: I know. It's the only thing keeping me sane at this point.

Brooke: That and the dragon blood I drink for breakfast every morning.

Annette: That's beet juice, honey.

I SETTLED into an empty spot in the last row, my lemon squares on my lap and my tote bag still slung over my shoulder, and scanned the station's meeting room. This was the oldest portion of the station by hundreds of years and had once served as the town's courtroom. The wide plank floors creaked, thick beams bisected the ceiling, and it was said these benches were older than the state of Maine.

The room held no more than twenty-five or thirty people and about that many were gathered together in small groups or bent over their phones or newspapers. Owen Bartlett and the other members of the town council were huddled together beside a long table at the front of the room. I knew from past experience they were reviewing tonight's agenda and the list of residents signed up to speak during the public comment portion of the meeting.

From the hallway, I heard Jackson's voice. "There's something going on out there. I don't know what it is but I don't like it."

"I hear you, sheriff," someone replied. "But we might be fighting the wind. The fence coming down, the noises. Probably nothing more than some strong breezes that they're hearing now because the windows are open. They're anxious folks, ya know?"

I leaned back against the bench, turning my head in the direction of the hallway to catch more of their conversation.

"It's not the wind," Jackson argued, his tone firm. "They have every reason to be anxious. Something isn't right at the inn and I want eyes on that property every hour until I tell you otherwise."

"Understood, sir," the other man said.

"I have to step into this meeting now," Jackson said. "Update me in an hour."

Still staring in the direction of the hall, I smiled when Jackson walked through the door, his hands fisted at his waist and a scowl on his face. "I'm here and I brought lemon squares," I whispered, holding up the container.

"You're amazing," he replied, dropping beside me on the bench. He motioned for me to lift the lid. "You didn't tell me you were coming. I would've walked you over if I'd known."

Jackson helped himself to a lemon square as I shrugged. "I didn't decide until just now," I said. "Is everything all right? I heard you in the hall."

He licked the lemon curd from his fingers, his head bobbing from side to side. "Just keeping watch on a few things," he replied. "Did you lock your doors when you left?" I nodded. "That's what I like to hear."

I crossed my legs. His gaze followed the movement. "Aren't you supposed to sit up front?"

"Even if I am," he started, his attention on my strappy sandals, "I'm staying right here." He leaned forward, tucking a curl over my ear. "You know we're giving them something to talk about. Right?"

"Mmhmm." I shot quick glimpses around me, taking stock. JJ Harniczek was in the front row, his hat on backward and his arms crossed. The Fitzsimmonses were on the far left, the Lincolns a few rows away. Neither family spoke to anyone else. The DiLorenzos were showing off pictures of their new grandson. I was surprised I didn't find Owen's boyfriend Cole among the people gathered for this meeting. Perhaps they reserved their public snuggling for bookstores. "They haven't stopped looking since you sat down and shoved your hand into my dish."

His shoulders brushed mine as he laughed. "You love it when I do that," he murmured.

"You're right," I said, grinning. "I do."

Jackson tipped his head toward the people seated in front of us. "You're all right with this?" he asked. "You're good with everyone and their auntie showing up at your shop tomorrow, digging for dirt?"

Still smiling, I nodded. They'd come. I'd smile but say nothing substantial. The Cove would light up with speculation. It would be a lot of chatter but it would also be fine. "I'm great. How are you?"

"I'm simple man, Annie. I have you and I have lemon squares. There's not much else I could ask for." Jackson sat back, his knee bumping mine as he spread his legs. "But there's one other thing I've noticed," he said under his breath, his gaze straight ahead as the council members took their seats. "Your tits are falling out of that dress."

I'd taken Brooke's advice and changed into a yellow sundress printed with blue pineapples, one with a deep v-neck. "Oh, you noticed that?" I asked.

A growl sounded in Jackson's throat as he folded his arms over his chest. "This is going to be a long meeting."

MRS. BALL STEPPED up to the podium. There was a Mrs. Ball in every town, I was sure of it. She lived in everyone's business, found enjoyment in nothing, and didn't appear to age. She was elderly when I was a little kid—back when she gave popcorn balls as Halloween candy—and she was elderly now but didn't look a minute older than she did thirty years ago.

"There is an urgent need for a stoplight on my street," she announced, waving a spiral-bound notebook as she spoke.

"A stoplight," Owen repeated.

"It's necessary," she continued. "I've been watching the stop sign at the end of my street for the past month and I've written down the license plate numbers of each car that's failed to come to a complete stop. Thirty-four license plates. That's how many cars I've spotted rolling past the stop sign in *one month*."

Owen stared at her for a beat, then said, "A stoplight would involve hiring a surveyor to gather data on the intersection and assuming the surveyor agreed with your assessment, the public works department would dig up both Willis Point Road and Long Cove Way to run the electrical and install the proper posts. I'm talking about weeks of construction where access to your street would be limited. Once that was finished, you'd have the glare of a stoplight coming through your windows night and day. Is that what you want? Is that how you'd like us to address an otherwise safe intersection?"

Mrs. Ball paged through her notebook for a moment. "Then I'd like to know how the town plans to address the lawlessness on Long Cove," she said with a sniff. "It's clearly out of hand."

Owen shifted his stare from Mrs. Ball to Jackson. "I'm certain the sheriff will put the appropriate resources into the issue," he said. Jackson nodded in agreement. "Anything else, Mrs. Ball?"

"Not tonight," she replied. "But I'll be back next month."

"I would expect nothing less," Owen said. He glanced to the clock and made a note on his pad. "Meeting adjourned."

With that, Denise Primiani swiveled around to face us from the next bench. Her gaze swung between me and Jackson, back and forth, a knowing smile pinned on her lips.

Like most of the people at this meeting, I'd known Mrs. Primiani my whole life. I'd been close friends with her daughters when we were younger, before they moved away. She loved true crime stories. Couldn't get enough of them.

Like most people at this meeting, Mrs. Primiani was reading all the way into Jackson's choice of seats. The only difference between her and everyone else was that she was a teacher at same junior high where my mother and sisters taught.

"How are your parents doing, Annette?" she asked. "I haven't seen your mom since school ended. Is she having a good summer?"

Well...shit. Now, I was going to have to tell my family about Jackson.

"Oh, you know," I said, nodding unnecessarily. "She's good. Enjoying the time off."

I was smiling but a pit of dread opened in my stomach at the notion of announcing my relationship with Jackson to my family. That required an uncomfortable sequence of events where I told Jackson about my very nutty, very judgey family, then told my family about Jackson, and also managed to avoid presenting him at my mother's Sunday dinner table for inspection and interrogation.

Those dinners were ridiculous. There was no singular reason why they reached the level of insanity that they did but that was how it went when my mother and sisters were together. They were loud and a little mean, and they fed off each other, every opinion bolder and stronger than the one before.

As a kid, I'd spent most of the meal ignoring the spirited discussions they carried on, focused instead on the book I'd snuck in and hid under the table. They preferred it that way. I'd always been too young to understand or I didn't know the people or topics being discussed well enough to comment. They made sure I knew that. They liked to keep me in my place.

Now that my sisters were married and had kids and teenagers of their own, the dinners were different. Still spirited, still ridiculous, but bigger and somehow louder. Still a little bit mean. Since opening the shop, I'd made a point of staying open on Sundays *and* manning the counter for the singular purpose of avoiding those dinners.

"And what have you been up to this summer?" Mrs. Primiani asked, shooting another purposeful glance at Jackson.

"Jackson Lau," he said, extending his hand. "I don't believe we've been properly introduced."

Goddammit. I tried my hardest to fight off a grin but lost that battle, smiling down at my lemon squares. Of course he'd take that opening.

"Jackson, this is Denise Primiani. She lives down on Old Sheepscot Point," I said gesturing between them. "Mrs. Primiani meet Jackson Lau, our new sheriff."

I didn't blame him. We were sitting here in front of all our neighbors, as official as a Facebook relationship status update. He had no way of knowing the connection between Mrs. Primiani and my mother and sisters, or that I was extremely conservative about the information I shared with my family.

"Looks like this sheriff has a sweet tooth," Mrs. Primiani said, grinning at my nearly empty plate of lemon squares.

"When it comes to Annette's baking, I certainly do," he replied. "You should try one."

She shook her head, scrunched up her nose. "Oh, I couldn't. I gave up sugar."

"I'm sorry for your loss," I said.

She smacked the back of the bench and let out a deep laugh. "That's a good one," she said. "I had quite the mourning period but I'm slimming down for a cruise this winter. It'll be worth it."

"I'm sure it will be," I lied. I couldn't stomach the idea of giving up sugar. "Send my best to your girls. I hope they're doing well."

"I will," she replied, sliding out of the bench. "And say hello to your mom for me. I can't wait to catch up with her."

That was local-speak for "We are going to talk about this juicy new bit!"

"I will," I said, forcing my enthusiasm. "Have a good night."

Jackson stretched his arm across the back of the bench, his fingers resting near my shoulder. After a moment, he said, "Don't you think you've tortured me enough for one night? Don't you think it's time you let me take you home?"

I turned toward him, my mind still on Denise Primiani and the pit of dread in my stomach. But when I met his dark eyes, I wasn't worried about my parents or my sisters. I didn't need to figure out how I'd tell them about my relationship or gird myself against their cutting commentary.

There was something about Jackson. It'd always been there but it seemed bigger now, brighter. And it wasn't just the desire to get naked. It was so much more.

It was as if he came upon me and took stock of me and my aggregate parts, and said, "This is nice, your calm, collected existence but wouldn't it better if we turned it upside down?"

That was exactly what he was doing and I didn't want him to stop for anything.

BAKING BLIND

***v. The process of partially or fully baking a pastry case, such as a
pie crust, without filling.***

Jackson

IT WAS a great day for disasters.

I didn't make my opinions on the matter known but I was convinced
the arrival of the full moon came with the surge of calamity. Most people
brushed off that kind of thinking as old wives' tales or other nonsense
but I was a believer. There was a restlessness in the air when the moon
was ripe, one I was feeling today.

First, the innkeepers, Cleo and Rhys Neville, reported more suspicious activity on their land. Their dogs had spent the night barking at
nothing, their goats and chickens were spooked, and one section of their
back fence kept coming down. Once again, I didn't find any evidence of
trespassers but that didn't ease their minds.

We walked their property together, righted their fence, and adjusted
their motion-sensitive flood lights. I promised to keep a deputy
patrolling their street for the next few days and put another call into my

contact at the FBI. Even if she knew nothing, it kept the Nevilles' case on top of her mind. It wasn't much but short of razing the woods behind the inn and planting a sharpshooter on the roof, there was nothing left for me to do.

Shortly after leaving the Nevilles, a dog fell into a decommissioned well in the forest on the far end of town. The well was well off the hiking trail and required use of the off-road vehicles to bring in the proper equipment. It took several hours but the pup was rescued and shipped off to the local animal hospital to inspect his injuries.

Then I fielded a call about a group of teenagers rigging up a barge of fireworks. I found them gathered around a rudimentary raft and enough explosives to blow a crater in the beach. As it turned out, they were planning a big send-off for their friends going away to college next week. I was certain they had a cache of beer with them but didn't go looking for it. Instead, I pawned this issue off on the firefighters.

On the way back to the station, I spotted an elderly man walking along the coast road. This was the wrong spot for an afternoon stroll. The road hugged the rocky shoreline, leaving no room for sidewalks or shoulders. Drivers found the speed limit irritatingly low but with one lane and miles of turns and bends ahead, it was necessary.

I sped up and stopped at the least dangerous spot, then jogged back toward the man. I didn't recognize him until I was a few feet away. "Judge Markham," I called. "Out for a walk today, sir?"

"No time for pleasantries," he replied, his arms pumping at his sides. He was slow going but he was going. "Lead the way, bailiff. I'm late."

The judge was dressed in pajama pants, a white undershirt, and a dark brown bathrobe. Shiny dress shoes slapped the asphalt as he walked. I fell in step with him. "Where are we headed, sir?"

Pausing then, he met my eyes with an impatient glare. "To court," he replied. "I'm presiding over an important trial today, bailiff. You should know that."

"Yes, of course," I replied, nodding as I squinted at him. Judge Markham didn't leave the grounds of his estate often. I was told he preferred keeping to himself and puttering in his garden. But this wasn't reclusive. This was unwell. "Allow me to drive you to the courthouse. We'll get there faster."

I gestured to my SUV up ahead and he gave me a brisk nod. "Yes, very good. Hurry now. This trial is important. You should know that, bailiff."

After securing him in the back seat, I radioed the station. "Any missing persons reports this afternoon?" I asked, my voice low to avoid rousing the judge.

Cindy was quick to respond. "No, sir. Nothing's come up since that pupper took a bath and those kids trying to blow us to kingdom come."

I glanced in the rearview mirror and found the judge fashioning his robe's belt into a necktie. "All right," I said. "I'll be back within an hour or so. Let me know if you hear anything else."

"You got it, boss," she replied.

I followed the coast road up to the Markham estate. From the street, I spotted Brooke running across the lawn and a handful of other people spread out behind the main house. As I pulled into the driveway, I rolled down the window. "Brooke," I called.

She stopped and then sprinted toward me. "If you're here for rela-tionship advice, this is the wrong time." She rested her hands on her hips and bent at the waist as she caught her breath. "My father took a walk around the garden but now we're not sure where—"

"I have him," I said, hooking my thumb over my shoulder. The judge was busy adjusting his robe.

She pressed her palm to her chest as relief washed over her. Then she yelled, "Oh my god, what? Where was he?"

I opened the door and stepped onto the gravel, forcing her back a few steps. I wanted to have this conversation with some degree of privacy. "He was hiking up the coast road," I said. "He tells me he's late for court."

She sagged, her eyes drifting shut for a minute. "He's always late for court." Just as quickly as she'd softened, her spine snapped straight again. "Lettie," she called. "The sheriff picked him up. Take him inside, would you?"

A tall woman wearing pale pink scrubs headed for the SUV's back-seat to collect the judge. Two more women joined her. He was delivering a ruling, too busy with his recitation to notice the people shuffling him into the house.

"We need to have a conversation about this," I said, gesturing toward the cluster around her father.

"I am not obligated to discuss anything with you, sheriff," Brooke replied, her fear and vulnerability quickly replaced with her usual brand of firepower. "Thank you for finding him. There's nothing else for us to discuss."

"Brooke, I am only trying to help you," I argued. "Has he wandered off before? Is it Alzheimer's? Dementia?"

"It's none of your fucking business and I don't need your help," she replied. "I have this under control."

"Excuse me, ma'am, but you don't," I replied. "He was gone long enough to make it a mile and a half from home and in that time, you didn't report him missing."

"He's never left the grounds before," she said. "I fully intended to contact the station if we couldn't find him on the property."

"Your property covers half the town," I argued. "With all due respect, ma'am, you should've called the minute he went missing."

She eyed me up and down. "He's home now. That's the only thing that matters."

"I have to disagree with you, ma'am. He was walking along one of the most dangerous highways in the state. Aside from the fact he could've been hit by a car, he could've tripped and fallen off a rocky cliff into the ocean." I gestured to the house. "It seems like you have assistance here but it wasn't enough this time and you're fooling yourself if you think it won't happen again."

Brooke ran her tongue along her upper lip and crossed her arms. "Thank you for bringing my father home. You can go now."

I stared at her, frustrated that she wouldn't use her good sense and let me help her protect him. "The next time this happens, call me immediately," I said, stabbing the air between us. There would be a next time, I'd put money on it. If the judge found a way to give his caretakers the slip today, he'd do it again. "Whatever territorial pride issue that's preventing you from recognizing reason won't help you the next time he's gone."

"Thank you again," she said, inclining her head toward the street. "I trust you'll show yourself out."

"Does Annette know about this?"

Brooke blinked at me, unmoved. That lady was a tough nut to crack. "I'm not obligated to answer that question," she replied. "You'd do well to keep Annette out of this and keep your private life separate from the professional."

With that, she stalked into the house and slammed the door behind her.

By the time I made it back to the station, it was late in the afternoon. I was tired and hungry, and in need of some good news. Hell, I'd be happy with no news if it meant I could grab a bite to eat.

Cindy greeted me with a fistful of messages and a folded newspaper. "Nothing urgent except Debbie Ball standing in the middle of the street yelling at cars again. She's been at it every day for the past week. She hasn't let up since the town council meeting," she said, tapping her finger on the papers. "But there's a nice write-up about our little Annette's bookstore, right here in the Portland paper. Fancy, huh?"

"Very fancy," I agreed, tucking the papers under my arm. "Thanks, Cindy."

"You got it, boss," she chirped. "I'm gonna take my break now if it's no trouble. Annette has a few books squirreled away for me. I'll only be a few minutes but I can wait if you need anything from me."

"Go right ahead. No trouble at all."

I headed into my office but left the door open. I dropped everything on my desk to scrounge for a snack. My search turned up little more than a bag of pretzels that seemed too flat to yield anything of substance.

I thumbed through the messages and returned several calls. While I listened to Mrs. Ball rattle off the license plate numbers of every car she spotted rolling the stop sign near her house, I paged through the newspaper in search of Annette.

"I'll send a deputy out to watch that intersection," I promised. "Bye now, Mrs. Ball."

Once I reached the Lifestyle section, I found Annette's smiling face. She was gorgeous as always but it was her confidence that radiated from the page. She had her arm resting on the counter inside her shop, piles of books at her back. I remembered her wearing that dress several weeks ago, the aqua one with the funky print along the hem. After the interview, I'd dragged her into the storeroom, ducked under the skirt, and offered my congratulations with my tongue.

A sidebar listed her top new releases of the past summer as well as her all-time favorites, plus recommendations for younger readers. The page was loaded with bright photos of Annette's shop and close-ups of her chatting with customers. They were great shots and Annette looked amazing. The article, that was another story.

The reporter went for the lady bookseller angle, favoring *lady* over *book*. I would've been on board with a good boost for women-owned businesses but the interview centered around her personal life rather than her career.

The reporter seemed to draw connections between Annette's favorite books and her marital status, writing, "It's no surprise this lover of all things Jane Austen is holding out for Mr. Right. When asked about her own experiences with romance, Ms. Cortassi demurred but later admitted she was 'very single.'"

I would've been all right with "single." I could've taken that punch and gone on fighting but "very single" knocked me out. I was on the ground, my eyes crossed and stars spinning over my head, and it took me a full minute of reminding myself that interview took place a *month* ago to get back up.

Blinking down at the newspaper, I skimmed the last paragraphs. Thankfully, I wasn't tempted to put my fist through a wall while reading but I still resented the hell out of this reporter. I had a mind to write a letter to the editor, complaining about that reporter's lack of profession-alism. Readers deserved better than reporters who saw nothing more than a woman's bare ring finger.

And I wanted to talk to Annette about this. About the *very*. We were going to get a few things straight, yes, we were. There was no *single*, no *very*, none of it. Even if the interview hadn't aged well, I wanted to hear that from her.

I pushed out of my chair and pivoted, facing Annette's shop. It seemed like she had some customers in there but I could go in through the back door and wait until she was finished. We'd talk, we'd make sense of this impasse, and then I'd take my woman home with me. Keep her home with me.

CURDLING

v. The condition when a food mixture separates into its component parts.

Annette

THE LAST THING I expected to see this afternoon was my mother and sisters marching through the village like they were storming the beaches. My hands froze over the stack of books on the counter as I watched them descend on my shop in near-identical outfits: yoga pants, neon sneakers, t-shirts emblazoned with the regional middle school's mascot, a fuckton of makeup.

"What do I owe you, dear?" Cindy asked, snapping me out of my surprise-visit-induced stupor.

"Sorry about that," I murmured, blinking down at the counter. I added the last of Cindy's selections and pivoted the sales screen toward her. "Twenty ninety-seven."

She thumbed a few bills from the purse she kept belted around her waist. Some would call it a fanny pack. Cindy wasn't one of those people.

She called it a cross-body bag and didn't have time for anyone who tried to correct her.

"I have twenty-one dollars and two pennies for you," she said, sliding the money toward me, "for a nickel back."

I bagged her books, my gaze continuously pinging over her shoulder at my family as they neared the shop. I was able to convince myself they were in town for reasons other than visiting with me. Perhaps they wanted ice cream from the local creamery or craved some fried fish goodness from The Galley. Better yet, they were getting their steps in with a harbor view today. All perfectly reasonable.

"I think you'll like this one," I said, gesturing to the newest in a series about a family of hunky, swoony California winemakers. "Steamy. Real steamy. But a lot of substance, too."

"I bet you're right," Cindy answered, her smile wide and her eyes glittering with the joy of getting lost in a new story. "If you don't mind, I'm just going to browse a bit more. Poke around. See if I can't blow the whole paycheck."

"Be my guest," I said with a forced laugh. I couldn't find any humor with my family on the sidewalk.

When the door chime announced their arrival, I played busy. My focus on the box of new releases in front of me, I called, "I'll be right with you. Just looking over next week's new titles. I know one of them is going to fly right off the shelves and I won't be able to—"

"We're not here to talk about books, Annette," Nella said.

"Well, not right now," Lydia added.

"But can we talk about that dress real quick?" Rosa asked, zigzagging her finger in my direction. "Because the cut is fine but the color is a crime against your skin tone. I swear to god, Annette, I'm going to clean out your closet one of these days and get rid of all the pastel. Baby shades don't work for you."

"You're right," Nella murmured.

Glancing up, I worked hard at pulling a surprised expression. It wasn't that I didn't enjoy seeing my family. I did. I also liked the time and space to mentally fortify myself for those interactions. And wine. I liked wine.

"Oh my gosh! What are you guys doing here?" I asked, holding my arms wide but staying behind the counter. Not in a million years was I acknowledging that comment about my dress. I loved this pale pink sundress and I wasn't parting with it for anything. My sisters could lapse into full-on Fashion Police mode on me and I didn't have one good shit to give about it.

I held a big smile while my sisters and mother exchanged wordless glances and tiny shrugs. It went on for a solid two minutes, long enough to catch Cindy's attention over in the romance section. She gave them a quick once-over and went back to her browsing. Whichever plan they'd hatched on the way here—because they always had plans—had gone to shit when they walked in.

Eventually, my mother asked, "Annette, are you dating Sheriff Lau?"

A shocked, breathy noise rattled in my throat, like I was gagging on a laugh. I hadn't been expecting this visit but I should've expected that question. I didn't look toward Cindy or the romance section. I couldn't meet her gaze for anything. "What? What are you talking about?"

"See? I told you it was ridiculous," Rosa said, giving my mother and sisters a sharp look. "Can we go now?"

I went back to fussing with the box in front of me. I wasn't lying, not exactly. I just wasn't confirming anything. It was an omission, for sure, but I needed more time to formulate my approach with my family. If I appeared disinterested and blew off their questions, I'd buy myself a month or two. That was what I needed to prepare Jackson for a Cortassi family dinner-slash-inquisition and pray he didn't run far and fast in the opposite direction.

"If you're not involved with him, well, that's—that's *good*," my mother said. "A relief, really."

"A relief?" I asked. I was glad I hadn't said anything. This way, I could hear what they really thought. I went on shuffling the contents of this box as if it required an extreme attention to detail. "How do you figure that?"

Rosa smiled as she stepped toward me. "We wouldn't want you getting hurt."

"Okay," I said, dragging the word all the way out. "Not sure about that but thanks."

"He's just out of your league, honey. It wouldn't work out in the long run," Rosa said. "Think about it. If you're honest with yourself, I'm sure you'll see we're right."

Ice shot through my veins, freezing me where I stood. Rosa wasn't one to make oblique comments so she wasn't saying that to hurt me. She was saying it because she believed it. Part of me believed it, too. I'd always believed it.

"And after everything that happened with Owen," Nella added. The cringe on her face said it all. She didn't have to say another word but she couldn't help but provide an annotated history of my missteps. "Where you kept trying to force it with him and he clearly didn't want that, and you didn't know how to recognize a brush-off when you saw one, and you spent a couple of years looking desperate? You don't want to do that again."

"You don't," Lydia agreed. "It doesn't matter what you two are doing. You shouldn't try to force it with the sheriff, Annette."

I jabbed a finger at them. "You're being kind of awful right now. You're welcome to rest this case at any time."

Nella folded her arms as she sent me a smug glare. She was good at that, being smug. I couldn't say it suited her but it was certainly a skill she possessed.

"We're telling you the truth," Nella argued. "We care about you. We wouldn't be saying this if we didn't."

"I mean, there are ways to get your point across without also being awful," I said, shrugging. "I'm just saying."

"Sometimes the truth hurts. It's a lot like getting your vag waxed," Rosa said. "And you seem really sensitive for someone who claims she isn't hooking up with the sheriff."

"Your sisters are right," Mom said, leaving no room for dispute. "Whatever you think is happening between you and the sheriff, it's time to let it go. You two aren't a good match."

"Not at all," Nella insisted.

"Cool," I deadpanned. "Not sure about all that but thanks for your concern."

I wanted to argue. Tell them they knew nothing about me and Jackson. Insist I was worthy of a man like Jackson. Remind them I'd never questioned them or their relative value when they were dating their now-husbands.

I wanted to cry. Walk away, sink down into a dark corner, and cry. The door chimes sounded and I answered Cindy's wave with one of my own.

"He needs a wifey-wife and you're not into the wifey gig," Nella continued. Goddamn, I wanted to throw a book at her head. "You don't cook, you don't iron, you're not into the whole happy home thing. There are too many nice girls around here who would do that for him. Don't make him believe he should settle."

"We're only looking out for you, Annette," Mom added. "We don't want to see you following that poor man around like you did with Owen. Like Nella said, it was desperate. You don't attract a man with desperation."

Their words stung but I wasn't going to let them see that. I wasn't going to let them see anything.

I wanted to argue. Tell them they knew nothing about me or Jackson. Insist I was worthy of a man like him. Remind them I'd never questioned them or their relative value when they were dating their now-husbands.

I wanted to cry. Walk away, sink dark down into a corner, and cry. Forget all the barbs and backhanded comments—the open-fist ones, too—and pour it out.

I wanted Jackson. I wanted to get lost in him and his unyielding comfort, and I wanted him to promise me they were wrong. But now I knew what they'd think about me and Jackson, together. What they'd say when I wasn't in the room. I'd always known it would be this way but hearing it from them cemented it for me.

I also wanted to school my family on gender roles in modern society. I didn't know where they got off with this line of thinking. It was moments like these that made me question my lineage.

Somewhere in the far reaches of my soul, I found an extra store of saccharine sweetness and forced the brightest damn smile of my life. "That's enough about crazy town gossip. What's for one day," I said, shaking my head hard. "What's going on with you guys?"

Rosa fluffed her ponytail with an exaggerated groan. "We've been setting up our classrooms all morning," she said. "My room was such a disaster."

Everything made more sense now. The workout gear, the freshest cut from the rumor mill. Denise Primiani wasn't getting any baked good from me for the rest of the year.

"I can't believe how much work I have left before the first day of school," Lydia said. "I'm going to be in my classroom nonstop for the next two weeks. Goodbye, beach. Goodbye, vacation."

"It's the same every year," Rosa snapped. "Stop thinking it's going to be different because you use colored tape to organize your boxes at the end of the year."

"Why was it so bad?" I asked. It was an honest question. I didn't understand why classroom setup was such a time-consuming experience every time August came to a close.

"Oh, Annette, you should've seen it," Mom said, rubbing her brow. "The entire building was painted over the summer and everything was in a pile in the center of my room. Chairs, desks, books, boxes, everything. It was like climbing Kilimanjaro just to get started."

"I was completely convinced I was going to die in a landslide," Nella added. "It's amazing that none of us are trapped under a pile of desks."

"It was bad but I didn't think I was going to die," Rosa said.

"The summers when they paint are the worst," Mom replied. "If I wasn't retiring at the end of this year, I would've painted the room myself and been done with it."

"That seems...difficult," I said.

"You have no idea," Nella said. She was wagging that finger again and I was working overtime to keep my expression easy. "Honestly, though. You don't know the first thing about getting a classroom ready for the first day of school. You have it so easy, Annette."

This book was practically begging me to chuck it at her.

"I sure don't," I replied. "Understand, that is. I don't understand."

Lydia dug through her purse, absently saying, "We have to go. We're meeting the rest of the English Language Arts department for vertical alignment planning and we're going to be late if we don't leave now."

"Oh, yeah," Rosa said, touching her fingertips to her temples. "Winnie Walton asked me if you could recommend some new young adult historical fiction books for her World War Two unit. I told her I wasn't sure if you knew anything about kids' books."

I could put up with some bullshit but this was one pile too many. "I do," I snapped. I flung my arm toward the left side of the shop. The one overflowing with children's and young adult books. "Plenty. Tell her to stop by or shoot me an email. I have tons of new titles her students would love."

Rosa blinked at the life-size Harry Potter cutout in the corner. "Yeah, I guess so," she murmured. "Huh. I've never noticed that."

"Rosa, you can have this conversation some other time. I'm grade chair this year," Nella said. "I can't be late for this meeting."

"Girls," Mom chided. "I'll meet you in the car." Shaking her head, she stepped away from my sisters and met me at the counter. "Annette, sweetheart, promise me you won't chase the new sheriff. If he's interested, he'll come to you."

"Mom," I said, laughing off her comment. "I get what you're saying. Loud and painfully clear. Okay?"

She tipped her head to the side, her lips folded together as she regarded me. "I want the best things for you," she said.

I believed that, too. She wanted me to be happy and have everything I wanted. The only issue was that she also believed I should lower my expectations and cram myself into a tiny, wifey box. Back when I started talking about opening a bookstore in Talbott's Cove, she insisted I'd be content working at the big chain bookstore outside town. She'd argued it would be easier, less stressful, more secure. I'd have a consistent paycheck and reliable health insurance, and I understood where she was coming from. That was my mother's way of caring—being extremely risk averse.

But it also had the effect of taking an axe to my sense of agency.

"I know you do, Mom," I replied.

She straightened a display of greeting cards and postcards before stepping back. "All right. Angie Dixon's son is moving back home next month. I'm sure you remember him. Since you're *not* dating anyone," she said pointedly, "I'll talk to her about setting you two up."

I reached out, trying to snatch that idea away from her. "Mom—"

"Don't worry about a thing. I'll take care of it all," she promised.

I stared after my mother as she exited my shop and hiked across the village. With her went a wave of adrenaline and I slouched against the counter. It wasn't always like this with my family. Most of the time, they ignored me, going about their inside conversations without noticing the outsider. But there were occasions when I had a clan of mothers, each one intent on babying me in her way.

It wasn't just the babying though. It was the minimizing, the way they confined me to that tiny cube and told me it was all I could have. Everything else, it wasn't for me. Too big, too small, too ambitious, wrong league. It left me hollowed out.

Abandoning the new releases, I trudged toward the storeroom. I needed some water and a brownie because brownies made everything better.

Instead of a brownie, I found Jackson leaning against the table. It was a casual pose, his arms folded across his chest, his long legs stretched out before him and crossed at the ankles, but it was his expression that had me frozen in the doorway. His head was tipped down, his gaze steady on the floor but distant, his jaw clenched. His collar was open at the base of his neck. I stared at the golden skin there for a long moment.

"I dropped by to say hello because I wanted to talk to you," he started, his tone sharper than any knife, "and I learned you're not dating anyone and your mother is fixing you up with other men."

I clasped my hands together and tucked them under my chin, the only shield I had from this war on two fronts. On the one side was my family and their insistence I wasn't meant for a man like Jackson. I could scrape the black-tarred stick of their words away—and I would—but I'd always know they believed he was settling with me. That he could—and should—do much better than the bookish chick who didn't own an iron. It didn't matter that they were wrong or that I'd discarded that notion as soon as they floated it. They'd never look at me and Jackson with anything less than exasperated hand-wringing and I wasn't sure I could continue scraping that away without leaving myself tender and raw in the process.

On the other side, Jackson wanted so much more than I could fathom. He wanted all the relationship bells and whistles but I didn't know how to operate the most basic bell and I couldn't find my whistles.

He was ready for all these things and I was busy constructing a bridge of spun sugar. It was a thin, fragile connection between me and all of my doubt and issues to his boundless belief in us.

In the middle of it all was me and the creeping notion that I wasn't meant for this man. What had I done to deserve him? Nothing. He happened to drag my drunk ass home one night and I'd employed my limitless talent of making it awkward. If not for that run-in, we would've gone along without seeing each other naked. I'd forced this, just as I had with Owen.

He pushed away from the table and paced toward me, all six-foot-something of him towering over me. I knew he wasn't attempting to intimidate me but I already felt so small after my family's visit that I couldn't help but shrink even further.

"If we're not together, Annette, would you care to explain to me what we are?"

20

———————————

PUNCHING DOWN

v. The process of pushing dough down, pulling the edges in on itself, and flipping it over after it has reached the point of doubling in size.

Jackson

"IF WE'RE NOT TOGETHER, ANNETTE," I started, gazing down at her, "would you care to explain to me what we are?"

She dragged her teeth over her lower lip and asked, "How much of that did you hear?"

"Is that the best you've got?" I asked. "I had to read about you being very single in the Portland paper and then I listened to you dodging every question about our relationship. I need you to do better."

She shook her head and pressed her clasped hands to her mouth. "I'm sorry. I am so sorry, Jackson. I wish I had the right thing to say but you've caught me at a bad moment and I'm fresh out of the right things. All I have is wrong. Actually, I came in here to gorge myself on chocolate. That's how much wrong I'm working with today."

I shoved my fingers through my hair as I stared at her, desperate for more. Just a bit. I only needed a hint that we were on the same team but I wasn't getting it. "Then help me understand," I replied. "Tell me why your mother is setting you up with Angie Dixon's son and you're not refusing. I want to understand this. I want a reason to stay instead of walking out right now."

Annette started to reply but stopped herself, her hands holding back the words. She blinked away, her gaze darting to the table behind me, the door, the boxes in the corner. I didn't understand what was going on here but I couldn't climb out of my mad to figure it out.

"I don't think I can give you what you need," she said eventually. "Not right now, maybe not ever. I mean, I don't even iron. I'm sorry. I'm sorry about everything."

"Were you planning to go through with that date?" I asked, my patience far past frayed. "At least tell me that much."

She buried her face in her hands. "My mother is always trying to set me up with people. I smile and nod, but nothing comes of it."

"Is that what you're doing now? Smiling and nodding, and letting me believe we're in a really fucking intense relationship? Because that's what it seems like today."

We stared at each other for full minutes but didn't move an inch closer to comprehending anything. And perhaps that was my biggest issue, beyond the very single, the refusal to acknowledge that we're together, the blind date. We didn't understand each other and we couldn't fuck our way out of it anymore.

That realization sank in my stomach like a stone. I couldn't stay here, not when I wanted to wrap her up in my arms and snap her out of that fifty-yard stare. And wasn't that a bitch? Even as she was pushing, pushing, pushing me away, I wanted her more than ever.

"If you ever figure out what you want, give me a call," I said, backing toward the door. With one hand on the knob, I raised the other in a wave. "And god help me, Annette, keep this damn door locked."

21

———————————

FERMENTATION

***n. The chemical change in a food during the baking process in
which enzymes leaven a dough and add flavor.***

Annette

I SPENT the rest of the day flying on autopilot. I didn't remember the people who came through the shop, what we talked about, or which books I sold them. But I made it through without spending more than a stray minute or two acknowledging the day's bruises.

When the storefront was closed for the evening, I dropped onto one of the toadstool-shaped pouf pillows in the children's section. There, in the shop's darkened quiet, I felt those bruises. The ones from my family barely registered. They were the mauve-gray shadows that came and went without much notice.

The one from Jackson—the one I'd caused—that was different. It was deep blue with angry red around the point of impact. I'd feel it in every breath and movement. The ache would rouse me from sleep. It would take months to fade and even then, the pain would pang through me without reason.

I thought about calling Jackson, explaining the mess he'd walked into this afternoon. But this fight wasn't about the mess. It was about me and all the trouble I had accepting love. Not just accepting it but cultivating it, defending it, keeping it. I knew that now, sitting on the toadstool in the dark long after he'd left be in the storeroom, but I didn't know how to fix it.

Knowing was one thing. Solving was a different one altogether.

I could call Jackson or go to his house and say, "Oh, hi there. Just so you know, my family verbally bitch-slapped me this afternoon and they'll always think you're too good for me. Needless to say, I was in a wonky place when you dropped in. Also, I'm kind of a mess because I can't make heads or tails of real, true affection and I don't know how to take what you're giving in a healthy way. Can you bear with me while I figure it out?"

I could do that but I didn't think I could manage if Jackson said no. And after the way I'd reacted to him, how could he respond with anything other than a resounding no? My family was awful to me and I was awful to Jackson. All that awful needed somewhere to go and I'd dumped it on the one person who *knew* me, *cared* about me, *chose* me.

Instead of reaching out to Jackson, I picked my phone up from the floor beside me. Swiping it to life, I found several messages from Brooke. Nothing from Jackson—my whole reason for keeping the device nearby —but that didn't surprise me. He'd made it clear he was waiting for my move.

Brooke: Can we talk?
Brooke: I can't leave the house tonight. Would you mind coming here?
Annette: Do you have wine?
Brooke: Of course.
Annette: Okay. I'll head over in a few minutes. I have to put myself together.
Brooke: Don't pretty yourself up on my account.
Annette: I wasn't planning on pretty but I do have to get off the floor and find my purse.
Brooke: Why are you on the floor?

Brooke: No. Don't answer that now. Just come over. I'm out on the porch with a bucket full of screw-cap pinot and cheese.

Annette: Bless you.

Brooke: To clarify, the cheese is on a plate with crackers and nuts. The wine is in the bucket. I don't eat cheese out of buckets.

Annette: That's probably for the best.

Brooke: Probably.

"BOTTOMS UP," Brooke said as she clinked her glass against mine.

As I sipped my wine, I stared out at Talbott's Cove. It wasn't dark yet but that shadowy space between evening and night that forced you to stop, look at the sky, and wonder how any other moment in a day could be so grand. Even now, as I sagged into this wicker rocking chair to lick my wounds and numb my emotional exhaustion, I couldn't help but love this little town.

"Nice night, huh?" Brooke remarked.

"Yeah," I said, motioning toward the horizon. Some summer nights in the Cove were unpleasant. *Unbearable* didn't begin to describe the combination of heat and humidity. But this, tonight, was the best the summer had to offer. Cool air with a gentle sea breeze. The scents of ocean and woods mingling together. Dragonflies swooping from flower to flower in the garden. Pinprick stars winking in the sky. "You have an incredible view up here."

"I'm sorry I haven't invited you to visit recently," she said, busying herself with the brie. "Things have been complicated since I came home."

I nodded. "Family is complicated. I know all about that," I added.

After a long pause, Brooke said, "I screamed at your boyfriend today. Maybe it wasn't screaming but it was a more assertive conversation than my usual."

"I'm not sure he's my boyfriend at the moment," I murmured.

"Wait. What? What's going on?" she asked, leaning on the arm of her rocking chair. "Is it because I yelled at him?"

"I don't think so," I replied, "but why were you yelling at him?"

She held up one finger. "You tell me your story and then I'll tell you mine."

"My mom and sisters paid me a visit this afternoon. It was one of their usual 'we love you so we're going to say terrible things' shows. I rolled my eyes so hard, I burned calories."

"About what?" Brooke cried. "I want to know about these terrible things so I can dispute each one."

"They've heard rumors about me and Jackson," I said. "They don't feel we're well matched."

"And why the fuck not?" Brooke asked, her brow crinkled. "Aside from being jealous that you snagged the prime rib while they have to go home to their ground beef, what's the complaint?"

"They claim Jackson needs a wife to iron his shirts and make casseroles for dinner." I pointed at myself. "And I'm not qualified on either count."

Brooke waved a hand in front of her face as she blinked, processing my response. "I'm sorry, I'm so confused right now. Are we saying that Sheriff Lau, the former badass lieutenant from the New York State Police, is capable of neither dressing nor feeding himself? Is that a correct summation of the facts as presented?"

I held up my hands. "Apparently, yes. They want me to get out of the way of the women who can do that for him, and also, I'm pathetic and embarrassing because all I do is follow around guys who don't want me."

I'd tried to keep a cavalier attitude about this. Tried to shake those barbs off. But my voice caught on those last three words and tears surged to my eyes. I refused to cry, not because I couldn't be vulnerable with Brooke but because my sisters didn't deserve that much of a reaction from me.

"And they hate this dress," I added.

"Honest to god," Brooke said, holding up her hand. "I want to throw rocks at them. Can we go now? Please? At least let me slash their tires. I've always wanted to do that."

"Maybe then you'd get arrested and I could force an interaction with Jackson," I said, sniffle-laughing.

"I'd get arrested for you any day. Twice on a day when Jackson was doing the cuffing," she said. "Okay so you've told me about the evil step-sisters—"

"They're not *step*sisters," I argued.

"I don't care," Brooke replied. "They act like evil stepsisters. You're their Cinderella. It's obnoxious and I want to go slash their tires after you explain why this means you're on the outs with Jackson."

I reached for the wine and topped off our glasses. "He overheard some of it. The part where I didn't object when my mother decided she was going to fix me up. Probably more. With my luck, I'm sure he heard the whole damn thing and tallied up all the times I let my sisters believe nothing was going on between us."

"Yeah, that was a brilliant move," she said.

"Thanks. Really, thank you. I needed someone to crystalize it for me."

Brooke leaned back in her chair and crossed her legs. "I'm just wondering why you didn't tell them to get the fuck out of your business. Even if Jackson hadn't heard anything, it would've addressed the issue of your people being shit-stirrers drunk on their own stew."

"Because it's easier to ignore them than engage," I replied. "Every family has its issues. Mine is chronically miffed by everything I do. Does it mean I'm going to cut them off, never talk to them again? No. Does it mean they're going to listen if I raise hell and insist they knock their shit off? Also, no. I have to make peace with who I am and who they are, and stop letting their issues impact me. It doesn't matter what they think about my clothes or my work, and it doesn't matter whether they think I'm good enough for Jackson."

Brooke traced the rim of her glass before saying, "The only difference between you and Cinderella is that Cinderella actively tried to get the fuck out of the attic when the prince came around with the glass slipper. You're sitting here with me and the bucket of wine. Seems like you've chosen poorly."

I gave her a bland face. "You asked me here to talk. Have you forgotten that part?"

"Not at all," she said. "But if you'd mentioned that you were due to follow up on some pressing matters with Sheriff Prime Rib, I would've understood." She brought her hand to her chest. "*I'm* a good person.

Unlike those sister bitches of yours, *I* actually care about you. I'm also living vicariously through your adventures with the man meat but I'm still a good person."

"A good person who yelled at Jackson today," I added. "What was that all about?"

Brooke glanced away, picking at the cheese plate between us. She blew out a breath, sipped her wine, then turned her attention back to the plate. She was quiet for a minute or two, focused only on freeing the grapes from their stems.

"I yelled at Jackson because he told me my dad isn't okay," she said slowly. "He's right. That's why I yelled at him. Dad isn't okay and I don't know what to do."

I reached over and gripped her hand. "I know, but we'll figure it out."

The details were hazy but I knew enough to fill in many of the blanks. I used to see Judge Markham in the village every day, but over the past two years, he seemed to fade away.

He used to walk down, pick up a newspaper, and read it cover to cover at DiLorenzo's counter while eating his standard order of fried eggs and with a side of pancakes. He'd always attended the town council meetings, often piping up with minutes-long monologues about laws and regulations, local history, and the ways things used to be around here. But he'd retreated into his gardens, ate his breakfast at home, skipped meetings. And then Brooke returned to the Cove, leaving a big career and a big life in Manhattan. As close as we were, she had yet to mention the reason for her return.

But it didn't matter whether I had the full story or not. Brooke was my friend and I could support her without getting a complete accounting of the issues.

"Are you sure?" Brooke asked, her voice watery.

"I am. I'm sure. Between the two of us, we can solve any problem," I replied.

"And Jackson. We need him," she added, blinking away tears. "You're gonna have to make things right with him because he's rather handy and I will continue to push for a sister-wife arrangement."

"I'll see what I can do," I said.

"You can do better than that," Brooke snapped. "You're fucking fabulous and when you're fucking fabulous, you take what you want without apology."

We stayed there, our hands clasped tight against the home-front battles ahead of us, and drained two bottles of wine. We ducked inside for the bathroom at one point, more cheese at another. We never circled back to her father, Jackson, or my family, instead devoting our time to discussing our shared affection for a retired collection of lip colors and whether we should make time to go shopping in Portland next month. She needed something fancy for her computer, I needed a deeper pie dish. It was the most superficial of conversations but we needed this kind of mindlessness tonight.

If friends were good for anything, it was softening life's hardest edges by doing little more than being there with a bucket of wine and easy chatter.

"I'm sad that sundress season will be ending soon," I said. "But I'm also excited for boot season. And long sweater season. It's more complicated than sundress season but it's basically a game of mixing jeans and leggings with boots and sweaters. Boots and long sweaters are the best."

Brooke gestured toward her faded orange running shorts and ratty Yale t-shirt. Only she could make that look like a style worth replicating. "Yeah, same."

"We'll get you some full-length yoga pants," I said. "Some boots, too. We'll call it shut-in chic."

"Speaking of shoes, I want to go back to that prince and the glass slipper," Brooke said, holding up a finger. "Can we talk about that? Not the part about you feeling like you deserve your sisters shitting on your love life or you pushing Jackson away because you've bought into their bullshit but the actual slipper. Who in their right mind would wear a shoe made of glass? Have you ever broken a heel?" She didn't wait for my response, instead barreling on. "It's fucking disastrous. It's like a high-speed blowout. One minute, you're cruising along. The next, you're swerving across five lanes of traffic and probably rolling over into a ditch. Add a glass heel to the mix and I'm done. Honestly, the most unrealistic part of Cinderella is not the fairy godmother or the sewing birds or the dude who doesn't recognize a woman he hung out with all night, it's the goddamn glass slippers."

"You feel very strongly about this," I said, laughing.

"Yes! My biggest fear is stepping on glass. Why the fuck would I put myself in a position to willfully stab myself in the feet?"

I grinned at her, shrugging. "It's just not your fairy tale, honey. Doesn't mean you won't get one."

22

———

CATALYST

n. An ingredient that helps bring about change without itself being changed.

Annette

THE SOUND of sirens pulled me from a deep sleep. I bolted upright, blinking into the darkness as I tried to remember where I was and how long I'd been asleep. It came back to me in pieces. The walk home from Brooke's house. Flopping onto my bed, fully dressed. Promising myself I'd get up, wash my face, and change into my pajamas after I cried for a few minutes. It seemed like a fair bargain since I hadn't cried once today.

But instead of shedding some dainty tears and moving on with life, I fell into spine-shaking sobs. It wasn't about Jackson or my family or the issues facing Brooke, but everything, all the hurts I'd socked away. I wasn't sure all that crying yielded anything more than a good emotional purge and accompanying headache, but that was fine. It was out and that was better than holding it in.

Pushing off the bed, my palm flattened against my forehead to keep the pounding at bay, I went to the window. It was unusual to hear sirens unless there was a fire but the engine doors were shut. Then I noticed lights flashing in the distance. Three SUVs raced out from behind the station and through the village. My heart flipped and then my stomach followed suit. Knowing Jackson was in one of those SUVs and rushing toward something potentially dangerous had me wide awake.

Since I was still dressed, I slipped on a pair of flip-flops, grabbed my phone and keys, and headed out. I wasn't alone. Sirens didn't blare at three in the morning without bringing the entire town to the streets. We were a nosy lot here in Talbott's Cove. And I couldn't go back to sleep without laying eyes on Jackson. I needed to know he was all right.

I made my way toward the station, exchanging confused shrugs and yawns with my neighbors. No one knew what was going on but everyone had theories. Car accidents, domestic disputes, wild animals at the back door. All of it was plausible.

Cindy lumbered over to me with a walkie-talkie clipped to the neck of her sweatshirt and her cane in hand, and held out a shawl. "Come on, now. Take this. You'll catch your death out here, dear."

I accepted the shawl and linked my arm with hers. "Thank you," I said. "Do you know anything?"

Her lips folded into a faint line as she shook her head. "Nothin'," she said. "But I know our sheriff was on patrol tonight, him and the other boys, too. He wanted all hands on deck."

"Does he do that often?" I asked, scanning the crowd again.

Cindy hummed to herself. "He's only been here a short time," she said. "I'm still learning his methods."

In other words, no.

"Don't pull that face," Cindy chided. "It took me twenty years to learn the last boss. I'm a slow study. Not like you, picking up new things like magic."

"Magic?" I asked, laughing. "No magic here."

"Don't be silly," she said, whacking my arm. "You taught yourself how to start a business and now you've been at it for how long? Six, seven years?"

"Almost seven," I replied.

"And don't forget about the baking. Good gravy, I've gained an extra love handle since you started visiting the sheriff. If you marry him, I won't fit into my bikini anymore."

"I've given up on mine," I said with a laugh. I wasn't touching that marriage comment with a marble rolling pin. "No one's complained yet."

"You've got yourself a good one," she said with a knowing grin. I started to joke about the firefighters lusting over her but she whacked my arm again. "Your sisters are boring and they wear too much makeup. What's with all the bronzer? It's just silly. Don't listen to them."

I glanced at her, studying the laugh lines around her mouth and eyes. "I try not to."

"Don't listen to your mother either. She's just as bad with the bronzer and she has a twig up her rear end. I don't know where it came from since your grandmother is such a saint but it's lodged way up there," Cindy continued. "But that sheriff of ours, you go on and listen to him. He knows his mind and he knows you're one in a million."

"I'm working on it," I said, bumping my shoulder against hers.

Flashing lights tore open the night as a caravan of law enforcement vehicles drove through the village. "They're coming back," Cindy said. "I'm going to head inside and put things in order. Who knows what they'll need when they get here." She stepped forward, her arm still linked with mine. "Let's go. You can stay in the sheriff's office. He'd hate it if I left you out here in the cold."

"Cindy, there's barely a breeze," I argued. "I'm fine out here."

She flapped her hands, nearly putting my eye out with her cane. "He'd want you inside."

Before I could respond, Jackson's SUV pulled into the parking lot with four deputies' vehicles immediately behind him.

"Time for me to skedaddle," Cindy called. She shot me a baleful glance and hobbled away. "Come on in when you're ready."

The crowd closed in as Jackson stepped out of his vehicle. He seemed well and unharmed, all limbs accounted for and no blood in sight. I gathered the ends of the shawl in my fist, holding it as tight as possible to keep me from falling apart with relief.

Jackson flattened his hand against the backseat door while he conversed with the deputies assembled around him. They seemed to be strategizing, motioning between themselves and toward the public safety building. It was the wrong time to fixate on the way his uniform trousers hugged his ass and thighs but I was doing it anyway. His posture—strong and assertive with his feet spread and shoulders back—made me salivate. I wanted to go to him and fix everything right now. I also wanted to rip my undies off but that was nothing new when it came to Jackson.

From behind me, I heard someone say, "It could be the Fitzsimmons boy."

"That's what I thought," another agreed. "Nothing but trouble, that one."

"He was never a nice boy," someone else chimed in. "Problems with him right from the start."

"It's these parents nowadays," a fourth voice added. "Too permissive. Always wanting to be friends. In my time, we said 'spare the rod, spoil the child.' No spoiling in my house and my boys turned out just fine."

"He's in rehab," an irritable neighbor said. It sounded like JJ Harniczek but I was too busy watching Jackson to turn around and verify my suspicions. "You should give the kid some credit. He's workin' at it, he's tryin' to kick the habit. Not easy shit. You think you're all so good and holy, why don't you save your judgment for your next talk with god, huh?"

After a pause, someone said, "Maybe it's Lincoln. I love the guy but he's an angry drunk."

"Nah, that's not true. I've never seen anything like that."

"Everyone knows there are problems in that house. Always fighting, always storming out. He put his fist through a window a few years back. You remember that, don'tcha?"

"It's not Lincoln," the irritable neighbor snapped. "You people need to knock this shit off. Might as well go back to bed so you can piss and moan in comfort."

"Who can sleep with all this noise? And the lights? My god, do they need to make such a racket?"

"Why won't they just open the door? What are they waiting for?"

"I heard they found him at the Nevilles' inn. Didn't get inside the house or anywhere near their baby, thank heavens, but had weapons on him."

"Those poor people. They've been through so much."

"I couldn't go on, knowing one of the men who killed my entire family was still on the loose. Couldn't do it at all. The stress alone would take me."

"Might not be loose anymore."

"The sheriff's been spending a lot of time out there recently. At that inn. He's kept a good eye on that place. Probably saved that family from another tragedy."

"I had my doubts about this sheriff but he's a good egg. Just hope he lasts."

"Quiet, quiet, something's happening," someone hissed.

The deputies closed in around Jackson while he opened the backseat door and reached in to collect the prisoner. They headed toward the station, Jackson walking with one hand on the prisoner's cuffed wrists, the other on his shoulder.

The questions and murmurs continued around me but I stopped listening when Jackson's gaze met mine for a heartbeat.

For that single second, everything was good and right and he was coming back to me and I'd fix everything.

But he looked away, turning his hard gaze and equally hard jaw toward the station and all my doubts returned. Then he disappeared inside.

The crowd lingered outside the station for a bit, trading theories and rumors as news trickled out from the Nevilles' neighbors. Some claimed the perpetrator was inside the inn, others insisted he was apprehended near the inn. It was said there was a cache of guns and knives found in the woods. It was also said there was a bag of rope and duct tape. There was talk of calling in the FBI, and then a hearty debate about keeping the feds out of our town.

No one knew all the details but one thing was decided: Talbott's Cove was keeping Jackson Lau. Any doubts the townspeople might've harbored toward this out-of-state transplant sheriff were gone. He was ours now.

And all I wanted was to call him mine.

LAMINATION

n. A preparation consisting of many thin layers of dough separated by butter, produced by repeated folding and rolling.

Jackson

I WAS dead on my feet. Hadn't slept in two days, couldn't remember my last meal or shower, and didn't know whose shirt I was wearing. My scruff was crossing into beard territory. I was shuffling along, coffee and adrenaline serving as my only sources of energy. There was no other description for my current state of existence.

Even if I managed to drag myself home now that the dust was settling, I couldn't bear an empty house. Every room was scented with memories of Annette and I couldn't go there without walking out and heading straight for her. I wanted Annette's comfort more than anything. I wanted it but I wasn't certain I could have it, claim it as my own.

I went on shuffling, pushing forward as best I could.

Prior to settling in Talbott's Cove, I believed life here would be slower. Without the mad hustle of the city, it had to be. Small towns like this didn't experience ongoing cycles of crime and violence.

To a degree, I was right about the pace of life. Instead of investigating assaults and homicides, my days were spent mediating neighborly disputes and fishing dogs out of wells. That change made all the difference for me. But this small town wasn't immune from anything.

The team of FBI agents parked in my conference room proved that.

They were busy collecting forensic evidence from the inn, poring over the logs of my recent visits with the Nevilles, and interviewing damn near half the town. They'd already transported the prisoner to a federal facility in Vermont, which was one burden off my small office. Talbott's Cove didn't have the type of high-security facility necessary to jail a suspect who'd twice slipped out of state custody.

I passed the conference room on the way to my office, saluting the agents with a brief wave. Some of my residents disagreed but I was thrilled to have the feds here. No pissing contests from me. To my mind, they had a broader set of resources at their disposal to build the case against the Nevilles' attacker and they were best suited to handle the matter.

A call came through just as I dropped into my seat. In the two days since apprehending the attacker, my phone hadn't stopped ringing. Between reporters thirsty for details and state officials offering assistance or insisting I make Talbott's Cove my home for the long haul, I'd talked myself hoarse. I appreciated the wave of support from outside the town but it was the local backing that truly mattered. I hated that it took the thwarting of a deadly attack to rally the Cove around me as sheriff but I wasn't complaining.

"Sheriff Lau," I answered.

"Listen up, sheriff, because I'm only going to say this once," boomed Brooke Markham's voice. "Get off your ass and go to her."

A surprise laugh burst from my lips. "Excuse me?"

"I told you to listen," she chided. "Honestly, if you weren't Grade A man meat, I'd be done with you right now."

"I see," I replied, not knowing what else to say. In need of a prop to occupy my hands, I reached for my lukewarm coffee.

"Actually, you don't see a damn thing," she said. "You don't realize that you and Annette are rowing at different speeds and instead of moving forward, you're turning in a circle. That doesn't mean you need to stop rowing, bro. It means you need to match her pace, let her build up the strength and stamina to meet you at your level. Stop focusing on her shortcomings and start acknowledging her progress."

I sipped the coffee. It tasted like dirt. "Thank you for this insight, Brooke."

"No. No, that's not how this is going to pan out," she said. "You're going to fix this shit."

On a sigh, I leaned my head against my palm. "How would you recommend I do that? If you haven't noticed, I'm in the middle of a major investigation here."

"My sources tell me the FBI has it under control and they'll be packing up by the end of the day," she replied. "You did your part, sheriff. You caught the guy. Now, go get the girl."

"Brooke, I admire your tenacity and loyalty to Annette—"

"You want to talk loyalty?" she interjected. "I'll tell you a little story about loyalty. Annette is my best friend in the whole world. She's my sister, maybe not by blood but by every other standard that matters. Believe me when I say I'd kill for her."

"Don't tell me that," I said, groaning.

"It's true," she cried.

"You still shouldn't tell me that."

"I'm just saying, I'd do anything for that girl. But her actual sisters? They're miserable, jealous cows. They went to her shop the other day and had full-on baby tantrums because they heard you two were together."

"Why would that matter to them?" I asked, sitting up straighter. "Why would they be unhappy with her?"

"Like I said, they're miserable, jealous cows," she replied. "They know you're prime rib and they don't want Annette to have you. They said shitty things about her being pathetic and desperate for chasing after you, and how she needed to get out of the way because you needed someone with a decent tuna noodle casserole recipe. And that, my friend, is why you heard Annette telling her mother you two aren't in love and getting married and having all the babies."

I slapped my hand on the desk as I pushed to my feet. "That's horseshit," I snarled. "Her sisters? Her *sisters* said this?"

"And this brings me back to my original point about loyalty," Brooke said with a cluck of her tongue. "I know I can call her on *her* worst day and she'll still show up for me. There's nothing I won't do for my girl and that's the reason for this call."

Pausing, I turned to gaze at the village outside my window. The sun shone at an angle that obliterated my view into Annette's shop but I still watched, waiting for a glimpse of her. I hadn't allowed myself that much since storming out the back door and now I couldn't look away. I was drawn to her like a force field, a magnetic pull I hadn't been able to ignore since my first morning in this seat. What made me think I'd ever be able to resist it? Resist her?

I couldn't and I didn't want to. I loved Annette all the way through and back again. I loved her warmth and the joy she found in things as simple as a beautiful blueberry or finding someone the right book. I loved her sweet and her fire, my very own Fireball shot. I loved the way she poured herself into her baking and her bookstore and her friends. And me. I loved that way she gave herself to me and asked nothing in return.

But that was the catch, wasn't it? She asked nothing in return. She expected nothing. Either she didn't know how to demand it or she didn't think she deserved it, and I'd failed to right that wrong in the most critical moment.

I wasn't about to fail again.

"Tell me what to do."

A throaty laugh came across the line. "Very good. Let's get started with short-term tactical responses and move on to longer-term strategic solutions. You'll want to write this down."

PARTIALLY SET

v. To refrigerate a mixture until it thickens to the consistency of unbeaten egg whites.

Annette

Brooke: Let's go to The Galley tonight.
Annette: Can't. I'm banned for life.
Brooke: No one has ever been banned from The Galley, certainly not you. Meet me there around 7, okay? Don't make me drink alone.
Annette: I love you but I'm not suited for mixed company. Maybe wine at your place?
Brooke: I want to be around people tonight.
Annette: And I wanted to try out a cream pie recipe tonight.
Brooke: Wait, did you talk to Jackson?
Annette: Not yet. Why?
Brooke: I mean...
Annette: Yes?
Brooke: Never mind. I've spent too much of life in the company of frat boys.

Brooke: Don't even think about ditching me. I'll go to your place and drag you out of the kitchen.
Annette: Understood but please be aware you're buying the drinks tonight.
Brooke: You got it, babe.

BEFORE LEAVING to meet Brooke at The Galley, I flipped through my calendar and counted the days since my last visit. Forty-two. I should've been able to estimate that without tapping my fingertip against each uniform square but I couldn't believe so much time—and so little—had passed since that night.

I remembered the chin-quivering ache that sent me in search of liquid pain relief. It'd seemed like a real, palpable hurt, something I could wrap my hands around. And maybe it was. Looking back on it, I could barely reach those feelings of sadness, loss, humiliation. They were there but they weren't the same as the rough stab of regret I experienced every time my thoughts wandered to Jackson.

I should've handled things differently. I knew that now. It was possible I knew it in the moment but I'd been rubbed raw by the interaction with my family and didn't say the right things. Rather, I ran in the opposite direction of the right things and now I was busy charting my way back.

There were no plans, no recipes for fixing things with Jackson. I'd spent the past couple of days paging through cookbooks and browsing foodie blogs to find the pastry that said "I'm sorry and I want to fix things but I'm also scared and don't know how."

Food was magical like that. With a single dish, one was able to say a million different things. *Welcome home. Congratulations. Marry me. Happy birthday. My condolences. Feel better. I'm sorry. I love you.*

I'd tested a few recipes last night in the hopes of stumbling onto the perfect combination of heart, comfort, and sweet. Chocolate zucchini cake, banana bread, éclairs. None of them were quite right and I couldn't go to Jackson until I had it right. Until I'd folded my love for him in with the dry ingredients and knew he'd be able to taste it in every crumb.

Before closing the shop for the night, I noticed a text from Brooke.

Brooke: Running late. Grab a seat at the bar and I'll be there soon.
Annette: Is everything okay?
Brooke: Fine. Dealing with stuff at the house.
Annette: We can reschedule. Or I can go there. Whatever you want...
Brooke: Stop it right now. I'll be there soon. Ish. Soonish.

WITH THAT KNOWLEDGE, I grabbed two new cookbooks and tucked them into my tote bag. Perhaps I'd find the Rosetta Stone of pastries in one of them. Once the shop was locked up, I headed to the scene of the original crime—The Galley. I returned, my head held high, and Owen and Cole showed up not more than two minutes after I settled into a seat at the bar.

Of course.

But it wasn't just my former fake flame and his boyfriend. The entire town—or so it seemed—was at The Galley tonight.

JJ Harniczek tossed a coaster in my direction, the cardboard square spinning across the bar top. "Long time, no see," he remarked. "Did it take you all this time to shake off the hangover?"

I reached into my bag for one of the books and set it in front of me. "I'm going to read my book until Brooke gets here," I said, tapping my palm against the cover. "We don't have to talk about vodka and other bad memories."

"Bam Bam's coming?" JJ asked with a hoot. "I'm really gonna need the sheriff tonight. One of you, well, that's one kind of trouble. The two of you? That's a lot more trouble. Should I call him now or wait until you're nice and sloshed?"

I didn't want to meet Jackson on these terms again. I didn't want him coming to my rescue and putting me back together when I was capable of rescuing myself, putting myself back together.

I gave JJ an unimpressed stare and opened my book. "Make yourself useful. Go pour me some pinot grigio," I said, flicking my hand toward the bottles lined up behind him.

JJ dropped his forearms to the bar and leaned forward. "You used to be a good girl," he said. "All prim and proper, keepin' your shoes shined and your nose clean." He eyed me, as if he was seeing me for the first time. "You're not so good anymore, are you?"

"I'm pretty sure pinot grigio is the official drink of good girls everywhere," I replied.

He shook his head as he pushed away from the bar. "You've changed since the last time your behind warmed that seat," he said. "Not so good anymore."

I didn't refute JJ's comment. I didn't want to address any changes—real or otherwise—that I'd experienced in the past forty-two days. Instead, I paged through my book, sipped my wine, and tried my best to keep from staring at Cole and Owen. Trying didn't equal succeeding.

I wasn't watching them out of morbid fascination or pointless jealousy. I was watching because I felt nothing for them. I had no emotional or romantic connection to Owen, not now and not then. There was little more than familiarity between us and my misplaced hope that familiarity would blossom and bear fruit.

That I'd survived for so long on so little only served to remind me that I was used to begging for scraps. I'd accepted those scraps as proof of affection, fondness, maybe even the inklings of love. I'd settled for those scraps, convincing myself they were plenty. That I could stitch together threadbare rags and form a connection worthy of my heart, my soul, my body.

When you were used to scrounging for scraps, real affection was tough to swallow.

Shortly after I requested a refill, Brooke arrived. She waved to me but found herself snared in a conversation on the opposite end of the bar. It wasn't uncommon for my neighbors to ask after her father and wax on about the time he said one thing or did another. She was always polite about it, answering questions with a pleasant-but-fake smile, nodding along as they reminisced about events she didn't recall. I didn't know how she did it, carrying the world and all its secrets on her shoulders. She made it seem effortless but I saw the cracks in the foundation.

I ordered a glass of wine for her and returned to my books. The minutes ticked by while Brooke kept that hollow smile plastered on her face and JJ peppered me with vague comments about behaving myself tonight, and then silence swept through the tavern. Glancing up, I found Cole and Owen cozied up in their booth, their heads bent together.

I smiled at them, wishing them well in this small gesture. They didn't need my acceptance or approval to love each other but I still wanted them to know we were good. No hard feelings, no awkwardness.

Returning to my cookbook, I got lost in an intricate linzer torte recipe that started with a detailed accounting of the cake's history and permutations through the centuries. It wasn't until the main door clattered that I looked up and found Jackson darkening The Galley's doorway. On a gust of wind, the door banged behind him again, drawing the attention of everyone in the tavern.

He stood there a moment, his shoulders nearly broad enough to brush the doorframe as he scanned the room, and then his gaze fell on me. His golden arms were bent at the elbows, his hands loosely gripping his duty belt. That pose had the fabric of his short-sleeved sheriff's shirt straining around his thick biceps and my lips parting on a sigh.

I found a deep store of confidence, one I wasn't sure I had anymore, and smiled at him. This wasn't how I'd imagined I'd see him again but here we were, no baked goods in sight and the entire town our audience. He blinked at me, once, twice, thrice before allowing the corner of his lip to turn up in response. I tipped my head toward the empty seat beside me, the one reserved for my best friend, and raised my eyebrows.

It was an invitation, one I hoped he'd take even if I didn't have the haziest idea what I was going to say or do if he joined me.

Jackson strode across the tavern, certain and bold, as if sent to collect me. It occurred to me that he was here for that exact reason. I peeked at JJ, who was reading the back of a whiskey bottle like it revealed the secrets to a long life.

"This will come back to you, Jedidiah," I hissed. "Don't think I'll forget."

"Can't imagine what you're talking about," he replied, watching as Jackson stopped at my side.

"Annette," Jackson said, his deep voice raking over my name. "I'm taking you home."

"Not until you settle up your tab," JJ called.

Jackson dropped some bills on the bar and pushed them toward JJ without taking his eyes off me. "I'm taking you home," he repeated.

"Can we talk first?" I asked, gesturing to the empty seat.

He shook his head once, a curt movement that had my edginess rising. He didn't want to sit, didn't want to talk...what was I missing?

"I am taking you home, Annette," Jackson said, each word crisper than the one before. Then, softly, "Please, beautiful. I need you right now."

And that was it. That was all I required to hop off the stool and gather my books.

"Give me that," he ordered, reaching for my tote bag.

I snatched it away with an exasperated frown. "I've got it," I said, swinging the tote over my shoulder. "It's two books and I can't let you pay for my drinks and carry my bag all on the same night. These people are going to think I'm a kept woman or something."

Jackson brought his hand to my lower back and bent to brush his lips over the shell of my ear. "That's exactly what I'd like them to think."

25

———

GLAZE

v. To brush food with milk, egg, or sugar before baking in order to produce a shiny, golden finish.

Jackson

I HADN'T EXPECTED to march through The Galley and claim Annette with the whole town watching us over their grilled swordfish, but Brooke was right. It was the best way to kill a whole lot of birds with one stone.

There was no credence to the suggestion Annette was the one doing the chasing, not when I made it clear to everyone watching she was mine.

There was no denying we had a history, one that transcended our roles of sheriff and bookseller.

There was no hiding the relief I felt when she climbed off that stool and I was certain everyone saw it on my face, too.

She'd played her part well with that flare of fire when I'd tried to relieve her of her bag. No one could argue there wasn't heat between us.

I knew Annette's family wouldn't be at The Galley but I also knew this would get back to them. And I wasn't done. No, we had another stop on our route before heading home.

"Jackson," Annette said slowly, glancing up at me, "can we talk now?"

I led her across the street, toward the alley behind her shop, and took her in my arms. I'd never believed the touch of another could soothe me down to my core but Annette, she was my balm.

"I missed you today," I whispered. "Yesterday, too. I don't want to miss you anymore."

She nodded, her head rubbing against my chest as she moved. "I missed you, too," she confessed. "But I have a lot of things to say and I think I should say them."

"Can you talk and pack at the same time?" I asked. "Because I meant it when I said I was taking you home now."

Annette stared at me for a moment, her wide, dark eyes blinking up at me as if I'd spoken another language and she needed time to translate. Eventually, she said, "I can't. I can't talk and pack, I have to say this now."

"Okay," I said. "Go ahead. I won't rush you."

She brought her hands to my chest, her gaze locked on the buttons running down my shirt. She bit her lip, hesitating before she spoke.

"I'm just learning how to do this. I'm—I'm going to make mistakes. I'm going to push you away because I don't know what to do with big feelings and big love but I want to get better at it. At this." She tapped her chest and then mine. "At us."

"I'm going to pull you right back," I said, scooping her up in my arms and backing her up against the building. I wanted her body pressed to mine but I also needed some help staying upright. "I'm going to want everything with you and you're going to have to tell me when to slow down. I can handle it, I swear. Just tell me what you need and promise you'll give me a chance to adjust."

"I love you," she whispered, a deep valley of awe in her words. "And I want to let you love me, even when it's scary and overwhelming."

"I've loved you since the first moment I set eyes on your ankles," I replied. "I saw you from my office and my heart broke free from my chest and climbed into your hands."

I kissed her then, fast and hard, just like we'd fallen for each other.

She tasted like wine and comfort, and I found myself rocking into the heat between her legs. I was exhausted and in desperate need of sleep but my cock was ready to go all night.

"Isn't this illegal?" she asked against my lips. "Public indecency or something?"

"That's why I'm trying to take you home," I said, groaning as the friction spiraled through me. "Quick. We're running upstairs and getting all the things you need for the next day or two. Your favorite whisk, the rolling pin you favor, aprons with flamingos on them, a few of those white dresses I like so much. Just the basics. Panties are unnecessary."

"Whisks, rolling pins, aprons," Annette repeated. "What am I making with those things?"

"Anything you want," I said. "Anything at all. I want you with me and not just for one night. I want you to stay. Stay for a long, long time, Annie."

She ran her teeth across her bottom lip, humming to herself. I was prepared for an argument, braced against her certain refusal.

"But no panties? Is that your way of getting around previous restrictions on touching my underwear? This is one conversation we can have while we pack, you know. We don't have to do this up against my building."

No argument. No refusal. Just me and Annette, trying our damnedest to do this thing. With or without undies.

"If you insist." With regret, I set Annette on her feet and let her lead the way to her apartment. "I'm just throwing out some ideas here but I think we can live happily with a no-panties rule. Seems mutually beneficial to me."

Annette shook her keys at me when we reached the landing outside her door. "See? Keys. For the lock. The one on the door."

I brought both hands to her backside and squeezed. "What? You think I'm going to reward you for seeing to the most basic safety procedures? No, beautiful. Not happening."

She hooked a glance at me over her shoulder, her eyes a pair of inky pools in the darkness and her lips pressed together in a pout. I couldn't resist that face. It was the same one she used on me that first night, when she didn't want to be alone in my bed.

"What if I asked nicely?"

I squeezed her ass, harder this time. "You better pack fast."

Annette pushed open the door and I followed her into the narrow apartment. She handed me a reusable grocery bag and gestured to the baking pans and tools piled high on the kitchen table. "You work on the kitchen goods and I'll grab some clothes. Don't mean to break your heart but I will be bringing undies. Not everything can be fun and naked games."

I pointed at her with a muffin tin. "That's false. Fun and naked games are the gift of adulthood."

She moved toward me, her saucy expression crumbling with each step. "I am sorry." She ran her hands from my shoulders down to my wrists before tangling our fingers together. The muffin tin clanged to the floor. "I didn't say what I meant and it hurt you, and I'm sorry."

I leaned forward, pressing a kiss to her forehead. "I didn't say what I meant either. Not what I truly meant. I'm sorry I left."

Annette nodded, her grip tight on my fingers. "You look tired," she said, her brows furrowed. "Jackson, tell me you haven't been working around the clock since that situation at the inn."

"I could use a good night's rest," I admitted. "It will be better with you."

"Give me ten minutes," she said.

"Then we can go home?" I asked. "We can do this?"

"We're going home." She bobbed her head, a wide smile telling me everything I needed to know. "We're doing this."

CARAMELIZE

v. To heat sugar until it is melted and brown.

Annette

"WHAT IS THAT?" Jackson murmured, his words vibrating against the tender skin at the junction of my neck and shoulder. "What is it and how do I make it stop?"

It took a minute to hear anything other than my need for him. We'd only just set my things down inside his home when we reached for each other and we hadn't been able to let go since.

After another trill, I leaned away, blinked, and glanced around his kitchen. After a long moment of concentrated listen-staring, I placed the noise. "It's my phone," I said, peering around him to see where I left my tote. Grocery bags loaded with kitchen tools littered the countertop, and my tote was hidden beneath it.

"The only person who needs you now is right here," he said.

"I know," I said, busy loosening his shirt buttons. "I'd rather ignore it but it just keeps ringing."

With a grunt, Jackson scooped me up and set me on the countertop. He kept one hand on my backside and used the other to dig through the bags and then upend my purse. He sifted through lip balms and tampons, coins and hard candies to find my phone trilling under my wallet.

"Where is the pepper spray I gave you?" he asked, holding the phone out of my reach. Brooke's picture flashed on the screen.

"I didn't have room for it," I said, grabbing for my phone. The ringing stopped but then quickly started again. "She doesn't know how to back down. She'll just keep calling. Better yet, she'll show up at the door."

"You didn't have room for it," Jackson said, still staring at the contents of my purse. "You have room for six different lipsticks but not one pepper spray." He turned his attention toward me, his eyebrow arched. "We'll talk about that later but don't doubt we'll talk about it."

"I'm sure we will," I said, taking the phone from him. "Hi, Brooke."

She didn't bother with pleasantries or preamble, instead launching right in. "Are you with him right now? I saw him walking you to his house with a bunch of bags but I need more information. Tell me everything."

"Yes, I'm with Jackson." I smiled up at him and his impatient scowl. "He took me home and I'm staying here. Me and all my stuff."

The scowl softened into a smile I couldn't help but return. "It's about time you came around to those facts," he said.

"It's my turn with you. Tell him to cut out the sweet sentiments for a minute," Brooke said. "What did he say? What did *you* say? What's happening now? I need to know!"

Jackson stepped between my legs, pushed my skirt up to my waist. "Wrap it up," he said under his breath.

"Are we still on for wine and lunch this weekend?" I asked.

"Wine, yes. I can live without food," she replied. "But don't think you're leaving me hanging until then. I need all the details. Living vicariously through you is the only thing keeping me from going full-metal Kate Chopin and *The Yellow Wallpaper*."

"I think you mean Charlotte Perkins Gilman," I replied. "You and Kate Chopin have other things in common."

Jackson dragged his fingers up my inner thighs, grinning as if he was unwrapping the gift he'd always wanted. He did that to me, he made me believe I was worth treasuring.

"Okay, whatever. Give me the literature lesson later," Brooke said. "Please get to the good parts. I'm growing old and weary over here."

With my gaze locked on Jackson, I said to her, "You were at The Galley. You saw him drag me out of there."

"Yes, kicking and screaming," she replied.

"I'm probably going to get naked in his kitchen. I might even spank him. Then we're going to bed where we plan to sleep."

"At least for a little while," Jackson murmured.

"This is completely unacceptable as far as key details go," Brooke seethed. "You better choose me as your maid of honor after all the shit you've put me through with this man. I'm going to give the sloppiest, sappiest toast at your wedding and I'm going to make those evil stepsisters of yours my bridal party bitches. And you're definitely buying the wine this weekend."

"Happily," I said, a giggle-moan ringing in my words as Jackson's thumbs brushed along the edge of my panties.

"Okay, all right, that's enough," Brooke said. "I can put up with a lot of things but I don't want to listen while he fucks you."

"He's not—"

"I don't care," she interrupted. "Something is going on over there and I don't need to be involved in it. We can talk *about* sex but we can't talk *during* sex."

"Love you, babe," I said.

"Love you back," Brooke replied.

I ended the call and set my phone aside before looking up at Jackson. "What happens now?" I asked.

I meant *right now* but I also meant everything after *right now*.

"Anything you want," he said, still stroking the edge of my undies. "Ask me for anything, Annette. I'll give it to you."

I brought my hands to his face, cupping his strong, square jaw and running my thumbs over his cheeks. His eyes were heavy and exhaustion pinched his brow. "It's my turn to put you to bed," I said, sealing that promise with a kiss. "And when I need it, you'll do it for me."

"That's all?" he asked.

"That's everything," I replied.

27

STRAIN

v. To separate solids from liquids

Annette

TWO MONTHS later

"IT HAPPENS LIKE THIS EVERY YEAR," I murmured, my chin tipped down as I tugged up my coat's zipper. "One day it's lovely and wonderful with cool, crisp autumn air and sunny skies"—I gestured to the dark sky overhead with my gloved hand—"and then there's a cold snap and the next ice age begins. That's the real problem with having homecoming in the fall. It needs to be a springtime deal so people aren't turning into icicles out here. I don't care if that screws up everything with football. It's what I believe."

Jackson murmured in agreement as he wrapped a flamingo scarf around my neck. He was in uniform tonight, wearing a thick, dark sweater over his tan shirt, and a coat over the sweater to ward off the wintry chill. That sweater—with the sheriff's office insignia embroidered on the arm and his name over his chest, worked like a charm for me. I wanted to rake my fingers down the knit, slide my hands under it—I wanted to peel it off him. I wanted to toss it to the floor and get my hands on his skin and keep them there until he couldn't take any more. And then I'd slip into that sweater and see how long it took him to rip it off me.

"I won't let you turn into an icicle," Jackson said, patting the scarf then untying it again. "You look cute. I like seeing you all bundled up."

"Don't get me wrong," I said. "I live for boots-and-long-sweater season but it's the transition between wearing sundresses and sandals all summer to wearing, you know, socks and jeans and then to coats and hats and scarves and mittens. The hats really get me. They fuck up my hair."

"Believe me," he murmured, his concentration locked on the scarf, "I'm suffering the loss of your sundresses, too." He met my gaze with a small smile. "But your ass is on fire in those jeans. I can't figure out whether I should pinch it, spank it, or bite it." He glanced up and down the sidelines. "There's also a fourth option but I'd rather not mention it here."

I waved toward the high school's football field and the cheerleaders warming up within feet of us. "Good call, sheriff. Tuck that one away for later. We don't need to stir up any more attention than necessary."

He followed my gaze to the stadium stands where my family sat, decked out in the high school's colors. "Fuck that," he whispered, bending toward me. "Let them watch."

He tipped my chin up and brushed his lips over mine. There were no secrets about us being together but I wasn't entirely steady with the eyes of the entire town—and my family—on us. I wasn't so self-centered that I believed all these people cared about the minutiae of my life but I was standing on the sidelines before the homecoming game, wrapped up in this big grizzly bear of a man's arms, all while the back of his coat proudly announced his title.

When we parted, I ran my gloved finger over his bottom lip to tidy up the shiny lip gloss left there. "You're a bad influence, sheriff."

"I am." Jackson ran his palms down my shoulders and arms before gripping my hands. "Where's Brooke tonight?"

I shook my head at him, gave him an *if you only knew* face. "She doesn't attend football games. She has a complex relationship with our alma mater."

"Knowing Brooke, that is unsurprising." Jackson brushed some stray snowflakes from my shoulder. A squall was in tonight's forecast. "We don't have to stay for the whole game."

I snickered at that. "No, we need to stay for the entire thing. Every last minute," I insisted. "It's the homecoming game. You have to do the coin toss thing. I have to crown the homecoming court. We have to stay through the end and we probably have to go back to someone's house for a little post-game potluck, too."

"I don't want a potluck," he grumbled, seizing my waist in his hands. "I haven't seen you all week. I want to take you home."

It had been a busy week. Jackson was in Augusta for a three-day law enforcement meeting, I had two evening events at the shop, and Brooke and I met up for dinner and drinks last night. I worked hard at making time for my friend, even when it would've been easier to cancel on her and spend the evening snuggled up with my man.

But I was determined to avoid that. She was there for me before Jackson I wasn't leaving her on the back burner now that I was with Jackson. She was the sister I chose and I wasn't about to forget that she chose me, too.

"You're seeing me right now," I said.

"Yeah, Annie, I am," he said, his voice gravelly. "And I'm wondering whether I was wrong about your fuck-hot ankles now that I'm seeing you in jeans. Goddamn, girl. The things you do to me."

I started to explain my fascination with his official sheriff's uniform sweater but I spotted my mother and sisters headed straight toward us. I wasn't sure where they'd left my dad and brothers-in-law but those men seemed to follow the old adage of being seen but not heard. Sometimes they went above and beyond with silence *and* absence.

"Oh. This is special," I murmured, stepping out of Jackson's embrace. I didn't go far but I didn't want them to see me pawing at him. They'd file it under my repeated acts of desperation and never let me forget it.

While I hadn't shut my mom or sisters out after their visit to my store a couple months ago, I wasn't seeking them out either. I accepted that there was a world of difference between me and the rest of my family and I wasn't about to change any of that. It didn't matter whether that difference sprung from choosing this profession over theirs or the tremendous gap in our ages or even my failure to be born a boy. It didn't matter at all.

Jackson swung his arm over my shoulder, tugging me closer. "Don't say a word. I've got this," he said under his breath.

"Got what?" I whisper-shrieked.

He shook his head once and held out his free hand to my mother. "Mrs. Cortassi. It's a pleasure to see you this evening," he boomed.

She accepted his hand but couldn't tear her constipated stare away from his hold on my shoulder. "The pleasure is all mine." She glanced away from me and gestured to my sisters. "I don't believe you've met my daughters. Rosa, Lydia, and Antonella."

He nodded toward each of them. "I've met my favorite," Jackson said, pressing a kiss to my temple.

My mother blinked at us for a moment as she struggled to process the picture before her. For my part, I was struggling to hold back a giggle. "Oh, yes," she said, eyeing me. "Yes, you have met Annette."

"Not only have I met her but I've spent the summer falling in love with her," he said. "Long before she knew it, months ago, I was falling for her."

In place of my bones was jelly. Even after two solid months of Jackson telling me he loved me—*and* saying it back—the accompanying rush of bone-melting heat hadn't faded.

"Oh my god," Nella muttered, curling her fist in front of her mouth.

My mother recovered, cooing, "Sheriff, you're such a sweetheart. We must have you over for Sunday supper. How about next weekend? Yes, next weekend. You're coming over. It's settled."

I wasn't sure whether my invitation was implied or they were hoping to get alone time with him.

Jackson glanced down at me, his hungry stare concentrated on my lips. "Does that work for us, beautiful?" he asked.

"It's fine," I said, my cheeks warming under his study. "I think. Probably."

His eyebrow arched up in question and I gave a quick shrug in response. I couldn't refuse with an audience.

"Now that I think of it, Annie and I have plans next weekend," he replied, turning back to my family. "Yes, I just remembered. We'll have to take a rain check." He motioned toward them. "Why don't we have you over to our place?"

"You and An-Annie," my mother repeated, stumbling over Jackson's nickname for me.

"Your place?" Nella asked. "You have a place? Together?"

"When did that happen?" Rosa asked.

Jackson smiled at me, nodding. "Back in August," he said, still staring at my mouth. "I'm not too proud to say I begged. I couldn't spend another night without her and I begged her to come home with me, stay with me." He patted his belly and shot them a quick grin. "And her baking, my god. I can't function without her pastries. But I'm sure you know all about her talent in the kitchen."

There were a great many wonderful things about Jackson. The list was long and remarkable, not unlike his...ahem. But the trait I most admired in him was his willingness to make a bold move on behalf of another. He looked after me when I was drunk and sad. He listened to the Nevilles when others had dismissed their concerns. He confronted Brooke about her father's issues despite her history of tearing those who crossed her in half. And now he was picking off my family's shady comments and straitjacketing them where they stood.

"Annette, you've been holding out on us," my mother chided.

Jackson blew out a sharp breath before saying, "Not at all. Everyone in town is a fan of her baking."

"Speaking of the town, how are you finding Talbott's Cove, sheriff?" Nella asked.

"It's a great place to call home," he said, his words wide with certainty. "But it wouldn't be half as great without this lady right here. I don't know what I'd do without her. She keeps me on my toes, I'll tell you that. But I'm not saying anything you don't already know, right?"

Nella looked like she was witnessing a live-action atrocity. Hands fisted at her sides, mouth hanging open, eyes bugging out. I loved my sister but it was amazing to see her furious over something as simple as this man professing his love for me. And my muffins.

"Sure," Rosa murmured, bobbing her head. "I guess...I guess I can see that."

Lydia had the decency to appear bored with the whole conversation, craning her neck around the stadium. "I wonder if they're selling nachos at the concession stands tonight," she mused, tapping a manicured finger to her lips. "I really want nachos."

My mother clapped her hands together. "About that Sunday supper," she said, her gaze swinging between me and Jackson. "We really must have you over. Give me a date. There has to be one Sunday when I can get you two at my table."

"That's very kind of you," Jackson replied. "But we'd be happy to host you. It would give us a chance to show you the house we're buying and the plans we have for remodeling. I'm sure you want to see the new displays Annette has at the shop, too."

I shifted a bit, pressing the side of my face into Jackson's chest to smother a laugh. My family had never once visited my shop to see new storefront displays. I rubbed my cheek against that sweater I liked so much and sucked in a lungful of his scent. He truly was one of the good ones.

"Yes, of course," my mother agreed. "How about—"

"Wait, wait, wait," Nella interrupted. "You're remodeling a house? Where?" She pointed at me. "Why all the secrets, Annette? What are you trying to hide?"

Jackson's chest rose and fell under my cheek. Rose and fell. "As I'm certain you can see, we're not hiding anything," he said.

Still directing her comments toward me, Nella continued, "Then why haven't you told us about any of this?"

Jackson and I glanced at each other, our half smiles mirror images of each other. "We didn't hear back about our offer on the house until yesterday so it's as new to you as it is to us. And Jackson was in Augusta and I had that author event on Wednesday, and we've been busy," I said, still looking at him.

"Really *busy*." He pressed a kiss to my forehead, my cheeks, my mouth. "Since Annette doesn't require your approval, I can't imagine you'd be anything but thrilled for her. Isn't that right?"

"We can be thrilled and ask questions at the same time," Nella argued. "The two are not mutually exclusive. This has happened rather quickly. Wouldn't you agree, sheriff?"

A low growl sounded in Jackson's throat as he tightened his hold on me. I had to hide my face again.

"Oh my god, Nella," Rosa murmured. "Can you stop trying to prove a point for a freaking minute? You don't have to be a bitch all the time."

"Who are you calling a bitch?" Nella snapped.

"What are we talking about?" Lydia asked, her eyes narrowed as she looked between us. "Never mind. Someone will tell me later. I'm going to get nachos."

My sister turned and walked away, not troubling herself with pleasantries.

"I want to hear about this house," my mother said, holding both hands at her side as if to hold down my sisters' comments. "Where is it? When will it be ready?"

"We put in an offer on the old Dickerson house," I said. "It's in bad shape but the land is incredible."

Incredible and private. When we started tossing around the idea of finding a place together, something new to us, one of the top requirements was a home that afforded us a degree of privacy. Our days were spent interacting with the community and sharing ourselves with this town but we also needed a place to close the doors and be alone.

We hadn't expected to find something as fast as we did but we couldn't pass up the ancient farmhouse with the woods at its back and the ocean shimmering in the front.

"And the view," Jackson added, his chin brushing the crown of my head. "The view's the best."

"The work will take several months but we figure we'll be moved in come springtime," I said. "Maybe summer. We'll see how the winter goes."

The school's marching band launched into the fight song as the players jogged onto the field. My mother gestured between her ears and mouth, indicating it was too loud to talk right now. She dropped a quick kiss on my cheek and gave Jackson a one-armed squeeze. She gathered up Rosa and the still-fuming Nella, and headed back to the stands.

When the referee beckoned to Jackson to lead the coin toss, he took my hand and led me to the center of the field with him. I hadn't expected to join him for this portion of the festivities but I didn't mind. If there was anyone left wondering about my man's relationship status, this moment cleared it right up.

Several players from each team huddled around us, watching as he popped the coin into the air and then slapped it down on the top of his hand. Instead of looking at the coin, he hooked his arm around my neck and pulled me in for a kiss.

Jackson's lips a breath from mine, he whispered, "Didn't seem like the right time to tell your family that you've come to your senses and agreed to marry me. We'll tell them when my parents come to visit in a few weeks. We'll have to invite Brooke, since she's been sitting on this info since last weekend. That will be fun. They can all be hysterical together."

A smile stretched across my face as I remembered us hiking around the Dickerson Farmstead, marveling at barely-standing barns, rows of apple trees marching into the woods, stone bridges over deep streams. We'd followed a path that led to a seaside cliff and watched the ocean rush over the rocky shoreline below. I was too busy counting the wild blueberry bushes lining the path to notice Jackson had dropped down to one knee.

I didn't remember his exact words but I remembered feeling chosen. *Worthy*. Those sensations didn't swamp my system like a bath in warm honey because he wanted to spend a lifetime with me but because I finally believed I deserved it.

I was worthy of a big, full, messy love.

I was worthy of living the life I'd imagined for myself.

I was worthy of skipping over the scraps and taking everything I'd ever wanted.

If I had it to do all over again, I would've remembered what Jackson said as he knelt before me, but I wouldn't have traded that burst of confidence—of knowing what I wanted and accepting it, too—for anything.

THANK you for reading *Hard Pressed!* I hope you enjoyed Annette and Jackson. Keep reading for a sneak peak of the next Talbott's Cove novel—Brooke's story—*Far Cry*!

"MY TAVERN ISN'T your hookup pool."

She cast her gaze from one end of the bar to the other. "I wouldn't call it much of a pool."

"Why can't you use Tinder like everyone else? Come on, sweetheart. Get yourself some apps and get the hell outta here."

"I hate apps," she replied.

"And I hate cilantro, but you don't see me passing on the tacos, do you?"

"No, I mean I *hate* apps," she said, holding up her phone. "I hate them so much that I don't have any." I snatched the device away from her and peered at the screen. "Look. No social media. No news or weather. No food delivery."

"The only delivery around here is DiLorenzo's and it's only when Denny's in the mood."

She sliced her hands through the air. "Irrelevant. I didn't have delivery apps when I lived in New York."

I hit her with a glare. "If you really wanted something, you'd download an app for it."

"And that's where you're wrong, Jed. If I really wanted something, I'd go out and get it." She waved her hands. "That's what I was attempting to do earlier."

I set her phone on the bar top. "You have the newest iPhone and you use it for what? Phone calls? Texting Annette?"

She tilted her head, schooling me with an expression that said I should know better. "Not that I owe you any kind of explanation but until recently, when my previous phone met with an unlikely end, I had one of the earliest models." She pursed her lips. I looked away to keep from staring at her there. "And yes, Jed, I use it to make phone calls and text my bloodless sister."

I blew out a breath as I reached for towel. All the glassware was dry, but goddamn, I needed something to keep my hands busy. "You come out with a lot of strange shit, BamBam, but that's the strangest."

"It's so great that you have opinions," she mused. "Even better that I don't give a single fuck what you think." She leaned forward, folded her arms on the lip of the bar. "Then again, I can't give a single fuck because I don't have any. Literally. I have no fucks because you cockblocked me."

"What d'you want from me, Brooke? An apology? You're not getting one. I kicked the guy out because he annoyed me. When you own the joint, you can do that."

"You kicked him out while also cockblocking me," she replied.

"Not that it'd matter to you, but I'm pretty sure he's married."

"'Not that it'd matter to you,'" she repeated. "Your dick isn't big enough to use that tone of voice with me. Check yourself, Jed."

"Sweetheart, you don't know the first thing about my dick."

Her blonde hair spilled over her shoulders as she leaned forward. "Oh, I know more than enough."

I twisted the towel around my fist. "Big talk from a girl trying to pick up tourists."

"Funny how it's only a problem when I do it."

I blinked at her. Dropped the towel. Swallowed down the words I wanted to say to her. Rounded the bar. I closed my hand around Brooke's bicep and tugged her off the stool. "Let's go," I murmured.

"And where, may I ask, are we going?"

I gave her only a clenched jaw in response as I yanked her around the bar and into the dim storeroom. I kicked the door shut behind us. I marched her toward a wall of empty kegs until her back met the cool metal.

"Excuse you," she said, glaring at my hold on her arm. "What do you think you're doing with your hand on me?"

"We both know you would've ripped my fucking ear off and kicked my balls into my gut by now if you didn't want my hand on you."

"Oh really?" she scoffed. "So, what? I'm *asking for it*?"

"You're asking for something, sweetheart."

I was right about that. She was looking for something. She was fishing.

And I was taking the bait.

. . .

FAR CRY **IS NOW AVAILABLE!**

Join Kate Canterbary's Office Memos mailing list for occasional news and updates, as well as new release alerts, exclusive extended epilogues and bonus scenes, and cake. There's always cake.

If newsletters aren't your jam, follow Kate on BookBub for preorder and new release alerts.

Visit Kate's private reader group, Kate Canterbary's Tales, for exclusive giveaways, sneak previews of upcoming releases, and book talk.

FAR CRY

ABOUT FAR CRY

Brooke Markham needs a man. A real good man.

But she's not looking for a keeper. She's too busy kicking ass, running an empire, and caring for her ailing father to spend time with men who want annoying things like relationships and commitment and...conversation.

Brooke knows what she wants and it's not a future with the growly barkeep.

JJ Harniczek needs money. A whole lot of money.

He's determined to launch his distillery, expand his tavern, and put Talbott's Cove on the foodie tourism map. But there's no way he's asking Brooke for a dime. Not before he takes her to bed and definitely not after.

JJ knows where he's headed and the blonde bombshell isn't about to change that.

Not until she changes his entire world.

For angry women.

CHAPTER ONE

BROOKE

Deferred Revenue: liability arising upon the prepayment for goods and services yet to be delivered.

September

I DIDN'T THINK I'd see the day it happened. I didn't think I'd cross this line.

But here I was, standing on my deck in the middle of a weekday, wearing the short kimono robe I'd lifted from a roommate years ago and wondering how my life was reduced to this. My hair was wet, my feet were bare. My thirty-fourth birthday lurked on the other side of today's sunset and I couldn't remember the last time I sat down to eat a meal.

And I'd jackhammered my orgasm right out of existence.

I never would've believed such a thing was possible if I hadn't spent the morning plowing through my toy box only to discover those toys weren't getting me where I needed to go. *Again.* The floor of my bedroom was littered with vibrators, some of them still buzzing away.

I'd hoped a shower would check some boxes on both the hygiene and gratification fronts. I was as clean as any person could be after aiming a steady blast of water at her clit until her hand cramped and her fingers went numb.

Clean and wet and crawling out of my skin.

By my math, it added up.

My best friend was living with her own personal Ken doll, bound to get engaged any day now, and she repeatedly rejected my suggestions of forming a sister-wife arrangement.

My job was a remote game of Battleship that involved shifting mind-blowing sums of money around the globe with the dual purposes of making more money and upstaging every banker boy who'd called me Blondie rather than Brooke.

My father was suffering from frontotemporal dementia and couldn't remember how to use a fork.

My mother was six years gone (icy driveway, lights out) and I couldn't remember the last time I'd spoken to her before she died.

I hadn't had sex—the kind that rearranged organs, made ears ring, and required a recovery protocol—since coming home two years ago to this tiny seaside village that looked like a postcard from coastal Maine and felt like a prison sentence against progress.

And I was trying to get off in my childhood bedroom, the one still decorated in cloyingly virginal shades of rose pink and mint green.

Even the best vibrators were no match for all that.

It wasn't an issue of taking matters into my own hands. My hands were managing this matter—until I'd desensitized the shit out of my clit. Nothing worked for me anymore.

That wasn't a fair statement. I couldn't say nothing worked when I hadn't tried *everything*. As far as buzzy buddies went, I had one in every shape, size, and horsepower. I was game for fingers, showerheads, and a rainbow of porn—but only the respectful, tasteful, feminist stuff.

If I could do it alone in my bedroom of childhood innocence, I'd done it.

With the small exception of good old-fashioned sex with another person.

I wasn't one for abstinence. Aside from my present drought, I hadn't gone more than a few weeks without since I was seventeen or eighteen. If I'd wanted to have sex, there was always a dick available for the catching. And that dick accounted for nearly half of my life.

It was no wonder the mechanical options failed me.

But catching some dick in Talbott's Cove, Maine was fundamentally different than doing it in my true hometown of New York City, an island designed for casual sex. Think about it: young people flocked there with the hopes of making it big, only to discover the real world was boring, cruel, and unfulfilling. Alcohol and drugs—legal and otherwise—were as common as coffee and bagels. Cabs and car services ran nonstop, making late-night visits easy and early morning escapes discreet. You had to put a concerted effort into *not* having sex under those conditions.

The most dangerous consequence of casual sex in the city was running into that person at a bar—worse, a bodega without the cushion of loud music and liquor—and making the snap decision whether to ignore or acknowledge. That was it. An awkward moment. New York City was beautifully efficient in its ability to absorb good and bad and everything in between, and spit out overripened cynicism.

Talbott's Cove offered no such mechanism.

There was no illusion of privacy here. Everything happened out in the open, even that which occurred behind closed doors. Lies festered and secrets didn't keep. Not when your neighbors lived in your back pocket and personal business was subject to public purview.

It wouldn't surprise me to find the demise of my orgasm in this week's edition of the Talbott's Cove newspaper and that was the exact reason I hadn't hoisted my dick-catching net and headed off to the area's man forest.

I didn't need to run into my second grade teacher and the high school softball coach while they discussed my sex life over honey-dipped crullers and coffee tomorrow morning at DiLorenzo's Diner. I didn't need my mother's friends sharing shock and horror at my wanton ways at their next bridge game. There was more than enough on my plate right now, and putting out small town slut-shamey fires wasn't the side dish I was willing to order, even if I didn't know how to experience shame much in the way some people didn't notice their bad breath.

But some things were worth an extra helping of local drama. "Fuck it," I murmured. "I need to find myself a man."

Before I could go hunting, I had to make my way inside, throw on some clothes, and run a comb through my hair. Instead of doing any of those things, I searched my bedroom for the phone I'd abandoned in the pocket of yesterday's shorts. Keeping track of mobile devices wasn't an aptitude of mine. In New York, I'd hired an assistant with the singular responsibility of holding my phone. In Talbott's Cove, I had no such luxury. If it wasn't in my pocket or tucked under the band of my bra, I was hopeless. But I'd vowed to do better following recent events.

Over the summer, one of Dad's home health aides texted me while I was on a video conference call with investors on four continents. She reminded me she had a personal thing and was due to leave early and other details I should've known in advance but didn't. That left me pitching my investors with my phone switched to silent and set face-down while Dad went unsupervised—*for two hours*. Since dementia functioned like a goody bag of jigsaw puzzle thoughts, Dad managed to get out of the house, leave the property, and walk his bathrobed ass two miles down the coastal highway while I closed a deal worth more than the state of Maine's annual operating budget.

Since I'd earned a sweet seven figures that day—and it was obviously the right thing to do—I doubled Dad's staffing and committed to keeping my phone visible at all times. I succeeded on the visibility front for a little while. Last month, I forgot my phone downstairs, and when I went looking for it I found my father using it as a sounding block for his gavel. He remembered all of his fifty-two years on bench but not that he had a daughter. Dementia was fun like that.

He'd cracked the screen to shards, but he had a lot of fun playing courtroom. Since there was no salvaging the device, I taped up the glass and let him keep it. His happiest, most calm moments always involved presiding over his courtroom.

As if those reasons weren't enough to keep me connected, Annette Cortassi, my best friend and this town's only redeeming quality, messaged me throughout the day. Usually between customers at the bookstore she owned in the harborside village. Today was no exception.

Annette: Did you ever watch that Netflix comedy special I told you about? The one where I strained a muscle laughing and couldn't pull a shirt over my head for a week because my side hurt so much?

Annette: I swear, it was worth the pain.

Annette: I'm going to assume by the delay in your response that you're either buying a country or dealing with some shit. Let me know when you're free and/or if I can help.

Annette: I can't do anything with buying countries, but...

Brooke: So long as I'm here, I'm not free.

Annette: Oh, would you shut up?

Brooke: You're more capable than you think. You could run a small country, no problem.

Annette: I'm going to stick to running a small bookstore. That's challenge enough for me.

Brooke: I don't buy countries. That's not what hedge fund management is about.

Annette: You say that, but it doesn't clarify your job to me at all.

Brooke: I oversee the investment and strategy of macro and long/short hedge funds with the objective of minimizing risk and maximizing profits.

Annette: Nope, that doesn't help either.

Brooke: People give me lots of money and I decide where to put that money to turn it into more money, and for my trouble, I keep a lot of that money.

Annette: That's a little better.

Annette: Let's talk about you now, Miss Brooke.

Brooke: We are talking about me. This entire conversation has been about me.

Annette: Any chance you're excited about your birthday weekend?

Brooke: That really depends on whether I have to acknowledge that I'm older.

Annette: You do not.

Annette: Once you hit 30, you don't have to acknowledge each individual year. You're a woman in your 30s and everyone knows better than to ask for specifics.

Brooke: It's not that I have an issue with this year. I just don't like the look of 34. It's obnoxious. I mean, 32 was cute. That was a cute year. Everyone is cool with 32. But 34 is that awkward phase after the early 30s and sliding into the mid 30s. It's not cute anymore. It's a nightly serum regimen and a living will.

Annette: I remember being young and my parents throwing a 40th birthday party for one of my uncles. It was over-the-hill themed. All black. A tombstone cake.

Annette: And here I am, 34 now, wondering what the fuck that was about.

Brooke: I could be wrong, but I think you'd light things on fire if anyone threw you an over-the-hill party, ever. Even if you were 95.

Annette: You're right. I would burn it down.

Brooke: I'd help.

Annette: But I don't mind gaining some pearls of wisdom as I age.

Brooke: Those pearls of wisdom are from me. They have nothing to do with age. It's who you know.

Annette: And aren't I lucky to know you?

Brooke: The best thing about being over 30 is blow jobs.

Annette: I'm going to need you to unbox that one, honey.

Brooke: No blow jobs after 30.

Annette: ...okay. I'm trying to follow you, but I'm not sure I am.

Brooke: I haven't given a blow job since I was 29.

Annette: I gather you're pleased with this?

Brooke: Don't pretend you like the feel of fuzzy balls on your chin or having that dick taste in your throat.

Annette: I'll say this. I enjoy reciprocity.

Brooke: Oh my god, stop it.

Annette: Stop what? It's only fair.

Brooke: And what do you do, darling deep throat, with all the jizz? Because that's a riddle I've never solved.

Annette: Are you asking me this literally or...?

Brooke: Swallowing isn't an option. I can't. I won't. That means I have to duck out of the way before he goes off like the Bellagio fountains or offer up my skin for the Jackson Pollock treatment. And you know what happens after that? On the off chance he's a considerate guy, I get to wait with a puddle of human fluids on my chest while he finishes with the convulsions and heavy breathing to fetch a washcloth. Entire minutes of my life go by while I'm marinating like tonight's pork loin.

Annette: You're so special.

Brooke: You go right ahead and enjoy your reciprocity.

Annette: I'll ask one more time. Are you ready for your birthday weekend? Because I have plans, lady. PLANS.

Brooke: If you're asking whether I'm ready to dance like I'm working hard for the money, then yes.

Brooke: I reserve the right to slap you if there's cake and singing involved.

Annette: So...that means we won't be going to that place we like, the one that isn't a karaoke bar but they still have the equipment and they always let us go to town on Britney and Christina songs?

Brooke: I did not say that. I don't want anyone singing AT me. There is a difference.

Annette: Mmhmm and the cake? I was under the impression you required a yellow cake with chocolate buttercream frosting, but it sounds like that's canceled too?

Brooke: I don't mind cake. I just don't want someone to walk up with a cake and put it in front of me while everyone stares.

Brooke: That shit is fucking awkward.

Annette: Right, right, right. Let me see if I have this straight. You want singing, but not at you. You want cake, but you don't want anyone presenting it to you. Is that correct?

Brooke: Mostly.

Annette: Ah. All right. I'll see what I can do about meeting these specifications, then.

Brooke: You're implying that I'm super high maintenance and I'd like to point out that while it's true, it's also very strange that modern tradition requires people to sit in front of flaming baked goods while others sing.

Annette: Sure, honey. Whatever you want. I'll just hide the cake and leave you to find it alone, without anyone watching or singing.

Brooke: Now you're just being absurd.

Annette: I'm absurd. Sure.

Brooke: I never should've told you my birth date.

Annette: Yes, you should have. You just don't want to be the center of attention in ways you can't control.

Brooke: Well...shit.

Brooke: I don't know how much of Annette Unfucks My Life I can handle today.

Annette: It's what you get. You unfucked my life.

Brooke: Did not!

Annette: I distinctly recall a conversation where you YELLED at me IN PUBLIC about how I am to proceed when there is a cock in my hand. I call that unfucking my life.

Brooke: You needed permission to have sex. I need...a field of lavender and sage, a wheelbarrow of crystals, a shaman, a priest, a psychiatrist, Marie Kondo, Cesar Millan, and Jillian Michaels.

Brooke: And some good dick. You don't even understand how much dick I need. The wheelbarrow I really need is a wheelbarrow of dicks. It's at crisis levels.

Annette: I understand the sage, lavender, crystals, and dick, but why do you need a dog whisperer? You don't have a dog.

Brooke: Cesar Millan just seems like the kind of guy who takes one look at you and tells you how to solve all your problems. Dog or otherwise.

Annette: And Jillian Michaels?

Brooke: She'd yell at me.

Annette: Isn't her thing yelling at people while they exercise? You don't exercise. At all.

Brooke: Yeah, but I'm sure she'd yell at me about anything I need for the right price.

Annette: And why do you need someone yelling at you?

Brooke: Same reason I need crystals and lavender. My life is a hot mess and I'm irrationally concerned about cakes and singing.

Annette: Mmhmm. Okay. And Marie Kondo?

Brooke: This house is full of stuff. It drives me bananas. For once, I'd like to open a closet and find it empty. One less pile of shit for me to deal with.

Annette: She's going to make you touch all the stuff and decide if it brings you joy.

Brooke: I'd really prefer she make those decisions for me.
Annette: Not how it works.
Brooke: All I want is one full day where I don't have to make the decisions or deal with the problems.
Annette: And you'll have it. Birthday weekend, my darling. No decisions, no problems.
Brooke: Will you be arranging the man meat as well?
Annette: Excuse me, what?
Brooke: That's what I thought.
Annette: What are we talking about?
Brooke: I need to get laid. Like, immediately.
Annette: Brush your hair and go to the Galley. It's apple, pumpkin, and leaf peeping season. I bet there are some tourists in town.
Brooke: The Galley? Really? Isn't that a little too close for comfort?
Annette: Allow me to stress this point one more time—pick up a tourist, not a townie.
Brooke: Yeah yeah I get that. But townies hang out there. Lincoln's ass print is permanently carved into his seat at the bar.
Annette: So what?
Brooke: So...one does not simply initiate a one-night stand with a Greek chorus of locals watching.
Annette: One is more concerned with neighborly gossip than self-care.
Brooke: We're calling hookups self-care now?
Annette: You need to take some time for yourself. You know what they say about oxygen masks.
Brooke: The bag might not inflate, but air is flowing?
Annette: Yours first, everyone else second.
Brooke: You're sure about the Galley?
Annette: Believe me. You'll find someone there.
Brooke: If I don't, can I borrow Jackson?
Annette: I'll share just about anything else with you, but not him.
Brooke: It would make things so much easier...
Annette: I know you think so, yes.

CHAPTER TWO

BROOKE

Derivative: a financial contract whose value is determined by the fluctuations in the value of underlying assets often used as an instrument to hedge risk.

"DON'T EVEN THINK ABOUT IT."

I stopped drumming my fingertips on my lips at the sound of his voice behind me. Rolled my eyes. Thought about throwing an elbow in his direction. "Think about what, exactly?"

Still concealed over my shoulder, he replied, "Whatever the hell you're cooking up, don't do it. Stop cooking. Give it up and get the hell outta my tavern."

I turned my head, but this dim corner of the Galley between the now-empty pay phone nook and restrooms didn't reveal more than JJ Harniczek's silhouette. Dark jeans, dark shirt, dark boots, dark mood. "You won't sell much beer with an attitude like that."

"I don't have the patience for games tonight, Bam Bam."

That goddamn nickname. It was my mother's fault. She was nearly six years gone, but I still blamed her for this shit. She'd been fanatical about initials. If there was a bare inch of fabric, metal, or glass, she wouldn't rest until it got a serving of initials. I could've lived with this fanaticism, but my name was Brooke-Ashley Markham and she had B.A.M. embroidered on my backpack, lunch box, scarves, mittens, socks, sweaters, everything. There was no escaping it, and even in first grade, JJ knew a tease-worthy nickname when he saw one.

I believed in karma and I knew it was real because JJ had been gifted the equally troublesome name of Jedediah Judson Harniczek. The torment flowed both ways. "I'm not playing games, Jed."

"You're at my tavern without your sidekick and you're hidden away back here, watching my customers like a jaguar licking its chops before an ambush. I'd say you're playing something." He stepped into the light, turned to face me. "And I'm not interested in having it tonight."

I gave him the *I'm just a sweet, innocent girl and I don't know what you mean* pout as I blinked up at him. He was tall and solid with a beard that meant business, only an ax short of achieving full lumberjack status. If you liked that sort of thing.

"Annette is home with Jackson and I had a"—I paused, searching for the right word to adequately describe my experience with involuntary edging—"frustrating day, one might say. I just want to have a drink and unwind like everyone else."

He crossed his thick arms. Scowled, blinked. "I seriously doubt that."

"Doubt all you want, but you're making me a drink. I'm sure you can manage a vodka gimlet with extra lime." I tipped my chin toward the bar. "I'll be over there. Thanks in advance, Jed."

I breezed past him and settled on a stool at the far end of the bar, a prime position. From here, I could scope out everyone seated around the three-sided bar without being obvious or drawing attention to myself. If I sat somewhere in the middle, I'd have to lean forward to check out the people on either side of me and I'd lose a good view of those seated at tables and in booths. There was no greater mark of an amateur dick hunter than getting caught in the process of assessing the territory. Eyeballing men required perfecting the air of disinterested disaffection— be bored and ignore everything around you.

As much as I hated to admit it, Annette was right about the Galley. There were a number of new faces here, and the locals were busy watching some sportsball game on the big-screen television suspended from the ceiling. I could've stripped to my skin and offered lap dances to anyone interested without snapping the loyalists out of their sportsball trance.

Come to think of it, that wasn't an awful idea. It was a quick method of assessing the *responsiveness* of this crowd.

"One vodka gimlet. Extra lime." JJ plunked a glass in front of me. He rocked back on his heels and spread his arms out wide, planting his hands on the edge of the bar top as if he was doing his best to keep from strangling me. He was never more than a couple of steps away from second-degree murder. "Drink up and go."

I knew that look well. Our interactions were fitting for people who'd known and teased each other since babyhood, shared one strange—and never spoken of since—kiss and some light groping the night after our high school graduation, and now found ourselves in the same small town we'd vowed to leave behind us forever.

With my gaze locked on JJ, I reached for the napkin dispenser stationed two seats to my left. One by one, I pulled out ten napkins. My collection formed a small paper plateau, a landform that seemed to anger the barkeep as it grew, if his quiet snarls were any indication. Once my supplies were in place, I made a show of mopping up the clear liquid that'd sloshed over the rim, down the glass, and all over my section of the bar. I was dainty about it too, using only the corner of a napkin as I tidied his mess.

And it worked.

"Fucking hell, Brooke, give me that." He gathered the used napkins in one hand, the glass in another. Without breaking his stare, he pitched the napkins into the waste bin and dumped the drink into the sink. "What do you think you're doing?"

I gestured to the empty—but still damp—space before me. "I was attempting to enjoy my gimlet until you ripped it away from me. Honestly, Jed. It was rather rude." He responded with a smirk that only highlighted the splattering of freckles across his face. Some were faint angel kisses, others were as dark as his hair. "May I have another?"

He nodded at the damp, empty space. "I'm short-staffed. I have pressing issues to handle. I don't have time for your games tonight—"

"Get a grip, Jed," I snapped. I drove my hand through my hair and sucked in a breath. "I'm not going to whip the townspeople into a fury and convince them to haul off and kill the beast. This obsession with my games, as you call them, is unhealthy. I take a lot of joy in busting your balls but if my presence in your tavern is truly disruptive to business, please escort me off the premises. Otherwise, I'd like a vodka gimlet, nice and limey, and a couple of moments where you aren't harassing me about my intentions. I realize I don't possess your barkeeping wisdom, but I cannot see how a nice lady enjoying a cocktail could incite the type of mayhem you're suggesting. But go ahead. Explain it to me."

JJ regarded me for a second, the hard gaze of his hazel eyes giving nothing away. At first glance, they appeared brown, but I knew they were hazel. He worked his jaw, rocked back on his heels, dropped his hands to his lean hips. He seemed poised to say something, but instead, he turned and retreated to the opposite end of the bar.

I stared at the strong, broad line of his shoulders. The dark, unruly hair gathered with a band at the nape of his neck. The jeans skimming his taut backside. It made for a pleasant, if not problematic, picture.

"Ah, the pleasures of small town living," I called after him. "I'd pay three times as much for a bartender to chastise me in Manhattan. Then again, the only time a bartender would chastise me in Manhattan was if I asked for a side of ice with my cabernet."

He didn't respond and I was content with forfeit by way of silence. It gave me an opportunity to evaluate my options. There were a handful of fresh faces, but the pickings were slim. Strategy was essential. The Galley was theatre in the round, wide and open for everyone to observe. I couldn't flutter around, visiting every guy with clean fingernails and no wedding ring like a hookup hummingbird. I needed an airtight plan of attack before my ass left this stool because I wasn't taking aim for a second shot.

That left me eyeing a late thirtysomething man who seemed promising on looks alone. No rings, no grubby fingernails, and no one seated beside him. Other out-of-towners were scattered around him, a stool or two separating them. This one was working the "dress shirt with an open collar" angle to his advantage, even if the shirt wasn't appropriately fitted. His hairline was a pair of cul-de-sacs and his brows needed a trim. But his hands were big, wrapping around his pint glass like it was a pixie stick, and that counted for something.

All things considered, my target was remarkably average. In these situations—and my entire life was composed of these situations—I always went for the average guy. The gorgeous ones knew they were hot shit and fucked like they were doing you a favor. While I was in desperate need of that exact type of favor, I wasn't interested in communicating it to anyone but myself.

A few minutes later, JJ set a fresh drink in front of me. He didn't speak, didn't look at me, didn't slow down for more than the delivery. "Thank you," I called to him.

His back to me, he lifted a hand in acknowledgment. This was how we did it: name-calling, senseless bickering, and low-key ultimatums followed by a cease-fire. He was going to his corner, I was staying in mine, all was well in Talbott's Cove.

I sipped my drink until the ice melted to the point of diluting the liquor, all while JJ pretended to ignore me. It was amusing of him to think I could miss those side-eye glances.

He circled back in my direction, busy organizing and polishing everything behind the bar as he went. When he edged toward me, his focus stayed on his work. I stayed focused on my work too. The work of poaching a man for the night.

Without glancing toward me, JJ asked, "Did you eat? Tonight?"

I swirled my glass, shook my head. "I don't think so."

His brows shot up. "How do you not know?"

"I don't know," I answered. "I don't keep track of these things."

"For fuck's sake, Brooke." Grumbling the whole way, he bent down, reached into a cupboard, and retrieved a small bowl. He set it on the bar and motioned for me to take it. "Eat."

I tipped the bowl toward me. Pretzels. "Thank you, no. I have no idea where this has been and who it's been with and I'm sure you know how people are about restrooms and hand washing and such."

He snatched the bowl away, dumped it in the waste bin, and set a fresh refill in front of me. He drilled his finger on the shiny hardwood surface. "Eat."

With an eye on my slowly balding target, I shook my head. "I don't like pretzels."

Again, he muttered, "For fuck's sake, Brooke."

My guy glanced at his watch and that was my cue. I leaned over the bar top, snatched a cocktail napkin and pen, and scribbled my phone number.

"No fucking way." JJ reached for a dish towel. "I warned you, Brooke. No games."

"Stay out of it, Jedediah," I replied under my breath.

"My bar, my business," he snapped, wrapping the towel around his palm.

"Why can't your business be stocking more than one shiraz? That would be smart business. Interfering with my Thursday evening is not."

I hopped down from my seat and made my way to the opposite end of the bar, my gaze steady on the visitor. I slipped between him and the empty seat to his right. No one looked good climbing up onto a stool, and standing at this angle allowed me a swift exit. It also gave him a clear view of my cleavage, not that there was much to see.

"Hi. I couldn't help but notice you," I said, brushing my palm over his forearm. "Visiting from out of town?"

From the corner of my eye, I saw JJ toss his towel to the floor. He pushed through the storeroom door with force, leaving it to slam shut behind him.

"Yeah, up from Manchester," the tourist replied. "New Hampshire."

"All by yourself?" I cooed. "You must love those autumn leaves. Or is it pumpkins you're after? Maybe apples?"

"Mostly leaves, but I think we're stopping at a pumpkin patch too." He dipped his head, laughed. "I'm meeting up with my—uh, a group of people. They left for dinner before I arrived, so I have some time on my hands."

JJ didn't last long in the storeroom. He returned with a case of wine and dropped it on the bar with enough force to rattle glasses and draw the attention of everyone seated there.

"Listen," I said, reclaiming the visitor's attention and forcing my lips into a flirty smile-pout. "I think you're really hot and I'd like to get to know you better."

"I'm really—me? Yeah?" he asked. "Okay. Yeah. I'm—"

I pressed my finger to his lips and dropped the napkin on the surface in front of him. Patted it twice. "Shh. Tell me later."

I stepped away from the tourist—and JJ—and sailed out of the bar without a backward glance.

Shot fired.

CHAPTER THREE

J J

Fungibility: the ability to interchange one asset with another, similar asset.

I STARED at the door for a solid minute.

Staring was safer than running through it, ripping it off its hinges, or throwing bottles of liquor at it. Those were the only options as I saw them.

Motherfucking Brooke Markham.

From behind me, I heard, "You saw that, right? That really happened?"

There were a lot of things I didn't have tonight. Not enough staff to cover the dining room and bar.

Another man said, "If I hadn't seen it with my own two eyes, I wouldn't believe it."

Not enough time to hammer out updated financial projections before meeting with my business partner tomorrow morning.

He asked, "Do you think it's legit? If I text this number, am I gonna find out it's the local pizza place?"

Not enough tolerance for out-of-towners here for an authentic autumn weekend in Maine. Especially the ones who took off their wedding rings while ordering a Moscow mule.

Other man replied, "A certified dime piece was sitting in your lap. Even if it is a pizza place, you're still winning."

And not even an ounce of patience for Brooke Markham and her bullshit.

He said, "I'm gonna text her. Can't pass up an opportunity like this one."

Something inside my head snapped. Whether it was the muscle keeping bad choices from overruling good sense or my tenuous hold on everything I'd tried to keep in check, the seal was broken.

I gave the door one last scowl before turning and snatching the napkin out of that asshole's hand. "Not a chance in hell."

For a second, he had the decency to look guilty. But assholes bounced back quick and this one was no exception. "Does this involve you?"

From the other end of the bar, two of my regulars, Bobbie Lincoln and Rhys Neville, shifted away from the televised baseball game. Their concerned expressions seemed to ask whether I needed assistance. I shook my head. I had this well in hand.

"Yeah, it involves me." *More than you'll ever know.* "Get the fuck out of here."

THE MAIN DOOR banged open five minutes before midnight and I knew it was Brooke before glancing up from the evening's receipts. No one flung a door quite like Ms. Markham.

I knew she'd come back. A masochistic part of me had spent the past four hours craving it. There was no other explanation for me leaving the door unlocked long after my last customer settled up for the night. But this knowledge was more than a basic understanding of her operating system. The air changed when she was around. It was charged, unpredictable, almost dangerous. No, *always* dangerous. There was no trusting this woman.

"You gonna fix those hinges for me?" I gestured toward the threshold with a roll of quarters. "Because I can see from here they're loose from the rough treatment you're giving them."

"Get me a screwdriver." She stomped across the empty tavern, her long blonde hair spilling over her shoulders and anger rising around her like a bank of coastal fog. If I knew anything about Brooke—and fog—I knew I wouldn't be able to see the hand in front of my face real soon. "I'll tighten them right up after you and I have a little talk."

I returned to my receipts. "Sorry, sweetheart, closed for the night."

She slipped onto her usual stool, the one near the end with a sniper's view of the tavern. "Would you care to explain to me what the fuck happened here, Jed?"

"Gonna need you to be more specific, sweetheart."

Brooke paused, laced her fingers together on the bar top. "I came in here earlier."

"That you did." I nodded as I shuffled the cash again. I couldn't even count when she stared at me like that. "Left without paying too."

"Put it on my tab."

"Last I checked, you haven't opened a tab." I shoved everything into a bank bag and finally shifted to face her. A feral smirk pulled at her lips and her brilliant blue eyes sparkled. I'd never seen anything more beautiful—or infuriating—than the wrath she kept simmering beneath the surface.

And it was a goddamn problem. Of course it was. Pissing her off made my damn day, but moments like these, when it was me and Brooke and all that fog rolling around us, made for a different kind of day.

"Then let me open one right now." She drew her narrow shoulders in, lowered her lashes, and peered up at me. I wanted to believe that move was pure and unpracticed, although Brooke got everything she wanted not because she deserved it but because she knew how to demand it. "I think you know I'm good for it."

So fucking dangerous.

I ran my palm over my head, tugged the hair knotted at the base of my skull. "Like I told you earlier, I don't have time for this." Didn't have the time, the mental fortitude, the goddamn strength. "Get to the point or get the hell outta here."

Every ounce of sweet drained from her. In its place was rock salt in the shape of an obnoxiously lovely woman. "What happened with"—she pointed to the empty stool where the stuffed shirt from Manchester had sat—"that one?"

I went in search of something to do—or break. Ice was the only thing I could shatter without creating more work for myself. I pushed back the top on the chill chest, speared the metal scoop inside. "Why the sudden interest in visitors to the Cove?"

I heard her snicker over the tumble of ice cubes. It was a halting breath that twisted into a brittle laugh. That rough, unsatisfied sound tightened my shoulders and locked my jaw. I wished I hadn't heard it because that reaction told me everything I needed to know about her in this moment. For starters, she didn't give a shit about the guy she'd tried to pick up for the night. Not surprisingly. Second, the *who* was far less relevant than the *what*. Finally—and this was the most important one— she was damn close to combusting. The only question was whether she wanted someone to light her up. Not the way that Manchester asshole would've done it, if he'd managed to fumble his way to that point. But really set her on fire. Make her burn—and glow.

"My interest in visitors is none of your business," she answered. "Since you've inserted yourself into my business, I'd like to know what you did with the gentleman I met earlier."

"'Met' is a rather civilized way of describing it, don't you think?" I snapped the chill chest shut, looked around, shrugged. "My tavern isn't your hookup pool."

She cast her gaze from one end of the empty bar to the other. "I wouldn't call it much of a pool."

"Why can't you use Tinder like everyone else? Come on, sweetheart. Get yourself some apps and get the hell outta here."

"I hate apps," she replied.

"And I hate cilantro, but you don't see me passing on the tacos, do you?"

"No, I mean I *hate* apps," she said, holding up her phone. "I hate them so much that I don't have any." I snatched the device away from her and peered at the screen. "Look. No social media. No news or weather. No food delivery."

"The only delivery around here is DiLorenzo's and it's only when

Denny gets tired of washing dishes and needs some walking-around money."

She sliced her hands through the air. "Irrelevant. I didn't have delivery apps when I lived in New York."

I hit her with a glare. "If you really wanted something, you'd download an app for it."

"And that's where you're wrong, Jed. If I really wanted something, I'd go out and get it." She waved her hands. "That's what I was attempting to do earlier."

I set her phone on the bar top. "You have the newest iPhone and you use it for what? Phone calls? Texting Annette?"

She tilted her head, schooling me with an expression that said I should know better than to pick at her spoiled little rich girl status. "Not that I owe you any kind of explanation, but until recently, when my previous phone met with an unlikely end, I had one of the earliest models." She pursed her lips. I looked away to keep from staring at her there. "And yes, Jed, I use it to make phone calls and text my bloodless sister."

I blew out a breath as I reached for a towel. All the glassware was dry, but goddamn, I needed something to keep my hands busy. "You come out with a lot of strange shit, Bam Bam, but that's the strangest."

"It's so great that you have opinions," she mused. "Even better that I don't give a single fuck what you think." She leaned forward, folded her arms on the edge of the bar. "Then again, I can't give a single fuck because I don't have any. Literally. I have no fucks because you cock-blocked me."

Why I thought I could carry on this conversation without submitting to her like every other object in her orbit was a mystery to me. Whatever it took to stand here without wanting to fist her platinum hair and bite her bow lips and give her the kind of fuck she'd never forget, I didn't have. And I'd looked. Fuck me, I'd *looked*. I'd spent the past two years searching.

"What d'you want from me, Brooke? An apology? You're not getting one. I kicked the guy out because he annoyed me. When you own the joint, you can do that."

"You kicked him out while also cockblocking me," she replied.

"Not that it'd matter to you, but I'm pretty sure he's married."

"'Not that it'd matter to you,'" she repeated. "Your dick isn't big enough to use that tone of voice with me. Check yourself, Jed."

Nothing about her words was particularly infuriating—no more than the rest of this conversation—but they sent me over the edge nonetheless. "Sweetheart, you don't know the first thing about my dick."

Her hair cascaded over her shoulders as she leaned forward. "Oh, I know more than enough."

I twisted the towel around my fist. "Big talk from a girl trying to pick up tourists."

"Funny how it's only a problem when I do it."

I blinked at her. Dropped the towel. Swallowed down the words I wanted to say to her. Rounded the bar. I closed my hand around Brooke's bicep and tugged her off the stool. "Let's go," I murmured.

"And where, may I ask, are we going?"

I gave her only a clenched jaw in response as I yanked her past the bar and into the dim storeroom. This was happening somewhere dark and private—and it *was* happening. I kicked the door shut behind us and marched her toward a wall of empty kegs until her back met the cool metal.

"Excuse you," she said, glaring at my hold on her arm. "What do you think you're doing with your hand on me?"

"We both know you would've ripped my fucking ear off and kicked my balls into my gut by now if you didn't want my hand on you."

"Oh really?" she scoffed. "So, what? I'm *asking for it*?"

"You're asking for something, sweetheart."

I was right about that. She was asking for something. She was fishing. And I was taking the bait.

I flicked a glance at her eyes, her lips. I hated how much I wanted to taste her. "Tell me what you're looking for."

Her eyes narrowed and her lip curled up in the way it always did when she was drowning in all the contempt and condescension she kept close. It wasn't meant to be hypnotic, but fuck me if I could convince my cock otherwise. "I don't need to tell you anything."

"Need? No. But you want to, Bam Bam." I shuffled closer to her, my lower body settling against hers. "Go ahead. Tell me what you want."

Her breath caught and that small proof she wasn't nearly as contemptuous as she pretended felt like a victory. But she wasn't letting me enjoy the win. Not even for a second.

"It's nothing you'd be able to manage."

I traced the neckline of her sweater, just barely brushing my fingertips over her pale skin as I went. Not a freckle or tan line to be seen. "Try me."

A beat of silence passed between us before I vaulted over a line I swore I'd never approach, much less cross. Not again. I shouldn't have done it. Shouldn't have dragged her back here to begin with—to this room scented with stale beer, and to the moment where everything between us changed—but I never should've bowed my head and closed my lips around the tender skin below her ear. It was a quick taste that turned into a kiss and then a scrape of my teeth less gentle than I'd intended.

But while I was tasting and kissing and biting her neck, Brooke was statue still. She didn't react, didn't move, didn't even breathe. She was dead silent until, "Do that again."

There it was, the single most important reason for staying far away from that line, and it was spoken with her special blend of entitlement and ice that burned the sense out of me.

I pulled back. "No."

Her lips flattened and her brow arched up. "Again."

"That's not how it works here, sweetheart."

She blinked, tipped her head to the side as if she hadn't heard me. "My universe isn't the one where I take orders, Jed."

"And my universe isn't the one where you get what you want simply because you want it." I kicked her ankles apart and pressed myself into the notch between her legs. Her body shuddered against mine in a violent, lingering jerk. A man who hadn't devoted entire years to observing this woman would've blown the whistle and called the game, but I knew we were just getting started. Brooke, the woman constructed from ice and salt and fire, was only warming up with sighs and shudders like these. "Go ahead. You don't like my rules, you're welcome to walk out of here."

She pouted. She whined. Then, "Again—*please*."

And I damn near died.

I pulled myself back from that free fall and brushed my beard over the curve of her neck. "That's it, that's right," I murmured.

She twisted her wrists out of my grip. I expected her to take that freedom and use it to pop me in the eye, but she dragged her palms down my back and curled her fingers around my belt. She used that leverage to pull me closer. *Fucking closer*.

I rocked my hips into the heat between her legs and dragged my lips up the slender column of her neck. She smelled like soap and flowery shampoo and her skin was softer than I'd imagined. Than I'd remembered. It was irritating as hell. I wanted to hate every second so I could discard this desire and move on with my life.

"If this is all you want, sweetheart, you went to an awful lot of trouble for a little necking."

"No one says necking, Jed. They haven't in fifty-seven years."

"Fifty-seven, huh?" She bobbed her head, humming in agreement. "What would you rather I say?"

"Say your mouth is auditioning for me."

I kissed down the line of her jaw, telling her, "I'm not auditioning for a fucking thing. Tell me what you want or go home."

"Mmhmm. Yes."

She sighed as I mapped her skin with my mouth, tipping her head back to grant me greater access. Now that I'd started, I couldn't stop thrusting against her. Couldn't keep myself from nipping and sucking her neck. Couldn't come to the realization this was a terrible idea. Couldn't. Wouldn't. Her grip on my belt tightened and she moaned like I was creating magic and then—

"Good night, Jed."

She slipped out of my arms and away from the kegs, and she marched her fine ass to the door while I stared after her once again.

There was no moving on. Not from this.

CHAPTER FOUR

BROOKE

Short Selling: the practice of borrowing and selling shares of stock based on expectations of declining value only to then repurchase those shares at a lower price to turn a profit.

"THAT WAS NOT THE PLAN," I said to myself for the fifth time since leaving the Galley. "Not the plan *at all*."

I stamped my foot on the sidewalk outside my father's house, but it didn't help. *Nothing* helped. Wasn't that the story of my life right now? No matter what I did, it wasn't getting better. And if I thought I'd been in rough shape earlier today, my current condition could only be expressed by wailing at the moon.

Shoving my fingers through my hair, I glared at the walkway that led to the door that would take me inside. Back to the place where nothing helped, nothing got better, and nothing ever would. I wasn't ready to go in and face that reality.

"Not yet," I murmured, turning away from the house.

Down the hill sat the village of Talbott's Cove, quiet and dark in the crisp September night. Harbor lights cast a golden glow over the water and surrounding homes and businesses.

There'd been a time when I loved being able to see the entire town and everything happening in it from my father's house. It wasn't until I'd returned home after years away that I realized isolation was the price paid for this vantage point.

I was alone, even with round the clock staff and my father and my best friend never more than a text away. I was so damn lonely and over-whelmed and resentful and—and I didn't want to be any of those things tonight.

I turned back toward the village. And I ran.

As I barreled down the hill toward the village, I didn't allow myself to think this through. If I started thinking now, I'd come up with several strong reasons why I should return home, plug into the Asia-Pacific markets, and forget about the feel of JJ Harniczek's hands on my body. And yet, as my shoes slapped the pavement, I allowed myself a pair of thoughts.

One: Running was awful. Why did anyone do this for sport?

Two: Would JJ be home yet or should I stop at the tavern first?

When I reached the town square, the tavern was dark save for a single light over the door. "All right. Onward," I said to the night air. "The things a girl has to do for some dick."

On days when the dementia wind blew a certain way, my father would sit by the bank of windows facing the village and recount the history of this town as he knew it. He was careful to note the exact years each road was constructed and structures that followed, and the reasons for all of it. JJ lived at the end of a narrow, bungalow-lined street set behind the harbor that was built in the mid-eigh-teen-hundreds. Better roads were needed around the harbor then, and as the lobstering trade took off more local housing was required.

This was the predominant thought in my head as I run-walked down the sidewalk at twelve thirty in the morning. The approximate age and purpose of this road. I had to mentally box that noise up and hide it in a brain closet when I reached JJ's house because dick and Dad's dementia monologues didn't mix.

I'd nearly caught my breath when I knocked on his door, but the bare chest and scowl he greeted me with stole it all over again.

Goddamn. When did he get all that ink and chest hair and muscle?

He raised his arm, braced it on the doorframe. An octopus wrapped itself around his bicep and over his shoulder, and a little round bird with a long beak lived on his flank. "What the hell do you want?"

I glanced down at his jeans. "Take off your pants."

His brows pinched together. "Come again?"

"I'd love to, but I'm going to need you to drop those jeans first." I ducked under his arm and stepped into his home. "I trust you have a condom or two."

JJ stayed rooted at the threshold while I explored the living room. Dark blue sofa, white walls, hardwood floors. There was art and photos too, but I didn't stop long enough to take them in.

"Two?" he called. "What gave you the idea I want to have sex with you twice? Or even once?"

I wandered into the dining room and circled the table. It was an old, battered, family-style table, and none of the chairs matched. I kind of loved that. A laptop and stack of file folders sat beside a glass of water.

"Your dick was on my thigh like it was drilling for oil thirty minutes ago," I replied. "I don't think I'm the one overselling here."

He pushed the door shut and flipped the locks, but didn't turn around for a long moment. When he did, he leaned back against the slab, his arms folded over his chest. Making me stare at him while he stood there with his tattoos and chest hair on display was the most outrageous thing he'd ever done to me.

"What are you doing here, Brooke?" His voice was low and rough but free of all the hostility he often aimed at me.

"I'm telling you what I want."

He rolled his eyes up to the ceiling. "And what's that, sweetheart?"

I gestured to his jeans. "Off."

Shifting on bare feet, he brought his hands to his belt. The fabric dipped, highlighting a trail of dark fuzz and muscular grooves. Now, that was truly outrageous. "I'm not playing another game with you."

"No games. No bullshit," I said, blinking away from the belt-to-belly button region. "Just you, me, a condom or two."

"Lose the sweater."

I reached for the hem. "Fine." It sailed through the air, landing in front of his feet. "Your turn."

JJ charged across the room and curled both hands around my waist. "Let's get something straight. You tell me what you want, I tell you what to do. You're not the one issuing orders here."

I glanced between us and grinned at the hard bulge trapped behind his fly. "I'm pretty sure I am." I reached up, traced the lines of the octopus strangling his arm. "Here's what's going to happen, Jed. You're going to take me to a room with a bed. Once we get there, you're going to drop these jeans and I'll do the same. When I'm satisfied with the condom situation, you'll fuck me." I smiled up at him. "I prefer to be on top, so that's how we'll do it."

"Yeah. All right. You'll get what you want, sweetheart." A smirk tugged up his lips. "This time."

I blinked. "Excuse you?"

"This way." He squeezed my waist and nudged me backward. When I didn't move, he said, "I don't have all night and like I said, I'm not playing around with you."

"And I told you this isn't a game." He stared at me, his hazel eyes cool and his expression stony. "It's up to you whether you believe me."

I turned with the intention of marching myself down the hall and making him appreciate all the amazing things these jeans did for my ass, but he wrapped his arm around my waist and pressed his chest to my back within two steps.

"You're a lot of work," he murmured, his lips on my neck. "An awful lot of work."

"And you love it."

"Not how I'd describe it."

JJ reached for the light switch when we stepped into his room, but I batted his hand away. It was as if he'd never done this before. "No. No lights, thank you. We don't need them."

"So much work."

He flipped open my button fly and yanked my jeans and underwear down my hips. "That was also unnecessary," I said, righting my panties. "These will stay."

His fingers traced the underwire of my bra while he kissed my neck just like he had at the tavern. It was rude, the way his lips and teeth pulled at my skin. Just...rude. Like it belonged to him and he was well within his rights to bite me simply because it pleased him.

"I don't know what you're used to, sweetheart, but I'm gonna need these off if you want me to fuck you."

"No, you don't. I'll pull them to the side," I answered. "That's all you need."

He barked out a laugh. "You have no fuckin' idea what I need."

If I tried to explain to someone the lengths and hurdles I was going through to get laid, they wouldn't believe me. They'd insist I was exaggerating because there was no one alive who'd prefer to argue about whatever-the-fuck while my shirt was off and I flat-out demanded sex rather than get his cock out. Apparently, I'd stumbled upon the exception to every rule.

"Then take your fucking pants off and show me." I shoved out of his arms and ripped off my jeans. They landed on the other side of the room, one leg snared on a lamp, but neither of us moved to right them. I climbed to the bed and kneeled in the center, hoping to hell he didn't notice that every inch of me was dotted with goose bumps and I was shaking like a virginal leaf. I couldn't explain either reaction, but I knew I needed him to help me fix it right now. "Come on, Jed. Show me what you need."

He stared at me for a moment that stretched long enough to make me wonder whether I'd completely miscalculated, but then he glanced down at his belt. Mumbling to himself, he loosened the buckle, lowered his zipper. He closed his fists around either side of the open placket, pausing and shaking his head before pushing his clothes to the floor.

I knew good dick when I saw it and that was it. The shaking, the goose bumps, they only intensified.

"On top?" JJ produced a condom from a nightstand drawer and ripped it open. "You're sure about that?"

I didn't respond until he'd rolled the condom down his length. "Very sure."

A noise sounded in his throat, like a husky hiss or a growl. "Brooke."

I couldn't stop staring at his cock. I hadn't looked away since it'd appeared. "Mmhmm?"

"Close your mouth, sweetheart, unless that's where you want me putting this."

I glanced up as he joined me on the bed. "Could you talk less? Your cock looks bigger when you're quiet."

JJ twisted his fingers around the side of my panties and jerked me down into his lap. I landed with his face in my cleavage and his other hand on my ass. He closed his teeth around the side of my breast, bit down hard enough to soak my panties. A moan slipped past my lips and a tremor moved down my spine as he rocked against my core.

"If you wanted a taste of my tits, you could've asked."

Another bite, another growl. "Are you taking this bra off? It tastes like fabric softener."

I braced my hands on his shoulders and straddled his lap. I shook my head. "Can't see why I should."

"How about the fact I've barely touched you and there's a decent chance you came from that alone." He drew his index finger along the leg of my panties, slowing to drag his thumb through the wet. "Push these out of the way or whatever the hell you're doing."

I kept one hand on his shoulder and my gaze on his face while I edged my panties to the side. "I sincerely hope you know how to use that thing."

As he thrust inside me and ripped a gasp from my lips, he met my gaze with a smug grin. I would've told him where to shove that grin, but I was stuffed speechless. There was so much dick inside me, I wasn't certain I could properly inhale. I flattened both hands on his chest to hold myself still while I adjusted to him. It was a sharp, stinging reminder that sex toys weren't the same as the real thing. They just weren't.

"What'd I tell you about closing that mouth, sweetheart?"

At least sex toys didn't have an obnoxious comment for everything.

"If you think your dick is getting anywhere near my mouth, we need to get you medical attention because you're suffering from delusions." I rocked forward and back several times as I tried to find a rhythm that didn't feel like it would end with a broken vagina. "Just be quiet and let me get comfortable. I need a minute. Okay?"

All I'd wanted was to resurrect my orgasm and look what it got me. If I was going to crack my vagina in half, I would've thought it'd happen with one of the vibrators that didn't concern itself with anatomical correctness, not the mouthy barkeep.

"Yeah. Okay." JJ tucked my hair behind my ears and held my face in his hands. "There's no rush, Brooke."

He ran his hands down my spine, moving his fingers in slow circles. It helped. I didn't know how, but it did. As the seconds ticked by, he started rolling his hips in tiny waves that matched the soothing pressure on my back. With each rise and fall, my body relaxed—and tightened.

"That's good, that's good." I dragged my tongue over my lips as I sank all the way down on his cock and moved with him. "Yeah, good, that's—*yes*."

He smiled up at me, nodding. "This is what you want?"

I didn't answer. I was busy finding my way, learning his body. And answering while impaled on someone's rolling-pin cock usually meant showing some vulnerability. I wasn't here for that.

"Brooke." He closed his eyes, turned his head to the side. Murmured and moaned into the pillow. "Fuck, Brooke. What am I allowed to do?"

This would've been better if we didn't talk. I wasn't here for that either. I needed to remind my body what sex was all about, realign my orgasm settings, and get back to my life. I would've been able to do all of that if JJ didn't insist on reminding me it was *his* dick I was riding.

"What is it you want to know, Jed? And what kind of question is that?"

He moved his hands from the small of my back and yanked my ass cheeks apart, forcing himself deeper inside me and ripping a gasp from my lips. This was officially more than I'd bargained for.

"I want to know what I'm allowed to do," he gritted out as he dragged a pair of fingers to my clit. "Am I allowed to touch you here?" With his other hand, he brushed his knuckles down my backside. "What about here? Can I have this?"

I stared down at him, blinking. His jaw was locked and the tendons in his neck pulled taut. Under my hands, his chest and shoulders felt like granite.

He abandoned my ass to cup a breast. "What about here? Can I suck you, pinch you, bite you?"

"You've already bitten me." It wasn't the cleverest thing I'd ever said, but it was the only response I could manage.

He started moving his hips faster. Harder. He held me like he didn't care if I broke. "And you seemed to enjoy it."

"*Enjoy* seems like a strong endorsement," I replied. I shifted my hands to the mattress, not wanting to rely on him to stay steady. "More like a means to an end."

JJ speared up and stayed buried inside me for a beat. A noise rattled out of me, some kind of gasp or cry. "Is that all you want?" His fingers circled my nipple and clit at the same time, and that cry kept breaking free. "An end?"

"It would be preferable, yes."

"And that's it? That's all you want?"

I rolled my eyes as best I could when stuffed three ways to Sunday and going cross-eyed from the clit-and-nip program. "Yeah, Jed. That's all I want."

He closed his fingers around my nipple, pinched hard. "And you usually get what you want."

A laugh shot out of me. "It's nice to think that, but no." I almost continued, almost added that I hadn't gotten what I wanted in such a long time. But that kind of statement invited questions I wasn't interested in answering. Definitely not while his balls slapped my ass.

"Then get what you need." He punctuated each word with a pinch. "Go ahead, sweetheart. Get it."

I didn't comprehend his command at first, but then he brought his hands to my hips and shuttled my body over him. He wanted me to get what I needed—from him. "Keep doing that," I said, rocking against him. "*Keeeeeep* doing that."

If I'd caught a look at myself in a mirror or window reflection, I was certain I'd hate the visual of him bouncing me on his dick and using me like a fuck doll, but I wasn't looking or caring. I was almost there, *close close close*, and I just needed a little—

"*Fuuuuck*. Brooke. Say something. Anything."

"This would be so much better if you didn't speak." I squeezed my eyes shut and held myself tight as the first bites of pleasure pricked at my cheeks, my lips, my shoulders. "Just shut the fuck up and fuck me."

Thankfully, JJ did exactly that. He hammered into me with no more conversation than the occasional curse or growl. It was quiet and his cock was great and this was what I needed to reclaim my orgasm. I made the completely unnecessary announcement "I'm coming" while my body refused to do anything but bathe in those sensations.

"I know, I know. You're right there," he murmured, his brows drawn tight and his forehead creased. "I can feel it, sweetheart. Keep going."

But there was nowhere to *go*. It popped and fizzed and now, it was over. "Yeah, I don't think that's happening."

Once again, he surged into me, his cock deep enough to nudge my vital organs out of place. This time he stayed there, his grip on my hips tight and his gaze burning my skin. "What do you mean by that, Bam Bam?"

Without giving it much thought, I clenched around him. JJ tossed his head back on a chorus of my name and colorful variations of *Fuck*, and I did it again. That was when it happened. When I tripped his kill switch. He didn't thrash or scream, but he came like a train running a minute behind schedule, all raw power and steam and a flat-out refusal to let me get away with anything.

But I was always getting away with something. Always playing. I couldn't do this unless I played a fuckton of pretend. Right now, I wasn't me and he wasn't him, and this was acceptable only under those circumstances. Except when he squeezed my waist, threw his head back, and released a mile-long breath as he pulsed inside me.

When he finished, I pushed up from his chest. His hands fell away from my hips and I crawled out of his lap. "Since this is finished, I should go now," I said. "As you've mentioned repeatedly, you don't have much time tonight."

"That's what you wanted?" He eyed me as if he didn't expect the truth. I wasn't convinced he'd earned the right to the truth. It wasn't something I shared often. "That's it?"

I turned in a circle but didn't see my sweater anywhere. I couldn't remember where I'd left it. "Yeah. This was good."

He balled the condom in a tissue, shot it into the waste basket. "Good?"

"That's what I said." And that was honest. It was good sex. The dick was well above average and the conversation was abysmal, and when factoring in the overall mechanics, it came out to an overall positive event. There was an entire corporate belief system about good being the enemy of great, but that kind of touchy-feely-organizational-behavior bullshit didn't hold much water with me.

"I don't believe you." He laced his fingers behind his head and pulled that smug grin again. "I don't think that was what you wanted and I don't think it was good for you."

I knelt down to grab one of my shoes from under the bed. When I stood, I said, "It was fine, but thanks for making this weird in the comments section."

"I'm not making it weird," he replied with a brisk shake of his head.

I gathered my jeans from the lamp and clutched them in my arms. I wasn't going to give him the satisfaction of watching me shimmy into slim-cut jeans while he lay there with his dick lengthening on his belly like a damn periscope. Men were the worst. Thank god I wasn't going to need one again for another two years.

"Then what the hell are you doing, Jed? Because it seems like you're telling me I'm bad in bed and that's strange because I know you enjoyed it just fine. It's also extremely rude, but that's your usual." He swung his legs over the edge of the bed and snagged me around the waist, but I stepped out of his reach. I wasn't doing that again. "Thank you, no. I'm going to find my sweater and go home, and we're never talking about this night ever again."

"Brooke." He pushed off the bed. As much as I wanted to erase these events from memory, the heaviness in his tone rooted me in place. He stopped behind me, his hands settling on my hips. His cock tapped the small of my back. "I'm not telling you you're bad in bed."

"Then what are you telling me?"

He plucked my jeans and shoes from my arms, tossed them to the floor. "You had it your way," he said, his beard scraping my shoulder as he spoke to my skin. "Now, it's my turn."

CHAPTER FIVE

J J

Elasticity: a measurement of shifts in demand for a product correspondent to price shifts.

IF I WAS GOING to ruin my life, there was no sense in half-assing it.

To be sure, I *was* ruining my life. Even as I kept telling myself this was a one-and-done situation, having sex with Brooke was suicide. I'd never come back from this. Never shake it off. And not because she was a spectacular lay—she was—but because she'd never let me forget how I bent to her will and gave her everything she wanted, even when I knew it was a goddamn mistake.

"Now it's my turn." I dragged my hand up her spine, stopping between her shoulder blades. I stroked her alabaster skin for a second before shoving her facedown onto the bed.

She went with an indignant shriek and, "You better watch yourself, Jed."

I climbed over her and straddled her thighs. Front row seat to the best ass in the state and my complete downfall. "Let me ask you this one more time, Brooke. What am I allowed to do?"

She huffed out the sigh of a woman who'd never been thrown on a bed and didn't want to admit she liked it.

"You're allowed to get the fuck off me," she replied.

I filled my hands with her ass cheeks, kneading and squeezing and separating while Brooke shot her most vicious scowl at me over her shoulder. "For such a mouthy, bratty woman, you're shit at asking for what you want."

"I just asked you to get off me."

I moved my hand between her thighs, but I waited, drawing circles on her leg with my thumb. I waited while her pale, narrow shoulders loosened and a breath whooshed out of her. Waited until she glanced at me from under that long curtain of platinum hair and those pale lashes, and tipped her stubborn chin up in the tiniest unspoken *yes* I'd ever heard.

So, this is how it's going to be.

Finally, I cupped her the way I'd wanted all night. The black panties she insisted on wearing were warm and wet. She pressed the back of her hand to her mouth when I brushed her clit over the fabric. "It's not that hard, sweetheart. You tell me what you want, I give it to you."

"Haven't I told you to shut up? You're the most conversational dick appointment I've ever had," she hissed. "It's a tragedy I don't carry ball gags with me anymore."

I gave her cheeks a harsh squeeze. It took real restraint to keep from tearing off those panties, leaning forward, and licking her. Just to know, once and for all, how Brooke Markham's ass tasted. "Maybe if you answered my fucking questions the first time I asked them, you could get the dick you came for."

"I distinctly recall you telling me you didn't want to have sex with me twice."

"You should take your own advice and shut up." I slipped my fingers under the fabric, inside her. We groaned at the same time. She fisted the bed linens, buried her face in the blankets. Worked damn hard at denying herself as she moved against my hand like she was made for it. "Fucking hell, Brooke. Let me take these goddamn panties off you."

She was panting as she found a rhythm on my fingers. Watching her like this—with my cock hard on the back of her leg and my hand between her thighs and her body writhing on my bed—made it easy to ignore the consequences. The price I'd pay for this.

"Fine," she snapped. "But don't you dare ruin them."

I hooked my free hand around the waistband, edged it down. "How could I ruin your precious underwear?"

"You're approximately two hundred and fifty pounds of lumberjack man," she answered. "I wouldn't put it past you to ruin some fine lingerie."

I couldn't identify anything fine about these panties beyond the delicate script lettering on the waistband reading *Agent Provocateur*. Shifting to my knees, I dragged the overpriced scrap of fabric down her thighs. Once it was free, I chucked it over my shoulder. Fuck her fine lingerie.

Slipping my fingers under the band of her bra, I said, "This too."

"*This*," she muttered, "is hand-sewn lace imported from France. Handle with care."

I flung that French lace clear across the room. I ran my hands up the back of her thighs, now well and truly obsessed with licking this woman. "I'm going to ask you one more time—"

"You've said that at least four times," Brooke interrupted. "Maybe you should save your breath. It's not getting you anywhere."

"Maybe you should answer me."

She folded her arms and rested her head there. She stared in my direction without meeting my eyes. I wasn't positive, but it seemed like she was studying my cock. I had no problem with that, not when her hooded-eye gaze was the most honest thing she could offer.

"Why? Nothing about this needs to be complicated or customized, Jed. It's not like I'm ordering a burrito bowl."

I braced my arms on either side of her, pressed my chest to her back. "Because"—I paused to scoop her hair off her shoulder—"it actually matters to me that you want this."

She lowered her eyes, pursed her lips, stayed silent for a long moment. Then, softly, "I do."

I grabbed her around the waist, jerking her up to her knees. Kept my lips on her back and her shoulders as I slipped my hand between her legs. Without any fancy underwear to slow me down, I was able to touch all of her at once. She jerked and gasped when I traced her clit, her seam, her ass. "You want me to fuck you like this?"

She nodded, hummed. "Yes."

"On your knees?"

She replied with another nod and a high-pitched noise I couldn't decipher. I'd call it a squeak, but this woman didn't squeak. She screeched and screamed and roared, and I wanted to hear all those things from her before the sun came up on this day.

Fisting my shaft, I said, "That wasn't an answer, sweetheart." I dragged the head between her cheeks, through her wet, stopping only to slap her clit. "On your knees, ass in the air, head down?"

It took her a second to find her voice, but when she did, she snapped out an impatient "Yes."

"You're sure about that?" Reaching for the table, I grabbed the other condom and rolled it on. "You know you don't get to call the shots from down there, sweetheart."

"The hell I don't," Brooke replied.

I took hold of her hips and filled her with one thrust. "Go ahead and try."

Jesus Holy Christ, she felt incredible. There was all the usual pussy goodness—hot, wet, tight—but that fire-breathing rage of hers made everything better. I couldn't shake the sense she'd let me fuck her until she couldn't walk right, but then she'd rip one of my kidneys out and keep it as a trophy.

She reached back, grabbed hold of my thigh. "If you don't move in the next zero-point-two seconds, I'm gonna show you what it looks like to call the shots from down here."

I eased out, sucking in a breath as I dragged my length over her folds. "You could do that," I said, staring at the place where her body yielded to mine. "But we both know you didn't come here for that."

Brooke muttered something into the mattress I couldn't understand. She was so damn angry about everything. Most of the time, that poor little rich girl fury clawed at my last nerves, but this was different. I couldn't explain how or why it was different, but I knew this night wasn't like the others. She needed something—or someone—and that need wrapped around the nerves dedicated to this woman in a way that compelled me to give her everything. Even if it meant trashing the life I'd established for myself to meet that need.

She rocked back, claiming the head of my cock. Even that inch of heat was enough to make me dizzy. Enough to start me thinking about the ways I'd take her the next time and the next and all the times after that. And that was only one of the reasons she was ruining my life.

"Is this some kind of art house film where you tell me you're going to fuck me in half and go to a lot of trouble to position me the way you want, but then stare off into space while you wonder where your one true love is tonight?" she asked. "Because that's the way this is unfolding."

I ran my hands over her backside, dug my fingers into her skin, spread her cheeks to get a better look at my cock pushing inside her. I watched as she stretched and opened around me, moving slow to aggravate her and amuse myself. "I'm just making sure you can handle this."

She laughed, causing her muscles to contract around me. For a second, my eyes rolled back in my head. "That's not going to be a problem."

"You sure about that?" I gripped her ass like I meant to mark it, pushed all the way inside her. She responded with a choked cry that shifted into a moan, a hum, and then a hungry, desperate whine. Her hands shifted, scrambling to fist around the blankets. To hold tight. "I don't know, sweetheart. You had a hard time handling me last time and I just lay there, as you requested."

"That's because after high school your dick grew up to be a freak of nature elephantine baseball bat that might actually destroy my uterus. Thanks for warning me about that, by the way."

She shot a withering look at me over her shoulder, but that didn't stop her from working herself on my cock. She was taking what she wanted. Finally. She was gorgeous like this, her face flushed, her hair everywhere. And on her hands and knees for me while I carved fingertip bruises into her ass.

"You're welcome." I brought a hand between her shoulders, pushed her head back down to the mattress. "Hush, now."

"Hush yourself," she yelled into the blankets. "Fuck me like you know how to do it or let me go home to my vibrators."

The mental picture of Brooke spread out on a bed, her knees bent and her hand working between her legs while a battery-powered hum and the sharp spice of her arousal filled the air, was enough to snap my thrusts into an urgent, primal rhythm. "You'd be there right now if that was what you needed, Bam."

I expected a retort, but not the one that came. A high, breathy whimper sounded in the back of her throat and— "I don't know what I need."

I paused, my hand still flat on her back and my cock as deep as she'd take me. I blinked down at her, ran my thumb over the bony ridge of her spine. This was how she did it, how she destroyed me. How I let her.

Leaning down, I licked a trail up her back, along those notches. Rested my forehead there, kissed her once—then again and again. Whispered into her skin, "Then let me show you."

I felt her nodding, felt her cry, "Yes, please," felt her clench around my cock like she never wanted to release me. Then, "For fuck's sake, Jed, *please*."

Once she spoke those words, we stopped having sex. It wasn't about anatomy or friction anymore. This was fucking, fast and frantic, as if we were trying to get away with something we knew was wrong but couldn't help wanting.

She thrashed beneath me, her eyes shut and her mouth open as I hammered into her. The bed creaked, scraped at the floor, pounded against the wall. She cried out; I growled. I flipped her on her back; she wrestled her way into my lap. She swore at me; I swore right back. Sweat clung to my brow, my hair came loose from its knot. We batted away pillows, blankets. The sheets were off, gone. She scratched; I sucked. Nothing was off-limits, and we pushed hard at those boundaries.

We were loud, messy, almost violent. It ended with shouts and roars certain to wake half this town, but I didn't care. I'd wake the whole fucking world to feel Brooke come apart on me again.

Without a doubt, I would. I ruined my life for her and I'd do that again too.

CHAPTER SIX

BROOKE

Break-Even: the level of revenues and expenses at which a project earns zero profit.

THIS WAS A MISTAKE.

The word *mistake* felt inadequate for my current situation. Mistakes were buying bubble bath instead of body wash, or closing a spreadsheet before double-checking it was saved. Mistakes were not running down a hill, through a village, and along a side street at midnight and demanding sex not once but twice from a man who despised me—and doing it on my damn birthday.

But I wasn't prepared to call this a disaster, not even when he locked his arms around my torso and fused his lips to my neck. Knowing Jed, he wasn't cuddling so much as debating whether he wanted to smother me with a pillow or bite my carotid artery open. No, this wasn't a disaster. Those left damages in their wake. The only damages here were the ones to my vagina and I'd invited those.

Not a mistake but not quite a disaster meant this was a problem teetering into crisis territory. I'd breach that threshold if I stayed in this bed—in this man's arms—for more than five minutes. That was the limit, five minutes. Enough time to catch my breath and plan my parting remarks.

"What's wrong?" he asked, his words sleepy. Almost scratchy.

I managed a small shrug in spite of his straitjacket hold on me. "Nothing's wrong."

"No, of course not. Your ass is always tight enough to bounce quarters off it."

"As a matter of fact—"

"Save it, sweetheart. We have argued enough for one night, don't you think?"

Something about that roughly spoken *we* scratched up my spine and sent me scrambling off the bed. "I think this is never happening again," I said as I gathered my things. "And we're never speaking of it either."

JJ propped his head on his hand, watching as I plucked my bra off the curtain rod. "Would you care to explain to me what just happened?"

Stepping into my panties, I said, "This is how it ends, Jed."

He went on lazing in the bed, the sheets gathered at his waist and his head bent as if I was a great curiosity. "Uh huh. Sure, Brooke. If that's what you want."

I gave him my back as I pulled on my bra. "Let me explain a few things to you, Jed."

He barked out a laugh. "No explanations needed. You came here with one thing in mind and you got what you wanted. Now it's over. I got that loud and clear, sweetheart."

I stared at the wall, a bitter smile twisting my lips as his rough, faintly Maine *sweethabht* washed over me. It wasn't meant as an endearment. It wasn't intended to hit me in my hardest, toughest spots and I wasn't supposed to like it.

Whirling around, I said, "Again, we are never speaking of this or repeating these events. We have altogether too much shared past and more than enough shared present. There shall be no hookup routine between us. No future dick appointments."

He ran his knuckles down his jaw, frowned at the mattress. "That's unfortunate. I was really coming around to the idea of you making a reservation for my cock."

A stiff, slightly manic laugh shook my shoulders. "That's funny. Really funny, Jed. But let me explain the facts of this matter to you." I held up my index finger. "One, this town is microscopic. There's no room for secrets here and we both know they don't keep."

"They sure don't." He blinked at me, the kind of intentional, pointed blink that suggested we were talking about different things. "Doesn't matter how hard you try."

"Whatever you're doing, stop." Forgoing all semblance of dignity, I wiggled into my jeans. "Second, I'm not interested in a repeat performance. This was fine and it's over."

"Yeah. Your pussy was adequate at best."

My jeans halfway up my thighs, I stopped to glare at him. "You're an asshole."

"Just following your lead."

Returning to my jeans, I murmured to myself, "I knew I shouldn't do this in my backyard."

"Right, because the entire town is your property."

Not bothering to look away from my button fly, I replied, "Unnecessary."

"Yeah? I'm being unnecessary?" He sat up, leaned against the headboard. The sheets pooled at his hips. "How about you going on a rant about how I'm not allowed any more *dick appointments* with you when I don't recall asking for this one?"

"Oh, so, now I forced you to have sex with me? Really, Jed? After you spent a goddamn hour asking me whether I wanted it, you're the one who didn't?"

His jaw worked as he glared at me. "That's not what I said."

"No, it's not what you said at all. You made a rude little quip about my pussy and then had the good sense to bring up my family owning the entire town." I jammed my feet into my shoes and wished like hell I could find my sweater. "This happened once—"

"Twice," he interrupted.

"—and it's not happening again."

He kicked off the sheets and swung his legs over the side of the bed. Still glaring at me as if he intended to draw blood, he stepped into his jeans and buckled his belt. "Seems like you're having some trouble understanding me, sweetheart. I'm not interested in fucking you again."

"Perfect." I stormed into the hallway and toward the front of the house with JJ right behind me. My sweater lay in the middle of the hardwood floor, a pathetic heap of cashmere and regret. I snatched it up, pulled it over my head. "I expect you'll keep these events private. There's no reason to share this with anyone."

From behind me, he said, "Least of all Annette."

Fuck. "As I stated, there's no reason to share this with anyone."

"Agreed."

He stepped around me, fetching his boots from beside the door. At some point in the past few minutes, he'd donned a shirt. A tiny part of me wished he'd left it off. When he tugged the boots on, I asked, "What the fuck are you doing?"

"A real piece of work," he said, laughing to himself. "I'm walking you the fuck home, Brooke."

I dropped my hands to my hips. "I'd rather you not."

"That's tough shit, sweetheart. It's almost four in the fucking morning. The last thing I need is you getting mowed down by a moose. That would really screw up village traffic and I got a big beer delivery coming in from Harpoon this morning."

"All right, Jed," I said as indulgently as I could manage. "You can keep an eye out for *moose*. You do that."

I flung open the door and stepped into the chilly night air. Early fingers of dawn poked at the horizon. I hugged my arms to my chest as I headed toward home, walking as briskly as I would in Manhattan. People around here didn't understand the sidewalk laws of the city. They favored leisurely strolls in these parts. They'd survive ten minutes in the city.

Behind me, I heard a whistle, a door shutting, and footfalls on the pavement. And also—panting? I glanced over my shoulder and found a dog walking beside Jed. "Where did you get a dog?"

He shoved his hands in his front pockets, shrugged. "She found me."

"Like, right this instant?"

Jed seemed to share a laugh with the dog. I didn't know much about dogs, but she looked like a Labrador or a retriever. One of those big, sturdy dogs who understood commands and herded children when need be.

"About three years ago," he replied. "She showed up behind the tavern."

I stopped to gaze at them as they caught up with me. "You're telling me there was a dog in your house—the whole time?"

"Yeah, Brooke." He touched his hand to my lower back, urging me forward. "Is that a problem?"

"Uh, no," I replied. "I just don't know how I didn't notice a dog."

"Butterscotch conks out around ten o'clock and doesn't wake up until I tell her it's morning. A band of pirates could've stormed my house and she would've slept through every second of it."

I glanced at him as we crossed into the village. "You named your dog Butterscotch?"

"I mean, look at her." He gestured to the dog's golden coat. "Also, she'll steal an ice cream sundae out of your hand if you're not careful."

"I suppose that fits," I conceded. "But I didn't know dogs ate ice cream."

We walked up the hill to my father's house—which sat on a parcel of land that'd been in my family for hundreds of years and covered almost half of Talbott's Cove—in silence. When we reached the entrance, JJ eyed the house and dropped his hand to Butterscotch's head, scratching behind her ears.

I spread my hands out in front of me. "As you can see, no moose."

He snickered. "You're welcome."

"Yes, Jed. Thank you. Your generosity is appreciated."

"Yeah, well..." His voice trailed off as he glanced toward the water. "Good night."

He turned to leave, but I couldn't let him go. Not without killing this with fire. "Jed?"

Stopping, he studied me with a wary smirk. "What is it, Bam Bam?"

"The next time I try to pick someone up at the tavern, you won't interfere." I offered him a sharp grin and marched up the walkway, not waiting for a response.

When I closed the front door behind me, he was still standing on the sidewalk with Butterscotch.

One last shot fired.

CHAPTER SEVEN

JJ

***Reserve: an accounting entry that properly reflects contingent
liabilities.***

BARRY O'CONNOR TURNED in a wide arc, his head tipped back and
his gaze fixed on the exposed beams overhead.

The beams, the birds' nests, the bursts of sunlight streaming in
through gaps in the roof. The old cider house presented my business
partner with plenty to see.

"You think this will work?" he asked, still staring at the remains of
the roof. "Or are you thinking we knock this popsicle stand over and
start from scratch?"

"I think this will work," I replied, working hard to keep the impatience out of my tone.

If I'd wanted to start from scratch, I would've shown him any one of
the many parcels of vacant land available in this town. This distillery
project wasn't about building something new. It was about building on
that which already existed.

Barry ambled to the far side of the cider house. He rapped his knuckles on a post, tapped his shoe against the cracked cement floor. "It's gonna need a lot of work," he said. "It might be cheaper to knock it down."

"But that forecloses the possibility of selling on the story," I argued. "No one makes a destination out of a new-construction distillery. That's no different than any number of breweries along the seacoast."

"That's only part of the pitch," he argued back. "Even with new construction, we still have the locally sourced angle, the Prohibition Era bootlegger angle, the charming small town angle. We have enough angles to do without the most expensive one." He frowned at a dark stain on the floor. "Was someone killed here?"

I shoved my hands in my pockets, ignoring the tug of well-used abdominal muscles. I couldn't think about Brooke or the things we did to leave me sore today. Not while I dealt with my part-time pain in the ass business partner. "Ever in the history of the cider house? Probably, yes. That I know of, in recent times? No."

"That's positive," he muttered.

Barry painted himself as a hometown guy, someone who grew up a handful of miles down the coast and cared about seeing this region thrive. These days, he lived in Boston and developed commercial real estate. He talked a big game about investing in Maine-based passion projects intended to grow the local economy, but a solid year after our first meeting and his verbal commitment to this distillery, he hadn't written a single check.

Each time we met, he insisted he needed one more thing before pulling the trigger. More detailed financial projections, preliminary approval from the town council for a liquor license, a site walk-through. It made sense—I was asking for tens of millions of dollars to make this happen—but I was growing tired of the hurry up and wait routine. I couldn't determine whether Barry was a flaky guy or not fully committed. His interest seemed to shift with the lunar cycle and that didn't fill me with much confidence.

"Tasting room," he announced, drawing invisible lines along the west side of the space. "We'd put the tasting room here. Keep it intimate, a little dark. Like a speakeasy. We want a space that evokes that air of secrecy and sin, you know?" He turned toward the ocean, facing east.

"Save the sunlight for the restaurant. We can add twenty percent to the price of everything on the menu when we're garnishing with ocean views like these." He pivoted, holding his arms open to the wide space. "And the rest of it, well, that's where you show off racks of distilling barrels. Make the work of a distillery part of its art."

Whether flaky or not fully committed, when Barry was on, he was all the way on. His instincts were solid, and ideas—an on-site display garden to emphasize the locally grown ingredients—strengthened my plans.

"Love it," I agreed. "Let's walk the perimeter." I gestured to the wide doors on the opposite end of the space. "Back when this was a functioning cider house, this is where the wagons came in from the orchards. As you can see, it would make for the perfect patio area. Big enough to host large events like weddings and live music. With the right setup, it could house summertime farmers markets, food truck nights, and festivals. Bring in some potted trees and bushes and it's small enough for cocktail parties or bridal showers."

Barry glanced around, nodding. "The ocean view is worth the price of construction."

I was counting on it. This whole thing was a gamble of unbelievable proportions and every time our meetings ended without an exchange of funds, the stakes increased.

"Why not cider?" he asked.

I frowned at him as we rounded the building. "I'm not sure I follow you."

"This is a cider house." He shook his hands at the structure, as if his point was obvious. I knew where he was going with this, but I wasn't copping to that. He proposed crafting something different every time we met. "We should make cider. The hard cider market is—"

"Declining," I interrupted. "It boomed three years ago and it's on the way down. Beyond that, it's more labor intensive. Gin and vodka are mainstays."

Opening a distillery hadn't crossed my mind until a few years ago, when a tourist insisted on buying all of my house-made gin. I'd never sold my honey-steeped liquor by the bottle before, but this woman wasn't exiting the tavern without it. She offered a deranged amount of money, an amount that made refusing even more deranged. Before leaving, her husband told me it was time to expand beyond fried seafood and beer if someone was willing to drop that kind of cash on a case of gin.

As I didn't enjoy unsolicited advice, I ignored his suggestion. I went back to tooling around with small-batch liquors in my spare time and convinced myself there was no place for a high-end gin joint in Talbott's Cove. But then the deranged woman's friends showed up. They'd heard about this scenic town and its artisanal gin, and they'd traveled here from Boston to see it for themselves—and buy a case of their own.

That was when I realized it wasn't isolated to opening an upmarket gin joint. These deranged people spent the weekend at the local inn, shopped all over the village, chartered sunset boat cruises around Penobscot Bay. They poured money all over a region reckoning with warmer ocean temperatures and permanent shifts in the fishing industry, with declining employment and rising hopelessness. If they came for gin, others would too.

"Right, right," Barry murmured. "And you're sure we can't get in on the hard seltzer market?"

"As a marquee product, no, we can't get into hard seltzers." How I managed to respond without snapping at him was a mystery. "We could work on adding a specialty seltzer to the menu once we have the right equipment in place."

"Yeah, something seasonal and locally inspired," he replied, snapping his fingers. "It would coincide with the rotating menu."

"We'd need dedicated equipment for seltzer," I added. "It requires testing."

Barry laughed as if developing a carbonated liquor beverage with organic ingredients was a simple task. "You can do that now. Test it out at your tavern. Do some market research."

I didn't respond to that. Instead, I steered Barry toward the northernmost tip of the property which backed up to a thick grove of maple trees. "This land makes for the perfect pollinator garden and apiary. It's the right distance from the primary outdoor spaces so we won't end up with bees buzzing around the clientele, but still close enough to include it in the educational walking tour."

"People fuckin' love bees," he mused. "Can't we do rum with bees?"

"Do *what* with bees?"

I marched away from the intended garden plot and toward the area I'd sketched out for deliveries and parking. The purpose of this meeting was to visit the site and then work through other elements critical to the business plan. We needed to make headway on licensing and zoning, as well as the paperwork necessary for overhauling a historical building. We needed to hire contractors, agree on budgets, and formalize partnership agreements with all the area farmers I'd tapped for this work.

"Rum," he repeated, jogging to catch up with me. "Doesn't Maine have a long, sordid history with the rum trade? Weren't there stories about rum barrels washing up on the shores after pirates and privateers intercepted ships? Capitalizing on a pirate connection would be a better way to leverage local history than the cider house angle."

I stopped at the front side of the building, dropped my hands to my waist and ignored Barry's presence for a second. After walking Brooke home, I'd managed three hours of fitful, furious sleep in which I'd dreamed about marching into the massive estate sitting atop the hill bearing her family's name and throwing her on the first bed I found. Telling her that, as long as she was in my tavern, I intended to interfere as much as I fucking wanted. I woke up with the kind of erection powered by regret and masochism. The kind that couldn't be helped.

That left me standing here, hot despite a brisk snap in the air, exhausted and aching all over. And I still had to put on a good face for the man with the money.

"Not sure about rum, Barry," I answered, exasperated as hell and working my ass off to keep it contained. I ran a hand over my head as I blew out a breath. I needed to chug some water and get a sizeable lunch in my belly if I was going to survive the rest of this day. "I think that was farther south. Cape Cod or Block Island Sound, maybe. I'll check into it, but you should know rum distilling also requires specialized equipment. The more we add, the higher the bill."

He considered this. "And it muddies the message. Are we rum or gin or cider? Who knows? Too confusing. You have to home in on one core competency."

I gave him a thoughtful look as I bit the hell out of my tongue. "Yeah, you're right about that."

Barry shifted to study the side of the building that would greet visitors. He lifted his arms, holding his hands out wide. "Down East Distillery," he announced. "The home of fine artisanal spirits."

I wasn't getting my hopes up, but— "This is the place?"

"This is it," he agreed, clapping his hands together. "Lots of history and local lore to play with. I love it." He smiled at me, the kind of grin that made me wonder whether he knew exactly how much he'd jerked me around this past year. "Let's do this thing."

RIGHT SMACK in the middle of the lunch rush—before I'd gotten around to eating or drinking much of anything myself—Sheriff Jackson Lau strolled into my tavern. Moseyed up to the bar and gestured for my attention as if I had all the time in the world for him. He kept the peace well enough, but he didn't have to do it with that holier-than-thou, merit-badging Boy Scout routine. Being the next best thing to Captain America had to get boring.

Regardless of my feelings about Lau, I had some trouble with his type. My record was clean and my closets free of skeletons, but I kept my distance from authority figures. More often than not, their power was like a penis. Always taking it out and waving it around, slapping people in the face with it, shoving it down other's throats. The worst of them would shove it right up your ass and then expect you to thank them for their service.

I met his gaze briefly before turning back to the taps. "What brings you in, sheriff?"

He rested an arm on the bar, leaned in close. "I need a moment of your time, Harniczek."

"Never would've guessed," I muttered. "As you can see, my hands are full. Sit a minute, order a sandwich. Then, we'll talk."

He offered a brisk shake of his head that annoyed the actual fuck out of me. "No can do, Harniczek. I'm on duty and have a tight schedule to keep."

Always by the book with this one. I glared at him as I loaded a tray with freshly poured beers. "Uh huh. Yeah. So, you want avocado on that BLT or no?"

The sheriff mulled this over as he settled onto a stool. "I wouldn't mind some avocado, if it's no trouble." When I shook my head, he continued, "And an iced tea, if you have any. I'm trying to cut back on the soda."

I reached for the pitcher of herbal tea produced by a local grower. They were hooking me up with juniper berries for house-made gin. I was experimenting with some tea-scented vodka too, but I wasn't convinced I could pull that one off in small batches. Wasn't convinced I could make it sound appealing either. "Is that so?"

"Annette brings a lot of sweetness to my life," he said, laughing. "In more ways than one."

"And that's why you're cutting back on the soda." This conversation was four minutes old and already far too long. "Got it." I punched his order into the point of sale system and kicked it up to the front of the queue. "That sandwich will be up in a minute. Mind giving me the general reason for your visit while we wait?"

I set a glass of tea down in front of him and grabbed the next set of tickets waiting for me. I glanced back at the sheriff while I lined up pint glasses under the taps. Waited. Cleared my throat. Waited a bit longer.

"Here's something you don't know," I said, lifting a pint glass in his direction. True to form, he waved me off. "I wasn't offering you a beer, sheriff. I understand you're a principled man and I'm not about to test those principles by pouring you a brew while on duty. Feeding you a sandwich is a big enough challenge. Now, since you're sitting here, I'm gonna teach you something. See this here?"

He followed my finger to the foam at the rim of the pint glass. "The head?"

"The proper term is barm," I said. "'Fill the barm to the brim but make it slim.' That's some bartender wisdom for you."

"I'll put that to good use the next time Annette and Brooke drag me out to trivia night," Lau replied. "It's always nice to have an ace in the hole with those two. They'll run roughshod if I'm not careful."

The mention of Brooke's name had me bobbling the trio of pint glasses pinched between my fingers. The idea of her and running roughshod...well, that was how my boots ended up soaked with beer. "Motherfuck," I hissed. I turned away from the sheriff to wash my hands. "It's brave of you to take on both of them at once. I wouldn't do that without an athletic cup and a case of Sauvignon Blanc."

"They're a package deal," he replied, shrugging. "If I didn't enthusiastically enjoy Brooke's company, Annette wouldn't have the time of day for me."

"And you do? Enthusiastically enjoy Brooke's company?" I added.

The sheriff paused long enough for me to take pleasure in his silence. Brooke wasn't for everyone. No one operated at her speed. Few could handle her. Even fewer understood her. I was positive I didn't.

"Your silence says it all, sheriff."

"No, you have the wrong idea," he insisted. "Brooke is a dear friend to Annette and she never ceases to amaze me with the things she says. But Annette worries about her and that makes me worry." I accepted a plate from one of my servers and set it in front of Lau. "I'm happy to have Brooke join us for trivia if that means fewer worries."

Nodding, I stepped away to revisit the drink orders I'd spilled on myself. It was important to keep the beer flowing, but it was also important to stop myself from asking why Jackson and Annette were concerned about Brooke. I had a few ideas on that matter and I could've compared notes all day, but she wasn't my problem.

Not. My. Problem.

"Why don't we step into your office," Lau suggested.

I glanced at his plate, clean save for some fries and a pickle. "You're as bad as the princess," I murmured. "Next time you come in here hungry, don't dick around with me, sheriff. Order a damn sandwich, you hear me?"

Standing, he counted out enough cash to cover four BLTs and tucked it beside the plate. "An excellent meal as always. Thank you."

I dropped the cash into the servers' tip drawer. I wasn't doing him any favors and he sure as shit wasn't doing me any.

"Make it quick," I said, waving him down the hallway toward my office. The hallway in which I'd found Brooke lurking last night. I needed to open a distillery just to work in a place free from her fingerprints.

I dropped into my desk chair while the sheriff sat across from me. "I'll make this quick," he said.

"Music to my ears," I muttered.

"Nathan Fitzsimmons is scheduled to leave rehab at the end of next month."

"Already?" I barked. The Fitzsimmons kid needed help. Real help. He needed professional people who knew how to help him unwind his addiction and live his life without going back to the pills again. "He's only been there, what—"

"Four months," Lau interrupted. "When he's discharged, it will be five."

"That doesn't seem like enough." I gripped the arm rests. That kid's parents went through hell trying to get him help. I couldn't count the number of times they'd checked him into detox. Couldn't count the number of times the sheriff's deputies were out at the Fitzsimmons house, hauling him away after a fight with his parents turned physical or they'd found him stealing the rug out from underneath them to pay for drugs. But I remembered the last time, when they decided enough was enough. "How does someone learn how to live a new life in only four or five months?"

Lau jerked a shoulder up. "Most opioid dependency programs are less than a month. Twenty-eight days, usually. This one treats both dependency as well as other mental health diagnoses. He was lucky to get a bed in this facility. It probably saved his life. Certainly kept him out of prison."

"That's great but how is he allowed to leave without—I don't know—going to some kind of transitional living or halfway house to help him back into the real world?"

"There are a slew of conditions to his release. He has court-ordered drug tests every week for a year as well as counseling, sobriety support groups, and regular meetings with his probation officer." Lau glanced down at the floor. "His PO believes he'll succeed, but he won't be able to do it alone."

Fuck me. Just...fuck me.

"The reason for your visit is revealed." I waited for Lau to deny it, but he only sat back with his hands folded in his lap. "I don't know how you'd like for me to help this kid. In case you haven't noticed, I run a tavern. It's not a good old-fashioned tavern because we don't put up travelers for the night, but we hold with the tradition of serving beer, wine, and spirits alongside food. That is no place for a young man making a run at sober living and I'm the farthest thing you'll find from a social worker."

"Think about it," the sheriff prompted. "Do you think he has any chance of succeeding if he goes back home to his parents' house? That's his only option right now and we both know that won't work." He ran his hand through his hair, huffed out a rueful laugh. "Trust me, I've already tried that angle and it's a nonstarter. I've also approached a number of other residents. I'm asking you a favor, Harniczek."

"What are you suggesting, sheriff? I'm not in the market for a roommate."

"Maybe not, but you do have that vacant apartment on the back side of this building," he answered. "If my understanding of your zoning and property tax filings is accurate, that is."

That goddamn power penis. I did not need this shit today. Not on a couple of hours sleep and not with my muscles humming with every move and a woman in need of some roughshod no more than a five-minute walk from this very spot. "You want me to put this kid up in an apartment above a tavern? You think that will support his recovery?"

"According to the probation officer, Nathan's dependency is isolated to opioids. He's never been a drinker and doesn't see alcohol as a coping mechanism."

"How convenient." I leaned back in my chair, blew out a ragged breath. I hated this. I hated the sheriff coming into my business and asking for help. More than all that, I hated knowing the kid was in a bind and no one was willing to stand up. "What about your girlfriend's old apartment? She's not living there anymore."

He ran a hand along his jaw, his brows drawing together as he nodded. "That was one of my first considerations," he said. "But five other people have been asking after that apartment and she doesn't own the building. It's not her call."

"Now, that's convenient."

"I'm also hoping you're in need of a dishwasher," Lau continued. "Nathan needs a job and one that won't get hung up on his prior convictions."

I touched a hand to my chest. "And you think I'm that employer? You also think I'm willing to hire and house a kid who has spent the past five or six years of his life hooked on drugs and hope he doesn't replace that addiction with booze? You've gotta be out of your damn mind, Lau."

"You could set him straight, Harniczek." The sheriff had the balls to give me one of those *I believe in you* nods reserved for the soccer coaches of small children. "He's pissing in a cup weekly, so we'll know if he's drinking. I'm sure you'd also notice any variations in your stock. If it turns out this situation is too complex for him, we'll find something else. But I've given this a lot of thought and I think it could work. You run a tight ship and you don't let anything slip through the cracks. You won't let him fuck up or fall off the deep end. You could give him the reset he needs."

"If I agree to this, will you stop waltzing in here and taking up my time during the busiest parts of the day?"

"I'll do my best." He shrugged. "Would it help if I brought some homemade muffins or brownies? I'm sure Annette would be happy to make something special for you."

I cocked my head to the side. "Could you fucking not?"

"What? Her muffins are amazing."

"I'm not discussing her muffins with you."

"All right." He held up his hands, let them fall. "No muffins."

"This better not blow up on me, Lau. My hands are full right now and I don't have time to big brother all over a recovering twentysomething. Like I said, I'm no social worker. If this starts going south, I'm expecting you to relocate this kid to your couch if need be."

"Let's hope it doesn't come to that," he replied.

"That's not an agreement, Lau."

He chuckled, but I wasn't sharing his amusement. "I can't guarantee my couch, but I can promise I'll step in if there's an issue."

"I suppose that's all I can ask," I said with a sigh.

The sheriff pushed to his feet. "Thanks for the talk. I'll follow up when I have more information from Nathan's probation officer. I'm on a tight schedule today, so I have to cut this short. I'm taking Annette and Brooke down to Portland for the weekend."

Despite knowing better, I asked, "What's the occasion?"

A wide grin split his face. "Didn't you know? It's Brooke's birthday today. The girls will be celebrating with spas and shopping and more club hopping than I'd prefer."

That information landed in my gut like a harsh blow. "Best of luck to you," I managed. "You'll have your hands full with those two."

"I will," he agreed, laughing. "But they'll sleep the whole drive back home on Sunday. It will be my only moment of peace all weekend." He moved toward the door, held up his hand in a crisp wave. "Thank you for taking the time to talk."

"Next time you need to sort out some community problems, could you do it around three or four in the afternoon? I'd appreciate it."

"I'll work on that as well." Lau pulled the door open. "Have a good weekend, Harniczek."

The door whispered shut, but I didn't return to the bar. I needed some time to think about Brooke-Ashley Markham and all the ways in which she'd ruined my life. On her birthday.

CHAPTER EIGHT

BROOKE

Coverage Ratio: a formula used to express the adequacy of earnings-based cash flow relative to meeting debt obligations.

Annette: Well?

Brooke: Well what?

Annette: It's been more than a few hours without an update from you. That's uncommon.

Brooke: ...and?

Annette: And I require an update!

Brooke: Since I'm responding to you now, it's clear I'm still alive.

Annette: Oh my god, you're a pain in the ass sometimes.

Brooke: Sometimes feels like an underestimation.

Annette: Did. You. Have. The. Sex.

Brooke: Yeah.

Annette: That's it? Just "yeah"?

Brooke: I'm not sure what you're looking for, my love. I didn't keep the condom or snatch some of his pubes for the scrapbook.

Annette: You found someone at the Galley?

Brooke: Oh yeah.

Annette: I told you!

Brooke: You have no idea how right you were about the Galley...

Annette: I notice you're not thanking me for that advice.

Brooke: I'll pick up the tab the next time we go out for lunch. That's your thanks.

Annette: You always pick up the tab. You slapped me the last time I tried to grab the check. If you recall, I had a welt on my arm all afternoon because you make more money than everyone in this entire town combined.

Brooke: Yeah, sorry again about that. I'd hoped Jackson would slam me up against his patrol car while cuffing me.

Annette: Is it a law enforcement fetish? Is that it? Because Jackson has a handful of deputies. I'm sure we could find one to slam you up against cars, walls, couches. Refrigerators are also great options.

Brooke: Considering I've known all those guys since they were toddlers, I'm going to pass. There's something about knowing Heath Carroll used to stuff his pockets with food from the cafeteria trash barrels that turns me off from a sexual relationship.

Annette: That was kindergarten.

Brooke: That's the problem with small town living.

Annette: Okay. Back to the sex. How was it?

Brooke: Rather good.

Annette: Did you sign a nondisclosure agreement or something? Why can't you tell me anything?

Brooke: I'm in a bad mood.

Annette: You had "rather good" sex last night. You shouldn't be in a bad mood.

Brooke: One night of good sex isn't changing my desire to burn shit down.

Annette: Why are you in a bad mood today? What's wrong?

Annette: This guy was decent, right?

Brooke: He was decent. Annoyingly so.

Annette: I can appreciate an annoyingly decent man.

Brooke: You should know. You're living with one.

Annette: Stop trying to change the conversation from you to me.

Brooke: It's nothing. I'm fine. I'm looking forward to the weekend.

Annette: You're so cute when you lie.

Brooke: I'm not lying. I'm actually looking forward to the weekend. I can't wait to get out of here for two nights.

Annette: Can I say happy birthday yet?

Brooke: Can we not make this about my birthday? Can't it be a girl's weekend away—with Jackson—and not dip the whole thing in birthday sprinkles?

Annette: Can I just send you a screenshot of the conversation we had about this last year? Because I have a ton of orders to get out the door before taking off for your birthday weekend and my argument hasn't changed.

Brooke: That seems like a lot of work. Scrolling through a year's worth of messages.

Annette: I am going to celebrate the fuck out of your birthday. You can't stop me, so you might as well join me.

Brooke: Why do you do this?

Annette: By this, I'm guessing you mean not letting you get back on your bullshit.

Brooke: No. I mean, why do you care so much?

Annette: Because there's nothing you can do that will ever push me away, so stop trying.

SAME STOLEN ROBE, same wet hair, same bare feet, same ocean view. But it was a different day and I had a new set of regrets to keep me company while the autumn sun heated my skin and dried my hair. A different kind of hollowed-out loneliness to keep me company.

It was unusually warm for late September. As the story went, I was born on a day much like this one. A bright, clear sky overflowing with sunshine while only the slightest hint of cool, crisp air lingered in the breeze. The trees were a riot of red, orange, and gold, and the barren grayness of winter seemed impossibly distant. The kind of day captured in postcards and photography books and B-roll footage.

It was the perfect miracle of a day for a perfect miracle of a baby to be born.

And I *was* perfect. Not in any of the ways that meant something, but in all the ways that'd made my parents happy. I was beautiful. My hair was platinum blonde and my eyes sapphire. My skin barely tanned, never freckled. I was tall and lean, but never so much that anyone took note of either. Add to that some high cheekbones, full lips, and luck of the draw facial symmetry and I was one beautiful baby who grew into a beautiful child and then a beautiful young adult whose awkward phase lasted all of a week. It was the easy, shallow kind of beauty that signified nothing.

I was a miracle too. As that story went, I was so much of a miracle, my parents named me twice. They'd known on that sunny day in September that I'd be their only child—the only one they'd carry out the hospital doors—and that was all the reason they needed to saddle me with two first names. They'd hoped their little miracle would fill all the voids they'd identified in their lives, mend their differences, and save their marriage. But babies never saved marriages. They didn't make up for falling out of love after two decades of bitterness and disappointment and they didn't fix the things that'd broken along the way.

I wasn't the perfect miracle they'd needed, but dammit, I'd tried to be. I tried to be everything, anything. Whatever it was, I did it until I couldn't do it anymore. Until rendering my entire existence down into the glue necessary to keeping a broken family together succeeded only in burning off every last bit of my miraculous shine. But it was a challenge I'd been born to best and even now—more than sixteen years after walking away from Talbott's Cove and dysfunction and miracles that weren't—I was still trying. Still failing. And still angry as hell that I had to hold it all together for everyone else.

The sour irony of this challenge was that no one outside my father's house expected anything from me. Most people looked at me and expected nothing more than my face. Once they tossed in the cutesy hyphenated name and the family known for settling in provincial Maine a full century before the Mayflower departed from Plymouth, the expectations ceased to exist. I didn't need to be generous or smart or capable. Pretty and privileged were impressive enough for the world, but underneath all this blonde hair and behind these blue eyes was a mind overqualified for my appearance. I wasn't supposed to say that, but it was the straight truth.

I wasn't the person anyone expected. I wasn't the version they wanted. More often than not, I wasn't the version I wanted either.

I dragged a hand through my hair, pushing it over my ear as I watched the water. I did this every day. Not the wet hair, bare feet, stolen kimono, whole life navel-gazing thing, but trying to find the farthest visible point from Talbott's Cove and imagining myself there. On cloudless days like today, I could wish myself all the way to Matinicus Island. It was nothing more than a slab of rock in the middle of Penobscot Bay, but goddamn, it wasn't here.

If I was there, I wouldn't have to be me.

CHAPTER NINE

JJ

Absolute Return: an asset's achieved earnings over a period of time.

OCTOBER

THE KID WAS PISSED and I couldn't say I blamed him.

"You want me to live in a bar? And work here too?" Nate asked the sheriff. He shifted the cardboard box he held to his hip and glanced around the tavern's empty dining room. "This was the *good* idea?"

"I recognize it's unconventional," Jackson replied, holding out a *listen to reason, son* hand. "However, I've heard time and again you don't see alcohol as a coping mechanism and Mr. Harniczek here—"

"Christ almighty, don't call me that."

Under no circumstances did I want to have a conversation with Sheriff Lau before ten in the morning. Not a single one and yet here I was, shoulder to shoulder with that shined-shoes, do-good motherfucker at nine fifteen.

I held out my hand to Nate, as he preferred to be addressed. "JJ, please."

"All right, *JJ*," Nate replied with a huff. "No disrespect, man, but I don't see how this is going to work. I'm pretty sure my father carved his name into that barstool right over there. Alcohol doesn't do shit for me, but after enough time around my father, I'd start gnawing on the wood just to get high off the varnish." He angled his body to face Jackson. "I know you're sticking your neck out there and pulling favors for me, but I can't stay in this town."

Jackson went for the *listen to reason* hand again. I rolled my eyes. "Let's not jump to any conclusions. You can—"

"Yeah, I can go to Portland or Orono or Macias, or literally anywhere but this town where no one leaves, no one changes, and no one forgets a fucking thing," Nate interrupted. He dropped the box, shrugged off his backpack. He brought his fingers to his temples, rubbing as he stared at the floor. "I appreciate you trying to set this up, but it's not gonna work. I'll find somewhere else to crash."

"Or you can decide it doesn't matter." I shoved my hands into my front pockets. "This place, these people. Your parents. You can decide whether any of it matters to you." Jackson and Nate turned toward me at the same time. "Will there be shitty moments when those things force their way into your life? Of course. My father dropped dead of a heart attack my last year of high school. If you ask anyone around here, they'll say I blew off college because of it. That wasn't the reason, but I have better things to do than chase down everyone's thoughts and waste my time trying to fix them." I bent down and picked up his box. It was much heavier than I'd expected. "Nothing good will come from running up to Orono or Macias."

He turned away from us, exhaling heavily as he went. "And staying here is that much better?"

Behind Nate's back, the sheriff and I exchanged glances. I shook my head, gestured to my watch. Jackson held up his palm and gave me a chastising stare. I tapped my watch again and hooked a thumb over my shoulder. He responded by shifting his gaze to Nate.

"We can't force you to do anything," Jackson started.

"No, you cannot," Nate added.

"And if you want to leave town, I'll do what I can to help you on your way." The sheriff tipped his head to the side as if he was about to impart some fatherly wisdom. I rolled my eyes at him. Again. "This place might not feel like home right now, but it's worth giving it a chance."

I stepped in front of Nate and clapped my hands together. "All right, kid, here's what's up. I have to run to a meeting on the other side of town. If you think the Cove never changes, you should come along and listen. After that, I'm gonna grab some lunch and run invoices for the month. Are you any good with envelopes?"

"Envelopes?" he repeated.

"Yeah, you know, folding a bill, putting it in an envelope, sealing it," I replied, miming the process. "Stamps, addresses, the whole thing. Can you manage that?"

He swung a gaze between me and Jackson. "Yeah, I can manage that."

"That's all I needed to know," I replied. "Let's put your things down and we'll head out." I shook the cardboard box as I stepped away from the dining room. "What do you have in here anyway? Bricks?"

"Books," he answered, trailing several paces behind me. "And I didn't agree to stay."

"All I want to do is put this box down and we can't leave it in the middle of my tavern where someone could trip over it. The last thing I need is a lawsuit." I elbowed the back room door open, motioned for Nate to join me. Jackson followed him, not that he was invited. "Where you rest your head tonight is your business, kid. Stay, go, transform into a seagull for all I care."

I led them past the microdistillery that'd served me well when I bottled a dozen or so batches of gin each week but now fit like a school uniform in May. We passed the lineup of empty kegs I couldn't look at without thinking about Brooke and the wicked things she'd said and the way her brow had crinkled when she wasn't getting exactly what she wanted. As I had for the past month, I kept going. Moved past it. Ignored the shit out of everything to put one foot in front of the other, through the ever-present reminders and up the steep staircase.

The apartment was freshly cleaned, but that didn't make up for the fact it was an attic with a bathroom. I went to set the box down on the round kitchen table the sheriff had lugged over from his girlfriend's old apartment, but Nate snatched the box from my hands.

"I've got it," he murmured, dropping the box beside the bed.

From the looks of the pastel rainbow blanket and small pillows with flamingos painted on them, those pieces were also courtesy of Annette's former residence. "Now that's handled, we have to hit the road." I glanced at the sheriff. "You good, man?" When he didn't immediately respond, I continued, "Okay, great. We'll see you around."

I'd almost reached the base of the staircase when I heard another set of footsteps behind me. I didn't have to glance back to know they belonged to Nate. "Where are we going?" he called.

I walked through the back room, the kegs on one side and the bottling setup on the other. I knew how to ignore a certain portion of this room, but I also enjoyed pressing that bruise. Not that one night with Brooke left me wounded, though her fingerprints were a mark I couldn't wash from my skin. Just as I savored the ache that came with remembering her touch, it also served as a reminder to stay far away from that woman.

Cutting through the alleyway exit, I pointed at my car and called, "It's not far, but we're heading out to Beddington to pick up some honey when we're finished."

"All the way to Beddington for honey?" Nate asked as he pulled the car door closed. "Do they have better bees up there?"

"Would you believe me if I told you they do?" We shared a glance as I paused before backing out of the alley. When he didn't say anything, I continued. "Do you know the old cider house?"

"Know it? I used to meet one of my dealers there. It's a great spot for that kind of action. Completely hidden from the street by the tree line."

"Good thing the sheriff nabbed him a couple of months ago."

Nate stared out the window. "Thorough, that sheriff."

I snickered. "Like you wouldn't believe." I turned down the potholed road leading to the cider house. "We're meeting a general contractor. He's going to show us all the construction issues that will require more time and money. Then, we're going to meet a plumber with his own list of issues."

Nate scanned the area around the cider house. The overgrown vegetation that'd once consumed the grounds was gone. Stakes with fluorescent tags outlined the planned walkways, patios, and gardens. Spray-painted arrows and dashes marked the underground locations of water, gas, and electric lines.

"What is this?" he asked.

I stared at the building and the hard-packed earth surrounding it. Save for text messages promising to follow up soon, I hadn't heard from Barry in a full month. Our last real conversation was right here, when he was seeing the site for himself. It was classic Barry.

"When we're done, it will put this town on the farm-to-cup tourism map with a craft distillery and dining venue. It's progress." I tipped my chin toward the building. "That's what I'm hoping it is." When I saw the contractor's truck rumble down the road, I stepped out of the car and waved for Nate. "You're welcome to come along. It might not be much entertainment, but it's gotta be better than kicking rocks."

He jogged around the back side of the car to join me. At the entrance to the cider house, he flattened his hand on the door, saying, "Hold up. It would really help my ability to process all of this if you could tell me when you're going to start hiding the knives and locking up the cough syrup."

Through his windshield, I watched the general contractor plow a glazed donut. I glanced back at Nate. "Correct me if I'm wrong, but I don't think anything would stop you if you were determined to start using again. Not me, not the sheriff, not a lock on the medicine cabinet." He dropped his gaze, banded his arms over his chest. "I'm running one business by myself while trying to get a second off the ground. I don't have the time to babysit you and even if I did, that shit sounds boring as hell. If you think I'm reporting back to Sheriff Lau or your probation officer or anyone else, you've miscalculated the time I have on my hands."

Nate hesitated before saying, "I don't know anything about bartending."

The contractor popped another donut in his mouth. Jelly, this time. "What do you know about?"

"Books. Poetry." He lifted his shoulders, dropped them with a sigh.

"The treatment facility I was at this summer had a gardening program. It was nice. Everyone tended their own piece of land."

Considering this, I shifted toward the ocean. Nate did the same. "And you learned something? From the gardens?"

"I learned that flowers and fruit are the last stages in a plant's life cycle," he answered. "That tons of growth takes place underground, where no one sees it. And that it might look like nothing is happening for so long that people wonder whether it's unhealthy or the soil isn't draining well or it doesn't belong in this climate, but that plant is busy gathering the strength to bloom. That's what I learned."

The contractor slammed his truck door shut and wiped his paws on the seat of his jeans. I raised a hand, waving him toward us. To Nate, I said, "I'll teach you what you need to know about mixing drinks and pulling pints. The rest of it is listening while someone tells you how their garden grows." I clapped him on the back. "If you stick around, that is."

CHAPTER TEN

BROOKE

Covenants: The conditions agreed to in the process of financing debt, intended to protect the lender's interests.

November

Annette: Let's go to the Galley tonight.
Brooke: This isn't a good night for me.
Annette: Tomorrow?
Brooke: Maybe not.
Annette: Come on…I realize it's not the swankiest spot, but we get to drink liquor and annoy JJ. That sounds like a great outing to me and we haven't been there in ages. Like, full months.
Brooke: I need to keep a handle on things around here.
Annette: Is everything all right?
Brooke: Yeah.
Brooke: No.
Brooke: I don't know.

Annette: It's okay, sweetie. We don't have to go out. I can bring some snacks and wine over.
Brooke: That works. Thank you for dealing with all my quirks.
Annette: Don't mention it. You deal with mine.

DECEMBER

Annette: I regret to inform you that I am dead.
Annette: I've died.
Annette: Remember me fondly.
Brooke: This is fascinating for me because I'm usually the one coming out with outrageous comments and you're the one saying, Uh huh. Okay. Care to unpack that for me?
Annette: Please don't enjoy my death.
Brooke: Let's start with this. Why are you dead and how did you die?
Annette: Allow me to set the scene.
Brooke: Should I pour a glass of wine for this?
Annette: It's not even 9 a.m. yet, so maybe not.
Brooke: Seems like an arbitrary reason, but okay. Set the scene.
Annette: It's early this morning. Before Jackson's alarm goes off. We're having sex and things are good. As far as pre-dawn sex goes, it's real nice.
Brooke: I don't even remember what pre-dawn sex is like.
Annette: Oh, honey.
Brooke: Ignore me. Carry on. Seriously, I need to find out how you died.
Annette: Like I said, real nice pre-dawn sex...until a sound emerges from my body.
Annette: It was a deep squelching sound. A cross between a deflating windbag and aggressively stirring macaroni and cheese.
Annette: And it might've been fine if it happened just once. But much in the way aftershocks follow an earthquake, there were several smaller but equally noticeable squelches.
Brooke: Some might call that a queef.

Annette: No. A queef is too dainty for this noise. This was aggressive. Like a vaginal cannon blast. I don't know how he stayed inside me.
Brooke: What did you do?
Annette: I died. Right there on the bed.
Brooke: How did Jackson handle it? Did he say anything?
Annette: He paused for a second and then said, Okay, back to business.
Brooke: I love him so much. Are you certain we can't negotiate a sister-wife agreement?
Annette: We are reserving a room for you in the new house, but I don't see any polyamory in our future.
Annette: Not unless Jackson is down at the station, rethinking his life choices on account of the noise violations from my downstairs.
Brooke: What was his expression? Did he look shocked or concerned or amused? He couldn't have been that mortified since he kept going.
Annette: I couldn't see his expression.
Brooke: Ah. All right.
Brooke: Well, so what? It was a queef. A super loud one. Given that you two live together, I'm sure there are other unpleasant things he's witnessed.
Annette: It's easier to keep up the charade than you might think.
Brooke: There's one bathroom at your place. There's no room for charades when you share a bathroom.
Annette: You're forgetting that my shop is a three-minute walk from the house and there's a perfectly private bathroom there.
Brooke: Oh my god, Annette. You're leading a double life. You can't marry this man if you've led him to believe you don't poop. It's deceptive and wrong. I won't let it happen.
Annette: It's irrelevant because I'm dead.
Brooke: You're not dead. You just don't like living through a moment where Jackson thinks you're anything but a delicate little lady who doesn't poop.
Brooke: We can look at this a few different ways.
Annette: Which is why I love you.
Brooke: First, certain positions can be noisier. That has nothing to do with you or him or anything other than the acrobatics.
Annette: It's never happened in that position before.

Brooke: Which brings me to my second point. Maybe Jackson has a really big dick and it just...you know...forces a lot of air in there.

Annette: It's his fault?

Brooke: Why the fuck not?

Brooke: But why does it have to be anyone's fault? All kinds of horrible things happen during sex.

Annette: Examples, please.

Brooke: I've done all of these things during sex: cut myself on a guy's gnarly toenail and bled all over his sheets, punched a guy in the nose, forgotten about a tampon, elbowed a guy in the eye, started my period, puked in a guy's lap because his dick smelled like a sewer, and peed the bed.

Annette: You peed the bed?

Brooke: I know, I know. I was young and I didn't know how to get up and go to the bathroom in the morning without waking the guy.

Annette: So...you peed the bed?!?

Brooke: No, I stayed in bed and held it. But then he woke up and wanted to have sex. Again, I was young. Like, 21. And I figured it was fine, I'd pee later.

Annette: But that wasn't how it worked out, huh?

Brooke: Nope. In the middle of sex, peed the bed. I told him it was some special girly juice from him being super good at sex.

Annette: Did he believe that?

Brooke: Sadly, yes.

Annette: That toenail story was disgusting.

Brooke: You don't even know. I insisted on getting a tetanus shot.

Annette: The most awful thing to happen to me during sex was this morning.

Brooke: You see? It wasn't that bad.

Annette: You say that but I'm still convinced it was pretty bad. It was explosive. Vagina cannon, I tell you.

Brooke: Perhaps you have a wide-set vagina. That, coupled with the really big dick and the position, could set the stage for a vagina cannon moment.

Annette: We're just going to blame Jackson, okay?

Brooke: Remember you're having good morning sex and I'm not, okay?

JANUARY

Annette: I want to redecorate the back room at the shop. It's really dreary and boring in there.

Brooke: You're just noticing this now?

Annette: Actually, yes. I've never used it as more than a place to store boxes because I handled business stuff in my apartment.

Brooke: If you tell me that Jackson keeps you on your back too much to handle your paperwork, I'm going to die.

Brooke: Not on the spot, but soon.

Annette: Helpful clarification.

Brooke: I'll wander into the woods and wait for the elements to claim me. That would be better than hearing about the sex life you won't share with me.

Annette: Sometimes I have trouble determining whether you're being serious...

Brooke: You're doing fine.

Annette: You do realize you're hot as fuck, right?

Brooke: What does that have to do with anything?

Annette: You're going to argue with me on this, but you're a good person too. You're a little psycho, but you're kindhearted about it.

Brooke: Are you...are you hitting on me?

Brooke: Although I have yet to act on it, I've always considered myself a Kinsey 2 or 3 but I thought you were MUCH closer to a 0 than this conversation suggests.

Annette: What?

Brooke: I love you, I really, really do, but I don't think I want our relationship to change and there are times when I really need some dick in my life.

Brooke: And this is one of those times.

Annette: What are we talking about?

Brooke: You were putting the moves on me.

Annette: I was not.

Annette: I was gently reminding you that you can get a sex life of your own and stop trying to insert yourself into mine.

Brooke: I'm definitely looking for some insertion.

Annette: ANYWAY.

Annette: If I mentioned to a few people that you're looking, you'd have a line at your door in 10 minutes.

Brooke: omfg stop.

Brooke: Talk about ugly storage rooms. Please.

Annette: Let me forage for you.

Brooke: I love you but oh my god no.

Annette: You don't trust me to find someone you'd like?

Brooke: If I needed to cover up a crime, you'd be the first person I call.

Annette: My fiancé, the sheriff, would have some...concerns...about that.

Brooke: I'd want you to clear my browser history, reset my phone, and discreetly dispose of my vibrators if I died suddenly.

Annette: And I'd want the same.

Brooke: I'd trust you to give me an at-home Brazilian wax.

Annette: That's special.

Brooke: But I don't want you matchmaking for me, dearie.

Annette: And why is that?

Brooke: Because you believe in love and relationships and knowing the person's name before you have sex with them.

Annette: You deserve that, you know.

Brooke: I recognize what you're doing. You're giving me all the shit I gave you.

Annette: You are the smart one in this relationship.

Brooke: But the difference between me giving you shit then and what you're doing now is you had a man carrying your panties with him as a good luck charm, and I am not the subject of anyone's obsession.

Annette: That did not occur.

Brooke: Mmmm agree to disagree. Let's get back to the storage room before I have to deal with the fallout over Dad rejecting whatever his caregivers made for dinner because all of his triggers seem to be food-related. Please.

Annette: I don't like bringing work home. I'd rather do it at the shop, but the back room is depressing. It needs some warmth and motivation.
Brooke: In my old office, in New York, I had a huge reproduction of a Georgia O'Keefe painting framed behind my desk. A complicated red flower. Actually huge. At least 5 feet wide, probably 8 feet tall.
Brooke: People (and by people, I mean men) would stare at it. As per male usual, they never knew what they were seeing.
Annette: Pussy power much?
Brooke: My workplace was filled with men who used their penises to activate touch screens. Men who insulted each other with stories of fucking each other's wives and mothers. Men who loved a good rape joke.
Brooke: You bet your ass I decorated with pussy power.
Annette: Where is it now? I'm not sure I have the wall space for a giant red vagina painting, but I like the idea.
Brooke: It's in a storage facility outside Manhattan.
Brooke: Along with the remains of my hold on reality.

CHAPTER ELEVEN

JJ

Collateral: assets which can be repossessed in the event of loan default.

THERE WERE a lot of things I didn't know about starting a business. It was no skin off my back to learn, as I'd been doing that since taking over the Galley from my aunt and uncle years ago. But there was a substantial difference between figuring out the food and beverage business as I went and banging my head into walls because it was better than making sense of building codes and licensing permit paperwork.

That was how I found myself chucking a binder at Sheriff Lau's head.

"Whoa there," he called, swerving in the doorway to avoid the offending binder. It hit the wall and thumped the floor. "Should I take that personally?"

I leaned back in my chair, regarding him as he stood before my desk. "Give it a try and don't tell me how it works out for you."

Finding no humor in my suggestion, he went on staring at me with a cool, flat expression I was certain he received with his badge and uniform. "Can I borrow a moment of your time?"

"Only if you intend on returning it." He offered more of that cool flatness in response and I wished I had another binder to throw simply for the purpose of snapping him out of it. "What do you need, sheriff?"

He settled into a chair, saying, "I've heard from several different people that you know how to stop Audee Netishen from shooting the deer and moose he lures onto his property."

"It's always something with that old fucker," I muttered. "I bet he's telling you it's legit because he's not hunting outside the state's season and bag limits, but protecting his home."

The sheriff nodded. "That's correct."

"And I bet he also has a peck or two of apples piled up on his property."

Another nod. "Also correct."

"He does that," I said, reaching for my glass of water. "He hires high school kids to harvest his apple trees every autumn, but then he leaves them in his damn barn three or four months. Because he's a crazy old fucker, he carts them all out in December and January, leaves a peck right in front of his house, and bags some deer from the comfort of his recliner. His wife sells the jerky at one of those big farmers markets up in Orono."

"Sounds like a lot of work," he said.

"Sounds like you don't know much about hunting," I replied. "I don't have an interest, but I grew up with it and I can tell you it's much easier to cart some apples out from a barn than it is to get geared up and sit in the woods all day."

"And that's how you know the magic word to getting Netishen in line?"

I barked out a laugh. "We used to be neighbors. My family lived next door to the Netishens for twenty years. My father planned his entire year around the season. He loved hunting, but he was a lot like you, sheriff. By the book." I paused, ran my tongue over my teeth. "He worked as a game warden until the day he died. Every time he saw Audee dragging those apples out of his barn, he told him he'd permanently lose his hunting license if he bagged so much as a goose. They had the same conversation two or three times each winter."

"That's all it takes?" the sheriff asked. "A warning?"

With as much patience as I could muster, I gestured at his sheriff's garb, saying, "From a game warden. Guys like Audee know the system better than the state does and they know you"—I pointed at his badge —"aren't pulling his license. Call the Augusta office and fill them in. They'll send a warden down."

He bobbed his head as he took in this information. "There are moments when I forget I'm still a newcomer here." He glanced up at me with the barest of smirks. "But then I'm sent here to get a history lesson and a shove in the right direction."

"No one in this town will give you a simple answer when the complicated one makes more sense to them," I said, laughing. "Give it a few years, you'll be doing it too."

"I suppose I should thank you for that lesson as well," he said.

"That one is on the house," I replied.

Jackson rested his hands on his thighs and took a moment to sweep a gaze over my office. It was piled high with boxes and crates, decades' worth of accounting ledgers, and an assortment of items branded with beer logos. Hats, t-shirts, paper coasters, frisbees, you name it. I meant to clean it out every time I couldn't find something, but never remembered to get it done.

"Since I'm here," he started, "I'm interested to hear how Nate is progressing."

And since you're here, I'm interested in hearing everything you can tell me about your fiancée's best friend. "You'd have to ask him that yourself," I replied. "You could, but he's not here right now."

The muscles in his jaw twitched. "Where is he?"

"I got enough problems of my own. I don't keep track of the kid's calendar too."

I shuffled the documents on my desk, looking for nothing but an exit from this conversation. I didn't care for the routine check-ins on Nate's recovery or the constant questions about his conduct and habits, and the sheriff wasn't the only one asking. The reemergence of Nate Fitzsimmons was something of a local legend now. It wasn't uncommon for customers to ask him highly personal questions or gape at him while he bused their table. Others gave him sobriety advice after ordering their meals and a special few made it their business to watch his every move and report back to me about behavior they found suspicious.

"Got it, got it," Jackson murmured. "I'd have to assume he's doing well enough if you've kept him on this long. Knowing how you operate, he would've been on the curb if there was an issue."

I didn't like the sheriff. We were cut from different cloth. But I couldn't deny that he was suited for his job. "What do you want? A performance review? He comes in on time, he does the work, and he puts up with all the assholes this town has to offer. He's fine. Leave him alone."

He nodded thoughtfully, as if this information put everything in a new light. "I see him at the gym in the morning." He shared a laugh with himself. "The mornings I manage to drag myself out of bed early enough to hit the gym."

I gave him a blank stare. "Ha."

"He seems to like the six a.m. yoga and meditation class," Jackson continued. "The weight room too. All the times I've stopped by, he's been very focused on the weights."

"Maybe if you shared your protein shake recipe with him, he'd share his workout plan," I replied. "I'm sure you'd hit it off once he forgets he's on probation and handing in a cup of urine every week and you're the head of the local law enforcement agency receiving those piss reports."

He blinked at me. "Point taken."

"Leave the kid alone. Let him work out without the sheriff spotting him." I took another sip from my water. "Don't you have better things to do? You're engaged, you're building a house, and you're in a power struggle with Audee Netishen. Isn't that enough?"

Jackson lifted a hand to his forehead, rubbed his brow. "Following up on Nate is much easier than building a house. The process is—I can't even explain how complicated and exhausting the damn thing is. And the ground is frozen, so there's nothing we can do until spring, but since we have that time to kill, we might as well change the plans seven or eight hundred times."

"Don't forget about the wedding," I added.

"I don't know whether I should be concerned or relieved that Annette has prioritized the house." He continued rubbing his brow. "I figure she wouldn't be driving herself nutty over closets and cabinets if she didn't intend to stick around." He glanced up at me, a look of pure dread on his face. "She wants us to visit a home design studio in Portland this weekend."

"Isn't that what you do best, sheriff? Escorting Annette and Brooke up and down the coast while they shop and brunch and whatever else it is they do?"

It was such a lame attempt at drawing information about Brooke out of him that I wanted to kick my own ass.

"We haven't seen much of Brooke lately. She has a lot on her plate." He frowned, glanced over his shoulder at the door. "Last I heard, she isn't available to compare bathroom flooring samples this weekend."

I drummed my fingers on the desk, considering my options while the sheriff and I stared at each other. They weren't good options. Everywhere I turned, I boxed myself into a new corner. I couldn't ask about Brooke and whether she needed some help without tipping my hand hard in that direction. I couldn't ask whether her father's condition was deteriorating because it was possible Jackson didn't know about it.

"Annette's baked a number of banana cream pies for Judge Markham these past few weeks," Jackson continued. "I'm told it's his favorite, but Brooke hates them. Can't stand the smell of bananas. The conversations Brooke and Annette have about those pies are, well, they're entertaining."

"It's always fun to be the target of Brooke's simultaneous love and hate."

Jackson pushed to his feet and opened the door, hooking a glance at me over his shoulder. "You would know, wouldn't you?"

And that was how I realized Jackson Lau was better at his job than I thought.

CHAPTER TWELVE

BROOKE

Prime Rate: the interest rate at which banks lend to their best customers.

FEBRUARY

Annette: Jackson just sent a million roses to the shop to celebrate six months of cohabitation.

Brooke: That sweet boy. Someone taught him right.

Annette: That's the truth.

Brooke: As you know, I love you dearly.

Annette: Yep.

Brooke: Do you think you could share with me some of the downsides of that cohabitation? Because I love you and don't want to hate you for having unlimited access to good dick and someone to take out the trash.

Annette: I wouldn't say it's unlimited access. He does work.

Brooke: And you've had sex in his office enough times to count on both hands, so let's not split hairs on that point.

Annette: Here's one. He prefers to store leftovers on plates covered in plastic wrap. He doesn't see why anyone would move food to a storage container when it's on a perfectly good plate.

Brooke: What a savage. Pyrex is life.

Brooke: Keep going.

Annette: He doesn't believe in expiration dates.

Brooke: What's that now?

Annette: Yeah, I bought a bunch of ricotta cheese in November. Two quarts. I wanted to try a new cheesecake recipe, but I never got around to it. It has since passed its expiration date, however, Jackson won't let me toss it because he believes it's still good. So, we have two quarts of aging cheese in the back corner of the fridge.

Brooke: That's an interesting belief system.

Brooke: What else?

Annette: He flat-out refuses to take any of my help when he's getting sick. I tried to give him some vitamins when he picked up that cold after the holidays and you would've thought I'd offered him heroin or a teacup of bleach.

Brooke: Men are the worst.

Annette: He won't admit when he's falling asleep. He likes to watch one of those sports news programs every night, though he's never seen an entire episode. He falls the fuck asleep. And god forbid I suggest he DVR it or turn off the television. It's right up there with illicit use of vitamin C.

Brooke: Yeah, you're a heretic.

Annette: Whenever it's snowing, he wakes up two or three times during the night to shovel. He says it won't accumulate as much that way. I understand that it's easier to shovel a few inches rather than a few feet, but first of all, we have a snow blower. Second, nothing good has ever come from going outside at three in the morning during a snowstorm.

Brooke: Literally nothing.

Annette: I don't even try to argue it with him. He's going to do what he's going to do.

Brooke: How do you manage?

Annette: He makes up for it in other ways.

Brooke: This guy has the good dick.

Annette: You're not wrong.

Brooke: Ugh this hasn't made me hate you less.

Annette: That's fine. You can hate me. It's that or put real effort into meeting men, I guess, and we both know you won't do that.

Brooke: Would you just shut up, please?

Annette: Since when have you refrained from giving anyone a pointed push?

Brooke: Yeah, because that's my thing. I'm the rude one. You're the nice one.

Annette: Only sometimes.

Brooke: Wait, are you referring to me or you?

Annette: Both seems like a fine answer.

MARCH

Annette: Can I be ridiculous and self-centered for a minute?

Brooke: You never have to ask permission to be ridiculous or self-centered as I am both with alarming frequency.

Annette: You're neither.

Brooke: Don't try to debate this with me. I'll win. I always win because I'm amazing like that.

Brooke: See? Ridiculous and self-centered.

Annette: Anyway...Jackson's sister is coming to visit next weekend.

Brooke: Rachel, right?

Annette: Yeah.

Brooke: Isn't she a teacher in some Grimms' fairy tale land?

Annette: By that, I assume you mean western Massachusetts.

Brooke: Same thing.

Annette: Right, well, Rachel who teaches middle school out in western Massachusetts is visiting next weekend and this is the first time I've spent more than a Thanksgiving meal with her.

Brooke: ...and you're freaking out about what?

Annette: The list is extensive.

Brooke: Start with the most absurd shit.

Annette: She doesn't like sweets and 90% of my life is baking with tons of sugar and I don't understand how anyone could exist without pie and cookies and cake and lemon squares.

Brooke: Proportionally speaking, your life is not 90% baking. You run a small business, babe. Baking is your passion project, your stress relief, your hand work.

Annette: I don't really care about the math.

Brooke: Of course. But, real talk, she's not going to ooh and ahh all over your sticky buns and that's okay. People like you for reasons entirely separate from the treats you shove in their mouths.

Annette: I don't shove anything in anyone's mouth.

Brooke: Oh, right. I forgot it's the other way around with you.

Annette: Shut up.

Brooke: Back to the freak out of the day. What's the next most absurd thing?

Annette: I feel like the house is a weird mix of 1990s-meets-vintage-thrift. I know that's the least of her concerns and she's not coming here to evaluate the style of the place we're renting while our house is being built, but I've never had guests in our home before and I want it to be nice.

Brooke: Would you like to move into the carriage house over here? It hasn't been updated since before my mother died, but you can play house there all you want.

Annette: Jackson would never go for that.

Brooke: It's funny how Jackson is the reason it won't work and not your own lunacy.

Annette: (eye roll emoji)

Brooke: What else is bothering you?

Annette: I just want her to like me.

Brooke: She absolutely will.

Annette: Sisters never like me.

Brooke: Your sisters are the heavyweight champions of cunt. They do not count as evidence.

Brooke: Rachel will adore you. She'll get a tattoo that reads "I'm With Annie" before the weekend is over but if you think for one second that this chick is replacing me as your bloodless sister, I will wage war.

Annette: I would never go to war with you.

Brooke: Because I know all of your weak spots?

Annette: Because we know each other's weak spots, but we'd never use them.

Brooke: No. We wouldn't.

Brooke: Would you like to continue freaking out or are you feeling better?

Annette: I think I'm okay.

Brooke: I know you're okay.

CHAPTER THIRTEEN

BROOKE

__Depreciation: the allocation of value over a period of time to account for the loss of value as an asset ages or is rendered obsolete.__

APRIL

ANNETTE STARED at her reflection in the mirror as she pivoted on the pedestal. "I'm not sure."

"Aren't you supposed to have an involuntary reaction? Something more interesting than a sneezing fit, but less troublesome than a seizure?"

She glared at me in the mirror. "This was your idea."

"You're the one who got engaged," I argued from my perch on the tufted white sofa. "Suggesting we find you a wedding dress doesn't seem ridiculous to me."

"But this," she cried, fisting the ball gown's heavy skirts, "this *is* ridiculous."

"Oh my god, yes." I drained my champagne. Everything in this bridal boutique was blindingly white and the dresses were questionably fashion-able, but at least the champagne was free. "Take it off immediately and return it to the America's Cup team. I'm sure they're pissed about someone stealing their sails."

"Perhaps a slimmer silhouette," the saleswoman offered as she flew to the racks. "Something form-fitting, like a column or mermaid."

Annette met my gaze in the mirror, shook her head. She blinked quickly as tears filled her eyes. That was my cue. "Sandra, you've been such a treasure today. We're going to pause here, but we'll be back when the bride has narrowed her ideas. Let's get her out of this giant cupcake, okay?"

Sandra stepped away from the sea of tulle and lace. "You're so lucky to have such a caring maid of honor," she said to Annette. "But *your* interests are my priority. What do *you* want?"

"I want to get out of this dress and never see it again," Annette replied.

"You are breathtaking in this dress," the saleswoman argued. "Look what it does for your figure. It's just magical." She smiled despite Annette's deep frown. "Let's try it with a veil!"

"I want to get out of this dress," she repeated.

The saleswoman shook her head. "Try to see it with your own eyes. Don't let the opinions of others"—a pointed glare in my direction as she went in search of a veil—"change your mind."

"My eyes are annoyed that I'm still wearing this," Annette replied.

I pushed up from the sofa and moved to my friend's side. Lacing my arm around her waist, I said, "I can have you out of this corset in thirty seconds flat."

"You should add that to your résumé. At least your LinkedIn profile." She patted my head. "It's strange being taller than you."

"Maybe, but now you're at the perfect height for me to nuzzle your boobs." I dropped my cheek to her chest. "I can see why Jackson wants to marry you. These are amazing."

"I know, they really are," she agreed with a laugh. "You can't hear it through the ten miles of satin fabric I'm wearing, but my tummy is rumbling like a thunderstorm."

I pointed to the front of the gown. "You pick up that end. I'll get the other end. We'll waddle back to the dressing room." The saleswoman appeared again, veils draped over her forearms and her hands outstretched as if she meant to help. "We've got this, thanks."

"Oh, well—"

"I wouldn't argue with her, Sandra," Annette interrupted. "She was president of Kappa Alpha Theta at Yale for three years and would've served a fourth year, but the bylaws didn't allow new pledges to take office."

The saleswoman trailed after us as we shuffled toward the dressing room. "Okay, but—"

"And she's the only female hedge fund manager in her firm's one hundred and nineteen year history," Annette continued. "She has a black belt in tae kwon do, speaks fluent French, German, and Mandarin, and consistently reels in the biggest catch during the bonito run. But, go ahead. Tell her she doesn't know how to properly exit me from this whipped cream avalanche."

I folded my lips together to stop myself from laughing. Once we'd wedged Annette through the dressing room door, I kept my gaze on the dress. I didn't dare look at my friend or the stunned saleswoman while I loosened the corset's lacing.

"I'll be right outside," Sandra said. "Shout if you need anything."

When the door closed, I said, "I don't speak German and I went fishing once when I was fifteen. I made Chad Bodger bait the hooks and then get the fish off the hooks because it looked horrible."

"So, you—what? Held the pole?"

"That could be the summary of my life right there," I said, giving the laces a yank. It was a wonder my girl could breathe. "I held the pole."

"But you do know tae kwon do?" she asked.

"No black belt, but I took a few martial arts classes when the guys in my office started raving about Krav Maga. They spent entire days chopping each other in the balls. I wanted to be able to poke them in the neck and have them fall to the ground and piss themselves."

"That's a noble desire." The dress fell away from her body and a breath rattled out of her. "I'm going to need some lunch now."

"Maybe we can talk about this wedding while we eat." I gathered the dress as she picked her way out of it. "You know, spitball some of the basics like colors, theme, venue. If you want to go crazy, maybe we'll even come up with ideas for the date."

Her back turned to me, Annette shrugged into her clothes. "I get it. Going dress shopping wasn't the best idea."

I slipped the dress onto its hanger. "That's not what I'm saying."

She bent at the waist to fluff her hair. "You're saying I can't choose a dress until I know when and where I'm getting married," she said, standing. "And you're not wrong, but dresses felt—I don't know—manageable. I figured we could drive down here and I could try on a dress and it would be perfect and then I'd have all the answers."

"You don't need all the answers," I said. "Let's get out of here before our friend Sandra busts in here and tries to sell you on some more meringue."

She frowned at the dress, brushed her fingers along the delicate fabric. "It is lovely," she said softly. "For someone else."

We left the boutique and headed straight for one of our favorite Portland breweries for lunch. Once we were settled with a flight of beers and three appetizers between us, I revisited the wedding topic. "You've been engaged for a couple of months now—"

"A couple of months is two or three," she interjected. "It's been more than two or three months. It's spring. Seasons have come and gone while I've been engaged."

"And I see we're sensitive about that," I said, laughing.

"A little bit," she conceded. "I just feel like I should have this sorted out by now." She laughed into her raspberry wheat. "If you asked my mother, she'd say I'm inexcusably far behind. She leaves me voicemails reminding me to make appointments with florists and bakeries and priests. But whenever Jackson and I try to decide on anything, we get derailed."

"Let's not call sex on the living room floor *getting derailed*." I shook my head. "It's punny, but we're better than that."

"There is that, but we're also trying to build a house and figure out how to live together without fighting over every little thing," she said. "The wedding is low on our list right now."

"And between all that living room floor sex and your mother, you're opting for the sex." I shrugged. "That's fair."

"My mother can't decide how she wants to handle this," Annette continued. "She's somewhere between wanting to make this bigger and better than my sisters' weddings, and being annoyed because I'm nothing like my sisters and won't go along with her daft ideas."

She went on venting about her mother's assortment of misguided wedding initiatives. I listened, nodding and sympathizing as best I could. Her mother wasn't my favorite person. She wasn't kind to my friend and I was waiting for an opportunity to call her on that shit. But beyond my frustrations with Mrs. Cortassi, I found myself wondering about my mother and how she would've reacted to me getting engaged.

I tended to believe my mother would've transformed into a steamroller, knocking me and my fiancé out of the way while she planned a showstopper of a wedding. It would be at home, of course, as she and my father were married there and she loved tradition when it fit her interests. She would've ordered the most opulent tent and bought all the flowers in New England. Every last one of them. The cake would be banana. Fucking banana. I'd wear whatever she told me to and style my hair as she instructed, and I'd do it without complaint or argument because I had to be perfect. Had to be perfect for her, for everyone.

It was macabre to think it, but I'd always known she'd die suddenly. My mother lived for putting on a show. It was always going to be the blink of an eye or a long, epic, slow process where she died but came back to life at least three or four times because everyone loved a good sob story.

"Shit," Annette murmured.

I glanced around the nearly empty restaurant, but couldn't locate a cause for concern. "What?"

"I'm going on about my mother and how I'd rather she go back to ignoring me." She gestured toward me. "And that's really insensitive of me."

"Oh, no, don't worry," I said, waving her off. "I'm fine. It never gets better, but it's okay. I don't think I want to get married anyway."

Annette gaped at me. "What? Since when? We've had no fewer than four thousand conversations about our fantasy weddings. You've already planned your groom's cake and you haven't even met him yet." She leaned forward, peering at me. "Why are you feeling all the feels today?"

"I'm not feeling all the feels." I busied myself with the beer flights, lifting and sniffing each glass before sipping. "This is your day to try on heinous dresses and have tiny panic attacks in them. This isn't about me and I'm *not* feeling the feels."

"I'll admit I had a tiny panic attack if you admit you're having deep, boggy feels."

I drained two different beers and shoved a slab of nachos in my mouth. "Fine," I said around the chips. "Feels."

"This is good. It's progress," Annette said, pointing at the empty glasses. "Drown them in beer and cheese." She nibbled a chip. "Was it the dresses or the wedding talk that did it?"

I shook my head. "Neither, I don't think. I don't know why I've had these—what did you call them?—boggy feels."

That was the truth. I didn't know where all these emotions came from or why they seemed to flood my waking moments, but I was lonely. Not alone, but lonely. Living with my father was like living with a ghost. In many ways, he was gone. He didn't recognize me, didn't call me by name, didn't remember his own name, couldn't care for himself. He hadn't experienced a good day in many, many days.

But he was very much alive. He was obsessed with banana cream pie and *Laverne and Shirley* reruns. He played Monopoly with one of his home health aides for six hours straight last week and required help to bathe and use the toilet. He was a living, breathing person but my father was gone.

Annette snagged another chip from the nacho plate. "Getting derailed might help."

JUST ONE MORE TIME, I promised myself as I headed toward the village that night. *There's nothing wrong with it as long as it's just one more time.*

When I reached the Galley, I stopped outside and stared up at the sign over the door. Scowled at it. I couldn't remember the last time I'd paid attention to the round logo with words arched over the top and a busty mermaid with a handful of wheat and berries—which made no sense whatsoever.

Aside from the logistical issues of a mermaid holding field crops, when did mermaids become things of admiration rather than animosity? The whole of history painted them as temptresses with fickle moods and violent methods. If they weren't seducing seamen into unchartered depths, they were gathering storms to toss those seamen and their ships into riptides and rocks.

It was never the sailors who encroached upon their sacred waters. Their warning songs and brutal storms were never acts of self-defense. The fishermen who reeled in mermaids and tortured them on ship decks weren't getting their due. Rather, it was the mermaid's fault for swimming too close to their nets.

She was asking for it.

And now, somehow, that mermaid represented beauty and whimsy and mystery, and that was splendid. But it didn't erase three thousand years of men blaming mermaids for their existence. And it didn't explain why this one was holding wheat and berries.

I found the tavern mostly empty when I pushed through the heavy door. Not surprising. This town marked its days by sunrises rather than sunsets, and anyone who worked on the water was tucked into bed by now.

Several familiar faces dotted the tavern, but the game playing on the television consumed their attention. Nate Fitzsimmons stood behind the bar, busy marking notes on a clipboard. No one noticed as I slipped into my usual seat on the far end.

I wasn't concerned about finding JJ. I'd put eyes on him when the time was right.

I checked my phone and then tucked it into my back pocket when I found no new messages. Jackson and Annette were watching a movie—rather, having sex while a movie played in the background—and my father was asleep. Barring any disasters, I'd have a couple hours before anyone noticed me missing.

Nate tapped his clipboard on the edge of the bar. He looked older than I'd remembered, with lines creasing his forehead, the edges of his eyes, his mouth. Tired too, but he'd bulked up since the last time I saw him. His shirt strained over his chest and his legs looked like tree trunks. "What can I get you?"

I hesitated. "What do you have for white wines tonight? Anything you'd find outside of this one-stoplight village where dreams go to die and conventional wisdom predates the Civil Rights movement?"

It took him a moment, but he chuckled. "Let me see what I can find. Are you looking for something dry or something sweet?"

The door to the storeroom burst open as JJ backed in with a keg in tow. "Nothing sweet about that one." To Nate, he said, "Put the empty out back with the others going to Allagash."

My chin propped on my palm, I watched while Nate removed one keg and JJ tapped another. He did it with an eye on the ball game and that was when I knew I really needed to have sex because there was nothing hot about him distractedly tapping a keg.

Still watching the game, he asked, "What brings you in here tonight, Bam Bam? Where's Annette?"

"It's just me," I said.

"Haven't seen you without your sidekick in months."

He had to call me on that. Had to make note of the fact I hadn't crossed the tavern's threshold without using my best friend as a human shield. Yes, I'd hidden behind Annette since leaving JJ on the sidewalk outside my father's house *months* ago. And it'd worked. She was a glowing bounty of goodness and light, and it wasn't unusual for her to shine like the center of the Cove's solar system.

As the moon to her sun, it was easier for me to fade into the background, especially now that she was engaged to the sheriff. The townspeople couldn't stop dousing her in well wishes and I was happy for her —and happy for the reprieve. While the endless familiarity often bothered the hell out of me, the folks around here were mostly kind and decent and they always asked after my father.

There was only one problem with those questions: no one knew about Dad's dementia. As far as this nosy, in-your-back-pocket town was concerned, Dad was involved in a single vehicle car accident a little more than two years ago which resulted in a badly broken leg and long-term mobility issues. They didn't know he'd emptied the contents of his refrigerator into the trunk before driving away, barefoot, and losing control of his car in the middle of nowhere, about eighty miles inland. They didn't know he'd been restrained and then sedated after punching a medical assistant in the mouth. And they didn't know I'd chartered a plane from New York City to get here as soon as possible, only for him to demand I keep his secret.

That was one of the last lucid conversations we'd shared, and it'd left me carrying a burden of unimaginable weight while those good, decent Talbott's Covians kept peppering me with their questions and concerns and prayers. So many prayers. Sooner or later, those prayers were bound to kick in. Right?

JJ shot a glimpse in my direction before testing the keg. "I was beginning to think you and Annette were joined at the hip."

"We would be if Jackson didn't mind me sleeping with them." I shrugged. "Strange as it is, he draws the line there."

JJ stepped away from the keg and turned to face me, his hands fisted on his hips. "What do you want, Brooke?"

"As I mentioned, some wine would be nice."

He shook his head. "I don't think so."

"Excuse you?"

"You heard me," he replied. We stared at each other until Nate returned from the back room and crossed between us. To the other man, he said, "I'm going to check on the small batches. Work on hustling Lincoln out of here before his wife comes looking for him. I'm not interested in staging any more domestic disputes."

"Amen to that," Nate muttered.

JJ spared me a glance that came across as one part irritation, one part impatience, and one last part interest. I could work with the aggregate. "Drink your wine and go home, Brooke."

He set a glass in front of me before turning on his heel and marching into the storeroom. Nate and I stared at the door swinging shut behind JJ. "Put this on my tab," I said.

Nate tucked a dishrag into his back pocket. "You don't have a tab, Miss Markham. Boss's orders."

"Your boss is needlessly rude." I slipped off the stool, yanked a twenty out of my bra and dropped it on the bar. He eyed the cash as if it was contaminated with boob sweat, which it was. "I need to have a talk with that boss of yours." I paused at the door to the back room, my palm flat on the slab. "Do me a favor, Fitzsimmons. Stay out here, even if you hear yelling and glass breaking and all kinds of mayhem."

He glanced at the cash again. "Is that supposed to cover mayhem?"

"It is if you interrupt." I didn't wait for him to respond, instead pushing into the dim room. The last time I'd visited, I'd missed the entire chemistry lab setup back here. There were tanks and beakers and devices I couldn't name. A floor-to-ceiling rack stood off to the side with a dozen rows of glass bottles, each bearing a scribbled label. "What the hell is all this?"

I heard an exasperated sigh before setting eyes on JJ. He crossed his arms over his chest and scowled as if he could warn me off with an angry pose and some bared teeth. He had the audacity to do all that while also wearing million-year-old jeans, a button-up with sleeves rolled to his elbows, and a goddamn tweed vest. He was so fucking grouchy and it made me want to push at him, poke and scratch that mood. I wanted to antagonize him until he pushed and poked and scratched right back. Until he snapped.

"Jesus Christ, Brooke, what do you want?"

I circled his work table, dragging my fingertips over the surface as I went. "Did you order that vest from the Bartenders of Brooklyn catalog?" I moved behind him, my fingers ghosting over his shoulders and earning me some major side-eye as I went. "It looks very official. I mean, Brooklyn as fuck, but also official."

He hooked his hand around the waist of my jeans as I passed him, jerked my body flush against his. "Admit it," he ordered, his teeth pressed to my neck and his palm low on my backside. *More of that, please. More more more.* "Admit you lied."

"I'm sure I don't know what you mean," I replied. "I'm also sure you have no business questioning my integrity."

His fingers followed the seam of my jeans down, between my legs. *More.* "You said never again, sweetheart, but look at you." His other hand slipped under my sweater, his knuckles brushing the underside of my breasts. "Admit it. You came out to play, didn't you?"

A fractional piece of me wanted to say yes, to surrender. To get what I needed. But the rest of me knew better than to surrender to any man.

"Just as soon as you explain why your mermaid is carrying wheat and berries."

"My fucking what?" he growled into my hair.

"Your sign, Jed. You have a mermaid on your sign and she's holding wheat and berries, and I shouldn't have to explain to you that neither grow close enough to the coast for mermaids to be in possession of either."

"Mmhmm." He palmed my ass and boosted me up onto the table. "You came here to argue about the plausibility of mermaids getting their hands on some fruit? That's what you want, Bam?"

I raked my hands down his tweed vest, laced my legs around his waist. "I'd like your signage to make sense, even if it is promulgating misogynistic mythology."

He planted his hands on the table, caging me in his arms. "I'll give you a fight if that's what you want. Just tell me, sweetheart."

I met his gaze, tipped my chin up. "Admit your sign—the one with the outrageously voluptuous mermaid—is inaccurate and illogical."

He bowed his head and bit the side of my breast through my sweater. "Meet me at my place in half an hour and we'll talk about the right kind of voluptuous."

"Are you mocking me?" I shoved him away from the sweater covering my barely B-cup breasts. "No amount of dick is worth dealing with a dickhead."

He rasped out a growl as he returned to my cleavage. "I haven't forgotten how much you liked the dick *and* the dickhead, Bam. You haven't forgotten either."

"You know what? I don't need this." I scooted forward to get off the table, but JJ fisted the hem of my sweater, held me in place. "I don't know what you think you're doing, but I don't need you for this."

"You wouldn't be here if that was true." He twisted my sweater around his hands until it tightened against my body. "I'm not mocking you and I'm not taking your shit either. I want your tits in my mouth and I'll debate some fuckin' mermaids with you while I do it if that's what you need to make it work in your head." He turned his hands once more, banding the cashmere under my bra like a tourniquet. He leaned close, his short beard tickling my neck, and pressed his lips to my jaw. "But if your ass isn't waiting for me at my house within thirty minutes, don't think you'll ever play this game with me again, Bam."

A gasp shuddered out of me as he tightened the sweater once more and kissed my cheek, right at the corner of my lips. Then he was gone, the door swinging behind him.

My fingers pressed to my not-quite-kissed lips, glanced down at the wrinkled, stretched-out mess he'd made of my sweater. "Look what you've done now."

CHAPTER FOURTEEN

JJ

***Compound Interest: interest paid on previously earned interest as
well as principal.***

"YOU'RE CLOSING UP, KID," I called to Nate as I blew into the bar.

I'd spent twenty minutes pacing the short length of the walk-in refrigerator. I'd solved all of jack shit in there. I stepped up to the point of sale system as I adjusted the unflagging bulge behind my zipper, but that didn't escape the notice of my bar hand.

"Did you hear me? You're closing."

He eyed me up and down before saying, "This seems like the type of situation where I should advise you to run far and fast in the opposite direction."

"From Brooke?" I asked, hooking a thumb over my shoulder toward the storeroom of ill-repute. "Nah, I've tried that. Doesn't help. She's the kind of storm you ride out."

"You're sure about me closing? I'm allowed to do that?"

I tapped the screen to run a day-end report. He'd been on the job more than six months now and I'd learned enough about him in that time to know he could handle more than his history of guilty pleas and rehab stays suggested. His humor was dark and his work ethic was mile-long, and he hadn't slipped up once since leaving his treatment program. "Why the hell not?"

Nate continued unpacking a crate of freshly washed glassware. "Would you like that in brief form or bullet points? Chronological order or degree of severity? My parents prefer chronological, if you were wondering."

I squeezed my eyes shut, rubbed my thumb across my brow. I knew everyone had their limits, but I couldn't understand why Nate's parents insisted on persecuting him for his mistakes while he worked his ass off turning his life around. It was a fine thing that they'd stopped coming in here, because that shit wasn't helping anyone. "This isn't the time to be self-deprecating. Just tell me whether you can handle the close-up checklist."

"Yeah. I have this under control." He glanced between me and the door. "I'd thank you for trusting me with the responsibility, but I don't think this decision has anything to do with me."

I closed my hands around the edge of the countertop, dropped my head between my shoulders. My entire body throbbed. Every last inch of me. This fucking *hurt* and I was the only one to blame. I could've stripped off Brooke's clothes and given us what we needed right there in the back room. All I needed was five minutes to finish her off and send her on her way.

But the same part of me throbbing from nothing more than her skin under my lips couldn't accept five minutes in a storage room. It'd taken me months to admit it to myself, but I wanted her naked between my sheets, mouthing off about everything, taking her sweet time as she struggled on my cock.

And I fucking hated that.

My life was too busy and my head too full to add the complication of Brooke-Ashley Markham. I had a tavern to manage, a distillery to open, a business partner obsessed with pirates and hard seltzers, a foster child bar hand trying to find his sea legs, and now that months had passed without her looking me in the eye once, Brooke was back and starved for attention. That was all she wanted from me—attention. Sex was part of it, sure, but not the entirety.

"If I didn't trust you, I wouldn't ask," I said to Nate. "This is your last chance, kid. Tell me if you're prepared to close."

He swung his gaze from side to side, a frown deepening as he scanned the tavern. "Can I call you if there's a problem?"

I didn't need the complications that came with Brooke. I didn't need the distraction or the drama, or the months-long sexual hangover that followed a night with her. But needs and wants were two separate, distinct creatures.

I folded my arms over my chest, gave a quick shake of my head. "There's not a chance in hell I'm answering my phone after I leave here."

Nate stared at the door to the back room, narrowed his eyes. "Is she still in there?"

"Probably not," I replied. "There's a delivery bay, an exit to the alley, and four windows. I'm sure she went through one of them. She's crafty."

"That's—well, okay." His brows arched up his forehead. "Yeah, all right. I can do this."

"You're a good man, Nathan." I clapped him on the back. "If everything goes wrong, just lock the doors behind you. Try not to start any fires or floods."

"I can do that," he replied. "I can lock the doors."

"Yes, you can," I called as I backed across the tavern. I was ready to sprint my ass home. "No fires, no floods."

I didn't wait for Nate's response, instead breaking into an easy jog through the village. It was late enough that most people were at home, zoned out in front of the television or tucked into bed, not minding the likes of me hauling ass for a woman who'd always demand but never appreciate that hustle.

And there she was, kicked back on my porch with her legs stretched out in front of her, ankles crossed. "That was thirty-nine minutes, Jed."

I stepped over her on my way to the door. "You can take your complaints up with my cock, Brooke."

"I'm merely pointing out you asked me to be here within thirty minutes," she continued. "Either you don't respect my time or this is some kind of dickhead power play, and I have to tell you, I'm not interested in either."

I opened the door, flipped on the lights, greeted Butterscotch with a head scratch. It was odd to find her awake at this hour. "It's always something with you, Brooke," I said, mostly to myself. The dog wasted no time on me, instead rushing to the woman's side as if she'd been waiting for her. *You and me both, Scotchie.* "At least the dog likes you. I'd have to say good night if she didn't."

Brooke glanced up from dousing the golden retriever in affection, smirked at me. "It's a wonder she likes you."

I kicked off my shoes, shrugging. "I feed her. Speaking of which, have you eaten?"

Brooke knelt down, raked her fingers through the dog's shiny coat. "Don't ask me questions like that."

"And why is that?"

Still focused on my dog, she replied, "You're not my keeper. It's none of your business."

"I was asking because *I* haven't eaten but this is a fine reminder you're an awful lot of work." I ran a hand over my head. "What are you doing here again?"

"Take your pants off and I'll show you." She stood up, sanded her palms together, and tipped her chin in the direction of my jeans. "You can eat after I leave."

"Or right now." I pointed at her jeans, her top. "Off."

She flicked a glance at my belt. "Same."

Neither of us moved. Butterscotch paced between us, alternately licking our hands and nudging our legs as she whined.

Brooke held out her palm and Butterscotch went to her. "Your dog wants you to stop screwing around."

I whistled, snapped my fingers in the direction of the kitchen. "Scotchie, go lie down." The dog gave Brooke one more lick before taking off for the kitchen. "Are you going to get what you came for or are you going to stand there and prove a point only you care about?"

"Why is your mermaid holding wheat?"

"Why did you move home from New York?"

That one landed like a slap across the face. It wasn't the reaction I'd wanted, not the one I'd intended, but she recovered quickly. "My question requires considerably less explanation, so you're welcome to answer first."

"You might think it's simple, but I reckon it's just as complicated as the one I want from you. There's some history, some family shit, and some laziness, and that's the answer."

She glared at me, the air between us heating and rippling with hostility with each breath. Then she charged toward me, her head shaking as she seethed, "You are the *worst*."

My back hit the wall as she reached for my vest, weaving her fingers between the buttons, dragging me toward her. I didn't doubt she'd tear it to shreds if she wanted. "And I keep good company."

I grabbed her waist, thumbed her fly open. I stared at her lips, and for a moment, I thought about kissing her. Nothing sweet or precious, but the kind of biting, brutal kiss she deserved—and wanted. I didn't doubt that for a second. She wanted me rough and rude, not giving a good damn whether I ruined her sweater or marked her skin. But I didn't kiss her. Not yet, not this time. Kisses were promises, even the vicious ones. Especially those.

"There's no confusion as to why you're here, sweetheart. Either get undressed or get the fuck out. I want your bare ass in my hands right now or we're not doing this tonight"—I shoved my hand down her panties and flicked her clit hard—"or any other night."

"What the fuck was that?" Brooke wailed.

"Exactly what you want," I replied, forcing her jeans down to her knees.

She yanked the vest open, sending at least one button flying across the room as it snapped free of the thread. I had her sweater over her head and off while she worked my shirt open. "Why the fuck did you stop wearing long-sleeved thermals?" she yelled. "You know, the ones without buttons? You used to wear those thermals every damn day unless it was summer, but no, you had to go and complicate your life with buttons."

The next time my cock wasn't throbbing a hole through my jeans, I planned to make sense of Brooke's accounting of my attire. But right now, I had her bra unhooked, but I couldn't discard today's fine lingerie until she gave up the button fight. "Would you fucking stop with the shirt?"

"You stop with the bra," she yelled. "Let me do this."

"Let go of the goddamn shirt. I'll take it off myself." I closed my fists around the delicate bra cups, tugged them apart. "If you think I won't rip this thing in half, you're not paying attention."

She dragged her gaze up my chest, to my face. "Don't you dare."

"Have it your way." I grabbed her hands away from the shirt and freed the bra from her arms. My shirt was quick to follow. "Just so you know, your way does not involve you fiddling with buttons for an hour."

I pinned her wrists behind her back and held them there with one hand. I shoved the other into her panties and strummed her clit as I walked her toward my bedroom.

"Rude," she muttered.

"Yeah, just the way you like me, Bam." I kicked the door shut and wasted no time yanking her jeans all the way off, bending her over the bed, pressing her cheek flat on the quilt. I traced the line of her panties from waist to hip to crotch. "What am I allowed to do? Or do you still not know what you need?"

"Bag up your meat and fuck me," she answered. "Don't act as if you know anything about me."

I fisted her panties, twisting the fabric until it wedged between her folds. She sent me furious glares over her shoulder, but she also squirmed like crazy to get the friction she wanted.

"You're cute like this," I said as I kicked off my remaining clothes and fished a condom out of my bedside table. "Never cuter than when you're bent over and snarling mad."

She wiggled out of the panties. "Is that supposed to be a compliment?"

I kicked her ankles apart and took my cock in hand, pressed it to her opening. Of all the things I hadn't been able to get out of my head in the past few months, the way her body opened to me was the most vivid. I remembered it like a punishment.

"It's true." Pushing that thought from my mind, I slammed inside her. I stayed there, my head bowed and every inch of me throbbing as she shifted beneath me. I listened to her uncomfortable gasps and frustrated sighs, holding myself steady as she adjusted to me. I thought I wanted this. I thought I'd enjoy watching her struggle like she did the last time, thought I'd get some satisfaction out of it. I didn't. I wanted to make it better, make it good for her. *So fucking good.* "It's true, Brooke."

"If you think calling me cute will soften me up, you're extremely confused."

"Not confused." I eased out of her, hooked my arms around her shoulders and behind her knees, and chucked her on the bed. "I know how to soften you up."

She went with a yelp and a curse—"Motherfucker!"—but her legs fell open when I crawled over her, a clear and welcome invitation.

I rested my weight on one arm as I fisted my cock, moving inside her with slow, easy rolls of my hips. She barely had half of me, but that half was heaven. There was a reason men were content with just the tip.

"This is better for you," I said. She licked her lips, hummed in agreement. "Then it's better for me."

"Don't bullshit me," she said, canting her hips up to take more. "The last thing in the world I want is your patronizing, nice guy bullshit."

"I don't know how I went from being the asshole to the nice guy, but I'm not patronizing you with any amount of bullshit, sweetheart." I dropped my forehead to her chest, ran my lips around her nipple. "Is this all right?"

Instead of speaking, she arched up, feeding me her small breast. I licked and sucked her nipple to a stiff peak while I snared the other between two knuckles. Now this, *this* was all right. She was wet like a river and all her tightly wound tension was melting away.

I couldn't claim to know everything about Brooke's mind or body, but I knew it took time for her to relax enough to enjoy this. She came to me with a head of steam and enough stress to form a diamond, and none of that disappeared when I dropped my pants. I couldn't argue it away and I couldn't fuck it away; I had to learn how to unravel it. I had to learn Brooke, and I was beginning to believe I wanted to make room for that challenge in my life. It was foolish and definitely in service to my dick, but I liked this. No matter what happened when it was all said and done tonight, it wasn't ending here.

"Your cock is not as great as you think," she said, her nails cutting into my biceps. "You need to do something with it. You need to move. You can't just stick it inside me and think you're done."

This fucking woman. Goddamn, I did not want to like her.

"And you can't just lie there and expect me to know what you want," I replied, giving her a slow roll of my hips. "Speak up, sweetheart."

"Keep doing that," she said, her head thrown back and her eyes closed. "Keep doing that and—*mmmm*."

"That is the right fuckin' answer, Bam."

BROOKE SIGHED at the ceiling approximately thirteen seconds after I rolled off her.

"Time for me to go. This was, well"—she glanced at me—"you know what it was. No need to explain."

My dick was half hard and still wet, and there was no reason for anyone to leave this bed. "Nah, you're staying right there."

"In fact, I am not. I'm leaving." She said this, but she remained where I'd left her.

"Give me two or three minutes." I moved my hand to her thigh, dragged my fingers over her silky skin. God, she felt good. "Don't move. The blood flow will return in my extremities and then I'm licking your pussy."

She shifted to her side, which put my hand between her legs. No complaints from either of us. "That's a real nice offer, but I'm leaving."

"Do I have to teach you how to enjoy that too?" I slipped a finger inside her, grinned at the way her eyes popped wide in response. "I don't mind, Bam. I'll put in the hours. I'll do the work."

"Your opinion of yourself is not proportional to the quality of your dick," she replied. "It would be nice if the two had a stronger correlation."

I brought my hand between her breasts, pushed her back down as I shifted to my knees. "Let's see how my tongue rates."

I was still shattered from the orgasm she snapped out of me like a sea witch's curse, but I wasn't passing up an opportunity to win an argument. Not a fucking chance.

I settled between her legs, careful to scratch my beard up her inner thighs as I found a comfortable position. She made some quiet noises, little gasps and whines that suggested she liked these moves, but the best indicator was the way her belly jiggled. There wasn't much to her, not an inch to pinch, but the area around her belly button was barely soft enough to telegraph every clench and release.

"I know it's lovely down there and I do put some effort into keeping things tight and tidy," she said, "but I was under the impression you were doing more than rubbing your beard all over my leg and making eye contact with my clit."

I blinked up at her for a second. I thought about arguing with her, but quickly determined the best course of action required no words. I shoved both hands under her ass, dragged her center to my mouth, and got my first real taste of her. Her clit was the most perfect little pearl. I couldn't stop circling it and sucking it while her body shook in my hands. That clit tasted like I was meant to obey it and fuck me if I wasn't ready to kneel.

In no time at all, I had her belly quivering and her most delicate flesh throbbing under my tongue. And since I was here, I was getting that ass too.

"Jed," she cried, her hands fisting around my hair. "Jed, I'm—almost —what—oh my, *fuck*."

The spasms crested and I backed off when she pulled my hair harder. I knew she could take more, but I wasn't going to tell her how to own and operate her body tonight. I'd save that for tomorrow night.

My head resting on her thigh, I looped an arm around her waist and pressed tiny kisses on her mound. "How'd I do?"

"This isn't the Olympic ice dancing qualifier. Stop waiting for a score every time you put on a show." She said this, but she also brushed her hand through my hair with more plain, transparent affection than she'd ever offered.

I flopped down beside her on the pillow. "When should I expect you again?"

"Expect me?" She sat up, an arm banded over her breasts as if I couldn't identify them in a blind taste test. "Why the hell would you *expect* me?"

"Because you'll be back." I dragged my gaze down the heart-shaped curve of her ass. "We both know you will be, so there's no sense in pretending otherwise. You're not a silly woman, Brooke. Don't play silly games with me."

"Is that because you believe I'm fond of your dick? Because I'd skip the victory lap if I was you. I can count the single guys in this dismal, hole-in-the-wall town on one hand and that includes old widower Lambertson, the Mulcaheys' grandson, who can't be more than twenty, and your little friend Nate, who is also too damn young for me." She climbed off the bed and stood in the middle of my bedroom, completely nude, and said without a hint of humor, "You're the least offensive option in the bunch."

I shouldn't have fallen for the obvious trap she laid, but I couldn't stop myself. Her words annoyed the shit out of me, so I laid a trap of my own. "Here's what I can't understand, Brooke. If you hate living here so much, why don't you leave? Go back to New York?"

She scooped a stray shirt off the floor, held it to her chest. She refused to meet my eyes. "I have my reasons."

"Such as? While you're at it, why don't you fill me in on why you came back here in the first place." I watched as she slipped my shirt over her head and took great pains to keep her gaze away from me. "I have some ideas, but I'd love to hear it from you, sweetheart."

"You don't get to call me that," she said, her voice barely audible. "And you don't know anything about me."

"You're not that difficult to understand, sweetheart."

"Uh, yeah, okay. Whatever. Believe what you want, but I don't have to sit here while you make all these accusations."

"I've accused you of nothing."

She snatched the only remaining pillow from the bed and winged it at my head while I pulled on my clothes. "It sounds like you're accusing me of something."

Tell me the truth. Tell me what's happening with your father and I'll help you. "Nothing you're not guilty of."

"Oh my god. I'm so finished with this." She pushed past me, into the hall. "What the hell is wrong with you? We had sex, that's it. You're not entitled to explanations. You don't have to go and explore issues and make sense of things." She stepped into her jeans, wrapped her sweater around her shoulders as if she'd planned on wearing it that way all along. "All you have to do is get your dick out and shut up, and apparently, that's too much to ask of you."

"It's a reasonable question, Brooke. You don't hide the fact you hate it here. What's the problem with asking why you stay?"

She shook her head and then flung the front door open. "Do not follow me."

The door banged shut behind her while I shoved my feet into shoes and whistled for Butterscotch. We stayed a fair distance behind Brooke, but that didn't stop her from tossing furious glances over her shoulder every few minutes.

"Why are you in such a rush?" I called. "It's the middle of the night."

"Oh, well, since you asked," she shouted back, "I'm going to get some work done. I'd planned on enjoying the post-orgasmic haze, but someone ruined that for me with a bullshit conversation that's none of his fucking business. I'm awake and I'm aggravated, so I might as well make some money."

"You could turn around and come home with me. You won't be aggravated when I'm done."

"One cannot be the source and the solution," she said. "I'm finished with you."

"For tonight," I added.

"Forever. I'm done with you *forever*. There are no circumstances in which you will ever see me naked again."

"You say that, sweetheart, and I know you think you mean it. But I also know you'll be back."

She stopped near the village, pivoted, and stared at me for a solid minute. Then, "Jed, I'd rather trip and fall into hot garbage in Midtown during a heat wave than get on your dick again."

Butterscotch galloped to Brooke's side and nuzzled her thigh. She murmured something to the dog and scratched her head, and they continued into the village side by side. They stayed together all the way up the hill to the Markham estate, Butterscotch's head brushing Brooke's hand every few steps.

I shoved my hands into my pockets and trailed behind them, content to follow—and wait.

CHAPTER FIFTEEN

BROOKE

***Marketable Securities:** financial instruments that can be readily converted into cash.*

Annette: Were you walking a dog last night?
Brooke: Good morning to you too.
Annette: Were you walking a dog in the middle of the night? Because one of Jackson's deputies swears he witnessed that exact thing and I... have so many questions.
Brooke: Can you describe the dog?
Annette: I didn't ask for details. All I heard was dog.
Brooke: Sounds unlikely.
Annette: And yet it wouldn't shock me if it was true.
Brooke: That says more about you than it does me.
Annette: Are you sure about that?

Annette: Did you walk any dogs last night?

Brooke: I did not, no.
Annette: Will you be walking any tonight?
Brooke: Can't see why I would...
Annette: I wasn't sure whether it's something new you're doing, like goat yoga.
Brooke: I'm not doing goat yoga. That sounds horrible. I don't want a goat in my face while I'm in downward dog, thank you.
Annette: But middle of the night dog walking? That's an option?
Brooke: Probably not.

Brooke: You know what's hard?
Annette: It feels like you're walking me into a dick joke.
Brooke: Ha. I wouldn't have this issue if I had some good dick available.
Annette: Go back to the Galley. That worked out well the last time.
Brooke: You don't fish in the same pond twice. It's a well-known proverb.
Annette: You just made that up.
Brooke: Maybe but I'm having real problems.
Annette: All right. Tell me what's hard.
Brooke: Trying to have some alone time with my new vibrator when Dad is taking a bath across the hall and having a loud conversation with his health aide about the town council being a pack of fools.
Annette: Yeah, that's rough.
Brooke: I'm almost certain he's referencing a council from the 1970s, but he's talking like it's today and it's messing with my orgasm.
Annette: Wait. Is the problem that you can hear him while you're visiting your amusement park or is it that he's talking like it's the 1970s?
Brooke: Honestly, a bit of both.
Annette: I'm sure you could leave the house, go to the Galley, meet someone, and fix that situation.
Brooke: Nah. I don't feel like putting pants on.
Annette: Also valid, but try some noise-canceling headphones.

Brooke: I've tried those and discovered dead silence is not an improvement over rants about lousy small town politicians.

Annette: Then put your damn pants on!

Brooke: You know what's funny? The idea of putting pants on in order to find someone to take them off.

Annette: You're stalling. Do not make me come to your house and dress you myself. I will. I'll also drag you down the street and force you to flirt with people at the Galley.

Brooke: omfg Annette, when did you get so militant?

Annette: Everything I know, I've learned from you.

CHAPTER SIXTEEN

JJ

*Fixed Costs: a cost that will remain constant regardless of the
amount of goods or services produced.*

BROOKE WAS in one hell of a rotten mood.

I knew it the minute she blew into the tavern, all thunder and lightning. I saw it in the scowl permanently twisted across her lips, the stiff line of her shoulders, the joyless chill in her eyes. It was the same way she'd blown out of my house four nights ago.

I cataloged her every movement as she swept across the tavern toward her usual seat at the bar. She worked hard at dodging my gaze, but that wouldn't last long. Once could be forgiven, twice was a mistake, three times was a pattern—and she was here for her third.

Turning away from the territory she'd claimed as her own, I sidled up to Nate. He was running the bar tonight and having a tough go of it. It was barely ten o'clock and we'd wasted more beer on foamy pours than I wanted to price out in my head. My pet project had also forgotten the ingredients to the most basic drinks—gin and tonic, anyone?—and looked damn close to melting down on several occasions, including this one. "How goes it, kid?"

Nate shook his hands at the taps. "Not great," he whispered, mostly to himself. "It's not great."

I glanced between him and the handles. "What's the problem?"

"That's a question I'd really like to answer, but I have no clue why I can't pour more than one beer at a time."

"Then don't pour more than one at a time." I clapped him on the back. "You run the ship, kid. It sails as fast or slow as you want, and these people"—I tipped my head toward the regular crew—"are just happy you're pouring them."

He closed his eyes, pressed the palms of his hands there. "I'm sorry."

"For what?" I asked. "For making some suds? That's nothing."

"For—it's just everything. You gave me a chance and I'm just fucking it up," he replied, still hidden behind his hands.

I turned in a half circle, scanning the bar and tavern. "That isn't reality, Nate. Look around. You have this under control." I elbowed him toward Brooke. "I'll handle these pours. Go get Miss Markham's order."

He dropped his hands to his hips. "Is it still on the house?"

I responded with a quick nod and pushed him in her direction. I didn't want to elaborate on that piece of legislation. It made sense to me in a convoluted way: any woman who shared my bed and consumed my waking thoughts drank for free. But more than that, I didn't want Brooke's money. She had a whole fucking lot of it, more than most people would see in ten lifetimes, and I wasn't prepared to mix that with sex. I didn't even like thinking about it. She didn't like anyone thinking about it either, but she came from old money and found a fuckton of new money for herself in Manhattan. No doubt about that.

Forcing myself to keep my focus away from Brooke, I went to work filling pint glasses. It gave me a moment to sweep a gaze over the corner of the bar closest to the television and gauge Bobbie Lincoln's degree of inebriation. As far as I could tell from beer-wet splotches on his shirt and his inability to simultaneously focus both eyes, he was far beyond his usual state. He seemed to be the only one getting more than foam from Nate's pours.

Lincoln was drunk every night of every week, but it tended toward pleasant, mild drunkenness rather than this evening's version of morose and increasingly hostile. He'd started bitching about sports to anyone who would listen, but the urge to instigate got the best of him and he'd transitioned to divisive political topics. No one was engaging—hell, I wasn't sure they were listening—but that didn't stop him from ramping up the rhetoric.

If I was smart, I'd ring the sheriff or one of his deputies to escort Lincoln home. But my bar hand spooked easily, and calling in the sheriff's deputies was certain to jangle his nerves even more. I didn't want to wash another keg down the drain. Add to those issues the fact I was short-staffed in the kitchen and playing phone tag with both Barry and the marketing coordinator he wanted to hire for the distillery's branding, and every aspect of the project was taking five times longer than planned.

And Brooke was in a ranty, pouty, jerky shoulders, rolling eyes mood. God, I wanted to fuck it right out of her. I would. But not yet. Not until I contained a few issues.

Once I'd cleared the pending beverage orders, I headed into the back room without glancing in Brooke's direction. Ignoring her served two purposes. First, it annoyed the hell out of her and I enjoyed nothing more than turning her screws. And second, I didn't trust myself to get a mouthful of her salty mood and not drag her out of that seat.

Free from the oppressive heat of Brooke's gaze, I fired off text messages to the Cove's innkeeper Rhys Neville, gently begging him to take Lincoln off my hands. When he agreed, I ducked into the kitchen to assess the situation there. The dinner rush was behind us, thank god, but running a kitchen without enough hands on deck was a nightmare. I checked the walk-in fridge for prepped goods, sent messages to suppliers to adjust tomorrow's deliveries, and returned to the back room. I took my time inspecting the kegs, bottled beer, and liquor stored in there.

When I emerged, I made a point of looking out across the dining room—and avoiding the devastatingly irresistible woman seated in her usual spot. I scanned the occupied tables, the patrons seated at the bar, the orders waiting to be fulfilled. I checked on Nate and found him managing a bit better now that he was out of the weeds.

Grabbing the day's inventory list from beside the point of sale system, I headed toward Brooke. I stopped two seats away from her, braced my forearms on the bar while I thumbed through the pages. It was enough distance to make it clear this mood didn't earn her my undivided attention. From the corner of my eye, I saw her fingertips tapping the walls of her glass in a quick, erratic rhythm.

"Here's what you're going to do," I said, flipping to another page. "Go to my house. There's a key under the mat at the back door. Get undressed and wait for me in bed."

"And how long will I be waiting, good sir?"

I lifted a shoulder, let it fall. Continued staring at the pages without seeing. "Until I get there."

"That's not going to happen," she replied. "I'm not going to wait around in your bed—naked—until you're content I've learned some kind of lesson."

"And why would I be teaching you a lesson, Brooke?"

The electricity behind her stare dragged my focus up, away from the inventory. I wished I hadn't surrendered to that pull because even with her forehead creased and a snarl on her lips, she was unreasonably beautiful. It was unfair for one woman to be granted so many gifts and advantages.

"I'm certain you have a reason or twenty-nine." She tossed her platinum hair over her shoulder and I had to draw a breath because the memory of those strands on my skin twisted my gut. "You've never lacked for reasons to resent me, Jed."

"We're not having this conversation," I replied.

She clasped her hands under her chin. "It seems that we are."

I leaned forward, lowered my voice. "And yet conversation is the reason you stomped out of my house in the middle of the night, swearing up and down you'd never be back."

"Hmm." She arched an eyebrow up as if granting me a point in this match. "Perhaps I should go to your house, lube up my preferred vibrator, and take matters into my own hands. I'm sure I'd learn a lesson from that." Another arched eyebrow. "Or perhaps the lesson would be yours."

I gathered the inventory, pushed away from the bar. "You're welcome to do that, Brooke, but you should think of it as tonight's appetizer. You'll get the main course when it's good and ready for you."

I HELD out for ninety-three minutes.

It would've been longer if Nate hadn't spilled a full tray of whiskey shots on my jeans and boots, but I could live with ninety-three minutes. It was enough time for Brooke to simmer down or boil over, and I was prepared for either version of her.

I wasn't prepared to find her curled up on my bed with Butterscotch tucked in beside her, fully dressed and fast asleep. Her hair was everywhere, mouth open, arms tucked inside the body of her sweater, one shoe on, one off. For an unreasonably beautiful woman, she slept like a blacked-out teenager.

Leaning against the doorframe, I watched her longer than I should have. My clothes were wet and reeked of whiskey—and everything else at the tavern. My body was exhausted from sixteen solid hours of work and my head ached from the hours I needed to catch up on distillery business. But I went on watching while she slept with my dog until watching wasn't enough. Until I had to touch her.

I pushed away from the door and stood by the bed. "Are you tired from being angry all the time? Or angry because you're so damn tired? Which one is it, Bam?" I tucked her hair over her ear, dragged the strands between my fingers. "And how can I make it better?"

Even as the words passed my lips, I knew I didn't mean them. I didn't want to help. Truly, I didn't want that trouble in my life. Helping people wasn't my thing. This town was packed to the gills with nosy neighbors who lived to help each other, one pot roast and diaper drive at a time. That wasn't me. It wasn't my place.

But Brooke was asleep in my bed. She came to me in that storm of a mood and she let it drop long enough to curl up with my dog, put her head down, and close her eyes. She came to me. She asked for me, albeit in her supremely fucked-up way. She needed me.

I stayed there longer than I should have, rubbing her hair between my fingers and studying this open, unpracticed version of her. Eventually, I stepped away to discard my liquor- and grease-scented clothes. I thought about showering the day away, but more than anything, I wanted to know how it felt to sleep beside Brooke. I pulled on a pair of flannel pajama pants and a t-shirt and slipped into the bed behind her. It took a bit of finagling with the blankets to get her underneath them without waking her and Butterscotch, but I managed. She must've been absolutely exhausted.

"Sleep well, Bam." I kissed her shoulder over her shirt and retreated to my side of the bed. A soft canine snore huffed out. "You too, Scotchie."

CHAPTER SEVENTEEN

BROOKE

Drawdown: the percentage loss from a fund's highest value to its lowest over a given timeframe.

I WOKE up to a tongue on my face.

I wasn't opposed to oral wake-up calls, but face licking wasn't my preferred form of oral. Call me particular, but I also preferred that tongue to belong to a human being rather than a dog.

"Good morning to you too," I said to Butterscotch. "What the hell am I doing here?"

"Scotchie," JJ whisper-yelled from the other room. "Leave her alone."

"It's fine, she's awake," I called back. I sat up and crossed my legs, and rubbed the sleep from my eyes. Blinking, I ran my hands through my hair and spotted the hazy outline of JJ in the doorway. "What happened? Why is it"—I glanced at the clock—"oh my god, why am I here at six in the morning?"

"You fell asleep." He wagged a spatula at me. "I let you stay asleep."

"Why the hell would you do that?" I cried. "I came here for a dick appointment, not a sleepover."

He crossed his arms over his chest. "You were out cold. Sorry, but I'm not fucking you while you're unconscious."

"It sounds like you want me to congratulate you for that. I'm not going to." I drove my fingers through my hair again, groaning. "Did it not occur to you that I needed to get home? That people might be looking for me?"

He pushed his tongue against the inside of his cheek. Stared at me. Waiting a long damn time to say, "Your phone is plugged in on the other side of the bed. If anyone was looking for you, they would've called. No?"

"Maybe I had to work," I continued.

"In the middle of the night, Brooke?"

I held out my hands. "The beauty of international markets is that one is always open."

JJ rolled his eyes and glanced over his shoulder. "Come get some scrambled eggs."

I followed him into the kitchen, calling, "I didn't come here for the breakfast buffet."

He held his hand over a cast iron skillet on the stove, nodded, and poured the contents of a glass measuring cup into the pan. Over the sizzle of the eggs, JJ said, "We've established that, sweetheart, but it seemed like you needed some rest." He jerked a shoulder up. "A good breakfast wouldn't kill you either."

Hipshot and arms crossed, I said, "It's not your place to tell me when I need to sleep or eat. Having sex with me a handful of times doesn't entitle you to make my decisions."

"How do you feel about marble rye?"

I blinked at him. "What are you asking me?"

He stepped away from the stove to retrieve two wax paper-wrapped loaves of bread. He lifted one of them. "I have a fresh loaf of marble rye from a husband and wife bakery over in Charlotte, Vermont." Lifting the other, he said, "They also sent a whole grain raisin walnut with my order, but I don't get the impression you're a fan of raisin bread."

I took the raisin bread from him and unwrapped the paper. "What? Just because I want you to wake me up and fuck me into a mild concussion, I can't like raisins?" I sniffed the bread. "That seems ruder and more judgmental than your usual."

He snatched the loaf out of my hands and set it on the countertop beside the stove. "I'm sorry that, rather than leaving you to stumble home with a sex-induced brain injury, I allowed you to sleep. It's terrible, I know. Can I make it worse by feeding you breakfast, Brooke?"

"Yes," I replied, surprising us both. "But I want the raisin bread, lightly toasted." I helped myself to his French press coffee and watched while he scooped the eggs onto a plate. "I'd also like a rain check for that dick appointment you missed."

"That *I* missed," he grumbled.

While he sliced the bread, I drifted into the adjoining dining room with my coffee. Binders, boxes, and file folders sat on several chairs. Architectural blueprints covered half the table, but I couldn't make sense of the plans. It seemed too big for a house and I couldn't imagine him tearing down the Galley and starting from scratch. It was a Talbott's Cove institution.

I was surprised I didn't notice any of this last night.

JJ came up behind me and set two plates on the table. "Your raisin toast," he said. "Sit, please."

I gestured to the blueprints. "What is this all about?"

He stared at the documents as he settled into his chair. After a moment, he replied, "I'll explain if you sit down."

Nodding, I dropped into the chair. He shot a pointed glance at the toast and I took a bite to appease him. "This is some quality raisin bread," I said. "Now, tell me what you're building."

He forked up a heap of scrambled eggs, still staring at the plans across the table. Eventually, he replied, "I'm building a distillery with a tasting room, restaurant, and event space."

Shocked, I gazed at him with the toast suspended an inch from my open mouth. "A distillery...and some other things? And where are you doing this? And how, exactly?"

His brows furrowed as he poked at the eggs. "Here in Talbott's Cove, on the site of the old cider mill, the one on the far end of the village. It's set back from the street, but close enough that people who come here for craft gin and vodka will stay for the bookstore, the gift shops, the inn, everything else." He took a bite, but still hadn't managed a glance in my direction. "It's contingent upon a million things. Inspections and feasibility studies and licenses and financing and my incredibly flaky business partner's daily whims."

I tore the toast into small pieces, bobbing my head as I considered this information. "You have a business partner? An accredited investor?"

And now he chooses to look at me.

"Yeah. Is that particularly surprising to you, Bam?"

I popped a piece of toast into my mouth. "It's not surprising, no. But I want to know who it is so I can look up his SEC filings."

He leaned back in his chair, layered his hands over his belly. "Why do you care? You're just here for the sex."

We gazed at each other for a moment that felt as heavy as midnight, and for once I yielded first. "Because this is my world. This is what I do. If you're working with someone who is promising to bring sizable capital investments to the table, I want to confirm whether this person is one of the good ones and he has a record of doing it right."

He tipped his chin up, studied me through narrowed eyes. "Again, why do you care? Why does he need to be one of the good ones, Brooke? As you've said, I'm the worst and this is a hopeless, dead-end town. Why does it matter whether we're doing it right?"

I hunched forward, flattened my hands on the tabletop. "You want me to confess something deep and meaningful, I can tell. Instead of doing that, why don't you run your business plan by me?"

He laughed into his coffee. "Isn't it a little early for a ritual beating?" For a minute, we ate in silence. Then he dropped his fork to the plate and said, "All right. Fine. Here's the quick version. Small-batch gin and vodka crafted entirely from locally sourced ingredients. Grains from nearby family farms, honey from an apiary in Beddington, juniper berries and herbs from growers all over New England. Clean, organic, sustainably produced."

"That's what you're brewing in the back room of the tavern?" I asked.

He bobbed his head as he sipped his coffee. "Yeah. It started out as an experiment, turned into a hobby, and now a solid percentage of the monthly profits come from distribution agreements with bars and restaurants all over the region."

"Nice. Word-of-mouth demand is the kind of proof point that opens more doors than any data set," I said.

He peered at me, frowning. "I thought you worked on Wall Street. Stocks and bonds and funds and...the rest of that stuff no one understands."

"Yeah, I do," I replied. Then, thinking better of it, I added, "I mean, I did. Obviously, I'm not there right now because I work out of my childhood bedroom as everyone truly aspires to do. My firm is at Broadway and Wall Street and they let me do this remote thing because being in New York City is not essential when one has a decent Wi-Fi connection, and I make a lot more money than their cadre of #MeToo miscreants. But yes, stocks, bonds, funds, and the rest of that stuff. Hedge funds, in particular. Before hedge funds, I managed a handful of different international market derivative desks. Derivatives trading bores the shit out of me, so I got the hell out of there. I spent a little time in venture cap, but I found all the idealistic people asking for money to be exhausting."

He polished off the rest of his eggs, wiped his mouth on a cloth napkin, and retreated into the kitchen without a word. Since this was JJ, I didn't question it. The boy liked to walk away and come back when it suited him. True to form, he returned with the French press and topped off my coffee.

"Thank you," I said. He waved me off as if he couldn't be bothered with my manners. "I want to hear the rest of your pitch. How does the cider house figure in?"

"The idea is to make a destination out of the production facility. Tasting room, restaurant, gardens, tours, the whole thing. The location has to be worth the trip and it has to photograph well because, like you said, word of mouth converts to social proof." He rounded the table and tapped his fingertips on the blueprint. "This is one of the proposed floor plans. This one allocates space to a fine dining restaurant as well as a fast-casual venue, both focused on showcasing the products and goods from local farming partners. I don't think we can sustain two dining facilities but my partner wanted to get an idea how it would look."

I couldn't make sense of the blueprint, but I nodded anyway. "If you get this right, it's going to be huge for the local economy."

"That's a big *if*," he said, laughing. "There's a lot of movement that needs to happen before the local economy feels a damn thing."

"And your investors? I know you mentioned a partner with a sense of whimsy and that troubles me. You shouldn't rely on someone like that. The kind of money I imagine you need is no problem for me. I'm willing to invest and—"

He brought his hand to my shoulder, drew it up my neck and into my hair. "I don't want to get into that with you. I need it to be separate."

"You need that separate from me?"—I tapped my chest—"Or *me*?"—I circled my hand between us.

"Yes and yes." He gathered my hair in his fist, held me steady as he barely brushed his lips over mine. It wasn't lost on me that we'd shared a bed and our bodies, but not a real kiss. This was the closest thing to it since high school and I didn't know what it meant that he was almost kissing me while asking me to stay the hell out of his business. "Please understand."

"I do, I mean, yeah, I get that. It's fine," I stammered. I did not get it and it was not fine. "You don't want to tell me who is bringing the capital to the table and I'm certain that makes sense to you, although I am going to offer you some suggestions because I invite myself into other people's problems. I know a number of investors who are big into food and beverage tourism ventures. I'm talking about people who open bars and restaurants every week, people who scout emerging foodie tourism markets, people who know the heartbeat of this business. Just off the top of my head, I can think of four or five investors who are actively looking for homegrown, niche market startups, especially ones with a sustainability angle. It's as easy as making email introductions if you're interested."

JJ was quiet while he rubbed his fingers over my scalp. I couldn't determine whether he was insulted or excited or his usual brand of grouchy. Then, "Thank you for...everything. I appreciate it. It's good to talk this out with someone who knows the town. But I have to say no. I'm all set."

I pressed my lips together and went right on staring at the blueprint I couldn't decipher. "Even if you won't take my money, I could help you. I could offer technical assistance on the financial side or connect you to talented branding and marketing people and"—I paused, glanced up at him as I found the words I never found for anyone else—"and I could fund this entire venture right now if you wanted to bail on that partner of yours. I could just *give* it to you."

He leaned forward, pressed his forehead to mine. Of all the touches we'd shared, this one made me feel the most exposed. "Bam, sweetheart, I'll give you all the rain checks for angry insult concussion sex you want. I'll let you bitch and moan about this town and I'll stop asking you why you came back, even though I think you want to get it off your chest. I'll set aside all the raisin bread I get from Vermont for you. But there is no way in hell I'd let you invest a penny in this project."

I twisted out of his arms as tears filled my eyes. I didn't know why I was crying, but I knew I had to leave immediately. "If you change your mind, you know how to find me," I called as I stepped into my shoes.

"Brooke, come back here and—"

I slammed the front door shut behind me.

CHAPTER EIGHTEEN

BROOKE

Duration: the measure of a bond price's sensitivity to shifts in interest rates.

Annette: Hello, madam. You're awake early. Or was it a very late night?

Brooke: I'm always awake early. I make a lot of money in China. Their morning is our night.

Annette: Yes, this is true. However, I don't usually see you walking through the village first thing in the morning. Because you're usually so busy with China.

Brooke: Oh, yeah. I just went out for a walk.

Annette: You went for a walk? Since when do you walk?

Brooke: I walk. I walk all the time.

Annette: Yeah, from one room to another. You don't walk for, you know, the practice of walking.

Brooke: Well, I went for a walk today. Fresh air, birds, sunshine. It was glorious.

Annette: I have several questions about this but I'd like to start with this—how dare you?

Brooke: How dare I what?

Annette: Do whatever you're doing without telling me!

Brooke: We cannot be those women who walk together in the mornings. Honey, no. I love you but we can't get a set of matching visors. That's not our look.

Annette: Let's presume it was a very late night. Let's also presume that it was a satisfying outing for you, even if it's not one you're willing to discuss with me.

Brooke: Why is it so hard to believe that I went for a walk?

Annette: If it was an early morning outing of the amorous variety, I applaud you. Morning sex for me is an experience made possible by virtue of already being in bed. Getting up and going out for sex at that hour is commendable. If we gave out awards for outstanding performances in getting some, you'd win in the Early Morning, Out of the House category.

Brooke: How much coffee did you drink today? You're wired, sweet pea.

Annette: You only deflect when I'm close to the truth.

Brooke: I'm worried about you. Go over to the pharmacy and get your blood pressure checked.

Annette: I'm keeping an eye on you, Markham.

Brooke: Don't stop with one eye. Use both of them. That's why you have two.

Brooke: This is going to sound ridiculous, but I'm asking anyway.

Annette: I'm here for it. Give me all the ridiculous.

Brooke: Where can I get really good fried chicken?

Annette: Quantify "really good."

Brooke: I have to tell you a story in order to do that.

Annette: I love your stories. I'm going to refill my coffee and sit down with a cupcake for this.

Brooke: Dad has been talking about his time in the National Guard recently. When I say recently, I mean it's the only thing he's talked about for the past week and I'm ready to start plucking my eyelashes out if it will make him stop.

Annette: Your father was in the National Guard? I didn't know that!

Brooke: Allegedly. I haven't done any digging to confirm or deny the story, but this is the first I've heard of his service.

Annette: Weird. Go on.

Brooke: It seems he enlisted after high school, trained with the state National Guard during college in Orono, and then spent a few months in Texas after graduation.

Annette: He was deployed to…Texas?

Brooke: It's hazy. Can't be certain. Dementia is a liar. This could be a story he read once upon a time or something he watched on television. It could be a mashup of things he believes to be true.

Annette: I know he's older than my parents, but not so old that he would've been down at the Alamo.

Brooke: Who fucking knows. But he claims he had the best fried chicken of his entire life while in Texas. In one retelling, it was near Galveston. In another, it was Plano.

Annette: And now he's craving some Texas-style fried chicken.

Brooke: It's not about the chicken, but it also is about the chicken. Right now, he wants that memory and the safety and familiarity that comes with it, but he can't access it without the chicken. For the past few days, he's been somewhere between aggressively angry and ugly cry sad at all times.

Annette: Oh, honey. I'm so sorry. You should've reached out earlier. I can help with things like chicken and whatever else. You have enough on your hands. Ask for some damn help, woman.

Brooke: I never know when these things will spin out of control. Sometimes they're quick blips.

Annette: I love you and I know you're trying your ass off, but it sounds like it spun out of control several days ago. Give me the context so I can help you fix this.

Brooke: As the story goes—and I can't believe I'm saying this—he and a bunch of other National Guardsmen brought a chicken to a shop where they fried it for them.

Annette: You mean a package of chicken from a butcher.

Brooke: That isn't the way the story was told to me, no.

Annette: They brought a live chicken to a fry shop?

Brooke: Maybe that's how it goes in Texas. Maine has general stores where you can buy ammo and wedding dresses.

Annette: Forgive me for being obvious, but have you tried any of the fast food chicken options?

Brooke: There are grease stains on the wall in the dining room and bits of chicken stuck in the chandelier. One of the home health aides is on personal leave because Dad stabbed her with a drumstick. My hair smells like fried chicken and I'm afraid I'll never wash that scent out.

Brooke: We've tried everything.

Annette: Then...we need to find a live chicken fry shop?

Brooke: I have looked, but as you know, certain parts of this region don't maintain much internet presence.

Annette: You need someone who knows how to fry chicken in volume and saves the oil.

Brooke: What does that mean, saves the oil?

Annette: It's a flavor thing. Trust me. I'll ask around.

Annette: I'll also see if anyone has a hen they want to sell.

Brooke: What does a hen cost? I'm sure I have the cash on hand, but I'm wondering what the going rate is for live chickens.

Annette: Let's work on finding a chicken and a fryer first, okay? Then we'll get into the economics.

Brooke: Good plan. Thank you.

Annette: You're welcome and stop letting it get this bad before asking for help.

Brooke: I'm trying.

Annette: Try harder.

Annette: Jackson and I are going to that pub in Northport tonight, the one with the Trivia Tuesday. Are you in?

Brooke: Ugh, no. I can't.

Annette: What's going on?

Brooke: I'm just swamped. I'm sorry. I know how Jackson loves it when I tell him he's wrong about everything.

Annette: Are you all right?

Brooke: Yeah, totally. Just a lot on my plate right now.

Annette: How's your father doing?

Brooke: No major changes. He's watching the original Hawaii Five-Oh and Quincy, M.E. and that's giving him something to talk about. I'm just torn between being really fucking happy I can stream these old shows and really fucking appalled at the shit that was acceptable back then.

Brooke: Also, the hairstyles. Did flat irons not exist until 2004?

Annette: I wouldn't know. They don't work on my kind.

Brooke: You curly-haired girls are all alike.

Annette: What's happening with work? Do you have any big pitches or, I don't know, whatever happens in your world?

Brooke: I have a number of SEC filings coming up.

Annette: We're not talking about college football, right?

Brooke: Securities and Exchange Commission.

Annette: Right. That SEC.

Annette: Are you sure we can't convince you to come along?

Brooke: Not this time. Have fun at trivia.

Annette: Have fun on your morning walk.

CHAPTER NINETEEN

JJ

Margin: the difference between the revenue produced by a good or service and the cost of production.

BROOKE-ASHLEY MARKHAM RUINED my life on an unseasonably warm night last September. She dismantled all the good sense I had with the simple command of "Take off your pants" and tore down the years of distance I'd put between us since high school. Since kissing her once and wanting more.

Now, she ruined my life with her hair on my pillow and my dog's affections and text messages that simply proclaimed, *I want you to fuck me tonight.*

As if I was just a cock waiting around for some pussy to invite me in from the cold for the evening. As if the only things we exchanged were soft and hard, yes and no. As if we weren't building a new world from the old, broken one behind us. As if we meant to stop.

And I let her do this. I asked for it. I went willingly, knowingly.

Same as I did every time she asked, I responded with, *I'll be home in forty-five minutes. Let yourself in.*

Brooke-Ashley Markham was ruining my life, and I didn't want her to stop.

CHAPTER TWENTY

BROOKE

Secured Debt: a debt which is covered by specific assets in the event of a default.

JJ GRABBED the backs of my thighs, pushed them to my chest. My ankles bounced on his shoulders as he slammed into me again. My body was stuffed and folded like tortellini, and all I could manage was, "What the hell kind of position is this?"

He turned his head, pressed his lips to my calf. He got what he deserved there, as I hadn't shaved my legs in *days*. "The kind that shuts you up long enough for me to use you the way you like."

I reached for sheets, blankets, anything to keep me anchored. "I'm not sure I requested *this*."

"The fact you have"—he rocked into me like he was trying to demolish walls—"something to say"—and dislocate my hips—"proves you want me to use you even rougher."

"No, Jed, not rougher," I begged. "No, I can't—"

"No?" He pulled out but kept his hands on my thighs, brushed his thumbs over my backside and the spot where my legs met my center. It was uncomfortable like this, contorted and empty. I wanted to be filled, moved. And yes, used. "You want me to stop? You've changed your mind?"

It hurt, this emptiness. It was an ache, deep and true, and I couldn't go on this way. I couldn't live another minute without him inside me. I clawed at his chest, reaching for as much of him as I could get. Anything I could get. "You owe me," I snapped. "You still haven't made up for the time when you didn't wake me up."

His thumb tapped my clit once, twice—and then he went back to kissing my damn leg. "Do better," he said. "I know you can do better than that."

"No, not when I'm still mad about it," I replied. "If I wasn't enjoying it, I would've woken up and told you as much. I wanted that one, Jed."

Scraping his beard up my leg, he laughed into my skin. "You know this isn't a punch card situation, right? You're not working up to a free fuck, Bam."

Still chuckling, he shifted my leg to kiss my ankle. My damn ankle. "Oh my fucking god, Jed. If you don't put that rolling-pin dick inside me and keep going right now, I'll leave here and set fire to the tavern."

I wasn't finished issuing that threat when he was seated all the way inside me and we were crying out, a chorus of groans, growls, wails. The way he bent me made it feel like his cock was everywhere. It was almost too much, but only almost. It reduced my world down to him, me, us. It emptied my mind and took away the itchy need to control anything.

"There you go, Bam." He grinned down at me as if I'd learned to tie my shoes and rewarded me with a slow, slow slide of him inside me. "That's how I want you."

"You like that?" I asked. "You enjoy the idea of me burning down the tavern?"

"I do," he admitted. "I want you so desperate that arson makes sense and then I want to fuck you so good all you can do is take it." He pressed two fingers to my lips. "No more talking. You're not the boss here. This isn't one of your conference calls."

I raked my nails over the octopus inked into his shoulder. He answered with a rumbly groan and I clenched around him without thought. "I hate you."

"Go ahead and let yourself believe that, sweetheart."

IT'D HAPPENED ONCE or twice and I'd written it off each time, never paying it any mind. It wasn't a big deal and there was no reason to create drama where none existed, so I didn't. It didn't mean anything. *This* didn't mean anything.

But as I lingered in JJ's bed more than thirty minutes after orgasms had been achieved and the condom was discarded, his arms tight around my body and my head tucked under his chin, the word *significant* pulsed behind my eyes. This was becoming significant, and I didn't know how to find space for more significance in my life. I didn't know whether I wanted to find that space.

He ran his palm down my flank, over my hip. "Are you good, Bam? Are you going to be able to walk all right?"

"Why? Are you tossing me out?" My words came out like the crack of a whip, much harder than I'd intended. "It's fine, I mean, I should go—"

"You really know how to wind yourself up," he murmured. "It's the middle of the night and it's snowing. You're not going anywhere but I want to know if you need a hot bath or something. This time was a little—"

"Savage?"

He shrugged, pressed a kiss to the crown of my head, my temple, the corner of my mouth. "Nothing wrong with savage if it gets you where you need to go."

"Tell me more about that, Jed," I joked, expecting him to say something about turning women into pretzels in order to give them black-out quality orgasms. "Where do I need to go?"

"You need to get out of your head," he replied softly. "So far outta your head, Bam."

Significant.

For the second time in far too recent history, tears filled my eyes. "I have to go," I said, fighting his embrace. "Seriously, this isn't one of those situations where I want you to hold me down and ignore my protests. I have to go."

"It's the middle of the night." He locked his arms around me, pinned my legs with his strong thigh. "It's snowing. It's been twenty minutes since you were semi-conscious and ten since you stopped shaking. You're not going anywhere."

I was prepared to argue, to kick and fight. To do all the things I usually did to keep people away.

But then he said, "And I don't want you to go, Brooke."

Resentful, overwhelmed, significant tears streaked down my cheeks and I turned my face toward his arm. "You don't get to say things like that."

"Why not?" he asked, his lips skating over my neck, my shoulder. "You're allowed to hate me just as much as I'm allowed to want you. It's always been that way."

"That is not how"—my phone's sharp, distinctive peal cut me off—"I have to get that."

Without argument, JJ untangled his limbs from my body. He watched as I scrambled off the bed to locate my device in the heap of clothes discarded on the floor. "Don't you have people who can answer your calls? I know you're important, but aren't you allowed a couple of hours when the world doesn't need your opinion on where to put money to make it grow faster?"

"This isn't work, it's my father," I shouted, snatching the phone from my coat pocket. I pressed it to my ear, still kneeling on the floor with the coat clutched to my chest. "What happened? What's wrong?"

The first thing I heard was crying in the background. High pitched sobs and wails that I would've recognized anywhere. Then, I heard the words. *Accident, inconsolable, bleeding.* I was certain the home health aide was speaking in full, thoughtful sentences, but I couldn't comprehend any of it.

"I'll be there in five minutes. Please try to keep him from injuring himself any further," I said, pushing to my feet. I ended the call and flattened the phone against my breastbone, my eyes shut as I searched for a calming breath.

"I'll drive you." Even with my eyes closed, I knew the sound of JJ stepping into his jeans and fastening his belt. The rustling that followed was the black thermal I'd ripped off him hours ago, the one he'd added back into the rotation after I'd complained about its absence. "You're not hoofing it through a spring snowstorm."

Unable to find that calm breath, I opened my eyes. I slipped into my clothes, stuffed my underwear and socks in a pocket. "That won't be necessary."

JJ held out my boots to me. "It wasn't a question."

"Neither was my refusal." Wobbling, I gripped his forearm as I jammed my bare feet into the rubber wellies. Gross, but necessary. "Stay out of it."

"Please put your outrageous arrogance aside for a minute and acknowledge when it makes sense to accept help," he said, following me to the front door. "The roads haven't been plowed and the sidewalks are buried under six inches of snow and ice. You can be right about everything else, Brooke, but you can't—"

I didn't wait for him to finish that thought. I walked straight into the storm.

CHAPTER TWENTY-ONE

JJ

Net Operating Loss: excess of business expenses over revenues.

ONCE AGAIN, Brooke was going to do what she wanted, how she wanted. It was up to me to decide whether I'd chase after her this time.

By the time I rolled up beside her, she'd waded all the way to the end of my street. Lowering the window, I called, "You're being ridiculous. Get in."

"Go home, Jed."

I wanted to let myself believe I wouldn't have followed her if it wasn't an emergency, but I didn't know about that. At this point, there wasn't much I wouldn't do for her, even when she insisted she didn't want it. And this was the tricky truth about Brooke: she *did* want it.

I pulled ahead of her, stopped the car, and stepped out into the snow. I pressed a hand to my heart and watched as she slipped and bobbled on the slick road, a fine layer of snowflakes crowning her head. Fickle, head-strong, and too fucking breathtaking for me to stand. And then I darted toward her, grabbing her around the waist and tossing her over my shoulder while she screeched and flailed. I dropped her into the back seat like a beautiful bag of potting soil.

When I settled behind the steering wheel, Brooke shouted, "That was unnecessary."

"I asked you nicely," I replied. "Several times."

"I know how to handle myself in a snowstorm," she argued.

I glanced at her in the rearview mirror as I drove through the village. "It's a good skill to have."

"I don't need anyone coming to my rescue."

I could hear her pouting. "Never crossed my mind that you would." I pulled into her driveway, turned off the car. Shifting to face her, I said, "I told you I wasn't letting you walk home alone in this storm and I didn't. I'm not letting you deal with this"—I hooked a thumb over my shoulder, toward the sprawling estate—"by yourself. Understood?"

Instead of agreeing outright, she climbed out of the car and said, "This is Vegas. What happens here, stays here."

I pocketed my keys and followed her to the door. "Everyone knows that mandate to be false."

She glanced at me, shrugged. "It's not false when I'm in charge."

I matched that shrug. "Whatever you want, Bam. I'm not going to fight you on the validity of tourism slogans."

Gripping the door handle, her expression tightened. Her lips parted as if she was ready to drop a counterstrike on me, but then she narrowed her eyes and said, "Promise me I can trust you."

"There's never been a time when you couldn't trust me," I replied. That wasn't good enough. The unyielding shine of her eyes told me so. She wanted me kneeling before her, pledging sword and skin. "Yes, I promise you can trust me, Brooke."

She pushed open the front door and we stepped into chaos. Every light in the house seemed to be lit. Competing televisions blared. The scent of fryer grease was thick in the air. People dressed in a rainbow of scrubs were everywhere, streaming in and out of rooms, moving up and down the front staircase, and they were all talking at once. A snowstorm raged outside, and it was the dead of night, but the Markham estate was hopping like Times Square.

Brooke jogged up the stairs, ignoring everything around her. I followed her into a room at the end of the hall where we found Judge Markham sitting up in bed, sobbing, with a gash on his forehead and blood running down his face and chest, smeared on his arms and hands. His shirt was soaked red, the bed linens much the same. Three health aides were positioned around the bed, their hands gloved and ready to block and tackle.

"Oh my god," Brooke whispered before quickly recovering. I ran my hand down her back, but she shook me off. To the aide closest to her father, the one with *Sherry* embroidered on her orange sherbet scrubs, she asked, "What the hell happened?"

"We think he fell out of bed and nailed his head right here," Sherry said, gesturing to the corner of the bedside table. "That, or he was sleep-walking. If that's the case, we're not sure where the injury came from. He won't let us get a good look at it. He was aggressive with Windy and Kayla when they tried to apply pressure and clean him up, which is why we called you."

"You should've called me regardless," Brooke said, not looking at the woman.

Before Brooke moved home, Judge Markham would come into the tavern almost every night. He'd sit at the same small table near the bar and order the catch of the day with a side of seasonal veggies. He drank one scotch on the rocks and requested the dessert menu on Fridays. He'd kept to himself, but the people of Talbott's Cove believed he belonged to them the way the sea and the sky belonged to them. The Markham family was a Talbott's Cove institution stretching all the way back to Talbott himself, and the Judge embraced that legacy. He weighed in on every local matter brought to his attention, recited town history, and lobbied for the region's development.

I'd watched him do this nearly every night, and I'd watched it slip away from him. It'd started with him forgetting his wallet four days in a row. Then, he yelled at one of my servers to turn off baseball reruns and switch to the football game—in July. Not long after that, he came into the tavern wearing slippers with his trousers, dress shirt, and tie.

Two months later, he crashed his car into a tree. Two months after that, Brooke moved back home. I knew it was bad, but I had no idea it was this bad.

Brooke grabbed a wad of gauze from the table and approached her father. "But *how* did this happen? Why weren't his bedrails up? There's no reason this should—"

She yelped when he slapped her hand away and kept slapping until I looped my arm around her waist and moved her back. The gauze fluttered down as he cried, settling on the sheets. She wrapped her hand around my arm and she kept it there.

"As you can see," Sherry started, "he's not receptive to touch right now."

"Maybe not, but we can't let him bleed until he cycles out of this," Brooke replied. "What are we supposed to do? I don't want to subject him to an ambulance and medics because it will end with sedation and we know how miserable he is when he's coming down from that."

"Can't be sure," I started, "but it looks like he needs a few stitches. At the minimum, a butterfly closure. I bet Yara Gwynn is"—I paused, not wanting to explain my knowledge of Yara's insomnia to Brooke at this moment—"able to come over if you need her."

Brooke glanced back at me, her brow wrinkled. "Who?"

"Yara Gwynn," I repeated. "She's the doctor who visits all the islands in the Bay. She lives down the street from the sheriff. Doesn't Annette know her? I assumed you all knew each other. She's strange. You'd like her."

"Annette and I don't socialize with other people." She shifted out of my arms, turning to face me. It was a wonder she'd let me hold her that long. "What kind of vampire is she that she wouldn't mind you calling at this hour?"

"The kind who makes house calls on remote islands for a living." I reached into my pocket and retrieved my phone. "I'll text her, if you want."

"Yeah. All right. That would be good." Glancing back to Sherry and the other aides, she said, "Let's see if we can't move him to a chair and get this bed stripped. Someone get an episode of *Matlock* going. He'll move for *Matlock*. Or *Murder, She Wrote*. He likes that Jessica Fletcher. He thinks she's a tough broad."

I stepped back from the action to message Yara. True to form, she replied instantly. The woman did not sleep unless she was on a boat. I glanced up from my phone as Brooke shepherded her father from the bed to a chair by the television.

"It might seem like a small matter, but it's dividing the town," he said, wagging a fist as he shuffled across the carpet. "There's nothing small about running a pipeline through someone's backyard."

"Not at all," Brooke murmured. "Did the people sue the town to bar the pipeline?"

It took me a minute to make sense of that question, but then I realized they were talking about an issue from years—maybe decades—ago. She was asking questions to which she knew the answer, leading him into the well-worn territory of Talbott's Cove political and legal history. It made sense there was a nostalgic comfort associated with those old stories, but nostalgia had to be bittersweet when losing your mind.

"Fifteen minutes," I mouthed, pointing to my phone.

"You better believe they did," he replied. "And I'll tell you something else, young lady, they won." He brushed the back of his hand over his forehead and wiped the blood on his pajama pants. "What's your name?"

I saw the split second where she wilted under that question. Her eyes were cool and distant and lines formed between her brows. "Brooke," she replied evenly.

"That's a lovely name," he said. "Do I know your family?"

She stared at me as she shook her head. "No, you don't know them. They're not from around here."

I arched my brows up, silently telling her, *We both know this isn't okay. We know you can't handle this on your own.*

She shook her head again. Instead of arguing with her, I waited by the front door for Yara. It was easier than watching small pieces of Brooke wither and die.

I saw headlights flashing through the first floor windows, and I held the door open for Yara. She bounded out of a souped-up Jeep, doctor's bag in hand, and climbed through the accumulated snow.

"Hey, JJ, hi!" she called, waving as she stomped her boots on the doormat to dislodge the snow. "Wild night, huh? You just can't predict the last snow of the season, can you? I always think it's over, I put the snow pants away, take the chains off my tires, and then poof! More snow. Can't even believe it."

I crossed my arms over my chest as I watched her shake off her coat. "How much coffee have you had tonight?"

"Oh, I don't know! Maybe a quart or two? Not much." She plucked her hat from her head, freeing her long black ponytail. "Why haven't I seen you around recently? Where are you hiding, sir?" She gave my chest a playful whack. "I don't even know what's happening in your life anymore. I've missed you."

"Hello."

One word. That was all it took. One word to snap me out of Yara's cloud of bouncy ball energy and drop the temperature in the house by twenty degrees. My girl was multitalented like that. "Brooke, this is Yara Gwynn. Yara, Brooke. Her father is the one with the injury."

"Thank you for coming." Brooke gestured toward the grandfather clock on the landing between the first and second floors. "Especially at this hour."

If she could've accompanied that gesture with a spray of ice from her hand, she would've. And I loved it. This frigid ray of jealousy was the highlight of my month.

Oblivious to the frost radiating from Brooke, Yara said, "That's what I do! That's what I'm here for!" She grinned at Brooke. "Okay, let's get going. Where's my patient?"

As I'd expected, Yara handled the shit out of the situation. She got on Judge Markham's good side by starting a *Murder, She Wrote* debate and managed to clean and patch the wound with some medical-grade Krazy Glue. She recommended feeding him some ice cream laced with two crushed sleeping pills and waited around to make sure he nodded off without incident.

For Brooke's part, she pretended I didn't exist for the entirety of Yara's visit. As much as I marveled at her transformation into a frozen block of resentment, I remembered how much I hated being invisible to her.

Once Yara was headed home and the Judge was secure in his bed, I dragged Brooke into the first room I could find. It was a bathroom, but I didn't give a damn. "Come on." I backed her up against the door, pressed my lips to her neck. "Ease up, Bam. It's just you and me."

"I have one question for you," she said. "How is it possible to have sex with someone who doesn't stay still for more than five seconds at a time?"

"You're so cute when you're jealous," I replied. "I've never seen this look on you before. I fucking love it."

She laughed, her whole body quaking against me. "I'm not jealous of anything. I'm merely pointing out that you know Dr. Gwynn more intimately than you might've suggested at the outset." She tilted her head back, batted her lashes as she hit me with an evil pout. Absolutely evil. "And she *misses* you, Jed."

I didn't stop to think before driving my fingers through her hair and kissing her as if I wanted to steal those words from her lips. She stayed rigid for a half second, but then all that ice melted away. She fisted my shirt, my belt, pulling me closer and forcing out the last of the distance between us. I held her, I kissed her, I drowned in her.

"Brooke," I rasped against her skin. "Talk to me, sweetheart. Tell me you're all right."

"I'm not talking about anything until you tell me something first."

I went back to her lips, kissing, biting, tasting her tongue. "Anything."

"When was the last time you got in Yara's snow pants?"

I ducked my head to her neck and kissed her there. I stopped short of sucking a mark into her skin. "About two years ago." *I could give you the exact date if you wanted it.* "Maybe a little more than that."

"Why weren't you surprised when you walked in here tonight?"

"Why did you think I wouldn't know?" I asked. "I've known since the day the Judge came into the tavern for dinner and asked whether I thought it was time for Nixon to resign. I've known since before you came home and since before his accident. I know you can't handle this on your own, but more importantly, you don't have to, Bam. You don't have to be the one picking up the pieces and holding them all together."

"Does everyone know? Is it the worst-kept secret in town?"

"I can't speak for the whole of the town, but I've never heard anyone suggesting anything other than the Judge is getting on in his years. People around here love him and they've granted him a wide berth. Even when he made odd comments or went out in town wearing mismatched clothing, they've assumed the best." When she bit her lower lip, I continued, "I'm telling you the truth, Brooke."

She nodded, but it was hesitant. "He made me promise I wouldn't let people watch him deteriorate and I wouldn't send him away. That's why —that's why I'm here. Why I do this."

"You can keep that promise without shouldering the world on your own. You could've shared this with me." When she started to protest, I swallowed her words with a kiss. "Don't you see? You've let me inside you, but not to any of the places that matter."

Her gaze dropped to my chest, and for a moment, I thought she was going to throw me out of her house. The possibility always existed. But instead of kicking me out, she pressed her face to my chest and let the dam break all over me.

"Bam," I said, pressing a kiss to her temple. There were more tears stored up in her little body than I would've thought possible. "I've got you, sweetheart."

"Will you stay?" she asked through her sniffles and hiccups.

"I'm not going anywhere." I gathered her in my arms and carried her out of the bathroom.

In the hallway, I heard the Judge snoring away like a chainsaw. It was a relief to know he was sorted for the remainder of the night. At the other end of the hall, I found Brooke's room and set her down on the bed. I curled up beside her, my arms tight around her body as she shook with sobs.

We fell asleep on top of the blankets, fully clothed. Somewhere between night and day, we reached for each other, discarding clothes and sliding beneath the sheets. Our bodies twined together, came together, stayed together.

CHAPTER TWENTY-TWO

BROOKE

Present Value: the current value of cash to be received in the future.

MAY

"WHAT ARE WE ORDERING?" Annette asked as she flipped over the menu. "Is it too early for sangria?"

"It's brunch," I replied. "By definition, it's not too early for anything."

"No, I mean, is it too early in the season for sangria," she said. "It's not appropriate to drink sangria until summer, but white peach sangria is on this menu even though it's too early to harvest peaches."

I set my menu aside and laced my hands on the table. I couldn't do this anymore. Not one more minute. "Can I talk to you about something?"

She peeked up at me, smiling. "We can totally skip the sangria. I was getting carried away with the idea of peaches. Would you rather have mimosas?"

"The sangria is fine—or mimosas. Or both. Order everything. I don't care," I said.

"Oooh, look! They have a blackberry mojito," she said. "You'd like—"

"I can't talk about mojitos with you right now because I have a standing dick appointment with JJ Harniczek," I yelled.

The server stopped at our table, glanced between me and Annette, and said, "I'll come back in a few minutes."

Annette blinked at me, her lips parted and the menu clutched to her chest. "Do...you have to leave?"

I pressed my fingers to my temples. "What are you talking about?"

"You said you have a dick appointment," she replied, jerking a shoulder up. "I'm wondering whether you need to leave or if this is taking place here." She glanced around, frowning. "The restrooms, perhaps? The back seat of a car? I don't know. I don't know how it is with you two."

I sat back, dropped my hands to my lap. And then I laughed, deeper and harder than I had in months. Tears clouded my vision as Annette joined in, rocking back and forth in her chair as her shoulders shook.

"I fucking love you," I said to her, mopping my cheeks with a napkin. "I mean it. I fucking love you, Annette."

"You should," she replied. "Now, start from the beginning and tell me everything. Just as you should have when it started. When was that, exactly?"

I glanced down at the menu. "It started last September."

The server returned to the table when Annette said, "It started in *September*? And you didn't tell me until *now*? I was prepared for you to say two weeks ago or maybe last month. *September*? You've hidden this from me since *September*?"

"Aaaaand I'll be back in a few more minutes," the server sang.

"No, don't go," I cried, clawing at the air in the server's wake. "She needs sangria. A really big pitcher of sangria. And a straw. Please. *Please*."

The server turned around, nodding. "Sangria," he said. "With a straw."

Annette glared at me, her eyes narrowed and her lips flat. "And one of those blackberry mojitos for the keeper of secrets."

"Sangria with a straw and a blackberry mojito." He gestured to each of us and then brought his palms together. "Can I interest you in a local creamery cheese plate or the rainbow chard dip with crudité and house-made breads?"

"Yes to both." I directed a pleading, hopeful smile toward Annette, but she held on to that glare. "And an order of fries for my very tolerant, very loving friend."

"Perfect." He glanced between us, nodding. "I'll get those orders in for you."

Once we were alone, I leaned forward to layer my hand over hers. "I'm so sorry."

"Just tell me why you've been hiding this from me since *September*."

"It was late September and it only happened once," I said. "It was actually your idea."

Laughing, she asked, "How was it my idea?"

"You told me to go to the Galley." I held out my hands toward her. "I went to the Galley."

"I specifically told you to aim for tourists," she said, still laughing. "I told you to steer clear of townies. How did you mix that one up?"

"Believe me, I tried. I brought my best game and JJ went ahead and cockblocked me," I replied.

"So, you slept with him?" she asked, shaking her head of dark curls at me.

"Yeah, that's basically what happened. I yelled at him and he yelled back, then I went to his house and told him to get naked and we yelled at each other some more," I admitted. "But it only happened the one time and I swore it wouldn't happen again. That's why I didn't tell you. I didn't want it to become part of the Talbott's Cove narrative."

Annette stared at her water glass for a moment. Then, "First of all, fuck you for suggesting I'd introduce any of your private affairs into the local lore. You know me better than that."

"You're right," I agreed. "You're right and I'm sorry."

"I'm not done with you," she said, wagging a finger in my direction. "Second, it's not cockblocking when a guy gets in the way of you having sex. You can cockblock a guy, but he can't cockblock you."

"That's true," the server said as he set a glass in front of Annette, filled it with sangria, and nestled the pitcher between us. "It's called clamjamming."

I stared up at him as he set the blackberry mojito in front of me. "Thank you for that insight," I said flatly. I turned back toward Annette. "Apparently, JJ clamjammed me. That is why I spent that evening expressing my frustration to him."

"That's reasonable." She reached for her drink. "It must've been good, right? Otherwise, it wouldn't have turned into a regular thing."

"It's not a regular thing. Except it is a regular thing. It is now." When she motioned for me to continue, I said, "Nothing happened for months and months, but then you suggested I go back to the Galley. You said something about getting derailed."

Annette pressed her hands to her cheeks. "I love how you're pinning the blame on me. That's adorable."

"I'm not blaming you so much as highlighting your influence on my life," I replied. "It happened a second time, and even though I promised myself it wouldn't turn into a regular thing, it did."

"Stop doing that! Stop telling yourself you can't have nice things. It's unhealthy." She rolled her eyes at me as she sipped her sangria. "You still haven't told me whether it's any good. I'm assuming it is, since you keep going back for more, but feel free to fill in the blanks."

"It's good," I conceded. "We argue all the time and he drives me crazy, but he's also—he's JJ. He insisted on going back home with me the night Dad fell out of bed and split his head open. He saw it all and...he was great. He helped out, he did everything I needed, and he stayed the night." I took a sip of my drink, shrugged. "But it's not a thing. It's not a relationship, it's not going anywhere. We're just two people who are super bored with Talbott's Cove and we happen to be in the same age band with complementary sexual interests. Of course, we're having sex. It's JJ or...who else, really? Either I hit up the widowers or start robbing cradles. However, the high school cross-country team jogs past the house every afternoon around four. A few of them are *men* and they've grown up *right*. There. I've said it. I'm not apologizing."

Annette propped her chin on her fist and stared at me, totally silent, for a full minute. Finally, she said, "It's unreal to be sitting in this seat."

"What is that supposed to mean?"

"It means I've been there, done that, and bought the t-shirt and I'm not letting you take the same trip. Now, listen. I know some people have casual sex and that's how they operate. I know you were that person at some point, but you're not that person right now. You are in a serious, heavy place in your life and while it might sound like a good idea to find someone light and casual to balance it out, that isn't what you need. You would've hopped on a hookup app and found a grad student from one of the college towns nearby if you really wanted casual and light."

I glanced around the restaurant in search of our server. This would've been an awesome time for him to appear with some cheese or unwelcome contributions to our conversation. "It's not?"

"Also," Annette continued, barely stopping for a breath, "JJ isn't a casual-sex guy. You might think he is—"

"Have you met Yara?" I interrupted. "Because I have."

Annette dismissed me with a wave. "Yara is a doll. We should invite her out with us sometime. Once you get to know her vibe, you'll agree."

"Her *vibe* wants to climb my man like a mainsail."

She steepled her fingers together. "Did you hear that? How you just went all possessive mama bear on a woman he hasn't touched since before you moved home? Because I did and I think it's time for me to rest my casual-sex case."

"I hear what you're saying and I know it sounds like I'm in this real deep, but he wants to keep it low-key," I argued. "He's working on expanding his business and he's doing all these things to help Nate and he's got too much going on for a serious relationship. He was there for me in a pinch, but that doesn't mean he wants to sign up for anything else."

Annette leaned in, whispered, "You, my darling, are full of shit. You are assigning opinions and attitudes to JJ that he probably doesn't possess and you are deciding how things are going to go down without asking what he wants." She stabbed a finger in my direction. "Have you even asked him?"

"I know you're trying to kick me in the ass the way I kicked you, but I'm not planning on staying here that long. I'm not having a heartfelt conversation with JJ about his wants and desires when I know damn well I won't be the one fulfilling them."

"That's news to me," Annette chirped. "What's your endgame? Are you moving your father to an assisted living facility? Are you leaving him in Maine or taking him with you to New York? What's the plan, Brooke?"

"I don't know," I replied. "I don't know, but I can't stay here forever. This isn't home for me anymore and I can't go inventing relationships where none exist because it's where I am right now."

"You'll have to forgive me," she said, tapping her index finger against her lips. "I didn't realize the relationship I thought I had with my maid of honor was a figment of my imagination."

"That's not what I meant," I said. "You know that, Annette."

"What do I know?" she asked. "In the past few minutes, you've announced you have no intention of staying in town and you have no real relationships."

"You are my other half. You're my soul sister. We don't have a *relationship*, no. We're way past that and you know it."

"Maybe I do know it." She lifted her shoulders. "Maybe I want you to be as honest with JJ as you are with me."

"I don't know about that," I said. "Sisters and misters exist on different planes. But I swear to you, Annette, I am going to rock the shit out of my maid of honor duties. Whatever it takes, I'm here for it. Bridal showers, bachelorette parties, dress fittings, cake tastings, seating charts —you name it, I'm there. I'm holding your dress while you pee."

"It's really convenient how you can commit to events that won't take place for twelve to eighteen months, but you won't commit to anything with JJ. Super convenient."

"Oh my god, Annette. Can we talk about sex now? Please. There are so many things I want to tell you. Is Jackson licking your ass? If not, go home and ask for that, pronto. You can thank me later."

"And here are the local creamery cheeses," the server announced.

"Right on time," Annette murmured.

Once we were alone with the cheese, I gestured toward her with a chunk of bread, saying, "His dick is unfortunately large."

She stared at the table, shaking her head. "I know I'm going to regret asking but...what's the threshold between fortunately and unfortunately large?"

"I haven't studied that in exact terms," I admitted. "I just know I've crossed it because there are times when I'm certain he's rearranging my intestines."

"That's really great for you. Not so much for your digestion, but it sounds like a good problem to have."

"Yeah," I said around a bite of cheese. "I mean, I've left his place feeling like I need to hold my vagina together because I'm sure he's hammered some dents into it and I don't want to risk it falling out."

Annette brought her fingers to her temples. "Oh my god, Brooke. *Oh my god.*"

"See," I replied. "You know what I mean."

She tipped back her glass, gulping the sangria. "I might, but I'm not going there with you."

"If I had sex with him every day," I continued, "I'd need a strict program of warm baths, physical therapy to keep that shit tight, and voodoo. And lube."

"It sounds like you have your priorities in order. That should be helpful going forward."

"Well, we're not going forward." I speared my knife into the goat cheese. "I'm riding out a phase."

"I see what you did there and it is hilarious," Annette replied lightly. "Riding out a phase. Nice."

"In all seriousness, how do you have sex every night and keep your vag from falling out? Wait, is Jackson's penis unfortunately small?"

Annette held up a finger. "First of all, it's more than enough."

"I figured as much. Those uniform trousers don't leave much to the imagination."

"It's great that you're inspecting my fiancé's trousers with such thoroughness," she said. "Thanks for that."

I shrugged. "I'm just looking out for you, love."

"Again, thank you," she said. "And second, we don't have sex every night."

"I'm sorry to hear that," the waiter cooed as he stepped up to the table. He shifted our plates and beverages to make room for the veggie dip and fries. To Annette, he said, "I hope things improve soon."

I reached into my wallet and pulled out two bills. "Here's one hundred dollars. Take this and exit yourself from this conversation." I glanced back at the table. "After you bring us another round."

He plucked the cash from my fingers. "Gladly."

I pushed the fries toward Annette. "Explain this to me. You're engaged, you live together, you can't get enough of each other—and you're not having sex every night? Why the hell not?"

"We don't need to," she replied. "Being with someone doesn't mean you have three-hundred-and-sixty-five days of sex. It means falling asleep beside them is just as meaningful as sex. Sometimes, more meaningful."

I stared at her, baffled. "You're steering me toward a long-term, committed relationship and *now* you're telling me it doesn't involve dick on the daily?"

As she hefted a handful of fries onto her plate, she replied, "That seems to be what I'm saying, yes."

"Are you out of your mind? Why would I entertain that sort of thing?"

"I love you," she said, laughing, "but you're crazy."

"I think you mean eccentric or free-spirited. Crazy has such negative connotations."

She grinned as she bit into the fries. "Mmhmm."

Holding out my hands, I leaned toward her. "Since we're here and we're having this conversation, I need your insight. Your married lady insight."

"I'm not married. We haven't even set a date yet. You know this, darling."

An exasperated grunt sounded in my throat. "You know what I mean."

"Yes, fine. I know what you mean." She fluttered her hands at me. "What do you need?"

I rubbed my thumb over my fingernails. "He does this thing where he waits for me."

"Waits where?" she asked around a mouthful of fries.

Still focused on my fingernails, I said, "You know. During sex."

There was a long pause and then, "Ah. Okay."

I glanced up at her, my lip snagged between my teeth. "Is that weird?"

She shook her head, waved her hands. "No, it's generous. It's *respectful*. Men who participate in sex like it's a team sport are the best kinds. Oh my god, the *best*."

I dropped my chin onto my fist. "I've never thought of it that way. The team sport way. I've always thought of it like an individual competition that happened to involve another person."

She grinned, her eyes sparkling. "Oh, so you're the selfish partner in the bed?"

I glanced away. "I guess so?"

"But JJ isn't selfish," she remarked. I shook my head. "I promise you, it's a good thing. It's awesome. Let it happen." When I didn't respond, she continued, "Do you know that expression, Big Dick Energy?"

I revisited the cheeses. "Ugh. Yes. Why?"

"Men who wait transcend that. They have a different kind of energy altogether. It's like Mighty Good Dick Energy."

I wagged a piece of cheddar at her. "Are you invoking Salt-n-Pepa right now?"

She shimmied her shoulders, arched her brows. "I am."

"Well done, madam." I smiled at her. I fucking loved this girl. "Well done."

Annette mimed a curtsey, saying, "To summarize, you have some Mighty Good Dick Energy on your hands. If you're careful, it's going to develop into some Mighty Good Husband Energy."

Skipping right over the husband comment, I replied, "It's not in my hands, Annette. A woman over thirty shouldn't be giving handies. Understood?"

She gave me a stiff, fake grin, the kind that made her eyes squint and her lips stretch into a thin, sarcastic line. "Sure. Let's make that the point of this discussion."

"Listen," I started, "I don't show up to meetings that can be held without me, you know?"

"I do. I really do," the server murmured. "And here's the blackberry mojito."

CHAPTER TWENTY-THREE

BROOKE

Capitalization: the sum of an organization's stock value, long-term debt, and retained earnings.

Brooke: I just found an unnaturally long hair on the back of my leg.
Brooke: I thought it was head hair I'd shed and it was stuck on my leg. When I tried to remove it, I discovered it was growing out of my leg. What the fuck is this about?
Annette: Welcome to your mid-thirties, love.
Brooke: I reject that explanation.
Annette: I'd like to reject it too, but I have a pimple on the inside of my nose and it feels like I'm driving a stake through my skull every time I touch it.
Brooke: This is some bullshit.
Annette: You have it easy. You're blonde.
Brooke: How? My unnaturally long thigh hairs are nearly invisible?
Annette: That's one benefit, but your grays will blend in. Mine look like tinsel.
Brooke: What are you talking about? You have no tinsel.

Annette: Oh, I have tinsel. Curly hair is forgiving, but when they come through, they shine like a disco ball.

Brooke: I'm not ready to start growing old. We'll do that in thirty or forty years, when we've bought a pair of cottages and wear matching track suits.

Annette: There's a difference between growing up and growing old. We're not growing old yet, my friend.

Brooke: Remember being twenty-one and thinking you were a grown-ass lady?

Annette: I remember being thirty-three and thinking that. I've learned a few things this past year.

Brooke: Right there with you.

Annette: I'm looking forward to those twin cottages and wearing stretchy pants every day. We're going to need rocking chairs too.

Brooke: Have you mentioned any of our plan to Jackson?

Annette: Not yet. I have to find the right moment. Have you mentioned it to JJ?

Brooke: Why would I do that?

Annette: I have to explain this to you as well?

Brooke: You don't have to explain anything. We have different perspectives on how long I'll keep this dick appointment.

Annette: No, my dear, you don't have a perspective. You have a good man who adores you and you reduce that to "dick appointment." I, on the other hand, have a clear vision of us living in our cottages and wearing our track suits while Jackson and JJ bicker about sports and politics and the color of the sky, but grudgingly enjoy each other's company.

Brooke: I don't want to fight with you about this.

Annette: Then stop pretending you don't care about him.

Brooke: Okay, so...should I pluck it? Cut it? Douse it in apple cider vinegar?

Annette: We're talking about the hair again? Not JJ?

Brooke: Yes, the hair. I wouldn't douse him in vinegar.

Annette: I didn't think so, but since you refuse to acknowledge your feelings for him, I wasn't sure. I'd pluck it because those things drive me nuts, but it will grow back.

Brooke: Then...vinegar?

Annette: I'm not sure how that would fix anything.
Brooke: Me neither! But the internet really likes that shit.

Brooke: I won't be able to get out of here for a few hours. Another one of Dad's caregivers quit.
JJ: What happened?
Brooke: Nothing. She just couldn't handle it anymore.
JJ: Are you all right?
Brooke: Of course.
JJ: You're sure?
Brooke: Yes. Don't make it seem like I can't manage some staffing changes. I can.
JJ: It's not the staffing changes I'm referring to when I ask if you're all right.
Brooke: Then what the fuck is it? Get to the damn point because I need to talk with the placement director at the nursing service to find a replacement.
JJ: Why do you expect more of yourself than professionals trained to handle these conditions?
Brooke: Why do you think you're entitled to ask those kinds of questions?
JJ: Consider it an objective observation.
Brooke: If you don't approve of the way I'm handling my father's care, you are welcome to fuck right off.
JJ: Got it. Get your ass over here when you're free.
Brooke: No. Not tonight.
JJ: Fair enough. I'll go there after I close up.
Brooke: That option isn't on the table.
JJ: I'm not fucking you on the sidewalk, sweetheart. Too damn cold, even in the springtime.
JJ: I'll be there by midnight and don't try to pull this bullshit.
Brooke: It's not bullshit.
JJ: It's not logical and you damn well know it.

I WALKED out of Dad's house in the middle of the afternoon. Just grabbed my shoes and walked the fuck out of there. I had no idea where I meant to go, but I knew I had to go somewhere. I couldn't stay another minute. Not in the house where things went from bad to worse, from severe to end stage. And not in the town where I didn't belong, not really. This wasn't for me, not a single inch of it.

Except for Annette. I couldn't live without her.

Also, Jed was growing on me in fascinating ways.

And I couldn't forget about Jackson.

The three of them were my de facto family, but I couldn't shake the sense that this wasn't where I belonged. Not this small town, not Dad's house, not this compressed, bitter version of myself. I didn't want to resent my father's dementia for stealing him away and leaving me with a living ghost. I didn't want to resent my father for making me promise to keep him at home, keep his condition quiet. I didn't want any of this.

I blew through the Galley's front door, not wasting a second on the fact I'd walked myself here without conscious thought, and marched up to the empty bar. When Jed spotted me, he stopped what he was doing, his hand paused over the knot at the nape of his neck. I loved it when those strands slipped loose. It checked a box I didn't know I had.

"You're going to light something on fire with that look, sweetheart," he said.

"What are you doing tonight?"

He dropped his hand, blew out a breath. "Don't ask me questions when you already know the answer. I don't have time for that."

"And I don't have time to repeat my mistakes but here I am."

He braced his hands wide on the bar. "Do you need to be hauled over my shoulder right now? Is that the kind of attention you need from me? Because that's what it sounds like, Bam."

"I need your dick paying extra-close attention to my vagina tonight. Do you think you can do that or is this another one of those instances where I'm supposed to intuitively know the answer?"

Nate sidled up beside Jed, swung an amused gaze between us. "I'll be here until closing, but I'm free after that."

Jed turned a glare in his direction. "Go somewhere else. Right now. Go and stay gone for ten minutes."

Nate glanced back at me. "It makes my day when you come in here and yell at him."

"Go away," Jed barked. When Nate pushed into the back room, Jed said to me, "I expect to find you in my bed tonight. Awake, please."

"Give me something worth staying awake for," I replied.

He pressed his fist to his mouth, but he couldn't hide his wicked smirk. My entire body clenched at that smirk.

"Bam, you don't know what you're asking for," he said.

"Explain it to me." I took a step back and then two more. I needed the distance. Without it, I'd vault my ass over that bar and drag him home right now. "Then make me regret it." I was almost certain those jeans of his were getting tighter by the second. "Don't make me wait." I hit him with a dick-eating grin and dodged Jackson at the door. To Jackson, I said, "It's a pleasure to see you, sheriff. Are you here in an *official capacity*?"

He responded with the same bewildered smile he'd been giving my innuendos for the past year. "Good afternoon to you as well, Brooke."

"You really don't know what you're getting yourself into," Jed called.

He was right about that. I didn't know what I was getting into with him, but I knew I could drop a few words on him and flash a feral stare and he'd be mine. Even if it only lasted a few hours, he could belong to me and I could pretend I belonged to someone too.

CHAPTER TWENTY-FOUR

JJ

***Due Diligence: the investigation of an organization or financial
opportunity prior to the consummation of an agreement.***

FOR NEITHER THE first nor the last time, I seriously contemplated running through a damn wall to stop Brooke from strutting out of my tavern with my balls in her back pocket. It wasn't about the balls. Goddamn, she could keep them if it meant I could keep her long enough to unravel the issues tying her in knots today.

"Harniczek. A moment, please."

"For fuck's sake, sheriff, why are you here?" I shouted, dragging my gaze away from the door and settling it on Jackson Lau. "In case you didn't notice, I just had a moment. I don't have one for you too."

Laughing, he dropped into a seat at the bar. "I have to admit I'm somewhat afraid of Miss Markham. I can't help but believe she'd reach into my belly and tear out my liver if I crossed her."

"You best believe she will."

"She might scare me, but you should know I won't stand for anyone screwing her over," he said.

Well, that was unnecessary. "It's funny you say that," I started, "because no one screws Brooke over. She can spot that shit from a mile away and she screws back a hundred times as hard. But it's not Brooke you're worried about here. It's me." When he responded with nothing more than his usual cool stare, I continued. "I don't dick women over, sheriff. Not my style."

"Then we won't have a problem," he answered.

That was really unnecessary.

Out of the fucking blue, Jackson said, "I've kept an extra set of patrols on the Markham estate since last summer. Every four to six hours, just to keep an eye on things." He gave me a meaningful nod. "If there's a need for Dr. Gwynn to make another house call during a blizzard, I expect you'll let one of my deputies escort her."

Without fail, the most annoying portion of the sheriff's lectures was when I realized we were on the same team. "Will do."

"The white-out conditions aside, I'm pleased the good doctor was on hand to assist when Brooke needed it. Not that Brooke would ever admit to needing help."

Instead of taking that bait, I grabbed a set of glasses, filled one with iced tea and the other with club soda. "To women."

Jackson tapped his glass against mine. "And their red flags."

"And the bulls who love them," I added.

"Too right," he murmured into his tea.

I drained the club soda in two gulps and went back to the taps for a refill. "Now, what the hell are you doing here? Did you miss lunch again?"

He waved me off, saying, "I'm curious about Nate's progress and whether you've noticed any signs of relapse. His probation officer sent a glowing report last week, raving about him meeting all the terms of his probation. I share that enthusiasm, but I know the realities of addiction. I want to hear your take."

I didn't care whether we were on the same team. I didn't have any patience for this shit. "You want my take, sheriff? Here it is. I believe in the kid and I believe in second chances. Third, fourth, fifth chances too. People can fuck up. People can do terrible things. And they can learn from them. No one should be thrown away or erased simply because they did the wrong thing. I don't care if they did the wrong thing for *years.* The minute they decide to turn it around, I'm gonna let them." I tossed a lime wedge into my glass with enough force to send half the liquid sloshing over the sides. "He didn't kill anyone, he didn't maim anyone. He harmed himself. Sure, he stole from his family. He hurt his relationship with his parents in ways that won't easily mend. But he's still alive and so are they. He gets another chance, and if he relapses, he gets another one after that."

Jackson regarded me for a moment and then said, "All right. I also have concerns about Bobbie Lincoln. He keeps drinking himself into trouble. Wandering down dark roads at night where he's bound to get hit by a car. Arguing with everyone who crosses his path. We're called out to that house at least once a month."

"It's not as simple as him drinking himself into trouble," I replied. "There's more to the story than you think."

He knocked his knuckles against the bar top. "That's why I'm here, Harniczek. Tell me the story. Let me help from my side while you help from yours."

"If you're looking for a buddy cop setup, you should know I'm not one for team sports."

"You make it sound like that should surprise me," he quipped.

I poured more iced tea into his glass. "When did you get a sense of humor?"

"It was probably around the same time you took up team sports with Miss Markham," he replied.

"Since that's a fully unacceptable line of discussion, let's get back to Bobbie Lincoln. All I can tell you is he's sorting through some issues. There's the unhappy marriage, the job that sucks the life out of him every day, the elderly mother-in-law who invited herself to move in a couple years back." I lifted my glass, motioned toward him with it before taking a sip. "I don't think the guy should be drinking it away to the point of walking in traffic but you can't fault him for bellying up to the bar if for no other reason than getting out of the house."

"I don't want to fault him either, but he picked a fight with a trash can outside the O'Keefe place shortly after one a.m. last night. The O'Keefes called the station thinking it was a bear. Lincoln pummeled the damn can until the boys rolled up. He broke both hands in the process."

He laced his fingers around his iced tea, glanced up at me. "Did you see him at any point?"

"I did, but he left before nine o'clock," I replied. "He had a couple of beers, bitched about the Red Sox, and took off before the fourth inning. If he was tanked enough to beat up some cans after midnight, he didn't get there on my watch."

Jackson lifted his shoulders. "I didn't expect so, but I think it's time someone had a conversation with Lincoln about getting help. I'm going to gather some resources and see about sitting down with him and his wife, but I wanted to give you the heads-up."

"What would it be like for you to leave an *I* undotted? Have you ever tried?"

"Is it safe to come out now?" Nate asked as he swept in from the back room. Seeing the sheriff seated at the bar, he stopped, glanced around the tavern. "First the blonde, now the cop. This is a lot of excitement for one afternoon." He fluttered his hand over his chest, but I knew his sarcasm was too dry for the sheriff to translate. "It's a lot for me to process."

Much too dry. "You're right about that, kid."

"My apologies." Jackson pushed to his feet, nodded at Nate and me. "I'll keep you updated on these matters. I expect you'll do the same." He stopped several paces from the bar, turned back toward us with a grin. "Give my best to Brooke when you see her tonight."

WHEN I MADE my way home that night, Brooke was awake and waiting in my bed as I'd requested. She was stripped down to her skin, her knees bent and her hand lazily moving between her legs. That picture was enough to incinerate me on the spot, but it was the screaming sadness in her eyes that slowed me to a stop.

Her legs fell open. "Make me regret this." My jeans hit the floor. "Make me regret it *all*."

There was no thought, no plan. Only Brooke and the absolute certainty I wouldn't allow her to regret anything, ever.

I wrapped her legs around my waist and watched while she taught me how her clit preferred to be treated, glancing away only long enough to snag a condom from the drawer.

"Keep doing that, Bam." With one hand on her waist and the other supporting her backside, I positioned myself at her entrance. "I want those fingers moving while I fuck you."

I thrust into her and that immediate wave of heat rolled up my spine and stole everything from my mind but Brooke. Everything but this woman and the way she was destroying my world.

"Maybe you should fuck me better," she said. "Then I wouldn't have to take matters into my own hands."

My hips moved in slow rolls, giving her the kind of deep, dragging slides of my cock I knew she loved. "You want that? Earn it."

Her eyes darkened at the challenge but it didn't stop her from trembling when I angled her hips to hit the soft spot that made her wild. "You're the *worst*," she said, her words dissolving into a beautiful moan. "The fucking worst, Jed."

"That's right, baby. The worst," I agreed. I shifted my hold on her, pressing my index finger to her back entrance. "You hate it when I tell you what to do, when I throw you on the bed, when I make those French panties of yours all wet, when I tease your ass. You hate it so much, Bam. *So much*. But you come on my cock like you think you can break me."

With her free hand, she parted her folds, exposing that perfect pink pearl and the place where her most intimate flesh stretched around me. Still rubbing her clit, she said, "Save the sermons. I'm the one doing all the work here."

"You want me to take over?" I asked, my index finger sliding between her cheeks. She clenched and, yeah, this was the kind of pain I wanted in my life. "You want to stop arguing and let me do this?"

She turned her face to the pillow, her eyes closed. "I want you to shut up and fuck me like I am the biggest mistake you've ever made."

"That's what it is for you, Bam? That's what you need? You've been getting it since the start. Never once has this been anything but a mistake." Brooke ground into me, her hips snapping to meet my thrusts while the headboard pounded the wall. "And never once did I think I'd be able to stop. You bring me this cocktease body and I'm gonna want it every damn time. Doesn't matter whether it's any good for me—"

"It's not," she whispered. "It's not, Jed."

"Doesn't matter," I said, bowing my head to drag her nipple into my mouth. "Doesn't matter. I'm not stopping. You hear me, Bam? You can't make me stop. Don't you try."

She blinked up at me, her sapphire eyes as clear as the dawn. "Don't stop. Please, don't."

"Never." She nodded, her hands still working between her legs. My balls were full and aching, and I was long overdue to empty myself into her. I gradually pulled out and then drove into her, lingering on that sweet spot, the one that felt deep and tender and *all fucking mine*. I stayed there as the cords holding her together frayed and she broke apart, as gorgeous and strong and fucking furious as I'd ever seen her.

CHAPTER TWENTY-FIVE

BROOKE

Initial Public Offering: a company's first sale of stock to the public.

Annette: Jackson just told me the most fascinating story!

Brooke: Let me guess. Someone was walking along Old County Road last week and they were struck in the leg with a golf ball. They contacted the sheriff directly because what else would you do about a non-event in the Cove? And the sheriff determined a few teenage boys were practicing their chip shots in their backyard. No charges were pressed.

Annette: Nope, not that one.

Brooke: Okay, let me think.

Brooke: Was it the car stopped between Jeffries Point Road and Main Street a little before midnight last night? The one where the guy had a craving for meatballs but wasn't sure where to go at that hour so he stopped in the damn intersection?

Annette: I hope you find this amusing, my dear.

Brooke: It's not amusing. It's the official Talbott's Cove sheriff's log. It's printed in the Talbott's Cove Times.

Annette: Wait, so...you read that? For funsies?

Brooke: No, I sure don't but my father does. Since he only knows how to read on the best of his days, I get to read those entries to him every bloody morning.

Annette: Wow. Okay. I hadn't heard about the guy with the meatballs.

Brooke: I want to know if he got any. The sheriff's log really needs to provide more follow-up details. Can you ask Jackson about that?

Annette: I'll see what I can do.

Annette: The story he did tell me involved you and JJ. Believe me when I tell you he was completely scandalized by the conversation he observed.

Brooke: Whatever he heard was out of context, I assure you.

Annette: There was no ultimatum issued? Nothing about giving you something worth staying awake? And he didn't offer up a semi-threatening response about making you regret that ultimatum?

Brooke: Pillow talk.

Annette: ...in the middle of a tavern?

Brooke: Um, okay, Miss Judgypants.

Annette: Stop it.

Brooke: I didn't realize you'd apply your contempt and condemnation like strawberry jam all over my toasty sex life.

Annette: No contempt, no condemnation. Just really amused to find your under-the-radar, no-strings, no-big-deal dick appointment is now an in-public, sexy-ultimatums-and-threats kind of relationship. If I had to guess, I'd say you'll be sharing a Netflix account within two months.

Brooke: Is that what couples do now? They share streaming accounts? What is this world we live in?

Annette: It's crazy, I know.

Annette: In other news, I have some fabulous ideas for double dates!

Brooke: I didn't understand a single word in that sentence.

Annette: Just you wait. I'll extract my vengeance for your months of secret-keeping.

Brooke: Fuck, you are evil. Diabolical. Why does anyone think you're the nice one?

Annette: Because I let them believe it.

Brooke: Wow. Just...wow.

Brooke: The Good Witch wasn't good, was she? It was an act and she had the right look for it.

Annette: And the Wicked Witch wasn't wicked, honey. She'd just taken too much of everyone's shit to play nice anymore.

Brooke: My sister-wife heard about the conversation we had at the tavern yesterday afternoon, from Jackson.

JJ: Please don't call her that. I'm sure it's some kind of appropriation and it also weirds me out.

Brooke: You don't like bloodless sister either.

JJ: What is wrong with her name? Why can't you simply say you talked to Annette?

Brooke: Because I'm cheeky like that.

JJ: All right. Fine. What are you trying to tell me?

Brooke: Jackson was a little concerned about the things he heard and passed that info along to (let me see if I do this right) Annette.

JJ: Yeah, I had a great chat with him after you left.

Brooke: You didn't mention that last night.

JJ: No, I was more interested in fucking you than recounting my conversation with the sheriff.

Brooke: I won't disagree with that logic.

JJ: Good girl.

Brooke: Don't tell me I can't use sister-wife when you toss around good girl. That one is just as bad.

JJ: Funny how you didn't object last night.

Brooke: All I wanted to tell you is Jackson told Annette everything he heard and now Annette is cooking up some devious double dates for us.

JJ: I'm not sure I want to ask but—what the actual fuck are you talking about?

Brooke: Don't worry. It'll be fine. She won't act on those threats.

JJ: Great. Have your ass in my bed before midnight.

Brooke: Excuse you.

JJ: Be a good girl and do as you're told.

Brooke: Oh, so you want to play?

JJ: Any day, Bam. Any day for you.

Annette: Hey, you two!
Brooke: omfg. Annette. What is this? A group text? Are you serious?
Annette: I'm inviting you both to a dinner party!
Jackson: We'd be thrilled to have you over.
Annette: Right! Yes! WE are inviting you two to a dinner party!
Brooke: What do you mean by "dinner party"?
Annette: Jackson and I want to have you over for dinner on Thursday and it's a party!
Brooke: That's enough exclamation points, lady. You're killing me.
JJ: What distinguishes dinner from a dinner party?
Annette: We're expecting you two at 7 on Thursday!
JJ: Will there be party hats at this dinner party? Is that what carries it over the line into party territory?
Jackson: We'll skip the hats.
Annette: Can't wait to spend time with both of you, together!
JJ: Are gifts exchanged at a dinner party?
Annette: And don't think you can get out of this!

Brooke: Any chance you have a food and beverage emergency you'll need to handle tomorrow evening?
JJ: Are you trying to get rid of me?
Brooke: I just don't want to do this.
JJ: I'm the last one to willingly break bread with law enforcement considering Lau is a pain in my ass more often than not, but I don't mind your sidekick Annette.
Brooke: I think I'm her sidekick, actually.
JJ: Either way, I'm guaranteed a good meal from her. That's more than I can say for you.
Brooke: Yeah, feeding people isn't one of my gifts or talents.

JJ: Aside from me joining in, how is this different from any other evening you'd spend with them?

Brooke: I'd rather not view it through that lens.

JJ: The logic lens?

Brooke: Call it what you want.

JJ: Should we bring something?

Brooke: How the hell should I know? See, this is how it's different. I've third-wheeled it with them plenty of times and never once worried about sacrificial offerings to the dinner party gods.

JJ: I was thinking more along the lines of a bottle of wine or something, or some flowers. Not so much in the sacrifice lane.

Brooke: Again, call it what you want.

JJ: I can grab a bottle of wine, gin, vodka. Two, even. A combo pack if you want to go wild. I have plenty in the storeroom.

Brooke: No, that's boring. Unimaginative.

JJ: Your confidence in me is inspiring.

Brooke: You don't need any additional confidence. You're doing fine.

JJ: Okay. We won't bring wine.

Brooke: I'll figure something out. Don't worry about it.

JJ: I wasn't worried.

Brooke: You're never worried.

JJ: That is untrue.

Brooke: You never worry about things that matter.

JJ: Yeah. Imaginative dinner party gifts for your best friend are the things that really matter.

Brooke: Exactly what kind of Meet the Parents shit are you trying to pull?

Annette: I haven't a clue what you mean.

Brooke: You have many clues.

Annette: Listen. There was a small bedroom accident this morning and I nailed my head on the footboard. I have a terrible headache and an obnoxious goose egg that customers won't stop asking about. I'm going to skip our slow-walk-to-the-conclusion routine and give you some real talk.

Brooke: How...did you hit your head on the footboard?

Annette: It was a reverse cowgirl accident.

Brooke: Paint the picture, honey. Talk me through this.

Annette: Okay, so I'm on his dick and things are fine until I reach down and start playing with his balls and...other points of interest in that vicinity. Things got a little rowdy and I lost my balance and flew head first at the footboard post.

Brooke: The bronco bucked you off?

Annette: Pretty much.

Brooke: You know, I am not having that kind of sex. I think I'm okay with that.

Annette: Since we've cleared that up, I'd like to remind you that you fight back against things, all the time. It's your way of insisting the people in your world prove how much we really love you. We have to get past many levels of you pushing us away in order to prove we actually want to be with you. Because you'd rather reject people than be rejected. So, yes, we're having this dinner party, and yes, you are attending. Because Jackson and I love you so much, we'll go find you and drag you to the event if you don't come willingly.

Brooke: This makes me sound incredibly high-maintenance.

Annette: Humans are high maintenance. Some are better at putting those requirements out there than others.

Brooke: This is scary for me.

Annette: I know. It will be all right. I would never put you in a situation where it wouldn't be all right.

Brooke: I don't deserve you.

Annette: You do. You deserve many good things.

Brooke: At this dinner party...can I ask Jackson whether he's going to outfit you in pro football gear before taking you to bed again?

Annette: He feels awful about this.

Brooke: Great, I'll capitalize on that.

AFTER SPENDING the entire afternoon in small, cluttered boutiques all along the seacoast that offered everything from scented candles to quilted tote bags to wind chimes, I'd found a gift and completed the inevitable transition into my mother. There was no other way to explain the cellophane-wrapped basket that required both arms to carry.

"Would you let me take that?" Jed asked for the fortieth time as we stepped up to Jackson and Annette's door.

I nudged his hand away when he tried to free the basket from my grasp. The cellophane protested these movements with a crackle. "There's no need."

"You can't see over it. You're going to wind up falling on your ass." He reached for the basket again and I batted him away, nearly losing my hold on it in the process. "What do you have in there? It's the size of a commercial food processor, Bam."

"It's not a food processor. She already has one of those."

"Great. So, what the hell is it?" he asked.

Before I could respond, the door swept open and Annette cried, "Come in, come in, come in."

Jed glanced between me and Annette several times. "No one mentioned anything about a costume party."

Annette touched her fingertips to the wide swath of Pucci-inspired fabric covering her forehead and woven through her dark, curly hair. "It was optional," she replied. "I'm not surprised Brooke kept that tidbit to herself. You know how she hates these sorts of silliness."

"I do not hate silliness one bit. In fact, I love when sex accidents necessitate silliness," I argued, stepping inside the house. "Here." I pushed the gift toward her and nearly succeeded in knocking her down. "This is for you. And Jackson too, of course."

"Of course," Annette said over the crinkle of cellophane. "But what the hell is this and why are you giving it to me?"

At a volume not far from screeching, I replied, "It's a hostess gift. For hosting us."

"Bam," Jed murmured as he skimmed his knuckles down my back. "Take a breath."

Annette plopped down on the sofa, setting the basket beside her. "Let's see how to open this," she said, examining the basket for entry points. The cellophane squealed under her touch. It was taped and tied and ribboned to death. There was no entry. "Hmm. I wasn't prepared for a puzzle tonight."

I pressed a hand to my mouth because *oh my freaking god*, why didn't I opt for a bottle of relatively silent wine with an obvious opening?

"For fuck's sake," Jed breathed, reaching into his pocket as he crouched in front of the sofa. He took hold of the ribbon-tied top, flipped open a Swiss Army knife, and cut the wrappings off at the head. He drew the blade down the sides and front, peeling back the layers as he went. "There you go."

Annette ran her hands over the carefully displayed items, prying each from the mess of paper grass filling the bottom of the basket. Still staring at the gifts, she said, "You must be deep in the feels." She hefted the serving platter up, studied it, turned it over. "Oh, my friend. You're *deep* in your feels, aren't you?"

Folding up his knife, Jed asked, "Do I want to know what that means?"

I blinked at her, my hand permanently fixed over my lips. Nodded once. Yeah, I was in my feelings. All of my feelings.

"This is silver," Annette announced, as if I didn't know.

As if I hadn't selected the most lovely, excessive gifts I could find because that was how I managed my deep feels. I bought ridiculous things and hoped I could store my conflicted emotions inside those objects as there was no room for them within me. That was the reason for most of the shoes in my closet and the Brooklyn townhouse I'd purchased a week after my mother's funeral.

"This is a silver platter that's big enough for a giant Thanksgiving turkey. I mean, a big ass turkey. I could feed the entire town off this platter. And it's *silver*." She set the tray aside and chose another item from the basket. "What do I do with this?"

"It's a wine canister," I said through my fingers. "You put, you know, a bottle of wine or champagne in there. Mineral water, maybe. To keep it chilled while it's on the table."

Jed chuckled as he ran a hand down his face. "You're somethin' special, Bam."

"Okay." Annette bobbed her head as she set the canister down.

It was the type of "okay" that also said "I'm going to let you think I agree with that" and "In case you didn't notice, this is ridiculous." My soul sister could get away with a packed "okay" and make it sound as pleasant as pie, but I knew what she was thinking. *I knew.* And I was relieved I'd talked myself out of adding an ice bucket to this purchase.

"These must be coasters. Silver coasters." She grinned up at me, saying, "I take it they were out of gold and platinum options."

Her snark snapped me back into this moment. "Nothing encrusted with jewels either. It was annoying. I wouldn't have this problem in New York."

She glanced back to the basket of silver, shaking her head. "No, probably not, though I appreciate the absence of monogramming. There's some next-level crazy at work here, but I admire your ability to draw the line at engraving 'Jackson and Annette' or some combination of initials. That's how I know this is from the heart."

"It is," I replied softly. Jed squeezed my shoulder. "From the heart, I mean."

"Get over here and hug me." Annette pushed to her feet and held her arms out as she crossed the room toward me. She gathered me up, folding me tight to her body. "Come into the kitchen. I made a cheese plate. We'll handle your feels tomorrow." Leaning away from me, she asked Jed, "Do you like cheese?"

He rubbed his hands over my shoulders as he kissed the crown of my head. "What's not to like?"

"I always knew I liked you," she said, laughing.

Behind me, I heard the door open and then close. Footfalls on the floor. "It's good you learn the truth now, Harniczek. There's no tearing these two apart. The best you can do is hold on and hope for some scraps, even if that scrap means being the ass-end of a group hug."

"I don't think you should be telling anyone how to hold on," I said to Jackson. "Not when you're throwing Annette off beds and nearly cracking her skull open."

"Cheese!" Annette shouted, taking me and Jed by the hands. "It's time for cheese. We're going into the kitchen, we're eating cheese, and we're not talking about bedroom injuries."

"Jesus, Annie. Tell me it's better," Jackson insisted.

"Is that not how dinner parties work?" Jed asked.

"It's fine. Stop asking," Annette replied.

"Well, I'm gonna ask," Jackson grumbled as he made a beeline for the refrigerator. As he swung it open, he jerked his chin toward Jed. "What'll it be? Beer or wine?"

Jed tapped my wrist. "What would you like?"

There they were again, emotions like storm waves against a sea wall.

"I've got Brooke covered, don't you worry," Jackson called. "Beer or wine, Harniczek?"

"Beer," he replied, staring at me with a half-smile that pried something loose inside me. At the rate I was going, it was probably a bone spur or a blood clot. "Thanks."

Jackson popped the tops on a pair of beers, setting one in front of Jed before he busied himself collecting white wine and two glasses. When he'd delivered the wine, he pointed his beer bottle at me and Jed. "All ribbing aside, what's the story here? When did this start?"

At the same time as I said, "Last month," Jed responded with "Last year."

I turned to face him. "That's a bit of a stretch, don't you think?"

He leaned close to me, bent his head, dropped his gaze to my neck. "Yeah, I think it was a stretch," he whispered. "Took some getting used to, didn't it, Bam?"

Heat washed over my face and down my chest. I wasn't sure, but it seemed as though I was blushing all the way to my toes. I'd never reacted that way before and I wasn't keen on doing it again. "You're right and it's good of you to open up about your complete inability to engage in foreplay."

He edged farther into my space, pressed his lips to the base of my throat. Without thinking, my hand went to the back of his head, my fingers sliding through his wavy strands. "You weren't complaining last night."

"That's because I started without you," I replied.

"As if I could stop you," he rumbled.

"That's enough cuddling in my kitchen for now," Annette called as she shoved her hands into oven mitts. "You're melting the buttercream off my cake."

When Jed swung an arm around the back of my chair, Jackson wagged his beer bottle in our direction again. "I suppose we can live without a firm date, though the lack of clarity is concerning."

"Would you stop it?" Annette said to him as she bent to retrieve a dish from the oven. "You're not working a case here, Jackson." She set the dish down, shucked her mitts. "Let's move this into the dining room. JJ, you grab the salad. Jackson, you're responsible for the pasta. Watch out for the sauce, there's a lot on there. I'm taking the bread basket and leaving the extra meatballs in the kitchen because those are for lunch tomorrow."

I held out my hands as the men followed her orders. "What should I bring?"

"The wine, sweetie. You bring the wine. I think you're gonna need it," she replied.

I didn't want Annette to be right about that.

For the first few minutes, we filled our plates and spoke only of passing one thing or another. It was perfect. Jed and I didn't contradict each other. He didn't lick my neck in front of our friends and I didn't touch his hair. No one was yelling and the buttercream was safe.

Then, Annette asked, "What's new at the tavern these days, JJ?"

"The beauty of the tavern is that nothing has been new for decades," he replied. "It saves me the trouble of telling people to go to hell when they complain about hating change."

"I can't fathom why you'd take the humble road now, but it's not true to say you have nothing new in store." I hit him with a stern frown before glancing to Annette and Jackson. "Since he's playing shy, I'll tell you about the distillery he's opening on the grounds of the cider house."

"Brooke," Jed murmured.

"You know the one, it's just north of the village," I continued, ignoring him. "And it's not just a distillery. There's a restaurant and a bar area to sample everything. Gin, vodka. All homemade."

"Brooke," he repeated.

"Oh, and it's all local. Farm to, you know, highball glass. There will be tours and something with bees and a space for parties and wedding receptions. Oh! That's where you can get married. Wouldn't that be perfect?" I asked them. "You can finally set a date."

"Brooke."

I shifted to face Jed and found him with his arms propped on the table, his fingers steepled in front of his lips. "What? What was wrong with that?"

"You're opening a distillery in Talbott's Cove," Jackson said, each word spoken as if he couldn't believe them. "I knew there was work underway on that site and I'd heard about zoning permits being approved, but I didn't realize people would be coming to town for the singular purpose of consuming alcohol."

Jed stared at me for a beat before saying, "Nothing was wrong. I hadn't intended to discuss all of this tonight. Some of it is public, but not all." He tipped his joined fingers toward Jackson. "True to form, the sheriff has seven thousand questions and he's already setting up his DUI checkpoints—"

"You're damn right I am," Jackson said.

"—but I hadn't expected that to be part of the dinner party festivities," he said. "Then again, I never know what the hell I'm getting into with you."

I heard my heartbeat in my ears, and once again a blush colored my skin. I searched for words to wield like the sharp side of a blade, but only dredged up more confusing emotions. Instead of figuring out these feelings and finding room for them, I wanted to pluck them from the air around me and stow them somewhere far away.

"It's strange that none of this was covered in the dinner party book I read." Annette sent a quiet laugh to her plate. Motioning to Jackson, she said, "You have to practice balancing work and life."

"Annie, you know I can't do that," he replied.

"Shush. It wasn't a question. These are our friends and this is my party and it's not time to get your sheriff on." She lifted her glass in Jed's direction. "Congratulations on this amazing project! I can't wait to hear more about the gin and the bees and the cider house. If we ever finish building this new home of ours, we'll be your first wedding."

"Don't start with *if*," Jackson remarked. "It's *when* we finish building the house. *When*."

"It's going that well, huh?" Jed asked him.

Jackson's answering eye roll and groan said it all. "We thought it would be fun to build a house. We thought it would be better to have everything the way we wanted it rather than fitting ourselves into an existing home. We thought it would cost less than renovating. We knew nothing. *Nothing.*"

"And you," Annette said, shooting Jackson a tolerant grin as she turned toward me. "You are just the most precious mess, aren't you? You can't even help it."

I flipped my hair over my shoulder. "If I have to be a mess, I'd rather be a precious one." While Jackson and Annette laughed, I glanced to Jed, mouthing, *Sorry.*

Jed reached under the table, curled his hand around my knee. "Don't sweat it, Bam."

I laughed. I sipped my wine. I moved pasta around my plate while the conversation turned to the usual suspects of sports, weather, small town politics, moose sightings. I worked hard at restricting my comments to neutral, widely available information. I wasn't worried about inciting another incident as much as I worried about another wave of emotions dragging me down, driving me to delirium.

That strategy worked well enough until Annette served thick wedges of chocolate cake slathered in chocolate buttercream and Jackson asked, "The three of you grew up together, right? There must be a lot of history."

There was no specific reason for that question to hit me like a tsunami, but it did. It took me to the ground and slapped me with reminders that my relationship with Jed was complicated and tangled up with Annette and my family and this town, and it wasn't as new as I wanted to believe.

Jackson was correct. We had a lot of history.

"Technically, yes, we grew up together," Annette replied, passing a gigantic piece of cake to Jackson. His brows arched up to his hairline as he accepted it. "We lived in the same town and went to the same schools, but we weren't in the same friend groups and we didn't really know each other until later."

Jackson waved a hand around the table, saying, "It's difficult to imagine a scenario where you're not as close as you are now."

"Imagine a scenario where we're the most immature, concentrated versions of our adult selves and that's high school for you," Jed replied. "Surprising absolutely no one, Annette was the model student and the teacher's pet, and she was friendly and outgoing enough that no one held any of it against her."

"She was the favorite. Sweet cheeks through and through," I added.

"JJ was a bit of a loner, but in an interesting, enigmatic way," Annette said. "I remember you going through a Kafka phase. I remember your jacket—"

"The leather jacket." He bobbed his head, a self-effacing smile on his lips. "God, that thing got some use that year."

"You wore it every damn day," Annette said. "Until the Hemingway phase, where you wanted nothing more than to be an ex-pat."

"That's a difficult goal to realize while living in Maine," he said, laughing.

"And then there was Langston Hughes and I think it wrapped up with a Dostoyevsky phase, right? Am I recalling that correctly?" Annette asked.

Before I knew what I was saying, I replied, "Yes, it was Dostoyevsky."

As slowly as someone could move while still moving, Jed turned his head toward me. "You remember that?"

"Yeah." I jerked a shoulder to make sure he knew it was a stray memory from long ago rather than proof of anything meaningful. "You wore a t-shirt with the book cover on the front and a quote on the back and—"

"'Love in action is a harsh and dreadful thing compared to love in dreams,'" he said.

"You wore it all the time." I stabbed my fork into the cake. I refused to take responsibility for knowing the book he glommed all over in high school.

"Yes, I can picture it now," Annette added. "You loved your tortured, broody writer types, didn't you?"

His gaze still locked on me, he said, "That's what happens when you have after-school jobs at the public library and the graphic design shop out near the highway. They had a full screen-printing setup there, which allowed me to experiment with quippy t-shirts before quippy t-shirts were popular."

"Harniczek was a loner with a library card. Annie was a sweet little cinnamon roll." Jackson's brows bent together. "Where does that leave Brooke?"

Annette beamed at Jackson, saying, "She was the princess."

"Oh my god," I muttered to myself.

"It's true," Annette chirped. "She traveled in an opalescent bubble whenever she decided to grace the small people with her presence."

"That doesn't even make sense." I shoved a bite of cake in my mouth. "For the record, I was friends with everyone. I hung out with all the different crowds. The last thing I wanted was to be that spoiled, snotty kid everyone expected me to be. No princess, no bubble."

"There was a party. Junior year, I think," Jed said, his gaze unfocused. "A bunch of chill, low-key kids put it together. Nothing big or special, just one of those times when we got some beers and built a bonfire on the beach. I remember when you arrived. You didn't pop out of a bubble, but damn, that's not far from the truth."

"What does that mean?" I snapped.

"It was a performance," he replied. "Wasn't that what you did in high school? Every day, you were on stage. You didn't want to be the spoiled, snotty kid, but you did want to be the center of attention. A princess of the people is still a princess. That was the role you played."

"Don't you think that sounds a little harsh?" Jackson asked.

Before Jed could respond, I jumped in with, "No, it sounds accurate. I'm sure I'm guilty of all—"

"We're not doing that, drama llama," Annette said.

"I don't think it's drama and I don't think you need to admit any guilt," Jed remarked. "We were kids who struggled and fought and bounced our ways into who we are today. You probably struggled and fought more than either of us."

"That seems overly generous." I went on hacking the cake to crumbs. "Like you said, still a princess."

I felt Jed's hand on my knee again, but I didn't look away from the plate in front of me. The table was silent, save for the metallic slide of

Annette's knife against the cake tray. She dropped another slice on Jackson's plate and then one on Jed's.

"Why are you giving me more cake?" Jackson asked.

"It's for you to eat," she replied.

"Do I look like I need to be fattened up, Annie?" he asked.

"Sorry, can't hear you over the pounding in my head. I have a terrible headache because some brute threw me off a bed," she quipped.

While Jackson and Annette volleyed back and forth about sex and cake, Jed edged closer, ducking his head to catch my eye. "I've hurt you and I'm sorry. That wasn't my intention."

"It's fine. Not a problem. We were kids, and kids are assholes. No sweat, right?" I glanced up at him and found his hazel eyes gentle and earnest. It was nearly enough for me to admit it *was* a role, it *was* a performance. I was a princess and I was marital glue and I was perfect. But admitting that—saying it out loud to another person and watching while the truth seeped in—was terrifying. It meant acknowledging I'd spent years rotating through personalities as I attempted to be the person everyone else expected me to be. It meant confirming I'd never kept close, true friendships before Annette. And it meant recognizing Jed saw through everything I put between me and the world.

"Don't do that," he whispered. "You've never pretended with me. Don't start now."

Annette yanked my plate out from under my fork and replaced it with a fresh slice of cake. "Try *eating* this one." Rounding the table, she said, "Remind me where you went after high school, JJ. You saw all the big places. Rome, London, Hong Kong, Paris, Cairo, all of that good stuff. Where else did you go?"

I snapped my head up, blinking at Annette and Jed. "When was this?"

"After high school. After graduation." He forked a chunk of cake from my plate, popped it in his mouth. "I headed out of town, picked up a job with a travel company, and gave tours around Boston for a few months. Don't make me tell you about the Freedom Trail. It's great and important, but I still hear that lecture in my sleep." He claimed another chunk, ate it. "After the company sprung me from Boston, I rotated throughout the United States and Canada for a year. I hear the Grand

Canyon lecture in my sleep too, but it gave me a chance to see every corner of the country."

"That sounds amazing," Annette said. "I always think I want to travel for extended periods of time, but I can't manage a weekend trip to Portland without packing my entire closet and then suffering because I forgot the one thing I actually needed."

"Yeah, you can't do that when you live on the road." Jed laughed as he stole another bite of cake. "After leaving North America, I spent a few more years touring overseas. Europe, Asia, Africa, Oceania. I had a chance to hit Central and South America, but I decided to live in New Zealand for a year instead."

I scowled at Annette across the table, but she didn't catch my meaning and scowled right back. She didn't realize I knew nothing of Jed's life outside Talbott's Cove. He saw me and he knew me, and I was busy floating around in my opalescent bubble, never bothering to ask him about his years away from this town.

"Why New Zealand?" Jackson asked. "I've always heard the best things about that country, but it wouldn't occur to me to move there for a year."

"And yet it occurred to you to move to Talbott's Cove from Albany," Jed mused. "I...I had time on my hands. I'd worked nonstop for six years at that point and I'd always loved touring through that part of the world. Always wished I had more time. Then, I had the time." He scraped up the last bite, careful to gather as much frosting as the fork would carry. "And New Zealand is as far away from this town as I could get."

"Did you stay in one city or wander like a proper nomad?" Annette asked.

"I spent some time in Wellington and then Christchurch. Everywhere in between. Later, I ended up on Stewart Island, on the far, far south end of New Zealand across the Foveaux Strait. A couple times each week, I took the ferry to Ulva Island to hike or read or whatever sounded good. They used rangiora shrub leaves as tickets. It was the most unbelievable experience of my life."

Jackson leaned back, crossing his ankle over his knee. "What did you do there? For *a year*?"

Jed lifted his shoulders, let them fall. "Lots of things. I wandered the

Rakiura Track on Stewart Island. It's about twenty-two miles and it's—it's beautiful. It's nothing like Maine, nothing at all. So, I walked. I took millions of photos. Probably more. I went to pubs and drank many times my weight in Speight's. I stared at the stars and birds and trees I'd never seen before." He gestured toward Jackson with his fork. "A little bit of everything, you could say."

"Why did you leave a place you loved so much?" My voice sounded rusty, as if I hadn't spoken in days. "What brought you here?"

"It was time." He draped his arm over the back of my chair. His fingertips barely brushed my shoulder. I edged toward his hand. "I loved everything about being there, but I also loved being half a world away—until I didn't love that distance anymore. As I explored the country and made my way through one town after another, I realized I missed this place. I missed Talbott's Cove. Part of it was nostalgia. At that point, I hadn't spent more than ten days here since graduation."

I jerked in my seat, bracing both hands on the edge of the table to hold steady. I stared at Jed but he offered nothing, no assurance he remembered the day we graduated from high school and the night that followed.

Those waves, they didn't stop.

"The other part of it was wanting a place in the ecosystem. While I tended bar all over New Zealand, I watched the way people in those towns interacted. How their universes functioned, how relationships grew roots, how people changed the places around them. At the same time, my uncle was dying of liver disease after drinking his way through fifty-plus years of owning the Galley. My aunt wanted it out of her hands and I wanted a spot in this ecosystem." He shifted his arm off the chair and onto my shoulders, tucking me into his chest. He pressed his lips to my ears, whispering, "This place called me home. I'm not sure of much, but I think it might've called you too."

I shivered as if I was standing naked in the cold. In a way, I was.

CHAPTER TWENTY-SIX

JJ

Long-Term Debt: a liability with a maturity greater than one year.

LATER THAT EVENING, after surviving a delicious but turbulent dinner party, I asked, "What happened that night? After graduation?"

Brooke glanced back at me over her shoulder. That movement sent her silky hair pooling on my chest and her bare body snuggling closer to mine. "What do you mean?"

Here she was, naked and satisfied in my arms, and even still, I hesitated. But I had to know. I wouldn't have broached the subject if not for the way she looked at me after dinner tonight. As if I'd done wrong by her all those years ago. "We were at that party at Peyton Woodmoore's place and we ended up behind the barn and—and I kissed you."

She forced a laugh. "Yeah. I know."

"But what happened?"

I watched as her brows lowered, eyes slanted to the side. "I still don't know what you mean. I'm sorry."

I should've stopped there, but I never stopped myself when Brooke came around. "You disappeared. You told me to stay there, behind the barn. You said you'd come back. I waited for—for fuck, longer than I should've. What happened?"

She teased a finger over the edge of the quilt, not meeting my eyes. "I don't know. I don't remember it well. There was a lot of beer and shots involved. *Bad* beer. *Bad* shots. I just remember you were gone a few days after that party."

This conversation was like waiting for a bus in the rain. Even if I leaned away from it, even if I hitched up my collar, I was still getting uncomfortably soaked. And I should've known not to wait for a bus in the rain, but now that I was here and wet, there was no sense turning back. "I decided to leave town after that night. I knew I wanted to go, and I knew that was the right time."

"Are you trying to say that was a product of me—what? Forgetting you behind a barn when I was young and drunk? That's why you went to Boston and you're still recovering from your Freedom Trail nightmares?"

"No," I replied. "I'd wanted to go. I'd wanted to go as much as you wanted the same thing."

A fast, breathy laugh shook her shoulders. "You're saying that me forgetting you behind the Woodmoores' barn gave you the push you needed to get the hell out of this town?"

I was quick to reply, "No." Then, "Maybe. I don't know."

Brooke turned over to face me, a gently smug smile pulling at her lips. "You're saying I wounded your tender teenage heart."

I stared at her, torn between coming in from the downpour and staying out here until I caught my death. "You did," I agreed. "I'd thought it meant something to you. I thought that one counted."

"Why? Because it took place behind a barn? After the official end of high school?" She wrapped her arms around my torso, pressed her nipples to my chest. "Or was there some other reason you wanted it to matter, Jed?"

I seized her waist, bringing us as close as we could get without a condom. "I was eighteen. My only reasons were 'because I want to' and 'because someone told me not to do that.'"

"Those are the same reasons anyone kissed me in high school, regardless of whether I was *performing*." She dropped her head to my shoulder.

"And then you took off on a journey around the world with your wounded heart in tow."

"Did it mean anything to you?"

She smiled down at my chest, brushed her hand over the ink on my arm and shoulder. I didn't expect her to respond. I figured she'd change the topic or deflect the question back on me, pick at my desire for youthful validation. But then, "You know what's really interesting? You thought I blew you off. You've spent all these years being bitter—"

"I haven't spent any years on bitterness. I left town. I got over it."

She pressed her lips to my sternum, humming. "Yeah, that's why you brought it up now."

"I brought it up," I replied, my tone growing impatient, "because your hair is everywhere and your bare ass is in my bed and I get to bring up whatever the hell I want under those conditions."

"Like I said, bitter." For that, I gave her backside a squeeze. "You thought I abandoned you behind a barn and—for a period of time—you had all these feelings about it. Feelings for which you blamed me." She burrowed against me, her head on my chest, her arms tight around my body, her face angled away from me. "And I thought we'd started something that night, but then you were gone."

I was wet from head to toe now, rainwater filling my shoes and blurring my vision. But it was possible I wasn't the only one waiting for this bus. "What do you mean?"

"I thought it meant something to you," Brooke said to my skin. "For the life of me, I can't remember what happened after I left you behind that barn but I thought...I thought it was real. You said you'd wanted to kiss me all night but had no intention of doing it in front of any of those assholes from our class. That was some advanced seduction technique, as far as high school went. I remember thinking I was going to have one of those glowy summer romances filled with beach blankets and ice cream cones and sunburned shoulders. I thought you were different, Jed, and then you were gone without a word."

I didn't know how we wandered into the land where all the bullshit fell away to reveal pure vulnerability, but I wasn't turning back yet. "I wounded *your* tender teenage heart."

When I brushed her hair away from her forehead, she glanced up at me. There was no smug smile, no contemptuous glare. It was Brooke, eyes wide and lips parted, free from all the space and show she put between herself and the world.

"Is that what I did, Bam?"

"A bit, yeah." She blinked away, pulled a small smile. "But what did we know back then? What did we know about anything?"

I chuckled. "We knew nothing."

"Not sure about that," she replied. "You knew you wanted to kiss me and you knew you wanted it to count."

"Still do." I traced the line of her lips, her jaw. "Do you still want a movie montage summer? It sounds like I owe you one."

"I'm more careful about sunburns now, but there's room on my beach blanket."

"Are you going to forget me behind a barn?"

"I will not," she replied. "Are you going to flee the state?"

"Only if you're coming with me," I said.

"Please," she scoffed. "You don't want to take me anywhere. You can't wait to get rid of me."

"That's not—no. No, I—" I knew what she was doing, but I had to stop myself. "No, I don't want to get rid of you, Bam."

She cocked her head, smiling up at me as she batted her lashes. "I'd ask if you intend to keep me, but I'm not a woman who can be kept."

And that was why I had to stop myself. It wasn't simple with Brooke. I couldn't tell her I was falling for her—no, fuck that. I'd fallen and I was long past the point of saving myself from her. It wasn't a matter of putting emotions into words, not for Brooke. She didn't trust either.

"Well, fuck," I muttered. "Here I was, thinking you could keep me."

She laughed, shook her head. "You're too busy redefining the entire tourism industry in Talbott's Cove to be anyone's house husband. It would never work."

I knew better, but I asked anyway. "Is that how you see it? That belonging to someone means giving up all of yourself?"

"I don't know," she said. "I don't know what it's supposed to look like. I don't know how to do it. This has meandered down some strange lanes, Jed. I...I don't even know what we're talking about."

"We don't have to talk about anything," I said, rolling her onto her back. "This is enough."

CHAPTER TWENTY-SEVEN

BROOKE

Basis Point: the smallest measure utilized for quoting interest yields.

Brooke: I hate you right now.

Annette: I cannot imagine why.

Brooke: You held me hostage.

Annette: I served you food and wine.

Brooke: You were a decent captor, I'll grant you that.

Annette: You entered into this captivity willingly.

Brooke: That is not my recollection of the events.

Annette: You need to calm down. We had a great little dinner party.

Brooke: Again, not my recollection.

Annette: Then tell me what you recall and I'll tell you why you're wrong.

Brooke: I'm going to ignore that condescending statement for a second while I enumerate the many issues with last night's events.

Annette: I'd expect nothing less.

Brooke: First, I agreed to this gathering under duress.

Annette: If inviting you over in a group text is the duress you're referencing, I'm calling bullshit.

Annette: Didn't you tell me about a time when you convinced a guy to
change his name?

Brooke: His name was terrible. I was doing him a favor.

Annette: You're making my argument for me.

Brooke: I didn't want JJ to think I was embarrassed or didn't want to be
seen in public with him. Or whatever lame shit guys come up with these
days.

Annette: So, you admit you're concerned for his feelings?

Brooke: I admit I'm going to slap you in the boob the next time I
see you.

Annette: That might sound like a threat to you, but my boobs are nice
and fatty. That would be like slapping a loaf of pumpkin bread.

Brooke: Even if I set the circumstances of the invitation aside, I'd like
to point out that the whole night was awkward as fuck.

Annette: It was not.

Brooke: The only way it could've been more awkward would be if you'd
spoken through a hand puppet or if I'd revealed to Jackson that you do,
in fact, poop.

Annette: Now you're just being ridiculous.

Brooke: Perhaps if you'd massaged Jackson's balls under the table, but
did it without trying to be covert. That would've knocked up the
awkward factor.

Annette: Considering I did that for no less than 15 minutes, I must've
been too covert.

Annette: Or, maybe—and hear me out—you're seeing this through hot
pink, heart-shaped, self-centered lenses.

Brooke: Of course I'm being self-centered. It's what I do best. I'm a
princess, apparently.

Annette: What I'm saying is you're seeing this from a perspective that
doesn't match up with reality.

Brooke: Pardon you and your suggestions of my looming insanity.

Annette: I'm trying to figure out where you diverged from that reality.
Was it the high school conversation?

Brooke: Fucking high school. Reason #841 why coming home isn't nearly as good as the movies make it seem.

Annette: I'm taking that as a yes.

Brooke: I never realized people regarded me that way.

Annette: I think you're hearing it differently than we're saying it.

Brooke: We're talking about six of one and a half dozen of another, my dear.

Annette: What about JJ's world travels? Did that push you into the hot pink zone?

Brooke: Why the fucking fuck didn't you tell me any of that? I thought you were my wingwoman. You sent me in blind!

Annette: If you'd given me any notice that you planned on going in, I would've provided you with the most current details.

Annette: But as it turned out, you went in without your wingwoman and decided to fly solo for months.

Brooke: You could've mentioned it during any of our conversations we've had in the past two years about the people in this town.

Annette: Is that how long you've been yearning for him?

Brooke: Oh my prickly pussy, Annette, I don't yearn for anyone.

Annette: You know exactly what I mean and I'm pretty sure you confirmed my suspicions.

Brooke: That I've had a burning desire for JJ Harniczek since I returned to this pastoral hamlet? On the contrary, that burning was from a bladder infection. Some cranberry juice and antibiotics, and I'm good as new. Nothing on fire here.

Annette: Mmhmm.

Brooke: Don't do that.

Annette: Sure. Okay.

Brooke: Do not do that.

Annette: Yep. I got it.

Brooke: I will walk into your bookstore and slap your boob if you don't stop it right now.

Annette: Stop what? I'm just thinking back to all those times we had drinks at the Galley and how you'd push JJ's buttons and how I thought it was just you getting some of your puppy energy out, but now I know you were pulling his pigtails.

Brooke: Allow me to repeat my original statement—I hate you right now.

Annette: Promise me you won't be a bridezilla. Swear to me that you won't scream at a florist over a precise shade of blush-pink peonies.

Brooke: Can't. Putting shoes on. Leaving the house. Coming to slap your boob so hard it slaps the other one for me.

CHAPTER TWENTY-EIGHT

JJ

Insolvency Risk: the risk that an organization will be unable to satisfy its debts.

EXACTLY FIFTEEN MINUTES after the midday rush wrapped up, Sheriff Lau marched into the tavern. If I had to guess, I'd say the man had a deputy keeping track of my patrons and notifying him when it was all clear. As much as it irritated me, I had to give him credit for respecting my terms.

"Sheriff. What brings you in today?"

He stopped, rested his arms on the backs of a pair of barstools. He glanced at me, then Nate. "If you have a moment to spare, I'd like to speak with you privately."

"You're in charge, kid." I passed a bag of limes to Nate. "These need to be washed and sliced." As I dried my hands with a dish towel, I caught the sheriff's raised eyebrow. There was no way in hell Nate missed that eyebrow or the meaning behind it. "When you're done with that," I continued, shaking my head at Jackson, "restock the oranges and olives. That should keep you busy for at least—"

"Nine, maybe ten minutes," Nate said. "I'll refill the ketchup bottles if I feel like getting really rowdy."

"Smart plan." Despite this situation being a pain in my ass, I liked the kid. I enjoyed his permanently dark, surly mood and I appreciated the way he was determined to prove everyone wrong. Add to that he'd taken it upon himself to plant the pollinator garden at the cider house in his free time and I was damn well ready to adopt him. At the minimum, I was getting between him and every shitty eyebrow the sheriff and anyone else in this town sent his way.

I led Jackson to my office and shut the door behind us. Immediately, he remarked, "He seems to be doing well."

I dropped into my chair, glared across the desk. "It's been months. Many months. You're not helping anyone with this."

Jackson, ever the Boy Scout, gave a chastened nod. "You're right. It seems like he's"—the sheriff paused, visibly sorting through his words—"he's back on his feet."

"You're fuckin' right he is," I yelled. "But if you come in here one more time and give him a visual pat-down, I won't be as pleasant when I say 'I told you so.'"

Holding up both hands, Jackson said, "Understood."

"Thank you," I replied. "Now, what the hell do you want?"

Jackson clasped his hands in his lap, inclined his head. "I don't have to tell you our women are best friends."

"Jesus Christ," I muttered to myself. "No, sheriff, you don't have to tell me they're best friends, but it would be good if you found a way to speak of them as something more respectful than 'our women.'"

"What's disrespectful about that?" he asked, his brows bent together and confusion rippling his features.

"Do I actually have to explain to you that they don't belong to us? I recognize there are shades of meaning here and the notion might give you some warm fuzzies, but I'd rather not reduce Brooke or Annette to possessions. In case it's not obvious to you, neither of them need us."

"No, that's plain to see." He bobbed his head in agreement, but he was busy deciding whether he understood my point.

"Listen, I'm not trying to bring down your worldview. I'm just trying to tell you there's a big difference between the things you say to Annette privately, when you're at home, when you're in your bedroom, and what you say to other people. It matters how you talk about women."

He ran his hand up the back of his neck, around the inside of his collar. "I thought I was good at this. The feminist stuff."

"You can be good at it while also accepting some feedback to get better," I argued. "I'm not saying you're a misogynistic piece of shit. I'm saying there's a better way to start a conversation about Brooke and Annette than minimizing them as 'our women.'"

"All right, let's try this again. Annette and Brooke are best friends. That's not about to change. I thought it might be different after we'd moved in together, after we got engaged. Don't know why I thought that," he added, laughing. "I think we have the privilege of taking part in their world. We need to find a way to deal with each other because they wouldn't blink an eye at dropping one or both of us if we ever tried to make them choose."

"That's the straight truth," I replied.

"They've made a family of each other and it's the only family they truly have," he continued. "You and I, we have a number of differences. We don't agree on many things. Hell, half the time I don't think we speak the same language. But it's in our best interest to get this right."

Pressing my fist to my lips, I stared at the sheriff. I didn't relish him being right, if for no reason other than my longstanding disdain for people telling me what to do. Authority figures had been grating on me as far back as my memories went. There was no clean genesis to my anarchist bent; I preferred to command myself, regardless of the outcome.

But Jackson wasn't the real authority figure here. It was Brooke. She was as much of an authority as anyone. I couldn't refuse his peace offering because—for the first time in my life—anarchy wasn't my answer.

"You're right about them making a family," I conceded. "I'm not about to take that away from Brooke."

"And you're not about to let her go," Jackson added. "Or did I misread things over dinner last night?"

Rolling my eyes, I leaned forward, folded my arms on the desktop. "Let's establish some ground rules, *friend*. Number one, you don't read shit into my relationship and I'll offer you the same courtesy."

Fighting a smile, Jackson said, "I can agree to that."

"Second, you're not the sheriff in social settings. You want to argue about drunks stumbling out of my distillery and raising hell on your streets, you save that for a conversation like this one."

"The badge doesn't come off because I sit down for a meal," he replied.

"You don't have to take the badge off, but I'd prefer if you kept a lid on your law enforcement crusades when we're gathered for a damn dinner party."

"Watch it. Annette spent hours making everything perfect for that party," Jackson snapped.

"And it was perfect," I replied. "I ate the leftovers for breakfast. But you have to know the proper times and places to pull the sheriff card."

He circled his hand, urging me to continue. "What else? This is your opportunity, Harniczek. Get it all out."

"We need to find something to discuss that isn't Nate Fitzsimmons or local law enforcement efforts because that's all we've ever talked about and I'm maxed out. Football, the last book you read, the weather, whatever the hell you want."

He stared at me for a long beat before saying, "I'll give it some thought." He continued staring because it wouldn't be a valuable conversation without slapping me with his power penis.

"Are we done here, sheriff? Or shall we play this game until someone comes looking for us? Nate can entertain himself with citrus fruit and ketchup all afternoon, but I'm sure your absence won't go unnoticed."

I expected him to leave without a word or make an ominous remark about keeping an eye on me, but he asked, "What have you heard about the kids hanging out near the old Walker farmstead?" He rattled off a few names. No surprises in that crew. "Every time one of my deputies swing by, they say the kids are being kids and there's no trouble beyond some minors in possession of alcohol. What do you think?"

It was good to slip back into the comfort of our long-established dynamic of sheriff and barkeep, where I kept a handle on under-the-table affairs in these parts and Jackson was the heavy when needed. We knew and enjoyed these roles and they were far less complicated than the ones we found ourselves in now, as the men in Brooke's and Annette's lives.

"I think it's probably a nonissue," I said. "If it's not one abandoned farm, it's another."

"Isn't that the truth," he replied. "So, how about those Rangers? Think they'll make it to the Stanley Cup?"

"That's enough." I pointed toward the door. "We've covered plenty of ground today, sheriff. We have to save something for tomorrow."

"Right," he agreed, pushing to his feet. "We should ask Annette to recommend some books for us. To keep the conversation going."

"We're not starting a book club, sheriff." I jabbed my finger toward the door again. "Not until I know we have compatible taste in reading material."

CHAPTER TWENTY-NINE

BROOKE

Arbitrage: any strategy that invests for the long-term in one asset and short-term in a related asset.

JUNE

I WAS angry about everything today. Everything, but also nothing.

There wasn't a singular source of my issues and that was also bothersome. I wanted to collect all these pebbles of fury and resentment, roll them into a big, craggy rock, and shove it out my front door. If I could push it away—or throw it at someone—I wouldn't have to lug this weight around anymore. I wouldn't have to be angry.

Instead of staying home and marinating in my mood like any normal person would, I filled my pockets with those pebbles and marched down to the Galley. The mermaid with her wheat and berries on the tavern's sign earned an apologetic frown from me on the way in. That poor girl deserved better.

I found the dining room and bar packed with customers, but my usual spot at the bar was open. *Small miracles*. Watching as Nate and Jed worked together pouring drinks, their backs to me, I slipped onto my stool with a contented sigh. Finding a new seat at the bar would've been the last straw in a day filled with last straws.

After sending a tray full of beverages off with a server, Jed made his way toward me. I didn't intend to stare at his bare forearms or the black shirtsleeves cuffed to his elbows or the way his belt buckle sat impossibly low on his waist, but I couldn't stop myself. Couldn't stop myself from noticing the heartbeat between my legs either.

Pointing at his watch, he asked, "What are you doing here at this hour? You don't come looking for attention until after the sun sets."

"That's the problem with the days getting longer. It fucks up my attention-seeking rhythms."

He stepped closer, folded his arms on the bar, leaned toward me. "What do you need, sweetheart? What can I get you?"

"I'd like to make a reservation with your dick," I said, edging closer. The freckles dotting his face caught my eye. I curled my hands around my biceps to keep from tapping my index finger to each one of them. "Later this evening, a seating for one."

Jed ducked his head, laughed. "No request required. You have a standing reservation."

"To think, I dressed, brushed my hair, and put on makeup," I mused, dragging a finger along the neck of my shirt. His tight-lipped gaze followed that finger and dipped to my breasts for a beat. He was still tight-lipped, but that gaze was hot enough to warm me all the way through. "Now, I find out I don't need to do any of it."

He ran his knuckles over the back of my hand. "Need to? No. Never. But you look good enough to eat, Bam."

"I might let you," I replied.

We stared at each other, the noises and people around us fading away. He closed his hand over my wrist. "Talk to me. What's going on with you?"

I glanced around him to watch Nate filling another tray of drinks. I shook my head. "You're busy."

"Shut the hell up and talk to me," he snapped.

"Think about that statement for a second, Jed. Just take a second with it and maybe you'll see why you're asking for the impossible."

Releasing my wrist, he stepped back, pointed a finger at me. "Your head is full of something." He reached for a glass and plucked a wine bottle from the chill chest. "Have you eaten? Never mind. I know the answer to that."

"I'd eat if there was something other than bananas at the house," I replied, grabbing hold of those pebbles again. "But Dad is back on his banana bullshit. This week, it's banana pancakes. It's the only thing he wants. The whole damn house smells like banana and I hate banana." I glanced at the wine he set in front of me. "What is this?"

He deposited a glass of water beside the wine. "It's the Sauvignon Blanc you like."

"I didn't ask for wine." I lifted the glass to my lips. "You're becoming rather presumptuous, Jedediah."

"Because bananas," he replied as he shifted toward the point of sale system. "Chicken Caesar salad, right? Extra croutons?"

I watched as he tapped the screen. "Yeah, sure," I agreed cautiously. "But since when do you know which wines I like and how I prefer my salad?"

Not looking up from the screen, he said, "I don't think I've ever seen you eat anything other than a chicken Caesar. It's the only thing you order here."

Raising the glass to my lips, I studied the way his shirt stretched across his broad shoulders and how it nipped in at his waist. Giving his jeans a thorough review was safer than articulating any of the thoughts in my head or my heart. It made better sense to objectify him than admit it mattered that he remembered the croutons.

Hell, I didn't know how I'd put that into words without sounding like a moron. "Thanks for remembering I like croutons."

Eyes narrowed and forehead wrinkled, Jed returned to my corner of the bar. "You have to stop with that face, Bam."

"Which face?"

"The one that's a cross between wanting to suck a dick and snatch a soul," he replied, his tone dark enough to bring goose bumps to my skin. "I can't get out of here for a couple of hours and there's no way in hell

I'm letting you sit there and make that face at me until then. Fix it now or you can eat your salad at home with Butterscotch."

I propped an arm on the bar as I pointed at him. "First of all—"

"Brooke-Ashley! Oh my goodness, I haven't seen you in months! How *are* you and where have you been hiding?"

Jed held my gaze for a long moment, his brows pinched and his lips falling flat as if apologizing for leaving me with Denise Primiani. The woman was old-school Talbott's Cove, through and through. She grew up here, taught in the town's public schools, gossiped like it was her job, and worked her ass off to look like a page out of an L.L. Bean catalog. The turtleneck and Bermuda shorts paired with duck shoes and the type of raincoat folks around here referred to as a "slicker" was fully on-brand. To be fair, Denise had been the first person to turn up at my father's house after his accident, a wagon of casseroles in tow. She'd talk about you behind your back, but she'd make sure you had enough beef stroganoff to get through a difficult time.

With a shrug meant to forgive his abandonment, I shifted to face her. "Denise, it's great to see you. As for me, I'm doing well. I've been here"—I shot a glance in Jed's direction and got a chuckle in return —"and there."

She touched her fingers to my wrist and gave me that close-mouthed smile that women used on each other to make it clear only one of them was capital-S Struggling. "But, how *are* you?"

Since I wasn't plugged into the local rumor mill, I didn't know why I was Struggling today. There was never any shortage of reasons—the unwell father often topped that chart—but there was also the matter of me moving back home. They understood my presence immediately after Dad's car accident, but they wanted to know why I was still here.

My neighbors took it upon themselves to fill in those blanks and that yielded some truly remarkable fiction. I'd lost everything—job, money, will to live, you name it. I'd been disbarred by the SEC, which wasn't a real thing that occurred, but that didn't stop anyone from saying it. I'd been the victim of a terrible crime—rape, attempted murder, kidnapping —and couldn't bear to live in New York any longer.

The ugly, horrible stories always beat out the obvious explanation.

"I'm great. Things are good. It's finally warming up around here ," I replied with as much breezy joy as a tampon commercial. "Every year, it seems like the winter is worse than the one before."

Still pity-smiling, Denise said, "And what about your father? How is he getting around? Is the leg improving at all?"

Jed cleared his throat as he set the salad in front of me. "What else do you need?" he asked, making no attempt to cut the familiarity from his tone. He shook out a cloth napkin and fussed with the silverware, setting each piece in its proper location while Denise watched. "More croutons?"

I laughed at the mountain of croutons rising up from a base of romaine lettuce, chicken, parmesan cheese. I laughed because it was ridiculous, but also because it stopped me from climbing over this bar and into his arms. I wouldn't have the right words, but I could put the pulse in my pussy to good use. "This seems like enough."

Under his breath, he said, "Fix your face." Then, to Denise, "What can I get you, Mrs. Primiani?"

She launched into a detailed story about eliminating sugar for a cruise, but then the cruise being canceled on account of an outbreak of some communicable disease on the ship, and now it was rescheduled for next year, and oh yes, she was still off sugar, so she'd like a dry red wine.

I figured she'd lost track of the unanswered questions in this time, but that wasn't the case. "What were you saying about your father, dear? I haven't seen him in ages, not even puttering around the garden. This time of year, I would've thought he'd be out." Before I could open my mouth to reply, she continued. "I can't tell you how much I miss talking through community issues with him. He'd sit right here, in this very spot"—she slapped her hand on the bar twice while Jed shook his head because no, Dad never sat at the bar—"and discuss the problems. He always knew how to get things done. It's such a shame he never ran for office. If we'd had him on the town council instead of Owen Bartlett with his liberal agenda, we wouldn't be in this mess."

"Which mess is that?" I caught Jed's eye on the other side of the bar and he shrugged, gave a quick shake of his head.

"Too many to count," Denise replied. "The taxes are outrageous while the schools are falling apart and packed to the gills. These children are leaving the cities in droves and overwhelming our classrooms. Do you see any roadwork being done? Not a bit. It's nothing like it used to be. It's not like that at all. They call it progress, but I call it a mistake." She leaned in close, lowered her voice. "And don't get me started on the drug and juvenile delinquency issues. We didn't have those problems in my day." Her eyes as wide as they could stretch without injury, she tipped her head toward Nate. "I hope you're keeping Judge Markham informed about these issues. I'm certain he'd want to know and make his opinion known."

I shoved a crouton in my mouth. "Mmhmm."

"You know what I should do? I should pay him a visit."

I shook my head. "No. No, not right now," I said around the crouton. This conversation needed to end by any means necessary. "Maybe a few months from now. We'll see how he's feeling, all right?"

"Oh, well—"

"Thank you for understanding," I continued. Still gnawing that chunk of crunchy bread. "I'm sure you can imagine the recuperation has been difficult and unpredictable."

"My sister-in-law fractured her hip two years ago and—"

"Please don't let me keep you," I said through a bold, brassy smile. "I know we could chat all night, but I'm sure you're meeting people and I'd hate to make them wait."

She wiggled her fingers at a group of women seated at a round table in the dining room. "How did you know it's my night out with the school girls?" she cooed. "We try to get together once a month, but we're lucky if we manage every other month."

Nodding, I went for another crouton.

"It was wonderful to see you, dear." Denise returned her hand to my wrist and resurrected the sad smile. "I'm so pleased you're getting on all right. Give me a ring if there's anything I can do for you and don't forget to pass my thoughts on to Judge Markham. See if you can't convince him to attend some of the town council meetings. We need him on our side!"

I went on grinning as she slipped off the barstool, but I wanted to gather those rocks in my hands, close my eyes, and throw them in every direction.

"HOW DO YOU DO IT?" I glanced at Jed as we walked toward his house later that night. "How do you, I don't know"—I shook my hands in front of me as if I intended to strangle something—"put up with this town?"

"Narrow it down for me, sweetheart. We could be talking about anything. What am I putting up with?"

"This entire town," I cried, a manic laugh winding through my words. "This small, insular, homogenous town where everyone is convinced the best days are behind them and the only solution is going backward. And these people who believe the old ways were best and refuse to acknowledge that progress might be a good thing." I stared at him in the darkness. "How do you do it? Because I can't deal."

Jed reached for my hand, layered it between both of his as we walked. "You had a shitty conversation with Denise Primiani. Who hasn't?"

"It's not one person with one shitty outlook," I replied. "It's the fact that many people share that outlook and feel comfortable announcing it."

"I understand what you're saying, Bam, but that's not a Talbott's Cove problem. That's everywhere and you know it." He shifted my hand to his waist while he unlocked the front door. "What's the Cove ever done to you?"

He pushed the door open and I stepped inside, kicked off my shoes. Butterscotch was quick to run up. "Look around, Jed. The Cove doesn't resemble the rest of the world. It's about as diverse as pasta salad. Noodles and mayonnaise and, if you're lucky, a few bits of color and spice."

"Pasta salad. Okay." His lips twitched as if he wanted to laugh, but he knew enough to hold back. "Owen Bartlett, the chair of the town council, is a gay man. That has to count for something."

"Sure, it counts, but the fact we're handing out brownie points for accepting a native son's sexuality is kind of ridiculous," I replied, pacing the length of the living room. "Not to mention, being able to name one gay man in the whole of this town and trying to pass that off as proof of Talbott's Cove forward evolution is absurd."

"Technically, we can name two because his boyfriend Cole lives with him now."

I held my arms up in celebration. "There we go. Two gay men equals a diverse, inclusive town. Check. Done. Problem solved."

"Perhaps I've mentioned once or twice how I'm working on bringing something new to this town." He perched his hands on his hips. "Jobs, tourists, money. Those things won't wave a magic wand over the town, but they'll get the tide turning."

"And you know I think it's an incredible plan," I replied. "Perhaps I've mentioned how I have money to invest."

"You know I can't do that, sweetheart. Keep your money."

I stopped pacing, stared at him. "Let me see if I have this straight. I can't complain about people with shitty opinions because they're everywhere. I can't complain about the pasta salad because you're solving that. And I can't invest in the distillery because you need a separation between cocks and stocks. Does that sum it up?"

Jed studied me for a moment, his gaze raking up from my bare feet, over my slim black pants and blousy top, stopping at my lips. He tilted his head to the side as if he'd settled a disagreement with himself and brought his hand to my back, resting between my shoulder blades. He nudged me forward, toward the hallway. Toward the bedroom. "You forgot to add in the piece about you rejecting all the local authority you possess by virtue of birthright."

"That's where your calculations are incorrect." I reached for his belt. "Just because my father leaned into the whole Markhams of Maine thing doesn't mean I can or should."

Growling, Jed yanked the shirt over my head. "You backed away from Denise's bullshit tonight. You didn't call her on any of it and you could have."

I scowled up at him as I unbuttoned his shirt. "Because I didn't want to start a brawl."

"A few well-chosen words and Denise would have a fresh perspective on so-called juvenile delinquents." He pushed my pants down to my knees and held my elbows as I wiggled out of them. "If we don't stick around and call out the bullshit when we hear it, this place will always be the same soggy pasta salad it's always been. It wouldn't be the worst thing in the world for you to put some of your family's leverage to good use."

"You're assigning me more power than I have on reserve, aside from the fact this isn't about me. This town hasn't seen a boom year in my lifetime but everyone is holding out hope we can find our way back to those good old days. If only we could slow down, back track over everything we've gained, and return to a time when the world was a simpler, more oppressive, more restrictive place, and then we'd be on the right track. You make it sound like I should—" I went flying through the air, landing on the bed with a shout. "What the hell was that for?"

Jed climbed onto the bed and settled over me, his knees tucked under my arms and his cock hard between my breasts. "That was for the look you've been giving me for the past few hours." He brushed my hair from my face and cupped my jaw. "It's time for you to suck some dick, sweetheart."

"What about snatching a soul?"

He took my hand, curled it around his erection. "You already did."

"I don't suck dicks," I replied as my hand shuttled over him.

He growled, low and guttural, just the way I loved. "You do now."

I shook my head, the movement causing me to brush my lips over his crown. "Probably not."

"Bam, you can't convince me you don't want this." His hips jerked as I stroked him harder. "I've watched you all night. I saw it in your eyes. Saw how you want to be completely merciless."

"You're selling this rather aggressively."

I shot him an indignant glare as I considered all the creative ways I could explain I wasn't meeting his dick-sucking needs. Instead of offering any of them, I opened my mouth, rubbed him against my lips. He was hot and thick, and throbbing in my palm, on my tongue.

His hand shot behind my head, urging me closer, rubbing my scalp. "Brooke. Fuck. *Fuck*."

I wrapped my tongue around his head and tasted the bead of fluid waiting there. It wasn't as unpleasant as I'd remembered. The muscles in his legs flexed, tightening against my torso as his body tensed. He twisted my name into groans, growls, and curses while his body arched and shuddered.

I wanted it this way. I wanted him begging and shaking, pulling my hair and trapping my body under his. I wanted him to want me even when I gagged, when my eyes watered, when I wasn't perfect.

Even when I told myself I didn't, I wanted him.

JJ THREW the car in reverse and hooked his arm over the back of my seat. I glanced down at my lap, a warm pulse moving through me as he backed out. It wasn't sexual. It wasn't about his body. It was care and competency and it turned me on, just the way it turned me on when I watched him tap a keg and mix a martini.

I didn't understand how something as simple as know-how could start me up, but I couldn't help it. I felt this as profoundly as filthy words whispered into my ear.

"What's wrong?" he asked, pausing at the end of the driveway.

"Nothing."

"Not nothing. Looks like you're annoyed." He considered me. "Or praying."

"Praying and annoyance are interchangeable in your book?"

"No, Bam. When it comes to you, everything comes with a side of annoyance."

"Or prayer?" I countered. I glanced down at the skintight jeans I'd selected for tonight's double date. We were meeting Jackson and Annette for dinner in the big city—as big as it got in Maine—Portland. The guys didn't know it yet, but they were also taking us dancing. "These are not the jeans of a woman who spends much time on prayer."

"Would you just tell me what your problem is? Goddammit, woman. Half the time you invent arguments just to give yourself something to do, I'm sure of it."

"Right," I deadpanned. "Because I have nothing better to do. Makes complete sense."

"You always have something better to do. That's not in question. It's whether you'd rather do that or start fires."

"Now I'm a fire starter?"

"As far as I can tell, that's how you spend the other half of your time."

I could've said something. I could've told him he looked good tonight or that I appreciated him doing this for me. I could've formed those words and sat there, vulnerable as fuck for a minute.

I didn't.

"It's rather cavalier of you to claim I'm inventing problems or starting fires when you were begging me to suck your cock less than"—I shot a pointed glance at the dashboard clock—"eighteen hours ago."

"Bam, sweetheart, if I were to apply that logic, you'd have to keep that pretty mouth of yours shut on a near permanent basis." He reached out, slipped his hand through my hair. "Since I know there's no way in hell to shut you up, why don't you tell me what's wrong."

"Nothing," I insisted as his grip tightened. "It was nothing. I'm fine. Seriously."

"I don't believe you." He loosened his hold on my hair only to gather up the strands again and twist them around his palm. "Would it kill you to be honest with me? Really, is it that hard for you?"

There it was. The quiet genius of JJ Harniczek. I didn't have to say anything for him to know everything or damn close to it.

I licked my lips, glanced away as much as I could given his grip on my hair. "Sometimes."

"What can I do about that?"

"It's not you."

He tipped his head from side to side. "Sure, that's a handy answer. But, as you mentioned, you're the woman sucking my cock. I'd like to make it better for you if I can."

"That starts with giving me plenty of warning. I'm not a swallower."

He shut his eyes, drew in a breath. He studied me as he exhaled. "I know, sweetheart. I'm sorry. That one got away from me." He leaned closer, bringing our foreheads together. Then, "Tell me you're all right and make me believe it."

"I'm honestly fine," I said, laughing. "I'm, um...I'm happy you're coming with us."

"You're not convincing me of anything," he replied.

"That's not my problem, Jed. Convince yourself."

"Answer me one thing." I murmured in agreement. "Are you coming home with me at the end of the night?"

"That depends," I replied. "Will you complain about me and Annette dragging you guys to some clubs after dinner? Are you going to give me shit about drinking tequila and dancing like it's my job?"

"Not at all," he answered.

"Will you complain if I dance with other guys?"

His lips pulled up at the corners. "That depends on whether you're coming home with me, sweetheart."

"And if I do?"

"Then I have no reason not to trust you."

CHAPTER THIRTY

JJ

Yield: the return on investment.

BROOKE WORE second-skin jeans and a satin bustier she'd hidden under a blazer during the drive and dinner. She made me watch from the sidelines while she and Annette knocked back shots and shook their asses all over the club's dance floor. That part was tough for Jackson. He couldn't handle the sight of men circling Annette and Brooke without snarling like a junkyard dog.

I did some snarling of my own, but it had nothing to do with the men she cast off with little more than a shake of her head. No, those snarls came from the expanding pressure inside my chest. Brooke-Ashley Markham ruined my life, but she also patched it up and put it back together. Nothing was the same, nothing sat in the proper order, but none of that mattered because I loved her. It was a long time coming, but here, tonight, I saw it up close and I felt the blunt force of it as she moved with the music.

"I'm going out there," rumbled Jackson.

I slapped an arm across his chest to hold him back but never took my eyes off Brooke. "You're not," I replied. "They have this under control."

He jutted a finger toward Annette and Brooke. "That's not under control."

I watched while a random dude pushed himself between them and made an attempt at grabbing Brooke's ass. My hands curled into fists and the pressure in my chest expanded with sharp points, but I waved Jackson off.

"Just wait," I murmured. "Give her a minute. Let her do this."

Brooke looped her arm through Annette's elbow as she rounded on the man. Her hair floated down her back and over her bare shoulders in loose waves, but that didn't soften the stare she sent in his direction. I couldn't hear the words she spoke to him but as I'd expected, they worked. He lifted his hands in surrender as she ticked off a list on her fingers. She mimed him stepping back, staying out of their circle. She wagged a finger at him and I was certain I saw the word *sorry* form on his lips. Then, she flicked her wrist and he bolted from the dance floor.

"Shit," Jackson muttered.

That woman is a motherfucking force to be reckoned with and I love her.

"I told you she'd handle it," I said, as smug as I fucking pleased.

"As impressive as that was, can we get out of here now?" Jackson asked miserably. "At this rate, I'm going to start making arrests or grow an ulcer. Maybe both."

"Soon," I replied. "Wait until they take their shoes off. That's when you know they're close."

After several minutes of silence between us, Jackson said, "We should've started that book club."

"The first rule of book club is you don't talk about the book club," I said, mostly to myself.

"That's interesting because the second rule of book club is you don't talk about the book club," Jackson added. "But there's no book club, so the other rules are irrelevant."

I shifted to face him, a laugh shaking my shoulders. "That wasn't bad, sheriff."

"High praise coming from you, Harniczek."

It wasn't long before Brooke and Annette left us in possession of their shoes, but they went a barefoot hour before calling it a night. They hugged for ten solid minutes before parting.

I drove her home, carried her tipsy ass inside, and led her to the bed I'd stopped calling *mine* in favor of *ours*. We found each other with unhurried touches and kisses, nothing like the first nights we'd shared together, when everything was over before it started.

"Thank you for coming along tonight," Brooke said.

"There was nowhere else I wanted to be," I replied.

"And thank you for keeping Jackson under control. He wanted to pull the sheriff routine all over the dance floor, I could tell."

"You're right about that," I said, laughing.

"I know group dates and dance clubs aren't your ideal evening out." She dipped her head, pressed a kiss to my neck. "Thank you for letting me and Annette have this."

"And thank you for letting me watch," I replied. "Do you know how much I loved seeing you kick ass out there? Fuck, you were amazing. Do you know? How much I love seeing you kick ass all the time? How much I love—I love you?" I heard a sudden inhale of breath from her, but now that I'd started, I couldn't stop. "You might not want me saying that. You might have reasons and arguments, but—"

"I love you too." She propped herself up on an elbow, lifted her hand to my cheek. Blinked down at me with those bright blue eyes and hair like heaven. "You're right. I didn't want those words because I don't know how. *I don't know how*, Jed, and I'm terrified I'll do it wrong."

I rolled her onto her back, settled between her legs. "You can't do it wrong, Bam."

"But you can," she argued, her hands warm on my chest. "You can. I've seen it, I've lived through it. My parents, they—"

"They're not us," I interrupted gently. "And we won't be them."

She reached up, loosened my hair from its tie. As strands fell to my shoulders, she raked her fingers over my scalp. "I don't know what I'm doing and it scares the hell out of me, but I know I love you."

Raw, fragile honesty from this woman was like a shooting star. I kissed her then because come the fuck on, how could I not? "That's all you need to know, Bam."

CHAPTER THIRTY-ONE

BROOKE

Discounting: calculating the present value of a future amount.

"WHAT IS THAT?" I grumbled to Jed's chest.

"What's what?"

I pushed up on an elbow, glanced around his bedroom with bleary eyes. Gentle rays of morning sun streamed in through gaps between the curtains. I blinked at the clock in an attempt to clear the sleep and lingering alcohol. As I blinked, the muffled sound echoed through the room again.

"That," I insisted. "Do you hear it?"

"Go back to sleep, Bam." He tugged me down, folded me into his arms so that I heard only his heartbeat.

I dozed for a bit—a few minutes, maybe more. But then there was a heavy knock on the front door.

Jed sat up, murmuring, "Who the hell is at my door first thing in the damn morning?" Not wasting time on boxers, he stepped into his jeans and zipped the fly. He left the top button and belt open. It read like a promise: he didn't intend to be clothed for long. I admired that promise. "I'll see what this is all about and be back. Stay here with the dog."

He nodded at Butterscotch, who was curled up in her bed and hadn't heard anything. "Yeah, I'm counting on her for guidance."

"It's too early for you to start with the comments, Bam." He snapped his fingers. "Come on, girl," he said to the dog. "You need to earn your keep."

For her part, she jumped up from her bed, galloped toward me, and rubbed her head against my outstretched hand.

"Good girl." With a smirk, he added. "Both of you." He disappeared into the hall only to return a moment later with my purse. "This is vibrating." When the pounding on the door continued, Jed called, "Calm the fuck down, we're coming." He tossed the bag onto the bed. "Turn off your alarm or whatever you have going. It sounds like a time bomb."

I swiped my phone to life, finding seventeen missed calls from Annette, a long line of texts asking me to answer her calls, and five voice-mails. There were other texts, other calls. The first ones came in two hours ago and they came from my father's house.

I gazed down at the screen as a ridge of icicles formed along my shoulder blades. My head swam. Goose bumps rippled over my skin. I knew I was clutching the device, but I couldn't feel it. I wasn't certain I felt anything more than cold. "Jed. Jed, can you come here?"

When the shape of him filled the doorway, I hadn't managed to glance away from the screen. He gathered a few things from the floor as he rounded the bed and settled on the edge. "Give me that," he murmured, snatching the device away and slipping it in his back pocket. "We need to put some clothes on you, okay? Jackson's here. He wants to talk to you for a minute."

Still silent, still staring down at my hand, I didn't react when Jed pulled one of his shirts over my head. Didn't ask why Jackson was here. Didn't complain when it took him several attempts to help me into leggings. Didn't argue when he lashed his arm around my waist and guided me toward the front of the house as if we were practicing for a three-legged race.

Jackson removed his Talbott's Cove Sheriff's Office ball cap, stepped toward me. "Brooke. I'm so sorry."

I didn't do any of those things because I knew my father was dead. He was gone and my first reaction was relief and I *hated* myself for it.

CHAPTER THIRTY-TWO

JJ

Useful Life: the estimate of the period of time an asset will be in use.

"THERE'S a shipment coming in from Trillium on Friday," I called over my shoulder as I moved through the storeroom.

"Tomorrow," Nate replied from behind me. "I talked to our rep yesterday morning because I noticed we're going through the summer brew faster than expected. He added a few units and bumped us to tomorrow's delivery."

"Even better," I said, pushing through the door to the bar. I tested the taps, checked the ice box, glanced at the garnishes. "Everything is in order."

"What did you expect?" he murmured as he made a note on his clipboard.

I lifted a whiskey bottle to the light, then another. "Did anyone give you trouble last night? Did Lincoln come in?"

"No trouble," he replied, still busy with his clipboard. "Lincoln pounded seven ginger ales and complained about the Sox for a couple of innings."

"Some things never change," I said. "When you get a chance, would you follow up with the beef supplier? We've been running low and—"

"Already done," he interrupted, looking up from his clipboard. "I know you're being thorough but what the hell did you think would happen when you left me to manage this place for a few days? Did you think I'd let us run out of burgers or beer?"

I turned in a circle, my hands on my hips and my mind racing. I needed to get back to the Markham house. I hated leaving Brooke this morning, but I had to run payroll and pick up my suit from the dry cleaner. Annette promised she'd stay with Brooke and assist with the funeral arrangements. Not that Brooke had allowed anyone to help her with anything in the four days since her father's death. She insisted on doing everything herself and I stood by, watching while she did it—and went on working her finance job as if nothing had happened.

"I expected you'd have it under control and you do," I said. "Thank you for handling things."

"No, man, don't start with that. Save your thanks." He pressed the clipboard to his chest, his arms banded over it. "There's no need." He jerked his chin toward the door. "You should get out of here while you can. I've got this."

"Call me if anything comes up. I don't care what it is or when it is."

"Go," he hollered.

"Going." My phone vibrated in my back pocket as I stepped out from behind the bar. I yanked it out, expecting to find Brooke or Annette calling, but it was Barry O'Connor. Of all the times for him to reappear. I waited until I stepped outside to tap the screen. "Barry. Hi."

"Hey, JJ. Is this a good time?" he asked. "I want to run a few things by you."

I paced away from the Galley and toward the harbor. "Ordinarily, this is a good time, but today is difficult. Can I call you next week?"

"Just five minutes," he said. "I'll make it quick."

I lifted my hand to my forehead, shielding my eyes from the day's intense sun. "All right. Go ahead. What's up?"

"Here's the thing, JJ, I'm trying to make a mark. I'm looking for the next great thing."

A seagull squawked overhead. "I'm aware of your aspirations."

"You're all systems go with this gin thing and it's so great, JJ. It's such a brilliant move. It's cool and hip, and going to take off like crazy in your neck of the woods." He drew in a breath, made a whiny noise in his throat. "But it's not for me."

"What?" I barked, confused.

"It's not for me. Small-batch liquor isn't my passion. It doesn't wake me up in the morning and keep me going at night. I want to steer my investments toward my passions, as I'm sure you can understand."

"What?" I repeated. Now I was annoyed.

"My attorney is drawing up dissolution papers today. He'll have them out to you tomorrow. Friday at the latest."

Again— "What?"

"As I'm sure you recall from the original agreement, the terms are generous," he continued. "There's a five-year grace period before repayment of the initial investment is required." He paused. Another seagull swooped by. "You have to know I labored over this decision for several months, JJ."

A dry laugh rumbled up from my chest. "It would've been nice of you to mention it sooner." A rough estimate of the upcoming construction and production expenses flashed through my mind. "You're not leaving me in the best position here."

"It's just business," he replied. "Look, JJ. I have another call coming in. Look for those papers from my attorney and—"

I ended the call and turned back toward the village. I swept my gaze over the place I'd hoped to redefine as the impact of losing Barry's investment landed in my gut like a brick. Lacing my hands behind my neck, I glanced up the hill to the ancestral estate where Brooke was undoubtedly approving the funeral reception menu while also moving money around the globe at the same time.

She could help. She could get me out of this mess.

But there was no way I could ask her for help. I wasn't going to add that dynamic to our relationship and I wasn't going to be another in a long line of people who expected something from her. If I intended to open this distillery, I was doing it without her saving the day.

CHAPTER THIRTY-THREE

JJ

***Current Liabilities: the sum of salaries, interest, accounts payable,
and other debt service requirements due within one year.***

LAYING Judge Markham to rest was a major event in Talbott's Cove. The flags were lowered and the local court closed. The entire town attended the funeral mass, many spilling out the congregation doors and onto the steps despite torrential rain. The firefighters and sheriff's deputies led a procession from the church to the family cemetery on the Markham estate, where he was to be buried alongside Brooke's mother and hundreds of years of ancestors.

Brooke put on an excellent show. She was gracious and genuine as she stood in the foyer of her father's house, accepting condolences from the hundreds, maybe thousands, of townspeople in attendance. She listened to an endless stream of stories, her hands clasped in front of her, and conjured the appropriate expressions and responses. But I knew it was a performance, and I knew she was heading for a crash.

Despite the best efforts of Annette, Jackson, and I, Brooke continued to refuse all assistance. She'd held us off since her father's death and we were running low on solutions. None of us wanted to force a confrontation or push her into a test of wills, but she couldn't keep going at this pace. She worked around the clock, rarely stopped to eat or sleep, and she hadn't shed a tear. I knew grief took many forms but I also knew this show couldn't go on forever.

When the line of visitors dwindled, Brooke stepped away from her post in the foyer. She joined us on the far end of the front porch, her sky-high heels clacking against the weathered wood in time with distant rolls of thunder. She looked regal in her sleeveless black dress, her hair twisted into a conservative knot and a string of pearls draped around her neck. She also looked exhausted and frail and painfully lonely.

Annette pushed a plate toward her, but she waved it off.

"No, I don't want anything." She ran a finger over her brow and closed her eyes for a moment. I rested my hand on the small of her back. "That's not true. The house smells like ham and wet hair, and I've heard the same six stories about five hundred times apiece. My feet hurt, my hair is frizzing around the back of my neck, and"—she tucked a finger under the belt cinching the dress at her waist—"this thing was a terrible choice."

"Okay, so," Annette started, "ham, shoes, people, and that belt. Anything else bothering you?"

"Many, many things are bothering me," she said, glancing out at the rain. "Very few of them can be improved."

"Let's start small," Annette said. "I can get you a pair of flats and some bobby pins for the frizz."

"There's nothing you need to do," Brooke replied. "No, that's not true. I want you to send everyone home."

"We can do that," Jackson replied. "Give me ten minutes, I'll shut this thing down."

"Ask the caterers to box up the leftover food," Brooke said, rubbing her forehead again. "Get rid of the ham, the roast, the lemon squares. All of it, I want it gone and I want everyone out. Tell the people whatever you want. It doesn't matter anyway." She cast another glance toward the heavy storm clouds overhead. "I'm going upstairs."

"I'll go with you," Annette offered.

"No." Brooke held up a hand, warning her off. "Thank you, but I want to be alone right now and I need you to handle the caterers."

We watched as Brooke marched away. When she stepped into the house, Annette said, "I'm going with her."

"The hell you are," I replied. "You're on catering duty. *I'm* going with her."

"She needs me right now," Annette argued. "You're great and all, but I'm the one who will get her through this."

"Not by yourself, no, you're not." When her eyes flamed with fury, I continued, "Look, I know it's been the two of you against the world for a time. It's not just the two of you anymore."

Jackson held up a hand in warning, but Annette brushed him off. "Okay. That's acceptable. But you need to know I will grind your bones to dust if you hurt her in the slightest way."

"Annie," Jackson grumbled.

"Understood." I gestured to the house. "Now, you fix the ham situation while I get her out of those shoes."

"Sex is not the answer," Annette called. "It's one of the answers, but not *the* answer. Not until after she gets something to eat and a good night's sleep."

I didn't respond, instead jogging inside and up the stairs. It took longer than it should have since the terrible weather meant the entire town was packed into this house rather than overflowing into the outdoor spaces. When I reached the landing, I yanked my tie loose and shrugged out of my suit coat, dropping both on the banister.

Brooke's door was shut but unlocked. The bedroom was as we'd left it that morning and it was vacant. I ducked my head into the bathroom and walk-in closet before noticing the deck door standing ajar. As I approached, I spotted Brooke on the far corner of the deck, staring out at the ocean while the rain washed over her.

"What are you doing out here?" I called, edging onto the deck. "You're soaked, sweetheart. Come inside."

She didn't respond, didn't react.

I crossed the deck and wrapped my arms around her shoulders. "Come on, Bam. You can't stay out here."

She didn't budge, didn't tear her gaze away from the water.

"I know, sweetheart. *I know*. This is fucking awful. It's one gut punch after another. Please, let me bring you inside. You're wet and shivering, and I can't watch you do this. It hurts too much."

I pulled her close, my arms around her torso as she swayed toward me. Then, she did it. She destroyed me all over again.

"I'm pregnant."

CHAPTER THIRTY-FOUR

BROOKE

Equity: the degree of ownership after all liabilities and debts have been satisfied.

THERE WAS a reaction to telling Jed I was pregnant. I was sure of it, though I couldn't make out the words. I couldn't hear anything beyond the whirling in my head, the incessant buzzing that came from realizing how much I resented my parents for expecting me to fix them, how much I hated every minute of caring for my father and rearranging my life to hold the shreds of his together, and how angry I was that he died alone too. No one ever let me say goodbye.

They all died, they all left me, but not before I stole the opportunity to leave them. And the staticky hum in my head was the sound of regret.

Jed gathered me up and brought me in from the rain. He stripped off my wet clothes and swaddled me in towels. I wanted my robe, the one I'd nabbed from that obnoxious roommate years ago, but I couldn't climb past the roar in my head to form words.

He tucked me into bed and climbed in beside me, his body warm and his grip certain. His hand raised to my face, he brushed tears from my cheeks. I hadn't realized I was crying.

"Brooke, are you sure about this?" he asked. "You've had a stressful week. That can throw things off, right? It could be that, sweetheart."

"I took a test this morning." I didn't recognize the watery sobs in my voice. "Then I made an appointment with a doctor."

"Why did you do that alone?" he whispered, his lips pressed to my temple. "Why-why didn't you tell me, Bam?"

"The appointment is on Tuesday. In Bangor." My body shook, quaking as the tears fell faster. "There's no such thing as privacy in this town."

"You're not doing that alone," he said. "You're not doing anything else alone. Do you hear me, Brooke? I'm going with you. I am *staying* with you."

I didn't say anything. I didn't think I could—and it didn't matter. Jed would leave me too. He'd leave and I'd have something new to regret.

CHAPTER THIRTY-FIVE

JJ

***Leveraged Buyout: the purchase of a controlling share in an
organization by its management using capital provided from
outside the organization.***

BROOKE DIDN'T WANT to talk to me in the waiting room at the
doctor's office. She flipped through a magazine, the pages moving at a
pace incompatible with reading. If there was anything to gather from
this morning—and every morning since the funeral—it was that I could
stay close if I didn't require anything from her.

It wasn't until that fire of hers cooled to embers that I realized how
much I needed it, thrived on it, savored it. *Loved* it. I missed her yelling
and cursing about every little thing. Missed her silver-tongued demands
and her piercing glares. Missed her fight most of all. This chilly silence
almost drove me to shake her out of it, to bait her the way she'd always
baited me. But antagonizing the woman I loved days after her father
died and she found herself unexpectedly pregnant struck me as
profoundly wrong, even if that was our first and finest mode of
expression.

I followed her into an exam room, staring at a wall of baby photos while the nursing assistant ran through a list of questions. I listened as I studied the round faces, desperate to glean some information, but I didn't know how to use any of it in a meaningful way. The first day of her last period sounded like a riddle no one saw necessary to solve for me.

So many little faces on this wall. Some bald, some with as much hair as I had today. Some smiling, some mad as fuck. *What will our baby look like?* I turned, stared at Brooke as that thought simmered in my mind. She sat on the exam table with her ankles crossed and hands balled in her lap. She glanced up at me for a fleeting moment, tipped her head to the side, and held her hand out.

Moving away from the wall, I stepped around the nursing assistant and stationed myself beside Brooke.

"It's fine. I'm fine," she said, her gaze glued to the floor as the nurse wrapped a blood pressure cuff around her arm. "You don't need to do this."

"I'm going to do it anyway," I replied.

The nursing assistant left parting instructions about changing into a gown and a promise the doctor would visit shortly. When the door closed, Brooke hopped off the table and turned her back to me as she undressed. She pushed her arms into the gown and shuffled back to the table, one hand fisted around the cloth to keep it closed.

"I've seen you naked. Don't hide your ass for my benefit."

"I know what comes next with these appointments," she said. "Covering my ass is all I can do to make this bearable."

"Is there anything I can do to make this better than bearable?"

"Do you want a baby right now?" she fired back.

"Do you?"

She was silent long enough that it seemed she didn't intend to respond. But then, she said, "I don't know."

The doctor bustled in, full of smiles and enthusiasm Brooke couldn't match. She dimmed the lights and dropped onto a short stool after instructing Brooke to lie back on the table. The sonogram screen flickered to life. Brooke grabbed my hand.

"There's your baby," the doctor chirped, circling a black and white area on the screen. "See that little strobe light? That's the heart. And this string of pearls? That's the spine. Based on these measurements and the dates you provided, you're about nine weeks along. Here, let's print out some pictures."

Brooke's grip on my hand tightened. There was no way to interpret the meaning behind that gesture, but I leaned down, kissed the top of her head. We'd figure this out.

THE FIRST HALF of the drive back to Talbott's Cove was agonizingly quiet until Brooke asked, "What do you want to do, Jed?"

As it turned out, I couldn't stop myself from antagonizing her. "Are you asking what I want to do right now, this morning? Because I need to get some breakfast and then run to a meeting at the cider house." I glanced over at her. "Or are you asking about something else, Brooke?"

"It's good of you to loop me in on your plans," she replied.

"I want to do whatever you want me to do," I said. "But I can't do that if you won't talk to me. I'll tell you this much, Brooke. Whatever you want to do, I'm going to support you. Whatever you want. There's nothing you can say to change my mind on that."

She reached into her purse and retrieved a water bottle. She took several sips before asking, "Who are you meeting at the cider house?"

I didn't want to have this conversation. I wanted the one about our baby and the rest of our fucking lives, but this one had to happen eventually. "I'm showing some potential investors around the site."

She whipped her head toward me. "Why? Is Barry renegotiating the terms?"

"You could say that," I murmured. "Barry decided to step away from this project. I've been reaching out to new funders."

I saw the exact moment she added up the pieces, her expression shifting like an unlocked door blown open by a gust of wind. "Why didn't you tell me? I've told you I am willing to connect you with other investors. Real, serious investors. People who do this every day rather than Barry's weekend hobby approach to business."

A humorless laugh tripped over my lips. "You've had your hands full, don't you think? I wasn't about to bother you with this last week."

"Why don't you trust me enough to let me help you?" she asked, her words losing their edge. "Why is that so terrible? Do you think I'd lead you around by the purse strings? Or that I'd lord it over you? What is so terrible about me? Why can't *I* help you? You're sitting here, saying you'll support me no matter what but I'm not allowed to do the same. I'm not allowed to help in the one way I'm able to because—because why? I can't be trusted because I ditched you behind a barn a long, long time ago? Because I can't react to death and babies and love the right way? Why am I terrible, Jed?"

"There's nothing terrible about you. Don't think that, please," I replied.

"There's nothing terrible about me but you don't want my money when you actually need it. When I could make a difference. Don't you see? You could focus on the things you do best rather than wasting your time on sales pitches and pacifying investors," she said. "Yeah, it makes total sense to keep me out of it."

I wanted to bash my head against the steering wheel. "Can we hold this discussion for later? None of this is about the distillery. Not at all. I want to talk about everything, but the next ten minutes isn't enough time to take it all apart."

She jerked a shoulder up, nodded. "I think it makes sense for me to go home now."

"Not a problem. We can talk more tonight, after I touch base with Nate. I'll drop you at home and then head to my meeting."

"I didn't mean my father's house," she said. "I meant it makes sense for me to go home to New York. I can manage anything that needs to be done from there. There's no reason for me to stay any longer than I already have."

"You're sure about that? Because I can think of several reasons for you to stay," I replied.

"You would say that," she mused. "You believe you belong here. You think this is a fine little pasta salad world. I, on the other hand, am long overdue for my exit. I stayed all these years and I killed myself to keep my father comfortable and honor his wishes, and what am I supposed to do now? Live in the house my family has been in since before electricity and indoor plumbing? Raise a kid with you when you don't trust me around your business? Why would I do that to myself? Why would I keep punishing myself that way? The Cove is a far cry from where I belong. If you can't see that, you haven't been paying attention."

"Brooke, I love you but I think you're angry and overwhelmed about a million other things and I don't know where to start with you when I have *minutes* to talk."

"And now I'm the irrational, emotional woman," she said. "How charming and predictable. I've always enjoyed being the villain in your story. Please be sure to keep that resentment going when I'm gone. The town needs some drama."

"You're being ridiculous," I said flatly. "You're also discounting all the relationships you've formed in Talbott's Cove. People care about you. *I* care about you."

"As great as that is, I'm the one who is pregnant and alone and living in a town where I don't belong," she argued. "I can't plan my life around you and a business you're hell-bent on launching in spite of the money I can provide."

I pulled into the driveway, killed the engine. "I don't have the time to explain to you the fifty ways you're wrong about all that, but I'll be back later and we're having this conversation."

She reached for the door handle. "No. We're not."

"Brooke—"

"Do the smart thing, Jed. Go to your meeting. Dazzle them with your ideas and your appropriately edgy vibe. Win them over and gain their trust. Take their money and build an empire on a pile of apple cores. Focus on that and I'll focus on myself, just as I always have. I'm going back to my empire, the one where I'm not your princess."

She slammed the door and I was out of the vehicle, chasing after her. I was going to be late and I didn't give a damn. I caught her elbow, yanked her back toward me. "You were never my princess," I roared. "Never once my princess. That girl belonged to everyone else. You"—I lifted my hands to her face, cupped her jaw—"you belonged to me." Her chin wobbled as her eyes filled. "It doesn't matter where you are. You're always mine."

"You don't even trust me enough to—"

"I trust you with everything, Brooke. *Everything.* I trust you with my life, my baby, my whole fucking world. Do you want to take over the finance side of my business? It's yours. But you're not giving me a penny. It doesn't matter whether this money is pocket change for you or I'm a fool for refusing it. You're done saving people, sweetheart. You're done sacrificing and stepping aside to make room for everyone else's needs. You're done resenting people for taking and taking and taking from you. So long as I'm in your life, you're done."

Fat tears rolled down her cheeks as she stared at me. "I'm going. I'm leaving."

I pressed my lips to hers in a hard, biting kiss that refused to say goodbye.

CHAPTER THIRTY-SIX

BROOKE

Bear Market: a steady, self-sustaining reduction in the market value of stocks and other market securities.

Brooke: Who is running the breakup pool?

Annette: What?

Brooke: The pool. I'm sure someone was taking bets on when things would fall apart with me and JJ, and who'd be the one to fuck it all up, and I'd like to congratulate the person who bet on me and today.

Annette: What happened, honey?

Annette: No, forget that. Where are you?

Annette: I'm walking out the door, so tell me where you are unless you want Jackson patrolling the streets for you.

Brooke: I'm at Dad's house. The door is open.

Annette: What can I bring you?

Brooke: Just bring yourself. That's all I need.

THE DOOR banged shut behind Annette as she said, "Tell me everything."

I glanced up at her from my spot on the foyer rug. I'd plopped down here after Jed dropped me off and hadn't found a reason to get up since. I didn't know where to go. Every room of this house was colored with overwhelming memories of the past two weeks, the past two years, and everything before that. The foyer was better.

Annette dropped to her knees, reached for my hands. "Say something, honey."

"I don't want to be here anymore," I said.

She bobbed her head in agreement, her dark curls bouncing with the motion. "Okay, we'll go to my house. There's plenty of room and you can stay as long as you need. I'll get some of your things. Don't move."

When she pulled away from me, I squeezed her hands. Tugged her back. "I meant I don't want to be *here*. I don't want to be in Talbott's Cove anymore."

Her sympathetic smile fell and that response cracked my heart open. She brushed her hands down my cheeks, wiping away tears. Again, I hadn't realized I was crying. "Here's what we're doing, sweetie. I'm going to pack a bag for you and we're going to head over to my place. Is there anything specific you'd like me to pack?"

"You don't have to do this. I'm fine. You have a bookstore to run. I'm just—" I shook my head, glanced away. "We had an argument. Jed sees things one way. I see them differently. Neither of us are willing to adjust our positions, so it ended. It was always going to end and now it has." I blinked at the wall of floral arrangements and suddenly understood the cloyingly thick scent around me to be white lilies. Every breath was soaked with lily until I tasted their perfume in the back of my throat. I scrambled to my feet, charged toward the door. "I have to get out of here."

"Wait," Annette called, but it was too late.

I fell to the grass, braced on my hands and knees, and emptied my stomach. She approached, gathered my hair from my face, stroked my back. She didn't say anything while I gagged and sobbed. When it was over, she wrapped an arm around my shoulders and passed me a wad of tissues. "I'm sorry you had to witness that," I said, accepting the tissues.

"What are sisters for if not holding your hair when you vomit?" She brought my head to her shoulder. *Goddamn. I had to tell her about the baby.* " Sisters are also good for helping you put your life back together when it shatters."

Knowing she was right, I said, "We'll go to your place, but just for tonight." I took her hand in mine. "Thank you."

"Anytime." She smoothed her hand down my spine. "I'm much shorter and rounder than you are, so while I'm happy to share all of my clothes, that won't work out well. I'm going upstairs to get your things. Stay here. Think easy, non-pukey thoughts."

I wanted to laugh at the idea of easy thoughts, but my stomach wasn't having it. "I'm not going anywhere," I promised. "Could you pick up my laptop too? I need to handle a few things in the morning and I don't want to come back here to do it."

She pushed to her feet and brushed blades of grass from her knees. "Of course. I'll be right back."

I stood and wandered down the walkway, away from the house—and the mess I left on the grass. Turning my gaze to the bright sky, I wondered whether I was supposed to know what I was doing yet. If I was supposed to know what to do now.

Annette chattered all the way to her house, recounting some incredible news hitting the book world today. She parked me in the living room while she put together some little nibbles, as she called them. I sat there, my hands flat on the cushions beside me while my head and belly swirled. The only solution that made sense to me was returning to New York.

It was what I'd wanted all along. It was the reason I kept my townhouse in Brooklyn and refused to apply for a Maine driver's license. Why I hadn't changed a single thing in my childhood bedroom, even after more than two years of hating all the mint green and pink. Talbott's Cove wasn't home anymore. Loving a grouchy barkeep couldn't erase that truth.

"We have a bit of brie, some sharp cheddar, those great herby raisin crackers you turned me on to, and some dark chocolate because it's necessary for my health and well-being." She set the tray down on the coffee table along with two wineglasses, and retrieved a bottle and corkscrew from her apron pocket. "But first, wine."

I stared at the glasses as she treated them to generous pours. "So, I'm pregnant."

She clutched the bottle by the neck. "*What* did you say?"

I scooped a handful of crackers off the tray and sagged into the sofa. "Yeah, that was my reaction too."

"Okay." She sat cross-legged on the floor, tucked into the coffee table. "Are you exercising your rights or investing in stretchy pants with a belly pouch?"

"No one boils it down quite like you, my dear," I said, laughing. "I don't know what I'm doing. I haven't decided anything." The video montage in my head played a constant loop of my father's house, Jed, New York, the obstetrician's office. Decisions waited for me at every turn. "I haven't decided anything, but you need to hold off on getting married this year. I love you to pieces, but I doubt my ability to host your bridal shower and bachelorette party without the aid of alcohol. And you know none of the male strippers will give a pregnant woman a lap dance."

She selected a chunk of cheddar from the tray. "How do you know this?"

I held up a hand. "Trust me. I know how it is with male strippers." I ate one cracker and immediately felt better. "And there shall not be a single photograph of me helping you into a dress or fixing your train while pregnant. I was angling for a Pippa Middleton-level maid of honor show-ing, but that's out of the question now." I rested my hand on my belly, even though I was annoyed at myself for doing it. There was nothing there yet. No kicking, no bump. Just an accident, a souvenir from the night Dad bashed his forehead on the nightstand and Jed threw me into his car like he was kidnapping me. "Assuming that, you know, I do this."

Annette poked at the dark chocolate, taking her time to find the perfect piece. "And JJ? What are his thoughts on *this*?"

I popped another cracker in my mouth. "He did everything right."

She nodded slowly. "But you had a big fight?"

"I don't know what comes next for me, now that I'm not taking care of Dad anymore." I motioned toward the windows looking out onto the village of Talbott's Cove. "When I first came home, I thought it was for a short time. I remember telling the partners in my firm that I'd be gone for three months. Six at the most. I thought I'd be able to handle everything in that time. It made perfect sense to me that I'd merely 'handle' dementia in a quarter or two." I ate another cracker. "It's a couple months shy of three years."

"Aaaaaaand you live here now. You have people here. People who consider themselves your family. In case I'm not being clear, I count JJ among those people."

"Yeah? Maybe?" I shrugged, shook my head. "We've yelled at each other while naked for months. What does that amount to? It's not a solid relationship. It's not the kind of family you bring a kid into and hope everything falls into place. The best thing for me is to go back to New York."

Annette's eyebrow arched up as she sipped her wine. "Brooke, you'd rather leave someone before they have a chance to leave you."

"I object to that generalization. Simply because I'm contemplating it now doesn't mean it's my primary mode of handling shit," I replied.

"You know I love you and you know I say this from a place of love. I'm not trying to burn you at the stake."

I pushed to my feet and marched into the kitchen for a glass of water. "No, only men who don't understand the first thing about women and believe the uterus is where we hide our witchcraft burn us at stakes," I called over the sink. "It's always them with the torches."

"But JJ isn't holding a torch, honey," Annette said. "And he doesn't think you have witchcraft in your uterus. If I had to bet, I'd say he thinks there's a baby in there and he's wondering whether it will be born with a full beard or just a goatee."

I returned to the living room but couldn't sit. "He thinks Talbott's Cove is a fantastic place to live. He's traveled the world and he *chose* to come back here."

"And I'd agree with him," she replied. "The Cove is not without fault, just like New York City and everywhere else in the world isn't without fault. But I'm happy here. If you'd stop resenting this town for a second, you might realize you're happy too. You might realize you resent it for reasons that have nothing to do with the town at all, but every-thing to do with your roots."

I stopped pacing, met her gaze. "I found you here—"

"I found *you*," she argued.

"We found each other," I said pointedly. "And I'm so thankful for that. For you. But it doesn't make sense for me to stay here, Annette."

"You'd rather leave than be left," she said. "You push, push, push. You make everyone prove they really want you by pushing so hard that only the most stubborn and defiant of us stick around. You make us prove how much we really want you by forcing us away and waiting to see if we'll return."

I banded an arm across my chest. "You make me sound like a manip-ulative psycho."

"No, honey. You're just like the rest of us. We're all dented and defective in our own little ways and we hold it together the best we can."

"You say that, but all I hear is 'manipulative psycho.'"

"Because you're not used to anyone wanting to help you hold it together. You don't know what it means to stick around and push through the discomfort of embracing something new and scary. You're not used to anyone seeing past all the barriers you put up and the ends to which you drive people."

"So...I'm just super fucked up. That's it, I'm super fucked up. Consid-ering that, I should definitely leave. I can't live in a small town where everyone knows I'm super fucked up and watch them tiptoeing around me. That would make me even more fucked up."

"We're all fucked up, Brooke. Sometimes, you lean into it. I'm only pointing it out so you don't walk away from something—and someone—good." She paused, sampled more of the chocolate. "You should know that if you leave, he'll follow. He'll abandon his distillery. He'll go to New York, he'll find a job that isn't the one he's poured his life into, and he'll do it because he adores you. But, honey, that's not what you want. I *know* it. I know it and I need you to know it too."

I dropped down on the floor beside her. "Okay—yeah—so what? I stay here and have a baby and live in my father's house? And we start a baby buggy power walking club for moms where we compare Kegel routines and bitch about our husbands leaving their dishes in the sink or pissing on the toilet seat?"

Laughing, Annette said, "You just married us off and got me pregnant in one little daydream. And opened us up to new friends. That's how deep you're in this, honey. That's how far you've thought this one out. We're talking to *other people*."

"But that's where this is going, isn't it? We'll be pregnant and our kids will be best friends and our husbands will learn to tolerate each other and we'll plan our group vacations to Disney World."

"You're absolutely right, my dear." She grabbed hold of my hands. "I'll wear something Snow White-inspired and I'll work on getting you into something Sleeping Beauty-ish. Jackson will scope out the wait time for each ride and formulate a plan around snacks and naps. JJ will wear the diaper backpack and insist on pushing the stroller too. That's his way, even though you won't let your youngest out of the Baby Bjorn."

"I won't let my youngest out of the fucking what?"

"The Bjorn. You know, it's the mommy-and-me equivalent of a wrap dress." Annette motioned as if I should know what she meant. I shook my head. "The fabric thing you use to wear the baby."

"That sounds like a terrible idea," I said. "While this Ghost of Uteruses Future moment is really fun and all, I am still processing the notion of—of any of this. I can't live here and get married and have a baby and dress up like Sleeping Beauty."

Still laughing, Annette asked, "Has JJ even asked you to marry him?"

"In which universe do I strike you as someone who waits for a man to propose? It sure as hell isn't this one. If I want to get married, I'll tell him. It's a conversation, not a surprise attack." I glanced at her and tried to swallow around the foot in my mouth. "I don't mean—"

She held up her hands. "Nope. It's fine. The surprise attack worked well in my situation, and to be fair, there was a conversation beforehand. Several of them. I didn't expect he'd be in such a hurry to go forward after those conversations, but you know Jackson. He likes efficiency. It's too bad we haven't been able to apply that same efficiency to wedding planning."

"Okay," I replied, unconvinced that I hadn't kicked the puppy of our friendship. "I'm not trying to—"

"I said it was fine and I meant that. We don't get bent out of shape over things like this, Brooke. We don't let little nonsense divide us. You're spinning too fast to see that right now, but believe me, we're okay."

I bobbed my head. "Thank you."

"Don't thank me," she replied. "And don't leave because you're scared. If you really, truly want to go, I'm not going to stop you. I won't ask Jackson to chase you down the interstate or close the airports. If this is what you want, I won't try to change your mind. But I'll miss the hell out of you. I'll miss having you down the street. I'll be sad I don't have the same relationship with you, but I'll be happy you're getting what you want. You deserve that."

I layered my hands over my belly over the little blob of cells inside me. "I don't—I don't know what I want."

Annette's eyes softened as she smiled. "Then stay here and figure it out." She lifted her hands. "Or leave and figure it out in New York. I'll be here for you either way. I can think of someone else who will be here— anywhere—for you too."

I wanted to believe that. I wanted to believe I hadn't killed the possibility of us with fire.

But I couldn't.

CHAPTER THIRTY-SEVEN

JJ

Liquidity: the ease and speed with which a purchase or sale can be completed.

IT WAS one of those unusually quiet nights at the tavern, the sort where I checked the town calendar for big events and stepped outside several times to confirm the lights were on. As far as I could tell, the golden combination of glorious July weather, late sunsets, and minimal responsibilities meant everyone was cooking out, going on evening walks, or coming up with reasons to avoid the indoors.

I couldn't comment on the weather or the sunset. I hadn't noticed either today. The only thing I knew was Brooke left town first thing this morning after turning off her phone and spending the night with Annette. Jackson was kind enough to pass that information along to me. Brooke, not as much.

But I knew it was coming when she wouldn't see me last night. Annette swore Brooke needed time to process the recent events and she'd take care of my girl, but I knew she was as good as gone. She needed to do this and I needed to let her. *Letting her* had its limits, however, and there were approximately twelve hours left on this experience before I hit mine. As much as she inspired me to club her over the head and drag her home, I wasn't letting it go down that way. I didn't want her to be alone right now and I wasn't letting her do this alone for one more day. If that meant following her around New York City, I'd be hot on her heels.

I checked my phone at the off chance I'd missed a call or message. Nothing new.

The door creaked open, and for a split second my heart pulsed into my throat thinking it was Brooke. God, it would be so good to see her. Hold her. Instead, it was Cole McClish, the better half of lobsterman and town council chairman Owen Bartlett. I kept watch on the door, expecting to find Owen close behind.

"It's just me tonight," Cole said, following my gaze. He gripped the back of a stool and cast wary glances at the stragglers seated around the bar. "Is this okay? Should I—"

"Sit your ass down," I barked. I flung a coaster across the bar top, dropped a menu beside it.

"Yes, sorry," he murmured as he settled into the seat. "What do you recommend?"

I stared at him. Blinked. Exhaled like a motherfucker. "Narrow that down, would you? I'm not going to sit here and recommend appetizers when you're only interested in red wines. I got better things to do with my time."

Cole glanced at the menu, a deep frown etched into his face. He was the newest Talbott's Cove import, all the way from sunny California. He was one of those tech sensations who'd earned his first billion before he was old enough to drink to his success. Somehow he'd found his way to our corner of the world and into Owen's heart. The two of them were damn near inseparable, which made Cole's appearance here even more unusual than the empty dining room.

He pushed the menu aside. "I could use a drink. How about a bartender's special? I don't have any strong preferences or aversions."

For a second, I thought about blasting him with some noise about having a drink menu for a reason, but I couldn't do it. I was tired as hell. I missed Brooke like I didn't think possible. If I stopped long enough to get my arms around the idea of Brooke being pregnant—and *gone*—and the distillery's uncertain future, my brain short-circuited.

"All right. Let's shake something up." I reached into a low cabinet for one of my small-batch gins and set to mixing the distillery's proposed signature martini.

Surprising the shit out of me, Cole scooped a handful of pretzels out of a communal bowl and shoveled them in his mouth. Then, he propped his arm on the bar, rested his cheek on his hand, and dragged the bowl in front of him. He selected individual pretzels, eating them one at a time as he said, "I stepped on Owen's overgrown toes tonight. That's why I'm here."

Not taking my eyes off him, I reached for a martini glass. "I'm gonna need you to be clear. Is this a metaphor or did you actually step on his toes?"

"It started when we were changing the sheets this morning," Cole said. "I told Owen he was doing it wrong—and he was. The fitted sheet was inside out and I merely told him this."

"Metaphorical, then," I said to myself as I filled the glass.

"We weren't finished with the sheets even ten minutes when Owen decides he wants to revisit a mistake I made last weekend," he continued. "I'd picked some berries in the woods near the house, but it turned out they weren't edible. They looked like wild blueberries. Like I said, it was an honest mistake. He didn't have to keep bringing it up as if I was an incompetent child who couldn't be trusted to play in the backyard without supervision."

I set the glass in front of him. "Not edible or poisonous?"

He closed his fingers around the stem, shook his head. "I'm not sure. Owen prefers an abundance of caution in all things."

I leaned back against the opposite countertop, crossed my ankles and peered at Cole. "Did he mention which kind of berry it was?"

"Pokeberry? I'm not sure. Something like that." He sipped his drink. "Oh. This is fabulous."

I warmed at the compliment. "Good to hear it, but those pokeberries are poisonous. A handful will kill a child. Two handfuls would take down either one of us."

Cole jerked a shoulder up and pulled a defiant frown. "Even so, it doesn't benefit anyone to treat your partner like a helpless fool and there's no sense bringing it up days later."

"Yeah, Owen should've gotten over the poisonous fruit you touched and brought home to eat much sooner," I replied. "It's outrageous to think he's ruminating over this incident."

"How do you know this?" Cole asked. "How do you know when it's a blueberry and when it's a poison berry? Owen said I should've noticed the color of the stalk."

"The pokeberry has a pink-purple stalk. Blueberries have a green stalk."

Cole shook his hands at me. "How do you know this? I don't think most people carry this kind of information with them. If I went back to Silicon Valley and asked around, I doubt I'd find anyone who knew these distinguishing characteristics."

"It's the sort of thing you learn when you grow up with Talbott's Cove as your backyard." I crossed my arms over my torso. It was all I could do to keep myself right here, rooted in this spot, rather than running and not stopping until I laid eyes on Brooke and convinced her we were in this together. "But, also, didn't you invent something where you can take a photo and the internet tells you what you're looking at?"

He set the martini glass down and leveled me with a glare. "Do not weaponize my tech against me." When he was satisfied that point landed, he continued, "Anyway, as I was saying, I must've stepped on all of his toes because it didn't end with the allegedly toxic berries. We had to dredge up the bad experience we had with the dog groomer and how Owen knew that person wasn't right for the job and I never listen to him and now we've traumatized the dog."

When he drained his glass, I picked it up, asking, "Another of the same or something different?"

"Surprise me," he replied. "I agree, Sasha was horribly groomed and we'll never go back to that shop. I understand that he's putting all his stress and anxiety about our poor girl's bad haircut—plus a dozen other things that have nothing to do with the dog—on me and I know he's doing that because he trusts me with that stress and anxiety, but some-times, it's tough to absorb it all."

On any other night, I would've tuned out this story the same way I tuned out all the others, picking up enough to chime in at the appropriate time with nods and murmurs of agreement. But listening to Cole only pressed the sharp edge of Brooke's absence deeper. It made me realize I wanted to argue with her about sheets and poisonous berries and dog grooming. Or, some version of that. I wanted to fight with her about everything, every day, and I wanted to do it until I ran out of days.

Goddamn, I should've told her that. I should've stopped and said that before I said anything else. I should've said nothing but that. As I shook Cole's next beverage, I shot a glance at the wall clock. It was too late to catch a flight to New York. The best I could do tonight was call or text.

Setting a fresh drink in front of him, I said, "This one is a little floral. The gin is steeped with beach rose. If it's too strong for you, I'll make something different."

He sipped, glanced at me over the rim of the glass, and sipped again. Then, "How is it I've lived here almost a year and I'm just now having a beach rose gin martini?"

I wiped my hands on a towel and busied myself with rinsing out the shaker. "I don't know your life, man. Maybe you should come in here more often. Get that boyfriend of yours to socialize a bit."

"That will be my next order of business after fixing his bruised toes," Cole replied. "I can't believe this drink. It's amazing. When you said floral, I thought I'd be choking down some hand soap, but this is the right kind of rose martini." He took another sip. "My original CFO from back in our startup days loves gin. He kept a trophy case of gin in his office. It was very strange. He lives on a chain of islands he bought in the South Pacific now. Rumor has it, he's building an end-of-days bunker. Not sure the South Pacific is the right place for that sort of thing, considering how oceanic it is." He lifted the glass up, studied it in the light. "I've missed the days of drinking good gin martinis with him."

I glanced at the clock again. "No hand soap served here."

Cole swirled the liquid in his glass. "Which brand is this? I'd love to send him some. He'd get a kick out of my tastes evolving for the better."

Against all my better judgment, I replied, "It's my brand. I distill small batches of gin and vodka in-house."

Not missing a damn beat, Cole said, "You need to develop a national distribution strategy."

Laughing, I said, "I've explored several expansion opportunities. They haven't panned out as of yet."

Giving me his best *that doesn't sound right* face, he asked, "What kind of opportunities and why didn't they pan out? Was it a licensing issue? Distribution? I know certain states have blue laws that go back to the Puritan days and those can create headaches, but it's a simple matter of locating your warehouse in a more legally friendly state."

"It's not that."

"Then...what is it? This is phenomenal liquor and there's no reason to keep it a secret. Why isn't it flying off the shelves?"

I wasn't one for sharing. Not my stories and not those of others. But tonight, with a near empty tavern and every vital organ aching for Brooke, I didn't have the strength to hold back. "It's not going anywhere because my financial backer bailed on an initiative to convert the local apple cider house into a distillery and gathering place with dining and event options."

Cole stared at me, bobbing his head slightly. "Who owns the property? The apple juice place, I mean."

"I do. It was cheap enough to grab on my own," I replied. "Rather, the *cider house* is owned by the tavern."

"One of these days, you can explain the difference between apple juice and apple cider to me, but not tonight," he said. "What's it going to cost to turn the apple juice place into the type of location that will yield the kind of traffic you want?"

A dish towel clenched in my fists, I gazed at him for a long moment. "It's great that you like my gin, but I don't want to talk about money with you."

"Why not?"

Because I hate talking about money with people who have more of it than I do. "Because this isn't the time."

He held up his hands, glanced around. "What better time than now? I'm enjoying your product and I want it to be widely available so I can enjoy more of it and brag to my friends about finding a hot new label before they did. This is the perfect time." When I didn't respond, he continued, "All I want is a loose estimate. I'm wondering what this sort of project costs. Consider it pure curiosity on my part. I could guess, but I shouldn't. Guessing gets me into trouble because I meander down long mental paths until five days have passed without me noticing it."

"You're not leaving until I tell you."

"No, definitely not," he replied with a laugh. "Owen needs more time to cool down and I want to know everything about this distillery."

With a sigh, I grabbed a cocktail napkin and scribbled a figure on it. I pushed it across the bar. "Consider your curiosity quenched."

Blinking rapidly, Cole stared at the napkin. "Characterize this amount for me. Is it bare bones, middle of the road, bells and whistles?"

I dumped several jiggers, stirrers, and mixing spoons into the sink, unconcerned with the bracing clatter of those items hitting the stainless steel basin. "Somewhere between middle of the road and bare bones."

He pushed the napkin back across the bar. "Write down the bells and whistles number. For my curiosity."

I pointed my pen at him. "You know something, McClish? Most people come in here, get a drink, watch the game. They don't tell me about the poison berries they brought home and they don't expect a business plan to garnish their martini."

"I've never once succeeded at doing the things most people do," he replied. "Everything that's ever gone right in my life is the result of following my own path, fucking it up along the way, and acknowledging that conventional wisdom doesn't work for me." He pointed at the napkin. "Since I'm not going to watch the game and you've already heard about my berries, why don't you write down that number and see what happens?"

"Fuck it," I mumbled, snaring the pen's cap between my teeth.

Cole didn't look at the napkin when I pushed it toward him. "What happened with the investment partner?"

"He liked the idea of building a food and beverage destination here, but he wanted to exploit every trend in the market. Ciders, seltzers, pirates." I ran the dish towel over the lip of the bar. "For better or worse, this place is about craft gin and vodka, and that didn't excite him enough. I'd rather see the distillery fail before getting off the ground than die a miserable, trend-chasing death."

Cole finished his drink and then reached into his back pocket, pulled out his phone. He tapped out a message, nodded at the screen, and tapped another message. "Expect a call from my aide-de-camp. Her name is Neera Malik and she'll need your bank information. She'll send some legal paperwork for you to sign. All boilerplate. Your basic covenants and restrictions and such. If you get it back to her tomorrow, you'll have the full amount"—he tapped his finger against the second figure, the bells and whistles—"by the weekend."

"What the hell did you just say?"

"Neera Malik," he repeated. "She'll call you—"

"No, I caught that much," I interrupted. "Why are you doing this? What are you getting out of backing my distillery?"

Cole scratched his jaw. "Why? Because Owen loves it here and I love Owen. This town desperately needs new ideas. Small places like Talbott's Cove are struggling because there's a painful absence of innovation. Nothing new has come to town in fifty years, maybe one hundred, and those things aren't new anymore. Hell, people have no real options beyond leaving. Change is fucking scary, but without it Talbott's Cove won't survive another twenty or thirty years." He glanced to his phone and typed out another message. "And what do I want? For starters, a case of gin each month. Beyond that, I want to connect you with branding and marketing people who know their shit. I'd like a seat on your board of directors, but I know fuck all about running a business so I'll keep quiet."

"That's it?" I twisted the towel around my hand. Untwisted it. "You drop some cash because you believe in Small Town, USA, sprinkle some marketing on top, and cross your fingers?"

He placed his phone on the bar, clasped his hands. "It seems like you want this to be more complicated. I can ask Neera to do that for you, but I have no desire to do that myself. I'm offering you a clean deal. Take it." He glanced at the clock, nodding. "I think Owen has had enough time to cool off."

"How do you know that? How do you determine the right amount of time?"

"I won't call myself an expert, but I think it depends on the size of the fight. We weren't yelling at each other about berries or sheets or dog grooming. We were yelling about time. I'm pushing a new product through beta testing and I've been spending unconscionable hours at my computer. The summer season is kicking Owen in the ass and he's exhausted. We had to get our frustrations out, even if that meant going hardest on the person we care about most." He slipped his phone in his pocket. "Owen needed a couple of hours to be angry, but once he works his way through it, he's done with it."

"And what if you go to him before he's done with it?" I asked for entirely selfish reasons.

"Then I give him the space he wants," he replied. "I've learned to accept that Owen works through things differently than I do and I can't expect him to hurry up because I'm ready to move on."

Cole tried to drop some cash on the bar, but I waved him off. "Don't drink this on the walk home," I cautioned, setting a fresh bottle of beach rose gin on the bar. "Thank you. I can't explain how much I appreciate this."

"No need for pleasantries. We'll thank each other when we've grown a new economic base for this town and my Silicon Valley friends call me the craft gin evangelist."

The door thunked shut and I caught sight of Owen Bartlett. "There you are." He charged across the room. "I've been looking all over for you."

"Found me," Cole chirped. "Look at this, it's gin flavored with beach roses. Do you know what those are? I'm sure you do. Maybe you can show me tomorrow because I have no idea. Also, it's amazing and I worked out a deal so we're getting a case of gin every month. Isn't that awesome?"

Owen smiled at me over Cole's head. "If that makes you happy, baby, then I'm happy."

"Can we go home now?" Cole asked.

"That's why I'm here. I came to get you," Owen replied.

"Good night," I called as they shuffled out, their arms tangled around each other. Watching them together hurt like I couldn't believe, but I had my phone out before the door rattled shut behind them.

This was the only thing for me to do—wrap my arms around her as best I could from hundreds of miles away and ask if she was ready to come home.

JJ: There are a lot of things I want to say. I've been trying to figure out the right place to start all day, but I don't think I know where it is.
JJ: Since there's no good place, I'll start with the thing I wish I'd said the yesterday.
JJ: I don't want you to leave, but I'm not talking about Talbott's Cove. You can go anywhere in the world. I want you to be where you're happy. But please don't leave.
JJ: I didn't tell you about losing Barry and his investment because I didn't want to bother you with it. I know it wouldn't have bothered you. Hell, it might've been a good distraction. But then everything happened with the baby, and the distillery was the last thing on my mind. I can't convince myself I should've added that to your plate, sweetheart. Not right then. I'm sorry it came out the way it did, but I'm not sorry for protecting you.
JJ: I'm going to keep doing that, you know. You'll hate it and you'll throw fire at me, but if I'm extremely lucky, you'll put up with it.
JJ: I think I'm extremely lucky, Brooke.

CHAPTER THIRTY-EIGHT

BROOKE

Hedge Fund: a pooled, collective investment vehicle used to yield aggressive returns.

I KNOCKED on Jed's door. At first, it was a polite knock. A light tap of the knuckles against solid wood. When that resulted in nothing, I put some muscle into it. A deep thunk vibrated across the slab and echoed down the street. Damn near bruised my hand in the process.

It was the middle of the night, the summer air heavy on my skin and cicadas hissing in the trees as if I required more recrimination. I did not. I knew where he kept the spare key, but it didn't feel right to let myself in, not when I'd escaped from the Cove before sunrise like a fugitive.

Even if I wanted to climb into his bed and tuck myself up against his body and sleep for the longest time, I couldn't do that. Not until I'd earned the right.

The door swung open to reveal Jed in black boxers, that delicious line of fuzz running down his belly and the octopus climbing his arm. Butterscotch galloped up, her tail wagging her entire body while her front paws danced. She jostled Jed out of the way and circled me twice, huffing and whining as she went. She nudged me over the threshold and into Jed's house.

"Okay, Scotchie, okay," I sang, my hands sweeping over her coat as she nuzzled my legs.

"My dog has never loved anything or anyone the way she loves you," Jed mused. "If you're not here to tell me something good, I hope you know you're gonna break the old girl's heart."

"I tried to go home today," I said, still dividing my attention between him and the dog. "I have a townhouse in Brooklyn. The Vinegar Hill neighborhood. I don't know if I've ever told you that."

He leaned back against the door. "Probably not."

"But I didn't have a key," I continued. "I'm sure I did at some point, but I couldn't find it today. I couldn't get in."

Jed crossed his arms. "Seems like an important detail."

"Not anymore," I replied. "I sold it. I sold my townhouse."

"Wait—how? In one day? What?"

I ran my hands through my hair, shrugged. "I know people. I know how to get things like this done and I wanted it done."

"You sold your place in Brooklyn," he murmured. "Now what? Buying something new?"

"That would be a smart investment," I said, pacing the length of his living room. "Generally speaking, real estate is the most stable, low-risk investment most people will ever make." I turned back toward him, my hand on my belly as it had been all day. "I'm not a stable, low-risk invest-ment. I'm a high-risk investment."

He stared at my torso for a second. Then, he tipped his chin up. "How do you figure?"

"I'm-I'm not going to pretend my head isn't a mess," I said. "I've been dragging a little red wagon's worth of issues around since forever. I'm still fucked up over losing my mother the way I did plus everything I went through with my father. I don't think any of that is going away right now." I shook my head, willing him to understand. "I am a high-risk investment, the kind of risk on which I'd never gamble. And I'm proof that babies don't make people happy. They don't make anyone fall back in love and they don't solve relationship problems. Babies can't fix their parents."

"I know, Brooke. I know that."

His gaze skated over me from head to toe as he stood silent. Eventually, he reached out, grabbed a handful of my dress, and yanked me up against him. Butterscotch protested with a series of yips and barks, wiggling her body between us.

"She wants to protect you," he whispered against my neck. "Can't say I find any fault there."

"I shouldn't have left the way I did. I shouldn't have said the things I did. I was wrong, although I had to go. Had to drive to Portland in the dark, wait for my flight there, wait on the ground at Teterboro, crawl through traffic in Manhattan and over the bridge, all to find out I couldn't go back to the place I'd thought was my home. I had to figure this out, Jed."

"I could've gone with you," he replied. "You could've figured it out with me right there beside you."

"Maybe that's true," I conceded. "But I don't think you would've let me sit on the grass at John Street Park and cry for an hour. You would've insisted I tell you how to fix it and I would've told you I wanted to fix it myself. We would've argued under the Brooklyn Bridge and solved nothing."

"That's where we don't agree. I want to fight with you. Every damn day of my life. I don't want a day to go by without feeling your fire. But understand this, Brooke. I don't want to fight you. I want to stand on the same side as you."

"I don't know how to do that, Jed. I don't know how to do any of this." I layered both hands over my belly, my eyes wide and pleading as I stood there, the farthest thing in the world from perfect. I was exposed and vulnerable, and terrified he wouldn't understand. "I am telling you I don't have the answers and I don't know what I'm doing, and I don't think I've ever been so—"

He pressed his lips to mine. "Beautiful." Another kiss. "Open." Another. "Real." And another. *"Mine."*

"But Jed, I'm—"

"Are you staying?" he asked. "Or am I going with you?"

"Staying. I'm working on getting used to that idea but I sold my townhouse so I'm running short on options at the moment."

"Are we still in this thing together?" he asked as he steered me down the hall.

I nodded. "Yes."

He tugged the dress up, over my head. "Are we still having a baby together?"

Another nod, a terrified gulp, a hand to my bare belly, and— "Yes."

He wrapped his arms around me, brought my head to his shoulder. "There's nothing to forgive. We'll argue, probably every damn day. We'll walk away, cool off, come back. We're in this."

I tapped my index finger against his sternum. "About the distillery—"

"Handled," he replied.

"Yeah? The meeting went well?"

His body shook as he barked out a laugh. "The meeting was a train wreck," he said. "But Cole McClish came into the tavern tonight and we started talking about gin. He sampled the beach rose batch and funded the entire launch on the spot." He pressed a kiss to the crown of my head, my temple. "You can blame Cole for robbing you of that bargaining chip."

"So, that's it?" I asked, glancing up at him. "Cole saved the day and you've accepted my apologies? It's that...simple?"

He dropped his hands to my ass, squeezing and grinding me against him. "If you really want to make amends and apologize for putting me through hell today, you're welcome to suck my cock."

I sighed. "I'm going to be someone's *mother*, Jedediah. Mothers don't suck cocks."

"And yet the term *motherfucker* exists," he mused as he relieved me of my bra.

"It's only available to those up to the task," I replied.

He dragged my panties down, his eyebrows arched. "Since I'm the one who knocked you up, I believe I'm uniquely qualified for this job."

"Can I make one request?"

His chin bumped my head as he nodded. "Anything you want, Bam."

"Take your fucking boxers off."

"All right. That's what you want? Not a problem." He drove his fingers through my hair and tipped my head back. "Don't think I'm throwing you on the bed. You deserve it, and fuck me, I want it like you wouldn't believe. But you ran off to New York City and you cried in a park and you're carrying my child. Right now, I need to hold you more than I need to give you a good toss."

I eased out of his arms, climbed onto the bed, and settled in the middle. "Come here. Come hold me." I nodded at his boxers. "After you drop the shorts."

His underwear hit the floor and then he was beside me, one knee between my legs and his arm under my shoulders as he skimmed a hand up my torso. He gazed at my belly for a long moment. "You're a real piece of work, Bam. The shit you put me through, my god." He rested his forehead between my breasts and released a jagged exhale. "Promise me you won't stop."

I reached for the knot at the base of his skull, pulled his hair loose. The unruly strands fell to my chest and I lashed my arms and legs around him. "Never."

He brought his hand between my legs. "What am I allowed to do?"

"Everything," I replied, arching into his touch. "Give me everything."

Our lips met as he pushed inside me, a chorus of groans and growls passing between us. To the corner of my mouth, he said, "You will tell me if anything is uncomfortable, Bam."

I hummed, canting my hips up to take more of him. "I will."

"You'll tell me to slow down." His hips rolled gently while he continued gazing at me. "I'm not letting you hurt tomorrow."

"And I'm not letting you give me a weak fuck," I replied. "I don't want you holding back. I know how to speak for myself and you know I will. Give it to me or get off me."

"I love you a whole fucking lot," he said, roping his arms around my torso.

"I love you just as much." Then, I felt a flutter on my foot—and wetness. "Jed, honey, oh my god, she's licking my foot."

He peered at me. "What are you talking about? Who?"

"Butterscotch." I gestured to the side of the bed where she had her front paws perched on the mattress and her tongue trained on my toes. "She's licking me like a popsicle. This seems incredibly strange but I can't move since I'm trapped under a lumberjack."

He glanced behind us as Butterscotch hopped onto the bed and plopped down right beside me, her face tucked into the crook of my elbow. "Oh, fuck." He snapped his fingers, pointed to her bed. "Scotchie, off."

She turned her head in the opposite direction and thumped her tail against his ass.

"What do we do now?" I whisper-screamed.

"I-I don't know." To the dog, he said, "Butterscotch. *Off*. Right now." She huffed out a sigh and nuzzled closer to me. "Looks like you're the boss, Bam."

"Butterscotch," I sang. Her ears perked up. "Go to your nest, pretty girl."

She licked my arm, shot Jed a disgusted glare, and jumped off the bed. She trotted over to her corner, circled her bed twice, and dragged a paw over the fleece surface. Eventually, she flopped down and started snoring.

"And here I thought I could keep you all to myself," Jed mused.

"I told you I can't be kept." I locked my legs around his waist and drove my fingers through his hair. "But that doesn't mean I can't keep you."

EPILOGUE
BROOKE

***Consolidation: the joining of two or more organizations to form a
new organization.***

A WARM, quiet laugh slipped out of Annette. *Again.* I wasn't keeping track but it was easily the fifth time she'd giggled to herself in recent memory and I wasn't having it. Nope. I was operating on a few non-sequential hours of sleep thanks to Elliott teething *and* hitting a growth spurt, and I wasn't having any more of this lady's random chuckles.

"For fuck's sake, Annette." I set down my foundation brush and glared at her in the mirror. "If you don't tell me why you have a serious case of the giggles, I'm going to assume Jackson put it in the wrong hole last night and you're just imagining the shocked-but-secretly-thrilled look on his face when it happened."

"It sounds like you're familiar with the shocked-but-secretly-thrilled expression," Annette replied.

"My familiarities are not the topic of this conversation," I said. "Will you just tell me what you're laughing about? Creepy-laughing at the bride on her wedding day has to be bad luck. You know I'm not one for tradition but you're making second guess this."

"And there it is," she said, laughing yet again.

"There is *what?*"

She jabbed an eyebrow pencil in my direction. "You, my dear, sweet, psychotic friend, are freaking out."

I turned away from the mirror to face her head on and folded my arms over my torso. "I'm what?"

"Freaking out," she repeated with a laugh. "You and JJ decided you wanted to get married, and since you've had less than a week to plan and think about this whole thing, you haven't had time to realize what this all means until now." She glanced at the clock beside the bed. "Half an hour before the ceremony. Right on time. You forget that I know you. I know you don't like being the center of attention unless you're in complete control."

The woman had some fair points. This wedding had been thrown together like a half-assed potluck but I happened to enjoy half-assed potlucks. Considering Jed was working insane hours to open the distillery in twenty-nine days and I still played financial Tetris *and* we had an infant with two teeth on the way, a voracious appetite, and a casual interest in naps, a half-assed potluck seemed like an outstanding achievement.

But I wasn't freaking out. I was too sleep deprived to manage a reaction at that level. Too sleep deprived and too full of ass-over-elbow love for all the unexpected things in my life now. Jed and Elliott and our friends and the little family we'd created here in Talbott's Cove. Unexpected. *So fucking unexpected.* I'd never once imagined this life for myself. I'd never imagined this...contentedness.

I was exhausted and I didn't recognize my body and, on most days, I was certain I didn't know the first thing about being a mother—let alone wife—to anyone. And I woke up every morning—or middle of the goddamn night—content.

What the fuck was that about?

Where did contentedness come from? And why did it come for me?

I'd wondered about that more than once in the months since my father's death and my son's birth. There were several occasions where I wondered whether I deserved it, whether I deserved any of this.

I'd wondered about it last weekend while Elliott slept on Jed's bare chest, his little hands curled into fists and his lips twisted as if he was angry about being tricked into napping.

I whispered, "How did I get all of this?"

He reached over, pulled me close to his side, and asked, "How do I get you forever?"

"Are you under the impression I'm going somewhere?"

He tucked a few strands of unwashed hair over my ear and smiled down at my milk-stained t-shirt. "It's not about staying or going. It's about...permanence."

I brushed a finger over Elliott's bald head. "This feels rather permanent, Jed. Not sure we could get any more permanent than having a child together."

"You're right. We'll always be connected because of him," Jed replied. "What about being connected because of us?"

I glanced up at him. "Are you waiting for me to propose?"

"Bam, I've been waiting for the past year," he replied. "If not longer."

We stared at each other for a moment. "No churches," I said.

He nodded once. "No banquet halls."

"No white dresses," I added.

"No tuxes."

"No bouquet tossing," I said.

"No cake smashing." He nodded again. "Just you and me—"

"And Elliott," I added.

"Of course Elliott," Jed agreed. "Neither of us have spent more than six hours away from him since he was born. The time we went out for the night and—"

"When he spit up directly into Jackson's mouth?"

Jed laughed. "So damn proud of this kid."

"You and me and Elliott," I said. "And Annette. Jackson too. And Nate."

"Cole and Owen," Jed added. "Maybe a few others."

I dropped my head to his shoulder. "Maybe."

He pressed a kiss to my head. "Backyard? Or the tavern? Because you know the distillery is a shit show for the next month."

"Backyard," I said.

"Then I'll see you in the backyard, Bam," he said. "Next Saturday."

"I can tell you with absolute certainty I am not freaking out," I said. "I'm having a normal reaction to you being strange while I'm trying to fix my face. I don't want look like I'm rocking an infant sleep schedule in my wedding photos, you know."

"The only reason you have a photographer is because my person was free today," Annette added.

"And I'm eternally grateful for you and your person," I replied. "Even if I'm certain there would've been plenty of photos without your person."

Annette stared at me for a moment. Then, "*Why* aren't you freaking out?"

I shrugged. "I don't know. Because I don't need to?"

She rolled her eyes. "Sure. Yeah. Go ahead. Be easy-going and breezy on your wedding day. As if that makes any damn sense."

"I think you want me to freak out so you can feel better about freaking out when it's your turn next month," I replied. "We both know you're going to lose all of your shit that day."

Annette propped her hand on her hip, frowning. "Not *all* of it."

"Most," I said. "Let's be real. You're going to need Jackson to put it in the wrong hole just to take your mind off things."

"I—I'm not talking about that," Annette said.

"Then what do you want to talk about? My calm, cool demeanor?" I asked, running a brush through my hair with more force than necessary. "Because I'm not calm and I'm not cool. I'm worried about whether Elliott slept enough this afternoon and whether he'll scream for six hours tonight like he did last night. I mean, aside from that, I worry about this kid every single day. For a million different reasons. Most of which are ridiculous things not worth worrying over but a lot of them involve not subjecting my kid to the kind of upbringing to which my parents subjected me. I can't decide whether this"—I skimmed my hands over the knee-length blue dress—"looks good but it seems too late to change. The only laundry I've done all week is the baby's and I don't have clean underwear so I'm not wearing any. I'm not sure but I'm guessing Jed is in a similar position. I can't remember whether I pushed through some sell orders yesterday and I don't know if we have enough plates for tonight. But walking out there and saying "I do" isn't a problem for me. The rings, the promises, the legal transaction? Those are the easy parts. Living them is harder but for right now, today, I'm too busy being happy to freak out."

Once again, Annette laughed.

I wagged my brush at her, ready to tell her what I thought about all these chuckles when I heard a watery gurgle-burp behind me. Annette smiled over my shoulder as I whirled around to find Jed standing in the doorway, Elliott nestled in the crook of his arm. He had the baby dressed in the infant approximation of shorts and a button-up shirt with a plaid bowtie. It was obscenely cute.

"I don't want to hear about it if you're not wearing underwear," Annette said to Jed. "Just keep that information to yourself."

He blinked at her as he bounce-rocked the baby. *Goddamn, that move was hot.* "All right," he said. He glanced at me, his gaze traveling over the lines of my body and the dress covering it. "Don't change."

"I know," I said. "It's too late—"

"No," he interrupted. "You're beautiful. Don't change." He shifted Elliott to his other arm. "Not right now, not ever. There's no reason for it."

I gripped the hairbrush tighter.

"I have to check on the cake," Annette whispered, sailing past me, past Jed. "I want to make sure it—I don't know—hasn't disappeared. Or something."

He crossed the room, stopping only when he was directly in front of me. Elliott cooed and rubbed a warm, slightly sticky hand on my cheek. So much for fixing my face.

"Did you hear all of that?" I asked.

"Was I not supposed to?" Jed asked.

I shrugged. "Nothing I wouldn't say to your face."

Jed brought his free hand to the back of my neck, pulling me forward and dropping a kiss on my forehead. "I wasn't sure if you were testing out your vows on Annette."

Shaking my head, I said, "I wouldn't do that because Annette would insist on making them poetic. She'd insert crying pauses."

"Like I said," he started, "don't change. Not today, not ever." He shifted his hand to cup my jaw, tipping my face up. "Were you serious about not having any underwear?"

"Mmhmm." I eyed him as my lips twisted into a grin. "It's probably time for us to get some help around here. Every day can't be this fun."

"Here I was, thinking marriage was all good times and bare asses." He matched my smile as he leaned in, brushed his lips over mine. Elliott squealed and tangled his fingers in my hair.

"Don't forget the hair pulling," I said, laughing despite the pain. For a baby, his grip was steel and the more I yelped in discomfort, the tighter he held and louder he joyfully babbled.

Once I was free and Elliott was more amused than ever, Jed asked, "You're sure you want to do this?"

"Are you?" I replied.

"Yeah," he answered. "Yeah, I am."

"Me too."

Elliott replied with a long string of baby gibberish.

"It's more than saying "I do" and being happy on one day," I said. "It's about—it's about working at it when it's difficult."

"I know," he replied.

"And it's about not resenting each other and not putting a child in the middle of your issues," I continued.

"I know."

"And it's—it's all the things that are complicated," I said. "It's compromising and getting through it and finding time and—"

"And we will," he said. "We'll compromise. We'll get through. We'll find time. We won't resent each other and this is the only way Elliott will ever be between us. I know it. I know you wouldn't let any of it happen and I know I don't want that to happen to us."

"Come on. Let's do this." I wrapped my arms around them. "Before Jackson and Annette defile the baby's room."

IT WAS a gorgeous day for a wedding.

With my dress gathered in my hands as gingerly as I could, I walked a circle around the outdoor ceremony setup. White chairs curved in a half-moon around the pergola and thick garlands of white hydrangea led the way down the aisle. With the ocean as the backdrop and a bright, shining June sky overhead, it didn't matter that the peonies filling the pergola were a slightly darker pink than I'd expected.

Satisfied, I traveled toward the tent constructed for this evening's reception. I moved between a pair of long, rectangular tables, each dressed with an assortment of linens, candles, and flowers. The design was simple without being plain, rustic without being rough.

On the far end of the tent, I spotted Owen Bartlett pacing a short route between the six-tier wedding cake and the dessert table. I headed in his direction.

"Are you ready for this?" I called, gesturing to the space around us.

He eyed my dress with a pleasant grin. "Are you?"

"I will feel much better when you tell me you have your portion of the events on lock."

He glanced at his small leather notebook. "This is my eighty-ninth wedding ceremony. I didn't think I knew that many people, but here I am, presiding over all these unions. It's surreal when I think about it." He patted the notebook. "I have this on lock, Brooke."

"I expected nothing less." I peered around him. "Where's Cole?"

"Where do you think? He's back in the distilling room, geeking out over the newest batches JJ has in the works." He shook his head as if he didn't relish his husband's obsession with Down East Distillery's research and development efforts. "Have you given any more thought to the proposals on the table? Mind you, I'm not trying to rush the process. Just curious. I get that from Cole."

As it did whenever the topic of my father's estate surfaced, a sudden pressure filled my chest. In the year since his death, my perspective on the home my lineage had kept for centuries evolved. At first, after collecting my things and moving them to Jed's house, I'd wanted to sell. Be done with the ancestral property and move forward. But it wasn't as simple as hanging a For Sale sign in the yard, not with generations of history packed into every corner.

After the summer ended and the loss wasn't as raw, Annette

convened a clean-out party disguised as another one of her double dates of vengeance. We managed to remove much of the recent history—leftover boxes of sterile gloves, dementia-proofed door handles, banana-flavored pudding mix—and that eased some of my tension. I didn't feel the need to avoid the property anymore but I didn't know what to do with it either. Not wanting to deal with that on top of growing a human being and reorganizing my entire life, I set it aside. Until the offers started coming in.

Most were easy to dismiss—the numbers were too low or the buyers weren't qualified—but each one forced me to think about how I wanted this to unfold. As much as I struggled with the truth, I couldn't walk away. I didn't think I could look at the house atop the hill without believing some part of me belonged there and some part of it belonged to me.

"I haven't made any decisions, though I am leaning toward the historic preservation proposal," I admitted. "I like their focus on expanding the gardens, converting the bedrooms into guest suites, and updating the outbuildings."

"And you retain ownership," he said, laughing.

"That always helps," I replied. "That proposal makes the most sense. Turning the house into a museum as other developers have suggested seems—I don't know—wasteful. The only people who will visit are elementary school kids on class field trips and that's not a punishment I'm prepared to administer. I'd rather reimagine it as an inn, a horticultural center, something like that."

"I understand, and I'm confident the town council will approve the zoning changes necessary." Owen jerked his chin toward the main entrance. "You should get back inside. People are going to arrive early. They're all chomping at the bit for a look at the place."

"As they should be," I said, motioning to the lush grounds. "This place is fucking amazing. Did you see that patio area over there? And the gardens? Holy shit. I didn't know gardens could look like that. It's hard to believe we're in Talbott's Cove." I swept an arm out. "A wedding with three hundred guests tonight? No problem. A grand opening next week? Got it covered. Farmers markets and food festivals and five different pop-up events the week after? Business as usual." I tapped an index finger to his suit coat. "Start planning for more stoplights, my friend. This town is never going to be the same."

A rare smile pulled at his lips. "What a remarkable gift it is to get on your good side."

Shaking off his words as I moved toward the doors, I called, "If I see Cole, I'll send him your way."

I slipped inside, careful to keep my steps silent against the concrete floors. It was wild to think this old cider house was ready for its debut after all these months of work and planning, all while welcoming a newborn baby into our lives.

As I ducked down the hall toward the distillery's offices and private rooms, I found Nate marching toward me. His sleeves were rolled to his elbows and his collar was open, a necktie dangling from his back pocket. All he needed was a tweed vest to complete his barkeep chic look.

"Where are you sneaking off to now?" he asked.

"Sneaking? Me?" I asked, feigning all the shock in the world. "Never."

We shared a laugh and I skimmed a glance over the fully grown man we referred to as our foster child. These days, he managed the Galley while also tending to the distillery's gardens. Much like Jackson and Annette, Nate was our family. He was part of us.

"Do you need anything?" he asked.

"You'd know if I did." I reached up, brushed some dust from his short beard. "What is this? Have you been rolling around in an attic? Don't you have better things to do, Nathan?"

"Rolling around on the floor," he replied. "I was fixing one of the refrigerators at the tavern."

"That doesn't sound like any fun."

Shaking his head, he said, "It wasn't, but I got it patched up. That's all I care about."

"The next time you're rolling around on the floor, please try to have fun while you do it." I patted his forearm. "Perhaps you'll meet someone who shares those interests this evening. You know what they say about single women and weddings."

Here I was, thirty-five years old, living in my hometown, and meddling my ass off as mothers have since the dawn of time. Even in my worst nightmares, I'd never imagined this would be my life.

And I wouldn't trade it for anything.

"Don't start with that again, Brooke," Nate warned. "I appreciate your concern, but I can't get involved with anyone. Not yet."

"I know, sweetie. I'm just saying this"—I circled both hands at his tightly bunched shoulders and stiff jaw—"might benefit from a night of rolling around on the floor with someone." Before he could respond, I held up a finger, silencing him. "Do you want me to explain how one-night stands work? I will. I'll give you the overview right now. Better yet, I'll grab Annette. We'll do it together."

"Please don't." Nate shook his head. "None of that is necessary. None of it at all. Not a single word."

"Let me know if you change your mind," I said, backing down the hall.

"I promise you, I won't," he called.

"But if you do," I shouted back.

"But I won't," he replied, his laugh echoing after him.

I stepped into the room designated for wedding preparations. Wrapped bouquets sat in low vases with just enough water to keep them perky. Hairspray and makeup littered the tabletop.

I glanced at my reflection in the mirror, smoothing my hands down the long dress. I never would've selected this style for myself, but Annette convinced me to try it on and the rest was history. I looked different now, my hips wider and my breasts fuller, but I recognized myself. I was my kind of perfect.

From the hallway, I heard, "Where is my wife? No, I've been out there already. This place isn't that big. I should be able to find one tiny woman without—"

The door opened and I met Jed's gaze in the mirror. My lips pulled up in a smile.

"There you are," he said, our son squirming against his chest. "I've been looking everywhere."

My husband's large hand covered the entirety of the baby's back, and if that wasn't enough to arouse me in the strangest ways, the burp cloth over his shoulder sealed the deal. Another bit of strange-but-true sources of arousal: my husband's wedding ring.

The baby, the towel, and the ring. *Fuck me.* It wasn't even fair.

"I heard you," I replied, holding out my hands for Elliott. "Is he hungry again?"

Jed crossed the room and shifted the infant to my arms. Elliott was a sweet, squishy ball of baby with my eyes and his father's hair and coloring.

"Much like everyone else around here, he just wants your attention." He leaned in, kissed my forehead. "This production is nice for Jackson and Annette, but I'm so fucking happy I married you in the backyard last month."

I never would've chosen this place or these people for myself, but now I couldn't imagine choosing anything else. "Me too."

THANK **you for reading *Far Cry!* I hope you enjoyed Brooke and JJ.**

Keep reading for a sneak peak of the next Talbott's Cove novel—*Rough Sketch!*

AFTER A THORNY PAUSE, I asked, "How is your meal?"

He bobbed his head as he savored a bite of dosa. "Excellent. Best I've had in—I don't know—years. And I think that was in Mexico City."

"Mexico City has amazing Indian food." I hummed in agreement. "Whenever I'm traveling, I try to sneak in stops at local Indian restaurants. I have an ongoing samosa study."

I watched a warm, cheerful smile brighten his face and crinkle his eyes. "What's this samosa study involve?"

I pressed the edge of my fork into the uttapam, suddenly and irrationally shy about my multi-continent cataloging of Indian cuisine. "I'm not sure whether it's an atavistic desire or callback to my childhood." I paused, studied my tray. "We didn't eat out when I was a child. We didn't have the money for restaurants and my parents didn't enjoy the local favorites. But on special occasions, my parents loaded us into the car and we'd drive to different cities in the area. Greenville, Spartanburg, Asheville. Athens, once. We'd always go out for Indian and meet the Desi people in that area. And now, well, I just—I tend to judge cities by the quality of their samosas...and other dishes."

He made a sound. A rumbly, growly, throaty sound. Somehow, I knew it was one of approval. "Yeah? Any surprises?"

"I'm not sure about surprises." I sampled the uttapam. I loved these savory pancakes topped with tomatoes and onions. That they constituted a traditional south Indian breakfast mattered little to me. If they were crisp and fresh, I'd eat them any time of day. "There are Desi people all around the world and many of them make superb food." I gave him a pointed nod. "Just as there are French and Brazilian people everywhere and some of them choose to carry on their cultures in most delicious ways."

"Point taken." He drummed my wrist again. This time, he went to the trouble of dragging his fingertips over the back of my hand and staring into my eyes while he did. *So damn arrogant.* "But I still want to know your favorites."

I thought for a moment. "Albuquerque. Egypt, outside of Cairo. Beijing. Then again, there are no bad meals in Beijing."

"Haven't been."

I tipped my chin down. "Now, that's surprising. I figured you'd gone everywhere worth going."

Shaking his head, he said, "South and Central America, sure. Western Europe, yes. Portions of Africa, mostly northern. As far as Asia and much of North America, I have a lot of ground to cover. I don't know much outside the southwest."

I pointed my fork at him. It was rude but I found myself wanting to be rude with him, just a bit. "You don't have much an accent."

He pressed his tongue to the inside of his cheek. "Neither do you."

"I grew up here." I waved at the table. "Not California, but South Carolina. I'm American."

"Doesn't South Carolina saddle its progeny with a loose-tongued twang?"

I thought back to my pre-college self. Before Stanford, the Bay Area, and Silicon Valley stripped the south from me. Not that I missed it. South Carolina was the place my parents lived but it wasn't fundamental to my identity the way some of peers held California or Colorado or Texas fundamental to their identities.

"Some. Doesn't Brazil do something of the same?"

"No twang with the Portuguese, *querida*." He chuckled, drew his index finger over my knuckles. "Whichever accent I had, I lost at boarding school."

I watched as he dragged a bit of naan through the remains of several dishes, blurring all sauces and spices into one savory scoop. "Tell me, Mr. Guillmand." I grinned as the name bristled over him. "How are you finding California?"

He seesawed his hand. "I got *here*, didn't I? I can handle a map."

"That's not what I meant, you unbearable man."

He shrugged, held up his hands, rested his leg between both of mine. His jeans were rough against my unadorned skin, almost overwhelming, but I kept that reaction off my face. He eyed the gulab jamun on my tray, pointed. "What's that? They smell like flowers."

"Rosewater." I tore one in half and offered it to him. He accepted, but not without curling his fingers around my wrist and eating from my hand. "It's similar to a doughnut hole, but for dessert."

He sucked the sweetness right off my fingers and he did it while the VCs gaped at us. More than one Slack channel was blowing up this evening. "Delicious," he murmured, seemingly immune to our audience.

"Mmhmm." I gulped back a groan. "If they weren't boiling hot from the fryer, I'd eat them before anything else."

Gus tilted his head to the side, brought my thumb to his lips. "I'd eat you before anything else, Miz Malik."

Join Kate Canterbary's Office Memos mailing list for occasional news and updates, as well as new release alerts, exclusive extended epilogues and bonus scenes, and cake. There's always cake.

Visit Kate's private reader group to chat about books, get early peeks at new books, and hang out with over booklovers!

If newsletters aren't your jam, follow Kate on BookBub for preorder and new release alerts.

ROUGH SKETCH

ABOUT ROUGH SKETCH

Smart, successful, and sitting pretty at the top of her game, Neera Malik has it all figured out.

Save for the small issue of Gustavo Guillmand.

The artist with a cult—and Instagram—following has a problem and it's not his preference for shirtless selfies.

No, he has an attitude problem, a minding his own business problem, an infuriatingly sexy problem.

They can't stand each other and they can't stay away from each other.

This steamy enemies-to-lovers office romance originally appeared on the Read Me Romance podcast. This edition includes a seriously extended epilogue beyond the podcast content.

For lady bosses who wear orange shoes with all their black dresses.

CHAPTER ONE

NEERA

***Scumble:** the technique of applying a thin layer of opaque to semi-opaque paint over another layer, often to mute or dull the previous layer.*

THERE WAS another bird on my desk.

A wooden one, but a bird nonetheless.

The fifth bird to find its way into my office in as many weeks.

I'd paid little mind to the first carving. It was a simple gesture, of that I was certain, and nothing more. Wasn't that what artists did? They created lovely things and shared them with people. There was nothing special about it.

But then they kept coming. No note, no explanation. Just one beautifully carved bird after another. Now I couldn't stop thinking about those blasted birds.

I had an idea who left them but I couldn't imagine *why* he was doing it, or how he gained entry into my office. It was no great mystery, and if I wanted answers, I had only to access the company's surveillance network. Snatching my tablet from my bag, I was ready to do exactly that. But my finger hovered over the icon, a beat of hesitation holding me back. Even if I confirmed my suspicions about the *who* and the *how*, the *why* would linger unresolved.

And I wanted to know *why*.

On a better day, I would've set the carving aside and gone on with my work. After spending the past week blocking and defending my boss against every asshole with an idea at the Aspen Institute's annual think tank festival, I had plenty of work waiting for me. That was on top of prepping for a business trip tomorrow, managing four pre-dawn crises, sitting through two waste-of-time meetings before noon, and enduring one unnecessary lunch meeting featuring a poor excuse for a Niçoise salad.

I was behind schedule, annoyed, and hungry.

Today wasn't one of my better days.

I set my tablet, bag, and tea on my desk and marched out of my office. As I reached my assistant's desk, I announced, "I'm stepping out for a moment."

"You just got here," Heath said.

"And I'll be stepping out now," I said, pausing at his desk. "Do you have any idea where I can find Mr. Guillmand at this hour?"

Heath tapped at his keyboard before swiveling to face me. "The artist guy?"

Swallowing a sigh, I said, "Yes." I caught myself before adding, *The one sneaking into my office and leaving sculptures all over the place.*

When it came to presiding over the company's rumor mill, Heath was unparalleled in his skill. That was half the reason he was my right hand. But I wasn't prepared to give him fresh material on Mr. Guillmand. Not until I knew why he was leaving birds at my door like some kind of praise-hungry house cat.

"Beats me," Heath replied. "Haven't seen the guy since that first day when he was introduced at the all-staff convocation last month. I hear he likes to hang out near the gardens but I've never seen him there."

"So, then," I started, drumming my fingers against my hips, "he hasn't stopped by? Hasn't asked to see me?"

"Nope."

Heath dug a purple carrot out of the feed bag he kept under his desk and bit into it. He grew his snacks at the community garden plot on the far side of the campus and foraged for wild mushrooms on the weekends. He was phenomenal at his job and knowledgeable about every facet of this company, but he was an unusual fellow. Around here, unusual was the norm. I barely registered it anymore. Quirky, eccentric types were standard issue in Silicon Valley. It often seemed that the people around here leaned into those quirks and eccentricities as if they were required elements of their personal brand.

Mushroom foraging. Cross-stitching. Throat singing. It was always something.

"Haven't seen him," Heath continued between bites. "Do you want me to call over to the studio?"

I shook my head, already moving toward the hallway. "No, thank you." I stopped, calculating the time it would take to reach the studio and garden. I hadn't formulated a course of action for handling Mr. Guillmand and wasn't certain I'd make it back to meet with the chief financial officer and his team as planned. "Reschedule my three o'clock meeting."

Not waiting for a response, I headed toward the stairs. For better or worse, my office was housed in the flagship building, the central hub of activity. It was a grand, glass-enclosed space bathed in warm California sunlight and scented with mossy green. With native trees and plants, and a softly babbling stream running through the atrium, it seemed our head-quarters grew up among nature rather than us bending the environment to our preferences. It managed to feel energetic and serene all at once. Not the ideal place for stomping or scowling.

On a better day, I would've stopped to properly greet the people who waved and called "Good afternoon" as I passed. It still wasn't that day. I could only manage a quick smile as I continued toward the doors, my hands balled into fists and my shoulders tight. I was getting to the bottom of this bird situation and resetting expectations with Mr. Guillmand.

I could manage damn near anything—a corporate coup d'état, large-scale foreign hacking attempts, lawsuits by the dozen—but something about this sculptor drove me straight over the edge.

On paper, Mr. Guillmand was exactly the type of rising star artist we wanted to celebrate and support with a yearlong residency. His accomplishments were in raw materials sculpture but several of his paintings fetched respectable prices in up-and-coming galleries. He favored striking new spins on origin stories and creation myths, his portfolio ranging from Popol Vuh, the history of the K'iche' people of the Guatemalan Highlands, to the Hopi's Fourth World story, to the Homeric Hymns. His global consciousness made sense. Born in São Paulo, boarding-school-educated in Switzerland, fine-arts-trained at UCLA—Mr. Guillmand was a citizen of the world.

It was said his father could trace his lineage to the French monarchy. At least the ones who'd escaped with their heads.

The man knew and respected culture, and despite his aristocratic upbringing, he lived an unpretentious life in northern Arizona. And his social media following numbered in the millions. It helped that half his Instagram posts featured him shirtless, smiling, splattered with clay.

Not that I'd dedicated much time to studying Mr. Guillmand's bare chest but it was difficult to vet his online presence without catching a glimpse or two. Perhaps more than that.

It didn't matter, of course. Plenty of pretty faces and washboard bellies belonged to obnoxious men who didn't know their place.

And this man, with his lurking and sneaking and bird-carving, didn't know his place. I realized it the day he arrived at the company's campus. He'd been arrogant, his arched eyebrow nothing short of contemptuous as he scanned the ten-thousand-square-foot studio built to his specifications and then turned his unimpressed gaze toward me.

It was a moment, an exchange over before it started, but it burned long enough to leave a bitter taste in my mouth. After that, I'd made a point of avoiding Mr. Guillmand's corner of the campus. Frankly, I had more important matters at hand than a condescending artist. I served as executive vice president and chief of staff to the company's founder. My days were packed with real priorities. The moods of one inconsequential man didn't rank among them.

"This isn't an effective use of my time," I murmured to myself.

I knew this, but I didn't turn back to my office. If there was one thing I did well, it was shutting down problems. I intended to do just that.

The campus was vast, many hundreds and thousands of times larger than the tiny offices we'd shared with two other start-up ventures back before our initial public offering. There were moments when I missed fighting for desk space and electrical outlets, and waging war on anyone who dared to microwave fish in the communal kitchen.

Most of all, I missed knowing every member of the team. We'd been a family in those early days, a scrappy little group willing to do whatever it took to get off the ground. With more than fifty-three thousand employees in offices all around the world now, we were a different kind of family.

And that scrappy little group was scattered to the winds. Most of the original outfit had moved onto new ventures and passion projects. Others left the company courtesy of a swift kick in the ass. Even the man who made me believe in the beauty and power of innovation, Cole McClish, had pulled up his Silicon Valley stakes and settled a world away in Maine.

It'd been Cole's idea to develop an artist-in-residence program. He argued it was small money for easy PR, and I bought that reasoning. I bought it, sold it to key stakeholders, and saw it through to fruition. It was a solid plan, but it never accounted for Mr. Guillmand's obnoxious birds invading my days.

Or his bare chest.

CHAPTER TWO

GUS

***Oiling Out:** the technique of painting a thin coat over existing layers, often to return colors to the shade when originally painted.*

I CLIMBED A TREE TODAY.

It wasn't my brightest idea, but I needed a new perspective on the hills and mountains in the distance, one I couldn't gain from the ground. If I was back home in Arizona's Rim Country, I would've hiked until I found the right vantage point.

Actually, no. Fuck that. If I was in Rim Country, I'd be scavenging for stone, clay, felled trees. I wouldn't be sketching ridgelines. I'd be doing something useful, not...whatever the fuck this was.

With a resigned sigh, I brought my charcoal back to the sketchbook. It was another in many pages of dark, smudgy scribbles. Flowers, trees, hills, clouds. Each more uninspired than the one before. If you'd asked me two months ago, I would've said my creative well knew no bottom.

That was before creating in captivity.

When the biggest, most recognizable internet firm in the world announced a residency at their California campus, complete with a hearty stipend, living quarters, and all the bells and whistles, I hadn't thought twice before applying. I never expected they'd select me. I figured they'd see my name, see my incoherent body of work, and move on to someone more suitable.

I'd made it through art school only because I hadn't known what else to do with myself and couldn't stomach working a nine-to-five. I wasn't classically trained, not really. I had no apprenticeships or residencies to my name and I'd rejected that path often. Regardless, I did well and I knew acclaim in small doses. A centerpiece sculpture in the New Mexico statehouse. Several community art installations across the Southwest. Exhibits in San Francisco and New York. A revolving collection featured at a new hotel in Vegas.

I made my way on my terms and that was essential.

But a slim part of me wanted this, wanted the stamp of approval. No matter how often artists said they did it for the craft, we also did it for the love. The adulation. It bit like a bug and the venom hooked you just as quick as it sucked the life out of you.

That venom had me up a tree in Silicon Valley, staring off at the natural world while my fingers scratched out the shape of the Santa Cruz Mountains. The lines started out soft, almost downy. Lamb's wool in shades of green, yellow, brown. Nothing like the Kaibab Plateau or Buckskin Gulch or the raw magnitude of the Mogollon Rim.

But I had to do this. I had to stretch my fingers, translate shapes into stories. I'd draw my way out of the driest spell in my thirty-six years, and eventually, I'd find a path back to the beginning. If I could do that, I'd learn how to create again. Even if I had to do it from inside a fishbowl.

I was betting on this. I couldn't stare at the walls or walk in circles anymore. I had to get out of my head and move my hands. I never went longer than a month without a new project taking over my existence. It always went that way—until now. An idea tickled the back of my brain until it consumed my every breath and thought. After submitting to that cycle for more than twenty years, I didn't know how to function without it.

I would've been rocking in a corner right now, scratching my skin off like a junkie in need of a fix, if not for a voluptuous, whip-cracking executive vice president. One frigid look from her and I felt the fire kindling inside me. *Fuck that.* It wasn't kindling. It was a goddamn wildfire. She brought to mind steel-tipped arrows and lush camellias and a dozen other contradictions.

And doves. Graceful, regal doves.

When I'd rifled through the warehouse-sized supply room after she deposited me in the studio on the first day of my residency, I hadn't intended to sculpt anything. But I'd happened upon some pale birch and the magic took charge. Two hours later, I had a dove in my hands.

Since then, I'd fever-dreamed a small flock of birds to life. Goldfinch, chickadee, sparrow, meadowlark, even a nice, plump dove. I'd decided it meant absolutely nothing. I wasn't sculpting birds that reminded me of her in peculiar ways for any profound reason. Muses came in all shapes and forms—music, weather, nature, women—and they went just as quickly. None of them meant a damn thing.

Save for the small issue of me gifting her those birds. All previous muses served *me* and my needs. I'd never served them. I didn't intend to change my ways now.

Except...I already was. I was crafting *by* her and *for* her, and that was the last fucking thing I wanted.

I shrugged off that inconvenient realization and went back to my mountain range. I had several pages filled with increasingly twisted interpretations of the geography. I couldn't sketch anything without traveling down a winding path and then turning it inside out. As far as my mind's eye was concerned, nothing was what it seemed.

These mountains were born of a blood feud, rock against rock, one rising up as the other bowed down. The Santa Cruz range stood as a tribute to the victor but also a reminder of its strength. The cost of that strength was in its scars. The terrible, rippled lesion of the San Andreas Fault served as a reminder of the fight.

Everything was a product of a long, blistering history. I couldn't see it any other way.

An airplane sliced my line of sight, its roar echoed by my growl at the interference. I glanced down at the sketch. The page was a mess of anthropomorphic earth at war with itself, line and smudge void of purpose and composition. If there was any vision here, I couldn't find it. Burning the whole damn thing would be the kindest solution by far.

I pocketed the charcoal and closed my sketchbook. "That's some real dog shit," I mumbled to myself.

I ran the back of my hand over my forehead as I frowned at the sunlight blanketing the cloudless sky. Today was the warmest since my arrival in early June, but a hot day in the Bay Area had nothing on Arizona's heat. I missed the wilderness and my place in it, but I could enjoy this temperate weather.

Then, I saw her in the distance, her dark skin shining in the afternoon sun like burnished bronze. She zipped down the sidewalk like a hummingbird starved for nectar. *Oh, fuck. A hummingbird.* "Speak of the fuckin' devil."

Miz Malik. She introduced herself that way, like some kind of prim, old-world maiden.

But there was nothing prim or maidenly about her. She wanted to play the part of the proper businesswoman, but heaven help me, she failed miserably. Anyone with lips like that would. Full, plump, dusky pink. Always pursed, as if she was biting that silver tongue of hers.

Luscious. Rubens was rolling in his grave and cursing the limits of his natural life for missing the opportunity to paint this voluptuous woman.

It was too bad she was so fucking insufferable.

The lady didn't know how to slow down to walk. If she'd ever stopped to smell the roses, I was certain she'd follow it up with a performance evaluation on the quality of their blooms.

But that hair. Dark and silky, just long enough to brush her shoulders. It shone like obsidian and spilled like a waterfall. My fingers itched to stroke those strands, feel it sliding between my fingers, carve an ode to it in stone.

I should've stayed in the tree. I should've kept my distance. Should've drunk in the sight of her and then attacked some wood.

I didn't.

Instead, I swung down from the tree and landed on the grass with a thud. "Good afternoon, Miz Malik."

The simple black dress she wore, the one designed for the singular purpose of showcasing her hips, defined entrapment. I couldn't stop myself from tracing the lines of her body with my gaze. I figured the dress hailed from a boutique for serious, reserved businesswomen, a shop that knew only the coolest hues of the color wheel. She didn't look serious or reserved. She looked like loosely restrained sin and the shiny persimmon shoes she wore only validated that. There was brightness and warmth inside her, but she kept it on a leash.

"What brings you out of the ivory tower?" I swiveled my head from side to side. "And where are your minions?"

She skittered to a stop, her hand pressed to her chest as she blinked between me and the tree.

"I—pardon me." She gestured to the oak. "Did you climb that tree, Mr. Guillmand?"

I tucked my sketchbook under my arm, dipped my hands into my pockets. "Yes, Miz Malik, I sure did."

She shook her head in tiny, tiny movements. All hummingbird. "Yes and—why?"

"Why not?" I shrugged. "What are trees for if not getting a look at the world from their vantage point?"

She shifted the hand on her chest to her forehead, murmuring, "That's a logical fallacy."

I turned away, wandering over the grass as she stared after me. "You never did answer my question," I called. She huffed out a snarl as I continued walking. "What are you doing out here on a nice day when you could be inside with the machines?"

I sensed her staring after me, a hot, unyielding glare. Here I was, walking away from her when most people devoured every word and bent eyebrow she offered. It was several minutes—excruciating minutes —before she abandoned the structure and comfort of the sidewalk, but even as the grass rustled under her steps, I still felt the heat of her gaze.

"And what are you doing out here when you could be in your studio? The one we designed to your exacting specifications, sir?"

On the other edge of this knoll sat a cluster of yucca and sacred datura. Like anything truly wild, they grew in disorderly clumps. I wanted to explore the ways they attracted and repelled each other and I wanted Miz Malik to follow me. I wanted her to see this because it was real and true and—fuck me—she needed some of that in her life. I couldn't say how I knew that but I did, as well as I knew I wanted her knees stained with grass, and dirt under her nails, and her dress—that proper, boring dress—ripped and wrinkled in the best ways.

As she came to a halt beside me, she announced, "I'd like to speak with you."

Her hands were on her hips and her lips were pulled tight, and goddamn me, I wanted to taste the cove where her neck met her shoulder. I couldn't pretend I'd be satisfied with one taste. Somehow, in the convoluted maze of human consciousness, I was able to find her desirable and aggravating all at once.

I wanted to fuck her and then I wanted to tell her to fuck off.

"Go ahead," I answered, my attention squarely on the yucca. "Speak."

"Would it be too much trouble for you to look at me while I speak?"

With all the impatience in my body, I shifted to face her. "Go on, Miz Malik," I drawled, an eyeroll tossed in for good measure. "You have my full attention."

She nodded in response, piercing me with another sharp stare. "I'm curious, Mr. Guillmand—"

"Gus, please," I interrupted.

"Gus," she repeated with a sigh, her shoulders rising and falling at the concession.

"Why are you so formal? No one else around here insists on the Mister and Ms. business. Should I curtsy too? Is that how you'd like me?"

She offered no reaction beyond a slow blink and that only agitated me further. This woman. She only bit so much of my bait.

"Mr. Gui—I mean, Gus," she said, her eyes fluttering shut as she corrected herself. "From what I hear, you aren't spending much time in your studio. Is there an issue with the space?"

"It's fine. Is there an issue with me spending time outside the studio or am I required to stay at my desk all day like the other worker bees?"

She waved at the open space around us. "By all means, enjoy the grounds."

"But spend more time in the studio," I added, crossing my arms. "Right? That's what you're trying to tell me. I'm on the clock and you want me churning out one masterpiece after another while the citizens of this strange corporate colony watch. You don't want an artist-in-residence, you want a dancing monkey."

"There is nothing further from the truth, Mr. Guillmand," she snapped, slicing her hand through the air as she spoke. "We appreciate and admire your talent. We want you to be comfortable. Even if that means spending most of your time swinging from the branches. My only concern is whether you have everything you need."

"Is that what got you out of the office, Miz Malik? Your *concern* for me? For my *needs?*"

"No, that's not the only thing." She glanced at the wildflowers, regarding them as if she'd never encountered such a sight in the hermetically sealed existence she called life. "I'm curious why you've gone out of your way to leave birds in my office."

I took a step toward her. "Is there a problem?"

She took a step toward me. "Is there a point?"

"Isn't that what I'm supposed to do here?" I stared down into her coffee-dark eyes. "Bring art to the people. Wasn't that the high-level objective of this gig?"

Another slow blink up at me, and then, "You are not required to literally deliver art to individual staff members. I apologize if that was unclear."

I scratched the back of my neck, humming. "Ah. I see. My misunderstanding."

"Very well."

Her gaze was locked on my eyes, but for a split second it flitted to my lips. It was nothing more than a glimpse but it struck me like a challenge —and an opening. Without allowing myself time to examine my actions, I reached out and curled my hand around her elbow. Heat coursed through me, a flash of fire a thousand times more powerful than anything else in the world.

She glanced down at my hold on her arm, up at me. "I'll leave the birds with my assistant. I'll ask him to work with the appropriate teams to get the pieces on display. If you need any help gathering the others— or whatever you've given staff members—we'll allocate someone with extra capacity this week."

She didn't know. She was the only one and she didn't know.

She gazed at my grip on her arm again, then over my shoulder, toward the office buildings. "Now that we've cleared these matters up, I'll be on my way."

I didn't get a chance to reply. She shook out of my hold and walked off with her persimmon shoes and plump lips, and didn't grant me even a passing glance.

This fucking woman.

CHAPTER THREE

NEERA

__Anamorphosis:__ a visual perspective technique that yields a distorted image of the work's subject when viewed from the typical viewpoint. However, it is employed such that when viewed from a specific angle, or reflected in a curved mirror, the distortion disappears and the image in the picture appears as expected.

I WASN'T one for knocking knees. I didn't wobble, I didn't waver. Few things struck fear in me.

But it wasn't fear that had me marching away from Gus Guillmand on unsteady feet. No, it was anger. True, kettle-whistling anger. That man was infuriating with his tree-climbing and word-twisting. It was anger and it was exasperation too. I wore a lot of hats around here, but riding herd on the artist-in-residence wasn't supposed to be one of them.

It was anger and exasperation, and an unwelcome jolt of attraction. That wouldn't do. I would *not*. I couldn't lust after someone like Mr. Guillmand, someone insufferable and argumentative and—and distressingly sexy.

I *could*, but I wouldn't.

It was anger, exasperation, attraction—rather unwelcomed—and a complete inability to focus on my work for more than three and a half minutes that had me clicking my online profile to *out of office* and packing my things well before my regular quitting time.

I told Heath I had some personal business to handle this afternoon and he smiled and nodded while munching a dandelion—leaf, stem, and flower. If I was a betting woman, I'd say the office would be brimming with theories as to whether I was leaving—whether by new employment or terminal illness—before tomorrow morning's first chai.

I tucked my hair back, put my earbuds in, and clicked on a podcast before boarding the company's commuter bus. Around here—and other civilized parts of the world—earbuds served as a clear Do Not Disturb sign. Today, it saved me from collegial conversation and mulling over my unlikely reaction to Mr. Guillmand.

Except I couldn't stop thinking about him. His grasp on my arm throbbed like a burn and I was hot everywhere. Our conversations were stuck on repeat in my mind. For the first time in my professional life, I was doubting the way I handled a situation. It was unclear to me how I could've better handled Mr. Guillmand, although one corner of my mind had *ideas* about *handling* him.

When the bus rolled into the Redwood City station, I'd resolved nothing. I was tired from all the emotional footwork and frustrated with myself for allowing the issue to consume this much of my day when topics of far greater value demanded my attention.

I tapped open a car service app as my colleagues disembarked. I was a ten minute walk from home but that wasn't where I wanted to go. I was in need of calm and comfort—and a mental reset—and right now, that meant crossing a bridge and crawling along the 580 toward West Berkeley.

THE CAFETERIA-STYLE RESTAURANT reminded me of Penn Station at rush hour. It was unbelievably loud and the crowd seemed to move as a collective body, swarming the front counter, surging toward open seats, scrambling to collect trays piled high with authentic Indian street food.

I loved it.

I gained as much peace from the atmosphere as I did the food. Perhaps that was a product of this great crowd and the anonymity that came with it. No one cared about me, my title, my connections, not when there was a fresh order of gulab jamun waiting for them.

I enjoyed my work and I was comfortable in my role but it was refreshing to live a moment or two without those pieces preceding me. *Yes*, that was it. Some comfort food and a reprieve from the world I managed, that was what I needed. Today's loss of equilibrium was a result of a busy week on top of a travel-heavy month on top of a turbulent year.

Mr. Guillmand was the unlikely product of my overdue need for some intense self-care. Nothing more.

One of the clerks behind the counter raised her hand, signaling for another customer. The waiting crowd heaved forward and an elbow connected with my upper arm. I covered the sting with my palm as I glanced to the side, in search of the offending elbow.

But it wasn't an elbow I found. It was a great wall of man, one barely enclosed in a black t-shirt, dark jeans, scuffed boots. One who seemed intent on invading every last inch of my world. I eyed him up and down, arching my eyebrow at his slicked-back hair and clenched hands. "Mr. Guillmand."

"Miz Malik." He loosened his fists and stretched his fingers, then shoved his hands into his pockets. "Of all the curry joints in all the towns in the Bay Area, what're the odds you'd walk into this one?"

"I could ask you the same," I replied, still rubbing my arm.

He tracked the movement, his dark brows knitting together as understanding flashed in his eyes. He slipped his fingers under my palm, pulled my hand away. But he didn't release me. He held on. "I'm sorry," he whispered, covering my bicep with his free hand. His thumb stroked my skin over my sleeve, his touch gentler than I'd imagined possible.

And I'd imagined. I didn't want to admit to myself—to anyone—but I couldn't stop imagining those charcoal-darkened fingers exploring my body. Leaving marks on my skin.

Forcing a smile, I shook free from his hold for the second time today, clasped my hands, and stepped back as far as the crowd would allow. It wasn't far. "It was an accident. Just a bump. I'm fine." I tipped my head toward the counter. "Enjoy your meal. The chole bhature is exquisite."

Mr. Guillmand hit me with a smile that could only be described as undeterred, and he edged back into my space. "Is that your order?"

"Hmm. Sometimes." I shot a glance at the menu board. I wanted a bit of everything. "Don't let me keep you, Mr. Guillmand."

He reached for my arm, curling his hand around my bicep. "Gus."

I didn't step back this time. I let him touch me and I let myself burn under that touch. "May I ask how you came to be here, in West Berkeley, *Gus*? This is a rather great distance from the campus and your living quarters."

His fingers slipped up the inside of my arm as he gazed at me, a curious, not altogether pleased grin pulling at his lips. "Slater Somethingoranother recommended it. The social media guy, the one who takes all the fake candid photos. He insisted I get out of Silicon Valley and he hooked me up with a list of local spots." His shoulders lifted and the gesture pushed the pad of his thumb into my soft tissue. Schooling my expression took serious work when I wanted to moan into his touch. "This is the only one I hadn't tried yet."

"Mr. Wend. Smart man, good taste." I gestured toward the counter when a clerk called for the next customer. His hand fell away. "Now, if you'll excuse me."

I wasn't excused for long. The neighboring clerk blindly beckoned for a customer and Mr. Guillmand stepped up beside me. We ordered separately but I couldn't stop myself from stealing glances at his profile. The way he flattened his palms on the counter drew my attention to the leather cuff on his left wrist. It looked worn, scarred but soft. I wanted to touch it, to run my fingertips over the raw edge and follow it along the topography of his wrist.

Ugh, no. Why, Neera, why?

I needed to recharge, not gain intimate knowledge of his body. I wanted an illogical smorgasbord of comfort food that would make my mother simultaneously cringe and roll her eyes: biryani, dahi puri, and uttapam, not an arrogant pain in my ass.

And yet I studied the sculptor's big, capable hands and asked, "Would you care to join me, Mr. Guillmand?"

A smug grin split his face, brightened his dark eyes. "I thought you'd never ask."

It was common courtesy. He was a visitor and a new member of the team, and it was common courtesy to share a meal with him given these circumstances. I was being a professional. That was all.

We stood shoulder to shoulder, waiting for our meals. We didn't speak, didn't touch. To my credit, I didn't retrieve my phone and fall down a fake-busy hole. No, I kept Mr. Guillmand in my peripheral vision as I gazed at the pickup window. It was better like this. I didn't hide, didn't prevaricate. I stared down tension until it cooled...or boiled over.

Our order numbers were called one after another. When I reached for my tray, Mr. Guillmand held up a hand, blocking me. "I've got this. You lead the way and I'll follow."

I spent no time considering the meaning behind his words even though I was certain I'd find plenty, instead occupying myself with picking my way through the eatery. Two seats opened up on the end of a long communal table and I quickened my pace to get there before anyone else.

I heard his coarse laugh over my shoulder as I hung my bag on the back of the chair. "Amused, Mr. Guillmand?"

He set our trays on the table. "Impressed. You're a vulture."

I brushed my hands together, glanced at the people seated nearby, sniffed. "What a vivid comparison."

"Like I said"—he passed behind me, his hand ghosting over my lower back, the pressure just enough to send my belly flipping—"impressed."

I sat, busied myself with unfolding my paper napkin and spreading it over my lap. My companion surveyed the diners around us, his gaze settling on the quartet of junior associates beside us from the venture capital firm Koos Blacke. They'd kept up their conversation about this fall's bonito run but made no attempt to hide their eavesdropping.

That was how I knew they were junior associates. Full associates and partners had perfected the art of invisible information gathering. Not that this meal offered information worth gathering, even for the Valley's virulent rumor mill.

"It's curious that we bumped into each other here," Gus commented.

"If you're implying anything other than happenstance, I'd suggest you reconsider."

"It wouldn't be the first time you've come looking for me today," he replied.

"That wasn't my intent this evening." I stared at him, my expression even. "How are you finding the Bay Area, Mr. Guillmand?"

He dropped his forearms on the table, hung his head, groaned. "You can't call me that."

My brows arched up. "And why not?"

His entire body sighed. Shoulders, arms, lips, chest. It moved like a skipped stone rippling over a pond. "My father is Mr. Guillmand." He focused on organizing the small plates on his tray. "I can't hear that name without my stomach dropping to my toes and turning around to figure out how the hell he's here when he's supposed to be back home in Morumbi."

"Is your relationship with him difficult?"

Gus shook his head. "Not difficult. Different."

"I would imagine being descended from the French monarchy does that to a bloodline."

He hit me with a flat stare. "So, you've heard about that."

I answered with a quick shrug and, "Did you think we'd bring you on without an extensive background check?"

"No. Of course not. But I didn't think *extensive* meant three hundred years of family history, and I didn't think you'd take time from your very busy, very important schedule to get my dirt."

I tipped my chin up. "I prefer to know who is in the building."

"Oh, yeah?" he challenged. "You review background checks and CVs for every intern? What about the guy who works the omelet station in the cafeteria? Or the lady who cleans your office? You know all of them, Miz Malik? You know their stories?"

"You're referring to Ido and Marian? Yes, I know them. I can't say the same for every intern as we have more than five thousand of them in offices around the world. However, I make a point of acquainting myself with the backgrounds of the interns on campus."

Gus dug into his meal, his gaze still fixed on me as he ate. Eventually, he asked, "Is this your way of telling me I'm not special, Miz Malik?"

"Do you need to be special?"

He bobbed his head as he speared a few chickpeas. "Doesn't hurt."

"Mmhmm. I see the royal bloodline runs thick with you."

He choked out a brittle laugh. "Says the kingmaker."

Again, my brows winged up. He knew something of my history as the right hand to brilliant leaders, as the second-in-command who consistently helped the first shine in spite of themselves. This man was robbing me of my poker face and I didn't care for it one bit. "It seems you've done some background study of your own."

Gus reached across the table, drummed his fingertips on the back of my wrist. "You like that, don't you? You like when someone digs up your dirt. You like being noticed. *Explored*."

I gave him a disinterested frown and returned to my biryani. What had I been thinking? What made me believe I could share a meal with this man and his arrogance and—and his hands?

We ate in silence for several minutes before he said, "You found my comment offensive."

"Not offensive. Rather, needlessly self-important."

"And that's an issue for you?" When I blinked at him, he continued, "I've been here for less than two months and I know everyone in the Valley is needlessly self-important. Compared to most of these motherfuckers, I'm Humble Henry."

"And yet you're the only one inserting yourself into my day and leaving a flock of birds behind."

He grimaced, cut his gaze to the VCs beside us. "Forgive me for doing my job in a manner that fails to align with your specific vision, Miz Malik."

I was prepared to volley back but stopped myself. My attention was my greatest asset and I wasn't paying it to this petty debate. "Let's set these issues aside for now. We can share one meal without contention. I'm sure of it."

He blinked at me as if he was surprised by this request. "Certainly."

After a thorny pause, I asked, "How is your meal?"

He bobbed his head as he savored a bite of dosa. "Excellent. Best I've had in—I don't know—years. And I think that was in Mexico City."

"Mexico City has amazing Indian food." I hummed in agreement.

"Whenever I'm traveling, I try to sneak in stops at local Indian restaurants. I have an ongoing samosa study."

I watched a warm, cheerful smile brighten his face and crinkle his eyes. "What's this samosa study involve?"

I pressed the edge of my fork into the uttapam, suddenly and irrationally shy about my multi-continent cataloging of Indian cuisine. "I'm not sure whether it's an atavistic desire or callback to my childhood." I paused, studied my tray. "We didn't eat out when I was a child. We didn't have the money for restaurants and my parents didn't enjoy the local favorites. It took them twenty years to fully embrace Lowcountry barbeque. But on special occasions, my parents loaded us into the car and we'd drive to different cities in the area. Greenville, Spartanburg, Asheville. Athens, once. We'd always go out for Indian and meet the Desi people in that area. Even if they didn't hail from the same region as my parents or speak the same dialect or cook the same ways, they were our people, our extended family. And now, well, I just—I tend to judge cities by the quality of their samosas...and other dishes."

He made a sound. A rumbly, growly, throaty sound. Somehow, I knew it was one of approval. "Yeah? Any surprises?"

"I'm not sure about surprises." I sampled the uttapam. I loved these savory pancakes topped with tomatoes and onions. That they constituted a traditional South Indian breakfast mattered little to me. If they were crisp and fresh, I'd eat them any time of day. "There are Desi people all around the world and many of them make superb food." I gave him a pointed nod. "Just as there are French and Brazilian people everywhere and some of them choose to carry on their cultures in the most delicious ways."

"Point taken." He drummed my wrist again. This time, he went to the trouble of dragging his fingertips over the back of my hand and staring into my eyes while he did. *So damn arrogant.* "But I still want to know your favorites."

I thought for a moment. "Albuquerque. Egypt, outside Cairo. Beijing. Then again, there are no bad meals in Beijing."

"Haven't been."

I tipped my chin down. "Now, that's surprising. I figured you'd gone everywhere worth going."

Shaking his head, he said, "South and Central America, sure. Western Europe, yes. Portions of Africa, mostly northern. As far as Asia and much of North America, I have a lot of ground to cover. I don't know much outside the Southwest."

I pointed my fork at him. It was rude but I found myself wanting to be rude with him, just a bit. "You don't have an accent."

He pressed his tongue to the inside of his cheek. "Neither do you."

"I'm American. I grew up here." I waved at the table. "Not California, but South Carolina."

"Doesn't South Carolina saddle its progeny with a loose-tongued twang?"

I thought back to my pre-college self. Before Stanford, the Bay Area, and Silicon Valley stripped the South from me. Not that I missed it. South Carolina was the place my parents lived but it wasn't fundamental to my identity the way some of my peers held California or Colorado or Texas fundamental to their identities.

"Some. Doesn't Brazil do something of the same?"

"No twang with the Portuguese, *fofinho*." He chuckled, drew his index finger over my knuckles. "Whichever accent I had, I lost at boarding school."

I watched as he dragged a bit of naan through the remains of several dishes, blurring all sauces and spices into one savory scoop. "Tell me, Mr. Guillmand." I grinned as the name bristled over him. "How are you finding California?"

He seesawed his hand. "I got *here*, didn't I? I can handle a map."

"That's not what I meant, you unbearable man."

He shrugged and held up his palms while he nested his leg between both of mine. His jeans were rough against my unadorned skin, almost overwhelming, but I kept that reaction off my face. He eyed the gulab jamun on my tray, pointed. "What's that? They smell like flowers."

"Rosewater. It's not typical but it's my favorite." I tore one in half and offered it to him. He accepted, but not without curling his fingers around my wrist and eating from my hand. "It's similar to a doughnut hole, but for dessert."

He sucked the sweetness right off my fingers and he did it while the VCs gaped at us. More than one Slack channel was blowing up this evening. "Delicious," he murmured, seemingly immune to our audience. Not that I cared much for them either.

"Mmhmm." I gulped back a groan. "If they weren't boiling hot from the fryer, I'd eat them before anything else."

Gus tilted his head to the side, brought my thumb to his lips. "I'd eat you before anything else, Miz Malik."

CHAPTER FOUR

GUS

Alla Prima: the act of creating a painting in a single sitting, often without any preparation or underpainting.

SHE'D FLITTED AWAY like a sandpiper on the shore. It happened faster than the blink of an eye, but she'd jerked her hand from my grasp, jolted out of her seat, and offered some boilerplate bullshit about enjoying the meal we'd shared and seeing me around the campus but needing to excuse herself right fucking now.

All while the taste of her skin lingered on my tongue.

And then she'd left.

The nonstop crowds prevented me from tracking her movement through the restaurant, but even if I'd wanted to follow her, I couldn't pry myself from this chair. If the heaviness in my cock wasn't enough to keep me seated, the weight of the world as it shifted on my shoulders was.

I wasn't one to process thoughts or emotions with words and I didn't have them now. But Miz Malik's departure left me with the definite sense I'd met my match.

I'd met her and she was delicious.

Slumped back, I folded my arms over my chest and scanned the crowd again. I'd missed the colorful art on the walls when I'd first arrived. I'd been busy gazing at the raven-haired beauty who'd appeared like an out-of-reach apparition intended to punish me for my basest desires.

Then she'd all but purred under my touch and I couldn't stop. Couldn't separate myself from her skin, even as that punishment closed in, loomed large. I'd scraped my teeth over her thumb and asked for it, damn near whispered, "Give me your worst."

I hadn't noticed signs for the adjoining spice market either. I'd noticed nothing but her dark, luminous skin and the way my palms pulsed with the boundless desire to touch her until I knew every secret her body would share. And I still wanted it. I wanted it all.

As if drawn by my true north, I jolted out of my seat and picked my way through the eatery until the crowd fell away and the orderly rows of a small grocery opened before me.

I found her pushing up on her toes to reach a jar on a high shelf. Her calves lengthened, the hem of her dress shifted up her glorious thighs. The backs of her persimmon shoes fell away from her heels as she stretched.

"Mr. Guillmand," she murmured. She didn't bother glancing in my direction. Didn't look away from the spices before her. "I see you've returned."

"Miz Malik," I said, her name nothing more than a sigh. "I believe you've been caught."

"Then," she panted, trying once more to grab the jar, "come catch me."

One urgent stride put me behind her but it was another step that aligned her full backside with my crotch. My hand found her hip, squeezed that supple curve. I traced the length of her arm from shoulder to fingertip as I tapped the jar. "This one?"

She nodded, hummed.

I retrieved the saffron, pressed the glass between her breasts. Her body stiffened but she allowed another hum, another nod. "Yes," she breathed. "That."

"You're such a good girl," I said, my words little more than a hiss as I spoke directly to the tender skin below her ear. "So fucking good, aren't you?"

"Yes," she whispered, her head bobbing once.

That was all she'd offer. A whisper, a nod. Nothing else. She didn't allow herself much but she allowed me far more. And now that I was here, I intended to take everything I wanted. Not because I was an egotistical bastard—despite Miz Malik's impression of me—but because she wanted me to take everything she had to give.

Hell, if she'd meant to cut me off, she would've left. She wouldn't be here, glaring at spices, *waiting for me*.

"Neera." My fingertips grazed her torso and found her nipple, stiff through her dress, and—if I wasn't mistaken—the hard nub of a barbell too. "Can you give me a single reason why I shouldn't pull up this skirt and taste your cunt right here?"

She swiveled her head from side to side, wiggled her fingers at her side. If my words stunned her, it didn't show. "None that I can think of."

I shifted my other hand from her hip, laced my fingers through hers. I placed her hand on her skirt, over the vee between her legs. Together, we stroked and circled until her head fell back on my shoulder and that hum was a beautiful moan. She rocked her ass against my aching cock. "Don't say things you don't mean, sparrow."

She fired a searing glance over her shoulder.

I had to mentally negotiate my way out of biting her neck for that look. Biting her neck, unbuttoning my fly, fucking her while a wall of spices crashed around us. I saw it in brutal oil paint like the exquisite disaster we were, a field of broken glass at our feet and a cloud of color and scent rising around us.

"Good girls don't get fucked in public." I licked my way up her neck, my face buried in her hair. If her cunt tasted anything like her neck, I wanted to drown between her legs. "Good girls don't let the world see them come."

She rocked against our joined hands and touching her over her clothes was no longer adequate. I needed much more. "You're baiting me."

"You're damn right I am, Miz Malik." I bunched her skirt in my fist, rucking it up inch by inch. "Is it working?"

A laugh rolled through her body before it burst over her lips. "I believe you know it is, Gus."

The portion of my brain dedicated to rational judgment quieted to a whisper as the hedonistic portion let out a primal roar. "Don't you ever want to do something bad, little sparrow?"

She dipped her chin, watching as the front of her skirt lifted just enough for our fingers to meet the damp fabric of her panties.

Anyone could've walked by.

Anyone could've heard her sigh in pleasure as we worked her clit.

Anyone could've watched my cock spreading the plump curve of her ass.

Anyone.

And she wanted it—*needed it*—that way.

"How do good girls feel about getting their fuck in the back of a Jeep?"

CHAPTER FIVE

NEERA

***Sfumato:** a technique in painting or drawing where the use of fine shading creates delicate, imperceptible transitions between colors and tones.*

"DON'T YOU EVER WANT," he started, his breath whispering over my ear, "to do something bad, little sparrow?"

I was nodding, purring in response before I could think better of it. And why did I have to think better of it? I did not.

"How do good girls feel about getting their fuck in the back of a Jeep?"

Again, I didn't think. Couldn't think. "I'd enjoy that now, please."

His index finger edged under my panties, between my folds. He thrummed my clit hard enough to cross my eyes and buckle my knees. I reached for him, anchoring myself with my fist tight around his belt. "What then?" he asked, his words rough, strained. "You ride this dick a time or two"—he pinched my clit between his thick fingers and I choked back a sobbing scream—"and then you're done?"

"Let's not get ahead of ourselves. I've only agreed to riding your dick once. I'll see how that goes before planning an encore."

His teeth pressed into my shoulder, just shy of biting the skin through my dress. He growled out a sigh, saying, "I'm parked around the corner, Neera. Let's go."

Gus took a step to the side, one arm locked around my waist with my dress in hand, the other working my clit. "Have you forgotten we're in a rather indelicate position?"

His fingers stroked my seam just enough to fray the last of my nerves. I was throbbing, bursting, *dying* with need.

"Haven't forgotten."

A small laugh tumbled past my lips. "If I'm to exit this establishment with you, I must ask that you release me."

"Is that the proper thing to do? Or is that what you want?" Before I could reply, Gus continued, "Because I think you want me to strip you down, spread you out on one of those long tables back in the restaurant, and fuck you until everyone—*everyone*—knows you're not even close to a good girl."

Without conscious thought, my body tightened against his words. "Yes."

Gus tugged my hand away from my center, sucked my fingers into his mouth. Before I could react to the sensation of his tongue against the pads of my fingers, he delivered a sharp slap—then a second, a third—to my pussy. The startled gasp I heard must've belonged to me but I couldn't process any thoughts beyond the need vibrating through my body. The clench in my core was real, spine-bending pain and I knew I'd do anything, anything at all to soothe it.

"Come now, little sparrow." Gus straightened my dress and ran his hands down my sides, raking his fingers over my nipples as he went. "You might be delirious from the idea of an audience but I'm not ready to share that much of you with that many people. Not yet."

Whether the walk to Gus's car was long or short, I couldn't say. I wasn't sure where I'd left the jar of saffron. The only sound between us was the slap of my flats against the sidewalk and the hum of the city around us. The summer sun was still high in the sky but I couldn't say whether the air was hot, cold, or wet because I was melting from the inside out. All I knew was the aching desire to be filled by him...and to be seen. I didn't want to examine that urge closely, didn't want to uncover its true meaning. But I wanted to feel filthy and depraved and—and gorgeously used.

By him. The man who irritated the hell out of me with his arrogance. The man who invented the art of condescending to me by saying little more than my name. *This* man. He was the one I entrusted with a desire so fresh and raw that I didn't know whether it'd lived dormant in me all this time or it was a product of his presence.

"This is what you want?" Gus stopped on the sidewalk, opened the black Jeep's back door, crowded me against it. His lips mapped my neck, jaw, cheeks, mouth. The hard line of his arousal bumped against my belly.

A breath caught in my throat and my entire body wavered as an emphatic *Yes* pulsed through my veins. But I steadied myself and hit him with a chilly stare. "Are your eyes bigger than your cock, Mr. Guillmand?"

"You get those panties off or I'll rip them off," he answered, his thumb and forefinger busy twisting my pierced nipple through my dress. "I will rip them right off you, sparrow."

I slipped out of his hold and into the Jeep, intentionally forcing my skirt up my thighs as I scooted over the bench until the lacy purple peeked out. "Yes, it does seem like you'll need to do that."

Gus glanced down the street, rocked back on his heels, and rubbed a hand over his brow as he murmured, "Fuuuuuck."

Then he lunged for me, his hands fisting around the delicate fabric and pulling it taut between my folds. The band cut into my hips, certain to leave marks, but I couldn't care about anything beyond the unchained gleam in his eyes. That was for *me*.

With nothing more than my panties as leverage, he dragged my body closer to the open door. Still rooted on the street, he bent over me and traced his nose along the waist of my panties. He whispered to my skin in a language I didn't understand and shredded the lace in one brutal tear.

When the cool evening air met my swollen skin, a shiver twisted through my body. "Gus." It came out as a pant, as a plea, and he required no further direction. His mouth covered my mound, sucking and licking until I was there, I was *right there*.

Until he stopped.

"No." His gaze skated up my body as my breath came in ragged, heaving pants. "No. Not yet."

I glared at him. "You are so fucking smug."

He straightened, tucked a thumb in his pocket, brought his knee to the seat. "I love the way *fucking* sounds on your lips." He climbed inside the vehicle, slammed the door behind him. "Will you say it again? Will you say it while you're on my dick?"

I reached for his belt buckle, careful to scrape my nails over the ridge of his erection in the process. He let out a howl. "Say please."

"I will." He pushed his jeans down once the belt and button-fly were loose. No underwear for Mr. Guillmand. With his hard cock in hand, he stared down at me. "I'll say, 'Please, Neera, get on my dick and ride it like you own it.'" He stroked his hand down his length once, twice, and then settled in the center of the bench seat. He patted his thighs and beckoned to me. "Now, sparrow."

I skimmed the ruined panties down my legs and crawled onto Gus's lap—as much as any full-figured adult woman could crawl in a back seat. I leaned against him, my back to his chest. His hands found my waist as I reached for his cock, dragged it through my slit. His answering growl was everything I needed to sink down onto him.

"Jesus. Fuck. Neera. Fuck." His fingertips brushed the tender skin below my belly button, moving back and forth. "*Fuck*, Neera, this cunt is going to kill me."

I found my balance by gripping the front seats but I couldn't find my breath. Not when I was full beyond belief. "Fine way to die," I managed.

"The finest, Miz Malik." His hips shot up, spearing me hard. "Let me hear you say it, sparrow. Tell me how much you love riding this dick."

Words were lost to me. They were gone, right along with my oxygen, my thoughts, my contempt for this endlessly arrogant man. All I could do was submit to the commands issued by his hold on my hips.

"You'll say it. Before this night is over, you'll say it," he whispered.

"Does your pride know no limit?"

Using the front seats as leverage, I sank down, grinding against him. Taking him inside me this way brought stars to my eyes. It straddled the line between pleasure and pain, but the strangled cry he choked out was worth it.

"I don't know," he replied. "Maybe you should spend the rest of the night searching for it."

He shifted his hands, sliding one between my legs and cupping my breast with the other. His touch was unbelievable, each pass of his thumb over my nipple sending a current of electricity straight to my center. The sounds of slapping skin against the chorus of sighs and grunts and the fireball of energy gathered inside me made me desperate to find my release—and his.

But I wasn't certain I could.

My body was enthusiastic about this activity. I was as turned on as I'd ever been. Gus met all of my most important criteria. The boxes were checked and this was the sex of gilded legends but I wasn't convinced I'd cross the finish line. Not without some additional intervention.

Huffing out a sigh, I said, "I'd prefer you spend the next five minutes using that ego of yours finding my orgasm."

"Look up, sparrow." Gus dragged his hand up my neck, lifting my head from where it hung between my shoulders. "Let them see you."

Two vehicles ahead, a man stood beside his car, his hand paused near the door handle.

He was watching us. Having sex. He was watching us having sex.

He was watching *me*.

"That's it," Gus growled. "That's what you need. Take it."

Everything inside me pulsed, a hard, heavy *whomp* that banished all doubt of getting mine. I was close—close enough to feel the first wisps of myself unraveling.

"He's watching you get fucked, Neera, and you *love it*."

I made eye contact with the man on the street. I didn't look away. "I—I—I don't know."

"You love it," Gus repeated. "He's watching you ride my dick like you were born for it."

"Like I own it."

Gus hummed in agreement. "He's watching *you*. He knows what you're getting, sparrow. He doesn't have to see your tits or your pretty cunt to know. And he knows it's all mine."

I was wet beyond belief. My inner thighs, Gus's hand, his cock—everything was soaked and slippery. His fingers tugged at the bar through my nipple, twisting it until I lost the ability to trace sensations back to specific portions of my body. Never in my life had I experienced arousal like this.

"Do you think he's hard, sparrow? Do you think he'll get in his car, rip his trousers open, and jerk off with you on his mind? In his rearview?"

I shuddered at his questions. I couldn't believe what he was asking me or what I was doing, but I nodded. "Yes."

He dragged two fingers down my pussy, tracing his cock as it moved inside me. "Should we show him what you look like when you're coming?"

I didn't have to think about that. "Yes."

"Then ask for it."

That quick, quiet command loosened something inside me and—and there it was, fraying like an overburdened rope until I was nothing more than a collection of fine, unbound threads. Like I was the sun and the stars and the moon, everything, all at once. My pulse pounded in my ears. I couldn't keep my eyes open. It felt like sunlight was streaming through my skin.

I was barely able to speak when I whispered, "Fuck me, Gus."

His answering growl was rough in the best ways. "I knew you'd say it."

CHAPTER SIX

GUS

Camaieu: *a painting technique where the artist creates the work using a single color, typically employing tints or shades to achieve to this effect. In particular, the painting's subject matter is often rendered in an unnatural color or hue.*

IT WAS ABOUT FUCKING TIME.

I didn't say it, but god help me, I thought it as I wrapped my arm around Neera's waist and plowed into her. I'd waited. I'd waited for her to find her confidence and her rhythm, and I'd waited for her to beg.

All of this waiting meant I was dangerously close to coming like a cannon shot before it was my turn. Traditional gentleman I was not, but I believed in ladies first. And this lady wasn't finished.

"Look at him watching you." I tightened my grip on her neck. It wasn't enough to cut off her air but sent a clear message. *Others can watch but I keep.* "He can't decide if he should jerk his dick right there on the street. That's what you're doing to him, Neera."

"What am I doing to *you*, Gus?"

She rolled her hips over me, pausing each time I bottomed out inside her. She liked feeling me deep inside her and—as evidenced by my semi-violent growling—she liked killing me with her cunt. But this didn't end with her simply getting herself off on my dick. No, I wasn't having that. This woman—this pain in my fucking ass woman—deserved to be taken apart and put back together in all the wrong ways, and I was damn well going to be the one who did it for her.

This was the one thing I wouldn't let her do for herself.

I lashed my arms around her torso and thrust up into her as her walls clenched around me, forcing a gasp and tiny shriek from her. "You know. You've known along. Leading me on with that peach-sweet ass and your bossy mouth. You haven't played like you don't know what you're doing to that guy so don't pretend you don't know what you're doing to me, sparrow. Don't try it."

"I make you want."

"More than want," I answered. I held her close as I pounded into her, unconcerned with whether the Jeep rolled over from the force. *"Need."*

"What do I make you need, Gus?"

Not for the first time, I wished she'd turned around when she'd nestled herself in my lap, giving me her wide, expressive eyes. It would've saved me from agonizing over every shift of her shoulders and bob of her head, every ham-fisted attempt at interpreting her words while I fucked the power of speech out of her. She wouldn't have enjoyed the gaze of her onlooker that had turned her body into hot, purring lava but I still would've made it good for her.

"You," I answered. "I need you, Neera." I'd tried to hold out. Fuck, I'd tried. But admitting I needed her blew it all to hell. If I couldn't ignore that truth, neither could my dick. "Tell me you're there. I need you to get there."

She didn't respond, not in words. She nodded, laced her fingers with mine, and turned her head enough for me to kiss her. There was a lot happening right now—I was coming like a fucking rocket, Neera was vibrating in my arms, some dude down the street was watching us, and my head was full of strange, clingy thoughts I'd never before entertained —and it seemed as though my body was caving in from the weight of it all. Just fucking imploding.

Minutes passed before I could tear myself away from her lips and take stock of my condition. I was surprised to find none of my bones or my internal organs were splattered on the windows. Also surprising—Neera didn't climb out of my lap the second she caught her breath. Surprising but welcome.

She traced the edge of my wrist cuff. "I'm afraid I'm unskilled in car sex etiquette. What is the appropriate next step?"

Always so proper, my Miz Malik. "But you assume I am skilled in car sex etiquette?"

I caught her side-eye glance and responded to it with a smirk.

She closed her eyes for a moment, sighed. Then, "I'm asking you what happens next, Gus."

That dollop of vulnerability from her was worth everything. *Everything*. "I have some ideas about that. I can't remember eating anything because I was too busy thinking about sucking on your neck. I bring this up because I know I'll require sustenance in order to survive the rest of the night with you. If I can interest you in a snack, I can promise I'll keep one hand in your panties while we eat."

"You rendered my panties useless, Gus."

"Mmm, yes. A fond memory." I reached for the shredded aubergine lace on the Jeep's floor and used them to mop up the wet we'd created between us. "Panties, no panties. You know what I'll do for you."

She tipped her head toward the windshield, where our onlooker was long gone. "Was that...all right?"

I shrugged. "If it's all right for you, it's all right for me."

"I've never done—I've never done any of that before."

"Doesn't make it any less all right, Neera." I kissed her cheek, her neck. "So, are you up for some food?"

She nodded. "I'd like that."

I gave her an exaggerated headshake. "I don't know what to do with you when you're being agreeable. Could you lapse into polite dictator mode for a second?"

Neera cleared her throat, squared her shoulders. "Mr. Guillmand, I'll grant you a short break, but after that time I must insist you revisit the day's priorities."

"Remind me what those priorities are, Miz Malik."

"There are a number of issues requiring your attention but chief among them is seeing what we can get away with in the parking garage at my building. Perhaps the elevator as well."

I responded with a solemn nod. "And remind me which floor you live on."

The corners of her lips crept up into a tender smile. "The fourth, but it's often empty." She jerked a shoulder up. "Everyone takes the stairs. They're busy closing their activity rings for the day."

"As am I." I lifted my hand to her cheek. Her skin was gloriously warm and soft like I'd never felt before. "I won't rest until I've handled those priorities, Miz Malik."

HOURS LATER, after refueling at a falafel truck, nearly dying when she sucked my dick in the parking garage but made me wait until fucking her in the elevator to get off, then repaying that favor by putting her Hitachi Wand to good, edge-tormenting use, and then fucking her against a city-view window, I propped myself up on an elbow and peered at her bedroom. "This isn't what I expected."

With her hair tousled and her lips swollen, she glanced up at me. "What did you expect?"

"Your shoes are persimmon, your lingerie is aubergine, there's a barbell through your nipple, and yet your walls are...*white*." I shook my head at the unadorned space she called home. "Tell me the truth. This is where you bring your slam pieces, isn't it?"

"Slam pieces?" she repeated, laughing. "What are you asking me, Gus?"

"A proper lady like yourself doesn't want random hookups at her house, so she keeps a place on the side." I shrugged as I ran my fingers over her belly, over her mound, between her legs. I cupped her there, my middle finger tapping her seam like it belonged to me. Not for the first time in the past ten hours, I considered the possibility it did. That I was tasked with keeping a part of her, if not the whole. "I'm asking whether this soulless box is your place on the side because I can't fathom you living here without wanting to throw a tomato at the wall for no reason other than needing to spruce up the joint. Not to mention, you're the boss of all the bosses and they pay you in gold bars. This isn't you, sparrow." I stared at her navel before continuing, "I'm also asking whether this was a one-night deal for you."

Neera pressed her palm to the center of my chest and turned her attention toward the greige draperies bookending the wall of windows beside her bed. The reverent stroke of her hand over my heart, the heat of her body against mine, the shy way she hid from the prospect of giving herself over to me. This fucking woman. She was infuriating and exasperating and adorable in ways I struggled to accept.

Most infuriating, exasperating, and unacceptable—she hadn't answered me. The woman rarely spoke without first curating her words, but even for Neera the length of this pause was remarkable.

Something was wrong. A bug in the code, as the computer-y types were wont to say.

Work wasn't the issue. My girl was brilliant. She was the boss. She knew how to compartmentalize.

She wasn't the issue. Regardless of whether she was sorting through a newfound desire to get caught in the act, this woman was rock-solid. She was bright and hungry and devious, and I saw the pieces she'd kept close and quiet.

Perhaps this *was* her crash pad and she did favor a one-and-done model. It was possible. Her nipple was pierced and she let me fuck her in broad daylight while a stranger watched. That she'd prefer casual sex wasn't beyond the realm of possibility.

It was possible but it didn't seem probable to me. Shoving a platinum rod through tender skin and early evening exhibitionism were serious business. They were commitments, and Neera managed her commitments with more righteous competency than I would've imagined possible.

All that pent-up competence meant nothing escaped Neera's notice and she saw everything *I'd* kept close and quiet too. She dug them out, dusted them off, and forced me to take a long look at them. She slow-walked me to the reality that my life was rich and full, but also lonely. That sparring with a worthy opponent was divine foreplay. That I craved the pleasure of being handled by a queen who'd happily behead me.

And she'd done it while being a contemptuous pain in my ass.

It was aggravating—and deserving of admiration.

I would've admired it until her legs were shaking and my name was the only word left in her vocabulary, but she was captivated by the curtains because she wasn't the issue and neither was work or exhibitionism or anything else on her side of the bed.

That meant I was the issue.

That had to be it and…the truth pinched a bit.

"Your silence doesn't bode well for me." When she didn't respond immediately, I continued, "Yeah. Okay. Message received. I'll see myself to the door."

I shifted away from her to fetch my jeans and get the fuck out, but she wrapped her hands around my bicep and tugged me back. I returned my hand to its home between her thighs.

"This isn't my side place. I do live here, regardless of whether I could afford more. And I would like to keep you as my slam piece…or something less ridiculous."

I stared down at her. I knew my expression was cooler than anything I felt for her but I was still chilled from opening my eyes to my emotions and waiting for them to be reciprocated. "Oh, would you? Is that how you want it, Miz Malik?"

With a smile, she stroked the nape of my neck. Her touch was generous, affectionate. *Heaven.* I found myself smiling back in response.

"That's how I want it," she answered. "But I have a question for you, Mr. Guillmand. Why all the birds?"

I gazed at her for a lengthy moment as I shifted between annoyance—she still drove me crazy—and confusion—how did she not know?—and then deep-spiraled adoration—how could I do anything but worship her? "Because you soar, sparrow. Because you're magnificent and free, and I could grow old watching you." I leaned in, dropped a kiss on her lips. "I carved those birds because of you and I carved them for you."

A blush colored her cheeks and she folded her lips together to harness a wild smile. Her restraint was beautiful, somehow bolder and warmer than the grin she attempted to hide.

Then her eyes crinkled at the corners. She ran her teeth over her bottom lip. "Have you ever been to Maine?"

"I haven't. That's—that's the East Coast, yes?"

She bobbed her head once. "Northeast."

"Ah." I sanded my knuckles over my stubbled chin. "Is that where you stable your slam pieces for safekeeping?"

Without batting an eye, she asked, "And if it is?"

"Then I'll pack my bags."

Her brows arched up. "My boss lives in Maine. I fly out there once a month. I'm due to leave in the"—she glanced at the clock, huffed out a quick laugh—"in a few hours. Perhaps you'd like to join me. I imagine you'll enjoy the seaside village where Cole and his husband make their home. Lots of trees to climb."

"You mock me and my process."

"I believe you've mocked my—what did you call it?—polite dictator mode," she replied with a hearty dose of indignation. "But I'm not mocking you at all. I fully support your process, Mr. Guillmand."

"You bust my balls, Miz Malik."

She reached between us, past the erection throbbing on her hip, to roll my sac in her palm. "You love it."

"In a bizarre and twisted way, I do." I didn't know what it was about this woman but—no, I knew exactly what it was. Neera was magic in the cloaks of an executive, an exhibitionist, an evenly matched sparring part-ner. "And you're taking me to Maine?"

A small smile warmed her lips as her hand shifted to my dick, stroking me in long, leisurely pulls. "If you wish to join me, yes."

"Little sparrow, I can feel your pulse on your clit. You're fucking right I'm joining you. I'm going to Maine. I'm going anywhere you go. That's how it's going to be."

Her brows furrowed. "That's a forthright position, Mr. Guillmand. Announcing how we are to proceed."

We. That glorious *we.* If I allowed myself a moment of wool-gather-ing, I'd be forced to acknowledge I'd never wanted for that *we.* Never inspected my life and came up with an empty space meant for a woman of Neera's caliber—or curves. Never desired permanence, never ached for possession.

And here I was, wanting, desiring, aching—taking.

With a sharp shove, I sent Neera sprawling on her belly. "Yes ma'am, Miz Malik. That's my position." I settled on my knees behind her and gripped her waist, bringing her luscious backside up where I wanted it. My hand met the heat between her legs. I coated my fingers in her arousal, painted it over her back channel before sliding one finger, then another, inside. "How do you feel about my *forthright positions* now, little sparrow?"

Her hands fisted around the white sheets as she rocked back, meeting each of my lazy thrusts. That sight alone made my cock as rigid as a two-by-four, jutting straight at her as if I needed help finding my way home. "Left side. Middle drawer. Gray bottle, hot pink label."

"Well, well, well," I murmured as I pulled open the nightstand drawer and retrieved the lube. "Prepared for everything, are we?"

"I see your brash attitude doesn't concern itself with logic."

Once I had the bottle uncapped, I drizzled it between her cheeks and over my cock. My hands moved as I readied us, but my mind was deep in the cave she'd unearthed inside me. I didn't know it was possible to experience this many powerful feelings for one woman—and experience them all at once. I wanted to know her, soothe her, annoy her, spoil her, protect her, see the world with her—and own every last inch of her body.

"Me? Brash?" I shook my head though she couldn't see it. "That seems an exaggeration."

She patted the mattress blindly until she found the Hitachi I'd abandoned a few hours ago, positioned it beneath her, and switched it to the lowest setting. My cock, shiny with lubricant and my own arousal, throbbed at the sight of her pliant and submissive in every way—but not at all.

Another wave of sticky, clingy thoughts crawled up my neck and damn near strangled me as I pushed inside Neera. If I hadn't been preoccupied with pocketing the desire to drop some heady declarations on her, I would've made a fine mess of us both and come within thirty seconds.

"If not for my preparedness, you wouldn't be fucking my ass right now," she replied.

"That's how it will work. You'll be prepared and I'll pick the positions." My words came in quick, gasping punches as I thrust into her. "That's not going to be a problem for you."

"Oh, it isn't?" she bit back.

"No, Neera. You like me this way." I reached beneath her, fumbled with the vibrator until it clicked onto the next setting. A curse slipped from her lips and it felt like she was levitating. Like we both were. "And I like when you give it right back to me."

I never went longer than a month without a project taking over my existence and though I hadn't known it until now, the same was true here. But this project wasn't a towering sculpture or myth translated onto canvas in the language of paint.

This project was the most important art I'd create, and for the first time I had the pleasure of sharing my vision.

CHAPTER SEVEN

NEERA

Trompe l'oeil*: a painting technique where objects are rendered with such verisimilitude, they force the viewer to contemplate the object's reality.*

Cole: I have many things to discuss with you when you arrive. I made a list.

Cole: But if you ask me about the Monarch Project, I'll curl into a ball and rock in a corner. Fair warning. I'm not ready. It's not ready. Nothing is ready.

Neera: No Monarch. Understood.

Neera: I am prepared for everything on this list.

Cole: That's your superpower. Anticipating the unknown and then kicking its ass.

Neera: Speaking of the unknown...

Cole: Now I'm nervous.

Neera: No need to be nervous, though you should know I'm traveling with Gus Guillmand.

Cole: Who?

Neera: The artist-in-residence.

Cole: Please tell me I'm not sitting for a portrait. I'm not so egotistical that I'd have a portrait painted.

Neera: No, he's traveling with me.

Cole: He's painting your portrait?

Neera: Also, no. He is with me.

Cole: With you?

Neera: Yes.

Cole: As in...WITH you?

Neera: WITH me.

Cole: Should I call over to the local inn for lodging?

Neera: Not unless you're uncomfortable with us sharing your guest room, in which case, don't derail your focus. I will see to the arrangements.

Cole: Oh. No, yeah, of course. Completely comfortable. That's cool.

Neera: Thank you.

Cole: Thank you for allowing me to observe this in action. The gratitude belongs to me.

Neera: Am I to interpret that as you believing I was otherwise incapable of forming amorous relationships?

Cole: I've never doubted your capability. You are audaciously competent with all things. I am, however, thrilled to find myself with a front row view of your personal life.

Neera: We've worked together for several years. You've had plenty of a view into my personal life.

Cole: That's a matter of perspective.

Neera: Perhaps.

Cole: Perhaps you're a closed book wrapped in chains and locked under ten magical spells.

Neera: Thank you for that vivid description.

Cole: Always. I can't wait to meet the lad.

Neera: I believe he's older than you.

Cole: Does that mean I can't refer to him as a lad? Because Owen convinced me to read a book about the Revolutionary War and in Alexander Hamilton's letters to John Laurens, he refers to the Marquis de Lafayette and George Washington as "the lads" and they were older than him. I checked.

Neera: I am certain you did.

Neera: Should I anticipate you at the airstrip?

Cole: Yes. I've told the lads at the tower to expect your arrival.

Neera: It's convenient, I see. Having your own airstrip and air traffic control tower.

Cole: Best piece of land I've ever bought.

I LAUGHED down at my phone before locking the screen. I hated to lean on the stereotype but there was something about boys and their toys. In this case, my boss and the long-abandoned cannery he demolished and repurposed as a private airstrip. He traveled no more than once each month but he kept a full-time ground crew because he loathed the hour-long drive to the region's other private airstrip.

Gus nudged my thigh with his knee, jerked his chin up in question from his seat opposite me on Cole's private jet.

"My boss," I supplied, tapping my fingers on the table between us. "He's rather fond of the runway he's built himself."

Gus nodded and returned to the sketchbook in front of him. It was angled up, away from my view.

It seemed we were running short on conversation today. When night had given way to morning, all of yesterday's freedom and courage and attachment had gone with it. The power and connection I'd felt hours ago was now replaced with awkward rigidity.

I'd slipped into checklist mode when I'd woken, busying myself with reviewing urgent issues and firing off messages while packing for this visit. I hadn't lingered in Gus's sleepy embrace or invited him into the shower with me. I hadn't spoken to him much at all.

It wasn't that I didn't want to speak to him. I kept a tight routine each morning. Cuddling—and conversation—didn't figure into that routine. I wasn't convinced it should. We'd shared one glorious night and I hurt in the best ways from it, but I couldn't up-end the order of my life on account of that night.

Routines aside, the ordered, strategic side of me doubted this. I doubted we could translate our animosity into more than highly spirited sex. I'd doubted Gus's desire to claim a place in my life. More than that, I doubted this hate-filled fondness of ours was meant for more than a weekend.

We were different people leading vastly different lives. We'd have our fun in Talbott's Cove and we'd burn bright for several days. Then, we'd return to the real world and burn *out*.

I shifted in my seat as the jet taxied down the runway, the pulses of last night aching low in my core. A noise rattled through me as I struggled to find comfort, part moan, part yelp. And now, it was his turn to laugh. My cheeks—my whole damn face—heated at the memories. But I wasn't embarrassed. I was overcome.

"All right?" he asked.

"Very well, thank you," I lied.

"Doesn't look like it," he replied.

"Thank you for that assessment, Mr. Guillmand," I snapped.

"That tart tongue of yours," he murmured.

We stared at each other through takeoff, a silent exchange of heat and knowledge and mutual irritation. As we climbed in altitude, I battled the urge to antagonize him. This wasn't a healthy means of communication, even if it was entertaining foreplay.

Gus tapped his pencil against his book's ring binding while he gazed at me, his eyes narrowed and a muscle ticking in his jaw. My belly swooped in response to that jaw. My toes curled, my chest lurched. His small, almost invisible reaction to me was enough to refill my courage, my power.

That was when I knew, when I truly believed this wouldn't outlast the weekend. Taking this much pleasure in a twitching jaw wasn't the foundation of a solid relationship.

Gus blinked away when the aircraft leveled off, revisiting his sketchbook. Not waiting for an invitation, I watched while he worked. He didn't appear focused, his gaze fixed on the windows dotting the opposite side of the aircraft while his hand moved the pencil over the page, seemingly independent from the rest of him.

From this angle, I couldn't see what he was drawing. And I wanted to know. Was it mindless doodling? Did professional artists *doodle*? Did they call it that? Or was this how he created—without looking at his work? I had no idea.

"May I ask what you're working on?"

He blinked up at me and then frowned at the page, shaking his head. "Nothing." With a laugh, he added, "Oh, that's right. You're entitled to all my work. I forgot I'm on the clock." He mimed checking off a box. "Must complete masterpiece before noon. On it."

"As I told you yesterday, that is not the case." I shot a pointed look at the pencil in his grip. "I asked because I was curious. About your work and—and how you do it. And I can't determine whether your comments are facetious or you aren't satisfied with this residency."

He tucked the pencil over his ear. "You want to talk about the residency?"

I folded my arms on the table between us. "If you'd indulge me."

"You don't want to talk about how I can see your barbell through that shirt?" He glimpsed at my breasts before shaking his head. "I'd rather indulge in the story behind that than anything associated with the dancing bear portion of my existence."

"I take that to mean you're not satisfied with the residency," I said. "How can I improve your experience?"

He yanked the pencil from its perch and bounced the eraser on the table. "You could start by unbuttoning that blouse."

I slapped my hand over his, stilling the pencil. "Give me five minutes of serious conversation and then I'll play your game for the remainder of the flight."

"You believe this is a game?" When I didn't respond, he continued, "We're not playing, sparrow. It's not a game when it's the way you're wired. You love our tug-of-war almost as much as you love your structure and goals. As much as I love interfering with them."

I ran the pad of my thumb over his knuckles. "If you know all about my wiring, you should know I don't stop until I've met my goals." I dragged my fingers over the back of his hand. "And you, Mr. Guillmand, are one of my goals."

"You scored this goal," he said, his words rough. "Several times over."

"Which means I've earned the right to know why you aren't pleased with this arrangement. With your residency," I added.

"The residency is fine. It's terrible but it's also fine." He turned his palm over, lacing my fingers with his. He stared at our hands as he said, "Silicon Valley is a man-made world. The lines between authentic and artifice are almost invisible and I can't wander here. I can't get lost. I hadn't realized that before coming here. I should've known but I didn't."

"I don't understand," I said. "Why do you want to get lost?"

As if it was the most obvious conclusion in the world, he replied, "That's how I find things."

"Is that why you climbed the tree?"

He laughed. "You're fixated on this tree, sparrow."

"Is it?"

He glanced up, met my gaze. "Yeah," he answered. "That's why I climbed the tree. I was trying to find something real." He paused, gifting me a warm grin. "And I did. I found you."

"I believe *I* found *you*," I replied. "How can I help you—what was it? —wander? How can I help you wander, Gus?" When he only blinked at me, I continued. "You might boil my last drops of patience, but I still want to help you succeed. Helping other people do their best work is *my* best work."

That grin morphed into a deep, full smile. "Wandering can't be helped," he replied. "Back home, I'd follow the land, the trees, the rivers and streams. I didn't plan where I was going or what I wanted to see. No goals, no structure. No thinking more than a few steps ahead. Definitely not management coaching."

"That sounds..." My voice trailed off as I searched for the proper description.

"Wonderful?" he supplied.

"Overwhelming," I replied.

"Not when you do it right." He knocked his knuckles against his sketchbook. "I can't do this without also doing that."

"I think I understand the origin of this conflict," I said. "You really do need to wander."

"Do you wander, Miz Malik?" he asked.

I glanced down at the sketchbook and then back up at Gus. "Not as often as I might like."

He gestured around the cabin. "What in the world is stopping you?"

"Having a private jet at my disposal doesn't mean I have the luxury of wandering whenever I wish," I replied. "My time is not my own."

He cocked his head to the side, his brow wrinkling as he asked, "When was the last time it was yours?"

I clasped my free hand around my phone. "I haven't slowed down in an age. That's the pace of things. It's an arms race."

He leaned over, pried my fingers from the device. Set it aside, just beyond my reach. "No, it isn't."

"I understand that's your view of the matter, but as someone who has lived in this world for—"

"Too long?" he asked. He gathered my hands between his, squeezing just a bit. "Too long without a break? What would happen if you gave yourself time to wander, Neera? Even if only for"—his shoulders lifted as he grinned at me—"this weekend?"

Yes, that was exactly what I was hoping to discover.

He traced the inside of my wrist, much as he had last night at the eatery. I felt the same intensity from him—from *me*—as last night. The power, the freedom, the courage, whatever it was, it was back. "Have you ever done anything like that? Like last night? Anything in public?"

I couldn't justify my need to know. Not in a manner that made sense. Gus was aware of the lines I'd crossed but he hadn't matched my confession with one of his own. And I needed it. I had to put this thing—this experience—into a quantifiable structure. I had to know what was happening, even while I knew it would flash and cool.

"Before last night, no. But I'm more than happy to be your accomplice." He dipped his head to meet my eyes before glancing to the back of the cabin. "Are you looking for an accomplice right now? Here?"

I followed his gaze to the nook where the flight attendant sat, her legs crossed and her iPad balanced on her thigh. I tossed the idea of her finding me in Gus's lap or with his hand up my skirt around my mind. It didn't zip through me like lightning, didn't quicken my pulse. "No. Not here." I gave him a disappointed frown. "It's not my plane. Doesn't feel good."

He barked out a laugh. "And if it was?"

"Then I might have a different mind about it," I replied. "There are other issues, but that's on the top of my list."

Seemingly content with that explanation, Gus lifted my hand to his lips and kissed my palm. Then, he popped the next two buttons on my blouse. "There. That's better," he murmured.

By my standards, this was indecent and unprofessional. By modern fashion standards, it was merely risqué.

And yet, I'd enjoyed sex in public places yesterday.

The brain was a complicated organ.

Gus asked, "Now that we have those matters settled, what should I expect from Maine?"

I was prepared to describe Cole and his husband Owen, the charming town where they made their home, and the routine of my monthly visits with them, but I stopped myself. "I believe you'll be able to wander."

CHAPTER EIGHT

GUS

Lightfastness: *the pigment's chemical stability under extended exposure to light and therefore, measure of a work of art's value and life expectancy.*

I WASN'T sure what I'd expected, but the whiplash of owning every intimate part of Neera last night and then barely owning her attention this morning had left me bruised and reeling. My ego took most of the hits but my hopeful heart didn't get out unscathed.

At first, I'd resolved to back off. Give her some space. It crossed my mind to dodge this trip altogether but the truth was, I needed to get the hell out of Silicon Valley. If Lucifer himself was offering rides, I would've hopped in with him.

I'd done an adequate job of backing off this morning. As best I could, considering. I'd put distance between us during the ride to the airport, I'd ignored her adorable expressions as she'd responded to emails and text messages, I'd kept my hands to myself. I'd wanted to lick her neck and twist the barbell teasing me through her shirt, but I'd done neither. Not until she'd insisted I tell her about the residency. When she'd asked me to stop playing games.

I couldn't see how any of this was a game, but I gave her what she wanted. That was when I knew I wasn't backing off, wasn't giving her an inch of space. No, this woman had me and now she was damn well going to keep me.

We landed at a private airstrip that was little more than a paved road in the middle of a forest and Neera was quick to inform me this was one of her boss's many passion projects. Since I didn't know what that meant and couldn't imagine wanting to know, I shrugged it off.

When we climbed down the jet's stairs into the warm evening air, a battered SUV drove across the tarmac. "That's Cole," Neera said over her shoulder. "Owen's probably back at the house."

Leaving the lights on and the engine running, Cole stepped out of the SUV, arms wide in welcome. A dog poked its head out the front passenger side window and barked its greeting. Cole's shirt was on inside-out and he had smudged Sharpie scribbles all over his forearm.

I held out my hand but he backed toward the vehicle.

"Come on, we'll talk in the car," Cole urged, waving us toward the SUV. "My husband will flay me if we're not on time to supper and it's possible we're already late."

I liked Cole immediately.

After we'd settled into the backseat, Neera said, "Cole McClish, Gus Guillmand. Consider yourselves formally introduced." She gestured to the dog smiling at us from the front seat. "And that's Sasha."

"Thank you for having me," I called to Cole. I reached forward and scratched between the dog's ears.

"Careful," Cole warned. "She'll be your best friend if she knows you'll give her the kind of attention she wants."

I was only partially certain we were talking about the dog with the hot pink lobster-printed collar and not the woman to my left, the one who'd nearly decimated me with her all-business demeanor this morning. I hadn't fortified myself for that, not at all.

"I told you when to expect us," Neera said to Cole as he drove across the tarmac. "How is it that we're late when we landed as scheduled?"

"Not sure," he replied. "There are a number of plausible explanations. There are some fascinating theories about wormholes and rips in the space/time continuum. All valid considerations."

"Would a valid consideration be that you told Owen we were arriving at a different time altogether?"

He bobbed his head as he drove straight toward the forest. "Also possible."

"Cole." Neera sighed and shifted toward me with a conspiratorial eyeroll. As if we shared eyerolls over her boss and his complete shortage of with-it-ness. As if she allowed me to possess enough of her to know her sighs, her glances, her moods.

I didn't. I knew that with crystal clarity. It didn't stop me from taking her hand and grinning in response. Because I wanted to. She drove me fucking crazy and I wanted to throttle her, but I also wanted to keep her as my one and only.

"I know, I know," he replied. He took a hard right turn onto a bumpy dirt road that sent Neera and I colliding on the bench seat. "I won't let it happen again."

"I'll copy Owen on my itinerary going forward," she said, steadying herself with a hand on my leg. I layered my hand over hers and slid it higher. Her brows arched up and her fingers rubbed the soft, worn denim between my thighs.

"That's nice but you know he doesn't believe in email," Cole replied. "Even though you're late"—this time, I was here for the shared eyeroll —"you've come at the perfect time. We're having the best summer weather right now."

He rambled on about the weather and the work project he didn't want to discuss while driving through the woods like he'd stolen this SUV. If he'd noticed that Neera and I had gone silent, he didn't mention it. I liked him even more.

I gestured to Neera, to my lap, and the swelling behind my button-fly. "Can you be quiet?" I mouthed.

She bit back a smile. Blushed hard enough for me to see it in the evening darkness. And then, shook her head. *No.*

"Not right now," she whispered back, a devious gleam in her eyes.

That's right, sparrow. Come back to me. Come back.

She never stopped stroking my inner thigh. My cock didn't get the attention it wanted, but there were days ahead of us before we were due to board that jet again. I'd get mine. I was sure of it.

"It might be fun," I whispered. Cole didn't notice us. He was going on about the market prices for different types of fish, of all things. "I don't imagine he'll notice."

"He won't," Neera replied, glancing toward the front seat. "But Sasha will."

Sure enough, the dog was staring at us over the seatback, her ears perked up and her tongue hanging out. "You never know, sparrow. You might like it. I know how you feel about back seats."

Neera pressed her face to my chest, smothering a laugh. I stole that moment to drag my fingers through her hair and suck in a lungful of her delicious scent. I'd missed this. Even after a day—but it wasn't a single day. It was a day plus every day since I'd arrived in California. Every minute, even the ones when she wasn't around and I couldn't resent her for claiming my attention and branding my dreams as her own.

No, this hadn't started yesterday. Not by a long shot.

IF MY LAST-MINUTE addition to this visit came as a shock to Cole or his husband Owen, they didn't let on about it. Instead, they welcomed me into their home and promptly put me to work carrying dishes to the table like I was an old friend.

I wanted to believe it was a product of their hospitality rather than experience with hosting a lengthy roster of Neera's suitors.

They made it easy for me to believe the former.

That was good news because any hint of previous men would've driven me to fuck the memory of them out of her on the kitchen table. Whether or not we allowed Cole and Owen to watch was an issue separate from the batch of jealousy I was brewing.

It was new to me, the jealousy. I had few experiences of this sort and couldn't decide whether my reaction was healthy and normal or proof I hadn't completely evolved from the cavemen. It was probably healthy. Completely normal.

Just like carving a flock of fucking birds.

Conversation hummed around me while I studied Neera from across the table. I didn't know how she did it, but she managed to slide between a friendly, almost sibling-like relationship with these men and full-on Miz Malik in all her strict, structured glory. It was strange to watch because I could almost see her settling the chief of staff hat on her head as she responded to certain questions from Cole.

It was strange and I adored that strangeness because I was wrong about Neera. She wasn't a taskmaster boss. She wasn't cold or detached. She wasn't any of the one-dimensional labels I'd slapped on her at the outset. She was everything, all at once, and the only label I wanted to slap on her now was *mine*.

"Does that work for you, Gus?"

I snapped out of my possessive thoughts and discovered Cole, Owen, and Neera staring at me expectantly. "I'm sorry. I didn't catch that," I said, glancing at each of them. I wasn't certain who'd asked the question.

"I believe this lad has a touch of jetlag," Cole announced.

"Jesus Christ, Cole. Enough with the lads, babe," Owen muttered, rubbing a hand over his brow. "We read one American Revolution book and look what happens."

"You're saying I should cancel the waistcoat and breeches order I placed?" he asked.

Still massaging his forehead, Owen asked, "It's a little early to be planning for Halloween, isn't it?"

"Sure," Cole replied. "If Halloween was the intended purpose. I just thought it would be fun to dress up and we could—"

"No," Owen interrupted. "Whatever the rest of that sentence is, no."

Stifling a laugh, Neera said, "Cole wants to get started on our agenda early tomorrow morning. Would that be all right? We're known to take over the table and have some spirited conversations."

"I have a whiteboard on wheels," Cole added.

"And it's hideous," Owen murmured.

"Sometimes, I drag out it out here and move the spirited conversation to the board," Cole continued. "It's better than paper or screens. Easier to scribble ideas and wipe them away when they're shit. D'you get that? You know, as an artist?"

I glanced at the Sharpie on his arm. "Yeah," I replied, nodding. "Yeah, I get that."

Owen shot me a pointed look. "My advice is to make yourself scarce. There's room on the boat if that's something you want to do."

"Allow me to translate my husband for you," Cole said. "The physical capacity of my lad's sailing vessel will accommodate another adult, however, the social-emotional capacity of the vessel is limited to one adult. If you choose to go along with him, please do not expect him to speak to you. Oh, and don't fall overboard. It's only adorable when I do it."

"It's a damn good thing you're adorable," Owen muttered. "And a damn good swimmer."

"Thank you for offering," I said. "We drove through a stretch of forest on the way, right? Are there any trails to hike as an introduction to the area?"

"Trails? Why ever would you need a trail when you enjoy getting lost?" Neera asked, a tease woven through her words.

"You know I enjoy getting lost," I teased back. "But only when I have a sense of the land." I glanced at the windows facing the water. Still darkness glinted back at me. "I'm not positive I could find my current location on a map and I definitely don't know what kind of wildlife I'll encounter in that forest. On this occasion, a trail is preferable."

"Whatever you do, don't eat any wild berries," Cole said.

Owen snort-laughed at that and said, "There are miles of trails right out the back door. You can't miss them." He ran his knuckles over his bearded jaw. "There's not much by way of wildlife in these parts around this time of year. A few woodchucks, a couple of foxes, some beavers, maybe a possum or two. Badgers. That's about it. Nothing noteworthy. It's a good time for hiking."

"You might even find a tree or two to climb," Neera added.

Owen nodded, saying, "Certain paths are better than others. I might have a trail map around. Stay here. I'll go look."

Cole tipped his glass toward Neera. "That means we're on dish duty. Wash or dry?"

"You use an unfathomable amount of soap. I can't stand by and allow that to happen," she said.

"Right, so, I'll dry," he replied.

Neera rounded the table, gathering plates as she went. She stopped beside me, leaned in close, and said, "You'll have a whole forest to roam. How's that?"

"You could roam with me," I said, resting my hand low on her back.

She shook her head. "Not tomorrow. Cole has a list. He grows anxious if we don't address his lists with expediency."

"But some other day?" I asked, hopelessly hungry for her attention.

She stretched to collect a plate from the other side of the table, the movement pressing her breasts against my face. I groaned into the glory of her body.

"Yes," she murmured. "Some other day."

"I'm holding you to that," I said.

She straightened, her arms loaded with dishes and utensils, and stared at me for a moment. Then, she said, "I hope you do."

AFTER THE DISHES were washed and dried, and I'd received an extensive explanation of the local terrain from Owen, Neera and I found ourselves closed up in a guest room. We were frozen in place, the bed between us and our feet rooted on the creaky hardwood floor as we gazed at each other.

I was gradually coming to grips with the fact we didn't always know what to do with each other. It was particularly obvious that we didn't slide between the assorted segments of our relationship with ease, not yet anyway.

Eventually, I asked, "What happens now?"

She studied the quilt on the bed. "To what are you referring, Mr. Guillmand?"

"You, Miz Malik, and me, in this room together tonight." I dropped my knee on the edge of the bed. "If you need an out or an opening, I'll give you one. I'll give you anything you want."

She glanced up at me, her lips pressed together in a sharp line. She was looking for the trap. "You'd do that?"

"This house is small, the floors are loud, and the walls are thin. I can't corner you the way I did at the spice market, not unless you want those two listening in." I tapped my fingertips on my leg as my words simmered between us. "I'm following your lead here, sparrow. You tell me what happens now and how you want it to go."

Her gaze on the quilt once again, Neera said, "I don't want Cole or Owen hearing—or seeing—anything. I know we played a bit on the ride here from the airstrip and after dinner but—but I don't want that right now. Not all of it, like yesterday." Shrugging, she continued, "It's not completely clear to me what I do want."

"You want to be exposed when it's anonymous," I supplied. "And when it's somewhat distant."

She nodded. That quilt must've been damn fascinating for the attention she paid it. Through the open window, I heard crickets and cicadas, water lapping the shore, wind rustling the trees. It was a calm, cool night and the sky was a dark velvet cloak studded with millions of jewels, just the way I liked it. And this woman, the one who had the world on a string and knew everything about everything, couldn't make sense of her needs.

I liked her most of all.

"Is that what you're craving?" I asked. "Some anonymity?"

"No," she replied. "That's not—no. That's not it." She started to shake her head but stopped herself. She lifted her chin, met my gaze. "Maybe it is. Maybe I don't want to be accountable. Even if it's dangerous. Even if it's reckless exhibitionist sex in a car. And maybe...maybe I don't know what it is."

"Then, let me help you find it."

She studied me as if she had to press my words through a sieve to understand them. Then, she held out her hand to me and said, "I'd like that."

I took her hand as she climbed onto the bed. We met in the middle. I shoved my fingers through her silky hair and tasted her lips for the first time in too long.

There wasn't going to be any headboard banging tonight. No sex toys, no up-market lube. No claw marks on my back, no hair pulling. Despite the possessive caveman in my head who'd wanted to sit Neera on my cock no fewer than ninety-six times today and even contemplated defiling the kitchen table, sharing a bed without the possibility of sex excited me more than anything we'd shared last night.

"Me too," I said.

THIS TIME, the jetlag was to blame.

I woke up much later than I'd intended and found the sun high in the sky and the waters of Talbott's Cove shimmering through the lace-curtained window. True to form, Neera had smoothed the sheets on her side, tugged her half of the quilt up, and nestled her pillows against the pine headboard exactly as we'd found them yesterday.

Once I'd checked the time—good fuck, it was almost noon—and posted a sleepy-face selfie to Instagram—that shit was follower wildfire—I made the bed and stumbled across the hall to the shower.

Cole and Neera were in the kitchen as promised. I didn't see them, but there was no missing the debate in progress. I spoke enough languages to get around this planet, but I couldn't make sense of a word they were saying.

While I waited for the shower to warm up, I studied the cramped bathroom with its vintage tiles and porthole window. Neera lived in a small, bland apartment and Cole and his husband had a bathroom straight out of the seventies. The better part of me admired the fact these people lived simply despite their staggering wealth. The smaller, grouchier part of me wondered how anyone with their money—not to mention a private airstrip for their private jet—could put up with a sluggish water heater.

My family didn't know the first thing about living simply. Though I'd never analyzed it deeply, I knew my desire to stay close to nature and make my own way was a reaction to them. They knew it too. Thankfully for all involved, my work earned me enough acclaim for them to regard me as an eccentric artist rather than a finger-painting nomad. Eccentric was fashionable; finger-painters and nomads were not. They weren't going to disown me or force me to eat my Christmas Eve meal in the potting shed, but me finding moderate success as an artist made it easier on them.

I washed and dressed as I knocked around the idea of Neera meeting my family. Traveling with me to Brazil, back home to the Morumbi district of São Paulo. Introducing her as my...as mine. They'd embrace her, I was sure of it. They'd see smart, savvy Miz Malik and they'd think she kept my ass in order.

I wasn't certain either of us were anywhere close to orderly.

I spotted Owen entering the kitchen from the back deck at the same time I came around the corner from the hall. A worn ballcap hid his eyes and the print on his t-shirt was long since sun-bleached away. He gestured for me to follow him around the island. Cole and Neera stood shoulder to shoulder at the far end of the table, bent over two iPads. They were deep in discussion, cutting each other off and jabbing fingers at the devices without noticing either of us.

"Heading out now?" I asked him.

"Been out, up the coast, off to the fish market, and back again," he replied. "My day's half over but I wanted to stop in and feed these two. If I didn't, they'd forget and then we'd have real problems on our hands. My husband is irrational when he's hungry." He pushed a glass of iced coffee in my direction. "I'm going to check a couple of traps soon, if you want to come along."

While I was interested in getting a view of the landscape from the sea and I knew Owen required no conversation, I needed to wander. A boat wasn't room enough to wander. "I want to take you up on that offer," I started, "but I think I'll stay on land today."

He nodded toward Neera and Cole on the other side of the room. "They'll be tied up for the next four or five hours. Go. I'll tell her you're settled."

I set off from the house with a backpack stocked with water, snacks, and enough sketch paper, pencils, and charcoal to occupy me for a month. Due to recent developments with a certain lady, I kept a small sculpting kit tucked into the front pocket. Couldn't risk encountering the urge to carve another bird without having the right tools on hand.

Salt water and forest scented the warm summer air and it tasted like rebirth. Once again, I knew who I was and how to exist in this world. I meandered down trails both marked and unmarked, sat on felled trees until my ass was numb, watched deer cavorting in the distance. I picked up branches and rocks, drew nineteen different renditions of the jagged coastline, walked through the town's picket fence neighborhood and heartbeat village. I stopped into a bookstore and bought reading material on the area's pre-Columbian history after talking with the shopkeeper, a delightful woman who seemed to have several graduate degrees'-worth of information to share.

Armed with new insight, I found a large, flat rock overlooking the shore and filled an entire sketchbook with the bounty around me. I didn't acknowledge the cramp in my fingers until reaching into my backpack for my spare sketchbook. I laughed at my stiff claw of a hand and hauled my ass off the rock. It was time to put the pencil down if I wanted use of this hand later—which I did.

I respected the hell out of Neera's boundaries and limits. I also respected my cock's desire to get inside her many more times before returning to California.

I picked my way through the woods and along the shoreline, collecting stones and stray bits of driftwood that intrigued me. I was busy turning a bit of old, knotted wood over in my palm when I bumped into a large outcropping of granite. I stopped, staring at the rock for a long moment. Earth and moss hid most of it, but the exposed portion angled toward the horizon, rough and harsh and amazing.

I wanted Neera to see this with me, if for no reason other than seeing the incredible things hiding in plain sight.

I turned in a circle as I looked up at the forest's canopy, imagining the way it would filter the moonlight, the shadows it would cast. The way Neera's dark skin would glow. I wanted her here. Draped over the rock. Kneeling, the earth staining her skin. Would she still savor being seen if the only ones watching the show were the animals and the trees and the sky?

That could be enough for her. I could be enough.

And this place, it could be enough for *us*.

CHAPTER NINE

NEERA

Craquelure: *the small cracks and delicate lines covering the surface of old oil paintings. These defects are the result of the paint and surface's shrinking and movement over time.*

OWEN STEPPED into the kitchen from the back deck, several grocery bags hanging from the crook of his elbow and a box clutched to his chest. "Babe," he called. "How's it going over there?"

"Not bad. Neera hasn't killed me yet," Cole replied, not looking up from his screen. "How was the water?"

"Good conditions. Swordfish for supper tonight," Owen stated, not looking up from his bags. "Brooke and JJ Harniczek too."

"I imagine we're only eating one of those things," Cole chirped.

"We'll see," Owen replied.

I admired their easy exchange of affection. They kept their own priorities and they did it without abandoning themselves or each other. I wanted that. I wanted the man in my life to know I valued his presence and I wanted to express that without setting aside everything else in *my* life to do it.

Cole shifted his gaze away from the screen, settling it onto me. "What else?"

I eyed the list he'd scrawled on the side margin of the town's weekly newspaper. "You have a few items here relative to the board of directors signing off on several initiatives, but we've addressed most of the pressing matters. I believe we're finished."

"Except for my Valley Forge," he replied.

"That was in the winter," Owen yelled. "You aren't camped out in Pennsylvania and no one has captured your capitol and you're not allowed to make any more American Revolution references, babe."

With a laugh, I said, "You mean Monarch."

Cole bobbed his head. "I fear the Battle of Monmouth is ahead of me."

"I don't understand your meaning," I said.

"He is saying it will end with a stalemate," Owen called over his shoulder from his position in front of the refrigerator.

Cole shrugged. "Something like that. I can see how the product will meet with mixed reactions."

"That's your view of all your projects before you release them," I replied. "You never believe they'll succeed. If I'm not mistaken, you have a history of assigning derogatory nicknames to your projects because you doubt them to such a great degree. There was—hmm." I tapped a fingertip to my lips as I thought. "There was the Shit on a Stick project. Then, the Deformed Snail Monster project. I believe there was a time when I saw something titled Worthless Splooge Sock. Does that sound right?"

On the other side of the room, Owen slapped his palm against the countertop as he doubled over in laughter. "Worthless Splooge Sock," he wheezed. "Cole. I love you."

"You certainly do," Cole replied with a smirk. To me, he said, "Yes, you're right. I struggle to see how my work will be received when I'm in the development and early testing phases. You're correct, but that doesn't change my relationship with this project. I need more time. I need you to create the cover necessary to justify more time without anyone kicking up a shitstorm about me getting slow and directionless now that I'm his full-time splooge sock."

"Oh my god," Owen panted. "I can't believe you said that out loud, Cole."

"What? Neera's family," Cole argued. "No secrets between us at this table." He shot me a pointed glance. "If Neera wanted secrets, she wouldn't have brought the artist man here and forced us to watch while he made heart eyes at her last night."

"I am not familiar with these heart eyes you speak of." I toggled to my email with the intention of drafting a message to the other vice presidents and the board of directors regarding Cole's request for more time. That was certain to be more pleasant than this conversation.

"You know, that emoji with hearts for eyes," Cole said.

"I know the *emoji*," I drawled. "It's the specific instance of Mr. Guillmand viewing me in such a light I'm disputing."

"I disagree with the majority of this conversation, but on the topic of Gus and heart eyes, there is no argument," Owen stated.

Cole pointed across the kitchen, toward Owen. "See? My husband is always right."

"Now, that's something I don't hear too often," Owen muttered.

I closed the lid of my laptop and sanded my palms together, desperate for a change in direction. My feelings *about* Gus and my feelings *for* Gus were complicated and contradictory. Much like Cole's Monarch, they weren't ready to share with anyone else. "How is that distillery you bought last summer? It opened recently, didn't it?"

"I didn't *buy* the distillery," Cole answered. "I merely invested in its startup. I'm a fan of startups, as you well know from the earliest days of launching that Shit on a Stick startup with me." He dropped back in his chair, folding his arms over his chest and stretching out his legs. "The distillery opened last month and it's doing well. Very busy, lots of good press, strong local energy."

"I have a love/hate relationship with my husband's newfound gin hobby," Owen remarked.

Cole hung his head, groaning. "Don't you start on that again."

"Start, please," I said to Owen. "What's the love/hate all about?"

Shrugging, Owen said, "I hate all the time he spends over at the distillery. He geeks out over the science of distilling and he samples everything. *Everything.* Twice."

"And what do you love?" Cole prompted, a smirk fixed on his face.

Matching that smirk, Owen said, "I love getting my husband back all nice and liquored up." He shook his head, chuckling. "Thankfully, Cole is an *I love you* drunk. Not too rowdy, hardly ever sloppy. But goddamn, is he snuggly."

"It's true," Cole replied. "I am extremely snuggly."

Before I could respond, the door from the back deck opened and Gus stepped inside. He was incandescent. That was the only word for it. He was alive and brilliant and glowing, his skin sun-kissed and his eyes gleaming, and I immediately wanted to lick that goodness right off him.

"Hello," he said, nodding at us.

I noticed several pine needles sticking out of his hair. I pressed my fist to my lips to conceal the broad, silly smile I couldn't restrain. "I take it you found yourself adequately lost," I said.

"More than adequate," he replied, gesturing widely. "The trees—and the rocks, these huge boulders—and the cliffs! Have you seen the cliffs, the ones just down the way? And how the ocean water sweeps into the cove and pounds the outcroppings? I could watch that all day."

"I see you stayed away from the berries," Cole said. "Since you're still alive, that is."

Gus's brows furrowed as he said, "No berries. Thanks for that advice."

"These two are wrapping up for the day," Owen said, gesturing toward the table. "They've passed the point of discussing anything useful and Cole finally acknowledged he needs an extension. Just in time too. I'm getting supper started now." He waved at us, shooing us away. "Stay if you intend to be useful. Leave if you don't."

"Allow me to translate my husband," Cole said, pushing to his feet. "None of us are useful. We couldn't be useful if we put our entire being into it. My husband wants to cook in peace."

I stood, piling my devices and folders. I couldn't stop sneaking glances at Gus. He seemed to carry sunbeams inside him. I'd never seen him appear this light and loose. I wanted to feast on it, savor it until I shared some of those sunbeams.

Owen nodded, adding, "And get this ugly whiteboard out of my kitchen."

"Yes, babe. Right away, babe," Cole replied with a salute.

"In that case, I'll get out of your way," Gus said. He ran a hand over his head, retrieving several pine needles in the process. "It seems like I need to shake the forest off before the meal too."

"Do you need any help?" I gestured toward him but quickly snapped my hand back, pressing it to my neck. Cole didn't bother stifling his bark of laughter at my question. "I mean, did you get very dirty in the woods?" Owen allowed himself a low chuckle and I squeezed my eyes shut at my poorly chosen words. The gleam in Gus's eyes was systematically robbing me of brain cells. "What I'm trying to say—"

"Yes, Miz Malik, I'm certain there's tree sap you'll need to scrub off me." He stepped toward the hall, waving for me to follow. "Come now."

With my things tucked under my arm, I followed after him. In the periphery, I was aware of Cole and Owen observing every second of this exchange. They'd watched me babble—a crime to which I was never victim. That was a horror show of the campiest caliber but it was a matter I'd manage on a different day. After Mr. Guillmand was dispatched from my life and I could employ some memory-editing technology on them. Until then, I was content—no, *eager*—to follow Gus into the bedroom and I was determined to understand the beautiful energy pouring out of him. I needed to know whether he felt the same, tasted the same, touched me the same.

He flattened himself against the door, holding it open for me but taking up too much space to allow me to pass without angling my body. "This way, sparrow," he said, his hand low on my back. He urged me over the threshold, my breasts brushing his chest as I entered the room. He groaned, closed his fist around my blouse. "*This way*."

Gus crowded me, his big body hot behind mine as I took care setting my things on the dresser. He smelled of dirt and pine and sweat, and never in my life had I considered the possibility I'd favor that scent. Until this moment, I wasn't certain I knew the true scent of pine, not the artificial one of industrial cleaners and car fresheners. This—and everything else associated with Gus—was entirely real.

He reached for my hand, turned my palm over, and gifted me a small, roughly carved bird. The wood was dry and dark, almost mottled. I stared at it for a moment, passing my thumb over the impossibly precise feathers. Then I turned away, breaking out of his hold, his scent, and set the bird on the bedside table.

He followed, crowding me once again. His fingers tugged the hem of my blouse loose, drawing me back toward his embrace.

"Neera," he said, my name nothing more than a sigh.

"I know," I murmured, shifting in his hold to meet his sharp gaze. I was electrified by him. Not the rush of being seen or heard or anything like that. It was Gus, pure and simple. He was the rush. "I know."

I brought my hands to his muscular arms, backed him against the wall. I smoothed my palms over his arms, his chest, his torso. All that pine and sweat, the hard muscle and warm skin. It was making me delirious. Then, I ripped his belt off. Yanked his button-fly open. Dragged his jeans down as my knees hit the floor. Still no underwear for Mr. Guillmand.

"Can you be quiet?" I asked. He nodded, driving his fingers into my hair. "Truly quiet? Not a sound?"

I needed that guarantee. Even if Owen and Cole knew we were in here and knew we were sharing this moment, I didn't want them hearing the specifics just as I didn't care to hear their marital convenings.

Still, my brain was a complicated place.

"Swallow me right now and I'll prove it, sparrow."

And I did. I took him all the way to the back of my throat. He tasted fresh and vital and earthy, like he was composed of the land itself. I brought a hand to his balls, cupping and tugging and brushing a thumb over his back channel. His hips surged as if my mouth conducted electricity. He dragged his t-shirt over his head, balled it up, pressed it to his face. A noise rattled out of him, muffled behind the shirt. It sounded like a groan, a growl.

The back of his head thunked against the wall as his hips moved faster, falling out of rhythm with my mouth. We kept trying and failing to meet each other, to match each other's pace, but this blowjob allowed for no artful choreography. My eyes watered, and the tears streaking down my face mingled with the saliva on my chin. His balls were heavy in my palm and my jaw ached, and though I'd never orgasmed as a result of pleasuring someone else, the clench in my center every time I squeezed my legs together seemed to suggest it was possible.

This act was a mirror to the moment: frantic, untidy, starved, raw, irrevocable.

I wanted to hold back a bit. Wanted something—*anything*—between us to be simple. What was simpler than a blowjob? Not much. But nothing we shared was simple. It wasn't pretty or tame or traditional. Never simple. It was a fucking mess and I didn't think we knew any other way.

Gus dropped the shirt and whispered something in another language as he gathered my hair in his fist. It sounded like a string of obscene curses. When our gazes locked across the planes of his torso and he looked at me with unguarded desire, I knew it was more obscene than I'd imagined.

I continued working my tongue along the underside of his cock while his entire body quivered.

He continued speaking, the words barely audible and fully incomprehensible.

He twisted my hair around his palm, tugging hard as the first hit of hot, salty liquid splashed my tongue. I swallowed as he hummed, gasped, shook. He gradually replaced those foreign words with my name, whispering, "Neera, Neera, Neera," as if it was equally obscene.

When the spurts ended and he slumped back against the wall, I bowed my head, resting my brow on his thigh while he rubbed the back of my neck.

"You know," Gus started, "I had it in my head that we had hot sex because we argued a bit beforehand. We don't need to say a fucking word and"—he barked out a laugh—"fuck, Neera. *Fuuuck.*"

A tight breath eased out of my chest and my shoulders sagged. I'd needed to hear that. I'd needed to know it.

"Thank you for—" A sudden burst of sound stopped my words. Dogs barking, several new people talking at once, a baby crying. We turned in the direction of the noise, listening as it continued. "I believe the rest of our party for the evening has arrived," I said, still kneeling on the hardwood floor.

"What do you think about this?" he asked. "This place."

I stared at the door separating us from the sound, my cheek pillowed on his bare leg. "I'm not sure," I replied. "It's different."

"So is a silent suck off but I can tell you right now I enjoyed it."

I studied the door again, quiet for a long beat while I eavesdropped on stray bits of conversation. "There's something charming about it," I answered. "Strange. Disarming. But also...charming." I shrugged, busied myself with smoothing the wrinkles in my shirt. "I didn't like it here at first. It seemed antiquated. Slow. Cole was slower too. I'd spent years adapting to his frenetic pace, his surges of hyper-focused activity and him expecting everyone else to move at that pace too. And then...he changed. He came here and he's still frenetic but it's manageable. It's—calm." I shrugged, glanced out the window. "To answer your question, Mr. Guillmand, I do like this. When I adjust to it."

"Me too," he replied, hiking his jeans up.

He didn't bother buttoning them while we shared a simmering gaze that spoke of quiet desires and filthy games. If he didn't fasten his jeans soon, this was bound to boil over. "Gus," I whispered. I didn't know what I wanted but I knew I *wanted*. Needed.

"Hand me my belt, sparrow." When I arched a brow at this command, he continued, "You're the one who threw it. The least you can do is fetch it now that you've decimated me with your mouth."

My palm braced on his washboard abs for balance, I pushed to my feet. I ran a hand through my hair. It was a tangled mess. I knew without finding my reflection in the mirror that my lips were swollen, cheeks warm, and eyes watery.

"There will be no mystery about our activities in here," I murmured, gesturing toward my face. I bent to retrieve the worn leather I'd ripped off him and glanced over my shoulder. "Typical. I did all the work *and* it shows. You—you're Instagram-ready as usual."

Yes, I'd seen his post from earlier in the day.

Yes, it was wholly unnecessary for me to bring it up.

Yes, I had strong opinions on the matter—opinions I shouldn't have entertained. The man was allowed to post all the suggestive content he desired and his audience was allowed to drink him in by the gallon. This was business as usual and I should've reined in my foolish reaction before it spiraled out in the form of catty off-handed comments. After all, I had no claim on him. There was no reason to assume he'd share anything about his bedmate of late with his followers.

No reason. No claim. And yes, I still wanted it.

"Should I step out to give you a minute?" he asked, frowning. "I'll tell them you're taking a call. I don't want to put you in an uncomfortable position."

He could've volleyed back with a smartass remark or a fun jab about me attacking him or rebuke me for criticizing his social media presence. But he didn't do that. I shook my head because the knot of emotion in my throat made it too difficult to speak. I crossed the room toward him, his belt in hand, and wrapped my arms around his torso. "I don't like you, Mr. Guillmand," I said to his chest. "Not one bit."

He pressed his lips to my cheek. I felt him smile. "No, you don't, Miz Malik."

I WASN'T A HUGGER.

People didn't greet me with a friendly hug and I preferred it that way.

As far as I was concerned, hugs were intimate gestures. They required a closeness that didn't have a home in the regular course of my life. It wasn't that I was incapable of engaging in that kind of closeness with others or expressing my fondness for them with physical touch. I simply preferred to do those things with other, less familiar gestures.

Talbott's Cove didn't do other, less familiar gestures.

No, hugging was a way of life here. Save for Owen and Cole who knew me well enough to know better, I was subject to unlimited hugs when I was in this area. Babies, adults, dogs—you name it, they hugged.

That was how I came to have an infant latched onto my cheek while also tearing my hair from the roots.

"Elliott, seriously, kid," Brooke Harniczek warned, prying his fingers open. "We can't do this to nice people. Neera's going to think you're a cannibal."

Outside on the deck with Owen, Gus shifted to face me, an amused smile pulling at his lips. He tipped his chin up. I did my best to return the smile despite the parents hovering around me and their baby.

"It's all these teeth he's cutting," JJ said, gathering his son under his arms while Brooke freed the last strands of my hair from his chubby palms. "I'm telling you, Bam, he needs more than milk, bananas, and avocado. We should give him a bone to gnaw on or something."

"Jed, we're not having this conversation while we extricate our child from his latest victim," she replied, sliding her finger into his mouth and breaking the suction on my cheek. I stepped back, grinning at baby Elliott as he sucked Brooke's finger while JJ cradled him. Those three rarely separated. It was unexpected—and sweet. "He can have a slab of prime rib if that's what he wants but first, we're dealing with the fact he tried to maul Cole's guest and it's not the first time he's done something like this."

"After all these years, I'm hardly a guest," I said, waving off their concern. I wasn't one for casual hugs and I didn't see that changing, but I wasn't upset about one zealous infant. If anything, he was a fine reminder that I was due to visit my gynecologist for a new IUD. "He's getting so big. How old is he now?"

"Almost seven months old," JJ replied, pride beaming from his deep grin. "Four teeth too."

"Don't I know it," Brooke muttered. "I'm so sorry he glommed all over you. He gets so excited when he comes here. The dogs, the uncles. Everything." She shook her head, only glancing away from her son for a moment. "I hope he didn't leave a mark. Is it okay? Did he get you?"

Again, I waved off the concern. "Nothing to worry about."

The deck door opened and Owen entered, a tray of grilled fish and vegetables in hand. "Have a seat, everyone," he called as he moved into the kitchen. Gus followed, closing the door behind him. "If you're pouring drinks, Harniczek, do it now."

"Already done," JJ replied, pulling out a chair for Brooke with one hand, football-holding Elliott in the other.

Cole, Gus, and I found our seats. Owen set the platters on the table and turned toward JJ, his arms outstretched. "I'll hold this little guy while you eat," he said.

"Are you sure?" JJ asked.

Owen nodded, plucking the baby from JJ's hold. "This is what uncles are for, yes. Sit, eat. I'll give him back when he needs to be changed."

JJ watched closely while Owen settled into his seat at the head of the table with Elliott perched on his lap. Eventually, JJ dropped into a chair beside Brooke, his gaze still fixed on his son.

Cole glanced up and down the table, frowning. "Why aren't Jackson and Annette here?"

"They're moving this weekend," Brooke answered. She glanced at me and Gus while she snatched JJ's plate away from him and proceeded to fill it with food. "You've met them, Neera. He's the sheriff. She's the little one with the curly hair. She owns the bookstore in town."

Gus bobbed his head, saying, "Yes. I met her today."

I shifted to face him. "What? When?"

He smirked. "When I was wandering. She explained some of the region's natural history and pointed me toward several books on the indigenous people."

"They're moving into the new place, Brooke? Their house is finished?" Cole asked.

"The paint is still wet but it's finished," she replied, handing the plate back to JJ.

"Took them long enough," Owen muttered.

"And Nate?" Cole asked, searching the table once again. "Where is he?"

JJ nodded as he sipped his drink. "Nate is moving into Annette and Jackson's old rental."

"Yeah, he's had enough of the tavern's attic," Brooke added. "Something about the low ceilings and tiny windows and the potpourri of beer and onion rings." She glanced back at us while she served herself. "He manages the tavern now that Jed lives and breathes gin. You'll meet him on your next visit."

Before I could swerve out of that commitment, Gus said, "That would be great."

"That kid needs a dog," Owen announced. Elliott was drooling all over his hand. Owen didn't seem to notice.

"The *kid* is much closer to thirty than he is twenty," JJ remarked. "We can't call him a kid forever."

"Can," Owen replied. "Will."

Cole shot an indulgent smile at his husband. "You think everyone needs a dog."

Owen nodded at the dogs seated beside him, Sasha and the Harniczeks' dog Butterscotch. Their tails thumped against the floor as they waited for scraps and attention. "It's true. I'm going to phone the kid after dinner and give him some info on the shelter where we adopted Sasha."

"I'm not sure he has time for a dog," JJ said. "But he loves Butterscotch."

"What's not to love?" Owen asked, using his free hand to scratch her head before moving on to Sasha. "Nate would do well with a dog. He needs someone counting on him."

"How is the distillery business coming along?" I asked JJ.

He ran a hand down his face, laughing. "Better than I'd expected. More tiring than I'd expected."

"Four teeth before seven months is part of the exhaustion," Brooke quipped. "Our kid likes to beat all expectations."

"My wife is correct. If he keeps going at this pace, I'll be able to put him to work pouring drinks some time next summer," JJ said. "Honestly, it's been incredible. We're closed one day per week now and that day is necessary to keep everything stocked and working properly. The real challenge is demand. We have a waiting list for events and distribution partners already. I didn't expect we'd get to this point for several years."

"I'm thrilled to hear it," I said.

"And I'm thrilled to drink it," Cole added.

Owen chuckled. "I'm thrilled you're a cozy drunk."

"How is your world, Neera?" Brooke asked. "It must be bizarre to go between Silicon Valley and Talbott's Cove. When I first came back here from New York City, I was fixated on all the overwhelming differences. I couldn't see the village without noticing the absence of yellow taxis and gridlock. It's quiet and everyone walks slowly and it is so freaking dark at night. Right? Do you notice these things?"

"There is some culture shock," I admitted with a laugh. "But Cole keeps me busy. I barely get time to notice the lack of noise and light when we're working together."

"I'm sure he does," JJ said. "It's not easy to keep track of this guy. I don't envy you."

Bristling, I forced a grin and lifted my drink to my lips. It was an innocuous comment—and one from a man who knew the realities of working with Cole—but it hit me the wrong way. When I boiled it all down, JJ was right. I kept track of Cole. My career was composed of helping men achieve great things by keeping them out of their own way.

At what point would I achieve something of my own? It wasn't a thought I entertained often. On most days, I was content—more than that, *satisfied*—with being the one who made things happen.

Suddenly, I didn't feel content today.

LATER THAT NIGHT, Gus and I were again closed up in the guest room. This time, we were getting ready for bed. Unlike the hedonistic moment we'd shared earlier, this was domestic and chaste. I tended to my extensive nightly skincare routine while Gus cleaned the remains of charcoal from his wrists and palms. I caught glimpses of him in the mirror as he hummed to himself and he circled a damp bit of cloth over his skin, focusing on the stains pressed far into the fine creases of skin.

"Let me ask you again," he started, "what do you think about all this?" He gestured to the door. "The family and the dogs and the baby and the total absence of business as usual. At least the business to which you're familiar."

"Regardless of my previous comments on the matter, you're expecting me to confess I hate it," I murmured. "That I prefer the clean structure of the Valley."

"And all its tightly branded bullshit? Yeah. I am anticipating that."

Instead of answering him, I asked, "What did you think of this evening's gathering?"

Frowning down at his palms, he replied, "I enjoyed it in spite of my expectations."

"Meaning what, exactly?"

"Meaning this isn't the norm for either of us," he replied. "You like your clean structure and I like my wide open spaces, and somehow both of us enjoyed that meal of chaos."

"It wasn't *chaos*," I argued. "It was emblematic of a different phase of life, one where animals and tiny humans are as relevant as the adults and their endeavors."

"Do you like that phase of life?" he asked. "The one with animals and —what did you call them?—tiny humans?"

I barked out a laugh. "I'm very happy for people who choose to bring children into the world and commit to raising them in loving families. My sister Talbia has two children," I added, almost an afterthought. "A boy and girl. They're young, four and six, if my memory serves. She adores them. She was meant to be a mother. She's a good daughter, as well. My parents live with her and her husband. She has what it takes to do those things and she's remarkably successful. The desire to nurture is not one I share."

"Isn't it, though?" he asked. "You gather up helpless creatures to save them from themselves. They aren't infants or the elderly, but you nurture them just the same, sparrow."

I glared at him. "You wouldn't say that to a male chief of staff."

"Probably not," he admitted. "But I only said it because you suggested your sister is the successful sibling based on her capacity for keeping her children and your parents tended."

"She *is* the successful one," I replied.

Behind me, Gus snickered. "You are fascinating, Miz Malik. Paid in gold bars, traveling on private jets, and debating measures of success."

"In her way, she is phenomenally successful. My life isn't meaningful and valuable because I earn a good living"—another snicker—"or travel comfortably. And her life doesn't lack meaning because her days are spent caring for her husband, her children, our parents. But I do know I wouldn't have the same success if I tried my hand at living her life."

"I'm sure you'd make a fine mother," he said.

"Don't do that. Don't patronize me," I replied. "Whenever a woman announces she isn't interested in motherhood, everyone jumps to convince her it's worth it, she'd be a natural, she'll regret missing out on her childbearing years when she's older. That doesn't account for the truth that some women aren't cut out for the task and others simply do not want the job."

"And you don't," he added.

I shook my head once. "I don't think I do, no."

"I respect that." With a nod, Gus tossed his rag to the floor and reached for my waist. "I know you said you wanted to keep it chill around your boss," he started, his lips on the back of my neck, "but, earlier...when we...*you* didn't—"

"I'm all right," I said, laughing. Talk about conversational whiplash. "There's no scorecard."

He tugged off his shirt, threw it in the same direction as his rag. "Maybe not but I believe in equality."

I eyed him in the mirror, my lips quirking up. "Do you?"

"Indeed. It's one of my top concerns. I don't believe you can be quiet, however. That's my secondary concern."

"What, may I ask, is your proposed solution?"

He shuffled toward the window, bending at the waist to peer out into the darkness. "I propose we take a stroll down the dock." He stood, glancing around the room before yanking a plaid wool blanket off the foot of the bed. "And we're taking this with us. I can handle my share of bug bites but splinters in my ass are a different story."

CHAPTER TEN

GUS

__Tenebrism:__ a technique employing extreme contrasts of light and dark used to increase emotion and drama.

ON OUR LAST day in Talbott's Cove, I woke up with the dawn. Neera was still asleep. I shifted toward her, wrapping my arms around her waist. I wanted to hold her close and savor this moment before it ended. I wasn't ready for the end, not in the least. I didn't even want to leave the bed because I knew every step away from this location was a step closer to the conclusion of us.

I couldn't explain it though I knew there was something magical about this town. For me, for us. It was more than the slower pace, more than the forest and sea. It was a place for wandering but also finding. It was roots—permanence—without losing any of the wildness that pumped in my veins. And I knew it was inside Neera too.

I continued to doubt my ability to find this town—hell, the state—on a map, but I wanted to stick around. More than that, I wanted Neera to stick around with me. I wanted to keep all of this.

WHY NEERA AGREED to come on a walk through the woods while the sun was still busy rising would always be a mystery to me. Regardless, I managed to get her out of bed and out of the house without attracting the attention of our hosts and that was a gift because I needed time with her. Time and space to make my case, make her see the things I saw.

We walked in silence for several minutes as I searched for the rock I'd noticed the first time I'd explored this area. I'd wanted her to see this and I'd wanted to see her here. It took several more minutes of heading in one direction, doubling back, starting off in another direction, retreating, and finally settling on the right path before that strange, wonderful outcropping.

"Isn't this amazing?" I asked as we circled the exposed rock. "There's so much I could do with this."

She blinked at the rock. "Sculpting, you mean?"

"Maybe but also—anything," I said. "It's marvelous to study. It's a story waiting to be told." I dropped my hands to her waist and steered her toward it. "Sit there for me. Please," I added when she gave me a baleful stare. I shrugged my backpack off my shoulders and retrieved a sketchbook and charcoal. "Please, sparrow."

She nestled on the upper slab, her legs tucked under her and her body angled toward the ocean. "Is this what you want?"

I stared at her, perched on the edge of a majestic rock as if she was presiding over this land. I flipped open my book as images flooded my mind's eye. "This is exactly what I want." Not missing her slight eyeroll, I continued, "I've learned a few things about this land since we've been here. The land and the people who have lived on it throughout time. I don't know those stories well enough to tell them yet, but I want to find my way there. I want to learn and I want to figure it out because when I came across this rock and saw it jutting out of the ground like it'd been thrown down from the heavens or shot out of hell, I knew I had to translate this story. I want to tell the story of this place."

She ran her fingers over the mossy ledge, saying, "I like this side of you. The hyper, driven side. I like that you've shared it with me and...I can't wait to see the story you tell."

Still staring at her fingers as they stroked the moss, I asked, "Will you tell me a story?"

"What kind of story?"

"A story of the future," I said, my gaze fixed on her hand while I sketched. "What comes next? Where do we go? *Who* are we?"

"That's a complicated story," she replied, twisting her hands together.

"I don't think it is." I flipped to a new page. "What do you want to do with your life, Neera? Tell me that."

I could feel her frowning at me for several heavy beats before she asked, "In what sense?"

"The rock you're sitting on has been here for at least twelve thousand years. Probably longer. I stumbled upon it a few days ago and I knew—I fucking *knew*—it deserved attention. It came from somewhere and it served purposes great and small and it's worth remembering." I turned the page, started sketching again. "What do you want from this life, Neera?"

She sucked in a breath and I knew the dam was breaking.

"I want to do something," she started, her voice smaller than I'd ever heard it, "something of my own."

"It's your turn to be *seen*, isn't it?" Another breath and I could almost see her heart swelling with the pleasure of recognition. "That's what it is. Recognition *of* you, *for* you. Not because of anyone else but because you're brilliant and talented and you've earned it."

She hesitated. "I think—"

"No," I argued. "You *know* what you want. Say it. Just fucking say it, sparrow. We're all alone out here. You and me and a rock that's nowhere near as tough as you. *Say it.*"

"I want to build something that will outlast me, something that will leave a mark." She ran her fingers through her hair, her lips pursed and her eyes unfocused on the horizon. "I want to get better, more accessible math and science and coding instruction in public schools. I want to make it more attractive to build technology that improves quality of life rather than that objective being secondary to profit and IPO valuations. I want to build windmill farms in developing countries and solar arrays in the desert, and I want to fund midwives and nurse practitioners in every small, impoverished town in this country. And it's not because philanthropy calls to my soul or I feel a need to give back after years of raking in exorbitant corporate profit. It's not about nurturing or any other maternal bullshit that gets pinned on women who put their energy into these endeavors. We need math instruction because we need talent. We need quality of life tech because the population of many developed nations is aging faster than the greater population is growing, and younger generations can't carry that burden alone. We need wind and solar and midwives because those developing countries and small towns represent talent pipelines and untapped markets. We need to create the world we want to do business in if we want to keep seeing those profits. And I want"—she shook her head as if this one was the true impossibility—"I want to make decisions rather than executing on someone's decisions."

"Then why don't you?"

"Because"—she slapped her palms against the stone—"because Cole needs me."

"I don't know shit about the internet—"

"Your Instagram engagement says otherwise," she quipped. "You know how to save the best moments for your followers."

I didn't know what I'd done wrong, but I knew it was something and I wanted to fix it right now. I glanced down at myself, considering my shirt. I pulled it over my head, rubbed a charcoal-darkened hand over my chest, and asked, "Better?"

She tipped her chin down. Her eyes answered for her. Yes, this was better. But she still frowned, asking, "Do you plan on posting a pic of this for your fans?"

"Only if I can also tell them this charcoal is a result of sketching the woman I'd like to call mine all morning. I haven't mentioned it to them yet because we haven't had the conversation and I'm not about to make announcements on social media without your prior knowledge."

"I—you—what?"

"I don't have to tag you if you don't want," I continued. "Business and pleasure can live separately for now."

"For now?" she repeated.

"Until it's professionally convenient for you. Until I'm no longer working under you—in the organizational structure sense, that is. Until you get to work on building some windmills." I turned the page. "Until you let the world see you, Neera."

"And you?" she asked. "Should I allow you to see me, Mr. Guillmand?"

"You should allow me to join you on your voyage, wherever it takes you. I'm a fine traveling companion, as I believe you've noticed."

She considered this, inclining her head in agreement. "You do pack more paintbrushes than pants."

"You say this as if it's a problem," I replied.

She didn't acknowledge my comment, only gazing back at the sunrise piercing the horizon. "We don't even know each other."

"Can you really say that after my cock has been in your ass?"

She ran her hand down her face, groaning. Now, that made for a beautiful picture. My hand could barely keep up with my mind. "Gus."

"Neera," I replied.

"We don't *know* each other," she repeated. "What if we—if we don't have compatible values?"

"I think we do," I said, my gaze still fixed on the page. "And if we don't, we'll adjust. We'll learn."

"You make it seem as though we have a long history of compromise," she murmured. "Which we do not."

"No, we don't," I agreed. "But we have a long history of yelling at each other and being obscene, and that has to count for something."

"It might," she conceded. "I'm not convinced it counts enough."

"Then I'll just love you harder," I said.

"You do not love me," she said. "I'm sorry, no. Not yet."

"But I will," I replied. "And you will too."

She stared at me as if she didn't understand the language I was speaking—which was possible. I'd been known to slip into Portuguese on occasion. French when I was very, very drunk. But I didn't think that was the issue here. No, I was making bold statements and backing them up with nothing more than a foggy belief that this might be *it*.

Eventually, she said, "Your residency—"

"I will complete it," I said with a sigh. I did not want to think about the Valley until absolutely necessary. "I imagine it will take you that long to find a suitable replacement. Rather, ten replacements who will deign to fill your shoes and struggle mightily."

"It will take that long to transition Cole," she said, mostly to herself.

"On that count, we agree."

"And then, what?" she demanded, setting her stare toward me. "You follow me from place to place while I—whatever it is I do in this fictional rendition of the future?"

I jerked a shoulder up, continued sketching. "Perhaps." Turned the page. "Perhaps I stay here."

"And what will you do *here*, Mr. Guillmand? You enjoy the forests and the shore and the dinners filled with dogs and babies now, but what happens after a few months? When you want to get lost somewhere new?"

"I don't imagine I will," I replied. I stuffed the charcoal in my pocket and tucked the book under my arm. "I think I'd like to build us a nest, sparrow."

EPILOGUE
NEERA

Sinking in: *a condition in which the paint medium absorbs into the underlying paint layer.*

Three years later

THERE WAS a bird waiting for me when I arrived home this morning.

I leaned a hip against the kitchen counter as I studied the newest addition to my flock. This one was stone, probably quartz or granite, and no bigger than an egg. This one had required time.

By now, I had more than a hundred of them and always a new one to welcome me home when I've been away.

Birds and a happy beagle we called Matilde.

"Hello there," I said as she tap danced at my feet. "Have you been good?"

She let out an indignant howl and I crouched down to receive my ration of kisses and irritable *where have you been?* yips.

"She's been hunting badgers again," Gus called as he shuffled down the stairs. From my position on the floor, I couldn't see him but I loved the sleepy drawl in his voice and the lazy way he thudded from one riser to the next. Sleepy, lazy Gus was one of my favorite iterations of this man. "She thinks it's her duty to thin the local population."

I gifted Matilde a meaningful stare. "Again?" She replied by nestling her head against my belly and frantically wagging her whole tail end. It was never just the tail. Always the whole back half of her body, wagging like it was making a wide turn.

"I tried to reason with her, particularly with respect to her commitment to leaving her trophies under the deck," he continued, stepping into the kitchen with both palms pressed to his eyes, "but she wasn't having it. She said it was her life's work and who am I to argue with that?"

I took Matilde's face in my hands, melting at her contagiously joyful grin. "We're not getting the hunter out of you, are we?"

"Owen appreciates it," Gus said, stopping behind me. "When I dropped by for dinner last night, he told me the badgers were gnawing on some of his nets last month. Digging up some of his cucumber plants too. Cole told me a long story about the Canadian fur trade. I don't remember the specifics. I was busy drinking his gin."

I gained my feet and stepped into his space, my arms closing around his lean—and delightfully bare—torso. He was still busy waking up, his skin warm and hair sticking in every direction, and he was mine.

"It seems I should ask whether *you've* been good?" I pressed my lips to my husband's neck. *Husband*. And I was his wife. Even after two years of marriage, that title still caught me like a blast of blinding sunshine after a week of dreary darkness. Of all the titles I'd collected in my life, *wife* wasn't one I'd expected. But now, I couldn't imagine living without it.

We'd stumbled into the nuptial conversation around the time Gus was finishing his residency back in Silicon Valley. Nothing about that year had been easy on us. I still couldn't believe we'd made it out intact. He'd moved himself into my apartment immediately following our return from Talbott's Cove, though neither of us were skilled at the art of cohabitation. We argued—*a lot*—and gradually learned the difference between disagreeing about issues of importance and instigating in the name of foreplay. Very, very gradually.

Once I'd announced my intention to step away from the company, my business travel schedule quadrupled as I was busy transitioning projects and management tasks at locations all over the globe. Even when I was in the office, my days started before sunrise and ended long past sunset, leaving us little time for both disagreement and instigation. Save for the weeks scheduled for visiting Talbott's Cove, I saw more of Gus's carved birds than I did of him during that period.

Thankfully, he'd discovered life beyond the stiff boundaries of the Valley and spent most of his time exploring everything from Big Sur to Half Dome. He'd stayed as far away from the campus as possible and, in that time, managed to create several spectacular sculptures which were now on display in the campus's flagship building. He'd claimed they were the worst thing he'd made since primary school. I disagreed but I loved him enough to know when to argue, when to instigate, and when to let him be wrong without telling him about it.

In addition to all the drama and exhaustion of that year, and our plan to move into a renovated farmhouse on the other side of the country, we'd decided to get married. The idea had first come up when Gus mentioned his O1-B visa was expiring and he was due to apply for an extension unless I'd rather save him the time and marry him.

We'd laughed for a minute because he hadn't meant to propose. He hadn't. Not after the year of constant bickering and separation and frustration over one thing or another. There were days when we barely tolerated each other and required some angry sex in semi-public locations to break through the tension. There were days when we doubted our plan to build a new life together in Maine because how could we do that when we couldn't agree on whether to run the ceiling fan all night, regardless of the weather. But I stopped laughing and I set all those issues aside, and I said, "Yes, I'd like that very much."

Two weeks later, we flew to Talbott's Cove. Owen conducted a brief ceremony in the forest which ended with, "I now pronounce you husband and wife. You may now adopt a dog."

None of these things were part of our plans but now, a little more than two years after our impromptu wedding, I couldn't imagine life without my husband and our heart-of-a-killer dog. The learning curve was steep but we'd scaled it together.

We still argued, still instigated. Still engaged in angry sex in semi-public places. But our world was different now and we didn't need the same things.

"I've never once been good." Gus slipped his hand down my back to squeeze my ass. He smelled like oil paint and pine needles, which meant he'd been painting in the barn. Unlike his former studio back in California, the barn was nothing more than a barn. Wooden beams, dirt floors, a single string of lightbulbs running down the center. The ocean-facing front was almost always bathed in bright sun, the forest-facing back was almost always shaded under the branches of old pines. It was uncomfortably simple and exactly the way he preferred to work. "How could I possibly start now? I wouldn't know where to begin."

"An excellent point." I dropped my cheek to his chest and inhaled. "Was the late night courtesy of the gin or the paint?"

"Gin, then paint," he replied, bringing his hand to the back of my neck and kneading the tense muscles there. Leaving Silicon Valley and launching a strategic philanthropy venture was exciting—and stressful as hell. Making the decisions *and* executing them kept my days busy and my hands full, though I savored this stress. I'd chosen it and I was the one to plot the course. "How was Cape Town?"

"Intense, but good." I hummed as his thumb found an especially tough knot. "More of that, please."

"More you shall receive," he murmured. "Tired, sparrow?"

I kicked my shoes off, shook my head. "Not right now. I took a nap on the flight."

"Good thinking." He edged my feet apart as he kneaded his thumbs down my back. I heard the rustle of fabric and felt his pajama bottoms drop to the floor. His hard cock slapped my belly, hot and hungry for attention. He dragged his stubbled chin over my neck, between the open collar of my blouse. "But you'll be tired when I'm finished with you."

Matilde slunk off to the sunny guest bedroom she'd claimed as her own while Gus freed me from my clothing. His fingertips drew patterns up and down my spine, and then lower, over my ass, slipping inside me.

"Miz Malik," he growled. "Oh, my beautiful girl. You are wet like the ocean."

"I have been away for nineteen days," I replied.

He offered another growl as he turned me, wrapping his arms around my waist, and walked me toward the living room, his cock nestled between my ass cheeks. A two-story wall of windows showcased all of Talbott's Cove and Penobscot Bay. He gathered several pillows from the sofa as we passed, tossing them to the floor in front of the window.

"Down," he ordered with a gentle shove.

I dropped to the floor and settled my knees on the pillows I'd selected for this precise purpose—but no one else had to know that. Gus joined me, an arm tight around my waist as he layered his body over mine. His erection slid through my slit and the early spasms of release danced up my legs, circled my ribs, prickled my scalp. *I am so ready for this.* When he finally thrust inside me, his cock gloriously thick and heavy, our cries echoed in the cavernous space.

"Your cunt missed me something fierce." He fisted my hair, angling my head to drag his teeth over my neck. "Did you play with it while you were gone? Did you open the curtains in your suite and spread your legs and tease this little clit until you came?"

"Once or twice," I replied.

Gus released my hair and reached down, slapping my mound as he slammed into me. "More than that," he said. Slapped again, and again. His chest tightened against my back, his muscles pulled taut, his breaths coming fast, his control eroding with each measured stroke. "More than that, sparrow."

"Did you miss me?" I asked.

He didn't answer right away, only delivering another fast, sharp slap between my legs. Then, "The next time you're alone in a hotel room with your legs spread, I expect a phone call. I want to hear it happening."

Gus pumped into me, his fingers swirling around my clit as he sucked my neck. "That can be arranged."

"Neera," he said, groaning. "Oh, fuck, I—*fuuuuck.*"

"Yes," I panted. "Tell me."

"You should've woken me up by sitting on my face."

"Next time," I promised.

"I fucking love you," he snarled. He came with a hoarse shout and his teeth on my shoulder, and I followed. We stayed there, quaking, panting, and I wanted this little moment to last forever.

"I love you too," I whispered.

He pulled out, and slapped my ass. "Welcome home, sparrow."

THANK **you for reading *Rough Sketch!* I hope you enjoyed Neera and Gus. Keep reading for a sneak peek of JJ and Brooke's story** —*Far Cry*!

"MY TAVERN ISN'T your hookup pool."

She cast her gaze from one end of the bar to the other. "I wouldn't call it much of a pool."

"Why can't you use Tinder like everyone else? Come on, sweetheart. Get yourself some apps and get the hell outta here."

"I hate apps," she replied.

"And I hate cilantro, but you don't see me passing on the tacos, do you?"

"No, I mean I *hate* apps," she said, holding up her phone. "I hate them so much that I don't have any." I snatched the device away from her and peered at the screen. "Look. No social media. No news or weather. No food delivery."

"The only delivery around here is DiLorenzo's and it's only when Denny's in the mood."

She sliced her hands through the air. "Irrelevant. I didn't have delivery apps when I lived in New York."

I hit her with a glare. "If you really wanted something, you'd download an app for it."

"And that's where you're wrong, Jed. If I really wanted something, I'd go out and get it." She waved her hands. "That's what I was attempting to do earlier."

I set her phone on the bar top. "You have the newest iPhone and you use it for what? Phone calls? Texting Annette?"

She tilted her head, schooling me with an expression that said I should know better. "Not that I owe you any kind of explanation but until recently, when my previous phone met with an unlikely end, I had one of the earliest models." She pursed her lips. I looked away to keep from staring at her there. "And yes, Jed, I use it to make phone calls and text my bloodless sister."

I blew out a breath as I reached for towel. All the glassware was dry, but goddamn, I needed something to keep my hands busy. "You come out with a lot of strange shit, BamBam, but that's the strangest."

"It's so great that you have opinions," she mused. "Even better that I don't give a single fuck what you think." She leaned forward, folded her arms on the lip of the bar. "Then again, I can't give a single fuck because I don't have any. Literally. I have no fucks because you cockblocked me."

"What d'you want from me, Brooke? An apology? You're not getting one. I kicked the guy out because he annoyed me. When you own the joint, you can do that."

"You kicked him out while also cockblocking me," she replied.

"Not that it'd matter to you, but I'm pretty sure he's married."

"'Not that it'd matter to you,'" she repeated. "Your dick isn't big enough to use that tone of voice with me. Check yourself, Jed."

"Sweetheart, you don't know the first thing about my dick."

Her blonde hair spilled over her shoulders as she leaned forward. "Oh, I know more than enough."

I twisted the towel around my fist. "Big talk from a girl trying to pick up tourists."

"Funny how it's only a problem when I do it."

I blinked at her. Dropped the towel. Swallowed down the words I wanted to say to her. Rounded the bar. I closed my hand around Brooke's bicep and tugged her off the stool. "Let's go," I murmured.

"And where, may I ask, are we going?"

I gave her only a clenched jaw in response as I yanked her around the bar and into the dim storeroom. I kicked the door shut behind us. I marched her toward a wall of empty kegs until her back met the cool metal.

"Excuse you," she said, glaring at my hold on her arm. "What do you think you're doing with your hand on me?"

"We both know you would've ripped my fucking ear off and kicked my balls into my gut by now if you didn't want my hand on you."

"Oh really?" she scoffed. "So, what? I'm *asking for it?*"

"You're asking for something, sweetheart."

I was right about that. She was looking for something. She was fishing.

And I was taking the bait.

FAR CRY **IS NOW AVAILABLE!**

Join Kate Canterbary's Office Memos mailing list for occasional news and updates, as well as new release alerts, exclusive extended epilogues and bonus scenes, and cake. There's always cake.

Visit Kate's private reader group to chat about books, get early peeks at new books, and hang out with over booklovers!

If newsletters aren't your jam, follow Kate on BookBub for preorder and new release alerts.

Talbott's Cove

Fresh Catch — Owen and Cole

Hard Pressed — Jackson and Annette

Far Cry — Brooke and JJ

Rough Sketch — Gus and Neera

Get exclusive sneak previews of upcoming releases through Kate's newsletter and private reader group, The Canterbary Tales, on Facebook.

ABOUT KATE

USA Today Bestseller Kate Canterbary writes smart, steamy contemporary romances loaded with heat, heart, and happy ever afters. Kate lives on the New England coast with her husband and daughter.

You can find Kate at www.katecanterbary.com